KT-215-956

STEP SISTER

C334365925

ALSO BY JENNIFER DONNELLY

These Shallow Graves
Revolution

The Waterfire Saga

STEP SISTER

JENNIFER DONNELLY

HOT
KEY
BOOKS

First published in Great Britain in 2019 by
HOT KEY BOOKS
80–81 Wimpole St, London W1G 9RE
www.hotkeybooks.com

Copyright © Jennifer Donnelly, 2019

All rights reserved.
No part of this publication may be reproduced, stored or transmitted
in any form by any means, electronic, mechanical, photocopying or
otherwise, without the prior written permission of the publisher.

The right of Jennifer Donnelly to be identified as Author of this work
has been asserted by them in accordance with the
Copyright, Designs and Patents Act, 1988

This is a work of fiction. Names, places, events and incidents are either the
products of the author's imagination or used fictitiously. Any resemblance
to actual persons, living or dead, is purely coincidental.

A CIP catalogue record for this book is available from the British Library.

ISBN: 9781471407970
also available as an ebook

1

This book is typeset using Atomik ePublisher
Printed and bound in Great Britain by Clays Ltd, Elcograf S.p.A.

Hot Key Books is an imprint of Bonnier Books UK
www.bonnierbooks.co.uk

To everyone who's ever felt that they're not enough

This is a dark tale. A grim tale.

It's a tale from another time, a time when wolves waited for girls in the forest, beasts paced the halls of cursed castles, and witches lurked in gingerbread houses with sugar-kissed roofs.

That time is long gone.

But the wolves are still here and twice as clever. The beasts remain. And death still hides in a dusting of white.

It's grim for any girl who loses her way.

Grimmer still for a girl who loses herself.

Know that it's dangerous to stray from the path.

But it's far more dangerous not to.

Prologue

Once upon always and never again, in an ancient city by the sea, three sisters worked by candlelight.

The first was a maiden. Her hair, long and loose, was the color of the morning sun. She wore a gown of white and a necklace of pearls. In her slender hands, she held a pair of golden scissors, which she used to cut lengths of the finest parchment.

The second, a mother, ample and strong, wore a gown of crimson. Rubies circled her neck. Her red hair, as fiery as a summer sunset, was gathered into a braid. She held a silver compass.

The third was a crone, crookbacked and shrewd. Her gown was black, her only adornment was a ring of obsidian, incised with a skull. She wore her snow-white hair in a coil. Her gnarled, ink-stained fingers held a quill.

The crone's eyes, like those of her sisters, were a forbidding gray, as cold and pitiless as the sea.

At a sudden clap of thunder, she raised her gaze from the long wooden worktable at which she sat to the open doors of her balcony. A storm howled down upon the city. Rain scoured the rooftops of its grand palazzos. Lightning split the night. From every church tower, bells tolled a warning.

"The water is rising," she said. "The city will flood."

"We are high above the water. It cannot touch us. It cannot stop us," said the mother.

"Nothing can stop us," said the maiden.

The crone's eyes narrowed. "*He* can."

"The doors are locked," said the mother. "He cannot get in."

"Perhaps he already has," said the crone.

At this, the mother and the maiden looked up. Their wary eyes darted around the cavernous room, but they saw no intruder, only their cloaked and hooded servants going about their tasks. Relieved, they returned to their work, but the crone remained watchful.

Mapmaking was the sisters' trade, but no one ever came to buy their maps, for they could not be had at any price.

Each was exquisitely drawn, using feathers from a black swan.

Each was sumptuously colored with inks mixed from indigo, gold, ground pearl, and other things—things far more difficult to procure.

Each used time as its unit of measure, not distance, for each map charted the course of a human life.

"Roses, rum, and ruin," the crone muttered, sniffing the air. "Can you not smell them? Smell *him*?"

"It's only the wind," soothed the mother. "It carries the scents of the city."

Still muttering, the crone dipped her quill into an inkpot. Candle tapers flickered in silver candelabra as she drew the landscape of a life. A raven, coal-black and bright-eyed, roosted on the mantel. A tall clock in an ebony case stood against one wall. Its pendulum, a human skull, swung slowly back and forth, ticking away seconds, hours, years, lives.

The room was shaped like a spider. The sisters' workspace, in the centre, was the creature's body. Long rows of towering shelves led off the centre like a spider's many legs. Glass doors that led out to the balcony were at one end of the room; a pair of carved wooden doors loomed at the other.

The crone finished her map. She held a stick of red sealing wax in a candle flame, dripped it onto the bottom of the document, then pressed her ring into it. When the seal had hardened, she rolled the map, tied it with a black ribbon, and handed it to a servant. He disappeared down one of the rows to shelve the map, carrying a candle to light his way.

That's when it happened.

Another servant, his head down, walked between the crone and the open doors behind her. As he did, a gust of wind blew over him, filling the room with the rich scent of smoke and spices. The crone's nostrils flared. She whirled around.

"You there!" she cried, lunging at him. Her clawlike hand caught hold of his hood. It fell from his head, revealing a young man with amber eyes, dark skin, and long black braids. "Seize him!" she hissed.

A dozen servants rushed at the man, but as they closed in, another gust blew out the candles. By the time they had slammed the doors shut and relit them, all that remained of the man was his cloak, cast off and puddled on the floor.

The crone paced back and forth, shouting at the servants. They poured down the dusky rows, their cloaks flying behind them, trying to flush the intruder out. A moment later, he burst out from behind one of the shelves, skidding to a stop a few feet from the crone. He darted to the wooden doors and frantically tried the handle, but it was locked. Swearing under his breath, he turned to the three sisters, flashed a quicksilver smile, and swept them a bow.

He was dressed in a sky-blue frock coat, leather breeches, and tall boots. A gold ring dangled from one ear; a cutlass hung from his hip. His face was as beautiful as daybreak, his smile as bewitching as midnight. His eyes promised the world, and everything in it.

But the sisters were unmoved by his beauty. One by one, they spoke.

"Luck," hissed the maiden.

"Risk," the mother spat.

"Hazard," snarled the crone.

"I prefer Chance. It has a nicer ring," the man said, with a wink.

"It's been a long time since you paid us a visit," said the crone.

"I should drop by more often," said Chance. "It's always a pleasure to visit the Fates. You're so spontaneous, so wild and unpredictable. It's always a party, this place. A regular bacchanal. It's so. Much. *Fun.*"

A handful of servants spilled out from a row between the shelves, red-faced and winded. Chance pulled his cutlass from its scabbard. The blade glinted in the candlelight. The servants stepped back.

"Whose map have you stolen this time?" the crone asked. "What empress or general has begged your favor?"

Still holding his cutlass in one hand, Chance drew a map

from his coat with the other. He tugged the ribbon off with his teeth, then gave the parchment a shake. It unrolled, and he held it up. As the three women stared at it, their expressions changed from anger to confusion.

"I see a house, the Maison Douleur, in the village of Saint-Michel," the crone said.

"It's the home of—" said the matron.

"A girl. Isabelle de la Paumé," the crone finished.

"Who?" asked the maiden.

"All this trouble for a mere girl?" asked the crone, regarding Chance closely. "She's nothing, a nobody. She possesses neither beauty nor wit. She's selfish. Mean. Why her?"

"Because I can't resist a challenge," Chance replied. He rerolled the map with one hand, steadying it against his chest, then tucked it back inside his coat. "And what girl wouldn't choose what I offer?" He gestured at himself, as if even he couldn't believe how irresistible he was. "I'll give her the chance to change the path she is on. The chance to make her *own* path."

"Fool," said the crone. "You understand nothing of mortals. We Fates map out their lives because they wish it. Mortals do not like uncertainty. They do not like change. Change is frightening. Change is painful."

"Change is a kiss in the dark. A rose in the snow. A wild road on a windy night," Chance countered.

"Monsters live in the dark. Roses die in the snow. Girls get lost on wild roads," the crone shot back.

But Chance would not be discouraged. He sheathed his cutlass and held out his hand. As if by magic, a gold coin appeared in his fingers. "I'll make you a bet," he said.

"You push me too far," the crone growled, fury gathering like a storm in her eyes.

Chance flipped the coin at the crone. She snatched it from the air and slammed it down on the table. The storm broke. "Do you think a *coin* can pay for what you've set loose?" she raged. "A warlord rampages across France. Death reaps a harvest of bones. A kingdom totters. All because of *you*!"

Chance's smile slipped. For a few seconds, his fiery bravado dimmed. "I'll fix it. I swear it."

"With *that* girl's map?"

"She was brave once. She was good."

"Your head is even emptier than your promises," the crone said. "Open the map again. Read it this time. See what becomes of her."

Chance did so. His eyes followed the girl's path across the parchment. The breath went out of him as he saw its end . . . the blotches and hatches, the violent lines. His eyes sought the crone's. "This ending . . . It's not . . . It *can't* be—"

"Do you still think you can fix this?" the crone mocked.

Chance took a step towards her, his chin raised. "I offer you high stakes. If I lose this wager, I will never come to the palazzo again."

"And if *I* lose?"

"You allow me to keep this map. Allow the girl to direct her own steps forevermore."

"I do not like those stakes," the crone said. She waved her hand, and her servants, who had been slowly edging closer to Chance, charged at him. Some were bearing cutlasses of their own now. Chance was trapped. Or so it seemed.

"There's no hope of escape. Give me back the map," said the crone, holding out her hand.

"There's always hope," Chance said, tucking the map back into his coat. He took a few running steps, launched himself into a somersault, and flew over the heads of the servants. He landed on the worktable with the grace of a panther and ran down its length. When he reached the end, he jumped to the floor, then sped to the balcony.

"You are caught now, rogue!" the crone shouted after him. "We are three storeys high! What can you do? Leap across the canal? Even *you* are not that lucky!"

Chance wrenched open the balcony's doors and leapt up onto its railing. The rain had stopped, but the marble was still wet and slippery. His body pitched back and forth. His arms windmilled. Just as it looked as if he would surely fall, he managed to steady himself, balancing gingerly on his toes.

"The map. *Now*," the crone demanded. She had walked out onto the balcony and was only a few feet away from him. Her sisters joined her.

Chance glanced back at the Fates; then he somersaulted into the air. The crone gasped. She rushed to the railing, her sisters right behind her, expecting to see him drowning in the swirling waters below.

But he was not. He was lying on his back, cradled in the canopy of a gondola. The boat was rocking violently from side to side, but Chance was fine.

"Row, my fine fellow!" he called to the gondolier. The man obliged. The boat moved off.

Chance sat up, eyeing the Fates with a diamond-bright intensity. "You *must* accept my stakes now! You have no choice!" he shouted.

The gondola grew smaller and smaller as it made its way down the canal. A moment later, it rounded a bend and disappeared.

"This is a bad state of affairs," the crone said darkly. "We cannot have mortals making their own choices. When they do, disaster follows."

The maiden and the mother stepped back into the room. The crone trailed them. "Pack a trunk," she barked at a servant. "I'll need quills and inks . . ." Her hand hovered over the bottles upon the table. She selected a deep ebony. "*Fear*, yes. *Jealousy* will be useful, too," she said, reaching for a poisonous green.

"Where are you going?" the maiden asked.

"To the village of Saint-Michel," the crone replied.

"You will stop Chance from taking hold of the girl?" asked the mother.

The crone smiled grimly. "No, I cannot. But I will do what we Fates have always done. I will stop the girl from taking hold of a chance."

One

In the kitchen of a mansion, a girl sat clutching a knife.

Her name was Isabelle. She was not pretty.

She held the knife's blade over the flames of a fire burning in the hearth. Behind her, sprawled half-conscious in another chair, was her sister, Octavia.

Octavia's face was deathly pale. Her eyes were closed. The once-white stocking covering her right foot was crimson with blood. Adélie, the sisters' old nursemaid, peeled it off and gasped. Octavia's heel was gone. Blood dripped from the ugly wound where it used to be and pooled on the floor. Though she tried to hold it in, a moan of pain escaped her.

"Hush, Tavi!" Maman scolded. "The prince will hear you! Just because your chances are ruined doesn't mean your sister's must be."

Maman was the girls' mother. She was standing by the sink, rinsing blood out of a glass slipper.

The prince had come searching for the one who'd worn it. He'd danced all night with a beautiful girl at a masquerade ball three days ago and had fallen in love with her, but at the stroke of midnight, the girl had run away, leaving only a glass slipper behind. He would marry the girl who'd worn it, he'd vowed. Her and no other.

Maman was determined that one of her daughters would be that girl. She'd greeted the royal party in the foyer and requested that Isabelle and Octavia be allowed to try the slipper on in privacy, in deference to their maidenly modesty. The prince had agreed. The grand duke had held out a velvet pillow. Maman had carefully lifted the slipper off it and carried it into the kitchen. Her daughters had followed her.

"We should've heated the blade for Tavi," Maman fretted now. "Why didn't I think of it? Heat sears the vessels. It stops the bleeding. Ah, well. It will go better for you, Isabelle."

Isabelle swallowed. "But, Maman, how will I walk?" she asked in a small voice.

"Silly girl! You will *ride*. In a golden carriage. Servants will lift you in and out."

Flames licked the silver blade. It grew red. Isabelle's eyes grew large with fear. She thought of a stallion, lost to her now, that she had once loved.

"But, Maman, how will I gallop through the forest?"

"The time has come to put childish pursuits aside," Maman said, drying the slipper. "I've bankrupted myself trying to attract suitors for you and your sister. Pretty gowns and fine jewels cost a fortune. A girl's only hope in life is to make a good marriage, and there's no finer match than the prince of France."

"I can't do it," Isabelle whispered. "I *can't*."

Maman put the glass slipper down. She walked to the hearth and took Isabelle's face in her hands. "Listen to me, child, and listen well. Love is pain. Love is sacrifice. The sooner you learn that, the better."

Isabelle squeezed her eyes shut. She shook her head.

Maman released her. She was silent for a bit. When she finally spoke again, her voice was cold, but her words were scalding.

"You are ugly, Isabelle. Dull. Lumpy as a dumpling. I could not even convince the schoolmaster's knock-kneed clod of a son to marry you. Now a prince waits on the other side of the door—a *prince*, Isabelle—and all you have to do to make him yours is cut off a few toes. Just a few useless little toes . . ."

Maman wielded shame like an assassin wields a dagger, driving it straight into her victim's heart. She would win; she always won. Isabelle knew that. How many times had she cut away parts of herself at her mother's demand? The part that laughed too loudly. That rode too fast and jumped too high. The part that wished for a second helping, more gravy, a bigger slice of cake.

If I marry the prince, I will be a princess, Isabelle thought. *And one day, a queen. And no one will dare call me ugly ever again.*

She opened her eyes.

"Good girl. Be brave. Be quick," Maman said. "Cut at the joint."

Isabelle pulled the blade from the flames.

And tried to forget the rest.

13

Two

The little toe was the hardest.

Which didn't come as a surprise. It's often the small things that hurt the most—a cold glance, a cutting word, laughter that stops when you enter the room.

"Keep going," Maman urged. "Think of what we will gain—a prince for you, perhaps a duke for Tavi, a home for us all in the palace!"

Isabelle heard the desperation in her mother's voice. She knew that the dressmaker had cut off their credit and that the butcher had sent a boy to the house with an overdue bill. She tightened her grip on the knife and finished what she'd started.

The blinding pain, the smell of seared flesh, and the sight of her own toes lying on the hearth were so horrible that for a few seconds Isabelle was certain she would faint, but then Adélie was at her side with gentle hands and soothing words.

A wad of soft cotton was brought. A fresh white stocking. Brandy. And the glass slipper.

Maman handed it to her. "Put it on. Hurry," she said.

Isabelle took it. It was heavy in her hands and cold to the touch. As she slid her foot into it, pain bit into her, sharp-toothed and savage. It moved up her leg and through her body until she felt as if she were being eaten alive. The blood drained from her face. She closed her eyes and gripped the arms of her chair.

And yet, when Maman demanded that she get up, Isabelle did. She opened her eyes, took a deep breath, and stood.

Isabelle could do this impossible thing because she had a gift—a gift far more valuable than a pretty face or dainty feet.

Isabelle had a strong will.

She did not know that this was a good thing for a girl to have, because everyone had always told her it was a terrible thing. Everyone said a girl with a strong will would come to a bad end. Everyone said a girl's will must be bent to the wishes of those who know what's best for her.

Isabelle was young, only sixteen; she had not yet learned that Everyone is a fool.

Three

Each step was agony.

Halfway down the hallway that led from the kitchen to the foyer, Isabelle faltered. She heard a thin, rising wail. Had it come from her?

"It's Ella," Maman said darkly. "Hurry, Isabelle. We must finish this business. What if the prince hears her?"

Just before the prince had arrived, Isabelle had locked Ella in the attic. Ella had wept. She'd begged Isabelle to let her out. She wanted to see the prince. She wanted to try the glass slipper.

"Don't be ridiculous," Isabelle had told her. "You didn't even go the ball. You'd only embarrass us in your ragged dress."

It was a cruel thing to have done. She'd known it even as she'd turned the key in the lock, but it hadn't stopped her. Nothing stopped her anymore. *God in Heaven, what have I become?* she wondered, as she heard another wail.

Maman eyed her closely, so closely that Isabelle felt she could see inside her.

"Let her out, Isabelle. Do," she said. "The prince will take one look at her and fall head over heels in love, like every other man who sees her. Do you want to be kind or do you want the prince?"

Isabelle tried, but could not find an answer. The choices Maman gave her fit no better than the slipper did. An image flashed into her mind, a memory from long ago. She, Tavi, and Ella had been playing under the ancient linden tree that shaded the mansion.

A carriage had pulled into the yard. Two men, associates of Ella's father—Isabelle and Tavi's stepfather—had gotten out. Being genial, well-mannered men, they'd stopped to chat with the girls, but what happened next had changed everything.

Isabelle wished she could go back in time. She wished she could stop what had been put in motion that day, but she didn't know how.

And now it was too late.

Who set us against each other, Ella? she wondered. *Was it those men? Was it Maman? Or was it the whole heartless world?*

Four

"Keep your weight on your heel. That will help with the pain," Maman advised. "Come now. Hurry."

She pinched color into Isabelle's bloodless cheeks and together they continued down the hallway.

The prince, the grand duke, and the soldiers who'd accompanied them were all in the foyer, waiting for her. Isabelle knew she must not fail as her sister had.

Tavi had fooled everyone at first, but as she'd walked out of the house to the prince's carriage, her heel had bled so much that she'd left carmine footprints on the ground.

No one had noticed the bloody tracks in all the excitement, but as Tavi had neared the carriage, a white dove had flown out of the linden tree. The bird had landed on the prince's shoulder and had begun to sing.

Blood on the ground! Blood on the shoe!
This false, heartless girl is lying to you!

The prince had paled at the sight of so much blood. The grand duke, a rangy, wolfish-looking man, had become furious

18

when he'd learned that his sovereign had been tricked. He'd demanded that Maman return the glass slipper, but Maman had refused. She'd insisted that Isabelle had a right to try the slipper, too, for the prince had decreed that every maiden in the kingdom could do so.

"Are you ready?" Maman whispered to Isabelle now, as they approached the foyer.

Isabelle nodded, then walked out to greet the prince. She'd glimpsed him at the ball, but only from a distance, and when he'd arrived at the mansion, Maman had quickly ushered her into the kitchen.

Now, standing only a few feet away from him, she could see that his eyes were the blue of a summer sky, and that his blond hair—worn long and loose and tumbling over his shoulders—was shot through with streaks of pure gold. He was tall and broad-shouldered. His color was high.

Gazing at him, Isabelle forgot her wound, her pain, her own name. She was stunned speechless. He was that handsome.

The prince was silent, too. He was staring at Isabelle intently, his eyes taking in every plane and angle of her face.

"Ah, do you see that? He recognizes his own true love!" Maman purred.

Isabelle shrank at her mother's lie. Everyone at the ball had worn masks that covered the tops of their faces. She knew what the prince was doing—he was searching the curve of her lips, the line of her jaw, and the tilt of her chin for traces of the girl he'd fallen in love with.

But that girl wasn't there.

Five

Isabelle and the prince continued to stare at each other. Awkwardly. Silently. Until Maman took charge.

"Your Grace," she said, pulling Isabelle down into a curtsy with her. "My younger daughter is the one you are seeking. The glass slipper fits her perfectly."

"I hope you are certain of this, madame," the grand vizier cautioned. "The prince will not look kindly on a second attempt to deceive him."

Maman bowed her head. "Please forgive Octavia," she said to the prince. "She is not a dishonest girl. Her only fault is that she was overwhelmed by love for you. What girl wouldn't be?"

The prince blushed at that. The grand duke did not. "May we see the slipper?" he asked impatiently.

Isabelle and Maman rose. Dread knotted Isabelle's stomach as she lifted the hem of her dress. All eyes went to her foot. To her immense relief, there was no blood. The stocking was as white as snow and the cotton Adélie had stuffed into it filled out the toe. The glass slipper itself sparkled with blue light.

"It fits," said the prince dully.

The grand duke and the soldiers—every single one—bowed to Isabelle.

"Long live the princess!" a captain shouted.

"Long live the princess!" the rest of the company echoed.

Hats were tossed up into the air. Cheers rose, too. Isabelle turned in a slow circle, astonished. For once, the admiration was for her, not Ella. For once, she felt proud, powerful, wanted. Only moments ago, she hadn't been good enough for the schoolmaster's son; now she was going to be a princess.

"We must travel to the palace, mademoiselle," the prince said to her, with a stiff smile. "There are many arrangements to make for the wedding."

He bowed curtly, then headed for the door, and Isabelle saw that his strong shoulders sagged and that the light was gone from his beautiful eyes.

The prince loves someone else; he longs for her, Isabelle thought. *If I go through with this, I won't be gaining a husband, I'll be taking a prisoner.*

She felt sick, poisoned by a thing she thought she wanted. Just like the time when she was little and Adélie had made a batch of tiny cherry cakes and left them to cool and she'd eaten every single one.

She turned to her mother, ready to say, "This is wrong," but as she did, she saw that Maman was beaming at her. For a few precious seconds, Isabelle basked in the warmth of her mother's smile. She so rarely saw it.

"I'm proud of you, child," Maman said. "You've saved us from ruin. I shall sell this gloomy house, pay off our debts, and never look back."

Isabelle's protests died in her throat. It was a terrible thing to break the prince's heart, but it was a worse thing to break her mother's. She did not, for even a second, consider what her own heart wanted, for a girl's desires were of no consequence.

Maman took Isabelle's arm and walked her out to the stone steps that swept from the mansion's front door down to its gravel drive. Isabelle could see a golden carriage drawn by eight white horses. The prince and the grand duke stood by it, waiting for her, deep in conversation.

Furrows marred the prince's brow. Worry clouded his eyes. Isabelle knew, as did everyone else, that his father was gravely ill and that a foreign duke, Volkmar von Bruch, had scented the old king's death and had brutally attacked villages along his realm's northern border.

Maman embraced Isabelle, promising that she and Tavi would follow her to the palace as soon as they could. And then, in a daze, Isabelle started for the carriage, but stepping down required that she put her full weight on her damaged foot. Halfway down the steps, the seared veins opened. She could feel blood, wet and warm, seeping into her stocking. By the time she reached the bottom step, it was soaked.

High above her, in the branches of the linden tree, the leaves began to rustle.

Six

The carriage was only ten steps away. Then seven. Then five.

A soldier opened the door for her. Isabelle kept her gaze trained straight ahead. The prince and the grand duke, still deep in conversation, weren't even looking at her. She would make it. She was almost there. Just a few steps. Three more . . . two . . . one . . .

That's when she heard it—the flapping of wings.

A white dove swooped down out of the linden tree and circled her. Maman, who'd been watching from the doorway, ran down and frantically tried to swat it away, but the wary bird kept itself above her reach. As it flew around Isabelle, it began to sing.

Blood on the ground! Blood in the shoe!
This is a girl neither honest nor true!

The prince stopped talking. He looked at the dove, then at Isabelle. His eyes traveled to the hem of her dress, which was stained with blood, then to the dark tracks she'd left in the dirt.

Isabelle slid her foot out of the glass slipper and took a step back from it. It toppled over, spilling more blood on the ground. The front of her stocking was bright red. Shame flooded through her.

"You cut off your own toes," the prince said, shaking his head in disbelief.

Isabelle nodded, frightened now as well as ashamed. She'd deceived him. God only knew what he would do to her. She'd heard grisly stories about palace dungeons, and heads stuck on pikes. Was that to be her fate?

But the prince didn't order his soldiers to seize her. There was no anger on his face, only sadness. And something else, something Isabelle had not expected to see—kindness.

"How did you stand the pain?" he asked.

Isabelle looked at the ground. Maman's words, spoken earlier in the kitchen came back to her.

Ugly . . . dull . . . lumpy as a dumpling . . .

"I've had a lot of practice," she replied.

The prince frowned. "I don't understand."

Isabelle lifted her head. She looked at his heartbreakingly handsome face. "No," she said. "You don't."

The grand duke joined them, fury sparking in his eyes. "I know battle-hardened soldiers who could not do what you did, mademoiselle," he said to Isabelle. Then he turned to the prince. "A girl capable of such an act is capable of anything, sire. She is unnatural. Unhinged. Dangerous." He motioned at a pair of soldiers. "Seize her."

Isabelle's heart lurched with terror as the two men started towards her, but the prince stopped them.

"Leave her," he ordered, waving them away.

"But, Your Grace, surely you will not allow a second deception to go unpunished," said the grand duke. "One is bad enough, but two—"

"I said *leave her*. She has crippled herself. What more could I do to her?"

The grand duke gave him a clipped nod. Then he addressed Maman. "I don't suppose you have any other daughters eager to cut off bits of themselves in order to marry the prince?"

"No," Maman said bitterly. "I have no other daughters."

"Then we shall be going," said the grand duke. "Good day, madame."

A fountain burbled in the centre of the drive. As the prince climbed into the carriage, the grand duke, who was still holding the velvet cushion, ordered a soldier to rinse the glass slipper off in the water. The soldier did, then placed it back on the cushion. Maman stood watching them, rigid with anger.

Isabelle, light-headed from her ordeal, sat down on a bench under the linden tree. She closed her eyes, trying to make her head stop spinning. She was dimly aware of the horses stamping, impatient to be off. Of bugs whirring in the afternoon heat. Of the dove, now cooing high above her in the branches.

But then a new sound rose above these others—urgent and piercing. "Wait! Don't go! Please, please, wait!"

It was a girl's voice. It was coming from the mansion. She was shouting. Pleading.

Isabelle opened her eyes.

The girl was running down the steps. Her hair was wild. Her dress was little more than rags. Her face and hands were streaked with soot. Her feet were bare.

But even so, she was astonishingly, achingly, breathtakingly beautiful.

It was Ella.

Isabelle's stepsister.

Seven

The grand duke gave Maman a deadly look.

"Is this another of your tricks, madame? Sending out a filthy serving wench to try the slipper?" he asked indignantly.

Maman's eyes narrowed as she regarded her stepdaughter. "Ella, how dare you!" she shouted. "Go back inside this instant!"

But Ella didn't even hear her. Her eyes were on the prince, and the prince's eyes were on her. He was already out of the carriage, hurrying towards her.

Watching them, Isabelle saw something she had never seen before. Not between her mother and stepfather, or her mother and father. It was raw and overwhelming. Powerful, deep, and true. It was love.

As Isabelle saw this love, intangible yet so real, she realized that Ella was the one the prince had danced with at the ball, that she was the one he longed for.

Envy's fine, sharp teeth sank deep into Isabelle's heart. Maman had done everything in her power to prevent Ella from going to the ball, yet Ella had found a way. Somehow, this girl who had nothing, had procured a coach and horses, a sparkling gown, and a pair of glass slippers. *How?* Isabelle wondered.

The prince and Ella stopped inches from one another. Gently, the prince touched Ella's face. His fingers traced the line of her jaw.

"It's you," he said. "I finally found you. Why did you run away?"

"Because I feared that once you discovered who I really was—just a common girl from the country—you would no longer love me," Ella replied.

"There's nothing common about you, Ella," the prince said, taking her hands in his. He turned to the grand vizier. "Bring the glass slipper," he commanded.

But to Isabelle's surprise—and everyone else's—the grand duke didn't budge. His lips were set in a hard line. Contempt darkened his flinty eyes.

"Your Grace, this girl is a *servant*," he said. "She wasn't at the ball. The guards would *never* let anyone dressed in rags into the palace. Why, the very idea—"

The prince cut him off. "The slipper. *Now.*"

The grand duke bowed stiffly. He walked towards the prince and Ella holding the velvet cushion out in front of him. When he was only a few yards away from them, the toe of his shiny black boot caught on something—a rock, he would later say—and he stumbled.

The glass slipper slid off the velvet cushion. It hit the ground. And smashed into a thousand glittering pieces.

Eight

The prince cried out in anguish.

The grand duke apologized, hand to his heart.

The soldiers shifted nervously, their swords clanking at their hips.

Maman laughed. Isabelle gasped. Only Ella was calm. It soon became clear why.

"It's all right. I have the other one right here," she said, smiling.

As everyone watched, she pulled a second glass slipper from her skirt pocket. She placed it on the ground and lifted her ragged hem. As she slid her small foot inside it, the blue light flared, and the slipper sparkled as if it were made of diamonds.

It fitted perfectly.

The prince laughed joyously. He swept Ella into his arms and kissed her, not caring who saw. The soldiers cheered once more. The grand duke wiped sweat from his brow. Maman turned away, hands clenched, and walked into the house.

Isabelle took it all in, wishing as she had a million times before that she was beautiful. That she was valued. That she mattered.

"Ella won," said a voice from behind her.

It was Tavi. She'd limped out of the mansion and was leaning on the back of the bench, holding her injured foot off the ground. She walked around to the front and sat down.

"Pretty always wins," said Isabelle bitterly.

As the two sisters were talking, a third person joined them—Ella.

Tavi gave her an acid smile. "How perfect," she said. "Here we are again. All three of us. Under the linden tree."

Ella barely heard her. She was staring at Isabelle's and Tavi's feet with a look of such deep sadness, it almost seemed like grief. "What have you done?" she asked, tears welling in her eyes.

"Don't you dare cry for us, Ella," Tavi said vehemently. "Don't you *dare*. You don't get to. You got what you deserved and so did we."

Ella raised her eyes to Tavi's. "Did we? Did I deserve your cruelty? Did you deserve these injuries? Is that what we deserved?"

Tavi looked away. Then, with difficulty, she stood. "Go, Ella. Leave this place. Don't come back."

Ella, her tears spilling over, watched as Tavi limped towards the mansion. Then she turned to her other stepsister. "Do you hate me so much, Isabelle? Still?"

Isabelle couldn't answer her; it felt as if her mouth was filled with salt. The memory she'd pushed down earlier surfaced now. She was nine years old again. Ella and Tavi were ten. Maman had been married to Ella's father for a year.

They were all together, under the linden tree.

Sisters.
Stepsisters.
Friends.

Nine

It was a summer afternoon.

The sky was blue; the sun was bright.

Roses tumbled over the stone walls surrounding the mansion. Birds sang in the spreading branches of the linden tree, and under them the three girls played. Ella fashioned daisy chains and made up stories about Tanaquill, the fairy queen, who lived in the hollow of the tree. Tavi did equations on a slate with a piece of chalk. And Isabelle fenced with an old mop handle, pretending to defend her sisters from Blackbeard.

"Time to die, pirate scum! *En garde!*" she shouted, advancing on Bertrand the rooster, who'd wandered close to the tree. She much preferred Felix, the groom's son, as a dueling partner, but he was busy with a new foal.

The rooster pulled himself up to his full height. He flapped his wings, crowed loudly, and attacked. He chased Isabelle around the tree, then she chased him, and on and on they went, until an exasperated Tavi shouted, "For goodness' sake, Izzy! Can't you *ever* be quiet?"

Unable to shake the rooster, Isabelle climbed up into the linden tree, hoping he would lose interest. Just as she'd seated herself on a branch, a carriage pulled into the drive. The rooster took one look at it and ran off. Two men got out of it. One was gray-haired and stooped. He carried a walking stick and a pink silk box with flowers painted on it. The younger had a leather satchel. Isabelle didn't recognize them, but that was not unusual. Men often traveled from Paris to see her stepfather. Most were merchants, like he was, and came to discuss business.

The men didn't see Isabelle, or Ella, who was well in under the canopy of branches, only Tavi, who was sitting on the bench.

"What are you doing there, little girl? Practicing your letters?" asked the older gentleman.

"Trying to prove Euclid's fifth postulate," Octavia replied, her brow furrowed. She did not look up from her slate.

The old man chuckled. He elbowed his companion. "My word, it appears we have a scholar here!" he said. Then he addressed Tavi again. "Now, listen to me, my little duck, you mustn't trouble yourself with algebra."

"It's geometry, actually."

The old man scowled at being corrected. "Yes, well, whatever it is, the feminine mind was not made for it," he cautioned. "You'll tax your brain. Give yourself headaches. And headaches cause wrinkles, you know."

Tavi looked up. "Is that how it works? Then how did you get your wrinkles? I can't imagine you tax *your* brain very much."

"Well, I never . . . Not in all my days . . . What a rude girl!" the old man sputtered, shaking his walking stick at her.

That was when Ella stepped forward. "Tavi didn't mean to be rude, sir . . ."

"Yes, I did," said Tavi, under her breath.

". . . it's just that Euclid vexes her," Ella finished.

The old man stopped spluttering. He smiled. Ella had that effect on people.

"What a pretty girl you are. So sweet and pleasant," he said. "I shall ask your papa to marry you to my grandson. Then you'll have a wealthy husband and live in a fine house and wear lovely dresses. Would you like that?"

Ella hesitated, then said, "Might I have a little dog instead?"

The two men burst into laughter. The younger chucked Ella under the chin. The elder patted her blond curls, called her a *pretty rose*, and gave her a bonbon from the pink box he'd brought for Maman. Ella smiled and thanked him and eagerly ate the sweet.

Isabelle, still up in the tree, watched the exchange longingly. She dearly loved bonbons. Mop handle in hand, she jumped down, startling the old man. He yelped, stumbled backward, and fell.

"What the devil are you doing with that stick?" he shouted at her, red-faced.

"Fighting Blackbeard," Isabelle replied as the younger man helped him up.

"You almost killed me!"

Isabelle gave him a skeptical look. "I fall all the time. Out of trees. Off horses. Even out of the hayloft once. And it hasn't killed *me*," she said. "Might I please have a bonbon, too?"

"Certainly not!" the old man said, brushing himself off. "Why would I give such a nice treat to such a nasty little monkey with grubby hands and leaves in her hair?"

34

He picked up the pink box and his walking stick, and headed for the mansion, muttering to his companion the whole way. His voice was low, but Isabelle—who still had hopes of a bonbon—followed them and could hear him.

"The one is a charming little beauty and will make a splendid wife one day, but the other two . . ." He shook his head ominously. "Well, I suppose they can always become nuns or governesses or whatever it is that ugly girls do."

Isabelle stopped dead. Her hand came up to her chest. There was a pain in her heart, new and strange. Only moments ago, she'd been happily slaying pirates, completely unaware that she was lacking. That she was less than. That she was a *nasty little monkey*, not a *pretty rose*.

For the first time, she understood that Ella was pretty and she was not.

Isabelle was strong. She was brave. She beat Felix at sword fights. She jumped her stallion, Ne, over fences everyone else was afraid of. She'd chased a wolf away from the henhouse once with only a stick.

These things are good, too, she'd thought as she stood there, bewildered and bereft. *They are, aren't they? I am, aren't I?*

That was the day everything changed between the three girls.

They were only children. Ella had been given a sweet and had preened under all the attention. Isabelle was jealous; she couldn't help it. She wanted a sweet, too. She wanted kind words and admiring glances.

Sometimes it's easier to say that you hate what you can't have rather than admit how badly you want it. And so Isabelle, still standing under the linden tree, said she hated Ella.

And Ella said she hated her back.

And Tavi said she hated everyone.

And Maman stood on the terrace listening, a dangerous new light in her hard, watchful eyes.

Ten

"Isabelle, I'm leaving now. I—I don't know if I'll ever see you again."

Ella's voice pulled Isabelle back from her memories. She leaned down and kissed Isabelle's forehead, her lips like a hot brand against Isabelle's skin.

"Don't hate me anymore, stepsister," she whispered. "For your own sake, not mine."

And then she was gone and Isabelle was alone on the bench.

She thought about the person she once was, and the person she'd become. She thought about all the things she'd been told to want, the things she'd crippled herself to get, the important things. Ella had them now and she had nothing. Jealousy burned in her, as it had for years.

Isabelle looked to her left and saw Tavi struggle up the steps to the mansion, limp across the threshold, and close the door. She looked to her right and saw the prince hand Ella up into the carriage. He climbed in behind her, and then he, too, closed the door.

The grand duke swung himself up next to the driver. He shouted a command at the soldiers ahead of him, all atop their horses now, and they started off. The driver cracked his whip, and the eight white stallions lurched forward in their harnesses.

Isabelle watched the carriage as it rolled out of the long drive, headed down the narrow country road, and crested a hill. A moment later, it was gone.

She remained where she was for quite some time, until the day grew cool and the sun began to set. Until birds flew to their roosts and a green-eyed fox loped off to the woods to hunt. Then she rose and whispered to the lengthening shadows, "It's not you I hate, Ella. It never was. It's me."

Eleven

"Hand over the eyeball, Nelson. *Now*."

A lively little black monkey, his face ruffed with white, scampered across the ship's deck. In one paw he clutched a glass eye.

"Nelson, I'm *warning* you . . ."

The man speaking—tall, well-dressed, his amber eyes flashing—cut a commanding figure, but the monkey paid him no attention. Instead of surrendering his treasure, he climbed up the foremast and jumped into the rigging.

The ship's bosun—one hand covering an empty eye socket—lumbered after the creature, bellowing for his pistol.

"No firearms, please!" cried a woman in a red silk gown. "You must *coax* him down. He responds best to opera."

"I'll coax him down, all right," growled the bosun. "With a bullet!"

Horrified, the diva pressed a hand to her ample bosom, then launched into "Lascia ch'io pianga," a heroine's aria of sorrow and defiance. The monkey cocked his head. He blinked his eyes. But he did not budge.

The diva's gorgeous voice, flowing over the ship's deck down to the docks, drew dozens of onlookers. The ship, a clipper named *Adventure*, had made the port of Marseille only moments ago after three weeks at sea.

As she continued to sing, another member of the amber-eyed man's entourage—a fortune-teller—hastily consulted her tarot cards. One by one, she slapped them down on the deck. When she finished, her face was as white as the sails.

"Nelson, come down!" she shouted. "This does not end well!"

A magician conjured a banana, tossed the peel over her shoulder, and waved the fruit in the air. An actress called to the monkey beseechingly. And then a cabin boy ran up from below decks, brandishing the bosun's pistol. The diva saw it; her voice shot up three octaves.

As the bosun took his gun and cocked it, a group of acrobats, all in spangly costumes, cartwheeled across the deck and launched themselves into the rigging. The monkey raced up the mast to the crow's nest. The bosun aimed, but as he did, a fire-breather spewed flames in his direction. The bosun stumbled backward, stepped on the banana peel, and lost his balance. He fell, hit his head on the deck, and knocked himself out. The gun went off. The shot went wide. And so did the flames.

Their orange tongues licked the lower edge of the rigging, igniting it with a whoosh, then rapidly climbed upward, devouring the tarry ropes. Terrified, the monkey flung himself from the crow's nest to the foremast. The acrobats leapt after him one by one like shooting stars.

As the last acrobat landed, a flaming drop of tar fell onto the fuse of a cannon that had been primed and at the ready in case of a pirate attack. The fuse caught; the cannon fired. The heavy iron ball whistled across the harbor and blasted a hole in a fishing boat. Shouting and swearing, the fishermen jumped into the water and swam madly for the shore.

Certain the *Adventure* was under attack, six musicians in lavender frock coats and powdered wigs took their instruments from their cases and began to play a dirge. They were nearly drowned out a moment later by the city's fire brigade, clanging down the street in a horse-drawn wagon.

The diva, at the end of her aria now, hit a high note. The fire brigade, pumping madly from the dock, shot fountains of water into the rigging, putting out the flames and dousing her and everyone else on deck. And still the diva sang, arms outstretched, chin raised, holding her note. The crowd on the dock erupted into thunderous applause. Hats were tossed high into the air. Men wept. Women fainted. And in the captain's cabin, every window shattered.

The diva finished. Sopping wet, she walked to the ship's railing and curtsied. Choruses of *Brava!* rang out.

The monkey scrambled down the foremast and jumped into the arms of his master. The amber-eyed man extricated the eyeball from the creature's grasp, polished it on his lapel, then gingerly put it back where it belonged. He had no idea whether it was right side up or upside down and the bosun, still unconscious, couldn't tell him.

The captain emerged from his cabin, brushing glass off his sleeves. He stood on the deck, clasped his hands behind his back, and surveyed the scene before him.

"Mr. Fleming!" he barked at the first mate.

"Sir!" the first mate barked back, snapping a salute.

"Who is responsible for this? Please do not tell me that it's—"

"The Marquis de la Chance, sir," the first mate said. "Who else?"

Twelve

Captain Duval was furious.

And Chance was doing his best to look sorry. It was something he was quite good at, for he'd had a lot of practice.

"What about the rigging you burned, the windows you broke, and the fishing boat you destroyed?" the captain thundered. "It will cost a fortune to replace it all!"

"Then it will be a fortune well spent!" Chance said, flashing his most charming smile. "I don't believe I've ever heard a more exquisite rendition of 'Lascia ch'io pianga' in my entire life."

"That is not the point, sir!"

"Pleasure is always the point, sir!" Chance countered. "It's not burned rigging and broken windows you'll remember on your deathbed, but the sight of a drenched diva, her gown clinging to every large and luscious curve, her magnificent voice soaring as the cannon fires and the flames climb. Let the bean counters count their beans, sir. You and I shall count moments of wonderment, moments of joy!"

The captain, having endured many such speeches during the voyage, pinched the bridge of his nose. "Tell me, Marquis. How did the monkey come to have the eye in the first place?"

"A bet was made on a hand of cards. I wagered the bosun five ducats against his glass eye. The foolish man took the eye out and placed it atop the coins. I ask you, Captain, have you ever met a monkey who could resist a glass eyeball?"

The captain gestured at Nelson, sitting atop Chance's shoulder. "Perhaps I should ask the monkey to pay for the damages?"

Chance reached into his satchel, lying on the deck by his feet, and pulled out a fat leather purse. "Will this cover it?" he asked, dropping it into the captain's hand.

The captain opened the purse, counted the coins inside it, and nodded. "The gangplank will be lowered shortly," he said. "The next time you decide to take a sea voyage, Marquis, please take it on someone else's ship."

But Chance wasn't listening. He'd already turned away to check that all the members of his retinue were above decks. Each and every person was needed. He was bound for the country. There were no opera houses there. No grand theaters or concert halls. Why, there were hardly any coffee houses, and very few patisseries, bookshops, or restaurants. He would not survive five minutes without his musicians, his acrobats and actors, his diva, ballerinas, magician, fortune-teller, fire-breather, sword-swallower, scientist, and cook.

"Wait! The cook is missing!" Chance exclaimed as he completed his head count. He looked at Nelson. "Where is he?"

The monkey pressed his paws over his mouth and puffed out his cheeks.

"Not again," Chance muttered.

A moment later, a short, bald man in a long black leather

coat with a red kerchief tied around his neck staggered up from the aft deck. He was rumpled and bleary-eyed. His face was as gray as week-old porridge.

"Seasickness," he said, as he joined Chance.

"Seasickness, eh? Is that how one says 'I drank too much gin last night' in French?" Chance asked, arching an eyebrow.

The cook winced. "Do you have to be so loud?" He leaned his head on the gunwale. "Why the devil are they taking so long with the gangplank? Where are we going anyway? Tell me it's Paris."

"I'm afraid not. Saint-Michel."

"Never heard of it."

"It's in the country."

"I hate the country. Why are we going there?"

Chance's hands tightened on the gunwale. He thought of the girl's map. Isabelle, her name was. He pictured the end of her path. The splotches of red. The violent lines etched into the parchment, as if a madman had made them.

And then he remembered that a madman had.

"It can be changed, her path," he whispered. "I can change it. I *will* change it."

"What path?" the cook asked. "What are you talking about? Why are you . . ."

His words trailed off. Something down below them had caught his attention. Chance saw it, too.

A swift black carriage was making its way up the bustling street that ran alongside the docks. A face was framed in its window—a woman's face, pale and wizened. She must've sensed that she was being watched, for she suddenly looked up. Her gray eyes found Chance's and held them. In her merciless gaze, he saw that no quarter would be asked in this fight and none given.

The cook took a deep breath, then blew it out again. "She's the reason we're here, isn't she?" he asked.

Chance nodded.

"That is *not* good. She's the worst of the three, and that's saying something. Why has she come? Why have we? Are you ever going to tell me?"

"To do battle," Chance replied.

"For what this time? Gold? Glory? Your pride?" There was a cutting tone to his voice.

Chance watched Fate's carriage round a corner and disappear, and then he replied, "For a soul. A girl's soul."

The cook nodded. "You should have said so. That's a thing worth fighting for."

The bleary look had left his face; a determined one had taken its place. He put his forefingers in his mouth and blew an earsplitting whistle. Then he strode off, bellowing at a hapless sailor, demanding that the man get the blasted gangplank down. The magician, the acrobats, and the rest of Chance's entourage, all milling about on deck, gathered their things and hurried after him.

Chance picked up his satchel, slung it over his shoulder, and followed his cook. If he had any hope of winning this fight, he needed to stay one step ahead of Fate, and already he was ten steps behind her.

Thirteen

Isabelle, sweaty, dirty, and bruised, leaned forward in her saddle and addressed her horse.

"Maman tried to sell you, Martin. Did you know that? To the slaughterhouse, where they'd boil your bones down for glue. I'm the one who stopped her. Maybe you should think about that."

Old, slow, and bad-tempered, Martin was also swaybacked, splay-toed, and nippy, but he was all Isabelle had.

"Come *on*," she urged him. She pressed her heels into his flanks, trying to get him to trot around the barnyard. But Martin had other ideas. He heaved himself into a sulky canter, then stopped short—sending her tumbling out of her saddle. She hit the ground hard, rolled onto her back, and lay in the dirt groaning.

It was the third time Martin had thrown her that morning. Isabelle was a skilled rider, but everything was different now. She couldn't get her weight right in her stirrups. There was no purchase where the toes of her right foot should've gripped the tread. Unable to balance properly, she had difficulty correcting when Martin reared, bucked, or simply stopped dead.

The falls didn't discourage her, though. She didn't care about the dirt in her face, the bruises, the pain. They kept her from remembering that Ella was gone. That Ella had won. That Ella had everything now and she had nothing.

She was still lying on the ground, staring up at the clouds scudding across the sky, when a face leaned over her, blocking them out.

"How many times have you fallen today?" Tavi asked. She didn't wait for an answer. "You'll kill yourself."

"If I'm lucky."

"Stop this. You can't ride anymore."

Fear pooled in Isabelle's belly at the very thought. It wasn't true. She wouldn't let it be true. Riding was all she had left. It was the only thing that had kept her going as her foot healed. As she got used to hobbling instead of walking. As the servants left. As Maman closed the shutters and locked the doors. As the weeds grew over the stone walls.

"Why are you here?" she asked Tavi. Her sister preferred to stay inside with her books and equations.

"To tell you that we have to go to the market. We can't put it off any longer."

Isabelle blinked at her. "That's not a good idea."

Word had spread. About the glass slipper and what they'd done to themselves to fit into it. About Ella and how they'd treated her. Children threw mud at their house. A man had pitched a rock through one of their windows. Isabelle knew they would only be inviting more trouble if they went to the village.

"Do you have a better one?" asked Tavi. "We need cheese. Ham. Butter. We haven't tasted bread in weeks."

Isabelle sighed. She stood up and brushed herself off. "We'll have to take the cart," she said. "We can't walk. Not with our—"

"Fine. Hitch up Martin. I'll gather some baskets," Tavi said brusquely, starting for the kitchen. She didn't like talking about their injuries. Ella. Any of it.

"Fine," Isabelle said, limping over to her horse.

She hadn't got used to her slow, lurching gait. Tavi's injury was not as severe. After it had healed, her stride had returned to normal. Isabelle doubted hers ever would.

"And, Izzy . . ."

Isabelle turned around. Tavi was frowning.

"What?"

"Behave. In the village. Do you think you can?"

Isabelle waved Tavi's question away and picked up Martin's reins. But the truth was, she had no idea if she could. She'd tried to behave. For years. In drawing rooms and ballrooms, at garden parties and dinners. With her hands knotted and her jaw clenched, she'd tried to be all the things Maman told her to be: pleasant, sweet, considerate, kind, demure, gentle, patient, agreeable, and self-effacing.

Occasionally it worked. For a day or two. But then something always happened.

Like the time, at a fancy dinner Maman had hosted, a cadet back from his first year at the military academy said that the Second Punic War ended after Scipio defeated Hannibal at the Battle of Cannae, when any fool knew it was the Battle of Zama. Isabelle had corrected him, and he'd laughed, saying she didn't know what she was talking about. After she got her favorite book—*An Illustrated History of the World's Greatest Military Commanders*—from her library and proved that she did, in fact, know what she was talking about, he'd called her an unpleasant name. Under his breath. Furious, she'd called him one back. Not under her breath.

Maman hadn't spoken to her for a week.

And then there was the time she'd attended a ball at a baroness's château, got bored with the dancing, and decided to take a walk. She never meant to get into a duel with the baron, but he'd found her admiring a pair of sabers mounted on a wall in the foyer and offered to show her his moves. She'd shown him hers, too, slicing several buttons off his jacket and nicking his chin in the process.

That time, Maman had given her the silent treatment for a month.

Her mother had said her behavior was atrocious, but Isabelle didn't think cutting off a baron's buttons was all that bad. She knew she was capable of worse. Much worse.

Just a few months ago, she'd been searching in her wardrobe for the pink parasol Maman insisted that she carry—*Pink enhances the complexion, Isabelle!*—and a pair of horrible silk slippers—*Too bad if they pinch, they make your feet look small!*—and had found a book on Alexander the Great that she'd hidden to keep Maman from taking it away.

She'd sat down on the floor of her bedchamber, rumpling her fussy dress, and had eagerly opened it. It was a relic from a happier time, a time before she'd been made to understand that warriors and generals were men, and that showing an interest in swords and warhorses and battlefield strategies was

50

unbecoming in a girl. As Isabelle had turned the book's pages, she'd found herself once again fighting alongside Alexander as he battled his way through Egypt. Tears of longing had welled in her eyes as she'd read.

Just as she'd been wiping them away, Ella had walked into the room carrying a silver tray. On it she'd placed a cup of hot chocolate and a plate of madeleines.

"I heard Maman shouting at you about the parasol and the slippers. I thought this might help," she'd said, setting the tray down next to Isabelle.

It had been a kind thing to do. But Ella's kindnesses only ever made Isabelle angry.

She'd looked at her stepsister, who had no need of parasols and pinchy shoes. Who looked like a goddess in a patched dress and an old pair of boots. She looked down at herself, awkward and gauche in the ridiculous gown, and then she'd picked up the cup of hot chocolate and hurled it at the wall. The madeleines had followed it. The silver tray, too.

"Clean it up," she'd ordered, a nasty glint in her eyes.

"Isabelle, why are you so upset?" Ella had asked.

Seething, her hands clenched, Isabelle said, "Stop, Ella. Stop being nice to me. Just *stop*!"

"I'm sorry," Ella had said meekly as she'd bent down to pick up the broken pieces.

That meekness should have mollified Isabelle, but it had only fueled her anger.

"You're pathetic!" she'd shouted. "Why don't you ever stick up for yourself? You let Maman bully you! You're kind to me and Tavi even though we're horrible to you! *Why*, Ella?"

51

Ella had carefully put the shards of porcelain on the tray. "To try to undo all of this. To make things better," she'd replied softly.

"You *can't* make things better. Not unless you can change me into you!"

Ella had looked up, stricken. "Don't say that. Don't ever change into me. *Ever.*"

Isabelle had stopped shouting, struck silent for a moment by the vehemence of Ella's words. And then Maman's footsteps had been heard in the hallway, and it had been all Isabelle could do to hide her book and grab her parasol before her mother was in the room, shouting at her to hurry up. They'd left for a garden party minutes later, one so mind-numbingly dull that Isabelle had forgotten her intention to press Ella for an answer. And now it was too late.

Martin, tired of standing still, nipped Isabelle's arm sharply, dispelling her painful memories.

"You're not much good at behaving, either, are you, old man?" she said to him.

She led the horse into the cool stone stables and removed his tack. She didn't need to tie him. Martin was a horse of few ambitions and running off was not one of them. Before putting his harness on, she gave him a quick brushing. It wasn't necessary; he hadn't been worked very hard, but Isabelle craved the feel of him under her hands, the velvet of his nose against her cheek, his gusty, grassy breath.

When she finished, she led him to the cart. As they walked through the stables, Isabelle glanced at the empty stalls. The pair of graceful Arabians that had pulled the carriage, and the huge Percherons who'd worked the fields, were gone, sold off after the groom left.

Though she tried not to, Isabelle couldn't help looking at the very last stall. It brought memories, too. The horse that had lived in it had also been sold. Years ago. Nero. A black stallion seventeen hands high, with onyx eyes and a mane like rippling silk. Riding him was like riding a storm. She could still feel his strength as he stamped and danced underneath her, impatient to be off.

She could feel Felix, too. He was sitting behind her, his arms around her waist, his lips by her ear, his eyes on the stone wall ahead of them. He was laughing, and in his laugh was a dare.

"Don't, Isabelle!" Ella had called out. "It's too dangerous!"

But Isabelle hadn't listened. She'd touched her heels to Nero's sides, and an instant later, they were galloping straight at the wall. Ella had covered her eyes with her hands. Isabelle had leaned forward in her saddle, her chest over Nero's neck, her hands high up in his mane, Felix leaning with her. She'd felt every muscle in the stallion's body tense, and then she'd felt what it was like to fly. She and Felix had whooped as they landed, then they'd streaked across the meadow and into the Wildwood, leaving Ella behind.

As quickly as they'd come, the images faded and all that was left was an empty stall with cobwebs in the corners.

Nero was gone. Felix, too. Taken away by Maman like so many other things—her leather breeches, her pirate's hat, the shiny rocks and animal skulls and bird nests she'd collected. Her wooden sword. Her books. One by one they'd all disappeared, each loss like the swipe of a carver's knife. Whittling her down.

Smoothing her edges. Making her more like the girl Maman wanted her to be.

Isabelle had cut off her toes, but sometimes she could still feel them.

Maman had cut out her heart.

Sometimes, she could still feel that, too.

Fourteen

"Six *sous*," the baker's wife said, her meaty arms crossed over her huge, freckled bosom.

"Six?" Isabelle echoed, confused. "But the sign says three." She pointed to a slate on the baker's stall with a price marked on it in chalk.

The woman spat on her palm, rubbed the 3 away and wrote 6 in its place. "For you, six," she said insolently.

"But that's double the price. It's not fair!" Isabelle protested.

"Neither is treating your stepsister like a slave," said the woman. "Don't deny it. You were cruel to a defenseless girl. Got your comeuppance, though, didn't you? Ella is queen now and more beautiful than ever. And you? You're nothing more than her ugly stepsister."

Isabelle lowered her head, her cheeks flaming. She and Tavi had only just arrived at the market and already the taunts were starting.

Taking a deep, steadying breath, she remembered her sister's directive: *Behave*. She counted out coins from her pocket and handed them over. The baker's wife gave her an undersized loaf, burned on the bottom, and a sneering smile to go with it.

"Serves her right," said a woman standing in line.

"Burned bread's too good for her," sniffed another.

The women stood there, nodding and pointing and making remarks, basting themselves in righteousness like geese on a spit, when just yesterday the first had slapped her small daughter so hard for spilling milk that the child's cheek still bore a welt, and the second had kissed her sister's husband behind the tavern.

No one jeers louder at a hanging than the cutthroat who got away.

"I hope you choke on it," said the baker's wife as Isabelle fumbled the loaf into her basket.

Isabelle felt anger kindle inside her. Harsh words rose in her throat, but she bit them back.

"I hope your ugly sister chokes, too."

At the mention of her sister—Tavi, who'd grown thin since Ella had left, who rarely smiled and barely ate—Isabelle's smoldering temper ignited.

The centrepiece of the baker's display was a carefully constructed pyramid of shiny brown rolls. Isabelle cocked her arm back and smacked the top off. A dozen rolls tumbled off the table and landed in the muddy street.

"Choke on *that*," she said to the spluttering baker's wife and her squawking customers.

The look on the woman's face, her shriek of outrage, her dismay—they all felt good, for a moment. *I won*, Isabelle thought. But as she limped away from the stall, she realized, with a sick, sinking feeling, that she hadn't won. Her anger had. Once again.

Ella would not have done that, she thought. *Ella would have disarmed them all with a sweet smile and soft words.*

Ella was never angry. Not when she'd had to cook and clean for them. Or eat her meals alone in the kitchen. Not even when Maman wouldn't let her go to the ball.

Ella had had a cold room in the attic and a hard bed; Isabelle and Tavi had blazing fires in their bedchambers and feather mattresses. Ella had had only a tattered dress to wear, while Isabelle and Tavi had dozens of pretty gowns. Yet day after day, it was Ella who sang, Ella who smiled. Not Isabelle. Not Tavi.

"Why?" Isabelle asked herself, desperate for an answer, certain that if she could get it, she could learn to be good and kind, too. But no answer came, only a pain, deep and gnawing, on the left side of her chest.

Had Isabelle asked the old wives of Saint-Michel, all sitting by the fountain in the village square, they could have told her what caused it. For the old wives have a saying: *Never is a wolf more dangerous than when he's in a cage.*

At the edge of Saint-Michel is the Wildwood. The wolves who live there come out at night. They prowl fields and farms, hungry for hens and tender young lambs. But there is another sort of wolf, one that's far more treacherous. This is the wolf the old ones speak of.

"Run if you see him," they tell their granddaughters. "His tongue is silver, but his teeth are sharp. If he gets hold of you, he'll eat you alive."

Most of the village girls do what they're told, but occasionally one does not. She stands her ground, looks the wolf in the eye, and falls in love with him.

People see her run to the woods at night. They see her the next morning with leaves in her hair and blood on her lips. *This is not proper*, they say. *A girl should not love a wolf.*

So they decide to intervene. They come after the wolf with guns and swords. They hunt him down in the Wildwood. But the girl is with him and sees them coming.

The people raise their rifles and take aim. The girl opens her mouth to scream, and as she does, the wolf jumps inside it. Quickly the girl swallows him whole, teeth and claws and fur. He curls up under her heart.

The villagers lower their weapons and go home. The girl heaves a sigh of relief. She believes this arrangement will work. She thinks she can be satisfied with memories of the wolf's golden eyes. She thinks the wolf will be happy with a warm place to sleep.

But the girl soon realizes she's made a terrible mistake, for the wolf is a wild thing and wild things cannot be caged. He wants to get out, but the girl is all darkness inside and he cannot find his way.

So he howls in her blood. He tears at her bones.

And when that doesn't work, he eats her heart.

The howling and gnawing—it drives the girl mad.

She tries to cut him out, slicing lines in her flesh with a razor.

She tries to burn him out, holding a candle flame to her skin.

She tries to starve him out, refusing to eat until she's nothing but skin over bone.

Before long, the grave takes them both.

A wolf lives in Isabelle. She tries hard to keep him down,

but his hunger grows. He cracks her spine and devours her heart.

Run home. Slam the door. Throw the bolt. It won't help.

The wolves in the woods have sharp teeth and long claws, but it's the wolf inside who will tear you apart.

Fifteen

Isabelle managed to finish her market shopping without further incident. There was a cutting glance from the cheesemonger and a few harsh words from the butcher, but she ignored them.

Now she was walking towards the village square. She and Tavi had decided to split up in order to finish their shopping faster, then meet back at their cart. Isabelle was headed there now, but the streets were unfamiliar to her and she hoped she was going the right way. Maman rarely allowed them to go to Saint-Michel. *Only common girls traipse through the village*, she said.

Isabelle was eager to get home. The rutted cobbles made for difficult walking and her foot was aching. Scents of the things she'd bought—slices of salty ham, tiny pickled cucumbers, a pungent blue-veined Roquefort—wafted up from her basket. Her stomach twisted with hunger. It had been weeks since she'd enjoyed such treats.

Isabelle made sure to keep her head down as she entered the square, hoping to go unnoticed. Though she couldn't see much looking at the ground, she could hear a great deal.

Villagers stood together outside shop fronts and taverns,

swapping rumors in tense voices. Volkmar von Bruch had raided another village. He was moving west. No, he was moving south. Refugees were everywhere. Good Queen Ella, God bless her, was trying to help. She had ordered noble families to open their manors and castles to children orphaned by the raids.

As Isabelle hurried on, she heard the sound of hooves on cobblestones. She turned and saw a group of soldiers approaching the square. Leading them was a tall man astride a beautiful white horse. Isabelle hobbled out of their way, joining the crowd at the fountain. No one bothered her; the people only had eyes for the soldiers. A loud cheer rose as they crossed the square.

"Bless you, Colonel Cafard!" a woman shouted.

"God save the king!" another bellowed.

The colonel sat tall and straight-backed in his saddle, eyes ahead. His dark blue coat and white britches were spotless, his boots polished to a high shine.

"At least Saint-Michel is safe," a man said as the soldiers passed by. Others agreed. Hadn't the king sent his finest regiments? Hadn't the good colonel set them up right outside the village in Levesque's pasture? Why, there were over two thousand soldiers in that camp. There was nothing to fear.

Though she was not cold, Isabelle felt a deep chill move through her. *Someone's just walked over your grave*, Adélie used to say when that happened.

She had no idea that the bloodthirsty Volkmar had advanced so far into France. Neither she, Tavi, nor Maman had left their home in over a month. The last bit of news they'd heard—that the old king had died, that the prince had been crowned king and Ella queen—had come from the servants before they'd departed.

Distracted by the villagers' talk, Isabelle did not see the pothole in front of her until she stepped down in it hard. A searing pain shot up her leg. She stifled a cry, limped to a lamppost, and leaned on it to take the weight off her throbbing foot. In agony, she glanced up the street hoping to see her cart, but there was no sign of it.

She did, however, see Odette, the innkeeper's daughter, walking towards her, tapping her cane over the cobblestones. Odette was blind and used the cane to navigate the village's winding streets.

Then Isabelle saw something else.

Cecile, the mayor's daughter, and her gaggle of friends were walking behind Odette. Cecile's eyes were crossed; her tongue was hanging out. She was waving her parasol in front of her as if it were a cane, mocking Odette. Her friends were giggling.

Dread gripped Isabelle. She knew she should go to Odette and defend her. But her foot hurt and she had no heart for another confrontation. She told herself that Odette didn't know what was happening. After all, she couldn't see Cecile, but she, Isabelle, could, and knew she would be the girl's next victim. She looked around anxiously for a place to hide, but it was too late. Cecile had spotted her.

"Isabelle de la Paumé, is that *you*?" she drawled, forgetting about Odette.

As Cecile spoke, Isabelle's eyes fell on the entrance to an alley. She didn't bother to reply but rushed down the narrow passage, heedless of the pain she was in. The alley was damp and smelled like a sewer. A rat darted out in front of her and someone nearly emptied a chamber pot on her head, but she managed to avoid Cecile and emerge on the very street where she'd left her cart.

Relief flooded through her. Tavi wasn't there yet, but Isabelle was certain she'd come soon. In the meantime, she could sit down. Her foot felt like it was on fire now. As she hobbled towards the cart, though, guilt pricked her conscience. She thought about Odette. Had Cecile left her alone? Or had she been so frustrated she couldn't taunt Isabelle that she'd tormented the blind girl twice as hard?

History books say that kings and dukes and generals start wars. Don't believe it. We start them, you and I. Every time we turn away, keep quiet, stay out of it, behave ourselves.

The wrong thing, the cowardly thing, the easy thing. You do it fast. You put it behind you. It's over, you tell yourself as you hurry off. You're finished with it.

But it may not be finished with you.

Isabelle had been in such a hurry to escape that she'd started for the cart without looking up and down the street.

"Isabelle, darling! *There* you are!" a voice called out.

Isabelle's stomach tightened. Slowly, she turned around.

Standing behind her, smiling like a viper, was Cecile.

Sixteen

Cecile, blond and haughty, strolled up to Isabelle. She was wearing a yellow dress, carrying a matching parasol, and trailing a dozen lesser girls in her wake.

"It's been *such* a long time, Isabelle," she trilled. "I *heard* about Ella and the prince. Tell us, what was the royal wedding like?"

There were snickers. Whispers. Pointed glances. Everyone knew that Isabelle, Octavia, and Maman had not been invited to Ella's wedding.

"Do you have your own room in the palace?" asked one of the girls.

"Has Ella found you a duke to marry?" drawled another.

"Who's marrying a duke? I wish I could!" said a third, smiling excitedly. She had just caught up with the group. Her name was Berthe. She was small and plump with prominent front teeth.

Cecile turned to her. "A *duke?* What would a duke want with *you*, Berthe? We'll find you a hunter to marry. *They* like fat little rabbits."

Berthe's smile slipped. Her cheeks flushed a bright, blotchy red. The other girls burst into laughter. They had no choice.

Cecile would remember any girl who didn't laugh. She would take it as a challenge and make that girl her next victim.

Under Cecile's pretty dress, under her silk corset and linen chemise, was a heart like a rotten log. Turn it over and the things living under it would scuttle from the light. Things like envy, fear, anger, and shame. Isabelle knew this because her own heart had become just like it, but unlike Cecile, she knew that cruelty never came from a place of strength; it came from the darkest, dankest, weakest place inside you.

Something in the street caught Cecile's eyes. It was a small rotten cabbage. She kicked it towards Berthe.

"Do it," Cecile commanded. "She deserves it. She's ugly. An ugly stepsister."

Berthe looked at the cabbage uncertainly.

Cecile's eyes narrowed. "Are you scared? *Do it.*"

Her challenge emboldened the other girls. Like a pack of hyenas, they egged Berthe on. Reluctantly, Berthe picked the cabbage up and threw it. It hit the cobblestones in front of Isabelle, splattering her skirts. The jeering grew louder.

Fear ran a sharp fingernail down the back of Isabelle's neck. She knew Cecile was only getting started. From deep inside her a voice spoke. *I am not afraid of an army of lions led by a sheep. I am afraid of an army of sheep led by a lion.*

In times of trouble, Isabelle heard generals in her head; she had ever since she was old enough to read about them. It was Alexander the Great who spoke to her now, and she realized he was right: Cecile's lackeys, desperate for her approval, would do anything she commanded.

Isabelle knew she could fight one girl off, even with a bad

foot, but not a dozen. She would have to find another way out of this.

"That's enough, Cecile," she said. Though she was in agony, she hobbled off, back towards the market, figuring that Cecile would tire of the game if she refused to play it.

But Cecile had no intention of letting her quit. She bent down and picked up a chunk of a broken cobblestone. "Stay where you are, Isabelle. Or I'll throw this at your horse."

Isabelle stopped in her tracks. She turned around. "You wouldn't," she said. This was a step too far, even for Cecile.

"I would." Cecile gestured to the others. "They all would." As if to prove her point, she handed the cobblestone to Berthe. "Throw it. I dare you."

Berthe stared at it; her eyes grew round. "Cecile, no. It's a *rock*," she said.

"Scaredy-cat."

"I'm *not*," Berthe protested, a quaver in her voice.

"Then do it."

Isabelle stepped in front of Martin's head, shielding him. Berthe threw the rock, but she hit the cart.

"You missed on purpose," Cecile accused.

"I didn't!" Berthe cried.

Cecile picked up another chunk of cobble and dropped it into her hand. "Go closer," she said, giving her a push.

Berthe took a few halting steps towards Isabelle, gripping the stone so hard, her knuckles turned white. As she raised her arm again, her eyes met Isabelle's. They were brimming with tears. Isabelle felt as if she were looking into a mirror. She saw the girl's anguish and recognized it; it was her own.

"It's good that you still cry," Isabelle whispered to her. "It's when you stop crying that you're lost."

"Shut up. I'm not crying. I'm *not*," Berthe said, cocking her arm back.

Isabelle knew that being hit by a rock would hurt. It could kill her. If that was her fate, so be it. She refused to abandon Martin. Eyes closed, fists clenched, she waited for the pain.

But it didn't come. Seconds slowly passed. She opened her eyes. The girls were gone, scattered like sparrows. Standing where Cecile had stood only a moment ago was an elderly woman dressed entirely in black.

Seventeen

The woman was gazing down the street, watching the girls hurry away.

Her face was etched with lines. Her snow-white hair was braided and coiled at the nape of her neck. A black ring graced one clawlike hand. She seemed to Isabelle to be the picture of frail old age, as brittle and breakable as a twig under ice.

Until she turned and bent her gaze upon her, and Isabelle felt as if she were drowning in the gray depths of those ancient eyes, pulled under by a will far stronger than her own.

"The one in the yellow dress, the ringleader, she'll come to a bad end," the woman said knowingly. "I guarantee it."

Isabelle shook her head, trying to clear it. She felt buffeted and unsteady, as if she were walking out of a heavy, roiling sea. "You . . . you chased them away?" she asked.

The woman laughed. "*Chased?* Child, these old legs couldn't chase a snail. I was coming to speak with you. The girls scurried off as soon as they saw me." She paused, then said, "You're one of the ugly stepsisters, no? I thought I heard them call you that."

Isabelle winced, bracing for a torrent of abuse, but none came. The woman merely clucked her tongue and said, "You are foolish to go out in public. Hard words cannot kill you, but hard rocks can. You must stay home where it's safe."

"Even ugly girls have to eat," Isabelle said, shame coloring her cheeks.

The woman shook her head dolefully. "People will not forget. Or forgive. An ugly girl is too great an offense. Trust me, I am old and have seen much. Why, I've seen a dishonest girl who stole a king's ransom of jewels be forgiven because of her pretty smile. And a violent girl who robbed coaches at gunpoint walk out of jail because of her long black lashes. Why, I even knew a murderous girl who escaped the gallows because she had full lips and dimples and the judge fell head over heels for her. But an ugly girl? Ah, child, the world is made for men. An ugly girl can never be forgiven."

The woman's words were like a knife between Isabelle's ribs. They pierced her so deeply, she found herself blinking back tears. "When I was small, I thought the world was made for me," she said.

"Children always do," the woman said sympathetically. "And lunatics. I'm sure you know better now, though. Do be careful. I doubt those girls will trouble you again but others may."

"Thank you, madame," Isabelle said. "I'm in your debt."

"You may be able to repay it," the woman said. She gestured at Isabelle's cart. "Might I trouble you for a ride? We arrived at the village inn last night, my maidservant and I, and have been trying since early this morning to get to my relatives' farm but can't find anyone to take us."

"Of course, I will take you, Madame . . . er, Madame . . ." Isabelle realized she did not know the woman's name.

"Madame Sévèrine. I'm the great-aunt of poor Monsieur

LeBenêt, who passed away a few months ago, God rest him. Tante Sévèrine, he called me when he was a boy. Tantine for short. And you must, too, dear girl. I wish to go to the LeBenêts'."

Isabelle brightened. "Nothing could be easier, madame. The LeBenêts are our neighbors. What a coincidence!" she exclaimed, happy that she could help this woman who'd been kind enough to help her.

"Yes, what a coincidence," said the old woman. A smile curved the corners of her mouth; it did not touch her eyes.

Isabelle explained that she had to wait for her sister, but as soon as she arrived, they would go to the inn and collect Madame's trunk and her servant.

"Tantine," the old woman corrected.

"Tantine," Isabelle repeated. "Would you like to sit while we wait?" she asked.

"I would. These old bones tire easily."

Isabelle helped her step up into the cart and settle herself on the wooden seat. She had warmed to this kindly old woman.

"Thank you, my child," said Tantine. "I think we shall be good friends, you and I."

"We're lucky our paths crossed," Isabelle said, smiling.

The old woman nodded. She patted her hand. "Some might call it luck. Myself? I'd call it fate."

Eighteen

It was just before noon when Isabelle and Tavi headed out of the village with Tantine seated between them. The sun was high and the August day was scorchingly hot.

Losca, Tantine's servant, a slight girl with a hooked nose, bright eyes, and ebony hair worn in a long braid, sat in the back of the cart on top of Tantine's trunk. She said nothing as she rode; she just watched the scenery go by, tilting her head and blinking.

Martin plodded up the road as slowly as possible, which gave Tantine plenty of time to tell the girls why she had come to Saint-Michel.

"It's this Volkmar business," she said darkly. "I live in Paris, you see, and he intends to take it. The king has fortified the city, but people are still leaving in droves. I plan to stay here with my relatives for the foreseeable future. It's the safest course. One must always follow the safest course."

"The LeBenêts will be so relieved to have you safe and sound with them, Tantine," Tavi said. "They must be worried about you."

"The LeBenêts have no idea that I'm coming," said Tantine. "We are not close. In fact, I've never met Madame LeBenêt.

It was my husband who was related to Monsieur LeBenêt. My late husband, I should say. He passed away recently, too."

Isabelle and Tavi expressed their condolences. Tantine thanked them.

"In his will, my husband left a sum of money to Monsieur LeBenêt," she added. "Now I am wondering what to do with it. I'm told there is a son, Hugo, but I know nothing of the boy. I would like to see if he is the sort who will bring honor to the family name before I bestow the inheritance on him."

I wish you luck, Isabelle thought. She'd known Hugo since they were children. He'd played pirates and musketeers with her and Felix a few times, always scowling behind his thick eyeglasses. In all the years she'd known him, he'd barely grunted three words to her. She doubted he'd grunt even one to Tantine.

As the sun rose higher, and Martin continued to grudgingly pull the cart past meadows, wheat fields, and orchards, the old woman continued to talk. She was just telling the girls about her elegant town house in Paris, when a scream, ragged and high, tore through the air.

Isabelle sat up straight. Tavi jumped. They traded wide-eyed glances, then quickly looked around for its source. Losca leaned over the side of the cart, craning her neck.

"There," Tantine said, pointing straight ahead.

A military wagon, pulled by two burly workhorses, had crested a hill and was rolling towards them. Even from a distance, Isabelle could see that the driver's uniform was blotched with red. As the wagon drew near, and she saw what it contained, she uttered a choked cry.

In the back, unprotected from the merciless sun, were at

72

least thirty men, all badly injured. Bandages soaked with blood were tied around heads and torsos. Limbs were missing. One man lay stretched across a wooden seat, his legs mangled. He was the one who'd screamed. A wheel hit a rut, jostling the wagon, and he cried out again.

By the time the wagon passed by, Tavi was clutching her seat and Isabelle's hands were trembling so badly, she had to squeeze Martin's reins hard to steady them. Tantine's mouth was set in a grim line. No one spoke.

Isabelle remembered her book, *An Illustrated History of the World's Greatest Military Commanders*. She and Felix had pored over it when they were little, looking at the hand-colored plates depicting famous battles. The pictures made them look glorious and exciting and the soldiers who'd fought them dashing and brave. But the suffering she'd just witnessed didn't seem glorious at all. It left her stunned and sickened. She tried to picture the man responsible for it. Volkmar. He was a duke, she'd been told. Did he wear medals on his uniform? A sash across his chest? Did he ride a horse? Carry a sword?

For a moment, Isabelle's vision narrowed. She no longer saw the road ahead of her, the stone walls that lined it, the roses that tumbled over them. In her mind's eye, a figure, tall and powerful, strode towards her across a battlefield. White smoke swirled around him, obscuring his face, but she could see the sword he held in his hand, its blade razor-sharp. A shiver ran through her, just as it had in the marketplace.

Tavi spoke and the image faded. "Where are they going?" she asked.

"To an army camp on the other side of Saint-Michel. I

heard villagers talking about it," Isabelle replied, shaking off the strange vision and the sense of dread it left behind.

"I've seen many such wagons on my way from Paris," said Tantine. "Ah, girls, I fear this war will not go well for us. Our king is young and untested, and Volkmar is ruthless and wily. His troops are fewer, yet they defeat the king's at every turn."

The three fell silent again. The only sounds were of Martin's plodding hooves, the creaking of the cart, and the droning of insects. Before long, they reached the turnoff to the LeBenêt farm. A dusty drive led to an old stone farmhouse. Threadbare white curtains hung in its windows; sagging shutters framed them. Chickens scratched around the weathered blue door.

The cow barn and dairy house, also built of stone, were connected to the farmhouse. Behind them, cattle grazed in a fenced pasture and fields bearing cabbages, potatoes, turnips, and onions stretched all the way to the edge of the Wildwood.

Losca was out of the cart before it stopped. As Isabelle helped Tantine down, and Tavi opened the back of the cart to get her trunk, Madame LeBenêt, threadbare and weathered herself, came out to greet them, if one could call it a greeting.

"What do you want?" she barked, the look on her face sour enough to curdle milk.

"We've brought your great-aunt, Madame," Isabelle said, nodding at Tantine. "She has come all the way from Paris with her maidservant."

Madame LeBenêt's eyes narrowed; her scowl deepened. "I have no great-aunt," she said.

"I am Madame Sévèrine, your late husband's great-aunt," Tantine explained.

"My husband never mentioned you."

"I'm not surprised. There was a family feud, so much bad blood—"

Madame LeBenêt rudely cut her off. "Do you take me for a fool? Every day now strangers fleeing Paris come to Saint-Michel pretending to be someone's long-lost this-or-that to get themselves food and shelter. No, madame, I'm sorry. You cannot stay here. You and your maid will eat us out of house and home."

Eat them out of house and home? Isabelle thought. *This little old lady? Her scrawny maid?* She ducked her head and fiddled with a buckle on Martin's harness. She didn't dare look up lest Madame caught her rolling her eyes.

The whole village knew Avara LeBenêt was a miser. Not only did she have bountiful fields, she had two dozen laying hens, ten milk cows, berry bushes, apple trees, and a large kitchen garden. She made a small fortune at the market every Saturday, yet all she ever did was complain about how poor she was.

"Ah, I am sorry to hear you have no place for me," Tantine said, with a crestfallen sigh. "I fear I shall have to settle the inheritance on another member of the family."

Madame LeBenêt snapped to attention like a pointer that had spotted a nice fat duck. "Inheritance? What inheritance?" she asked sharply.

"The inheritance my late husband instructed me to bestow upon your late husband. I thought to possibly give it to your son, but now . . ."

Madame LeBenêt slapped her forehead. "Tante *Sévèrine!*" she exclaimed. "Of *course*! My husband often spoke of you!

And with *such* fondness. You must be exhausted from your travels. Let me fix you a cup of tea."

"She should be on the stage," Tavi said to Isabelle.

Madame LeBenêt heard her. "What are you two waiting for?" she snapped. "Fetch her trunk!"

With great difficulty, Isabelle and Tavi managed to slide the trunk off the cart and carry it into the house. Isabelle hoped Losca might help them, but the girl was peering intently at a grasshopper on the scraggly rosebush near Madame LeBenêt's door, completely absorbed by it. Madame directed Isabelle and Tavi to place the trunk in a small bedroom, then hurried into the house to start the tea. When the girls returned to their cart, they saw that Tantine was still standing by it.

Tavi climbed back up into the cart and sat down, but Isabelle hesitated. "Will you be all right here?" she asked.

"I'll be fine," Tantine assured her. "I can handle Avara. Thank you again for the ride."

"It was nothing. Thank you for saving me from certain death at the hands of Cecile," Isabelle said wryly.

She turned to leave, but as she did, Tantine caught hold of her hand. Isabelle was surprised by the strength in those gnarled fingers.

They stood there for a moment, staring into each other's eyes, perfectly still. Fate, a creature with no heart and no soul, who walked with the dust of Alexandria on her shoes, the ashes of Pompeii on her hem, the red clay of Xi'an on her sleeves. As old as time. Without beginning or end.

And a human girl. So poorly made. Just tender flesh and bitten nails and a battered heart beating in a fragile cage of bone.

Isabelle had no idea whose fathomless eyes she was gazing into. She had no idea that Fate meant to win the wager she'd made, no matter the cost.

"We must be going, Tantine," she finally said. "Are you sure you'll be all right?"

Fate nodded. She gave Isabelle's hand one last squeeze. "Yes, and I hope you will, too. Be careful of those fleeing Paris, child," she warned. "Not all refugees are harmless old biddies like me. Some are scoundrels, just looking to lead young girls astray. Be wary. Close your shutters. Bolt your doors. And above all, trust nothing—*nothing*—to Chance."

Nineteen

Many hours later, on a blue damask picnic cloth, in a field well south of Saint-Michel, a diva, a magician, and an actress sat under an oak tree eating fruit and sweets.

Around them, musicians played. A juggler tossed flaming torches into the air. A sword-swallower gulped down a saber. And three noisy capuchins leapt to and fro in the branches of the oak while the fourth sat on the picnic cloth, eyeing the diva's pearls.

"Watch out. The little robber is planning his next theft," the magician warned.

"Nelson," the diva cautioned, wagging a finger at the monkey. "Don't even think—"

Her words were cut off by a loud bellow. *"Now?"*

"No!" came the shouted reply.

The three women turned towards the source of the racket. Chance, hands on his hips, was standing by a large, painted carriage. He'd flung off his coat. His white ruffled shirt was open at the neck, his long braids gathered up and tied with someone's shoelace. Sweat beaded on his brow.

Standing on top of the carriage, and on top of each other's

shoulders, were four acrobats. The bottommost had rooted his strong legs to the roof; the topmost held a telescope to her eye.

"Go," Chance commanded a fifth, gesturing to the carriage. "Tell me what you see."

A moment later, a wiry boy was climbing to the top of the human tower.

"Anything?" Chance shouted as the boy took the telescope from the acrobat under him. "You're looking for a village called Saint-Michel. It has a church with a statue of the archangel on it . . ."

"I can't see it!"

Chance swore. "You're next!" he said, to a second wiry boy.

"*Another* one?" the diva said, turning away. "I can't look."

Chance and his friends were lost. The driver had been navigating on instinct and had taken a wrong turn. He'd had no road map to consult; Chance didn't like them. They spoiled the fun, he said. Now evening was coming down, the village of Saint-Michel was nowhere in sight, and Chance was hoping his acrobats could spot it.

The diva helped herself to a macaron from a pretty paper box in the centre of the picnic cloth and bit into the sweet. Its brittle meringue shattered; crumbs fell into her cleavage. The monkey scampered over and fished them out.

"Nelson, you fresh thing!" she cried, swatting him. Nelson threw his furry arms around her neck, kissed her, and shot off. Had she not been so annoyed by his antics, she might've noticed that he was trailing something through the grass.

"The crone's already there. I feel it," the magician fretted, threading a silver coin in and out of her long, nimble fingers.

"If she finds the girl before Chance does, she'll poison her with doubt and fear," said the diva.

"But this Isabelle, she's strong, no?" the actress asked.

"So I've heard," said the magician. "But is she strong enough?"

"He thinks so," the diva said, nodding at Chance. "But who can say? You know what it takes to break free of the crone. It's a battle, as we who have waged it well know. And battles inflict wounds."

She pushed up her sleeve. An ugly scar ran from her wrist to her elbow. "From my father. He came after me with a knife when I told him I would not enter a convent as he wished but would go to Vienna instead to study opera."

The magician pulled the neck of her jacket open to show her scar, livid and shiny, just under her collarbone. "From a rock. Thrown by a priest who called me a devil. Because the townspeople liked my miracles better than his."

The actress's hand went to a gold locket pinned on her jacket, over her heart. She opened it and showed the others painted miniatures of a girl and a boy.

"No scar, but a wound that will never heal," she said, tears shimmering in her eyes. "My children. Taken from me by a judge and given to my drunken husband. Because only an immoral woman would exhibit herself upon a stage."

The magician pulled the actress close. She kissed her cheek and wiped her tears away with a handkerchief. Then she balled the handkerchief up and pressed it between her palms. When she opened her hands again, it was gone and a butterfly was sitting in its place.

As the three women watched, the butterfly took wing, carried aloft by the breeze.

It flew past a little monkey playing with a rope of pearls. Past a violinist and a trumpeter, a cook, a scientist, and three ballerinas, all with scars of their own.

Past a man with amber eyes, raging at the falling dusk. Swearing at the treacherous roads. Building his teetering human tower taller and taller.

A smile, small but defiant, curved the magician's full red lips. "That's what we do with our pain," she said, watching the butterfly rise. "We make it into something beautiful."

"We make it into something meaningful," said the diva.

"We make it matter," whispered the actress.

Twenty

As night came down, Fate sipped a cup of chamomile tea with Madame LeBenêt, Chance tried to find his way to Saint-Michel, and Isabelle, standing in her kitchen, cast a worried glance at her sister.

Tavi was doing what she always did in the evening: sitting by the hearth, a book open in her lap. But the furrows in her forehead looked deeper tonight, the shadows under her eyes darker.

Always bookish and inward, she'd become even more so since Ella had left. Sometimes Isabelle felt as if she were watching her sister fade like cooling embers, and that one day soon she would turn to ash and blow away.

The two girls were a year apart in age and looked very much alike. They both had auburn hair, high foreheads, a smattering of freckles across their noses, and eyes the color of strong coffee. Tavi was taller, with a lean figure; Isabelle was curvier. But it was their personalities more than anything else that set them apart. Tavi was cool and contained; Isabelle was anything but.

As Isabelle arranged slices of ham, apple, bread, and cheese on a plate to take upstairs to her mother, she wondered how to draw her sister out. "What are you reading, Tav?" she asked.

"*The Compendious Book on Calculation by Completion and Balancing* by the Persian scholar Al-Khwarizmi," Tavi replied, without looking up.

"Sounds like a page-turner," Isabelle teased. "Who's Al-Khwarizmi?"

"The father of algebra," Tavi replied, looking up. "Though some believe the Greek mathematician Diophantus can also lay claim to the title."

"That's a funny word, algebra. Don't you think?" Isabelle asked, eager to keep her talking.

Tavi smiled. "It comes from Arabic. From *al-jabr*, which means 'the reunion of broken parts.' Al-Khwarizmi believed that what's broken can be made whole again if you just apply the right equation." Her smile dimmed a little. "If only there was an equation that could do the same for people."

She was about to say more, but a voice, shrilling from the doorway, cut her off.

"Isabelle! Octavia! Why aren't you dressed? We're going to be late for the ball!"

Maman stepped into the kitchen, her lips set in an icy frown. She was wearing a satin gown the color of a winter sky and a plume of white ostrich feathers in her badly pinned-up hair. Her face was pale; her eyes were feverishly bright. Her hands fluttered around her body like doves, patting her hair one minute, twining in her pearls the next.

Isabelle's heart sank at the sight of her; she had not been right since Ella left. Sometimes she was her competent, imperious self. At other times, like tonight, she was confused. Lost in the past. Convinced that they were going to a dinner, a ball, or the palace.

"Maman, you have the date wrong," she said now, giving her a soothing smile.

"Don't be silly. I have the invitation right here." Maman showed Isabelle the printed card she was holding, its ivory surface smudged, its edges bent.

Isabelle recognized it; it had arrived months ago. "Yes, you do," she said cheerily. "But you see, Maman, that ball has already taken place."

Maman stared at the engraved words. "I—I can't seem to read the date . . ." she said, her words trailing off.

"Come. I'll help you undress. You can put on a nice comfortable nightdress and lie down."

"Are you quite certain about the date, Isabelle?" Maman asked, her tyrannical tone giving way to a bewildered one.

"Yes. Go back to your room now. I'll bring you your supper," Isabelle coaxed, taking her mother's arm.

But Maman, suddenly vexed again, shook her off. "Octavia, put that book down!" she demanded. "You'll ruin your eyes with all those numbers." She strode across the room and snatched the book from Tavi's hands. "Honestly! What man ever thinks, *Oh, how I'd love to meet a girl who can solve for x?* Go get *dressed.* We cannot keep the countess waiting!"

"For God's sake, Maman, stop this!" Tavi snapped. "That ball was ages ago and even if it wasn't, the countess doesn't want us anymore. Nobody does!"

Maman stood very still. She said nothing for quite some time. When she spoke again, her voice was little more than a whisper. "Of course the countess wants us. Why wouldn't she?"

"Because she *knows*," Tavi said. "About Ella and how we treated her. She hates us. The whole village hates us. The whole *country* does. We're outcasts!"

Maman pressed her palm to her forehead. She closed her eyes. When she opened them again, the febrile brightness had receded and clarity had returned. But something else was there, too—a cold, menacing anger.

"You think yourself very clever, Octavia, but you are not," she said. "Before the prince came for Ella, I had five offers of marriage for her. *Five.* Even though I turned her into a kitchen girl. Do you know how many I've had for you? Zero. Solve *that* equation, my dear."

Tavi, stung, looked away.

"What, exactly, do you expect to do with all your studying?" Maman asked, waving the book in the air. "Become a professor? A scientist? Such things are only for men. If I cannot find a husband for you, who will keep you when I'm no longer here? What will you do? Become a governess to another woman's children, living in some cold attic room, eating leftovers from her table? Work as a seamstress, stitching day and night until you go blind?" Maman shook her head disgustedly. "Even in rags, Ella outshined you. She was pretty and pleasing, and you? You make yourself ugly with your numbers, your formulas, your ridiculous equations. It must stop. It *will* stop."

She walked to the hearth and threw the book into the fire.

"*No!*" Tavi cried. She leapt out of her chair, grabbed a poker, and tried to rescue it, but the flames were already blackening the pages.

"Finish dressing, both of you!" Maman ordered, striding out of the room. "Jacques! Bring the carriage!"

"Tavi, did you have to upset her?" Isabelle asked angrily. "Maman!" she called, running after her mother. "Where are you?"

She found her trying to open the front door, still calling for the carriage. It took Isabelle ages to get her back upstairs. Once she had her in her bedroom, she helped her undress and gave her a glass of brandy to calm her. She tried to get her to eat, but Maman refused. Eventually, Isabelle managed to get her into bed, but as she was pulling the covers over her, Maman sat up and grabbed her arm. "What will become of you and your sister? Tell me?" she asked, her eyes fearful.

"We'll be fine. We'll manage. Stepfather left us money, didn't he?"

Maman laughed. It was a tired, hopeless sound. "Your stepfather left us nothing but debts. I've sold the Rembrandt. Most of the silver. Several of my jewels . . ."

Isabelle was exhausted. Her head hurt. "Hush, Maman," she said. "Go to sleep now. We'll talk about it tomorrow."

When she returned to the kitchen, she found Tavi kneeling by the hearth, staring into the fire. Isabelle took the poker from her hand and tried to pull the book out of the grate, but it was too late.

"Stop, Isabelle. Leave it. It's gone," said Tavi, with a hitch in her voice.

Isabelle's heart ached for her. Steady, logical Tavi never cried. "I'm sorry. I just wanted to help," she said, putting the poker down.

"Do you? Dress my hair, then," Tavi said brokenly. "Rouge my cheeks. Make me pretty. Can you do that?"

Isabelle didn't reply. If only she could make Tavi pretty. And herself. How different their lives would be.

"I didn't think so," said Tavi, staring at the ashes of her beloved book. "I could solve all the Diophantine equations, extend Newton's work on infinite series, complete Euler's analysis of prime numbers, and it wouldn't matter." She looked at Isabelle. "Ella is the beauty. You and I are the ugly stepsisters. And so the world reduces us, all three of us, to our lowest common denominator."

Twenty-One

Deep within the Maison Douleur, a tall grandfather clock, its pendulum sweeping back and forth like a scythe, ticked the minutes away.

Maman and Tavi were both in bed, but Isabelle couldn't sleep. She knew she'd only toss and turn if she tried, so she stayed in the kitchen and sat by the hearth, picking at the supper she'd fixed for Maman.

Once, she welcomed the night. She would climb down the thick vine that grew outside her bedroom window and meet Felix. They would gaze at the night sky and count shooting stars, and sometimes, if they were still as stones and lucky, they would see an owl swoop down on her prey or a stag walk out of the Wildwood, his antlers rising over his noble head like a crown.

Now the darkness haunted Isabelle. She saw ghosts everywhere. In mirrors and windows. In the reflection of a copper pot. She heard them in the creak of a door. Felt them fluttering in the curtains. It wasn't the darkness that was haunted, though; it was Isabelle herself. Ghosts are not the dead, come back from the grave to torment the living; ghosts are already here. They live inside us, keening in the ashes of our sorrows, mired in the thick, clutching mud of our regrets.

As Isabelle stared into the fireplace at the dying coals, the ghosts crowded in upon her.

She saw Ella, Tavi, Maman, and herself riding in their carriage. Maman was complimenting Ella luxuriantly. "How pretty you look today!" she purred. "Did you see the admiring glance the mayor's son gave you?"

Other images flickered to life. Maman frowning at Tavi's needlework, telling her she should practice until she could sew as nicely as Ella. Maman wincing at Isabelle's singing, then asking Ella for a song.

Envy, resentment, shame—Maman had rubbed these things against Isabelle's heart, and Tavi's, until they were raw. Maman was subtle; she was clever. She'd started early. She'd started small. She knew that even tiny wounds, left untended, can fester and swell and turn a heart black.

More ghosts came. The ghost of a black stallion. The ghost of a boy. But Isabelle couldn't bear these, so she stood up to carry her plate to the sink.

The clock struck twelve as she did, its chimes echoing ominously throughout the house. Isabelle told herself it was time for bed, then remembered that she hadn't locked the door to the stables or closed the chickens in their coop. With all the upset Maman had caused, she'd forgotten.

As she hobbled back to the fireplace to bank the coals, a darting movement caught her eye. A mouse had ventured onto the hearth and was digging in a crack between the stones. As she scrabbled furiously, two tiny mouselings scurried to her side. An instant later, the mouse stood up on her hind legs, squeaking in triumph. Clutched in her paw was a small green lentil. She bit it in two and handed the halves to her children, who nibbled it greedily.

Guilt's thin, cold fingers gripped Isabelle as she remembered how that lentil got there.

Ella had overheard Maman telling Isabelle and Tavi that the prince was holding a ball and that all the maidens in the realm were invited. She'd asked if she could go, and in response, Maman had picked up a bowl of lentils and thrown them into the fireplace.

"There were a thousand lentils in that bowl. Pick them all out of the ashes and you can go," she'd said, a cruel smile quirking her lips.

It had been an impossible task, yet Ella had managed it. Isabelle had just discovered how: the mice had helped her. When she had presented the full bowl, Maman had snatched it out of her hands, dumped it out on the kitchen table, and counted the lentils. Then she'd triumphantly announced that one was missing and that Ella could not go to the ball.

What was it like for Ella to be so alone, to have no friends except for mice? Isabelle wondered. Then, with a sharp stab of pain, she realized she didn't have to wonder—she knew.

The mouselings finished their meal, then looked at their mother, but she had nothing more for them. She'd eaten nothing herself.

"Wait!" Isabelle said to the mice. "Wait, there!" She hurried back to the supper tray but moved so clumsily that she scared the creatures. They scampered away.

"No! Don't go!" Isabelle cried, heartbroken. She snatched a piece of cheese off the tray, then limped back to the hearth, but the mice were nowhere to be seen.

"Come back," she begged, looking for them. *"Please."*

Kneeling by the fireplace, she placed the cheese on a hearthstone. Then she sat back down in her chair. Waiting. Hoping. But the mice did not return. They thought she meant to hurt them. Why wouldn't they? That's what she did.

Unbidden, voices from the market echoed in Isabelle's head. Tantine telling her that people wouldn't forget or forgive. Cecile calling her ugly. Worst of all, the words of the baker's wife: *You were cruel to a defenseless girl.*

Remorse curled around Isabelle's heart like a snake and squeezed. Tears spilled down her cheeks. Her head bowed, she did not see the shadow fill the kitchen window. Or the hand, pale as moonlight, press against it.

By the time Isabelle lifted her head again, the shadow was gone. Wiping her eyes, she stood. The barn and the chicken coop were still waiting for her. She shuffled to the door, lit the lantern that was resting on a hook next to it, and walked out into the night, sorrow hanging off her like a shroud.

Had Isabelle waited just a few more seconds, she would have seen the mother mouse creep out of the shadows and back to the hearth. She would have seen the hungry creature pick up the cheese. She would have seen her, whiskers quivering, blink up at the window where the shadow had passed.

Then shudder. And run.

Twenty-Two

Isabelle was glad of her lantern.

The moon was full tonight but had disappeared behind clouds. Once, she could navigate the grounds of the Maison Douleur in the dark, but it had been a long time since she'd ventured outside after midnight.

The outbuildings were located to the west of the mansion. Isabelle followed the path of flat white stones that led over the lawns, around the linden tree, through a gate in a wooden fence, and down a gentle hill.

Bertrand the rooster opened one suspicious eye as Isabelle shined the lantern into the chicken coop. After a quick head count, she latched the door and continued to the stables. Martin was dozing in his stall. He woke briefly as she checked on him, snorted with irritation, then settled back into sleep. Isabelle secured the stable door and started back for the mansion.

It was as she was closing the gate that it happened.

Out of nowhere, the gentle night breeze stiffened into a vicious wind. It ripped her hair loose, slammed the gate shut, and snuffed out her lantern. And then it was gone.

Isabelle pressed a hand to her chest, startled. Luckily, the wind had also scattered the clouds. Moonlight now illuminated the white stones snaking across the grass, making it possible for her to find her way. As the path carried her past the linden tree, the tree's leafy branches swayed in the breeze, beckoning to her.

Isabelle walked closer to the linden tree, thinking of the dove who had warned the prince of her deception. Was it roosting in those branches now? Watching her? The thought made her shiver.

She put her lantern down and stared up at the tree, remembering the days she'd spent climbing in those branches, pretending she was scaling the mast of a pirate ship or the walls of an enemy's fortress, going higher and higher.

The ghosts she'd tried to banish earlier crowded in on her again. She saw herself as a child, fearlessly threading her way through the tree limbs. She saw Tavi with her slate and her equations, and Ella with her daisy chains. They had been so innocent then, the three of them. So happy together. Good, and good enough.

The remorse that had squeezed her heart now crushed it.

"I'm sorry. I'm so, so sorry," she whispered to the three little girls, aching with longing and loss. "I wish things were different. I wish *I* was."

The leaves murmured and sighed. She almost felt as if the tree was speaking to her. Shaking her head at her own foolishness, she went on her way.

She'd only taken a few steps when she saw it . . . a movement in the darkness.

Isabelle froze. Her heart stuttered with fear.

She wasn't alone.

Someone was standing in the shadow of the linden tree.

Watching her.

Twenty-Three

The figure stepped out of the darkness.

Isabelle, her heart still battering against her ribs, saw that it was a woman—tall, lithe, pale as bone. Long auburn hair floated around her shoulders. She wore a high crown of twining blackbriar. Living forester moths, their blue-green wings shimmering, adorned it. A yellow-eyed hawk sat perched on her shoulder. Her own eyes were emerald-green; her lips black. The gown she wore was the color of moss.

The woman was clutching a struggling rabbit by the scruff of its neck. As Isabelle watched, she lifted the animal to her face, breathed its scent, and licked her lips. Her sharp teeth glinted in the moonlight.

Isabelle had never seen her before, yet she recognized her.

When Ella was small, she'd woven fanciful tales about a magical creature who lived in the hollow at the base of the linden tree. She was a woman sometimes, and sometimes a fox. She was a wild thing, majestic and beautiful, but sly and fierce, too. Isabelle had always thought Ella's stories were just that—stories.

Until now.

The woman gave her a smile, the same smile she'd given the rabbit right before she snatched it from a patch of clover. Then she started towards her, step by slow step.

Everything inside Isabelle told her to run, but she couldn't; she was mesmerized. This was no gossamer-winged creature sipping dew from flower petals. Nor was she a plump, cozy old godmother, all smiles and rhymes. This was a being both dark and dangerous.

This was Tanaquill, the fairy queen.

Twenty-Four

"You summoned me," the fairy queen said, stopping a foot away from Isabelle.

"I—I didn't. No. I don't think. D-did I?" Isabelle stammered, saucer-eyed.

Tanaquill's eyes glittered darkly. Her teeth looked sharper up close. She had long black talons at the end of her fingers. "Your *heart* summoned me." She laughed drily. "What's left of it."

She pressed a pale hand to Isabelle's chest and cocked her head, listening. Isabelle felt the fairy queen's talons curve into the fabric of her dress. She heard the beat of her heart amplified under Tanaquill's palm. It grew louder and louder. For a moment, she feared that Tanaquill would rip it, red and beating, right out of her chest.

Finally, Tanaquill lowered her hand. "Cut away piece by piece by piece," she said. "Ella's heart was not."

How would she know that? Isabelle wondered and then, with a jolt, it came to her: "It was *you*," she whispered in amazement. "You're the one who helped Ella get to the ball!"

She and Tavi had tried to puzzle out how their stepsister had acquired a coach, horses, footmen, a gown, and glass slippers.

And how she'd escaped from her room after Isabelle had locked her in it when the prince had come to call. Now she knew.

"A pumpkin transformed into a coach, some mice into horses, a lizard or two for footmen . . . child's play," Tanaquill sniffed. She regarded her rabbit again.

Isabelle's pulse quickened. *If the fairy queen can make a coach out of a pumpkin, what else can she do?* she wondered. For a moment she forgot to be scared. Hope kindled inside her.

"Please, Your Grace," she said, "would you help me, too?"

Tanaquill tore her gaze from the rabbit. "It was easy to help Ella, but I cannot help a girl such as you. You are too full of bitterness. It fills the place where your heart used to be," she said, turning away.

Isabelle lurched after her. "No! Wait! Please wait!"

The fairy queen whirled around, her lips curled in a snarl. "For what, girl? Ella knew her heart's deepest wish. Do you?"

Isabelle faltered, frightened, but desire made her bold. A dozen wishes welled up inside her, all born from her happiest memories. In her mind's eye, she saw swords and books, horses, the Wildwood. Summer days. Daisy chains. She remembered a promise and a kiss.

Isabelle opened her mouth to ask for these things, but just as the words were about to leave her tongue, she bit them back.

All her life, everything she'd wanted, everything she'd loved . . . they were always the wrong things. They got her into trouble. They broke her heart. They weren't for her; the world had said so. So why ask for them? They'd only bring more heartache.

There was one thing, though, that could fix everything. It

could make people stop hating her. It could make her what Maman wanted her to be, what the baker's wife and Cecile and the villagers and the old merchant and all the suitors who came to the house and the whole entire world demanded that she be.

Isabelle looked Tanaquill in the eye and said, "I wish to be pretty."

Tanaquill growled low in her throat and Isabelle felt as if she'd given the wrong answer, but the fairy queen didn't refuse her. Instead, she said, "Wishes are never simply granted. They must be earned."

"I'll do anything," Isabelle said fervently.

"That is what all mortals say," said Tanaquill with a scornful laugh. "They'll do *anything*. Anything but that which must be done. Only one thing can rid you of the bitterness inside. Do it, and perhaps I will help you."

"I'll do it. I *swear*," Isabelle said, clasping her hands together. "What is it?"

"Find the lost pieces of your heart."

Twenty-Five

Isabelle blinked. "Find the pieces of my heart?" she repeated, as if she hadn't heard the fairy queen correctly. "I—I don't understand. How do I find pieces of a *heart*? How did Ella?"

"Ella did not have to."

Isabelle scowled. "Of course not. I bet all *she* had to do was smile."

Her words, prompted by resentment, were tart and disrespectful. Tanaquill's emerald eyes hardened; she turned away.

Panic exploded inside of Isabelle like a dropped glass. Why could she *never* control herself? "I'm sorry. Tell me what the pieces are. Tell me how to find them. *Please*," she begged, running after her.

Tanaquill relented. "You know what they are."

"But I don't!" Isabelle protested. "I have no idea!"

"And you must find your own way to them."

"How? Show me," Isabelle implored, growing desperate. "Help me."

Still clutching the struggling rabbit, Tanaquill bent down by the base of the linden tree and, with her free hand, raked through the small bones scattered in the grass around it. She picked up a small, slender jawbone that had belonged to a darting, wily animal—a weasel or marten—and the empty half shell of a walnut, and gave them to Isabelle. Next, she reached into the thick blackbriar climbing the linden tree's trunk, drew a spiky seedpod from between its sharp thorns and handed that to her, too.

"These gifts will help you attain your heart's desire," Tanaquill said.

Isabelle looked down at the things she was holding, and as she did, the emotions she'd tried to hold down spiked like a fever, weakening everything strong and sure inside her. Her blood felt thin, her guts watery, her bones as crumbly as old mortar. The apology she'd made only moments ago was forgotten. Angry, jealous words burst from her lips.

"Gifts? *These* things?" she cried, staring at the bone, the nutshell, and the seed-pod. "You gave Ella a beautiful gown and glass slippers! A carriage and horses. *Those* are gifts. You've given *me* a handful of *garbage*!"

She looked up, but Tanaquill had turned away again. As Isabelle watched, the fairy queen disappeared into the hollow in a swirl of red hair and green skirts. Isabelle hobbled after her, but as she did, a thin, high-pitched scream rose, and was abruptly cut off—the rabbit's death cry. She took a wary step back.

Her gaze returned to the objects in her hand. The fairy queen was mocking her with them, she was certain of it, and that certainty was painful to her.

"Ugly," she said as her fingers touched the jawbone. "Useless," she said as they brushed the nutshell. "Hurtful," she said as the seedpod pricked them. "Just like me."

She would toss the objects into the hearth in the morning. They could at least help kindle a fire. She shoved them into her skirt pocket, then walked the rest of the way to her house, convinced that there was no help for her, no hope. There was only despair, heavy and hard, weighing on what was left of her cutaway heart.

Most people will fight when there is some hope of winning, no matter how slim. They are called brave. Only a few will keep fighting when all hope is gone. They are called warriors.

Isabelle was a warrior once, though she has forgotten it.

Will she remember? It does not look good. Then again, few things do in the dead of night. The small dark hours are the undoing of many. Candlelight throws shadows on the walls of our souls, shadows that turn a mouse into a monster, a downturn into disaster.

Should you ever decide, in those small dark hours, to hang yourself, well, that is your choice.

But don't hunt for the rope until morning.

By then you'll find a much better use for it.

Twenty-Six

As Isabelle made her way upstairs to her bed, Fate made her way through the Wildwood.

Spotting a fallen tree, she stopped, plucked a centipede from the rotted wood, and bit off its head. "Perfect," she said, licking droplets of black from her lips. "Bitter blood makes bitter ink."

As she dropped the still-writhing body into the basket she was carrying, she looked up into the high branches above her and said, "I need wolfsbane. Keep an eye out for it. A sprig of belladonna would be helpful, too."

A raven, perched in a pine bough, flew off and Fate resumed her stroll. A plump brown spider went into the basket, a mossy bat skull, white queen of the night flowers, speckled toadstools—all ingredients for the inks she was making.

Fate was prodding the bleached rib cage of a long-dead deer, hoping to scare some beetles out of it, when her raven flew down and landed beside her. A moment later, a girl stood where the bird had been, bright-eyed and blinking, wearing a black dress. She dropped a purple bloom into Fate's basket.

"Ah! You found the belladonna. Well done, Losca. Its berries give a nice luster to the darker inks, like *Doubt* and *Denial*.

Of course, I must get the girl's map back before I can make changes to it. Chance thinks *he* can redraw it, but that may prove more difficult than he anticipates. Have you seen any sign of him yet?"

Losca shook her head.

"He'll come. I've never known Chance to back out of a wager. I shall win this game, but not without a fight. He often gains the upper hand, however briefly, through sheer unpredictability. Mortals lose their heads around him. They start to put stock in their hopes and dreams, the poor fools. He *actually* makes them believe they can do anything." She clucked her tongue. "And he has the cheek to call *me* cruel."

Fate walked on, poking and digging, glad to be out of dour Madame LeBenêt's uncomfortable house for a few hours. Losca followed her. Absorbed in the hunt for ingredients, they didn't realize they'd reached the edge of the Wildwood until they heard voices.

"What's this?" Fate muttered, peering between the branches of a bushy tree. She soon saw that a shallow, grassy hill sloped away from where she was standing and flattened into a broad pasture. Stretching across it, as far as the eye could see, were neat rows of white canvas tents. Here and there, fires flickered. A horse whinnied. Someone played a sad, sweet tune on a violin.

Fate drew the hood of her black cloak up over her head. She was curious to see Colonel Cafard's encampment up close.

"Take this," she said, handing Losca the basket. As she did, she noticed that the tail of a small snake was hanging from the girl's mouth. Fate glared at her. "What have I told you about eating the ingredients?" she scolded.

Shamefaced, Losca sucked the tail into her mouth and swallowed it, like a child with a string of spaghetti.

"Stay close and don't make any noise," Fate cautioned. Losca nodded.

The two hugged the edge of the camp to avoid being seen. Though it was late, men were huddled around the fires, unable to sleep. They talked of Volkmar and what they would do to him once they got hold of him. Fate heard bravado in their voices but saw fear in their eyes. A grizzled sergeant sat among them, trying to raise their spirits by regaling them with tales of battlefield glories—until a scream, ragged and raw, rang out, abruptly ending his tale.

Fate heard the flapping of wings, then felt a weight descend on her shoulder. The basket Losca had been carrying lay on the ground.

"Now, now, child. There's nothing to be afraid of," she murmured, stroking the bird's back.

She picked up the basket, then sought out the source of the scream. Her search led her to the far side of the camp, where its hospital was located. There, men lay on cots, writhing and moaning, some mortally wounded, others delirious with pain and fever. A surgeon and his assistant moved among them, cutting and stitching, administering morphine, mopping drenched brows.

A woman moved among them, too.

Graceful and slender, she wore a gown the color of night with flowing sleeves and a high neck. Her long dark hair hung down to her waist. She was out of place among all the soldiers, impossible to miss, yet no one seemed to notice her.

A man cried out. He called for his sweetheart, then begged to die. The woman went to him. She knelt by his cot and took his hand. At her touch, his head rolled back, his eyes opened to the sky, his tortured body stilled.

The woman rose, and Fate saw what the soldier had seen—not a face, but a skull—its eyes yawning black pits, its mouth a wide, mirthless smile. She nodded at Fate, then moved off to another soldier, a boy of sixteen, crying for his mother.

"Death is busy tonight," Fate said somberly, "and has no time for pleasantries."

Fate had seen enough; she turned away and headed back to the enveloping darkness of the Wildwood. When she reached the trees, she cast a last glance over the camp and the sleeping village beyond it.

"Volkmar's out there. I feel him," she said. "Hiding in the hills and hollows. Coming closer every day. What will be unleashed upon these poor, innocent people?"

The raven shook out her feathers. She clicked her beak.

"Who is responsible? Ah, Losca, must you ask?" Fate said heavily. "This is *his* fault, of course. All his. Will that reckless amber-eyed fool ever learn?"

Twenty-Seven

Isabelle, still bleary-eyed from sleep, her hair in a messy braid, pulled a clean dress over her head and buttoned it.

She'd slept badly, kept awake all night by images of Tanaquill. By the time the sun had risen, she'd convinced herself she'd only dreamt the fairy queen. Such creatures did not exist.

But as she picked up yesterday's dress off the floor, meaning to put it in her clothes hamper, something fell out of one of its pockets. Isabelle bent down to pick it up. It was roughly two inches long, black, and covered with small thorns.

It was a seed-pod.

She thrust her hand into the pocket and fished out two more objects—a walnut shell and a jawbone. A shiver moved through her as she remembered how she got these things. The dark creature she'd met by the linden tree was no dream.

I wish I was pretty, she'd said to the fairy queen. And the fairy queen had told her to find the lost pieces of her heart.

Isabelle examined the three gifts one by one. Tanaquill said they would help her, but how? It was no clearer to her now than it had been last night. *Maybe they're meant to turn into something*, she reasoned. Hadn't Tanaquill said that she'd transformed a pumpkin and mice for Ella?

She turned the nutshell over in her hand. *This could become a pretty hat*, she thought. Running a finger over the jawbone's tiny teeth, she imagined that it might turn into a lovely hair comb. Next she regarded the seed-pod, but couldn't imagine how the knobby, spiky thing could ever turn into anything pretty.

Frustrated, Isabelle shoved the three objects into her pocket, then tossed her dirty dress into the hamper. She put her boots on and made her way downstairs. She'd had enough of the fairy queen's mysteriousness for the moment. There were chores to do.

As she walked across the foyer to the kitchen, a rich, bitter scent wafted towards her. *Tavi's up and she made a pot of coffee*, she thought. *I hope she's scrambled some eggs, too.*

Gone were the days when she would come downstairs to a full breakfast set out by the servants. Whatever she and Tavi wanted now, they had to make themselves.

Finding enough to eat in the summer wasn't difficult. The hens were laying, the fruit trees were heavily laden, and good things were growing in the garden. But what would happen come winter? A few days ago, Isabelle had decided to try her hand at pickling vegetables and Tavi had promised to help. Today seemed like a good day to start. The garden was full of cucumbers and they'd bought salt during their trip to the market. If her efforts were successful, she would put the pickles in the cellar for the cold months. She pushed open the kitchen door now, eager to see what her sister had made for breakfast.

As it turned out, nothing.

Except a breathtaking mess.

Twenty-Eight

Tavi was sitting at the long wooden table, peering through a magnifying glass.

The tabletop was littered with plates and bowls, all containing food, but everything was rotten. A slice of bread was furry with mold. A bowl of milk had curdled. A plum had shriveled in its skin.

"What are you *doing*, Tavi? This is disgusting!" Isabelle exclaimed. Her sister often conducted experiments, but they usually involved levers, ramps, and pulleys, not mold.

Tavi lowered her magnifying glass. "I'm hunting for very small, possibly single-celled, organisms," she said excitedly. "I set all of this out on a high shelf in the pantry a few days ago. I selected a high shelf because warm air rises, of course, and speeds the organisms' growth. Just look how they've progressed!"

Isabelle wrinkled her nose. "But *why*?"

Tavi grinned. "I'm glad you asked," she said. "The dominant theory of disease proposes that sickness occurs when miasma, or bad air, rises from rotting matter and is breathed in. But *I* think it occurs when some kind of organism, one invisible to the human eye, is passed from a sick person to a healthy one." She gestured at the stack of books on the table. "Why, just read Thucydides on the Plague of Athens. Or Girolamo Fracastoro in *De contagione et contagiosis morbis.*"

"I'll rephrase my question. Why hunt for organisms *now*? We're supposed to be pickling cucumbers today. You promised to help me."

"That's exactly why I'm conducting my research," Tavi replied. "When you mentioned preserving food, I began to wonder about the processes involved—mechanical, chemical, biological."

"Of course you did," said Isabelle, suppressing a smile. Her happiness at seeing color in Tavi's cheeks and fire in her eyes far outweighed her irritation over the mess. Only one thing could pull Tavi away from maths and that was science.

Looking at her sister, Isabelle wondered how anyone could ever call her ugly. She longed to tell Tavi that the intensity in her eyes and the passion in her voice made her catch her breath. The same way a falcon in flight did. A still lake at dawn. Or a high winter moon. But the sudden lump in her throat wouldn't let her.

"Take jam, for example," Tavi continued. "Heat is applied to fruit and sugar is added, correct?"

Isabelle swallowed. She nodded.

"Is that why jam doesn't spoil? Does the heat kill organisms? Does the sugar play any role? And what about pickling? Does vinegar inhibit organisms' growth? Depending on the type of organism you have, and what it colonizes—milk, cabbage, dough, or a human body—you could end up with cheese, sauerkraut, bread, or the Black Death!" Tavi said gleefully. "But what *is* that organism, Iz? That's what I'm dying to know. Aren't you?"

"No. I'm dying to know when you plan to stop theorizing about pickles and help me make some."

"Soon, soon!" Tavi said, picking up her magnifying glass again. "I made coffee. Help yourself," she added.

Isabelle shook her head. "No, thanks. I've lost my appetite. I'm going to feed Martin and let the chickens out."

Isabelle walked to the kitchen door, but halfway there, she turned and looked back at her sister, who was still peering through her magnifying glass, and thought, *Tavi is so smart. Maybe she can help me figure out what I'm supposed to be searching for.*

Isabelle's hand went to her pocket, she started to hobble back to the table, but then she stopped. Tavi was so logical, so skeptical, she probably wouldn't believe in Tanaquill. And if she told her about the fairy queen, she'd also have to tell her what she'd wished for and she was ashamed to admit that she'd asked to be pretty. Tavi would scoff. She'd mock.

As if sensing that Isabelle was still there, Tavi looked up from her work. "All right," she huffed impatiently. "I'll go."

"Go where?" Isabelle asked, puzzled.

"To the stables. The chicken coop. That's what you're about to ask me to do, isn't it? Abandon my scientific investigations to do the oh-so-important work of shoveling horse manure?"

"Don't rush," Isabelle said, glad she'd decided against telling her about Tanaquill. *Sarcasm is the weapon of the wounded*, she thought, *and Tavi wields it lethally.*

111

As Tavi scribbled figures in a notebook, Isabelle took the egg basket from its hook. Then she grabbed a clasp knife from a shelf, dropped it into her pocket, and left the kitchen. A minute later, she was making her way down the hill to the coop. As she neared the bottom, a fox—green-eyed, her coat a deep russet—darted in front of her. She paused, watching the creature lope across the grass.

In the stories Ella had spun, Tanaquill had sometimes taken the form of a fox. *Is that her?* Isabelle wondered. *Is she watching me? Waiting to see if I carry out her task?*

She didn't have long to wonder. Just as the fox disappeared into some brush, a shriek, high and bloodcurdling, ripped through the air.

There was only one creature who could make such a terrible sound.

"Bertrand the rooster," Isabelle whispered as she set off running.

Twenty-Nine

The shriek came again.

That fox is no fairy queen, Isabelle thought. *It's a chicken thief. And it sounds like another one is still in the coop.*

She, Tavi, and Maman depended on their hens for eggs. Losing even one would be disastrous.

Isabelle kept running, as fast as she could, heedless of the pain her bad foot caused her.

"Hang on, Bertrand!" she cried. "I'm coming!"

The rooster was a fierce creature with sharp, curved spurs on his legs. He'd chased Isabelle up a tree many times. But he was no match for a fox.

Or a wolf, she thought. Her blood ran cold at the very idea. She'd been so frightened for Bertrand and the hens, she'd hurried to the coop without grabbing so much as a stick to defend the henhouse, or herself.

As she ran past the stables now, flushed and panting, her eyes fell on the coop. She saw that the door was open and hanging off its hinges.

She also saw that it was no fox that was stealing her chickens, no wolf.

It was a man—dirty, thin, and desperate.

Thirty

The man was holding a cloth sack. It was moving and clucking. On the ground near the coop lay Bertrand, his neck broken.

Anger shoved Isabelle's fear aside. "What have you done to my rooster?" she shouted. "Put those chickens down!"

"Ah, forgive me, mademoiselle!" the man said with an oily smile. "The house is shuttered. I had no idea anyone lived here."

"Now you do. So leave," Isabelle demanded, gesturing to the road.

The man chuckled. He stepped out of the coop. His eyes swept up and down Isabelle, lingering on her hips, her breasts.

The opportunity of defeating the enemy is provided by the enemy himself.

This time, the words in Isabelle's head were not Alexander the Great's, as they had been when she faced down Cecile, but Sun Tzu's—a Chinese general who'd lived over two thousand years ago.

She put the words to good use. While the man ogled her, she eyed him back and determined that he was unarmed. No sword hung from his waist, no dagger protruded from his boot.

She also saw that she'd left a pitchfork leaning against a tree, a few yards behind him. All she had to do was get to it.

His gaze shifted from her to her house. "Why are you out here all alone? Where's your father? Your brothers?"

Isabelle knew better than to answer that question. "Those chickens are all my family has. If you take them, we'll starve," she said, trying to appeal to his better nature.

"And if I don't, *I'll* starve. I haven't eaten a proper meal in weeks. I'm a soldier in the king's army and I'm hungry," the man said righteously.

"What kind of soldier leaves his barracks to steal chickens?"

"Are you calling me a liar, girl?" the man asked, taking a menacing step towards her.

"And a deserter," said Isabelle, holding her ground.

The man's eyes narrowed. "And if I am, what of it? We are led to battle like lambs to the slaughter. Volkmar knows the king's every move before the king himself knows it. The others can die if they wish. Not me."

"You can take a few eggs if you're hungry," Isabelle said, adamant. "Put the sack down."

The man laughed. He nodded at the pitchfork behind him. "Or what? Or you'll come after me with that rusty tool you've been eyeing? Have you even held a tool before today?" He took another step towards her and with a leer said, "How'd you like to hold mine?"

"Go. *Now*. Or you'll be sorry," Isabelle said, ignoring his ugly joke.

"I'm taking four chickens. That's how it will be," he said.

Fury flared in Isabelle. Her mother and sister were not going to go hungry so this thief could gorge himself. But what could she do? He was standing directly in front of the pitchfork now, blocking her access to it.

I need a weapon, she thought, looking around desperately. *A rake, a shovel, anything.*

Remembering her clasp knife, she dropped the egg basket she was still holding and plunged her hand into her pocket. A pain, sharp and startling, nipped at her fingers. She gave a small cry, but the deserter, who'd gone back into the coop, didn't hear her.

She pulled her hand out of her pocket and saw that her pointer and index fingers were sliced across the tips and bleeding. Stretching her pocket wide, she peered inside it, thinking that the knife must have come open, but no. An object, white, slender, and smeared with her blood, jutted up at her. She realized it was the jawbone Tanaquill had given her. She pulled it out of her pocket and saw that its tiny teeth were what had cut her. With a screech, the angled portion of the jaw suddenly straightened in her hand, making her gasp. The end that had hinged to the animal's skull fattened into a hilt. The other end lengthened into a blade, its edge serrated with the razor-like teeth.

To her astonishment, Isabelle found that she was holding a sword, one that was finely balanced and lethal. As she was marveling at the weapon, the man reemerged from the chicken coop. Immediately, she advanced on him. "You're going to put my hens down and leave. *That's* how it's going to be," she said.

He looked up, laughing, but his laughter died when he

saw the fearsome sword in her hand. "Where did you get that?" he asked.

But Isabelle was in no mood for questions. She struck at him, and the blade bit, opening a gash in his arm. He yelped and dropped the sack.

"That was for Bertrand," Isabelle said. Her blood was no longer running cold. She felt like she had fire in her veins.

The man pressed his palm to the wound. When he pulled it away, it was crimson. He raised his eyes to Isabelle's. "You're going to pay for that," he snarled.

"Isabelle? What's going on? Is that . . . is that *Bertrand*? What happened to him?"

"Stay back, Tavi," Isabelle warned. Her sister had picked the wrong moment to appear.

"Get out of here. *Go*," she said to the man, keeping her sword trained on him. When he didn't move, she charged at him again. He stepped back just in time. Slowly, he raised his hands. "All right," he said. "You win."

He's leaving, Isabelle thought. *Thank goodness.*

Which was exactly what he wanted her to think.

Isabelle had been so outraged to discover a man raiding the coop, she hadn't noticed the satchel in the grass a few feet away or the sword lying next to it. The man lunged for his sword, pulled it free of its scabbard, and turned to face her, his weapon drawn.

Fear sluiced down Isabelle's spine like cold rain through a gutter. Her nerve almost gave way. He had been a soldier in the king's army, trained in the use of a sword. She had dueled with Felix. As a child. With a mop handle.

117

"I'm going to slice you to bits. When I'm finished with you, the vultures will carry you off, piece by piece. What do you say to that, you stupid little bitch?"

Isabelle swallowed hard. Deep inside her, the wolf, asleep under her heart for so long, opened his eyes.

She hefted her sword and stared the man down. "I say, *en garde.*"

Thirty-One

There are those who believe that fear is an enemy, one that must be avoided at all costs.

They run at its first stirrings. They seek shelter from the storm inside the house only to get crushed when the roof falls in.

Fear is the most misunderstood of creatures. It only wants the best for you. It will help you if you let it. Isabelle understood this. She listened to her fear and let it guide her.

He's faster than you! it shouted as the chicken thief rushed her. So she retreated under low-hanging tree branches, that scratched his face and poked his eyes, slowing him.

He's stronger than you! her fear howled. So she led him over the tree's knobby roots, and made him trip.

She parried every thrust and jab the deserter made, and managed to land another blow herself, swiping a bloody stripe across his thigh. Cursing, he scuttled back, away from the tree, pressing on his wound. Out of the corner of her eye, Isabelle saw Tavi trying to get around them, to get to the pitchfork.

No, Tavi, no! she silently shouted.

But it was too late. The man saw her, too, and went after her.

"Run, Tavi!" Isabelle screamed, breaking from the cover of the tree to chase after him.

He heard her and pivoted. Now he had her out in the open. With a roar, he ran at her, swinging for her head.

"No!" Tavi screamed.

Isabelle caught his blade with her own. The crash of steel sent shock waves down her arms.

Using all her strength, she managed to turn his blade, stumble away from him, and open a few feet of distance between them. The man wiped sweat from his face, then charged her again. He feinted left, then lunged right. Isabelle jumped back, but caught her heel on a jutting rock and fell. Instinctively, she rolled to her right as she hit the ground. Sparks flew as her attacker's sword struck the rock.

As Isabelle staggered to her feet, the man raised his sword once more. Winded, the muscles in her arms screaming with exertion, Isabelle lifted her weapon high to block him again, but he was stronger and sure-footed, and she knew that this time, the force of the blow would knock her sword right out of her hands. She would be defenseless when that happened, completely at his mercy. She braced herself for the worst.

But just as the man swung at her, a gunshot ripped through the air. Isabelle dropped into a crouch, her heart hammering. The blade whooshed over her head harmlessly; the sword fell to the ground.

Where did the shot come from? she wondered wildly.

She looked up at her assailant. He was holding his sword hand up. Blood was running down his palm. Two of his fingers were gone. He wasn't looking at Isabelle, but at something, or someone, behind her. His eyes were huge.

"I'm leaving. I—I swear," he stammered. "Please . . . let me take my things." He raised his wounded hand in surrender and picked up his sword with his other one. Backing away step by step, he scooped up his belongings and ran.

Isabelle put her weapon down and her hands up. A sword was no match for a gun. Chest heaving, she stood, then slowly turned around, certain that another deserter had come up behind her and was pointing the pistol straight at her head.

Or maybe a burglar. A brigand. A cold-blooded highwayman.

Never, for a second, did she expect to see a monkey wearing pearls.

Thirty-Two

It took Isabelle a full minute to believe what her eyes were telling her.

A small black monkey with a ruff of white around his face was sitting a yard away from her. A rope of pearls circled his neck. He was brandishing a small silver pistol.

As she stared at him, he hammered the pistol on the ground, peered down the barrel, then scampered off around the side of the stables, still holding the firearm.

Isabelle pressed a hand to her chest, trying to calm her pounding heart.

"Tavi!" she called out. "Be careful!" She took a hesitant step forward. "There's a monkey . . . he—he has a gun . . ."

"I see him!" Tavi called out, rushing to Isabelle's side. She'd got hold of the pitchfork and was clutching it for dear life.

Isabelle's foot was throbbing, but she limped after the monkey nonetheless, worried that he might shoot himself with the pistol, or Tavi, or her.

"Monkey? Little monkey, are you there?" she called out, following the creature's path.

The monkey ran out screeching from a water trough, bolted

across the drive, and made a beeline for a birch tree. A woman, her hair swept up with jeweled combs, her bosom rising up out of her sprigged gown like brioche, was standing at the base of the tree, looking up into its branches. She turned as she heard the monkey's screech.

"*There* you are, Nelson! Give me the pistol! You'll kill someone!" she scolded. The monkey darted around her and climbed up the trunk. Three more monkeys were already in the tree. The four made a game out of tossing the pistol back and forth while the woman stood below, shaking her fist at them.

Isabelle blinked. *I'm hallucinating. I must be*, she told herself. She squeezed her eyes closed and opened them again. The woman was still there.

"Are you seeing this, too?" she asked her sister.

Tavi nodded, speechless.

Isabelle approached the woman carefully, hoping she wasn't here to steal chickens too. She didn't think she had another sword fight in her.

"Madame, pardon me, but what are you doing in our stableyard? With a monkey?" she asked. "How did you get here?"

"How do you think?" the woman called over her shoulder, hooking her thumb behind her. "How else does one convey oneself to a godforsaken backwater in the middle of nowhere?"

Isabelle's eyes followed the direction of her gesture. Her mouth dropped open. There, standing a little way down the drive, but with a clear view of the chicken coop, was the most magnificent carriage she had ever seen.

Thirty-Three

In front of the enormous, painted coach, four dapple gray horses stood, tossing their heads and stamping their hooves.

Up high in the driver's seat sat a man wearing a jade-green jacket and pink trousers. A teardrop-shaped pearl dangled from one ear. He nodded at Isabelle and Tavi.

Goggle-eyed, they nodded back. Behind the driver, a dozen trunks were lashed to the carriage's roof. On top of them sat a troop of acrobats, one of whom was juggling knives blindfolded. Next to her a fire-breather blew lazy smoke rings; a magician caught them and turned them into coins. Musicians held their instruments as if at a concert hall awaiting their conductor. Isabelle was spellbound.

The carriage door opened, and a man stepped out. Isabelle glimpsed a pair of mesmerizing amber eyes, a sweep of black braids, the flash of a gold earring. The man started to clap. The others joined him. The applause was thunderous. Then the man waved his hand and it stopped.

"That was quite the duel, mademoiselle!" he said to Isabelle. "We saw you from the road and pulled in to help, but before I could even get my door open, Nelson took matters into his own hands. Paws, I should say. Though I shouldn't have left my pistol lying on the seat. Have you ever met a monkey who could resist a silver pistol?" He suddenly snapped his fingers. "Forgive me, I haven't introduced myself."

He took off his hat, bowed, then straightened again, and with a smile—one so beguiling that in a single day in Marseille it had inspired three sea captains to set sail for Cape Horn, a duchess to run off with her gardener, and a man named Montgolfier to invent the hot-air balloon—said, "The Marquis de la Chance, at your service."

As the words left his lips, the musicians shot to their feet atop the carriage and played a rousing fanfare.

The marquis winced. Turning to them, he said, "A bit much for the country, don't you think?"

The music stopped. The French horns looked down at their shoes. The trumpeter polished an imaginary speck off his instrument.

Isabelle, who'd dipped a curtsy, and pulled a stunned Tavi down with her, now rose. "Isabelle de la Paumé, Your Grace. And this is my sister Octavia. We are . . ." *What?* she wondered. *Shocked? Stunned? Utterly astonished?* ". . . *pleased* to make your acquaintance."

"I wonder if you could tell me how to get to the Château Rigolade," the marquis said. "I'm under the impression that it's somewhere around here, but we're a bit lost. I won it."

"You *won* it?" Tavi echoed, clearly baffled.

"Yes, in a game of cards. I needed somewhere to go. I and my household." He gestured to the carriage. "Paris is chaos at the moment, with that beast Volkmar on the rampage. And I require peace and quiet. I'm writing a play, you see."

"You're a playwright, sir?" Isabelle asked.

"Not one bit," the marquis said. "Never even put pen to paper before. But I'm always doing things I can't do. Otherwise, I'd never get to do them."

As Isabelle tried to follow that logic, the marquis said, "Now, about the château . . ."

Isabelle quickly gave him directions. "It's not far. Turn left at the end of our drive. Follow the road for a mile. When you come to a fork in the road . . ."

The marquis's eyes lit up. "A fork in the road! How wonderful! I *love* forks in the road! They lead to opportunity!"

"Change!" shouted an acrobat.

"Adventure!" trilled a musician.

"Excitement!" crowed the fire-breather.

Isabelle looked between the marquis and his friends uncertainly. "Yes, well . . . when you come to *this* fork, make a right. Keep on for another half mile or so, and you'll see the drive. The château itself sits on a rise. You can't miss it."

"We are forever in your debt," said the marquis. "But before we leave, I would like to offer you a bit of advice . . ."

The marquis walked up to Isabelle and took her hands in his. She caught her breath. His touch felt like lightning had just ripped through the air. Like she'd stolen a bag of diamonds. Found a chest full of gold.

But as they stood close, Isabelle saw that the merriment that lit his eyes, the ebullience that animated his every movement, the teasing challenge that sparkled in his voice, were all gone, replaced by a sudden, unnerving ferocity.

"You are good with a sword, but not good enough," he said to her. "Practice. Become faster. Better. There are worse creatures afoot in France than chicken thieves. Far worse. Promise me, young Isabelle. *Promise me.*"

It seemed very important to him that she learn to protect herself. She had no idea why, but he was clearly not going to let go of her until she agreed to his demand. "I—I promise, Your Grace," she said.

"Good," the marquis said, releasing her. "Now, if you ladies will excuse me—"

Ka-blam!

Another bullet whistled through the air. It hit the weather vane on top of the barn and sent it spinning. It sent Tavi running for cover.

It also spooked the horses.

Whinnying and wild-eyed, they lurched forward in their harnesses, wrenching the carriage around the circular drive so violently that it went up on two wheels and teetered there for a few heart-stopping seconds. The driver threw himself across his seat. Everyone on the roof leaned over. The marquis ran for the carriage, caught hold of the open door, and hung his full weight on it. Finally, the wheels slammed back down. The carriage careened under the birch tree, and as it did, the monkeys dropped out of the branches onto its roof. The marquis, safely inside now, stretched across the magician and the cook and leaned out of the window.

"Thank you!" he shouted. "Goodbye!"

"Goodbye, Your Grace!" Isabelle and Tavi called back.

They stood by the stables waving until the carriage sped

down the drive, turned into the road, and disappeared.

In all the commotion, they never saw the monkey unhook the pearls from his neck, stretch a furry arm out over the carriage's roof, and drop them into the grass.

Thirty-Four

After the excitement of the morning, the rest of the day passed slowly for Isabelle, full of chores outside of the mansion, and inside it, too.

Nightfall found her sitting at her kitchen table. Tavi had made them a delicious omelet with tarragon in it. Isabelle had cleaned her plate and was now staring at the sword the fairy queen had given her, lost in thought.

She'd hung the sword on a hook by the door. Tavi had asked her where she'd gotten it. Isabelle had fibbed and said she'd found it in a trunk in the stables some time ago, and had grabbed it as soon as she'd seen the chicken thief.

Tanaquill's voice drifted through her mind. *Cut away piece by piece by piece* . . . She'd said the word *piece* three times. *Is that a clue?* Isabelle wondered. *Are there three pieces that I'm supposed to find?* "We should wash the dishes, Isabelle," Tavi said now.

"Yes, we should," Isabelle agreed, but she made no move to do so.

Tavi followed her gaze. "You've been frowning at that sword all through supper. Why?"

Isabelle's frown deepened. "I've been wondering, Tav . . . what is a heart, exactly?"

"What a strange question. Why are you asking?"

"I just . . ." Isabelle shrugged. "Want to know."

"A heart is a four-chambered, pump-like organ that circulates blood throughout the body via rhythmic contractions."

"I meant *besides* that. In poems and songs, the heart is the place where goodness comes from."

Tavi gave her a long look. "Are you writing poetry now?"

"Yes! Ha. Yes, I am. How did you guess?" Isabelle said brightly. It was another fib and she felt bad about telling it, but it *was* the perfect cover for asking what she wanted to know without mentioning why she wanted to know it. "In my poem, the main character—"

"Do poems have main characters?"

"This one does, and she's lost her heart. Or rather, pieces of it. I need to find them. In the poem, I mean. For my main character. What would you say pieces of a heart could be?"

Tavi sat back in her chair, an expression of grave concern on her face. Then she picked up a candleholder that was standing on the table, and moved the flame past Isabelle's eyes.

"What on earth are you doing?" Isabelle asked, shrinking away from it.

"Seeing if your pupils dilate and contract properly. I'm worried you've taken too many falls off Martin. Hit your head once too often."

Isabelle rolled her eyes. "I *haven't* lost my wits, if that's what you're suggesting. Answer my question, Tavi. Theoretically."

"Well, let's say—theoretically—that it was you we were

130

talking about. I'd say that sword you've been staring at is a piece of your heart."

Isabelle stubbornly shook her head. "I don't think so. No."

"Why not? You used to love swords. You loved fencing and . . . and Felix. Why, the two of you—"

"Yes, I did," Isabelle said, brusquely cutting her off. Tavi's words were salt in a deep wound that had never healed. "And what did it get me? Felix made a promise and then he broke it. And me along with it."

"We're not talking theoretically any more, are we?"

Isabelle inspected her hands. "No," she admitted.

"I'm sorry. I shouldn't have mentioned him."

Isabelle waved her apology away. "Whatever the pieces of my heart are, they don't include him. Or swords."

"Then what do they include? And how are you going to find them?" Tavi asked.

"I don't know," Isabelle replied. She thought hard then said, "Since a heart is where goodness comes from, maybe I could do some good deeds."

Tavi burst out laughing. "Do good deeds? *You?*"

Isabelle glowered, offended. "Yes, *me*. What's so funny about that?"

"You've never done any!"

"Yes, I have!" Isabelle insisted. "I gave Tantine a ride to the LeBenêts' the other day. That's a start."

"Oh, Izzy," Tavi said softly. She reached across the table for her hand and squeezed it. "It's too late for good deeds. People shout at us. They throw rocks at our windows. Mean is all we have left. And all we can do is get better at it. Good deeds

131

won't change anything."

Isabelle squeezed back. "Maybe they'll change *me*, Tav."

Tavi rose to wash the dishes then, and Isabelle, seeing how dark it was getting, said she'd help her right after she locked up the animals.

"Take the sword with you," Tavi cautioned. "Just in case."

Isabelle did. As she lifted it off its hook, she wondered again how the fairy queen's gift would help her attain her heart's desire. She was glad to have had it, for it had helped save her life today, but pretty girls twirled parasols and fluttered fans. They didn't swing swords.

And yet, when Isabelle got outside, and felt how the sword's hilt fit so perfectly in her hand, how the blade was so finely weighted, she couldn't help but take a swipe at a rosebush, then smile as several pink flowers fell to the ground. She decapitated two lilies as she walked, then whacked a blowsy blue hydrangea off its stalk.

"The marquis told me to practice," she said aloud, almost guiltily, as if some unseen person had accused her of enjoying herself.

Dangerous characters were afoot. She was making sure she could defend herself, that's all.

It was magical, the sword. Incredible. Breathtaking. She couldn't deny it.

But it wasn't her heart.

And it never would be.

She wouldn't let it.

Thirty-Five

As Isabelle fenced in the darkness, Chance, comfortably installed in the Château Rigolade, peered down at the flask of silvery liquid he'd concocted.

All around him, his retinue busied themselves. Only the magician was nowhere to be seen.

His attention focused on the flask, Chance was barely aware of the people around him. The silver liquid was simmering on a burner in the centre of a diabolically complex distilling system. Its color was shimmering and rich, but Chance was not satisfied.

His scientist had set up the apparatus on the enormous table in the centre of the château's dining room just after they'd arrived. It was surrounded by brass scales, presses and expellers, a mortar and pestle, and apothecary jars containing all manner of ingredients.

Chance reached for one of the jars now. He removed its stopper, extracted a piece of yellowed lace, and dropped it into the flask. A spoonful of dried violets was added next, followed by a cobweb, a scrap of sheet music, a crumbled madeleine, and numbers pried off a clock face.

The liquid bubbled and swirled after each addition, but Chance was still not happy. He combed through the jars, searching for one last ingredient. With a triumphant *Aha!* he found it—a pair of shimmering moth wings. As he dropped them into the flask, the liquid transformed into a beautiful faded mauve.

"Perfect!" he declared. With a pair of tongs, he carefully lifted the flask off the flames and set it on a marble slab to cool.

"I need a name for this ink," he said to the scientist, who was working across from him. "A name for the feeling you get when you see someone again. After many years. Someone lost to you. Or so you thought. And you remember them a certain way. In your mind, they never age. But then suddenly, there they are. Older. Changed by time. Different, but exactly the same."

The scientist looked up from his work. He peered at Chance over the top of his glasses.

"This person meant something to you?" he asked.

"Could have. Might have. Almost did. Would have," Chance said. "If the timing had been right. If you'd been wiser. Bolder. Better."

The scientist, spare and rigorous, not a man given to flights of fancy, put a hand over his heart. He closed his eyes. A wistful smile played across his lips.

"Wonderfulness," he said. "That's the name."

Chance smiled. He wrote *Wonderfulness* on a paper label, stuck it on the bottle, and carried it to the far end of the table. The map of Isabelle de la Paumé's life lay rolled up there. One never knew when a reunion might be called for. It was important to be prepared for any contingency.

Other inks he'd created were scattered around the map. There was *Defiance*, a swirling red-orange ink made from ground lion's teeth mixed with bull's blood. *Inspiration* was pale gold, made from black tea mixed with cocoa, a pinch of dirt from a poet's grave, and four drops of a lunatic's tears left to ferment in the light of a full moon. And *Stealth*, the color of midnight, was composed of owl's breath, hawk feathers, and the powdered finger bones of a pickpocket.

Are the pigments bold enough, the formulas strong enough, to draw new paths? he wondered as he set the bottle of *Wonderfulness* down. He'd tried to make ink before, many times, but had never been able to devise tints powerful enough to undo the crone's work.

Dread jabbered at the edges of his mind now. He poured himself a generous glass of cognac from a crystal decanter to silence it. After draining it in one gulp, he sat down in front of the map. As he unrolled it, smoothing it flat, he couldn't help but marvel at the beauty of the Fates' work. Their parchment was the finest he'd ever seen, their inks exquisite, the quality of their drawing unparalleled.

Isabelle's full name was at the top of the map, hand-lettered in Greek, the Fates' native tongue. Covering the rest of the parchment was the richly colored landscape of her life. Chance saw her birthplace, other towns she'd lived in, Saint-Michel. He saw the peaks and valleys, the sunny plains and the dark woods through which she had crossed. He saw her path, a thick black line, and the dotted, dashed, and hatched lines of lives that intersected hers.

But it was what Chance could not see that so unnerved him.

135

Thirty-Six

"Are they ready?" he called out impatiently.

The scientist, polishing a pair of wire-framed eyeglasses with a soft cloth, nodded. He brought them to Chance.

"They're powerful?" asked Chance, taking them.

"Very. I ground the lenses myself. The left gives you hindsight; the right, foresight."

Chance held them up to the light. "Pink?" he said as he looked through the lenses. It was not his favorite color.

"*Rose*," William corrected. "It's hard to look at mortal life any other way. View it through clear lenses and it breaks your heart."

Chance put the eyeglasses on, hooking the curved ends behind his ears. As he gazed at the map through them, he caught his breath. The entire parchment looked like the pages of the clever little books paper cutters made for children in which everything popped up.

No one, certainly no mortal and not even Chance himself, possessed the Fates' sharpness of vision. They drew with such painstaking detail that most of their art was impossible to see with the naked eye. Chance had stolen many maps from the three sisters, but never before had he been able to view their work so clearly.

All along Isabelle's path, the moments of her life stood out in vibrant three-dimensional scenes. He saw her as a child, fencing with a boy. He saw her standing in front of a mirror in a fancy dress with tears in her eyes. And he saw her at the village market, just a few days ago, arguing with the baker's wife.

"You're a genius," he whispered.

The scientist smiled, pleased.

But Chance did not return the smile. His pleasure in the power of his new eyeglasses to show Isabelle's past so clearly was tempered by the knowledge that they would also reveal the details of her future. He already knew what lay at the end of her path, for he'd seen it when he was in the Fates' palazzo, but he didn't know exactly when it would occur.

He might have weeks to prevent it, even months. Then again, he might have only days.

His eyes darted to the bottom of the map, seeking the answer to his question. The legend was there. It explained that an inch equaled a year and gave Isabelle's birth date.

The Fates' seal was there, too. The crone put one on every mortal's map when she completed it by dripping melted red wax onto the bottom of the parchment and pressing her skull ring into it. The resulting impression was a death date, for the closer a mortal came to the end of her path, the darker the skull turned, deepening from bloodred to black.

The skull on Isabelle's map was a somber burgundy, streaked with gray.

"She has only weeks left. *Weeks*," Chance said. He pressed

a shaky hand to his head. "How the devil am I going to undo this?" he muttered.

He snatched his quill off the table, dipped it in *Defiance*, and started to draw Isabelle a new path, one that led away from her terrible fate. The ink shimmered brightly on the parchment.

"Ha! *Defiance*, indeed!" he crowed, encouraged.

But an instant later, the ink started to fade and then disappeared completely; the parchment had sucked it in like desert sands absorbing rain.

Chance took another tack. He dipped the quill into *Defiance* again and tried to cross out what lay at the end of Isabelle's path, but no matter how much ink he scribbled, stippled, hatched, and dripped onto the parchment, Isabelle's fate still showed through, like a corpse bobbing to the surface of a lake.

Swearing, Chance threw the quill down. He took his glasses off and put them on the table. This was a disaster. His inks weren't strong enough to draw so much as a detour, never mind counter the violent reds and slashing blacks that had been put there not by the Fates, but by one whose power to change paths was growing stronger by the day.

The scientist looked up from his work. "What's wrong?" he asked.

Chance was about to reply when a loud, insistent pounding at the door stopped him. It echoed through the château, shaking the furniture and rattling the windows.

The cook, who had just walked into the dining room from the kitchens, set down the silver tray of pretty cakes he was carrying. He hurried out of the dining room, through the chateâu's grand foyer, to a window at the side of the door. "Destiny calls," he shouted back to the others, glancing out of it.

The sword-swallower held up his hands. "Everyone stop talking!" he whisper-shouted. "Maybe she'll go away!"

"Don't be ridiculous. She knows we're here," said the diva. "The whole village does. We don't exactly blend in."

The knock came again. Chance groaned with frustration. A visit from the crone was the last thing he needed.

"Open the door," he finally said. "Let her in. But keep an eye on the map, all of you."

Thirty-Seven

"My dear marquis," said Fate as she walked into the hall, a raven on her shoulder. "What a handsome home. And what . . ." She paused, walked over to the table and examined the distilling apparatus. ". . . *interesting* furnishings. Making gin, perhaps? Perfume?" She tapped a finger to her chin. "Or, possibly, ink?"

Chance gave her a curt bow. "My dear madame," he said. "To what do I owe the pleasure of your visit?"

"Why, neighborliness, of course," Fate replied. "We are dwelling in the same village, are we not? We must keep relations cordial."

She slowly strolled around the enormous hall, taking it in. As she did, the members of Chance's entourage stopped what they were doing and eyed her, intrigued.

"This *is* a magnificent château," she said enviously. "I wish my accommodations were half as nice."

"Are you not staying at the village inn?" Chance asked.

"I was, but now I'm staying with . . ." She smiled, inclining her head. "Some long-lost relatives."

As she continued her stroll, her eyes fell on Isabelle's map.

"Don't even think about it," Chance said. "You won't make it to the door."

Fate clucked her tongue. "I hope you haven't made a mess of my work," she said, running her gnarled fingers over Isabelle's path.

As her hand neared the end of the path, it stopped short, as if it had hit an obstacle. Fate's mouth twitched. Her gaze sharpened. And then, as if remembering that eyes were upon her, she quickly rearranged her expression back to one of bemused coolness.

Did I imagine it? Chance wondered. The cook was standing on the other side of Fate. He gave Chance a quick, barely perceptible nod. *He saw it, too*, Chance thought. *What does it mean?*

"Why do you even bother?" Fate asked airily, turning to Chance. "You've brewed up a new batch of inks, but I doubt they're any match for mine. What I draw cannot be changed. Not by you."

"But *they* can change it," Chance said. "With a bit of luck, mortals can do incredible things."

Fate gave him a patronizing smile. "And some do. But one needs determination to change one's fate. Courage. Strength. Things most mortals grievously lack. One needs to be exceptional, and the girl Isabelle, most assuredly, is not."

"She has courage and strength. A tremendous will, too," Chance countered. "She just needs to find them again."

Fate's smile turned brittle. "As usual, you are meddling where you should not. Let the girl enjoy what little time she has left. You will break her heart by encouraging her to want things she has no business wanting. Girls die of broken hearts."

Chance snorted. "Here are the things girls die of: hunger, disease, accidents, childbirth, and violence. It takes more than heartache to kill a girl. Girls are tough as rocks."

Fate paused, as a cat does before sinking its teeth into a mouse, then said, "But Volkmar is tougher."

Guilt bled into Chance's eyes. He turned away, trying to hide it, but Fate had glimpsed it and she circled him for the kill.

"Volkmar certainly changed *his* fate, didn't he?" she said. "But he *is* an exceptional mortal. Exceptionally ruthless. Exceptionally cruel." She nodded at the map. "It's his work, that ugly scrawl at the end of Isabelle's path, as you well know."

The scientist squinted in confusion. "I don't understand . . . *Volkmar* redrew the girl's map?"

"Not with quills and inks as I do, but with the sheer force of his will," Fate replied. "He is so bold, so strong, that he is able to change his fate. And by so doing, he changes the fates of thousands more."

"So his actions have compelled your inks to redraw his map," the scientist reasoned. "And the maps of those whose lives he touches."

"Precisely," said Fate. "Volkmar wishes to rule the world and begins his cruel campaign in France. One by one, villages and towns will fall to him as he tightens his noose around Paris. Saint-Michel will fall, too, and with such savagery that the young king will have no choice but to surrender. Volkmar will slaughter Isabelle in cold blood. Her sister. Her mother. Their neighbors. Every last person in this poor, forsaken place."

A gasp rose from several people in the room. The diva uttered a cry.

Fate turned to her, affecting an innocent expression. "Did you not know? Did he not tell you?"

The diva, tears welling, shook her head.

"That is *enough*, crone," Chance growled.

But Fate, her gaze still on the diva, ignored him. "Why, my dear, don't you see?"

"I said *stop*."

But Fate did not. Eyes shining with spite, she walked to the diva and took her hands. *"That* is why your marquis is so desperate to change Isabelle's fate. Because he himself brought it about!"

Thirty-Eight

It was utterly silent in the grand hall.

Chance stood still, fists clenched, heart seared by shame and regret. No one else moved, either. No one spoke.

Until Fate, circling back to him, said, "I have come, however unwillingly. I accept your stakes. We will play our old game. You know the rules . . . neither can force the girl's choice. Or buy it. She may take what is offered or not."

Chance nodded stiffly. As Fate looked at him, something like sadness darkened her eyes.

"If you loved these mortals, you would leave them—"

"To your tender mercies?" he spat.

"—alone."

"It's because I love them that I won't. They deserve a chance. Some of them never get one. This girl will."

"But will she take it?" Fate asked.

"Thank you for your visit, but I must get back to work," Chance said brusquely.

Fate laughed, shaking her head. "She *won't*. Humans are what they are—dreamers, madmen, but most of all, fools."

She let herself out of the Château Rigolade and disappeared

into the night, but her laughter, harsh and mocking, lingered in Chance's ears. He slammed the door shut after her and leaned his forehead against it. After a moment, he faced his friends and attempted to explain.

"There was a party . . ."

The cook shook his head. "There always is."

". . . in a castle in the Black Forest. There was a sumptuous dinner. I drank a good deal of champagne. After dinner, there was a card game. The stakes were high."

"How high?" the cook asked.

Chance grimaced. "One million gold ducats."

The cook swore. "You never learn, do you?"

"I didn't know then who he was . . . *what* he was. I didn't know what he was planning. I never dreamt—" His closed his eyes against the crushing pain he felt. "Once he had the money, he used it to dark advantage. He built up his army, marched on France. Everything he's done is *my* fault. I created him."

Chance lowered his head into his hands. The diva hurried to his side; she squeezed his arm.

"Volkmar created himself," she said. "He had a choice. He could have used his fortune for good, not ill."

Chance groaned in despair. He felt so weary. His bones ached. His heart hurt. Everything seemed pointless. All his energy seemed to have drained out of him. "The crone is right," he said, sagging into a chair. "Mortals are fools. I should walk away. Leave them to their own devices. I mean to help, but too often I wreck things. And people."

"But you always tell us that one person can make a difference," the diva countered. "Isabelle might be such a person. If Volkmar

145

can change his fate, and the fates of thousands more, why can't this girl do the same?"

Chance gave a joyless laugh. "Isabelle can barely *walk*."

The diva sat down heavily. Everyone looked leaden and defeated. No one spoke.

Until the magician strode in from the night through a pair of glass doors that opened onto the terrace. She was wearing riding boots, breeches, and a close-cut jacket, all in black. Her lips were rouged. Her color was high. She was holding a dark flower in one hand.

"It took me a while, but I found the night orchid you wanted. For *Courage*."

Chance shook his head. "I won't be needing it any more. My inks don't work."

The magician looked from Chance to the others. "What happened? Did somebody die? Why are you all sitting around like mushrooms?" She made a face. "It *stinks* in here. Like surrender. Failure. And rot." Her eyes narrowed. "It's the *crone*. She's been here, hasn't she? Who let her in?"

The cook sheepishly raised his hand.

"Never, *ever* do it again," the magician scolded, opening the rest of the terrace doors. "She's like sulfurous gas from a fumarole. Bad air from an old mine. She poisoned you. Made you think you have to accept things rather than fight to change them."

She pushed the cakes off the silver tray, opened the neck of Chance's shirt, and fanned him with it. Then she strode over to the cook and slapped his cheeks.

"Snap out of it!" she ordered. "If the inks don't work, then we'll find something that does."

A breeze blew through the open doors, freshening the room. Chance blinked, then looked around as if he were waking from a deep sleep. A little spirit trickled back into him.

"There *was* something on the map. Something—" he started to say.

The cook snapped his fingers. "Something that bothered the crone. I caught that, too. If it's not good for her, it's very good for us."

Chance was back at the table in a flash with the cook right behind him. He put his glasses back on, then trailed his finger over Isabelle's path, searching for whatever it was that had rattled Fate.

He moved past the day Isabelle cut her toes off, past Ella leaving, to where Volkmar's brutal line started, and beyond, to where it finished, and then he went back and retraced the line, but he didn't see anything he hadn't seen before. Even with the glasses, he couldn't see as clearly as the Fates.

And then he did see something.

It was faintly etched. But it was *there*. A detour. Newly made. "Yes!" he shouted, clapping his hands together.

"What is it? *Speak*, man!" the cook said.

Chance ripped his spectacles off and handed them to him. The cook put them, squinted at the map, then grinned. "Ha!" he cried. "No wonder the crone's face looked like a bucket of sour milk! That path—"

"Isn't Fate's work, or Volkmar's . . . it's *hers*. Isabelle's. Her actions redrew her path," Chance finished, his eyes dancing. "I was right. She *can* change. She *will* change. We're going to win this game. We're going to beat the Fates."

"Easy. It's only a start. Let's not get cocky," the cook cautioned.

"It's *more* than a start," Chance insisted. "Did you see where it led?"

The cook peered at the map again. "It looks like a tree . . . an old linden . . ." He took the glasses off. "Bloody hell," he said, turning back to Chance. "Do you know who that is?"

"Tanaquill," Chance said.

"The fairy queen?" the magician asked, joining the two men. "Chance, she's—"

"Very, very powerful," Chance cut in.

"Actually, I was thinking *murderous*," said the magician.

"Did Isabelle summon her?" the cook wondered aloud. "For what purpose?"

"I doubt it was to invite her to tea," said the magician, with a shiver.

"I can't quite make that out. The glasses aren't powerful enough, but I think Isabelle asked her for help," said Chance. He ran his hands through his braids, then pointed at the cook. "I'll need a gift. I can't go empty-handed. Are there any rabbits in the larder?"

"I used the last ones for the stew we had tonight. I have pheasants, though," he replied, heading for the kitchen.

"I'll take them," said Chance.

"You're going to look for Tanaquill *now*?" the magician asked. "It's nearly midnight!"

"I don't have a choice," Chance said. "Fate saw that detour, too. She's hunting for the fairy queen as we speak, I'm sure of it. I've got to find her first." He sped off after his cook.

The scientist, his face etched with worry, picked up the rose-tinted glasses and polished them. "She'll eat him alive," he said.

The magician stared after Chance, a worried look on her face. "You're right," she said. She patted her hip, making sure her dagger was there, then added, "I'm going with him."

Thirty-Nine

The fairy queen was standing in a clearing in the Wildwood, an enormous yellow-eyed owl perched on her forearm.

It was well after midnight, but the darkness only set off her vivid presence. Her russet hair was braided and coiled. A circlet of antlers adorned her head. She wore a dress that shimmered like a minnow, and over it a cape of gray feathers held together at the neck by a pair of large iridescent beetles, their powerful pincers clasped.

Chance had found her by following her magic. It left traces, silver drops that gleamed on the forest floor, then slowly faded. As he and the magician watched, hidden in a copse of birch trees, Tanaquill stroked the owl and whispered to him, heedless of the sharp, curved beak that could crack bone and rip out hearts, of the curved talons that could flay hide.

"Ready?" Chance whispered. The magician nodded, and they both stepped out into the clearing.

"Hail mighty Tanaquill!" Chance called out. "My search is at last rewarded. It's an honor to be in your presence."

Tanaquill laughed. It was the sound of the autumn wind swirling dead leaves around. "You've been in my presence for a good half hour, cowering behind the birch trees. I smelled you. And your pheasants."

Chance approached her, with the magician close behind him. "Please accept them, Your Grace, as a small token of my esteem," he said with a bow, holding the birds out.

With a sneer, Tanaquill refused them. "Leave them for the vultures," she said. "They like dead things. I prefer my tribute living. The heart beating, the blood surging."

She put a hand on Chance's chest. Leaning in close to his neck, she breathed in his scent, licked her lips. Chance was enthralled by her beguiling green eyes, like a mouse transfixed by a snake. He'd let her come too close.

The magician saved him. She pulled him away, then stood in front of him, her hand on the hilt of her dagger. Tanaquill snarled like a fox who'd lost a nice fat squirrel.

"Why are you here? What do you want of me?" she asked.

"Your help. I want to save a girl. Her name is Isabelle. You know her. I have her map. Drawn by the Fates. It shows that you spoke with her."

"And just how did you come to possess the map?" Tanaquill asked. "The Fates guard their work closely."

Chance explained. As he finished, Tanaquill made a noise of disgust. "I want nothing to do with your foolish games," she said, walking away. "I do not serve you or Fate. I serve only the heart."

Chance took a desperate step after her. He couldn't let her slip away. He was certain something important had passed between her and Isabelle. Something he could use to help the girl.

"Volkmar comes closer to Saint-Michel with each passing day," he said.

"What of it?" said Tanaquill with a backhanded wave.

"He has rewritten Isabelle's fate. In blood. But she can change it. If she can change herself."

Tanaquill's laughter rang out through the Wildwood. "*That* selfish, bitter girl? You think *she* can best a warlord?"

"It is not only the village, and the mortals who live in it, that will fall. Volkmar plunders and burns everything in his path. The Wildwood and all that dwell in it . . . they will not survive him, either."

Tanaquill stopped. She turned around. Sorrow and anger warred in the depths of her fierce eyes. Chance saw her distress. And pushed his advantage.

"Please, I beg you. What did Isabelle say to you?"

"She asked for my help," Tanaquill said at length. "She wishes to be *pretty*." The fairy queen spat the word.

"And did you grant her wish?"

"I told her I would help her," Tanaquill replied in such a way that Chance had the distinct feeling she was evading his question. The fairy queen continued. "I also told her that she would have to earn my help by finding the lost pieces of her heart."

"Those pieces . . . what are they?" asked Chance.

"Why should I tell you? So you can find them and drop them into her lap?"

"So I can give her a *chance*. That's all I ask. A chance at redemption."

Tanaquill smirked. "Redemption? Would that be for the girl? Or for you?"

Her words cut Chance. He flinched, but his gaze did not falter. His smile was no longer golden, but naked and vulnerable. "Both, if I'm lucky," he said.

Tanaquill's eyes held his. Her gaze was piercing. Then she said, "Nero, a horse. Felix, a boy. Ella, a stepsister."

As soon as the words had left the fairy queen's lips, Chance shot the magician a look. She nodded, then melted away into the woods.

"Thank you, Your Grace," Chance said fervently. He took her cool, pale hand in his, lifted it to his lips, and kissed it.

Tanaquill growled, but there was little threat in it. "What happens next is up to the girl. Not you. Not Fate," she warned as Chance released her.

As if on cue, Fate walked into the clearing. "Ah, Tanaquill! Well met by moonlight!" she said. She gave Chance a smug smile. "Taking the night air, Marquis? A bit stuffy in the château?"

Chance's stomach sank to his boots. *How much of our conversation has she overheard?* he wondered anxiously.

Fate had a basket on her arm and a raven on her shoulder. "Are you hunting mushrooms, too?" she asked the fairy queen.

"I know why you've come," the fairy queen said, ignoring her question. "But I'm afraid your adversary here"—she nodded at Chance—"has beaten you to the draw."

Fate's smile soured. Chance let out a shallow breath of relief. Perhaps she had not overheard them.

"Leave the girl alone, Tanaquill," Fate said. "This is not your fight, and she is not worth your efforts. Stick to the woods. Go hunting."

The fairy queen whirled on her, snarling with fury. Fate stumbled back. Her raven squawked.

"Do *not* patronize me, crone. I have been summoned by a human heart and am not so easily put back in my box," Tanaquill warned. "You could no more contain me than you could contain a hurricane. I am older than you. Older than Chance. Older than time itself."

She waved her hand. There was a high-pitched shriek, a blur in the air. The raven never saw the yellow-eyed hunter coming. The owl tore the bird off Fate's shoulder and drove it to the ground. Then it lifted its wings over its prey and screeched at Fate, daring her to take it.

Fate did not. She stood still; her body was tense. Her eyes—back on Tanaquill—were calculating, like those of a lioness who wishes to attack a rival but is not certain of a win.

Tanaquill saw her wish. "I would not if I were you. Have you forgotten what I am? I am the heart's first beat and its last. I am the newborn lamb and the wolf that rips out its throat. I am the bloodsong, crone." She tossed a glance at the struggling raven and smiled. "So much for your box."

And then she was gone, vanished into the darkness, and her owl with her. And where the raven had been a girl sat, her chest hitching, her trembling fingers hovering over the gouges on her neck.

"Up, Losca," Fate ordered. "Go back to my room. Wait for me there."

Losca stood. She stumbled out of the clearing on unsteady legs.

"That owl could've killed the poor girl. Why don't you pack

up, before someone else gets hurt?" Chance said gloatingly. "I've as good as won this wager."

Fate regarded him coolly. "Go back to your château, Marquis. Get some rest. You'll need it. I believe you have a horse to find. A boy. And a stepsister, no?" she said, walking away.

Chance swore, furious. The crone *had* overheard his conversation with Tanaquill.

Fate stopped at the edge of the clearing, turned back to him, and, with a poisonous smile, added, "Unless *I* find them first."

Forty

Tavi stood by the kitchen door, cradling a bowl of fresh-picked plums, her white apron and the skirts of her blue dress fluttering in the morning breeze. She cast a skeptical eye over the contents of the large basket Isabelle had placed in the back of their wooden cart.

"But what if the orphans don't *want* eggs?" she asked.

"Of course they will," Isabelle said, adjusting a buckle on Martin's harness. "Orphans don't have much. They'll be happy to get them."

Tavi raised an eyebrow. "Do you even know where the orphanage is?"

Isabelle shot Tavi a look. She didn't reply.

"Do you have your sword with you?"

"I don't need it," Isabelle said.

The truth was that she didn't have it. She'd woken up this morning, two days since she'd used the sword to fight off the deserter, and had discovered that it had turned back into a bone, as if it had sensed that the danger has passed. She'd put it back in her pocket with Tanaquill's other gifts.

"And exactly why are you giving away our much-needed eggs?" Tavi pressed.

"Because it's a nice thing to do. A good deed."

"Still trying to find the pieces of your heart?"

"Yes," Isabelle said as she climbed into the cart and settled herself on the seat.

"Have you figured out what they are?"

Isabelle nodded. She'd been thinking about it nonstop. "Goodness, kindness, and charitableness," she replied confidently. "I'm working on the charitableness piece today."

Tanaquill said that Ella hadn't had to search for the pieces of her heart. *Because she never lost them*, Isabelle thought, as she lay in bed last night. *Ella was always good, kind, and charitable. Maybe Tanaquill wants me to be those things, too.*

"Izzy, I was serious when I said not to ride any more. Have you been?"

Isabelle, who was leaning forward gathering Martin's reins, sat up and looked at her sister. "You *still* think this is all because I hit my head?"

"I think this is all very strange," Tavi said, carrying her plums into the kitchen.

Isabelle watched her go. "I haven't lost my mind. Things will get easier, you'll see," she said quietly. "Things are always easier for pretty girls. People hold doors for you. Children pick flowers for you. Butchers hand you a free slice of salami, just for the pleasure of watching you eat it."

And then she snapped Martin's reins and set off.

Forty-One

Isabelle found the orphanage, tucked down a narrow road behind the church, without any trouble.

It was run by nuns and housed in their convent. An iron fence enclosed the building and its grounds, but the gate wasn't locked. Isabelle pushed it open and walked inside, carrying her egg basket.

Children dressed in rough gray clothing were playing games in a grassy courtyard. A sweet-faced boy approached her. A few of his friends followed him.

"Here, little boy," Isabelle said. "I brought some eggs for you."

The boy took a few hesitant steps towards her. "My name's Henri," he said, giving her a close look. "And yours is Isabelle."

"How did you guess?" Isabelle asked, kneeling down and smiling.

"I didn't. Sister Bernadette pointed at you when she took us to the market. She said we mustn't ever be like you. You're one of the queen's ugly stepsisters. You're awful and mean."

Isabelle's smile curdled. Two of the little girls who'd trailed the boy stepped forward. They started to sing.

Stepsister, stepsister!
Ugly as an old blister!
Make her drink some turpentine!
Then hang her with a melon vine!

Before Isabelle even knew what was happening, the children had all joined hands and were dancing around her like imps, singing:

Stepsister, stepsister,
Mother says the devil kissed her!
Make her swallow five peach pits,
Then cut her up in little bits!

They let go of each other's hands when they finished their song and backed away giggling.

Isabelle decided to leave before they were inspired to sing another verse. "Here, take them," she said, thrusting the basket out to Henri. "They're nice fresh eggs."

"I don't want them. Not from *you*," said Henri.

Isabelle felt a current of anger move through her, but she clamped down on it.

"I'm going to leave the basket here," she said. "Maybe one of you can take it inside."

Henri gave her a sullen shrug. He looked at the basket of eggs, then turned to his friend. "Do it, Sébastien," he said.

"You do it, Henri," said Sébastien. Henri turned to a little girl. "Émilie, *you* do it."

Isabelle gave up. They could argue about who was going to

159

carry the basket inside without her.

But that's not what the children were arguing about.

Isabelle had only taken a few steps when she felt a pain, sudden and shocking, right between her shoulder blades. The force of the blow sent her stumbling forward. She caught herself and spun around.

The children were laughing gleefully. Isabelle reached behind over her shoulder and touched the back of her dress. Her palm came away covered in yellow slime.

"Which one of you threw the egg?" she demanded.

No one answered her, but Henri sauntered up to the basket, picked up another egg and, before Isabelle could stop him, launched it straight at her head. His aim was excellent. It hit her right between the eyes.

Isabelle gasped. "Why, you . . . you little *troll*!" she shouted as egg ran down her face.

That was all the others needed to hear. They converged on the basket, grabbed eggs, and pelted her with them as hard as they could.

Isabelle should have run straight out of the courtyard and back to her cart. But Isabelle was not one to turn tail. She lunged for the basket, grabbed an egg, and threw it at Henri. Her aim was not as good as his, for she was still blinking egg out of her eyes. The egg went wide and hit little Sébastien instead, right in the back of his head. He tripped, fell down in the grass, and started to howl.

Isabelle threw another egg and pegged Henri in the shoulder. As she grabbed a third from the basket, three more hit her—one in the face. She lobbed the one she was holding just to get rid of it, so she could wipe her eyes again. Though she couldn't see where it landed, she heard it hit with a loud, wet splat.

"Great God in Heaven, what is going *on* here?" a voice shrilled.

Isabelle blinked; she opened her eyes all the way and discovered that it was not a child that her egg had hit, but an old woman who was dressed all in white and wearing a rosary around her neck.

Isabelle watched in horror as eggshell slid down the front of her spotless habit, then fell to the ground. Globs of yolk dripped onto the toes of her shoes. The old woman looked at the mess on her clothing. She looked at the children around her, at Henri, rubbing his shoulder, at Émilie, staring at her stained pinafore and sobbing piteously, at little Sébastien, sitting up in the grass now, wailing, "Isabelle, the ugly stepsister . . . she a-a-*attacked* us!"

Then the old woman looked at Isabelle. Her eyes, set deep in her wrinkled face, blazed. Her nostrils flared.

"Oh, dear," Isabelle whispered, pressing her hands to her cheeks. "Oh *no*."

It was Sister Claire, the head of the convent, the ancient and venerable mother superior, and she was *furious*.

Forty-Two

The iron gate slammed shut behind Isabelle with a loud, ringing clang.

Shamefaced, she looked back through the iron bars. "I'm so sorry," she said miserably.

"Never, *ever* let me see you anywhere near this orphanage again!" Sister Bernadette shrilled, wagging a finger at Isabelle from the other side of the gate. "The mother superior's fifty-year vow of silence broken . . . *fifty years*! All because of you!"

The nun turned on her heel and stalked off, leaving Isabelle by herself. Still cringing, she hobbled to her cart and climbed up to the seat. Martin looked back at her over his shoulder.

"Don't even ask," Isabelle said to him.

She wanted to get home desperately, but she was so overcome with regret for what she'd done that she leaned over, put her head in her hands, and groaned. Her mind replayed every dreadful second of what had happened after she'd hit the mother superior in the chest with an egg.

"You should be *ashamed* of yourself!" the old woman had shrieked. "Throwing eggs at *children*! Making poor orphans *cry*! Wasting desperately needed food while a *war* rages! Never, in all my days, have I witnessed such egregious behavior. I didn't want to believe what I'd heard—I closed my ears to the gossip—but you, Isabelle de la Paumé, are every bit as awful as everyone says you are!"

As she had been shouting at Isabelle, two nuns that had followed her into the courtyard had been frantically gesturing at her. One had held a trembling finger to her lips. The other had shook her head, saucer-eyed. "Sister, your *vow*!" she'd said.

To show her piety and devotion, Sister Claire had made a solemn oath of silence five decades ago. Through superhuman effort, she had kept the vow, never uttering a word, communicating with the other nuns through writing only. When she'd realized what she'd done, the old woman had clapped a hand over her mouth and fainted on the spot.

"I-I think she's *dead*!" Sister Bernadette had cried.

The minute they heard that, the children—every single one of them—had started wailing in earnest. Alarmed by their noise, a dozen nuns had come running. One had had the presence of mind to sit Sister Claire up and chafe her wrists. A moment later, the old woman had come to. That's when Sister Bernadette had ushered Isabelle out.

"Oh, Martin," Isabelle said, now sitting up. "I threw eggs at *children*. Ten-year-olds. Eight-year-olds. I think one was *five*."

She thrust her hand into her skirt pocket, feeling for the bone, the nutshell, and the seedpod. They were still there but felt more like curses now than gifts. Throwing eggs at orphans was no way to earn the fairy queen's help. She fervently hoped that Tanaquill would not find out about it.

Isabelle made her way home as quickly as she could. Luckily, she met no one else on the road. As soon as she pulled up to the stables, she untacked Martin, brushed him, and left him loose outside to graze. Then she held her head under the pump at the water trough to rinse the egg off.

A few minutes later, she strode into the kitchen, her hair sopping wet, her face red from the cold water, her clothing a filthy mess.

Tavi was stirring a bubbling pot of plum jam. Her eyebrows shot up when she saw her sister. "Looks like charitable pursuits aren't all they're cracked up to be," she said.

Isabelle held up a hand. "Don't."

"Where's our basket? Did someone poach it?"

"Just . . ."

"Now I'll have to scramble to find another one."

". . . *stop*!" Isabelle yelled, covering her ears. She hurried out of the kitchen and went upstairs to change her clothing.

It was a relief to step out of her dress, which was as stiff as meringue. She poured water from the pitcher on her bureau into a basin, wet a cloth, and removed the last traces of egg from her neck. A few minutes later, she was standing in the hallway, doing up the top buttons on a clean dress. As she walked towards the stairs, a voice from behind her said, "Where have you been, Isabelle?"

Isabelle's heart sank. *Not now, Maman*, she thought. She still had Martin to deal with and the day's long list of chores. She did not have time to persuade her mother that there was no ball, dinner, or garden party to ready themselves for.

Tavi had just come up the stairs carrying a tray with a cup of tea on it for their mother. "She went walking," she said, taking Maman by the arm and leading her back to her room.

"Really, Octavia?" Maman trilled, pressing a hand to her chest. "With whom? A chevalier? A viscount?"

"No, the Duke of Egg-ceter!" Tavi said, winking at Isabelle over her shoulder.

Isabelle scowled, but she was grateful to Tavi for distracting Maman. It allowed her to slip down the stairs and out of the house without any further questions.

Martin needed to be put in the pasture. She made her way back to the stables, got his halter, and walked over to him.

"Well, Martin, I'm clean. You're brushed. That's something," she said. "Perhaps the rest of the day will be peaceful and quiet." She gave him a wry smile. "After the morning's disaster, what else could possibly go wrong?"

The horse was standing in front of the stables in the shade of a tall birch tree, his head down. As Isabelle walked over to him, she noticed that he was intent upon something in the grass. He nosed at it, then raked his hoof over it.

"What have you got there, old man? Some chamomile?"

She knew he loved to eat the tiny white-and-yellow flowers that grew around the stables, but as the horse raised his head, Isabelle saw it was not chamomile flowers that had captured his interest.

Dangling from Martin's mouth was a priceless pearl necklace.

Forty-Three

Isabelle and Martin cantered up the winding, tree-lined drive of the Château Rigolade.

After she'd gotten over the shock of seeing her horse about to swallow the valuable pearls, Isabelle had grabbed the necklace out of his mouth, wiped the spit off, and put it in her pocket. The necklace belonged to the marquis or one of his friends, she was certain of it. The little monkey—Nelson—had been wearing it when he shot the chicken thief.

Whoever owns it must be worried sick, Isabelle thought. Each pearl was as big as a hazelnut.

As Isabelle reached the top of the drive, she looked for the stables, thinking she could hand Martin to a groom and then ask to see the marquis, but the drive led straight to the château itself, with its burbling fountains, its rosebushes, oak trees, and manicured lawns.

Isabelle could see no one—not a maid or footman or gardener, not the marquis nor any of his friends. She felt awkward sitting on her horse in the middle of a nobleman's drive, so she decided to knock on the château's front door, but as she got down out of her saddle, she heard music coming from behind the château.

It came to a slow, disorderly stop, as if one of the players had made a mistake, then it started again.

Isabelle followed the sound, leading Martin around the side of the building, to the back. The lawns there sloped down to a clearing framed by towering oak trees. At the very end of the clearing, a good distance away, was a partially constructed stage. Isabelle could just make out a man up on a ladder, his back to her, hammering boards into place.

Closer by, on the château's shaded terrace, members of the marquis's retinue appeared to be rehearsing a play. The musicians sat in chairs on one side of the terrace, wincing as their conductor angrily upbraided them. Actors roamed the other side. Some held scripts, others brandished fake swords and shields. Trunks, open and spilling costumes, stood nearby. Four monkeys chased each other in and out of them, skirmishing over glass beads and foil crowns.

Isabelle limped towards the terrace, nervously twisting Martin's reins. Several women looked up as she approached. They were older and sumptuously dressed, and she felt dull and drab in comparison. She recognized the diva, elegant and imperious; the magician, who was biting into a peach and somehow making it look mysterious; an acrobat spinning a plate on her finger; and an actress wearing a red wig and holding a scepter.

The magician was the first one to speak to her. "Isabelle, isn't it? You're the one who gave us directions, no?" Her eyes flashed with mischief. "I've been asking around about you. I hear you're one of the queen's ugly stepsisters."

Isabelle shrank at her words. These splendid women knew who she was; they wouldn't want anything to do with her.

The magician saw her discomfort. "Now, now, child. Ugly's not such a bad a thing to be called. Not at all!" she said, tossing the peach pit. "We've all been called it at one time or another, and it hasn't killed any of us," she added, wiping juice off her chin with her palm.

"In fact, we've been called far worse," said the actress.

The others chimed in. *Difficult. Obstinate. Stubborn. Shrewish. Willful. Contrary. Unnatural. Abominable. Intractable. Immoral. Ambitious. Shocking. Wayward.*

"Ugly's nothing," said the diva. "Pretty . . . now *that's* a dangerous word."

"Pretty hooks you fast and kills you slowly," said the acrobat.

"Call a girl pretty once, and all she wants, forevermore, is to hear it again," the magician added.

She drew a long silk cord from inside her jacket, tossed one end over a high tree branch overhanging the terrace, and secured it on a lower one. Then she jumped up onto a chair under the tree and knotted a loop in the other end of the cord.

"Pretty's a noose you put around your own neck," she said, doing just that. "Any fool can tighten it on you and kick away your footing. And then . . ." She lost her balance and teetered back and forth on the chair. Arms windmilling, she fell. The cord caught with a sickening twang. Her body spun in circles. Her legs kicked wildly.

Isabelle screamed, certain the woman just killed herself, but the magician slipped out of the noose, landed on her feet with a whump and burst into laughter.

"That's a *horrible* trick," the diva scolded, as Isabelle pressed a hand to her chest. "You've frightened the poor girl to death."

"What a dreadful welcome," said the actress, scowling at the magician. She turned to Isabelle. "Can I get you a cup of tea, my dear? A slice of cake?"

"N-no. No, thank you," Isabelle said, trying to calm her thumping heart. "I must get back. I came because I found something, or rather my horse did, that belongs to you, I think." She pulled the necklace from her pocket and handed it to the diva. "It was lying in the grass near our stables."

The diva gasped. "I thought it was gone forever!" she exclaimed, hugging Isabelle. "Thank you!" She fastened the pearls around her neck, then patted them. "The marquis himself gave these to me. I'm sure he'd like to thank you, too. Go to him, won't you? I believe he's down in the clearing with the carpenter."

Isabelle's gaze swept over the lawn, down the hill, to the stage. It looked like a long walk and her foot was aching. "Would it be all right if I rode him across the clearing?" she asked, nodding at Martin.

"Of course!" said the diva. "And, Isabelle?"

Isabelle hoisted herself into the saddle, then turned around. "Yes?"

"You'll come back, won't you? To see our play when it's done?"

"I would love to," Isabelle said shyly.

"Splendid! We'll send you an invitation. Goodbye!" said the diva, waving her off.

"Goodbye," Isabelle said. She clucked her tongue at Martin and headed across the lawn.

The diva watched Isabelle go, her smile fading. She was

joined by the magician and the actress. The three stood in silence, brows furrowed. Nelson lowered himself from a tree branch to the diva's shoulder.

"Are you *certain* you found the right one?" the diva finally said.

The magician nodded. "I'm positive. It took me three days to track him. Over hill and dale. Through four other villages. Turned out he was right under my nose the whole time."

"Boy hunting. Your favorite sport," the actress said tartly.

The magician's full lips curved into a wicked smile. "They *do* smell delicious."

"Fate knows what we know," the diva said. "Chance has to stay one move ahead of her. This better work."

"Yes. It better," Chance said, coming up behind them. "I just looked at her map . . ."

The magician turned to him, worry flashing in her eyes. "Her death date . . ." she said.

"The skull . . ." said the diva at the same time.

Chance nodded grimly. "It just turned two shades darker."

Forty-Four

Martin plodded his way across the clearing, pausing now and again to rip up a mouthful of grass or take a bite out of a shrub.

"Can you *behave*?" Isabelle scolded, tugging on his reins. "Just for once?"

As they drew closer to the theater, Isabelle looked at the framing. She could see that it was going to be a small but gracefully built structure, complete with apron, wings, and an arch.

The carpenter, she noticed, was still up on his ladder, hammering away. He was slender and tall and wore his thick brown hair tied back. His white shirt was soaked with sweat; his blue trousers flecked with wood shavings. Eager to find the marquis, she glanced around the theater, at the piles of lumber in front of it, the workbench littered with saws and drills, but she didn't see him.

He's not here; he can't be, she reasoned. *He's too colorful, too boisterous, to overlook.*

Her gaze drifted back to the carpenter. There was something familiar about the slope of his shoulders and the easy way he stood on the ladder, lost in his work, careless of the danger.

For a moment, she was certain she knew him, but then she shook her head at the very notion. Maman had never allowed her to speak to workmen.

She decided to speak to this one, though, in case he knew where the marquis was.

She had just leaned forward to call out to him when disaster struck. An enormous raven swooped down out of a tree and struck at Martin, beating its wings in his face, raking its sharp talons across his nose.

Martin shied, terrified, but the bird kept at him. He gave a shrill whinny, spun around and bucked, trying to kick the bird away. Isabelle lost her balance and pitched headfirst out of the saddle. Her boot caught in the stirrup as she fell and was pulled off, ripping her stocking and opening her wound. She landed facedown on the ground with a bone-jarring thud. Martin trotted off towards the trees, still kicking at the bird.

For a few seconds, everything went white. But then her senses came back and, with them, the pain. It was exquisite, but she was glad of it. She knew that it was only when you couldn't feel anything, like your legs, that you were in trouble.

Groaning, she rolled over onto her back. A moment later, she opened her eyes and was startled to see a face peering down at her. Though it was blurry and distorted, it looked like a boy's face.

Or maybe, she thought, *I'm dead and it's a saint's face. Like the ones in the village church with their high, carved cheekbones and sad, painted eyes. Or maybe it's an angel's face. Yes, that's it. An angel's face, tragic and kind.*

"Am I dead, angel?" she asked, closing her eyes again.

"No. And I'm not an angel."

"Saint?"

"No."

"Boy?"

"Yes.

There was a pause, and then the boy said, "People lose toes all the time, you know. Arms and legs. Eyes and ears. It's no reason to kill yourself. That's what you're doing, isn't it? Trying to kill yourself?"

Who are you, boy? Isabelle wondered. But he didn't give her the chance to ask.

"You're lucky your foot came free of the stirrup," he continued. "You could've been dragged. Broken a leg. Or your neck. Martin's a horrible animal. Why aren't you riding Nero? He would have chomped that bird in two."

How did the boy know Martin? And Nero?

Isabelle forced her eyes open. Slowly they focused on the boy's face. Now she knew why his eyes had looked familiar. Why she wondered if she'd seen him before. She had. Every day of her childhood. Climbing trees. Dueling with mops. Playing pirates.

She still saw him every night in her dreams.

"Blackbeard," she whispered.

"Anne Bonny," the boy said with a bow. And the softest, saddest of smiles.

Forty-Five

"It's been a long time, Pirate Queen."

Isabelle didn't trust herself to speak. She wasn't sure what would come out of her mouth. She just nodded as best she could given that she was lying flat on her back.

He's older, she thought. *Taller. He has cheekbones now and stubble on his jaw. His voice is deeper, but his eyes are exactly the same, that faded indigo blue. Artist's eyes. Dreamer's eyes.*

She longed to reach up and touch the face she knew so well, to run her fingers over the edge of his jaw, his lips. To ask how he got the tiny scar above his right cheekbone.

"Felix," she said, sitting up.

"Isabelle."

"It's so . . . um . . ." She cast about for a word. ". . . *wonderful* to see you again."

Felix gave her a worried look. "Maybe you shouldn't get up. I saw the fall. You hit your head. Can you see straight?"

"I'm fine," Isabelle said, standing up. Then she yelped. Pain, sharp and hot, shot up her leg as she put her weight on her bad foot.

"I think you should sit," Felix said, his eyes on her foot.

Isabelle followed his gaze. Her white stocking had a bloom of red on it. The pain from the fall had been so intense, she hadn't even realized she was bleeding. Felix took her hand and the warmth of his touch, the feeling of his skin against hers, made her feel woozy all over again.

He led her to a stone bench under a tree. She sat, glancing around for Martin. He was munching grass in the shade, his reins looped over his neck.

"He has a few scratches on his nose. Nothing terrible," Felix said.

"Thanks. I'm fine now. I won't keep you," Isabelle said, forcing a smile. "You have a theater to build."

"I do. And the marquis wants it done quickly. He's paying us—my master and me—well for it."

"Your master?"

"Master Jourdan. The carpenter in Saint-Michel. He hired me a month ago."

Isabelle digested this. Felix was back in Saint-Michel. She didn't know if she should be happy about that, excited, furious, or all of the above.

"So you're a carpenter now," she said, trying to sound nonchalant. Instead, she sounded ridiculous. *He's sawing boards and hammering them together for God's sake!* she chided herself. *What else would he be?*

Felix nodded. "I learned the trade working for other carpenters. In other villages."

"You were always carving, I remember that. You wanted to be a sculptor. Like Michelangelo."

"I wanted a lot of things," Felix said quietly, looking down at his scarred, work-roughened hands.

An uncomfortable silence descended. Isabelle longed to break it. She longed to shout at him, to tell him she wanted things, too. To ask him why he lied to her. But pride prevented it.

Felix looked up. His eyes met hers. They drifted down to her bloodstained stocking.

"I heard about it," he said. "All of it. The prince. Ella. The glass slipper."

Isabelle looked up. The bird that had spooked Martin was perched on a branch above them. "You know, I've never seen a raven that big," she said, trying to change the subject.

Felix glanced at the bird; then his gaze settled on her again. "Why did you do it? Why did you hack off half of your foot?"

Isabelle blanched. "Ever hear of something called small talk, Felix?"

"I never made small talk with you. I'm not going to start now. Why did you do it?"

Isabelle didn't want to talk about it. Not with him. But Felix was not going to let it go.

"Isabelle, I asked you—"

"I *heard* you," Isabelle snapped. She felt cornered.

"Then *why*?"

Because you left. And took everything with you, she thought. *My dreams. My hopes. My happiness.*

But she couldn't admit that to him; she could barely admit it to herself. "To get something—*someone*—I was supposed to want," she finally said.

Felix winced. "You did that to yourself for someone you were *supposed* to want?"

"You know what Maman is like. I couldn't fight any more. Not after I'd lost all the things I lov—" She bit the word off. "Not after I'd lost all the things that were important to me. Not after I became an ugly stepsister."

"Ugly? Where did that come from? I never thought you were ugly," said Felix. "I liked your laugh. And your eyes, too. I liked your hair. I still do. It's russet. Like a red squirrel."

"I have hair like a squirrel?" Isabelle said in disbelief. "Is that your idea of a compliment?"

"I love squirrels," Felix said with a shrug. "They're scrappy. And smart. And beautiful."

With that, he put his bag down again and knelt by Isabelle. Then he lifted the hem of her skirt and pulled her stocking off.

"Hey!" she cried. "What are you doing?"

Felix held her heel in his hand. "My God," he said, his voice catching.

Isabelle was horrified. The scar was livid and raw; part of it was split open and dripping blood. She tried to pull free of his grip, but he was too strong.

"Let go!" she cried, trying to cover her foot with her skirt.

"It's bleeding. I have bandages and medicine. I'm always cutting myself."

"I don't care!"

"Let me fix it."

"No!"

"Why?"

"Because . . . because it's mortifying!"

Felix sat back on his haunches. "I've seen your feet before, Isabelle," he said gently. "We used to wade in the stream

177

together. Remember?"

Isabelle clenched her fists. It wasn't embarrassment over her bare feet that was bothering her. It was that Felix saw more than her feet; he saw inside of her. He'd always been able to do that. And she felt scaldingly vulnerable under his gaze.

"Just let *go*!"

"No. You got dirt in the wound," Felix said, setting her heel down. "If we don't do something, it'll get infected. And then you'll have to cut off your entire leg. I don't think even *you* could manage that."

Isabelle slumped down, defeated. She'd forgotten how stubborn he could be. Felix walked to a nearby tree and picked up the leather satchel and canteen of water that were lying at the base of it, then carried them back to Isabelle.

He opened the canteen and doused the wound. Then he unbuckled his satchel and dumped out its contents. Chisels came spilling out. Pencils. Carving knives. A rasp. Rulers.

And a tiny soldier, about two inches high.

Isabelle picked it up. "Did you make this?" she asked, glad to have something to talk about other than the mess she'd made of her foot. And her life.

"I carve them in my room at night," Felix said. "I've made a small army complete with rifle companies, fusiliers, grenadiers, their commanders . . . It's almost complete. I just have a few officers to carve."

"What are you going to do with them all?" Isabelle asked.

"Sell them. To a nobleman for his sons to play with. A wealthy banker or merchant. Whoever can pay my price."

Isabelle regarded the little soldier closely. "He's incredible,

Felix," she marveled. Beautifully carved and intricately painted, he was so lifelike that she could see the buttons on his coat, the trigger on his rifle, and the determination in his eyes.

"It makes a change from building coffins," Felix said ruefully. "I sometimes think we'll need to cut down every tree in France to make enough to bury all the dead."

Isabelle put the soldier down. "Is it that bad?" she asked quietly.

Felix nodded.

"What's going to happen to us?"

"I don't know, Isabelle."

Some boys would have told her a happy story about how the king's forces would win, of course they would, so as not to upset her feminine sensibilities. Not Felix. He had never sugarcoated things. She'd always loved that about him.

At least that hasn't changed between us, she thought wistfully. *Even if everything else has.*

He continued to sift through his things until he finally found what he was after—a folded wad of clean linen strips and a small glass vial. He tipped a few drops of the vial's contents onto Isabelle's wound. It burned. She howled. He paid her no attention and carefully bandaged the wound.

"You're welcome," he said when he'd finished. Then he pulled the boot and stocking off her other foot.

"Felix," Isabelle said. "You can't just go around peeling girls' stockings off. It's inappropriate."

Felix snorted. "I don't find feet very exciting. Especially not sweaty ones. And anyway, I *don't* go around peeling girls' stockings off. Only yours."

He pulled her legs straight and placed her feet together, side by side, heels on the ground.

"What are you *doing*?"

"Maybe something, maybe nothing," he said, taking measurements, then jotting them down on a scrap of paper with a nub of pencil.

When he was done, he put her stockings and boots back on. Then he stood and said that the marquis was a kind employer but an impatient one, and that he'd better get back to work. Isabelle stood, too, and convinced him that she was fine to ride home. Together they walked over to Martin.

"Hello, you old bastard. Miss me?" Felix said to the horse.

Martin lifted his head. Pricked up his ears. And bit him. Felix laughed. "I'll take that as a yes," he said, patting the horse's neck.

Isabelle noticed that his eyes had become shiny. *Old horses still make him cry. That hasn't changed, either*, she thought. *Or made it any easier to hate him.*

She climbed into her saddle once again and took up Martin's reins. "Thank you, Felix. For fixing me up," she said.

Felix, scratching Martin's ears now, didn't respond right away. "*Loved*," he said at length.

"What?" Isabelle asked, sliding her feet into her stirrups.

"Earlier, you said, *Not after I'd lost all the things that were important to me*. But you were going to say, *Not after I'd lost all the things I loved*."

"What if I did?" Isabelle asked warily. "What does it matter?"

"It matters because once I thought . . ." His eyes found hers. "That I was one of those things."

And suddenly, Isabelle lost the small amount of composure she'd been struggling so hard to hold on to. How *dare* he, after what he'd done.

"And people say *I'm* heartless? You're cruel, Felix!" she shouted, her voice cracking with anger.

"Me?" Felix said. "But I didn't—"

"No, you didn't. And that's where the trouble started. Goodbye, Felix. Yet again."

Isabelle turned Martin around and touched her heels to his side. Martin must've sensed her upset, for he obeyed her command immediately and launched into a canter. They were across the clearing in no time.

Isabelle rode away without once looking back.

Just as Felix had.

Forty-Six

In the Wildwood, Fate bent down to a patch of mushrooms, slender-stalked and ghostly in the pale light of a crescent moon.

She plucked a plump one. "*Amanita virosa*, the destroying angel. Horribly poisonous, Losca," she said, handing it to her servant. "And essential when making any ink with a greenish hue such as *Jealousy*, *Envy*, or *Spite*."

Fate had brought some inks with her from her palazzo, and she'd been making more, but she needed to get Isabelle's map back in her clutches before she could use them. *Getting Isabelle in my clutches would be helpful, too*, she thought. *How can I convince her of the folly of struggling against her fate when I never even see her?* Chance had contrived to meet the girl twice already. Fate knew she needed to pull Isabelle firmly into her orbit, but how?

"Making ink tonight? Even though you don't have a map?" said a voice from the darkness.

Losca squawked with fright. Fate, not so easily startled, turned around. "Chance?" she called, peering into the shadows.

There was a whoosh, and then a brilliant, blazing light. Three flaming torches illuminated Chance, his magician, and his cook.

"How uncharacteristically optimistic of you," Chance said baitingly.

Fate gave a contemptuous laugh. "How does the skull look? The one on Isabelle's map? Has it grown any lighter?"

Chance glowered.

"I didn't think so."

"I'm winning," Chance said, jutting his chin. "I've given her one piece of her heart back. The boy loves her and she loves him. Love has altered the course of many lives."

"I hear that meeting didn't go quite to plan," said Fate, with a coiled smile. "I hear they didn't exactly fall back into each other's arms."

"Next time I see that raven, I'm going to shoot it," Chance growled, casting a menacing glance at Losca.

"You've won a battle, not the war," said Fate dismissively. "It's easy to love the lovable. Can Isabelle love when it hurts? When it costs? When the price of love may be her life?"

"Mortals aren't born strong, they become strong. Isabelle will, too."

"You are many things," said Fate, shaking her head. "Most of all, you are ruthless."

"And you are dreary, madame," Chance said hotly. "So dreary, you'd have everyone in bed at eight with a cup of hot milk and a plate of madeleines. Can't you see that the courage to risk, to dare, to toss that gold coin up in the air over and over again, win or lose, is what makes humans human? They are fragile, doomed creatures, blinder than worms yet braver than the gods."

"Challenging the Fates is hard. Eating madeleines is easy.

Most mortals choose the madeleines. Isabelle will, too," Fate said.

As she spoke, the moon disappeared behind a cloud.

"It's getting late. Past midnight already," Fate said. "There are dangerous creatures afoot in the woods at this hour, and I and my maid must return to the safety of Madame LeBenêt's farm."

Fate's shawl had settled in the crooks of her arms; she drew it up around her shoulders. Her gray eyes settled on the three burning flames held aloft by Chance and his friends. Suddenly, she smiled.

"It's so dark without the moon. So hard to find one's way. Might I beg a torch from you?" she asked.

Chance hesitated.

"Come, now," Fate chided. "Surely you wouldn't deny an old woman the means to light her way home?"

Chance nodded and the magician handed her torch to Fate.

"Good night, Marquis," Fate said. "And thank you."

Chance watched her as she started off, her torch held out in front of her, her maid scurrying behind her. He could not see her face, nor hear her voice as she walked away. Had he, he might've realized how foolish he'd been.

"Yes, there *are* dangerous creatures afoot tonight, Losca," Fate said to her servant. "And none more dangerous than me."

Forty-Seven

The drunken man swayed back and forth as violently as if he'd been standing aboard a small boat in rough seas.

The bottle of wine he'd guzzled, the one that had made him feel so happy only an hour ago, now sloshed around like bilge inside him.

It was *somebody's* fault, what had happened to him. It had to be. He wasn't quite sure whose, but he would find out and then that somebody would pay.

He'd lost his job that day. For stealing from his employer. And then he'd gotten drunk on borrowed coins and had staggered home. His wife had thrown him out of the house after he'd told her there was no money left to feed their children. "Go to hell!" she shouted at him. And now here he was, stumbling down a lonely road in the dead of night, halfway there already.

But wait . . . what was this? People? They were jeering, yelling. They were throwing handfuls of mud. At what?

The drunken man hurried closer on his unsteady legs and saw that it was a house—no, a mansion. The moon had come

185

out from behind a cloud, and the drunken man could see that it was shuttered and dark.

"What are you doing?" he asked a boy, short and loutish, with small eyes and bad teeth.

"The ugly stepsisters live here," the boy replied, as if that was the only explanation needed. Then he picked up a rock and lobbed it at the front door.

The ugly stepsisters! The drunken man had heard of them. He knew their story. *What nerve they have*, he thought. *Being mean when girls are supposed to be pleasant. Being ugly when girls are supposed to be pretty.* It was an insult. To him! To the village! To all of France!

"Avenge it," whispered a voice from behind him.

He whirled around, lost his balance, and fell on his face. It took him a few tries to get up, but when he was finally on his feet again, he saw who'd spoken—a kindly old woman, dressed in black, with a basket over her arm and a raven on her shoulder. She was holding a torch.

"What did you say, grandmother?" he asked her.

"Here you are out on the street, penniless and alone. And there they are in a big, comfortable mansion. Each one an uppity shrew, just like your wife. How they shame you, these women. You should avenge their insolence."

The drunken man turned her words over in his head. A light, dull but dangerous, filled his bloodshot eyes. "Yes. Yes, I will. This instant!" he said, thrusting a finger into the air. But then the finger sank down again, little by little, until it hung limply at his side. "But how?"

"You look like a clever fellow," the old woman said.

"Oh, I am, grandmother, I am," he agreed. "You won't find any man more cleverer than me."

The old woman smiled. "I know you'll find a way," she said. And handed him the torch.

Forty-Eight

Isabelle, legs tucked underneath her in a window seat in her bedroom, was blinking up at a silvery crescent moon that was playing peekaboo behind filmy, drifting clouds.

She was so tired, but she couldn't go to bed. She hadn't even undressed.

People had come again tonight, to shout and jeer and throw things at the house. They would stop after a while, when they saw that no one was coming to the door, when they finally grew bored, but until then, she would not sleep. Until then, she would remain wakeful and watchful, peering out between the slats of her shutters every so often to make sure the crowd did not drift too far into the yard, or go down the hill towards their animals.

Isabelle hoped the noise woudn't wake Maman and upset her. Tavi would be fine. Unlike Isabelle's window, which faced the front yard and the drive, hers overlooked the back gardens. She wouldn't hear a thing.

Isabelle yawned. Her body craved sleep. She'd worked from the moment she'd arrived home from the Château Rigolade to sundown, only stopping for a bite to eat at midday.

She'd scrubbed the kitchen floor. Beat the dust out of rugs. Washed windows. Swept steps. Weeded the garden. Pruned the roses. Did anything and everything to keep from thinking about Felix, to keep from remembering his kind eyes and lopsided smile. His gentle hands. The way tendrils of his hair, worked loose from his ponytail, curled down the back of his neck. The stubble-covered line of his jaw. The freckle above his top lip.

Stop it, she told herself. *Right now.*

It was treason, this wanting. How could you long for the very person who'd hurt you worse than you'd ever been hurt in your entire life? It was like longing to drink a glass of poison, pick up a cobra, hold a loaded gun to your head.

She forced herself to think about something else, but soon regretted it, for only memories of the day's other disaster came to her. The taunts of the children at the orphanage rang in her ears. So did the outraged shriek of the mother superior.

She was no closer to finding a piece of her heart, and Tanaquill's gifts weighed heavily in her pocket, reminding her of her failure.

She still had hope, no matter how fragile, of becoming pretty. She just had to find another way of earning the fairy queen's help.

Tavi made jam, she thought now. *I could bring some to an elderly shut-in . . . if only I knew one. I could knit socks to bring to Colonel Cafard's soldiers . . . but I never learned how to knit. I could make some soup and bring it to a sick person, or a refugee, or a poor family with lots of children . . . but I'm not a very good cook.*

Still looking out of the window, Isabelle heaved a deep sigh. "How'd you do it, Ella? How did you always manage to be so

189

good? Even to me?" She leaned her weary head against the wall. Shouts and laughter and ugly words drifted up to her from outside. She knew she mustn't sleep but she didn't think there would be any harm in closing her eyes. Just for a minute.

Isabelle was out instantly. As she drowsed, she dreamt of many things. Of Tanaquill. The marquis. The magician dangling from her silk noose. A monkey in pearls. Felix.

And Ella.

She was here again, in the Maison Douleur. She was standing at the hearth, wearing a threadbare dress. Her face and hands were smudged with cinders. Isabelle was so happy to see her, but Ella wasn't happy. She was pacing back and forth fearfully.

"Wake up, Isabelle," she said urgently. "You need to leave."

A fire was burning in the hearth, and as she spoke, it grew. Its flames curled around the sides of the hearth and up to the mantel. Isabelle coughed. It hurt to breathe. Her eyes stung. Smoke, thick and choking, billowed through the air. Tongues of flame licked the walls and ceiling. The room began to blacken and curled at its edges, as if it were not a real room at all, only a picture.

"Isabelle, wake up!"

"I *am* awake, Ella!" Isabelle cried, turning in frantic circles. The flames were devouring everything in their path. An oil lamp exploded. Windowpanes shattered. The curtains ignited with a thunderous whoosh.

"Go, Isabelle! *Hurry!*" Ella shouted. "Save them!"

And then Isabelle watched, horrified, as the flames engulfed her stepsister, too.

"Ella, no!" she screamed, so loudly that she woke herself

up. Her heart slammed against her ribs. She could still feel the heat of the fire, hear wooden tables and chairs crackling in the flames. It was hard to see; her vision was blurry from sleep. She rubbed her eyes with the heels of her hand, trying to clear them.

"It was so *real*," she whispered.

She stood. The floor was hot beneath her bare feet. Her eyes were stinging. With a sickening jolt of fear, she realized it wasn't sleep that had blurred her vision; it was smoke.

The fire . . . it wasn't a dream. It was real. Dear God, it was *real*.

Terror sent her flying across the room. "Maman! Tavi!" she screamed, wrenching open her door. "Get up! Run! *Run!* The house is on fire!"

Forty-Nine

"Isabelle?" Tavi murmured. "What is it? What's—" She didn't get to finish her sentence.

"Fire!" Isabelle shouted, pulling her bodily out of her bed. "Get out! Go!"

She ran out of Tavi's room and down the long hallway that led to her mother's chamber.

"Maman! MAMAN!" she called, bursting through her doors.

Maman was not asleep. She was seated at her vanity table, trying on a necklace.

"Stop shouting, Isabelle. It's unladylike," she scolded.

"The house is burning. We have to go," Isabelle said, grabbing her mother's hand.

Maman wrenched it free. "I can't go out like this. I'm not dressed properly."

Isabelle took her mother by the wrist and half cajoled, half dragged her down the hallway. At the top of the stairs, they met Tavi. Her arms were full of books. She was gazing down the stairwell at the conflagration below, paralyzed by fear.

"It's all right, we can make it," Isabelle said. "Look at the door, Tavi. Not the flames."

Tavi nodded woodenly, then followed Isabelle as she started down the steps. Windows shattered in the heat. Air ran into the house through the broken panes, feeding the fire, bellowing flames into the foyer. The three women had to cross it to get to the front door, and safety.

"We can do it. Stay close," Isabelle said.

"I don't want to go outside!" Maman protested. "My hair's a fright!"

"It'll look far worse burnt to a crisp!" Isabelle shot back, tightening her grip.

Isabelle continued down the curving staircase, pulling Maman behind her, forcing Tavi to keep up. By the time she got to the foyer, the flames were halfway across it.

"What do we do?" Tavi shouted.

"We run," Isabelle replied. "Go, Tavi. You first."

Head down, Tavi bolted across the floor. Isabelle heaved a sigh of relief as she watched her disappear through the front door. Now it was her turn. She tightened her grip on her mother's wrist and took a few steps across the floor.

As she did, a gust of wind blowing through a shattered window billowed a burning drapery panel at them. Isabelle instinctively raised her hands to protect herself against it, letting go of her mother.

Maman saw her chance. With an animal cry, she shot back up the stairs.

"Maman, *no*!" Isabelle shouted, darting after her.

She found her back in her room, frantically brushing her hair. Isabelle tore the brush away from her. "Look at me!" she said, taking her mother's hands in her own, forcing Maman to meet her eyes. "The fire is destroying the mansion. You *must* come with me."

Maman stood. She raked her hands through her hair. "What will I wear? What, Isabelle? Tell me!" She picked up a gown off the floor, and a pair of shoes, and clutched them to her chest. Then she lifted her heavy mirror off its hook on the wall. The gown and shoes fell to the floor as she did. "No!" she cried, snatching at them. She lost her grip on the mirror. It toppled forward, pinning her to the floor.

"Stop this!" Isabelle pleaded, pushing the mirror off her.

But Maman would not. She abandoned her finery but took hold of the mirror once more and carried it out of her room. She made it to the landing before dropping it again. It fell to the floor with a loud, echoing boom. Weeping, she sat down next to it.

Isabelle glanced over the railing. Her stomach clutched with fear as she saw that the fire was climbing the walls to the first floor. It was licking the staircase, too.

"Maman, we cannot take the mirror," Isabelle said, her panic rising.

But her mother only stared at the glass sorrowfully. "I can't leave it. I'm nothing without it. It tells me who I am."

Isabelle's heart was battering her ribs. Everything inside her was telling her to run. But she did not. Instead, she sat down next to her mother.

"Maman, if you don't leave the mirror, you will die."

Her mother stubbornly shook her head.

"Maman," Isabelle said, her voice breaking, "if you don't leave the mirror, *I* will die."

Would it matter to her mother if she did? Isabelle didn't know. She was nothing but a disappointment. Was there ever a time she'd pleased Maman instead of making her angry?

Maman looked at Isabelle. In the icy depths of her eyes, something was shifting and cracking. Isabelle saw it and saw that her mother was helpless to stop it. "You are strong. So strong," Maman said. "I saw that in you when you were a tiny baby. It has always frightened me, your strength. I would rock you in my arms and wonder, *Where is there a place in the world for such a strong girl?*"

Below them, a giant wooden ceiling beam gave way. It crashed down to the foyer, bringing much of the second floor with it. The noise was deafening. The dust and smoke it threw into the air were blinding. Isabelle covered her head with her arms and screamed. When the dust cleared, she peered over the railing again and saw a jagged, gaping hole in the foyer floor, next to the stairwell. In the darkness, with fire raging all around it, the hole looked like the gateway to hell.

"Maman . . . *please*," she begged.

But her mother, still gazing at the mirror, didn't seem to hear her.

Isabelle's stomach squeezed with terror. But another emotion rose inside her, pushing the terror down—hatred.

How many times had her mother summoned her to her room, stood her in front of that very mirror, and looked over her shoulder? Frowning sourly at the way her dress bunched here or puckered there? Disapproving of her freckles, her crooked smile, her wayward hair?

How many times had Isabelle lifted her eyes to her own

reflection only to see a miserable, awkward girl looking back at her?

That mirror, and all the others in her house, had stolen her confidence, her happiness, her strength and courage, over and over again. It had stolen her soul; now it wanted her life.

From deep within the house, another window exploded. The sound of breaking glass told Isabelle exactly what she had to do. She stood, tore the mirror from her mother's hands, and, with a wild yell, threw it over the banister. It hit the stone floor below and shattered into a million glittering pieces.

"No!" Maman screamed, reaching through the balusters. She stared into the flames for a few long seconds, then looked at Isabelle helplessly.

"Get up, Maman," Isabelle ordered, taking her hand. "We're leaving."

Together they started down the stairs once more. When they got to the bottom, they saw that most of the foyer floor was gone. Only a narrow strip remained, running along one wall and supported by burning joists. One misstep, and they would fall to a fiery death.

Isabelle led Maman along what remained of the floor, hugging the wall the whole time. When they got close to the door, they had to jump across a two-foot gap where the floor was gone completely, and then they were outside, and a sobbing Tavi was running to them.

Isabelle quickly pulled her mother and sister away from the inferno to the sheltering safety of the linden tree. From under its branches, their clothing singed, faces stained with soot, their arms around each other, the three women watched as the fire raged, collapsing the Maison Douleur's walls, bringing its heavy slate roof down, destroying everything that they owned, their past and their present.

"And, with any luck," whispered an old woman, dressed all in black and watching from the shadows, "their future."

Fifty

As the sun rose the next morning, Isabelle stood under the linden tree, gazing at the smoldering heap that had been her home.

Her dress was soaked. Tendrils of wet hair stuck to her skin. A heavy morning rain had doused the fire, but not before a strong wind had swept glowing embers across the yard, to the chicken coop and the open window of the hayloft.

Tavi had wrenched the door of the coop open and had chased the birds out of the yard to safety. They were gone now, vanished into the woods. Isabelle had got Martin out before fire took the stables. He stood under the linden tree with them, shaking raindrops out of his mane. Tavi and Maman sat huddled against the linden tree's trunk, asleep under some horse blankets Isabelle had managed to save from the stables.

Everything in the mansion had been destroyed. Clothing. Furniture. Food. Any paper money Maman had had was ashes, any coins or jewelry had likely melted or were hopelessly buried under piles of hot stone and smoking beams.

Not one neighbor had come to help them. To see if they were hurt. To offer food or shelter. They were utterly alone.

Destitute. Friendless. That terrified Isabelle even more than the fire had.

Chilled from the rain, numb inside, Isabelle did not know what they would eat that day or where they would find shelter that night. She did not know how to take the next step. She could not see a way forward.

She stood, cupping her elbows, mutely watching wisps of smoke spiral up into the air for over an hour. Until she heard the sound of hooves and the creak of wagon wheels, and stepped out from under the tree to see who it was.

"Isabelle, is that you?" a voice called. "My goodness, child! What happened here?"

Isabelle saw an old horse and an even older farm wagon, piled high with cabbages, creaking towards her. Holding the reins was Avara LeBenêt. Seated next to her, her face creased with concern, her dark eyes as bright and busy as a vulture's, was Tantine.

Fifty-One

"It was a fire," Isabelle said dully. "It took everything."

Tantine pressed a wrinkled hand to her chest. "That's terrible. Just terrible, child!"

"What goes around comes around," sniffed Madame LeBenêt.

"How did it start?" Tantine asked.

"I don't know," Isabelle said, pressing a hand to her forehead. "I woke up, and the downstairs was in flames."

"It must've been a spark from the fireplace. Or an ember that rolled out of the grate," Tantine said. "Where is your mother? Your sister?"

"They're under there, asleep," Isabelle replied, pointing to the linden tree.

"This is dreadful. You're soaking wet. Cold, too, from the looks of you. Have you nowhere to go?"

Isabelle shook her head but then had a thought. "Perhaps the marquis could help us. His château is so big. All we would need is a room in the attic. We could—"

Tantine paled. She shot to her feet, startling Madame LeBenêt and Isabelle. "Absolutely not!" she declared. "I won't hear of it. The marquis is a man of loose morals, my dear. He lives with several woman, not one of whom is his wife. I will not stand by and see two young women corrupted by that scoundrel!"

"But he seems so very—" *Nice*, Isabelle was going to say.

But Tantine held up a hand, silencing her. She turned to Madame LeBenêt. "They must stay with us, Avara. We are their closest neighbors."

Avara LeBenêt nearly choked. "*Three* more mouths to feed, Tantine? With a war going on and food so scarce?"

Isabelle thought of the rows of cabbages in the LeBenêts' fields. The plump chickens in their coop. The branches of their plum trees bent to the ground with heavy fruit. She did not relish the idea of accepting charity from this harsh, stingy woman, but she knew she had no choice. *Please, Tantine*, she begged silently. *Please convince her.*

"It's a burden, yes," Tantine allowed. "But you are an unselfish woman, Avara. A woman who always puts others first."

Madame LeBenêt nodded vigorously, as one does when accepting praise, or anything else, that does not belong to one. "You're right. I *am* far too kind. It's my undoing."

"Look at what you will gain from the arrangement: three desperately needed farmhands," Tantine said. "All yours have joined the army. Only Hugo remains because of his poor eyesight. Your cabbages will rot in the fields if you can't get them to market."

Avara looked Isabelle up and down. Squinted. Worked a piece of food from her teeth with her thumbnail. "All right," she finally said. "You and your family may come to the farm and I will feed you, if"—she held up a finger—"*if* you promise to work hard."

Isabelle nearly wept with relief. They could dry themselves

off. Warm themselves by the farmhouse's hearth. Maybe there would even be a bowl of hot soup for them.

"We will work *very* hard, Madame. I promise," she said. "Me, Tavi, Maman, Martin . . . all of us."

Madame LeBenêt shook her head. "No, absolutely not. The offer does not include your horse."

Isabelle looked from Madame LeBenêt to Tantine pleadingly. "But I can't leave him here," she said. "He's old. He needs his oats. And a dry stall to sleep in."

"You see, Tantine? I'm being taken advantage of already," Madame LeBenêt said, flipping a hand at Isabelle.

"I doubt the animal will eat much," Tantine assured her. "And you can use him, too."

Madame relented. "I suppose that's true," she said. She gestured at her own cart horse. "Louis here is on his last legs."

Because you worked him to death, Isabelle thought, looking at the poor bony creature. *And you'll do the same to us.* The realization sat heavily on her.

"It's settled, then," Tantine declared with a satisfied smile.

"Get yourselves to the farm," Madame LeBenêt said. "Find Hugo. He's cutting cabbages. He'll show you what to do." She snapped her reins against Louis's haunches. "Tantine and I must take this load to market."

"Thank you, Madame," Isabelle said as the wagon rolled off. "Thank you for making room in your house for us."

Madame LeBenêt snorted. *"House?"* she called over her shoulder. "Who said anything about the house? You three will sleep in the hayloft and be glad of it!"

Fifty-Two

Fate stared at the stingy portion of weak coffee in a cracked mug on the table in front of her. And the hard heel of bread to dip into it. There was a small pitcher of cream next to the mug. No sugar. No biscuits. No warm, pillowy brioche.

"Perhaps I was too liberal with my use of *Smallsoul* on Avara LeBenêt's map," she said to herself, drumming her fingers on the table.

Smallsoul—a dusty, dry black ink—was versatile. It could prompt miserliness, or, if applied properly, shrink the soul. It was also useful in curbing the artistic impulse, but one had to be careful; a little went a long way.

Fate closed her eyes and imagined a delicate porcelain cup of steaming espresso brewed from dark, oily beans. A plate of buttery anise biscuits. A velvet-covered chair for her old bones to sink into.

Ah well, it wouldn't be too much longer before she left Saint-Michel for good. Progress was being made. A drunken fool had burned the Maison Douleur down for her, and Isabelle and her family were now destitute. They were stuck here on the LeBenêts' farm, which meant Fate could control the girl. Chance no longer had the upper hand.

She rose now, moved to the old stone sink, and dumped the coffee down the drain. She rinsed the cup, dried it, then walked outside. Avara and Hugo were already in the fields; Isabelle, Tavi, and their mother, too. The three women had been here a week already.

As Fate bent to admire the late-summer blooms on a straggly rosebush struggling up the wall of the house, Losca landed above her on the roof.

The crone smiled, delighted to see the sly creature. "Where have you been? Impaling field mice with that sharp beak? Snatching hatchlings from their nests? Pecking the eyes out of dead things?"

Losca shook out her feathers. With barely contained excitement, she started to chatter. The crone listened, rapt.

"Two hundred miles west of here? Volkmar's moving quickly; that's good. The sooner this is behind us, the better."

Losca bobbed her head. Then chattered again.

Fate laughed. "That's *two* pieces of good news! The horse is with a widow, you say? And the stables are crumbling?" The crone nodded. "She probably doesn't have much money. A few coins should do the trick. I can't do the deed myself—too much blood—but I know a man who can. Well done, my girl! Chance found the first piece of Isabelle's heart, and put the boy right in her path, but the horse is one piece he won't find. And without all three, she won't gain Tanaquill's help."

She reached into her skirt pocket. "Here we are!" she said, pulling out a gangly spider. She tossed it to Losca, who greedily snapped it out of the air.

Fate started for the barn. She would ask Hugo to hitch up

a cart so she could go to the village and set her plan for the horse in motion. She was pleased, certain that it would only be a matter of days, a fortnight at the most, before she was ready to leave.

Volkmar was coming closer.

And she wanted to be long gone when he arrived.

Fifty-Three

Isabelle straightened—her face to the sun—and stretched, trying to ease her aching back.

Her callused hands were as filthy as her boots. The sun had bronzed her arms and added freckles to her nose and cheeks, despite the old straw bonnet she wore. Her skirts were hitched up and knotted above her knees to keep them from dragging in the dirt.

"Isabelle, Octavia, does my hair look all right? What if a countess or duchess should pay us a visit?" Maman asked anxiously.

"Oh, I'm sure one will, Maman. After all, cabbage patches are a favorite destination of the nobility," Tavi said.

"Your hair looks lovely, Maman. Pick up your knife now and cut some cabbages," Isabelle said, shooting her sister a dirty look.

As she did, she noticed that Tavi, who was one row over but well behind her, was bent over a cabbage, peering at it intently.

No vegetable can be that interesting, Isabelle thought. "Tavi, what are you doing over there?" she asked, jumping over her row to her sister's.

"Nothing!" Tavi replied quickly. "Just cutting a stem!"

But she wasn't. She'd pressed a large outer leaf flat and was using a sharp stone to scratch equations across it.

"No wonder you're behind!" Isabelle scolded.

Tavi hung her head. "I'm sorry, Isabelle," she said. "I can't help it. I'm so bored I could cry."

"Bored is better than dead, which is what you'll be if we don't eat, *again*, because we haven't filled the wagon," Isabelle scolded.

Madame LeBenêt had decreed that the three women must load the farm's large wooden wagon with cabbages every day or there would be no supper for them.

"I'm sorry," Tavi said again.

She looked so miserable that Isabelle softened. "You and I can go without a meal or two, but not Maman. She's getting worse."

Both girls cast worried glances in their mother's direction. Maman, sitting on the ground, was patting her hair, smoothing her tattered dress—the same silk gown she'd been wearing the night of the fire—and talking animatedly to the cabbage heads. The hollows in her cheeks had deepened. Her eyes were lackluster. There seemed to be more gray in her hair every day.

Since their arrival at the farm, she'd only slid deeper into the past. The few moments of clarity she'd had on the stairs of the Maison Douleur as it had gone up in flames had not come again. Isabelle blamed it on the trauma of losing their home and all their possessions, and on the hard life they now lived. But she knew there was more to it, too; Maman felt she had failed at a mother's most important task—seeing that her daughters made good marriages—and that failure had unhinged her.

Isabelle had startled awake their first night of sleeping in the hayloft certain that a mouse had run across her cheek, but it was Maman. She'd been sitting in the hay beside her, smoothing the hair off her face.

"What will become of you?" she whispered. "My poor, poor daughters. Your lives are over before they've even begun. You are farmhands with dirty faces and ragged dresses. Who will have you now?"

"Go to sleep, Maman," Isabelle had said, frightened.

Her fearsome mother was fading before her very eyes. It had often been hard living with Maman. Hard coming up against her constant disapproval. Her anger. Her rigid rules. But no matter what, Maman had seen to it that the bills were paid. Widowed twice, she'd still managed to keep a roof over their heads and food on the table. Now, for the first time, Isabelle had to do it. Sometimes with Tavi's help, often without it. That was hard, too.

They had arrived at the LeBenêts' a week ago, after salvaging what they could from the barn—horse blankets, two wooden chairs, two saddles and bridles. Miraculously, their wooden cart had not burned, but it had taken them hours to extricate it because part of the barn's roof had fallen on it. After loading it with their things, they hitched up Martin and rode to the LeBenêts'. By the time they arrived, Madame and Tantine had returned from the market. Madame had put them straight to work.

They'd learned how to cut cabbages, dig potatoes and carrots, slop pigs, and milk cows.

Tavi had proven herself even less capable around animals than she was around cabbages, so Madame had given her the cheesemaking tasks. It was her responsibility to tend the milk in the wooden vats in the dairy house as it soured and curdled, stirring the curds gently with a long wooden paddle, then setting them in molds to ripen into cheese. It was the one job Tavi did with enthusiasm, as the transformation milk underwent to become cheese fascinated her.

Their days were long and hard. Meals were meager, comforts nonexistent. Beds were horse blankets spread over hay. Baths were taken once a week.

With a wry smile, Isabelle remembered asking Madame if she could bathe at the end of her first day on the farm.

"Certainly," Madame said. "The duck pond's all yours."

Isabelle had thought she was joking. "The *duck pond*?" she'd repeated.

"You were expecting a copper tub and a Turkish towel?" Madame had said with a smirk.

Isabelle had walked to the pond. Her hands were blistered. Dirt had worked itself under her nails. Her muscles were aching. She stank of smoke, sweat, and sour milk. Her dress was so filthy it was stiff.

The banks of the pond afforded no privacy and Isabelle was too modest to strip off her clothing in plain view of others, so she'd simply removed her boots and stockings, placed the bone, nutshell, and seed-pod in one of her boots, then waded in fully dressed. She would take off her dress in the hayloft and let it dry overnight. Her chemise would dry as she slept in it. The one dress was all she had. The gowns in her wardrobe, the silks and satins Maman had carefully chosen to impress suitors, were nothing but ash now.

The pond was spring-fed, and the water was so cold it had made Isabelle catch her breath, but it also numbed her torn hands and sore body. She'd undone the dirty ribbon that cinched her braid, ducked her head under the water, and scrubbed her scalp. When she'd surfaced, Madame had been walking by.

"The tables have turned, haven't they?" she mocked, looking a sodden Isabelle up and down. "If only your stepsister could see you now. How she would laugh."

"No, I don't think so," Isabelle had said, wringing the water out of her hair.

"Of course she would!"

Isabelle shook her head. "I would have. But Ella? Never. That was her strength. And my weakness."

She ducked under again. When she came back up, Madame was gone.

She'd watched swallows swoop through the air for a bit, and listened to the frogs and crickets. She thought about Tanaquill and the possibility of help she'd offered, and it seemed as far away as the stars. How could she find the pieces of her heart when all she did, day after day, was cut cabbages? She thought about the people who had burned down her house, who would never let her forget that she was nothing but an ugly stepsister.

Maybe there is no help for me, she'd thought. *Maybe I have to find a way to live with that.*

That's certainly what Tantine counseled. *Ah, child,* she'd said the night after the fire. *Our fates are often hard, but we must learn to accept them. We have no choice.*

Maybe the old woman was right. A feeling of hopelessness

had descended on Isabelle ever since she'd arrived at the LeBenêts' farm. Her life was cows and cabbages now and it seemed like that was all it would ever be.

"It's noon already and you don't even have half the wagon filled," said a voice a few rows over, pulling Isabelle out of her thoughts.

Isabelle's spirits, already heavy, sank even lower. Here was someone who made Tantine look like a devil-may-care optimist.

It was Hugo, Madame LeBenêt's son.

Fifty-Four

Isabelle's shoulders rose up around her ears. "I *know* we haven't filled the wagon, Hugo. Thank you," she said tartly.

Hugo blinked at her through his thick eyeglasses. "I'm just saying."

"Yes, you are."

There were many unpleasant things about their new lives. Hunger. Exhaustion. Sleeping in the hot hayloft. Mucking out cow stalls. Raw, blistered hands that cracked and wept. Nothing, though, was more unpleasant than the hulking, surly Hugo. He was home instead of off fighting because his poor eyesight prevented him from joining the army. He didn't like Isabelle or Tavi and took every chance he could to make that clear.

"You don't get that wagon filled, you won't get any soup tonight," he said.

"You could help us. It would go faster. We'd get done that way," Tavi said.

Hugo shook his head. "Can't. Have to sharpen the plow. And then—"

"Hugo! Hey, Hugo!" a voice called, cutting him off.

Hugo, Isabelle, and Tavi all turned to see a wagon trundling down the drive. Two young men were riding in it. Isabelle knew them. They were soldiers under Colonel Cafard's command. They worked in the camp's kitchen and came every day to pick up vegetables.

"You've got to help Claude and Remy now," Hugo said. "Both of you. My mother said so. That'll take a good hour. You're going hungry again tonight."

Hugo said this without malice or glee, just dull resignation. Like an old man predicting rain.

"You could give us some of your supper. You could sneak it up to the hayloft after dark," Tavi suggested.

"It's soup. How am I supposed to sneak soup?"

"Bread, then. Sneak us some bread. Wrap it up in your napkin when no one's looking and put it in your pocket."

Hugo's face darkened. "I wish you'd never come here. You're always thinking of . . . of *things*," he said. "You shouldn't do that. Girls shouldn't. It's up to the man to think. It's up to *me* to think of sneaking you bread."

"Then think of it! Think of sneaking us cheese. A bit of ham. Think of *something* before we starve to death!" Tavi snapped.

"Hugo! Where are the potatoes?" Claude called out. "Cook says we're supposed to get potatoes and carrots today. Hello, Isabelle. Tavi. Madame de la Paumé."

Maman, still talking to the cabbages, stood. "Your Excellencies," she said with a reverent curtsy. "You see, girls?" she added grandly. "It pays to keep up appearances. The pope has come to visit us. And the king of Spain."

Claude and Remy gave each other puzzled looks.

"Never mind," Isabelle told them.

Hugo nodded in the direction they'd come. "That's quite a cloud you kicked up on the road," he said to the boys. The road was half a mile from where they stood, and a tall hedgerow blocked it from their view, but above it, they could all see a huge mass of dust rising into the air.

"That's not us," Remy said. "It's more wounded."

Hugo took off his glasses and cleaned them on his shirt. Then he put them back on and gazed at the dust cloud again. It rose higher and higher in the sky, swirling like a gathering storm. "Must be a lot of them," he said.

"Wagons for miles," said Remy. "As far as you can see." He looked down at the reins in his hands. "We're losing."

"Come on, Rem. That's only because *we're* not there yet!" Claude boasted, elbowing him. "I'll send Volkmar running back to the border with my sword up his ass!"

Remy mustered a smile, but it was a wan one.

Isabelle knew that both boys were being sent to the front soon. She wondered if she would see them again. Would they, too, be carried back over rutted roads in a rattling wagon missing pieces of themselves? Or would they end up in hastily dug graves, never to see their homes again?

They'd talked a little over the last few days, she, Remy and Claude, as she'd helped load their wagon. She'd learned that Claude, olive-skinned and dark-eyed, came from the south, from a family of fishermen. Remy, fair and blond, was from the west, a printer's son, who had hopes of not only printing books but writing them one day. They had no more wanted to be soldiers than Isabelle had wanted to marry the prince. But the choice to fight was not theirs to make, no more than the decision to cut off her toes had been hers.

Leaving Maman with the cabbages, Isabelle and Tavi helped the boys. Hugo decided to pitch in, too. When the last potato sack had been hoisted in, Remy and Claude climbed back into their seats.

"See you tomorrow," Hugo said, squinting up at them.

Claude shook his head. "Someone new will come tomorrow. We're heading out, me and Rem."

It was quiet for a moment; then Hugo said, "Then we'll see you when you get back."

Remy swallowed hard. Then he reached inside his shirt and pulled a silver chain over his head. A cross was dangling from it. "If I don't . . . if I don't come back, could you get this to my mother?" he asked Isabelle, handing it to her. He told her his surname and the town where he was from. He looked very scared and very young as he asked, and Isabelle said it wouldn't be necessary and tried to hand the cross back, but he wouldn't take it. Instead, he thanked her.

"It's nothing. I . . . I wish I could do more to help you, to help all the soldiers," she said.

Remy smiled at her. "What could you do? You're a girl," he teased.

"I'm good with a sword. As good as you are. Maybe better. I've been practicing."

"Girls don't fight. Stay here and cut cabbages for us, all right? Soldiers need to eat."

Isabelle forced a smile and waved them off. They trundled out of the farmyard and down the drive. She was back in the cabbage rows by the time they turned onto the road.

For several long minutes, she watched them go, holding her harvesting knife as if she were gripping the hilt of Tanaquill's sword. A terrible longing took hold of her as she did, a yearning buried so deep inside her, she couldn't even name it any more. It was a hunger deeper and more ferocious than the need for mere food, a hunger that sang in her blood and echoed in her bones.

Isabelle turned away and, with a heavy sigh, bent her back to the cabbages. She, Tavi, and Maman had many more to cut if they were going to eat tonight.

As she worked, she worried about empty wagons and empty bellies.

She needn't have, though. The stomach is easily satisfied.

It's the hunger in our hearts that kills us.

Fifty-Five

It was dusk, Isabelle's favorite time of day.

And she was spending it in her favorite place, the Wildwood.

Isabelle had ridden Martin across the LeBenêts' land and dismounted as soon as they'd reached the woods in order to give the old horse a rest. As they made their way through the trees, Isabelle took a deep breath of the clear forest air. It had been years since she'd set foot in the Wildwood. She'd forgotten how intoxicating the scent of the forest was—a mixture of damp, rotting leaves, resiny pine needles, and the dark, mineralish waters of the rocky streams they crossed. She took note of all the familiar markers as she walked—the giant white bolder, the tree felled by lightning, a stand of white birches—though she could have found her way blindfolded.

Finally, she reached her destination—a hidden bower far within the woods. Everything was just as she remembered it—the leafy canopy, the shaggy berry bushes, even the little heart. It was still there on a mossy bank, shaped of stones and walnut shells. Some were missing, but most remained, bleached by rain and snow.

Isabelle sat down on the soft moss and touched one of the

stones. She had tried her best to not think of Felix since her visit to the marquis's, but now everything came rushing back. She could see him, and herself, right here, just as they were the day they'd made the heart.

They'd been best friends. Soul mates. Since the day her mother had married Ella's father and had brought her and Tavi to live at the Maison Douleur. He was the groom's son and had loved horses every bit as much as she did. They'd ridden over hill and dale together, through streams and meadows, deep into the Wildwood.

From the start, Maman had disapproved. Two years ago, when Isabelle had turned fourteen and Felix sixteen, she'd declared that Isabelle was too old to be acting like a hoyden. It was time to give up riding and learn to sing and dance and do all the things that made one a proper lady, but Isabelle wanted no part of that. She'd escaped with Felix every chance she got. She'd adored him. Loved him. And then, one day, she'd discovered she was in love with him.

They'd ridden into the Wildwood and had stopped at the top of the Devil's Hollow, a wooded canyon. As much as they liked to explore, they knew better than to venture down into the Hollow, for it was haunted. Instead, they'd flung themselves down on the mossy bank and had eaten the cherries and chocolate cake that Isabelle had filched from the kitchen.

As they were finishing, and Felix was wiping cherry juice off Isabelle's chin with his sleeve, they'd heard a twig snap behind them.

Slowly, they'd turned around. A red deer had walked up behind them. She was only a few yards away and with her were twin fawns, still wobbly on their spindly legs. Their blunt black noses were shiny and wet, their soft coats dappled white, their dark eyes huge and trusting. As the doe grazed and the fawns stared at the pair of strange animals sitting on the bank, Isabelle had felt like her heart would burst with joy. Never had she seen anything so beautiful. Instinctively, she'd reached for Felix's hand. He'd taken it and held it and hadn't let go even after the deer had gone.

She'd looked down at their hands and then up at him questioningly, and he'd answered her. With a kiss. She'd caught her breath and laughed; then she'd kissed him back.

He'd smelled like all the things she loved—horses, leather, lavender, and hay.

He'd tasted like cherries and chocolate and boy.

He'd felt safely familiar and dangerously new.

Before they'd left, they'd made the heart together. Isabelle could still see them, side by side, placing the stones and shells . . .

"What a pretty picture," said a voice at Isabelle's side.

Isabelle jumped; she gasped. The images were swept away like rose petals in the wind.

Tanaquill laughed. "Ah, mortal happiness," she said. "As fleeting as the dawn, as fragile as a dragonfly's wing. You poor creatures have it, you lose it, and then you spend the rest of your lives torturing yourselves with memories until old age carries you off in some slow, bloodless death." She wiped a crimson smudge from the corner of her mouth with her thumb and licked it. "Better a quick and bloody one, if you ask me."

"You . . . you could see what I saw?" Isabelle said, her heart still jumping from her scare.

"Of course. The heart leaves echoes. They linger like ghosts."

Tanaquill was dressed in a gown of shimmering blue butterfly wings, their edges traced in black. A wreath of black roses adorned her head; several live butterflies had lighted upon it, their gossamer wings slowly opening and closing.

"Have you found the pieces of your heart yet, Isabelle?" the fairy queen asked.

"I—I need a little more time," Isabelle replied, hoping Tanaquill wouldn't ask why. She did not want to tell her how badly wrong her trip to the orphanage had gone. "I think I know what they are now, at least. Goodness, kindness, and charitableness."

Isabelle hoped Tanaquill would be delighted that she had at least figured out what the pieces were, even if she hadn't found them yet, but the fairy queen was not.

"I instructed you to find the pieces of *your* heart. Not someone else's," she said coldly.

"I'm trying. I really am! I—"

"By throwing eggs at orphans?"

Isabelle looked at her boots, her cheeks flaming. "You heard about that," she said.

"And your wish . . . is it still to be pretty?"

"Yes," said Isabelle resolutely, looking up again.

Tanaquill turned away, growling, then she rounded back on Isabelle. "I watched you as a child. Did you know that?" she said, pointing a taloned finger at her. "I watched you duel, swing out of trees, play at being generals . . . Scipio, Hannibal, Alexander the Great. None of *them* wished to be pretty."

Frustration sparked in Isabelle. "Alexander didn't have to be pretty," she retorted. "*His* mother didn't make him wear ridiculous dresses or dance minuets. Alexander was an emperor with vast armies at his command and a magnificent warhorse named Bucephalus. I'm a girl who can hardly walk. And that's *my* magnificent warhorse." She nodded at Martin, who, in his greed, had pushed himself so far into a blackberry thicket, all that was visible of him was his bony rear end. "He and I won't be invading Persia anytime soon."

Tanaquill looked as if she would speak again, but instead she froze. She scented the air, then listened as an animal does, not only with her ears, but with her flesh, her bones.

Isabelle heard it, too. A twig snapping. Footsteps kicking through the leaves.

The fairy queen turned back to her. "Try harder, girl," she said. "Time is not on your side."

And then she was gone, and Isabelle was alone with whoever was coming. Few people ventured this far into the Wildwood at dusk. Isabelle remembered the deserter who'd tried to steal her chickens. He'd tried to kill her. He'd try again, she was certain.

Cursing herself for being stupid enough to ride so far from safety with no sword, no dagger, not even a clasp knife, Isabelle looked around frantically for a weapon—a tree limb, a heavy rock, *anything*. Then she remembered Tanaquill's gifts. She dug in her pocket, hoping that one of them would transform into something she could use to defend herself, but they remained a bone, a shell, and a seedpod.

Isabelle knew she was in trouble. She was about to run for Martin, to try to ride out of the woods fast, when a figure emerged from the dusk, and her traitor heart lurched.

This was no chicken thief making his way towards her, but he was still a deserter.

"The very worst kind," Isabelle whispered.

Fifty-Six

Felix didn't see her at first.

He was too busy looking up, squinting into the dusk. At what, Isabelle couldn't guess.

He tripped over a tree root, righted himself, then did a double take as he saw her. After the initial shock of surprise wore off, a wide grin spread across his face. His beautiful blue eyes lit up.

Don't be happy to see me. Don't smile. You don't get to, Isabelle said silently.

"Isabelle, is that you?" he called out. "What are you doing here?"

"Talking to fairies," Isabelle replied curtly. "What are *you* doing here?"

"Looking for a downed walnut tree or at least a nice, thick limb."

"Why?"

"I need walnut to carve my commanders. For my army of wooden soldiers. Usually I can find scraps from furniture we make in the shop." The light in his eyes dimmed a little. "Only we don't have any orders for desks or cabinets right now. Just coffins. We use pine for those."

He shrugged his satchel off his shoulder and put it on the moss bank. Then he sat down next to Isabelle.

"I heard about your house. I'm sorry."

Isabelle thanked him. He asked how living at the LeBenêts' was going. Isabelle told him it was better than starving. Their conversation might have continued in terse questions and answers had the bushes nearby not shaken violently.

Felix started at the sound

"It's only Martin," Isabelle said.

"Let me guess . . . blackberries," he said, laughing. "Do you remember when he ate the entire bucketful we'd picked for Adélie?" He leaned back as he spoke, and his hand came down on one of the stones in the heart.

He turned around, lifted his hand. "It's still there . . ." he said, looking down at it.

His eyes sought Isabelle's, just for an instant, and what she saw in their depths made her catch her breath—pain, as deep and raw as her own.

She hadn't expected that. She hadn't expected him to remember the heart and wondered if he'd remembered other things that had happened here. If he did, he wasn't sharing his memories. His eyes were elsewhere now, their depths hidden from her. He'd opened his satchel and was digging through it furiously.

"I have something for you," he said. Quickly. As if he were trying to change a subject that no one had brought up.

He pulled out the same tools of his trade Isabelle had seen when he'd emptied his bag at the marquis's, but he was taking out other things, too. Strange things. A human hand. Half a face. A set of teeth. Two eyeballs.

Isabelle's own eyes widened in horror.

Felix noticed. He laughed. "They're not *real*," he said, picking up the hand and offering it to her.

Isabelle took it, half expecting it to feel warm. The painted skin was so lifelike. "Why do you have them?" she asked.

"I made them. I make a lot of body parts now, what with all the wounded men in the army camp. There's such a demand for them that Colonel Cafard won't let me enlist. I tried, but he said I'm more valuable to the army working for Master Jourdan than I would be working for him."

Plus you can't shoot straight, Isabelle thought, remembering the time they'd been allowed to fire her stepfather's pistols. He'd hit everything but the target.

Felix continued to dig in his satchel, then finally he pulled out an object and put it in Isabelle's lap. "There. That one's for you."

Isabelle put the hand down and looked at what he'd given her. It was a leather slipper, thin and finely stitched, with a gusset and laces above the arch. She picked it up. It was heavy.

"What is it?" she asked.

Felix didn't reply. Instead, he took the slipper from her, opened the laces, and pulled out whatever it was that had made it heavy. As he put the object into Isabelle's hands, she saw that it was a block of wood, carved in the shape of toes. Each was well delineated, separate from its fellows, sanded to smoothness.

"Toes . . ." she said wonderingly.

"*Your* toes," Felix said, taking them back from her.

"That is an unusual gift. Most girls get sweets. Or flowers."

"You were never most girls. Are you now?" he asked, an edge to his voice. He put the wooden toes back inside the slipper, then wadded a bit of lambswool he had in his satchel in after them. "Try it," he said, handing the slipper back to her.

Isabelle hitched up her skirt and took her boot off. She put the slipper on, then started to tie the laces.

"That's not tight enough," Felix said. "It has to fit like a glove." He leaned over her, pulled the laces tighter, and knotted them. "Stand up," he said when he'd finished.

Isabelle did. The slipper fit better than a glove; it fit like her own skin. She put her boot back on.

"Take a step. But be careful. Don't forget that you reopened your scar when you fell off Martin," Felix said, shoveling body parts back into his satchel.

Isabelle clenched her fists. He was making her want something badly. Yet again. What if the slipper didn't work? What if it hurt? What if it only made things worse? He had a talent for making things worse.

"Come on, Isabelle. You're braver than this. Take a step."

His voice was challenging, goading, and Isabelle bridled at it. He saw the fear in her, and she didn't want him to. Gingerly, she put her foot down, holding her breath. It didn't hurt. She exhaled. Took a step. And then another. The weight of the carved toes was perfectly balanced. The tight fit kept the toes snug up against the rest of her foot. Nothing slipped or rubbed. She'd never expected to walk without a limp again, and now she was. Her gait was smooth and easy.

Happiness flooded through her. She walked briskly back and forth.

"Take it slow," Felix cautioned.

She ran back and forth.

"Isabelle."

She jumped up on the mossy bank and jumped down again. Balanced on her new foot. Twirled. Lunged. Laughed out loud. Giddy and excited, she forgot herself. Forgot to be awkward. Forgot to be angry.

"Thank you, Felix. Thank you!" she said, and then she impulsively threw her arms around him.

She didn't see Felix's eyes fill with longing as she hugged him. She didn't know that just for an instant, he pressed his cheek against her head. She felt his arms stiffen at his sides, though. She felt him pull away from her.

Hurt, she took a step back.

"Isabelle, I can't—" Felix started to say.

"Can't what? Get too close?" Isabelle asked, her voice raw. "No, you shouldn't. I'm broken. And broken things draw blood."

"Either I back away or I wrap my arms around you. And then what?"

Isabelle couldn't believe what she'd just heard. "Is that some kind of rotten joke, Felix?" she asked angrily. "You should leave. Go. As far as you can."

"I already tried that," Felix said.

And then he reached across the space between them and cupped her cheek. Isabelle grasped his wrist, meaning to push it away. Instead, her fingers curled around it. She leaned into his palm, his nearness, his warmth, melting her defenses.

"Don't," she said. "It's not fair."

"No, it isn't."

"You said you loved me, but you didn't. It was a lie. How could you do that? How could you lie to me, Felix?"

Felix kissed her then, his lips sweet and sad and bitter, and Isabelle kissed him back, clutching handfuls of his shirt, pulling him to her. He broke the kiss, and she looked up at him, her eyes searching his, confused.

"That's how much I didn't love you," he said, his voice husky. "How much I still don't."

And then he picked up his satchel and walked away, leaving Isabelle alone in the gathering gloom.

"You're walking away?" she called after him. "Again?"

"What should I do? Let you break my heart a second time?"

"Me?" she sputtered. *"Me?"*

Isabelle paced back and forth, furious. Then she picked up a walnut that had fallen from the tree, round and green in its husk, and threw it at his back.

She missed him by a mile.

Fifty-Seven

"I would like to book a carriage," Fate said to the girl behind the desk. "To Marseille. In a week's time. I was told I could make the arrangements here."

She was standing in the bustling lobby of the village inn. Travelers were coming and going. A cat in a wicker cage was yowling. The child holding the cage was crying. Her harried mother was trying to quiet them.

"Yes, madame," said the girl. "How many passengers?"

"Just myself, my servant, and our trunk. My name is Madame Sévèrine. I'm staying with the LeBenêts."

"Very good, madame," the girl said with a nod. "I shall make the arrangements and send a boy to the farm to confirm them." She folded her hands on the desktop.

Fate frowned. She did not want her request forgotten or bungled. "Is that all? Shouldn't you write it down in a ledger?"

The girl smiled. She touched the side of her head. "This is my ledger. I cannot write. Do not worry, madame. I will see to the carriage."

Fate had been so distracted by all the noise, she hadn't noticed that the girl's pale blue eyes gazed straight ahead, unseeing.

Ah, yes, the innkeeper's daughter . . . Odette, she mused. She tried to recall the details of the girl's map, and vaguely remembered an unhappy life. *Denied her true love, was it?* she wondered. Well, whatever fate she'd drawn for her, Volkmar had undoubtedly altered it. The girl would end up a casualty of war, like the rest of the villagers.

Fate thanked her and turned to go, eager to leave the rackety inn. How good it felt to know she'd soon say goodbye to Saint-Michel, and the unpleasant business that had brought her here. Things were about to get more unpleasant. Markedly so.

"Leaving so soon?" said a voice at her elbow. "You must be feeling very confident. I can't imagine why."

Fate's good mood turned rancid. "Marquis," she said, regarding him. "Always a pleasure."

Chance was elegant in a black hat, butter-yellow jacket, and buff britches. He offered Fate his arm, and together they left the inn.

"Where is your coach? I'll escort you to it," Chance said.

Fate pointed down the street at Losca, who was sitting in the driver's seat of a wooden cart, holding Martin's reins. "There it is. It's every bit as comfortable as it is stylish."

Chance laughed, and they set off. He inclined his head towards hers as they walked. "Just because you burned down Isabelle's house," he said in a low voice, "doesn't mean you win the wager. We established rules, remember? Neither of us can force the girl's choice."

Fate affected an innocent expression. "Surely you don't think that *I* had a hand in that?"

"Two hands, actually," said Chance. "Clever move, inviting

them to the LeBenêts' farm. But I can invite them to live with me, too. And I will."

"You can, but they won't come. I've told them that you're a man of dubious morals."

"I shall go to them, then," Chance countered.

Fate smiled smugly. "No, I don't think so. I hear there's a lovely young baroness who lives in the next village . . ."

"Is there?" Chance said lightly, brushing invisible lint off his jacket.

"She's very fond of card games. And likes to bet kisses instead of coins—a proclivity her husband strenuously frowns upon."

"You can hardly blame *me* for what happened," Chance said, aggrieved. "She never so much as *mentioned* a husband!"

"The baron is a good shot, I'm told."

"Very," Chance said ruefully. "He put a hole through my favorite hat."

"Word got to Madame LeBenêt. And the girls' mother. I made sure of it. They're scandalized. I wouldn't set foot on the farm if I were you," Fate said. She changed the subject. "What were you doing at the inn anyway?"

"Sending a man to Paris to fetch me some decent champagne," Chance replied. "Plus a wheel of Stilton. Good strong tea. And the broadsheets." His warm eyes found Fate's chilly ones. "The country is beastly. We must at least agree on that."

"Indeed," Fate said heavily. "I recently sent to Paris myself for a few little luxuries to brighten the dreariness of life with Madame LeBenêt."

"Is it that bad?"

"The woman is so stingy, she uses the same coffee grounds

ten times. I would sell my soul for a good pot of coffee." She chuckled. "If I had one, that is. Ah, Marquis, if these mortals only knew, if they had the merest understanding of the grave, and of the eternity they will spend lying in it, they would eat chocolate for breakfast, caviar for lunch, and sing arias as they slopped the pigs. The worst day above ground is better than any day under it. Ah, well. We'll soon be away from this place. At least *I* will."

They arrived at the cart. Chance tipped his hat to Losca. "I wouldn't be so sure," he said. "My magician was in the Wildwood last night and witnessed a rather romantic interlude. That's one piece of her heart found, two to go."

Fate regarded him and with an acid smile said, "Finding pieces of a heart takes time. How is the skull looking? You know the one I mean, don't you? At the bottom of young Isabelle's map? How much time does she have left? Is it weeks? Days?"

Chance pressed his lips together. The muscles in his jaw tensed.

"*Days*, yes. I thought so," Fate purred. She patted his arm. "Do enjoy your champagne."

Fifty-Eight

Bette, chewing her cud, blinked her patient brown eyes.

"Good girl, Bette," Isabelle said, patting the cow's rump.

She sat down on a low wooden stool, leaned her cheek into the cow's soft warm side, and started to milk her. Bette's slow breathing, the rhythmic sound of the milk squirting into the wooden bucket, made a tired Isabelle feel even sleepier. She'd barely closed her eyes during the night. Images of Felix had crowded her brain. His angry words had echoed in her head.

How could he accuse her of breaking his heart, when he had broken hers?

Isabelle's memories dragged her back in time to a place she did not want to go. After their kiss in the Wildwood, when they first realized they were in love, she and Felix had decided to run away. They both knew Maman would never allow them to be together, so they'd made a plan: They would take Nero and Martin and ride to Italy. Felix would find work in Rome, as an apprentice in the studio of a sculptor. Isabelle would spend her days giving riding lessons, and in the evenings, she and Felix would visit the city's ancient ruins, walking where the Caesars had walked, treading the same roads their armies had marched down.

And when Felix was a sculptor himself, famous and very wealthy, they would travel to Mongolia and race horses with chieftains. Watch eagles hunt in the Russian steppes. Ride camels with the Bedouin. Discover the whole wide wonderful world.

But Maman had found out about their plans. Enraged, she'd fired Felix's father and sent his family packing. Before they'd left, though, Felix had climbed up the vine to Isabelle's bedroom window and had sworn that he would come back for her. They would meet in the Wildwood. He needed a few days to help his family find a place to live, he said, and then he would leave a note in the hollow of the linden tree telling her when.

Isabelle had packed a bag and hidden it under her bed. Every night, after Maman had gone to sleep, she'd climbed down the vine and dashed across the yard to the linden tree, hoping to find Felix's note. But it never came.

Summer gave way to autumn and then winter. Icy winds and deep snow prevented her from stealing out of her room at night, but by then it didn't matter; she'd given up. Felix had meant the world to her, but she'd meant nothing to him.

How many nights had she cried herself to sleep, with Tavi rocking her? Ella had somehow found out, too. She'd been nicer than ever to Isabelle, but Isabelle, heartsore and miserable, had been nothing but mean in return.

And now Felix was back. Making a slipper for her. Making her think he still cared for her. Holding her and kissing her in the Wildwood, and then behaving as if she were to blame for what had happened. Or hadn't.

And here she was, distraught and losing sleep over someone who, no matter what he did, or said, still didn't care enough to tell her why he'd walked away. It was foolish; *she* was foolish. She had more important things to worry about. She lived in a hayloft. She owned one dress. Her mother regularly mistook a cabbage for the Duke of Burgundy.

Bette lowed impatiently. Isabelle hadn't realized it, but she'd milked the cow dry. With effort, she pushed all thoughts of Felix out of her head and picked up the milk bucket. Bette was the last cow that needed to be milked that evening and Isabelle was glad. The day's chores felt endless, and she was eager to finish.

She picked up the milk bucket and hurried to the dairy house. Lost in her thoughts, she didn't hear the angry voices arguing inside until she walked through the doorway.

"You're an idiot!"

"No, *you're* an idiot!"

Hugo and Tavi were standing only a foot away from each other, shouting. Isabelle banged her pail down and got between them.

Through the barrage of rude remarks and gestures, she was able to ascertain that Tavi had added things to one of the cheeses as she set it into its mold last night. Honey from the farm's hives. Sediment from an empty wine cask. A dash of vinegar.

"But that's not the way it's done!" Hugo thundered. "Did you see it? It's ugly. It doesn't look like the others. It has spots. And a strange smell. It's different!"

"Is it so bad to try something new?" Tavi thundered back. "All I want to do is see if and how the substances affect the flavor. Honey, wine dregs, vinegar—they all contain different microorganisms—"

"What are you talking about?"

"Microorganisms?" Tavi repeated. "Single-celled life-forms? You know . . . Leeuwenhoek? The father of microbiology?"

Hugo gave her a blank look.

"Microorganisms acidify the milk," Tavi explained. "They curdle it. Cheese becomes cheese through the process of fermentation."

Hugo stuck out his chest. "Cheese becomes cheese through cheeseification," he said truculently.

Tavi blinked at him. Then she held up her hands. "Fine, Hugo," she said. "My point is, that if we alter just one factor of the . . . *cheeseification* process, even slightly, we vary the result."

"So?"

"So we might very well come up with something other than bland, boring white cheese. Wouldn't that be exciting?"

"I wish you had never come here."

"That makes two of us."

"You're changing things. Why do you have to do that?"

"I wonder if anyone said that to Da Vinci or Newton or Copernicus." Tavi put her hands on her hips and affected a put-upon voice. "Oh my *God*, Nicolaus. Did you *have* to make the Earth orbit the sun? We liked it so much better the other way!"

"They were men. You're a girl," Hugo said, glowering. "Girls don't change things. They bake things. And sew things. They wipe things, too. Like tables. And noses."

Tavi picked up a cloth and scrubbed Hugo's face with it. "And asses," she said, stalking off.

Hugo swore. He kicked at a floorboard.

"She likes to do experiments," Isabelle said, hoping to mollify him.

"I saw the cheese. It's ruined," Hugo said. "My mother will throw a fit."

"Maybe Tavi's right. Maybe it'll turn into something amazing," Isabelle said. She picked up her pail and poured the milk into a vat. "It'll be fine. You'll see."

But Hugo's thoughts were not on the cheeses anymore.

"She'll never get married," he said. "No man wants a woman who won't do what she's told."

Isabelle bristled. "Tavi doesn't want a man. She wants maths," she said, defending her sister.

"Maths won't get the two of you out of here. A man would, though. And I'm going to see if my mother or Tantine can find one," Hugo said, stalking off. Isabelle rolled her eyes. "Good luck. If Maman couldn't manage it, I doubt they will."

Alone now in the dairy house, Isabelle ventured to the back, to see the cheese that had caused all the upset. It was on a rack on the left side of the room. She spotted it immediately.

Hugo had called it ugly, but Isabelle found it interesting. Its odd green spots, its lopsidedness, the pungent smell it gave off—they all set it apart from the other cheeses, which seemed dull and smug to her in their sameness.

"You might do something with yourself," she said to the cheese. But her hopes were not high. Being different was not something that was tolerated in cheeses.

Or girls.

Fifty-Nine

The evening was warm and clear. The setting sun was painting the sky in brilliant shades of orange and pink; the scent of roses hung in the air.

It was calm. It was peaceful. Isabelle prayed it would last.

Tavi and Hugo were sitting side by side on a wooden bench, in the shade of the barn. Working silently. Neither had spoken to each other since their fight in the dairy house yesterday.

At least they're not yelling any more, Isabelle thought.

She and Maman were sitting on the grass across from them. They were all shelling beans into a wide bowl for a soup Madame planned to make. Isabelle glanced up at Tavi and Hugo every now and again. She was eager to keep the peace. She knew that their being here was Tantine's doing, not Madame's, and definitely not Hugo's. Staying here depended on working hard and not making themselves objectionable. She would remind Tavi of that tonight when they went to bed.

She and Tavi slept next to one another now in the hayloft. They talked before they fell asleep, much more than they had when each had had her own bedchamber in the Maison Douleur. Last night, Isabelle had told her sister about meeting Felix in the Wildwood and had showed her the slipper.

"I *thought* you were walking better," she'd said. "And?" she'd added expectantly.

"*And* nothing. There is no *and*." Isabelle had decided to keep the argument, and the kiss, to herself.

"That's too bad. I always liked Felix." Tavi had gone silent for a bit; then she'd said, "Just wondering . . ."

"Wondering what?"

"If you were still searching for the pieces of your heart. Because I'd say that he's definitely—"

"Not one," Isabelle had said firmly, turning on her side.

"The bowl is full," Hugo said now, dispelling Isabelle's thoughts.

She stood and stretched. "I'll take it inside to Madame and get—"

Another one, she was going to say, but her words were cut off by a hair-raising scream.

She and Tavi looked at each other, alarmed. Maman dropped the bean pod she was holding.

The shriek came again. It was coming from the dairy house and was followed by a single shouted word: "Huuuuuuuuuuugo!"

Hugo leaned back against the barn wall and groaned. "It used to be quiet here. It used to be nice," he said. "Well, maybe not nice, but definitely quiet. Whatever my mother is screeching about, it's because of you two. I just know it."

Another shriek was heard. "Hugo, come on!" Isabelle said, tugging at his hand. "It sounds like she's hurt!"

She started running towards the dairy house; the others were right behind her. When they arrived, they saw that Tantine was already there.

239

"I was in the kitchen . . . I heard screaming. Is someone hurt?" she asked, a hand pressed to her chest.

Before anyone could answer her, Hugo pushed the door to the dairy house open and stepped inside. The others followed. As Isabelle entered the room, an eye-watering stench hit her.

"What *is* that?" she cried.

"It's a monster!" Madame LeBenêt shrilled. "It's an abomination!"

She was standing at the back of the room, among the ripening cheeses, pointing at one.

Isabelle ventured closer and gasped as she saw the offender. It *was* a monster—wrinkled, misshapen, furry with mold.

"God in Heaven, the *smell*!" Tantine said, pressing a handkerchief to her nose.

"Like dirty feet."

"Rotten eggs."

"Like a sewer."

"Like a dead dog," said Hugo.

"A dead dog that's been rotting in the sun for a week," Isabelle added.

"And sweating," Hugo said.

"Technically, dogs don't sweat," Tavi pointed out. "At least, not in the way human beings do. Dogs especially don't sweat when they're dead."

"This dog does," Hugo stated. "Look at it!"

In the short time that they'd all been standing there, beads of clear yellow fluid had erupted from the cheese. They were rolling down its sides and dripping onto the floor.

"That does it. I want you three out. Tonight!" Madame shouted.

A grin lit up Hugo's face.

Isabelle's heart lurched. "No, Madame, please!" she begged. "We have nowhere else to go!"

"Your sister should've thought of that before she ruined my cheese!"

"Now, Avara," Tantine soothed, taking her by the arm. "Let's not be hasty. The girl made a mistake, that's all."

"It was an experiment, actually, not a mistake," Tavi corrected, peering closely at the cheese. "I'll need to modify my hypothesis."

"Out!" Madame sputtered. "Tonight!" She turned to her son. "Hugo, take that—that sweaty dead dog out of here this instant before it contaminates the other cheeses. Throw it into the woods or toss it into a pit!"

Tantine ushered Madame to the door. As Madame stepped outside, Tantine turned to Isabelle. "Help Hugo clean up this mess, child. I'll set things to rights." She patted Isabelle's cheek, then hurried after Madame.

Isabelle pressed the heels of her hands to her forehead, trying to think. This was a disaster. What if Tantine couldn't bring Madame around? What if she still insisted that they leave?

"Happy now?" Tavi asked a still-grinning Hugo. "You got rid of us. Be sure to throw some dirt over our bones after we starve to death in a ditch."

"I . . . I didn't think you'd *starve*," Hugo said, his grin fading.

"What *did* you think we'd do?" Tavi asked.

"Don't blame this on me! It's not *my* fault. You're the one who makes things hard!"

"For whom?"

"Can't you make yourself likeable? Can't you even try?"

Something shifted in Tavi then. She was always so flippant, trailing sarcasm behind her like a duchess trailing furs. But not this time. Hugo had pierced her armor and blood was dripping from the wound.

"Try for whom, Hugo?" she repeated, her voice raw. "For the rich boys who get to go to the Sorbonne even though they're too stupid to solve a simple quadratic equation? For the viscount I was seated next to at a dinner who tried to put his hand up my skirt through all five courses? For the smug society ladies who look me up and down and purse their lips and say no, I won't do for their sons because my chin is too pointed, my nose is too large, I talk too much about numbers?"

"Tavi . . ." Isabelle whispered. She went to her, tried to put an arm around her, but Tavi shook her off.

"I wanted books. I wanted maths and science. I wanted an education," Tavi said, her eyes bright with emotion. "I got corsets and gowns and high-heeled slippers instead. It made me sad, Hugo. And then it made me angry. So no, I can't make myself likeable. I've tried. Over and over. It doesn't work. If I don't like who I am, why should you?"

And then she was gone. And Hugo and Isabelle were left standing in the dairy house, awkward and silent. Isabelle reached for the mop and bucket, which were kept near the door, to clean up the mess pooling under the sweaty dead dog.

"Well done, Galileo," Hugo muttered under his breath.

But Isabelle heard him. "She could be. She could be Galileo and Da Vinci and Newton all rolled into one if she had the chance, but she never will. That's why she's the way she is."

She took a tentative step towards him. "Hugo, don't make us go. Please."

"You don't understand. There's a reason I wanted . . ." He swore. "Never mind."

"What reason? What are you talking about?"

Hugo shook his head. He moved towards the door.

"Where are you going?" Isabelle asked.

"There's an old wooden tea box in the barn. It's lined with lead. Hopefully it will contain the smell. I'm going to put the dead dog in the box, put the box in the wagon, then drive until I find an old well to throw it down. Maybe I'll throw myself down it, too, while I'm at it."

Isabelle watched him go, a fearful expression on her face. This was terrible. She would go to Tantine. As soon as she and Hugo had this mess cleaned up. If that woman hadn't succeeded in changing Madame LeBenêt's mind, they would be homeless. Helpless. As good as dead.

Sixty

Just before dawn, in the Wildwood, a fox stalked her meal.

The object of her attention, a red squirrel, was on the forest floor, busily collecting fallen nuts.

Hugging the lingering shadows, the vixen crept close. She tensed, teeth bared, but just as she was ready to spring, a huge, tufted owl landed on a branch above her, shaking the leaves noisily.

With a frightened squeak, the squirrel dropped her nuts and ran for her nest. A second later, the vixen was gone, too. In her place stood an auburn-haired woman in a dusk-gray gown. She spun around violently. Her green eyes flashed.

"That was my *breakfast*!" she shouted at the bird.

Creatures great and small scurried to their dens at the sound of her voice. Deer hid in the brush. Songbirds spread their wings over their young.

But the owl was not bothered. Let the fairy queen rage. He had chosen a nice high branch for his perch. He hooted at her now.

Tanaquill narrowed her eyes. "For *this* you rob me of my meal?"

The owl continued to speak.

"What of it?" Tanaquill growled. "Fate and Chance, Fate and Chance, one moves, the other countermoves. As if living creatures were nothing more than pieces on a game board. Their doings are no concern of mine." She turned her back on the bird and, with a swirl of her skirts, walked away. But the owl called after her, hooting harshly several times.

Tanaquill stopped dead. "A stallion?" she said. Slowly, she turned around. "Fate did this?"

The owl bobbed his great gray head.

Tanaquill paced back and forth, dead leaves rustling under her feet. The owl clicked his beak.

"No, I'm *not* going to tell Chance," she retorted. "He'll buy the horse and gift wrap him for the girl. I'll deal with this myself."

Tanaquill licked her lips. Her sharp teeth glinted in the pale morning light. "Isabelle has regained the first piece of her heart, though she refuses to admit it. Courage will be needed to regain this, the second piece." She snapped her fingers. "Come, owl. Let's see if she still has some."

Sixty-One

The village had almost forgotten about Isabelle.

Saint-Michel was so crowded with weary, bewildered refugees frantic to buy food, that the baker's wife, the butcher, and the cheesemonger had better things to do than taunt her.

She had found herself selling vegetables at the market with Hugo this morning because Madame, who usually went with him, was busy tending a sick cow. Tavi was more likely to conduct an experiment with the cabbages than sell them, so the task had fallen to Isabelle. Although she hadn't relished the idea of returning to the village, she undertook the task without complaint. Somehow Tantine had convinced Madame to let them stay, and a deeply relieved Isabelle was determined not to give her any reason to change her mind.

She and Hugo had been swamped with customers from the moment they'd pulled into the market square. The refugees, all living in tents, or wagons in the surrounding fields, clamored for cabbages and potatoes. Isabelle had no idea where they'd all come from, so she asked them and they told her.

Volkmar had stepped up his attacks on the villages surrounding Paris, they'd explained. They'd seen their farms pillaged, their homes burned. Many had escaped with only their lives. The king fought bravely, but his troops were being decimated. The grand duke had been seen riding throughout the countryside with a train of wagons, calling on citizens who possessed weapons of any sort—guns, swords, axes, *anything*—to donate them to the war effort. The queen traveled with him, searching for orphaned children and spiriting them to safety.

Some of the refugees were thin and sickly. An elderly woman, trailing four grandchildren, begged Isabelle for any leaves that had fallen off the cabbage heads. Isabelle gave her a whole cabbage and didn't charge her. The woman hugged her. Hugo saw the exchange. He frowned but didn't stop her.

Someone else saw her do it, too.

"That doesn't change anything, Isabelle," said Cecile, walking up to the wagon. "You're still ugly."

Isabelle felt herself flushing with shame. The village *hadn't* forgotten about her. It never would, not with Cecile around to remind everyone. She tried to think of something to say, but before she could get a word out, Hugo spoke.

"It changes things for the old woman," he said.

Isabelle glanced at him. She was grateful he'd come to her defense but also surprised. She knew he didn't like her much. From the set of his jaw, the hardness in his eyes, she guessed he liked Cecile even less. She didn't have long to wonder why, because another refugee, an old man, shuffled up to the wagon and asked for a pound of potatoes.

"Don't buy from her!" Cecile said as he handed over a coin. "Don't you know who she is? Isabelle de la Paumé, one of the ugly stepsisters!"

The old man laughed mirthlessly. The laugh turned into a deep, racking cough. When he could speak again, he said, "There's nothing uglier than war, mademoiselle," then shuffled off with his purchase.

Cecile snorted. She looked as if she'd like to say something clever and cutting, but cleverness was not her strong point, so she flounced off instead.

An hour or so after Cecile left, Isabelle and Hugo sold the last cabbage. Isabelle gathered the loose green leaves from the bed of the wagon, handed them to a small, barefoot boy in a threadbare shirt, and told him to take them to his mother to boil for a soup. Then she took off the canvas apron Hugo had given her to wear—its single pocket full of coins—and handed it to him.

But Hugo shook his head. "Hang on to it. Here's mine, too," he said, untying his own apron.

"Why? Where are you going?" Isabelle asked, taking it from him.

"I . . . uh . . . I need to do an errand. Head back without me. I'll catch up." He rubbed the toes of his boots on the back of his trouser legs as he spoke, then spat on his hands and smoothed his unruly hair.

Isabelle thought he was being very mysterious. She carefully folded both aprons so that no coins could drop out and tucked them underneath the wagon's seat.

"And, Isabelle?"

"Yes?"

"If you do get home before me, don't tell my mother about my errand. Say I went to fix a fence in the pasture or something."

Isabelle agreed to his request, more intrigued than ever. Then Hugo tugged on the sides of his jacket, took a deep breath, and went on his way. Isabelle climbed into the driver's seat and snapped the reins. Martin started off. They'd finished early at the market and she was glad. It meant she could get a head start on the rest of the day's work.

She'd only just driven out of the square when she spotted Hugo again. He was helping Odette across the street. She'd taken his arm. Her face was turned towards his. She was wearing a pretty blue dress. Her strawberry-blond hair was pinned up in a soft bun. A pink rose was tucked into the side of it.

She must be going to a party or a wedding, Isabelle thought. *I bet she got lost and Hugo is helping her find her way.*

It was a nice thing for him to do. Odette didn't have an easy life. Most of the villagers were good to her, but a few—like Cecile—were not.

Who knew he had it in him? Isabelle thought, softening towards Hugo, but only a little.

A few minutes later, she was heading out of the village towards a fork in the road. To the right was the way back to the LeBenêts'. To the left was the river and the various businesses that were not allowed to operate within the village because of the smells they made or the fire risk they posed—the tannery, the blacksmith's, the dye works, the slaughter yard.

Isabelle was so lost in her thoughts—wondering if Tavi managed to get the morning milking done without causing problems, and if Maman was cutting cabbages or conversing with them—that she didn't see the animal sitting directly in the centre of the fork, watching and waiting, as if it were expecting her.

By the time she picked her head up and realized a fox was blocking her way, it was too late.

Sixty-Two

The fox ran at Martin, her head down, her teeth bared. She dove under him and wove in and out of his legs, snarling and snapping, nipping at his hooves.

Terrified, Martin bolted to the left, ripping the reins from Isabelle's hands. The wagon lurched violently, throwing her across the seat. She managed to right herself but could not recover the reins.

"Stop, Martin! Stop!" she screamed, but the horse, crazed by fear, kept going. The fox followed, running at his side, snarling. The wagon banged down the rutted road to the river, with Isabelle holding on to the seat for dear life. They sped by buildings and work yards. Men tried to wave Martin down, but no one dared get in front of him. And then the river came into view.

He's not going to stop! Isabelle thought. *He's going to gallop straight off the dock. We're both going to drown!*

And then, as quickly as she'd come, the fox was gone and an exhausted Martin slowed, then halted a few yards shy of the water. Isabelle stumbled out of the wagon on legs that were rubbery, her breath coming hard and fast.

"Shh, Martin, easy," she soothed, stroking his neck. "Easy, old man."

Martin's eyes were so round, Isabelle could see the whites. His lips were flecked with foam; his coat with lather. She bent down to check his legs. There was no blood; the fox hadn't bitten him. She found the reins, tangled in the traces, and freed them. Then, taking hold of his bridle, she slowly turned him around. Miraculously, the wagon was intact.

Isabelle's breathing slowed little by little as they walked back up the road. They passed the tannery and then the dye works. Some of the workers asked if she was all right.

"If I were you, that horse would be the next one to come through these gates," a man called to her as they approached the slaughter yard.

Isabelle glanced at him. He was leaning against the fence, smoking. Blood dripped off his leather apron onto his shoes. Isabelle heard a desperate cry coming from a frightened animal on the other side of the fence. She looked away; she didn't want to see the poor hopeless creature.

"That horse is no good," the man said. "He could've killed you."

Isabelle ignored him, but Martin didn't; he looked right at him. His ears pricked up. His nostrils flared. He stopped dead. A smell hit Isabelle then, a rank, low stink of blood and fear and death, moving like a wraith through the iron spikes. Martin smelled it, too. He was trembling. Isabelle was worried he would bolt again.

"Come on, Martin, *please*. We have to go," Isabelle said, pulling on his noseband.

But Martin refused to budge. He planted all four hooves into the dirt, raised his head high, and let out a whinny so loud and piercing, so heart-rending, the Isabelle let go of his bridle.

And that's when she realized that Martin wasn't looking at the man; he was looking past him, at a horse on the other side of the fence. She took a step towards the yard, slowly, as if in a trance, and then another. Martin called out again, and the horse behind the fence answered.

"Don't," the man said. "It's not something a girl should see."

But Isabelle did see. She saw a flash of darkness between the bars. Wild eyes. Lethal hooves. There were four burly men around the animal, but they couldn't subdue him. Even though they had ropes and weapons and he had nothing, they were the ones who were afraid.

Martin had a friend once. He was magnificent. Tall, strong, and fearless. If Martin had been human, he might've hated him for being everything that he, Martin, was not. But Martin was not human and so he loved him.

Horses never forget a friend.

Martin had smelled his friend. And heard him. A horse as black as night and ten times more beautiful.

Martin knew that horse. He loved that horse.

And so did Isabelle.

She wrapped her hands around the iron bars and whispered his name. *"Nero."*

Sixty-Three

Isabelle ran.

Along the fence. Past the man, who was yelling at her to stop. Through the gates. And straight into hell.

Two sheep who'd jumped out of their pen were running through the yard, bleating, ducking their pursuers, desperate to escape. Cattle lowed piteously. Fresh carcasses were being hung to bleed out; older ones were being quartered.

And in the centre of it all, a black stallion fought for his life.

Death's servants, four burly men, circled him. One of them had managed to get a rope around the horse's neck. Another had caught one of his back legs, throwing him off balance. A third man caught the other back leg. The horse went down. He made a last, valiant attempt to get up, then lay in the mud, his sides heaving, his eyes closed.

The fourth man was leaning on a sledgehammer. He gripped its wooden handle with both hands now and lifted the heavy steel head.

"No!" Isabelle screamed. "Stop!"

But no one heard her, not over the bleating of the sheep and bawling of the cattle.

Isabelle ran faster, shouting, pleading, screaming. She was only a few feet away from the horse, when her foot came down in a puddle. She slipped and went sprawling.

Spitting filth, Isabelle picked up her head in time to see the man lift the sledgehammer off the ground and raise it high, spiraling it around his body, the muscles in his strong arms rippling.

A ragged scream burst up from her heart and out of her throat. She launched herself, half crawling, half stumbling through the mud and blood and threw herself on the horse's neck.

Just as the man swung the sledgehammer.

Sixty-Four

The hole the sledgehammer made was deep.

Isabelle knew this because the man who'd swung the tool forced her to look at it. He grabbed the back of her dress, yanked her off the horse as if she were a rag doll, and dropped her in the mud. She landed on her hands and knees.

"Do you see that sledgehammer? Do you see what it did?" he shouted at her.

Isabelle nodded even though she could only see the handle. The head was buried in the ground.

"That could've been your *skull*!"

The man, a burly giant, was shaking like a kitten. He'd swung the sledgehammer with all his might and then, in the space of a heartbeat, a girl had thrown herself in its path. He'd wrenched his body to the left at the last possible instant, swinging through and hitting the ground instead of the girl.

Isabelle stood up. Her dress was smeared with gore. Her face streaked with it. She didn't care. "Don't kill my horse," she begged. *"Please."*

"He's *my* horse. I bought him. You don't want him. He's too wild."

"I *do* want him."

"Then you can pay me for him. Four livres."

Isabelle thought of the money tucked under the wagon's seat and had to fight down the urge to run and get it. But she was not a thief.

"I don't have any money," she said miserably.

"Then find some, girl, and fast. You've got until tomorrow morning. We open the gates at seven sharp. Be here on time, with the money, or he goes."

Isabelle nodded. She told the man she'd be back. She told herself that she'd think of something. She'd get the money. Somehow.

"Let him up," she said, looking at her horse.

No one moved.

"Let. Him. *Up*." It was not a plea this time, but a command, and the men heard it. They removed the ropes they'd used to restrain him.

As soon as he was free, the horse got to his feet. He blinked at Isabelle, then slowly walked to her. He sniffed her. Snorted in her face. Tossed his proud head and let out a whinny.

Isabelle tried to laugh, but it crumbled into a sob. She leaned her cheek against his, knotted her dirty fingers in his lank, tangled mane. Nero had been sold away. She'd thought she'd never see him again. Now here he was, but he would be gone forever if she couldn't get hold of four livres.

"I will get you out of here. I swear it," she whispered to him.

"You have to leave now. We have work to do," the man with the sledgehammer said.

Isabelle nodded. She patted Nero's neck, then walked

out of the yard.

One of the men who'd roped the horse—a boy, really—closed the gates after her. He lingered there, watching her go. In that moment, he would've done anything she asked of him. Followed anywhere she led. He would have died for her.

He could not know it then, but the image of the girl, straight-backed in her dirty dress, her face streaked with filth, would stay with him for the rest of his life. He looked down at the knife in his hand and hated it.

Behind him, the others talked.

"Was that one of the de la Paumé girls? I thought they were ugly."

"What, you think she's *pretty*? Dirty as an old boot? Bold as a trumpet?"

"No, but—"

"I pity the man she ends up with."

"She has guts, I'll give her that."

"Yes, she does. Imagine if every girl had such strength . . . and learned of it!"

"Better hope they never do. What would our world become, eh?"

"Ha! A living hell!"

"No," the boy whispered. "A paradise."

Sixty-Five

The door to Madame's kitchen was open. Isabelle took a deep breath and walked inside.

The day was bright, but Madame's house was dark. It took a few seconds for Isabelle's eyes to adjust. When they did, she saw that Madame was standing at her kitchen table kneading bread.

"I'm back. I have your money," Isabelle said, placing the aprons on the table.

Madame wiped her hands on a dish towel, eager to count her coins, and caught sight of Isabelle. "What happened to you? You're *filthy*!" she squawked.

Isabelle began to tell her. Madame listened for a few seconds, but the lure of money was too tempting. She unrolled the aprons, dumped out the coins, and counted them. Tantine was sitting nearby in a rocking chair, knitting. Unlike Madame, she listened intently to every word.

When Isabelle finished her account, she said, "I need to buy my horse back. Nero. I need to bring four livres to the slaughter yard tomorrow or they'll kill him."

"Yes, so? What has that to do with me?" Madame asked

absently. She had eight columns of coins stacked already and still had half the pile to go.

"Please, Madame. It's only four livres. I've worked very hard for you."

Avara stopped counting. She looked at Isabelle aghast. "You're not asking *me* for the money, are you?"

"I will pay you back."

"Absolutely not," Madame said. "It's not just the four livres, you know. You've already put me in the poorhouse feeding that old nag of yours, Martin. Another horse will bankrupt me."

She said more, but Isabelle had stopped listening. She crossed the room and knelt by Tantine.

"Please, Tantine. I beg you," she said.

The old woman put her knitting down. She took Isabelle's dirty hands in hers. "Child, you said this creature was sold to the slaughter yard because he is unmanageable, no? What if he were to throw you? I could never live with the guilt. An unruly stallion is not a suitable animal for a young lady."

Isabelle saw that there would be no help for her here. She rose and started for the door.

Tantine arched an eyebrow. "Where are you going?" she asked.

"To the Château Rigolade. To see the marquis. I thought he might lend me—"

"No. I forbid it," Tantine said sharply.

"But—"

Tantine held up a hand, silencing her. "If you will not consider your own reputation, Isabelle, at least consider my family's. As long as you reside here, you are not to set foot near the Château Rigolade."

"Indeed!" Madame chimed in.

Isabelle lowered her head, devastated. "Yes, Tantine," she said.

"Instead of worrying about horses, worry about cabbages. They are not going to harvest themselves," Madame scolded. "See that the wagon is filled up again for tomorrow."

Isabelle left the house and drove the wagon out to the fields. All the way there, she racked her brain. There had to be a way to get the money. She refused to give up. By the time she'd unhitched Martin and had led him back to the barn, her head was high again. Her eyes were glinting. As she put him in his stall, she gave him an extra helping of oats.

"Eat up, Martin, you'll need your strength. We have a job to do tonight," she told him.

Martin pricked up his ears; he liked a bit of intrigue. Much more than he liked pulling cabbage wagons.

Isabelle had come up with an idea; it was desperate and risky. She would have to get her sister's help to pull it off. Hugo's, too, which would be more difficult. But he owed her; she'd said nothing about his errand.

As she brushed Martin, Tanaquill's words, spoken when they'd met in the Wildwood, came back to her. They rang out so clear, so true, it was as if the fairy queen was standing right next to her. *Find the pieces of your heart. Not someone else's . . .*

Nero was a piece of her heart. She knew this with an unshakable certainty. When she'd ridden him, she'd been braver than she ever thought she could be. It terrified her to admit this, because she knew if she lost him again, it would kill her.

"Nero is not going to die. We won't let him," Isabelle said, patting Martin's neck. "Get some rest, old man. We leave after dark."

Sixty-Six

"How hot does a fire have to be to melt gold?" Isabelle asked.

"Very," Hugo replied.

"One thousand nine hundred forty-eight degrees Fahrenheit," said Tavi. "One thousand sixty-four Celsius."

"Had that right on the tip of your tongue, didn't you?" Hugo said.

"What should I have on the tip of my tongue? The words to some silly love song? A recipe for meatballs?"

"Yes," Hugo said. "Both of those would be good things for you to know."

Tavi rolled her eyes.

The three were walking down the lonely stretch of road that led from the LeBenêts' farm to the Maison Douleur in the darkness. Isabelle had decided to search the ruins of her old home in the hopes of finding something of value. She knew she could not move charred beams and heavy stones alone and had begged Tavi and Hugo to help her. Tavi had agreed because she knew how much Nero meant to Isabelle. Hugo had because he'd made Isabelle promise that if she found more than one valuable thing, she would use it to find somewhere else to live.

Isabelle had owned a few pieces of jewelry. So had Tavi. Maman had owned many. When the Maison Douleur burned, they'd all assumed that the fire had destroyed them, but they'd never actually looked. Now Isabelle was hoping that she could unearth a necklace, or perhaps a silver serving spoon, a gold coin—*anything* that she could barter for Nero's life.

Martin trailed behind them on a lead. No one was riding him. He would need all his strength for what was to come. Hugo had a heavy coil of rope on one shoulder. He and Tavi were both carrying lanterns.

"Did you ever think about making sauerkraut with your cabbage?" Tavi asked. "That way you could have something to sell at the market in the winter."

"Did you ever think of leaving things just the way they are?"

"No. Never. You can't make wonderful discoveries that way."

Hugo snorted with laughter. "Like the sweaty dead dog?"

Tavi shot him a look. "Whatever happened to it, anyway?" she asked.

"It's still in a box in the wagon, under the back seat. I haven't found a good place to chuck it yet. Someplace where it won't kill someone. I'm hoping to find a bubbling lava pit one day. Or a dragon's cave. Or the gates of hell."

Tavi looked at the side of his face. "You're funny, Hugo. Who knew?"

Hugo was silent for a moment; then he said, "Odette. She knows."

"Odette from the village?" Tavi asked.

Hugo nodded.

"How does she know you're funny?" asked Isabelle. She

remembered seeing him helping Odette across the street earlier at the market.

"Because we're in love. And we want to get married."

Tavi and Isabelle stopped dead. Martin did, too. But Hugo kept walking, his hands clenched.

"Does your mother know?" Tavi asked, running to keep up with him. Isabelle and Martin trotted after her.

"That I'm funny?" Hugo asked.

"*No*, Hugo," Tavi said. "About Odette."

"Yes. I told her. A year ago."

"Then why haven't you married her yet?" Isabelle asked, catching up.

"My mother won't allow it," Hugo said forlornly.

Isabelle and Tavi exchanged glances of disbelief. Never had Hugo spoken so many words at once, or with such emotion.

"Hugo . . ."

"Don't make fun, Tavi. *Don't*," he warned.

Tavi looked stricken. "I—I wasn't going to."

"Odette practically runs the inn. She keeps all the reservations straight. She makes the best onion soup you've ever tasted. And her apple cake . . . I would fight the devil himself for a piece of it. But my mother says a blind girl can't run a farm. She says she'll be useless, just another mouth to feed. She only sees what Odette isn't, not what she is."

Tavi put a gentle hand on his back.

"This world, the people in it—my mother, Tantine—they sort us. Put us in crates. *You* are an egg. *You* are a potato. *You* are a cabbage. They tell us who we are. What we will do. What we will be."

"Because they're afraid. Afraid of what we *could* be," Tavi said.

265

"But we let them do it!" Hugo said angrily. "Why?"

Tavi gave him a rueful smile. "Because we're afraid of what we could be, too."

A silence fell over them then, as deep and dark as the moonless night.

Hugo was the first to break it. "What am I going to do? Can one of you tell me?" he asked. "She's everything to me."

"I can't believe you're asking us," Isabelle said. "I thought you hated us."

"I do hate you. But I'm desperate and you're smart."

"Marry her anyway," Tavi suggested.

"Live at her house," Isabelle said.

"There's no room for me there. Her family lives in a little cottage behind the inn. She has so many brothers and sisters it's bursting at the seams."

"There has to be a way. We'll think of something. We *will*," Tavi said.

Hugo nodded. He mustered a smile. But Isabelle could see that he didn't believe her.

They walked on down the road in silence, uncertain and aching. Hugo aching for Odette. Tavi aching for formulas and theorems. Isabelle aching to be pretty. Or so she told herself.

But alongside the ache, perhaps because of it, was a determination, too.

Neither Isabelle, Tavi, nor Hugo knew if any of them would ever be able to show the world what they were, not what they weren't. They didn't know if they'd be able to save their hearts from breaking.

But tonight, maybe, just maybe, they could save a horse. A

difficult creature who didn't know how to be anything but what he was.

They hoped for him, deep down inside. All three of them. Because they didn't dare hope for themselves.

Sixty-Seven

Hugo let out a low whistle. He was standing at the top of the front steps to the Maison Douleur holding his lantern out in front of him. The steps had survived the fire, but nothing else.

Isabelle and Tavi were standing next to him.

It was much worse than Isabelle remembered. Parts of the house which were still standing the morning after the fire had since collapsed. The roof, three of the walls, the floors and ceilings, had all crashed down. Only the back wall remained upright. Stone, mortar, and wooden beams lay tangled in treacherous, teetering piles.

"We're going to have to move slowly or we'll bring rubble down on our heads," Hugo said.

That was not what Isabelle wanted to hear. They'd had a late start. Madame and Tantine had stayed up late; Hugo hadn't been able to sneak out until eleven thirty. Isabelle had to be back at the slaughter yard with something of value by seven, they hadn't even begun to search yet, and now Hugo was saying they'd have to go slow.

Fear chattered at her, telling her that there wasn't enough time. That the rocks were too heavy to move, the beams too large. That even if she dug to the bottom of the ruins, she wouldn't find a thing of value, that the flames had taken it all.

As she stood there, at a loss how to begin, or even where, a loose rock tumbled down off the back wall into a pile of debris with a loud crash. It made her jump. It felt as if the Maison Douleur was warning them off.

Isabelle thought of Nero, standing in the slaughter yard staring into the darkness. She walked back down the stairs, climbed into the remains of her home, and refused to listen.

Sixty-Eight

"Hup, Martin! Hup, boy!" Hugo shouted, urging the horse on.

Martin leaned into the rope harness and pulled with all his might.

He was tired. They all were. They'd been searching for hours, crawling over charred debris with their lanterns, moving whatever stones they could by hand, and using Martin to move heavy beams, but they'd found nothing.

"Come on, Martin! Hup!"

Martin dug in, and the beam slid out of the rubble and across the grass. Hugo patted him and unknotted the rope.

"Anything?" he called out.

"No!" Isabelle shouted back.

Sighing, a weary Hugo turned Martin around and together they walked back to the ruins. Isabelle and Tavi were busy digging in what had once been their drawing room. Moving one thing often loosened something else. More than once, they'd had to jump out of the way of falling roof tiles or a chunk of lath.

Although no one knew it, the beam Hugo and Martin had just slid out into the yard had also destabilized debris. It had been supporting the pile of burned timbers Isabelle was picking around. Her back to the pile, she didn't see it shudder, then start to slide.

But Hugo did. "Isabelle! Look out!" he shouted, lunging for her.

He grabbed her arm and yanked her out of the way. She stumbled and fell against him, knocking him off his feet. They both hit the ground. The timbers crashed down near them. The jagged edge of one caught Isabelle's shoulder, slicing an ugly gash into it.

Tavi screamed. She clambered to Isabelle and Hugo and helped them up.

"That's it. We're finished here," she said, her voice quavering. "I'm sorry we didn't find anything. I'm sorry for Nero. But there's nothing here. Oh my God, Isabelle. Look at your shoulder!"

Tavi made her sister leave the ruins and sit down under the linden tree. There, she pressed a handkerchief against her wound.

Isabelle didn't want to sit. "I'm all right," she said, taking the handkerchief from Tavi. "I'm going back. Just one more time . . ."

"No," Tavi said. "You could've been killed. Hugo could've been. We're leaving."

Hugo had joined them. He lay down in the grass, spent. Tavi sat next to him. Isabelle reluctantly joined them.

"Are you all right?" Tavi asked him. He nodded, his eyes closed. "Thank you for saving Isabelle. I couldn't bear it if anything happened to her. To either of you." Her voice caught.

"It's all right," Hugo said. "We're both fine."

"No, it's not all right. I thought you were both dead. Oh, Hugo, I . . . I shouldn't have done it."

"Done what?"

"Called you an idiot. In the dairy house the other day. I'm sorry. Mean is all I've got, you see, so I'm always trying to get better at it."

Hugo gave her a tired smile. "You have more than mean, Tavi. A lot more. I'm sure if you lived a hundred years ago, *you* would've been the one who discovered that circles are round. Not Newton da Vinci."

Had Isabelle's attention not been entirely focused on the ruins, she might've seen that a bit of treasure had already been gleaned from the ashes—Tavi's newfound readiness to apologize for bad behavior, Hugo's willingness to speak sweet words instead of sullen ones. But Isabelle had only one thought in mind—saving Nero, and time was running out.

With a groan, Hugo stood. He picked up his rope, coiled it, and slipped it over his shoulder. "The sky's starting to lighten," he said. "My mother will be getting up soon. I better be in my bed when she comes to wake me."

Tavi stood, too. She turned to Isabelle. "Come on, Isabelle. Get up. It's time to go."

Sixty-Nine

Isabelle rose. Her hands were scraped raw, her shoulder was bleeding into the sleeve of her dress.

She looked at her sister and Hugo and Martin as they started down the drive, but instead of following them, she picked up her lantern and walked back into the ruins.

Despair swirled down on her like a thick fog, but she refused to give in to it. Or to give up.

As she bent down to move a timber, she felt something tug at her hem. Certain she'd snagged her skirts on a nail, she looked down, ready to yank them free, and saw that it wasn't a nail.

It was a mouse.

The creature's tiny paws were sunk into Isabelle's hem. She was hanging on to it with all her might, her back feet were half off the ground.

"Shoo!" Isabelle said. "I don't want to step on you."

But the mouse would not let go.

Her claws must be caught, Isabelle thought, reaching towards her to free her. But as she did, the mouse released the hem. She stood upright on her hind legs and squeaked.

Isabelle recognized the little creature. It was the same mother mouse she'd seen digging for lentils in the cracks between the hearthstones, the one for whom she'd left some cheese.

"Hello," Isabelle said. "I don't have any food for you. I wish I did. I—"

The mother mouse held up a claw, like a parent silencing a prattling child. She squeaked again. And then once more.

There was only a whisper at first. A low rustling, like a breeze whirling through the grass. But then it grew louder, more urgent, pushing in at Isabelle from all sides of the ruins.

Isabelle raised her lantern high and caught her breath, astonished. All around her, standing on stones, crouched on timbers, their whiskers twitching, their black eyes glinting in the light, their tails curled above them like question marks, were mice. Hundreds of them.

At another squeak from the mother mouse, they all disappeared into the ruins. Isabelle heard scrabbling, scritching, squeals and yelps.

Mystified, she glanced at the mother mouse.

"Where did they go?" she asked. "What are they—"

With a look of annoyance, the mouse held up her paw again. She was listening intently, her large ears quivering.

Isabelle listened, too, but she didn't know what she was listening for. She looked up. The stars were fading. The darkness was thinning. She had little time left.

And then a series of shrill calls rang out from the ruins. The mother mouse squeaked excitedly, hopping from foot to foot. She waved Isabelle close and pointed.

Isabelle put her lantern down and knelt on the ground, the better to see what the mouse was pointing at. As she did, another mouse, brawny and tall, emerged from the ruins. He was wearing something on his head. It looked like a crown.

"Is he your king?" Isabelle asked, completely perplexed now. "You want me to meet your king?"

Other mice reappeared from the ruins. They responded to Isabelle's question with strange little noises that sounded like laughter. The mother beckoned the large mouse over. He eyed Isabelle warily and shook his head. The mother mouse stamped her foot. The large mouse came.

He took off his crown with both paws and held it out to Isabelle. Not sure what else to do, Isabelle took it from him, then held it up to her lantern. A small cry escaped her as she saw that it wasn't a crown, not at all.

It was a gold ring.

Seventy

Isabelle's heart flooded with gratitude. For a moment, she couldn't speak.

She recognized the ring. Maman had given it to her. The band was thin. The stone—an amethyst—was small. Still, it had to be worth four livres. Maybe more.

"Thank you," she finally managed to say.

Two more mice emerged from the ruins dragging something behind them. They presented it to her. It was a bracelet made of small gold links; a little gold heart with a ruby in its centre dangled from one of the links. Her father had given it to her. It was covered with soot, but that could be wiped away.

The ring would pay for Nero. The bracelet would buy her freedom. She could sell it and use the money to rent a room in the village for herself and her family. They could be free of Madame, her cows, and her cabbages.

Humbled by the gifts, Isabelle placed her hand on the ground, palm up, in front of the mother mouse. The mouse hesitated, then climbed on. Isabelle lifted her up until they were eye to eye.

"Thank you," she said again. "From the bottom of my heart,

thank you. You don't know what this means to me. I'll never be able to repay you."

She kissed the mouse on the top of her head and gently set her down. Then she got up, clutching her jewels, and headed out of the ruins.

The sun was peeking over the horizon now. Songbirds were welcoming the dawn. By the time Isabelle reached the road, she was running.

Seventy-One

"You came back," the burly man said as he unlocked the gate. "I didn't think you would. Do you have my money?"

Isabelle, who had reached the gates only a minute before he had, was bent over, her hands on her knees, struggling to catch her breath. She'd run the whole way from the Maison Douleur to the slaughter yard without stopping.

"I have this," she said, straightening. She dug in her pocket, pulled out the ring, and handed it to him.

He handed it back, aggrieved. "I said four livres, not a ring! Do I look like a pawnbroker?"

Panic seized her. Never for a second had she considered that he might not accept it. "But it—it's gold. It's worth more than four livres," she stammered.

The man waved her words away. "I'll have to sell it to the jeweler. He's a tightwad. It's a lot of trouble."

"*Please* . . ." Isabelle begged. Her voice broke.

The man glanced at her, then tried to look away but couldn't. Her face was streaked with soot. Her dress was soaked with sweat. One sleeve was stained with blood.

"Please don't kill my horse," she finished.

The man looked past her, down the street. He swore. Muttered that he was a soft touch, always had been, that it would be his undoing. Then he pocketed the ring.

"Go get him," he said, nodding towards the yard. "But be quick about it. Before I change my mind."

Isabelle didn't give him the chance.

"Nero!" she cried.

The horse was standing at the far end of the yard, tied to a post. His ears pricked up when he heard Isabelle's voice. His dark eyes widened. Isabelle ran through the mud to him and threw her arms around his neck. He whickered, then nudged at her with his nose.

"Yes, you're right. We need to get out of here," Isabelle said. She quickly untied him and led him across the yard.

In her haste to get to him, she had not seen the other horses in the yard. But she did now. There were two of them.

They must've come in after I left yesterday, she thought. They were bony, fly-bitten. Their coats were dull, their tails full of burrs. She looked away. There was nothing she could do.

More men had arrived. The burly man was now making coffee over a small black stove in a ramshackle shed. The others stood around, waiting for a cup, but soon they would pick up their sledgehammers and knives and start their work.

Isabelle led Nero past them and out of the gates.

As she was about to lead him away, she glanced back at the horses. No one had fed them or given them water. Why would they? Why waste food on animals that were going to die? They were old, used up. Worthless. Hopeless.

Isabelle squeezed Nero's lead so tightly her hands cramped.

The bracelet, the one she was going to use to buy her freedom from Madame, and Tavi's and Maman's, weighed heavy in her pocket. It weighed even heavier on her heart.

Isabelle looked up at the sky. "What am I doing?" she said, as if hoping the clouds might answer her. Then she tied Nero to the fence, took the bracelet from her pocket, and walked back inside the slaughter yard.

"What a fool Isabelle is," many people would say. "What an idiot to throw her bracelet away on a lost cause."

Never listen to such small-souled folk.

The skin-and-bones dog who shows up at your door. The broken-winged bird you nurse back to health. The kitten you find crying at the side of the road.

You think you're saving them, don't you?

Ah, child. Can't you see?

They're saving you.

Seventy-Two

Isabelle, her head down, walked up the road from the slaughter yard, past the outskirts of Saint-Michel, trailing the three horses behind her.

Madame is going to kill me, she worried. *She didn't even want Martin, who earns his keep. What will she say when she sees Nero and these two poor wrecks?*

And then a more disturbing thought occurred to her. *What if Madame is so angry, she threatens to throw us out again?*

Isabelle hadn't considered that possibility when she was bargaining for the horses' lives—all she'd cared about then was saving them—but it loomed before her now. Tantine had been able to talk Madame into letting them stay after the sweaty dead dog disaster, but Isabelle doubted she would be able to save them a second time.

"Isabelle? Is that you? What are you doing?"

Isabelle looked up at the sound of the voice. She mustered a broken smile.

"I don't know, Felix. The mice found a ring for me, and a bracelet. And I was going to get us all away from Madame and her blasted cabbages. But I traded it all for Nero and these other two. I couldn't let them die. Oh, God. What have I done?" she said all in a rush.

Felix, who had been sent to the blacksmith's for nails, tilted his head. "Wait . . . that's *Nero*? What mice? Why are you bleeding?" he asked.

Isabelle explained everything.

Felix looked away as she spoke. He swiped at his eyes. Isabelle, nervously kicking at the dirt, never saw the silver shimmer in them.

She was just finishing her story when a noisy group of boys, trooping up from the river, interrupted her.

"Let's see here . . . are there three horses or four?" one called out.

"Three horses and one ugly, horse-faced girl!" another shouted.

They all hooted laughter. Isabelle winced.

"Get out of here before I kick your little asses," Felix threatened, starting towards them.

They scattered.

"Don't pay any attention to them," he told Isabelle. "What they said . . . it isn't true."

"Then why do they say it?" Isabelle asked quietly.

Felix looked at her. At this girl. Who was weary and dirty, bloody and sweat-soaked, but defiant. This girl. Who was leading three helpless creatures that nobody wanted away from the slaughter.

"That's not the question, Isabelle," he said softly. "The question is, why do you believe them?"

Seventy-Three

"Nelson, Bonaparte, Lafayette, Cornwallis!" Chance shouted. "You've been right all along, gentlemen! I shall never ride inside again!"

Chance was standing atop his carriage, legs planted wide apart for balance, as it thundered down the road to Saint-Michel. A card game was starting shortly, in a room above the blacksmith's shop. He didn't want to be late. His four capuchins were with him, chasing each other back and forth, screeching with delight.

"Faster, faster!" he shouted to his driver.

"Any faster and we'll be airborne!" the driver shouted back.

Nelson picked that moment to snatch the scarf Chance had tied pirate-style around his head—his hat had blown off miles back—and ran to the back of the roof with it. Chance gave chase, and as he did, he saw a rider cantering over the fields the bordered the road. She was nearly parallel with his coach.

It was a young woman. Her skirts were billowing behind her. Her hair had come free. She rode astride like a man, not sidesaddle. Her head was low to her horse's neck, her body tensed in a crouch. She jumped a stone wall, fearless, completely at one with her magnificent black horse. With a shock of delight, Chance realized he knew her.

"Mademoiselle! Isabelle!" he called. But she didn't hear him.

"That's Nero, it must be," he said to himself, his pulse leaping with excitement. "She got her horse back!"

He snatched his scarf back from Nelson and waved it, finally getting Isabelle's attention. She did a double take, then laughed. Chance, never able to resist a bet, a contest, or a dare, pointed up ahead. There was a church in the distance, at the top of a hill. He cupped his hands around his mouth. "I'll race you!" he shouted.

Isabelle grinned. Her eyes flashed. She tapped her heels to her horse's side and he lunged into a gallop. Effortlessly, he jumped a fence, two streams, then streaked across a field. She was leaving Chance in the dust, but as she reached the end of the field, a hedgerow loomed—a tall, thick wall of scrubby trees and brush that separated one farmer's field from another. It was a good five feet tall and at least a yard deep.

"Huzzah, my fine fellows!" Chance declared to the monkeys. "Victory is ours! She can't jump that. She'll have to . . ."

His words died in his throat. *Go around it*, he was going to say. But Isabelle was not going around the hedge. She was headed straight for it.

"No, don't! It's too high! You'll break your neck!" Chance called out. "I can't watch." He covered his eyes, then opened his fingers and peered through the slit.

Isabelle's hands came up the horse's neck, giving him his head. The stallion closed in on the hedge. He pushed off with his powerful back legs, tucked his front hooves under, and flew over it. Chance didn't see them land—the hedge blocked his view—but he heard them. Isabelle let out a loud whoop, the horse whinnied, and then he carried her the rest of the way up the hill.

She was trotting him in circles, cooling him down, as Chance and his driver pulled into the church's driveway.

"Mademoiselle, you are dangerous! A foolhardy daredevil! Completely reckless!" Chance shouted angrily, his hands on his hips. Then he smiled. "We shall be the very best of friends!"

"*I'm* reckless?" Isabelle said, laughing. "Your Grace, you're standing on top of your carriage!"

Chance looked down at his feet. "So I am. I'd quite forgotten." He looked up again. "My monkeys were having all the fun, you see, and I thought, why should they? Tell me, where did you get that stunning horse?"

"I rescued him. He was mine and then he wasn't and then I found him in the slaughter yard. It's a long story."

Slaughter yard? Chance thought, outraged. *I bet that miserable crone had something to do with it.*

"What's his name?" he asked nonchalantly.

"Nero."

Ha! Chance crowed silently. It was all he could do not to dance a hornpipe on the top of the carriage. *Her horse . . . a second piece of heart returned to her!*

He had been watching Isabelle's map closely and had noticed that two new lines had appeared on it. One veered into the Wildwood and crossed Felix's path. The other careened to the slaughter yard. Chance had not been able to guess why Isabelle had made the second detour. Now he knew.

The boy, the horse, Chance thought, *all that's needed now is the stepsister.*

285

Chance knew that if he was going to help Isabelle find the third piece, he needed to keep her here with him for a bit, to keep her talking and hopefully edge his way around to the topic of Ella. Fate had forbidden Isabelle from going to the Château Rigolade and had banned him from visiting the LeBenêts' farm. This was the first opportunity he'd had to speak with her since Nelson had shot the chicken thief.

He sat down on top of the carriage and dangled his legs over the side. "You ride him as if you raised him," he said, reaching a hand out. Nero walked over and allowed Chance to scratch his nose.

"I did raise him," Isabelle said, patting his neck. "I got him when he was only a colt. For my eleventh birthday. He was a gift from Ella's—I mean, from the *queen*'s father—my stepfather. Tavi and I, we're the queen's ug—"

"You're her stepsisters, yes. I know. My magician told me. What an incredible gift. Was Octavia not jealous? What about Ella?"

"Tavi was given a leather-bound set of Isaac Newton's *Mathematical Principles of Natural Philosophy* the month before for her birthday. She wouldn't have noticed if our stepfather had given me a herd of elephants. And Ella was never jealous. She was afraid of Nero, though. Afraid I would kill myself on him." Isabelle smiled wistfully, remembering. "She worried every time I galloped off on him. Usually with Felix. Your carpenter. He was one of our grooms . . ."

"Oh, was he?" Chance interjected lightly.

"Ella threw her arms around us every time we returned and kissed us, as if she was afraid that one night we wouldn't come back . . ." Her voice trailed away. "She was always so sweet, so kind."

Chance saw his opportunity. "You miss her," he said.

Isabelle looked down at the reins in her hands. "Every day. It's a hard thing to admit."

"Why?"

Isabelle laughed sadly. "Because she certainly doesn't miss me. She hates me."

"You know this?"

"How could she not?"

"Because you are bold and dashing. Who would not love such a girl?"

Isabelle shook her head. "You are kind, Your Grace, but you don't know me. I was . . . I was not good to her."

"I know cavalry officers who wouldn't jump that hedge. I know a brave soul when I see one."

Isabelle gave him a questioning look. "Are you saying I should—"

"Try to see your stepsister? Try to make amends? Why, child, you read my mind!"

"Do you think she would see me?" asked Isabelle, hesitantly. And hopefully.

Chance leaned forward, his elbows on his knees. "I think we all make mistakes. What matters is that we don't let our mistakes make us."

The church bell began to toll the hour—eight o'clock. Chance grimaced. The card game had likely started. "We must part ways, I'm afraid. I have business in the village. Paris is not far, young Isabelle!"

He jumped down and opened the carriage's door. Once inside it, he lowered the window, leaned out, and slapped the door. The driver turned the horses, heading them back towards the road.

Chance and Isabelle waved goodbye to each other, and then Chance fell back against his seat.

Things were going well. Isabelle was forging some paths of her own. The horse was hers. The boy, too. Or rather, he *would* be if they could stop sparring with each other. And now Isabelle was going to try to see her stepsister.

Chance should have been elated at this thought; but he was troubled. He had Isabelle's map. He looked at it daily, and no matter how much progress she made, the horrible wax skull at the bottom continued to darken. He guessed Isabelle had only a handful of days left before the skull turned black.

Finding Ella and gaining the fairy queen's help . . . these things were her only hope. And his.

Chance leaned out of the window again, searching for Isabelle. He spotted her galloping back over the fields, growing smaller and smaller.

"Go, you splendid girl," he whispered. "Ride hard. Ride fast. Make the road your own. *Hurry*."

Seventy-Four

Madame LeBenêt slammed the bread dough on the table as if she meant to kill it.

"Twice, Tantine!" she said resentfully. "Not once, but *twice* those girls have taken advantage of my kind nature. First the cheese, now the horses!"

"Isabelle has a soft heart, Avara. Just like you," Tantine said.

Her voice was soothing, her expression placid, but inside she was livid. Things had been coming together so well, and now they were falling apart. That damned stallion was supposed to be dead, not happily grazing in the LeBenêts' pasture. Fate had bought him from a poor widow, then sold him to the slaughter yard, telling them he was too wild to ride, a killer, and must be put down.

And if the very fact that he was alive wasn't bad enough, at the midday meal, which had been the usual thin and tasteless affair, Isabelle announced that she would be riding to Paris tomorrow to try to see her stepsister. Fate had to pretend to be happy about Isabelle's wish for a reconciliation. Avara hadn't pretended at all, but Isabelle had promised to do the morning milking before she left and to be back in time for the evening

289

one. Plus it was Sunday, supposedly a day of rest, and so there was little Avara could say about it.

The horse, the boy, now the stepsister—was Isabelle forging the paths to them herself? Or had Chance drawn them on her map? He still had it, of course. What if he'd somehow learned how to make stronger inks? Fate shuddered to think of the chaos that rogue would unleash with such power at his fingertips.

"Three horses she brings here from the slaughter yard. *Three!*" Avara fumed, driving the heels of her hands into the dough so hard the table rattled.

Fate could bear no more of Madame's tirade. "Have you seen Losca?" she asked, rising. "I have some mending for her."

"She's probably in the garden. Seems to be her favorite place," Avara replied. "Now *there's* a girl who causes no trouble. She's quiet, helpful, and she eats like a bird."

Avara said more, but Fate, already outside, didn't hear her. Losca was indeed in the garden. She was sitting in the tomato patch, pulling fat green caterpillars off the plants and stuffing them into her mouth. Her cheeks were flushed. The neckline of her dress was soaked with sweat. She looked exhausted.

"Where have you been?" Fate asked.

Losca, her mouth full, couldn't reply. Instead, she picked up something lying on the ground next to her and handed it to her mistress.

Fate's eyes lit up when she saw what it was—Isabelle's map.

"You *wonderful* girl! How did you manage this?" she asked.

Losca swallowed her caterpillars, then explained to Fate, in her high, harsh voice, that she'd flown to the Château Rigolade early that morning before the household was awake.

She'd squeezed through an open bedroom window and had silently glided down to the dining room. The map had been lying open on the table there, but Chance was slumped over it, snoring.

A decanter of cognac stood on the table nearby him. Playing cards and a pile of gold coins were next to it.

Staying in her raven form, in case she had to escape quickly, she'd clasped a corner of the map in her beak, then carefully tugged it out from under Chance, inch by inch, until it was free. Chance had grumbled and twitched in his sleep, but he hadn't woken. After rolling the map with her beak, Losca grasped it in her talons and flew back out of the window. Landing in the tomato patch hadn't been her intention but flying for miles with the map had made her so ravenous, she'd felt faint.

"Rest, Losca, and eat your fill," Fate said. "This fine work of yours deserves a special reward. We shall go walking in the woods tonight to see if we can find a dead thing crawling with nice, juicy maggots."

Losca smiled and went back to snatching caterpillars.

Fate hurried to her room and spread the map out on her table. With a bent, shriveled finger, she traced Isabelle's path. Relief washed over her face as she saw that though Isabelle had forged detours, the main path of her life was unchanged and so was its ending. Chance had not managed to alter them. The wax skull was the bluc-black of a crow's wing. In four days, five at the most, Fate estimated, it would turn as black as the grave.

Yet Fate knew that now was not the time for complacency. What if the girl actually managed to get an audience with her stepsister? What if Ella forgave her and invited her to live in the palace?

"Perhaps it's time to hurry things along a bit," Fate mused aloud. "Perhaps I can shorten four or five days to one."

She sat down at her table, picked up a quill, and dipped it into an ink bottle. With sure, practiced movements, she hatched in new contours to the existing landscape. When she finished, she highlighted the hills in *Doom*, a murky gray, and shaded the hollows with *Defeat*, a purple as dark and mottled as a bruise.

As she worked on the map, Losca walked into the room. She had recovered from her exertions. Her eyes had regained their bright beadiness; her cheeks their usual pallor.

"Ah, Losca! I'm glad you're here," Fate said.

She explained to her that Isabelle was riding to Paris tomorrow, and that she wanted her to fly out early in the morning and lay a little groundwork for the girl's trip. When she finished speaking, she returned to Isabelle's map, but instead of rolling it up and putting it away, she scowled. Something was still missing.

She reached for another ink, bright red *Destruction*, and stippled it liberally over Isabelle's path.

"Yes," she said with a satisfied smile. "That should get the job done. Perhaps instead of trying to stop the girl from changing her fate, it's time to send her rushing headlong towards it."

Seventy-Five

The fox ran ahead of Isabelle.

Then she stopped and sat on a tree stump at the side of the road, as Isabelle, riding Nero, caught up to her.

"It was you, wasn't it, Tanaquill?" she said, stopping Nero a few feet from the stump. Unlike Martin, he was not afraid of foxes.

The fox blinked her emerald eyes.

"You chased Martin past the slaughter yard so that he'd see his old friend. You gave Nero back to me. Thank you. He's one of the pieces, I know he is."

The fox lifted her snout and yipped.

Isabelle nodded. "I guess I've been wrong all along. About the pieces being goodness, kindness, and charity. You said my heart had been cut away piece by piece by piece, but things can't be cut away if they weren't there to begin with."

The fox licked her paw.

"I'm on my way to Paris now. To see Ella. I think she's a piece, too," Isabelle ventured, waiting for the fox's reaction. But if the fox agreed, she gave no sign.

"Nero made me a better person. He gave me courage," Isabelle continued. "And Ella? If I was ever good, even a little bit, it is because of her."

The fox flicked her tail.

"Tavi thinks Felix is a piece, too. But he's not. I *know* he's not. Can you tell me what it is? Give me a hint? A nudge? *Anything*, Your Grace?"

The fox turned her head and gazed down the road intently, as if she saw something, or heard something there. Isabelle followed her gaze, but could see nothing. She turned back to the fox, but the creature was gone.

"I'm talking to foxes now. That's almost as bad as talking to cabbages," she said, then she and Nero continued on their way. They'd put a good six miles of the twenty-mile trip behind them, and the whole way, Isabelle had been wondering if she was crazy.

Everyone thought that going to see Ella was a terrible idea. Tantine said the guards would never let her through. Tavi said Ella wouldn't want to see her. Madame said she'd probably be robbed and murdered and left in a ditch before she got halfway there.

Only Maman thought the trip was a good idea. She'd told Isabelle to find a duke to marry while she was there. And, of course, the marquis wanted her to go.

Her resolve wavered for a moment, but then she pictured the marquis as he'd looked as he'd stood on top of his speeding carriage, the wind snatching at his braids and billowing his jacket out behind him.

Most would have been screaming in terror; he'd been laughing, his head back, his arms outstretched to the sky.

She remembered his sparkling amber eyes, and how, when he trained them on her, he made her feel as if luck itself was on her side, as if anything was possible.

And then she clucked her tongue and urged Nero on.

They'd been cantering for a mile or so, when they saw a man walking along the side of the road ahead of them. It was a quiet Sunday, and they'd barely seen anyone else, just a few wagons and a carriage.

Isabelle didn't think anything of the man, until they got closer to him and she realized that she knew the slope of his shoulders and his easy, loping gait. She recognized the satchel slung over his back and the battered straw hat on his head.

It was Felix.

Isabelle's stomach knotted. She didn't want to see him. Whenever they were together for more than two minutes, bad things happened. They argued. Shouted. He kissed her, then walked away. He could be incredibly kind, and carelessly cruel.

Isabelle decided to gallop straight past him, pretending she didn't realize who he was, but then he suddenly turned around, having heard a rider come up behind him, and her chance was lost.

"Isabelle," he said flatly as he realized it was her. It appeared he wasn't eager to see her, either.

"Hello, Felix," she said coolly. "I'm on my way to Paris. I'm afraid I can't stop."

"That's a shame."

The baiting note in his voice irritated Isabelle. She scowled, but Felix didn't see her reaction. He wasn't looking at her any more; his eyes were on Nero.

The horse's ears pricked up at the sound of Felix's voice. He trotted up to him, sniffed him, then gave a gusty snort.

"Thanks, boy," Felix said, laughing as he wiped horse breath off his face.

His harsh expression had melted. Isabelle knew Felix loved Nero and Nero returned the love. He lowered his head, inviting Felix to scratch his ears. Prickly Nero, who shied from anyone's touch but Isabelle's, who was far more likely to bite or kick than behave.

Turncoat, Isabelle said silently.

"Why are you going to Paris?" Felix asked.

"To see Ella."

Felix glanced up at her from under the brim of his hat. "An audience with the queen. That doesn't happen every day. When did she summon you?"

Isabelle hesitated. "She didn't, exactly. Summon me, that is."

"So you're just dropping in on the queen of France?"

The skeptical tone of his voice shook Isabelle's confidence, and it irritated her even more. It made her wonder, yet again, if the marquis's idea wasn't, perhaps, a little bit insane. And if she wasn't, too.

"I'm going to *try* to see her," she corrected. "I need to. There's . . . there's something I need to say to her."

"Isabelle?"

"What?"

"Whatever you have to say to Ella . . . *say* it, don't yell it. There are guards in the palace. Lots of them. With swords and rifles. Don't throw things, either. Not eggs. Not walnuts."

"Where are *you* going?" Isabelle asked huffily, keen to change the subject. Obviously, Felix had heard about the orphan incident, too.

"Also to Paris," Felix said, running his hand over Nero's neck and down to his shoulder. "I'm delivering a face," he continued. "Well, half a one."

"Another war injury?" Isabelle asked, her pique forgotten for the moment.

Felix nodded. "Shrapnel took the left cheek of a captain. His eye, too. He can't go out. People stare. They turn away from him. I made a half-mask to cover the injury. I hope it helps."

Isabelle was about to say that she was certain it would, but he spoke before she could.

"Nero's sweaty," he said, frowning. "You should get down and walk for a bit. Give him a rest. You've got miles to go before you reach Paris."

"Are you telling me how to take care of my own horse?" Isabelle asked. But she leaned forward and felt Nero's shoulder, too.

"Yes."

Isabelle, simmering, didn't budge.

"Afraid?" Felix asked her, a taunt in his voice.

"Of what?"

"That I'll kiss you again."

Isabelle glared at him, but she jumped down because he was right, damn him; Nero *was* a little sweaty.

"*You're* the one who's afraid," she said testily as she pulled the horse's reins over his head and led him.

"Oh, am I?"

"You must be. Every time you kiss me, you run away."

Felix scoffed at that. Which was a mistake.

The rude noise, the dismissive look on his face—they brought Isabelle's simmering anger to a boil. She stopped dead in the middle of the road, hooked an arm around his neck, and pulled him close. The kiss she gave him was not sweet or soft; it was a hot, hard smash, full of fury and wanting.

She kissed him with everything in her, until she couldn't breathe, and then she let go. Felix stumbled backward. His hat fell off.

"Run. Go," she said, gesturing to the road. "That's what you do."

Pain twisted in his blue eyes. It hurt Isabelle to know that she'd put it there, but she couldn't rein in the anger she felt towards him. It had been pent up for so long.

"Why, Felix? Just tell me why," she demanded. "You owe me that. Did you change your mind? Did you find yourself a better girl? A pretty girl?"

Felix looked as if she'd run a sword through his heart. "No, Isabelle, I didn't," he said. "I waited. Alone in the woods. Night after night. For someone who swore she would come but never did. I waited until it turned cold and I had to leave the Wildwood, and Saint-Michel, to find work. I thought *you'd* changed your mind. Found a rich boy. Some nobleman's son."

Uncertainty skittered over Isabelle's heart like mice in a wall.

"That's not true," she said slowly, shaking her head. "After Maman found out about us, and made you and your family leave, you said you'd come back for me. You promised to leave a message in the linden tree, but you didn't."

Felix raked a hand through his hair. He looked up at the sky. "My God," he said. "All this time . . . all this time you thought that I . . ."

"Yes, Felix, I did. I thought you loved me," Isabelle said bitterly.

"But, Isabelle," Felix said. "I *did* leave a note."

Seventy-Six

Isabelle shook her head.

She felt as if she'd ventured out onto a pond that wasn't frozen solid, and now the ice was cracking under her.

"You *didn't*," she insisted. "I checked. Every night."

"And I waited every night. Right where I'd told you I'd be. Where we saw the deer and her fawns."

"No, it's not true," Isabelle said, but with less conviction.

"It is. I *swear* it."

"What happened to it, then?"

"I—I don't know," Felix said, throwing his hands up. "I don't see how anything *could* have happened to it. I was worried about it blowing away, so I put a stone on top of it to weigh it down."

It can't be true. He must be lying, Isabelle thought. *None of this made any sense.*

And then it did. The ice broke and a freezing shock of truth pulled Isabelle under.

"Maman," she said. "She was so watchful. I bet she saw you hide it. I bet she took it and burned it."

Isabelle felt like she was drowning. The hurt, the sorrow, the bitterness—all the emotions she'd carried for years, emotions that had been so real to her, she now saw were false. But a new one threatened to overwhelm her, to catch her and tangle her, suffocating her in its cold depths—regret.

She saw herself running to the linden tree night after night, hoping in vain for a note. She saw Felix, waiting for her in the Wildwood. And then both of them giving up. Believing the worst of each other. And of themselves.

"Oh, Felix," she said, her anguished voice barely a whisper. "If only I'd found the note. What would our lives have been like if I had? We'd be in Rome now, and happy."

"Maybe we'd be living by a turquoise sea in Zanzibar. Or high up in a mountain fortress in Tibet." He laughed mirthlessly. "Or maybe we'd be dead. Of starvation. Exposure. Or sheer stupidity. We didn't exactly plan the trip out. I had a few coins saved up. You were going to bring some hard-boiled eggs and ginger cake."

Isabelle desperately wanted to kick free, to surface, to find something hopeful in the dark, roiling water and use it to pull herself out. Could she?

She put a hand on Felix's chest. Over his heart. And then she kissed him.

"Are you going to walk away again?" she asked afterward, leaning her forehead on his chest. "Don't. Promise you won't."

"I can't promise that, Isabelle," he said.

She looked up at him, stricken, and tried to pull away, but he grabbed her hand and held it fast.

"I'm leaving Master Jourdan's. And Saint-Michel. I'm leaving France," he said, all in a rush.

"I—I don't understand . . ."

"I'm going to Rome, Isabelle. To become a sculptor like I always wanted to." He lifted her hand to his lips and kissed it. "Come with me."

Seventy-Seven

Isabelle and Felix walked down the road in silence, Nero clopping along behind them.

Half an hour had passed since he had asked Isabelle to go with him to Rome.

At first she'd laughed, thinking that he was making an impulsive joke, but she'd soon learned that he was serious.

"I have a place with a master sculptor," he'd explained. "He wrote to me a month ago. I'll be doing the worst jobs, the ones no one else wants to do, but it's a start. I've given my notice, bought my passage."

"Felix, when . . . how . . ." Isabelle said, dumbfounded.

"I've been saving money from every job I've had for the past two years," he'd told her. "From all the feet and hands and eyes and teeth I've carved on the side. And from my wooden army. I sold it. A nobleman in Paris bought it. He's already sent the money. I've only three officers left to finish. As soon as I send word, his servant will come to collect it." He paused, then said, "It's enough. To buy you a passage, too. To rent an attic room somewhere. Come with me."

Isabelle wanted to say yes more than she'd ever wanted

303

anything in the entire world, but it was impossible and she knew it.

"I can't go, Felix. Maman has lost her wits, and Tavi's head is always in the clouds. If I leave, who will take care of them? We're barely surviving as it is. They won't last a week without me."

"I can't get you back just to lose you again," Felix said now, dispelling the silence. "There must be a way. We'll find it."

Isabelle mustered a smile, but she couldn't imagine what that way might be. "I have to go," she said. Felix was spending the night in the city, at the home of the captain for whom he'd made the mask, but she needed to get to Paris, and get back to Saint-Michel, by evening.

"Stay with me for one more mile. There's the sign." Felix nodded ahead at a whitewashed post ahead of them. "We're nearly halfway there."

"All right," Isabelle relented. "One more mile."

A moment later, they passed the post. On it, a bright, newly painted sign pointed left to Paris. Another pointed right to Malleval. With barely a glance at it, Isabelle and Felix headed left.

Had their emotions not been running so high, had they not been so distracted by talk of Rome, had they not stopped, right in the middle of the road, for another kiss, they might've noticed that the white paint on the signs was not just new, but still wet. And that black block letters ghosted through it—Paris under Malleval, Malleval under Paris.

They might've seen boot prints around the base of the signpost, and freshly disturbed dirt a few feet away from it. Had they cared to dig in that dirt, they would've found two empty paint pots and two used brushes—all of it stolen earlier that morning from a nearby farmer's barn.

But they did not see any of these things, and so continued on their way.

As soon as they were out of earshot, the coal-black raven, who'd been perched out of sight on a leafy branch, flapped her wings noisily and flew off.

There was no need to stay. Her mistress had told her so.

The girl, and the boy with her, would not be coming back.

Seventy-Eight

It was the smoke that first got Isabelle's attention.

A burned-hay smell. Sharp and out of place on the summer breeze.

Farmers burned their fields to rid them of weeds and stubble in autumn, when the harvest was in. Not in August.

"Do you smell that?" she asked Felix.

"I do," he said, looking around for the source of the smoke.

Nero whinnied uneasily. He pulled at his reins. Isabelle realized nothing around her looked familiar. She had been to Paris before, several times, on shopping trips for dresses with Tavi and Maman, but she did not recall the huge apple orchard on the right side of the road. Or the old, tumbledown stone barn on the left.

"We took the right road, didn't we?" she asked Felix, realizing that she'd barely glanced at the signpost.

"I'm sure we did. I remember seeing the sign for Paris pointing left. That's the way we went."

They walked on. A few minutes later, they spotted another signpost. A man was sitting under it, his back against the wooden post, his head down, clearly taking a rest. He was wearing the

306

rough clothing of a farmer—battered boots, long pants, a red shirt. His straw hat was tilted over his face.

As Isabelle and Felix drew closer, they saw that there was only a single sign on the post, and that it read *Malleval*.

"That *can't* be right," Felix said. "Malleval's in the opposite direction."

Isabelle decided to get an answer. She handed Nero's reins to Felix and approached the resting man. "Excuse me, sir, will this road take us to Paris?"

The man didn't answer her.

"He's sound asleep," Isabelle said.

She hated to wake him, but she needed to know where they were. She didn't have time to waste.

"Sir? Excuse me," she said. But the man slept on. Isabelle bent down and gave his arm a gentle shake. His hat fell off. His head lolled sickeningly to the side. His body toppled over like of sack of meal.

That's when Isabelle realized that he wasn't napping, and he wasn't wearing a red shirt. He was wearing a white shirt that had turned red. His throat had been cut from ear to ear. Blood had cascaded from the wound down the front of his body. Some was still trickling out.

Terror broke lose inside her. "Please, somebody help! In God's name, help!" she screamed.

Felix was at her side in an instant. The blood drained from his face as he saw the murdered man. He grabbed Isabelle's arm and pulled her away. Nero, hearing her screams and scenting blood, grew wild-eyed. Isabelle took him from Felix and tried to calm him. Felix shouted for help again. But nobody answered them. Nobody came.

The breeze picked up and so did the scent of smoke. The bitter smell was like a slap; it brought Isabelle back to her senses. She realized how stupid they'd been.

"Whoever killed this man might still be nearby," she said to Felix. "And we've just let him know we're here."

"If that signpost is correct, Malleval will be close," Felix said. "We'll be safe there. We can tell them what happened. They'll send someone to get this poor man."

Casting a fearful glance around, Isabelle put her foot in the stirrup. Felix boosted her up into her saddle; then she pulled him up behind her.

"Go," he said, closing his arms around her waist.

Isabelle spurred Nero on. He galloped the mile or so down the road towards the village, but as it came into view, he stopped, raised his head, and let out an earsplitting whinny.

Isabelle's eyes widened. One hand came up to her chest.

"No," she whispered. "God in Heaven . . . *no*."

There would be no help from the villagers of Malleval.

Not now, not ever.

Seventy-Nine

Isabelle slid out of her saddle, then staggered through the wheat fields at the edge of Malleval like a drunk. Felix followed her.

Nero stood in the road where they'd left him, his reins trailing in the dust.

Lying in the dirt, amid the stubbly stalks of cut wheat, were bodies. Men's. Women's. Children's. They had been shot and stabbed. Many in the back. There was a man with a gaping hole in his side, still clutching his pitchfork. There lay an old woman, a bayonet wound in her chest.

Dark gray smoke swirled over them. The village's homes, its stables and barns, all had thatched roofs, and they were burning.

Isabelle started to shake so hard that she couldn't stop. Her legs gave way. She fell on her backside next to a dead mother and her dead child. A low keening sound moved up from her chest into her throat, then rose into a wild howl of pain. Thick, strangling sobs followed it. She folded in on herself, clutched at the dirt, and wept.

Sometime later—minutes? An hour?—Isabelle heard voices. Men's voices. She picked up her head and looked around. It wasn't Felix; he was carrying an old woman who was bleeding

309

badly through a field, running with her towards one of the only houses that wasn't burning.

And then Isabelle saw the men. They were soldiers. They'd gathered at the far edge of the field. They were talking and laughing. Some held the reins of their horses; others sacks full of plunder.

One of them turned. His gaze fell on Isabelle and an ugly grin spread across his face. He started towards her through the swirling smoke, through the falling ash, like a demon from hell. Two others made as if to follow him, but he waved them back. She was to be his sport, his alone. She'd never seen the man before, but she knew him. From rumors and stories. From a vision she'd had when a wagonload of wounded soldiers had passed by her on the road to Saint-Michel. He held a sword in one hand, a shield in the other. He wore no coat. His leather waistcoat and white shirt were streaked with blood. His black hair, shot through with silver, was pulled back. A scar puckered one cheek. His eyes burned with dark fire. He was Volkmar.

Inside Isabelle, under her heart, the sleeping wolf woke.

Eighty

Isabelle was terrified. She was going to die; she knew that. But she would not run; she would face Volkmar down.

She scrambled to her feet, praying that Felix would stay with the old woman inside the house, and searched for a weapon. There had to be *something* she could fight with—a pitchfork, a shovel, a hay rake. She would aim for Volkmar's neck if she could. His thigh. His wrist. She would do her best to make him bleed.

Volkmar closed in. He was only twenty yards away now.

"How did I miss this little rat in the wheat field?" he said, raising his sword.

And still, Isabelle was defenseless. Her heart kicked in her chest. Her blood surged, pounding in her ears. But over it, she heard another noise. It sounded like fabric tearing. She felt a weight, sudden and heavy, pulling at her clothing.

She glanced down and saw that her pocket had torn open. Because the nutshell inside it was growing.

Isabelle quickly pulled it out before it ripped her dress apart. As she did, it flattened and expanded until it was half her size. Leather straps appeared on the side facing her. She realized she was holding a shield. She snaked her arms through the straps and raised it over her head.

In the very nick of time.

A split second later, Volkmar's blade crashed down upon it. Isabelle was strong now, her arms well-muscled from endless farm chores, and she managed to hold the shield firm. Without it, the blow would have cleaved her in two.

She thrust her hand into her pocket again, remembering Tanaquill's first gift. Her fingers closed around the bone. She pulled it out, and as she did, it transformed into the same fearsome sword she'd used to fight off the chicken thief.

"Coward!" she spat at Volkmar. "Murderer! They were innocent people!"

The horror and grief had receded. She felt as if she were made of rage now.

Volkmar's grin twisted into a snarl. Her words had enraged him. A stab through the heart would be too good for her now. He would aim for her neck instead, and send her head flying.

He swung high, just as she'd known he would. She ducked, and his blade passed over her head. Her legs pistoned her back up. The tip of her sword caught his side and ripped a jagged gash up his rib cage. He bellowed in surprise and staggered backward.

Isabelle's heart was pounding like a war drum. Her blood was singing.

Volkmar touched his fingertips to his wound. They came away crimson. "The rat has sharp teeth," he said. Then he charged again.

Isabelle knew she had one chance left. She had to do better than a flesh wound.

She lifted her shield, raised her sword, but before she could use them, a bugle blast was heard. Two men came galloping across the field from her left. A riderless horse trailed them.

"The king's cavalry is coming!" one of the men shouted. "Jump on! Hurry!"

The horsemen swooped close. The riderless horse slowed to a canter. Volkmar threw his weapons down and caught the horse by his bridle. He ran alongside the animal for a few strides, then launched himself into the saddle. And then the three riders were gone, vanished into the smoke.

Isabelle lowered her sword and shield. As she did, they turned back into a jawbone, a walnut shell. She put them in her pocket. Seconds later, forty soldiers on horseback galloped into the village. They surrounded Isabelle and asked her what had happened. She told them, pointing in the direction in which Volkmar had gone and urged them to hurry.

The captain shouted commands at his men and they charged off.

Isabelle watched them go, longing to ride with them and chase down Volkmar. Then, sickened and spent, she looked for Felix. He was ministering to a dying man now, bare-chested, pressing his bunched-up shirt to the man's side, trying to keep the last of his life from leaking into the dirt.

As Isabelle watched him, kneeling among the obscene harvest of the dead, his body smeared with blood, his face streaked with tears, a pain, piercing and deep, made her cry out. It was worse than any that had befallen her that day. Her hand went to her chest. She bent double, her breath rapid and shallow, willing it to pass.

Inside her, the wolf, denied his rightful work, bared his sharp teeth and tore into her heart.

Eighty-One

The jagged scream tore apart the placid afternoon.

It was followed by a loud, heavy smash, and the sound of running feet.

Fate, peeling apples at the kitchen table, looked up, alarmed. Avara, stirring a soup at the hearth, dropped her ladle into the ashes.

"What the devil is going on out there?" she shouted. "Hugo! Huuuugo!"

Fate and Avara reached the door together and saw an earthenware bowl lying in pieces on the stone steps. Bright green peas were scattered all around it. Two hens had rushed over and were greedily pecking at them.

Fate soon saw that it was Maman who had screamed and Tavi who'd dropped the bowl. They were running down the drive. Two figures were walking up it. Felix was shirtless. His long brown hair, damp and lank, hung down his back. His trousers were stained with blood. His gaze was inward, as if focused on something only he could see. His arm was around Isabelle's neck, possessively, protectively, as if he was afraid she would be snatched away from him. The skirts of Isabelle's dress were

315

smeared with crimson. Sweat and dirt streaked her face. Her hair, flecked with ash, had tumbled loose from its carefully pinned coil.

"God in Heaven, what happened?" Avara shouted. She skirted the broken mess on the steps and joined the others. Hugo walked out of the stables, wiping his hands on a rag. He dropped it and broke into a run when he saw Isabelle and Felix.

Fate remained in the doorway. "It *can't* be," she hissed. "How is she still alive?"

Realizing that it would look callous for her to remain where she was, Fate hurried down the drive, too. Maman was in tears, pressing Isabelle's face between her hands one minute, asking the name of the brave knight who was with her the next. Tavi was shushing her.

Felix apologized for being bare-chested and filthy. He'd left his blood-soaked shirt in Malleval and had tried to douse himself clean under the village's pump, he said, but the water had only washed away so much. Then he told what had happened to them. How they'd ended up in Malleval after Volkmar had slaughtered its people. How Isabelle had somehow found a sword and shield and had faced him down. How they'd abandoned their plans to go to Paris and had made the long walk home.

It was quiet when they finished. No one spoke.

Then Tavi, her voice quavering with anger, said, "You could've been *killed*, Isabelle. What were you *thinking*?"

"That I wanted to kill Volkmar," Isabelle said in a flat, grim voice. "That I wanted to cut into his black heart and watch him bleed to death at my feet. That's what I was thinking." Silent

316

and hollow-eyed, she led Nero into the stables and started to untack him.

They all watched her go, then Hugo turned to Felix and said, "Come inside. Sit down. Have something to drink."

Felix shook his head. "I'm going to the camp. To warn Colonel Cafard. The sooner I get there the better."

Hugo insisted on driving him. He'd been just about to leave for the camp, he explained. The cook had sent for milk. Men had left for the front that morning. Every wagon in the camp had been needed to carry tents, arms, and ammunition. Not one was left to fetch food for those remaining.

Felix thanked him and asked to borrow a shirt. Usually Avara would have balked over such a request, badgering Felix not to stain it or wear out the elbows, but she didn't utter one word of protest. Worry crinkled the skin around her eyes. Her gaze drifted over her fields, her orchards, her cattle, her son.

Fate knew what she was thinking, what they were all thinking: Malleval was only ten miles away. "Volkmar won't come here," she soothed, the lie rolling smoothly off her tongue. "He wouldn't dare, not with Colonel Cafard camped right outside the village."

Avara nodded, but the furrows remained. "You're right, Tantine. Of course you are," she said. Then she took a deep breath. "Octavia, you broke my bowl! Do you have any idea what bowls like that cost? Clean up the mess and get the rest of the peas shelled!" But her voice lacked its usual vinegar.

Tavi bent over the pottery shards. She made a sling of her apron and put them in it. Maman helped her. Avara returned to her soup.

And Fate remained outside, watching as Felix shrugged into Hugo's shirt, then climbed up on the wagon seat next to him. As the two boys headed down the drive, her bright eyes searched the farmyard for Isabelle. They spotted her by the pond. She'd led Nero to the water; he'd waded in up to his shoulders and was drinking his fill.

Isabelle followed him in, fully clothed except for her boots and stockings. As Fate watched, she submerged herself. When she came back up, she sat down on the bank and rubbed at the bloodstains on her dress, then scrubbed at her hands, roughly, furiously, as if whatever was on them would never come off.

When she was finished, she lowered her head and wept. Even at a distance, Fate could see her shoulders shaking, her body shuddering.

How on earth did Volkmar fail to kill her? she wondered. *She's just a girl. Crumpling under the bloodshed she witnessed.*

Fate meant to get an answer to her question. Pleading tiredness after all the upset, she abandoned the bowl of apples she'd been peeling, closed herself in her room, and took Isabelle's map out of her trunk. She moved quietly. Losca was asleep in a trundle bed, her head tucked under her arm.

Fate smoothed the map out on her table, sat down, and looked it over.

She had tried to shorten Isabelle's path to her death, and it hadn't worked. Was it her inks? Maybe the ingredients hadn't been the best quality. The light was bad in this room; perhaps her artistry had suffered as a result.

But no, it was neither of these things. Fate's expert eyes found the problem. She had drawn a new path for Isabelle, a shortcut through Malleval to Volkmar, and Isabelle had followed it—most of the way. Just shy of the end, however, she'd turned off the shortcut and made her way back to her old path.

Fate sat back in her chair. She drummed her fingers on its arm. *Have I underestimated her?* she wondered.

Isabelle had refused to abandon her mother in a burning house. She'd saved three horses at the expense of her own freedom. She'd taken on Volkmar. This wasn't the same girl who'd stood by as Maman turned Ella into a servant, or who'd locked her stepsister in her room when the prince had come to call. Why, she was even walking taller these days, more confidently.

At least she failed to see Ella, Fate thought with some relief. That was the day's one bright spot.

But the boy—the first piece—he was worrisome. He'd had an arm around Isabelle as they'd walked up the drive. They seemed to have grown closer. Fate consulted Isabelle's map again, poring closely over the detour she'd made, then she pounded her fist on the table. The noise startled Losca awake. She sat up, bright-eyed and blinking.

"They reconciled!" Fate fumed. "He made a slipper for her. *That's* why she was walking taller. He even asked her to go with him to Italy!" She peered at the map again. "She told him she could not . . . That's good. But he promised to find a way." She shook her head in disgust. "What if he does? What if Isabelle *leaves*?"

Fate rose; she paced back and forth. "That cannot happen," she said. She knew she had to find a way of keeping Isabelle in Saint-Michel, but her bag of tricks was rapidly emptying.

319

Warm from her pacing, she moved across the room to open her window. It was a casement frame with metal hinges, one of which had developed an unpleasant squeak.

"I must get after Hugo to fix that," she muttered.

Hugo.

Fate whirled around. She rushed to her desk and scrawled a hasty letter on a piece of parchment.

"Up, girl!" she barked at Losca when she'd finished.

Losca rose. She smoothed her dress.

"Take this to Monsieur Albert, head of the bank in Saint-Michel. He'll be at home, eating his Sunday dinner. I need a good sum of money. More than he has in his vault. It'll take him a day or two to get it, no doubt, and we must move quickly. Hurry now! Go!" Fate said.

She walked Losca out of their room, through the house, past Tavi shelling peas, and down the drive, giving her directions to Monsieur Albert's. The girl set off running, the letter clutched in her hand.

Fate watched her until she disappeared down the road, then started back to the house. A movement caught her eye. It was Isabelle. She was in the pasture, riding Nero. She'd rigged up a scarecrow. His body was made out of branches; he had a cabbage for a head. He was propped up on a fencepost she'd sunk into a soft patch of ground. She was brandishing something in her right hand. Fate squinted and saw that it was an old sword that had belonged to Monsieur LeBenêt and had hung in the stables.

As she watched, Isabelle charged the scarecrow, sword raised high, and lopped his head off. She turned Nero sharply and charged again. The scarecrow lost an arm. Then his torso was hacked in two. Fate did not like what she was seeing.

Her expression darkened further as she passed by Tavi again and saw that she was using the peas she'd shelled to form equations. Her eyes lingered on the girl.

A few weeks ago, after the incident with the cheese, Hugo had come to her complaining bitterly about Tavi, asking Fate to get her married off.

Back then, Fate had thought the idea unnecessary, but perhaps it was time to act on Hugo's suggestion now. With a few slight modifications.

A wedding would be such a joyous affair.

"For everyone," Fate whispered darkly. "Except the bride and groom."

Eighty-Two

"Once again from the top. With feeling, please!" Chance shouted.

He was standing in front of his stage, a glass in one hand, watching his players rehearse. They were doing a terrible job. Missing cues. Mangling lines. Torchlight playing over his face revealed new creases engraved around his eyes.

"Louder, please!" he yelled, raising his hand, palm up. "I can barely hear you!"

The fortune-teller shouted her lines. The actress and diva joined her onstage and ran through theirs. Chance clapped out a quick tempo to speed them up.

One of the footlights, lacking a glass chimney, had been placed too far upstage. The fortune-teller's skirt brushed it. The fabric caught. The sword-swallower shouted at her, waving his hands. He hurried to stamp the flames out. Frightened by the fire, the fortune-teller ran, but not before the sword-swallower's foot came down on her hem. There was a sound of cloth tearing, and then the fortune-teller found herself standing centre stage in her petticoat.

The fire-breather, up in the rigging, peered down to see what was going on, lost his balance and fell. His foot got tangled in a rope that was attached to a painted backdrop. The backdrop shot up and smashed in the rigging. Splintered pieces rained down, knocking off the diva's wig and the actress's crown. The fire-breather dangled, his head only inches from the stage floor.

Chance closed his eyes. He pinched the bridge of his nose. Isabelle's map was gone. Fate was undoubtedly redrawing it to speed the girl to her doom. And what was he doing? Presiding over a disaster of a play.

Chance opened his eyes. "Someone cut him free, please," he said, gesturing to the fire-breather, who was still hanging upside down, spinning in slow circles like a human plumb bob.

"You tell him," hissed a voice from behind Chance.

"No, *you* tell him."

"Where's the cognac? Let's refill his glass. Bad news always goes down better with a glass of cognac."

"I really think *you* should tell him."

Chance turned around. "Tell me what?" he asked.

The cook and the magician were standing there, solemn-faced.

"Isabelle never made it to Paris," said the magician. "She didn't see Ella."

Chance swore. He turned and threw his glass against a tree. All the actors stopped what they were doing. A hush fell over the company.

Chance tilted his head back. He covered his eyes with his hands. He felt he was only one teetering step away from defeat.

"This play is it," he said, lowering his hands. "My last move. It's all I have left to convince Isabelle that she can make her own path. If it fails, then I've failed. And Isabelle is doomed."

The actors all started talking at once. Then yelling. Pointing fingers. Shaking fists. The noise grew louder and louder.

Until the fortune-teller, still in her petticoat, took charge. "Quiet, everyone!" she shouted, stamping her foot. "Places! Start again from the top . . ."

"Good girl. Put your heart into it," the magician urged her, walking to Chance's side.

"Deliver those lines like Isabelle's life depends on it," said the cook, joining them.

Chance nodded gravely. "Because it does."

Eighty-Three

"Octavia! Isabelle! Wake up!"

Isabelle sat up groggily. She'd been fast asleep. *Did someone call my name?* she wondered.

"Wake *up*, girls! I need to speak to you!"

It was Madame LeBenêt. Isabelle reached for her dress, pulled it over her head, and hurried to the edge of the hayloft, fumbling with the buttons.

Madame was standing by the ladder, hands on her hips. "Come to the house," she said brusquely. "Bring your mother."

Isabelle remained where she was, staring over the ledge, blinking stupidly.

"What are you waiting for? Get the hay out of your hair and get a move on!" Madame barked.

She turned on her heel and strode out of the barn, and Isabelle felt as if she was walking right over her heart. Panic rose inside her. She wondered what they had done. Was it the horses she'd saved? The bowl Tavi had broken? *Madame is going to turn us out*, she thought. *We've angered her once too often.*

"Tavi, Maman, get up. Get dressed. Madame wants us," Isabelle said, trying to keep her voice from trembling.

When they'd finished dressing, the three women made their way down the ladder and across the yard to the house. Isabelle smoothed her hair when they reached the door, then knocked.

"Come in!" Madame yelled.

With her heart in her mouth, Isabelle stepped inside. Tavi and Maman followed her.

Tantine was at the table, setting out cups. Madame was pulling a large copper frying pan off a trivet in the hearth. She carried the pan to the table, then gave it a knock with the heel of her hand. A fluffy yellow omelet flipped out onto a serving plate.

"Ten eggs in that!" she grumbled. "That's ten I can't sell."

"Now, now, Avara," Fate chided.

There was a pot of hot black coffee on the table with a jug of rich cream to pour in it, sliced bread, a dish of fresh butter and another of strawberry jam. Isabelle, who—along with Tavi and Maman—had been subsisting on stale bread and thin soup, felt her stomach twist painfully. She desperately hoped that Madame would give them something to eat before she sent them packing. Gazing at so much delicious food was torture to the hungry girl; she turned away and distracted herself by looking around the room.

Isabelle had only been inside Madame LeBenêt's house a handful of times and had never lingered. Now she had time to take it in. The room where they were standing—both kitchen and dining room—was small and low-ceilinged. There were no pictures on the gray stone walls, no flowers in a vase, no rugs on the floor, nothing warm or welcoming anywhere. She felt a rush of sympathy for Hugo, living in a cold, loveless house, with a mother who rarely, if ever, spoke a kind word.

"Sit down, girls," Madame said impatiently, waving them towards the table with the wooden spoon she was holding.

Isabelle and Tavi exchanged confused glances.

"Sit down? There at the table?" Isabelle asked.

"You mean us?" Tavi said.

"I said *you*, didn't I?" Madame replied.

"No, you said *girls*," Tavi pointed out.

Madame gripped her wooden spoon as if she wanted to throttle it. Tantine, who'd finished setting the cups out, ushered the three women to the table.

Isabelle had no idea what was happening. Was Madame going to let them stay? Or was she giving them a good breakfast before she threw them out to ease her conscience? She didn't have to wait long to find out.

As everyone settled around the table, Madame counted the pieces of bread that had been sliced from the large wheaten round. "That's two pieces per person. *Two!*" she said, glowering. "Tantine, you will ruin us."

"Avara, serve the breakfast, please," Tantine said, her teeth gritted.

Madame, lips pursed, dished out the omelet.

"I should explain why we invited you here," Tantine said as she passed the bread. "This breakfast is a bit of a celebration. As you know, my late husband left a small legacy to Monsieur LeBenêt. Since monsieur passed away, it was left to my discretion whether to bestow it upon a member of his family. I'm pleased to say that I've come to a decision—the money will go to the next LeBenêt male—Hugo."

Hugo was speechless. He sat there like a trout, mouth open, unblinking, until his mother kicked him under the table. "Thank you, Tantine!" he finally said. He puffed his chest out and leaned so far back in his chair, he almost fell out of it. At a dirty look from his mother, he sat forward again, bringing the front legs of the chair down with a crash.

"This is *great!*" he crowed, slapping his hands down on the table. "This means I can . . ."

Isabelle had never seen him so animated. Neither had his mother, apparently, for her look changed from one of disapproval to one of suspicion.

"You can do what?" she asked.

Hugo hunkered down in his chair, a furtive look on his face. *Marry Odette*, Isabelle thought. *But he's too scared to say so.*

"I . . . um . . . I can . . ." he stammered. Then he brightened. "I can have some money!"

"Use it to buy a brain!" Tavi said under her breath.

Tantine continued. "The legacy is enough to secure the future of this farm and continue the LeBenêt line, which is what my dear husband wished. But . . ." She held up a finger. "Fortune is only *good* fortune if it is shared, and I mean to see that you are *all* well taken care of. Not just my family, but also you, Isabelle, and your family. You are three women alone in the world. You cannot go on living in a hayloft. What kind of life is that for you? What will happen to you come winter? And so I have taken steps. I have made arrangements."

Tantine picked up her coffee cup and took a sip. Isabelle's hands tightened on her napkin. Hope leapt inside her. What had Tantine done? Was she giving them some money, too?

She'd mentioned the hayloft—had she found them something better? Isabelle was afraid to ask, lest she'd got her hopes too high, but she had to know. "You found us a new place to stay, Tantine?" she ventured. "A room somewhere? A tiny house?"

"Yes, child. A house and something more," Tantine said, lowering her cup.

Isabelle glanced excitedly at Tavi and then Maman. "What is it?" she asked.

Tantine settled her cup into its saucer. Beaming at Isabelle, she said, "A husband!"

Eighty-Four

Isabelle's blood froze in her veins. Her body went rigid in her chair; she was unable to move. "What do you mean a—a *husband*, Tantine?" she asked in a small voice.

"Why, just what I said, child—a man! A tall, strapping man in breeches and boots! Just what every girl wants."

"*Isabelle?*" Hugo said, looking surprised. "But I thought . . . I thought Tavi would marry first. She's the oldest."

Tavi said nothing at all; she was shocked speechless.

Maman, however, was overjoyed. "This *is wonderful* news!" she exclaimed. "Who is he? A baron? A viscount?" She looked from Tantine to Avara and back again, but they gave her no answer. "No? Well, no matter. A squire is acceptable, too. After all, these are difficult times."

"Will the wedding be soon?" Hugo asked.

"Within a matter of days," Tantine replied.

"*Yes!*" Hugo crowed. "Tell us, Tantine," he urged, rocking back in his chair again. "Who is it? Who will Isabelle marry?"

Tantine leaned across the table and covered one of Hugo's hands with her own. "Why, dear boy, haven't you guessed?" she asked. "It's *you!*"

Eighty-Five

Everything happened at once.

Hugo fell over backward with an earth-shaking crash, hitting his head so hard he knocked himself out. Maman slumped into a faint. Tavi jumped up to revive her at the same that Madame jumped up to tend to Hugo. They smacked heads, then staggered back, dazed.

And Isabelle squeezed her coffee cup so hard it broke, splashing hot coffee all over her hands. She didn't even feel it. She could hardly breathe. Her heart was pounding; it was beating out the name *Hu*-go, *Hu*-go, *Hu*-go over and over, like a funeral march.

Isabelle could not believe Tantine had done this. Moments ago, she'd been hopeful, believing that the old woman would help them find a new place to live. Now she felt like an animal in a trap. *Why* had she done this? Isabelle had never shown the slightest interest in Hugo, nor he in her.

"Tantine, I can't . . . Hugo and I, we don't . . . we never . . ." she said, struggling for the right words.

Tavi, who was chafing her mother's wrists, came to her aid. "But Hugo and Isabelle can't stand each other! It's a terrible idea, Tantine. This is the eighteenth century, not the tenth. She doesn't have to do it!"

"Girls, girls, calm down! Of course, Isabelle doesn't *have* to marry Hugo. She doesn't have to marry *anyone*," Tantine soothed. "But how unfortunate it would be if she didn't. You see, there are one or two things I may have neglected to mention. Hugo's legacy? It only goes to him if he marries. How can he continue the family line without a wife? And really, what girl wouldn't want to marry such a fine boy, especially one with a farm and fifty acres?" She paused. Her eyes caught Isabelle's and held them. Isabelle felt as if she was being pulled helplessly, hopelessly, into a cold gray abyss. "Isabelle is certainly free to refuse the proposal," Tantine continued. "She is also free to leave the farm and find herself, and her family, another place to live."

Isabelle felt the gray depths close over her and pull her down. She fought her way back up. She had to find a way to navigate between the two impossibities Tantine had presented.

"Madame," she said, turning to Hugo's mother. "I am nowhere near good enough for your son."

"True enough," Madame allowed, through a mouthful of omelet. "But as your own mother said, these are difficult times and one cannot be choosy. You are not a pretty girl, but cows don't care about looks and neither do cabbages. You're a hard worker, I'll give you that, and that's what counts on a farm. Plus, you're strong and sturdy, with a good pair of hips to carry sons and a fine bosom to suckle them. You'll breed well, I think."

Isabelle flushed a deep red, unaccustomed to hearing herself talked about as if she were a broodmare.

"There! We're all settled, then, aren't we?" Tantine said cheerfully, shoveling more omelet onto Isabelle's plate. "Now, eat your breakfast, child," she admonished. "You'll need your strength. You have a wedding to prepare for. I'm thinking next Saturday. A week from today. That's time enough to make the necessary preparations. What do you think, Avara?"

Isabelle didn't care what anyone thought. She looked at the cold wobbly omelet on her plate. Nausea gripped her. She got to her feet. "Pardon me, please," she said, hurrying towards the door.

"She probably needs to collect herself. Shed a tear of joy or two in private," Tantine said knowingly. "Brides-to-be are *such* emotional creatures."

Isabelle wrenched the door open, ran outside, and vomited her breakfast into the grass.

Eighty-Six

"A week," Isabelle said hollowly, leaning against the barn wall. "That's all I've got."

"We'll think of something," Tavi said. She was sitting on the same bench as Isabelle. "There has to be a way out of this."

Hugo, who had regained consciousness, was sitting between them, his head in his hands, his elbows on his knees, groaning.

Breakfast was over. The dishes had been cleared away. Maman, inconsolable that Isabelle was marrying a farm boy, not an aristocrat, had taken to the hayloft. Madame was tending a sick hen. Tantine had retired to her room. Isabelle, Tavi, and Hugo were busy veering between panic and despair.

"There's no way out," Isabelle said miserably. "Either I go through with it or we starve to death."

Hugo picked up his head. "I can't do it. I just can't. Why did you two ever have to come here? *Why?*" He groaned again.

"Stop it. You sound like a calf with colic," Tavi said irritably.

"You could at least show some sympathy. I'm in a terrible spot," Hugo huffed. "It wasn't supposed to happen this way."

Tavi's eyes narrowed. "What do you mean, *happen this way?*" she asked.

Hugo looked alarmed. And guilty. "Nothing," he quickly said.

But Tavi didn't buy it. "You know something about this. Tell us."

Hugo looked trapped. "I—I told Tantine that you had to go. I asked her to matchmake. To find a husband for *you*, Tavi," he admitted. "I thought if you got married, you'd leave and take Isabelle and your mother with you. I wanted you to leave because I can't stand you, but also because I thought I might have a better chance of convincing my mother to let me marry Odette if you were gone. She'd be more agreeable if there were fewer mouths to feed." Hugo glanced from Tavi to Isabelle. "That's, um . . . that's what I thought."

"So this is *your* fault!" Isabelle said angrily. "You were going to ruin Tavi's life, but you ruined mine instead!"

Tavi rubbed her temples. "Do us a favor, Hugo, don't think any more. Just don't," she said.

"I won't," Hugo said fervently. "I promise. Just get me out of this mess, Tavi. *Please.* I can't marry Isabelle. I want Odette. I can't stop dreaming about her. I have that feeling."

"What feeling is that?" Tavi asked.

"The feeling that you want to own someone body and soul, spirit them away from everyone else, have them all to yourself forever and ever and ever," Hugo said dreamily. "It's called love."

"No, it's called *kidnapping*," said Tavi.

A pit of hopelessness opened in Isabelle's chest as she listened to Hugo. She lowered her head into her hands.

Tavi saw her. "I'll do it, Isabelle," she said impetuously. "I'll marry him."

"Oh, Tav," Isabelle said, leaning her head on her sister's shoulder.

"I'd do it. I would. I'd sacrifice myself for you," Tavi bravely offered.

Hugo turned to look at her, offended. *"Sacrifice?"* he said.

Isabelle was deeply touched. She knew her serious, sober sister didn't talk just for the sake of talking. If she said something, she meant it. "You *would* do it, wouldn't you? You'd take on a fate worse than death for me."

"Worse than *death?*" said Hugo.

"It is. Just picture the two of us married," Isabelle said to him. "Milking cows and making cheese for the rest of our lives."

Hugo paled. "Together. In the same house. In the same kitchen," he said grimly.

"In the same bed," Tavi added.

"Good Lord, Tavi, stop!" Isabelle said, mortified.

"I'm just adding that aspect of things into the equation."

"Well, don't!"

"I bet you snore, Isabelle. You look like the type," said Hugo.

"Oh, do I, Hugo? Well, I bet you fart all night long."

"I bet you drool on the pillow."

"I bet your breath stinks."

"I bet your feet stink."

"Not as much as yours do. Only three-quarters as much, in fact."

"Eating breakfast together. Dinner. Supper. Staring at you across the table for the next twenty years. Thirty. Fifty, if we're really unlucky," said Hugo.

"Fifty *years*," Isabelle groaned. "My God, can you *imagine* it?"

Hugo, his face as white as lard, said, "There *must* be a way out of this."

Isabelle expected him to say something awful here, to deliver some stinging insult. But he didn't. Instead, he gazed down at their two hands and said, "You terrify me, Isabelle. I've never met a girl like you. You're a fighter, fierce as hell. You never quit. You don't know how. I've never seen anyone cut cabbages so fast just to get a bowl of my mother's horrible soup. You don't need anyone. You certainly don't need me." He looked up. "I don't want to marry you, either, Tavi. You're not scary. You're just weird."

"Thanks," Tavi said.

"I don't want a fierce girl. Or a weird girl. I want a sweet girl. A girl who makes me her whole world, not one whose only ambition is to turn the world upside down." He slumped against the barn wall. "Tavi, can't you figure this out?"

"I'm trying. Hard as I can."

Hugo sighed. "Where's Leo Newdanardo when you need him?" he asked.

Tavi laughed humorlessly. "Where, indeed?"

Eighty-Seven

"I just want you to know, that no matter what you might've heard, it's not true. I swear to God it's not."

Felix was in his master's workshop carving a regimental insignia on the lid of a fancy coffin, a lieutenant's coffin. He slowly turned around.

"What have you done now, Isabelle?" he said, a smile twitching at the corners of his mouth.

Isabelle, fretting the hem of her jacket, looked down at the sawdust-covered floor. "I got engaged to Hugo."

Felix's chisel hit the coffin lid with a loud thud. *"What?"*

Isabelle's head snapped up. "But it's not my fault!"

Two other men working in the shop lifted their heads, casting curious glances in Isabelle's direction.

Felix, his cheeks coloring, grabbed Isabelle's hand and pulled her after him. Through the long workshop, past coffins on trestles, and workbenches littered with tools, out of a door at the rear of the building and into the adjoining stables, where the master kept his delivery wagon and the team of workhorses that pulled it.

As soon as he closed the door behind them, Isabelle, talking a million miles a minute, told Felix what had happened, and how Tantine was pressuring both her and Hugo to marry within the week.

"We're going to come up with a way out of this, Felix. Me, Hugo, Tavi . . . we're all trying to figure out a solution," she said. Glancing at the open stable doors, she added, "I—I have to get back to the market. I left Hugo alone with the wagon and it's busy this morning . . ."

Ever since the breakfast at Madame's, two days ago, Isabelle had been desperate to see Felix, tell him what had happened, and that she had no intention of going through with betrothal, before he heard it from someone else. Tantine had been telling anyone who would listen about the wedding. She'd ordered a fancy cake from the baker, informed the priest that his services would shortly be required, and had even offered to pay for a wedding dress.

All the while Isabelle had been talking, Felix had been silent, his arms tight to his sides, his gaze slanted down. He didn't move, or speak, even after she'd finished.

"Felix? Felix, say something," she begged now, worried that he was hurt or angry.

"He'd make a decent husband."

Isabelle blinked, speechless.

"He's not so bad."

"Then *you* marry him!"

"All I'm saying is that maybe you should think about it."

Isabelle took a step back, devastated. She felt betrayed by his words, confused by the strange, sad look on his face. Only a moment ago, he'd appeared shocked to hear that she and Hugo were betrothed. Now he was telling her she should consider

339

going through with the marriage.

"Felix, why would you *say* that?" she asked. "Hugo doesn't love me. He loves Odette. And I don't love him. I—I love you."

Her words were a knife to his heart. She could see they were and it killed her.

"Should I not have said that? Is the boy supposed to say it first? Is that the rule?" she asked, utterly bewildered. "I never seem to be able to follow the rules. Maybe if I knew what they were I could, but I thought you . . . I thought we . . ."

"Sit down," Felix said, motioning to a wooden bench.

"I'm *not* marrying Hugo!" she said angrily, tears smarting behind her eyes.

"All right, Isabelle. You don't have to. You *won't* have to."

What does he mean by that? Why is he being so strange? she wondered.

Felix soon answered her questions.

As she sat, he reached into his vest and pulled out a small leather purse, tightly cinched across the top. He knelt down by her legs, opened the purse, and poured its contents into her lap.

Six shiny gold coins glinted up at her like a promise.

"Take them," he said. "It's enough to get yourself to Rome. To get your sister and mother there, too. You can find a small room. Live cheaply. You'll be safe there, Isabelle. Far away from this war."

"What do you mean *Take them?* Why would I take your money? And why did you say *I'd* be safe? What about you?"

"I'm not going to Italy."

Isabelle's head started to spin. "I—I don't understand, Felix. Just a few days ago, you said you *were* going. You said you wanted me to come with you . . ."

Felix looked down. "Yes, I did. But things have changed."

"You're regretting it. You don't want me. You don't love—"

Felix cut her off. "I do love you. I always have and I always will," he said fiercely. "More than my life."

"Then *why*?"

Felix took her hands in his. His blue eyes found hers.

"Isabelle," he said. "I enlisted."

Eighty-Eight

It was suicide.

Felix was a dreamer, an artist, not a fighter.

Isabelle tried to pull away. She tried to reason with him, but he tightened his grip on her hands and would not let her speak.

"I had no choice," he said. "Not after Malleval. I can barely work. I can't sleep. I see the dead in my dreams."

Isabelle remembered the smell of smoke in the air, the bodies in the field.

"Can you blame me?" he asked her.

Her anger, her arguments—they all fell away. "No," she said. "I can't."

"Remember your book? *An Illustrated History of the World's Greatest Military Commanders*? In all the stories we read, the best warriors went to war reluctantly. Volkmar is a different creature."

"He's not a warrior, he's a murderer," Isabelle said, her voice hardening.

"What if he raids Saint-Michel? How could I live with myself if I did nothing to stop him?"

"When do you leave?" she asked.

"In four days."

Isabelle felt the breath go out of her. "So soon?" she said when she could speak again.

"The recruiting sergeant wanted me right away, but I told him I needed a little time. I have a coffin to finish. A hand, too. And a general for my army of wooden soldiers."

Isabelle looked down so that Felix wouldn't see her eyes welling. The gold coins were still in her lap. She scooped them up, dropped them into the purse and cinched it shut. "I'll wait for you. You'll come back. You *will*," she said, handing it back to him.

But he wouldn't take it.

"You've seen the wagonloads of wounded coming back to camp just like I have," he said. "And the wooden crosses blooming in the fields next to it. We both know I'm not much good with a rifle."

"Felix, no, don't say these things," she pleaded, leaning her head against his.

His words hollowed her out. She had just found him, and now she was losing him again. Could the fates be so cruel?

"Go, Isabelle. Go for both of us. Leave Saint-Michel. And cows and cabbages. Leave Hugo and a life you don't want. There's nothing here for you. There never was."

"There was you."

Felix let go of her hands. He stood. His eyes were shiny, and he didn't want her to see. He was a soldier now. And soldiers didn't cry.

"Will I see you again? Before you go?" she asked.

"It's hard, Isabelle," he said.

She nodded. She understood. It *was* hard to say goodbye to the person you loved. It was excruciating.

"I'll write," he said. "If I can."

While you can, you mean, Isabelle thought. *Before a bullet finds you.*

He turned to go, but she snatched at his arm and stopped him. Then she took his face in her hands and kissed him. Kissed him until she'd filled her heart with him. And her soul. Kissed him enough to last her a lifetime.

When she finally stepped away from him, her cheeks were wet, but not from her own tears. Felix shook his head; he pulled her back. Crushed her to him. And then he was gone. And Isabelle was all alone.

She pictured Felix on a battlefield. Running through mud and smoke. She heard the sound of cannon firing, the thunder of charging horses, battle cries and death screams. She saw Volkmar, crazed by bloodlust, swinging his fearsome sword.

Wrenching emotions took hold of her. Heartbreak. Anger. Terror. Grief.

And one more. One that had appeared in a haze of green, like a bad fairy furious that she hadn't been invited to the party. One that Isabelle was quite familiar with, though she didn't understand why she felt it now.

Jealousy.

Eighty-Nine

"There used to be so many spiders in here. Now I never see one. Don't you think that's strange? No spiders? In a *stable*?"

"Incredibly strange, Hugo," said Isabelle distractedly as she hung up Martin's harness.

She and Hugo had just returned from the market. They'd driven the empty wagon out to the fields, ready to be loaded again in the morning; then they'd walked Martin back to the stables. After putting him in his stall with oats and fresh water, they cleaned his tack and put it away.

Hugo frowned. "You've been very quiet. You barely said a word the whole way home from the market. Is something wrong?"

Yes, whatever was left of my heart was just ripped out, Hugo, she thought. *That's what's wrong.*

All she could think about was Felix and the gold coins he'd given her. She hadn't decided what to do with them. At first, she thought she would hide them and hold on to them, as if by not spending them she could make sure he returned from the war.

She would marry Hugo and sacrifice her happiness if it meant Felix survived. But as she thought about it, she saw that holding on to a bag of coins couldn't guarantee his life, and that she would be sacrificing Hugo's happiness, too. And Odette's. Maybe Tavi's and Maman's. And she realized she didn't have the right to do that.

By the time Martin turned up the drive to the LeBenêts', she'd made a decision—she would tell Hugo and Tavi about the money and they would figure out what to do with it together.

"Hugo, stay here for a minute, will you?" she said now.

"Why? Where are you going?"

"To get Tavi. I'll be right back."

Isabelle found her sister in the dairy house. She made her come with her back to the stables, then she led them both into an empty horse stall and told them to sit down in the hay.

"Why are we hiding in a horse stall?" Hugo asked.

"So no one sees us. Or hears us."

Tavi gave her a questioning look. "This is all very mysterious, Isabelle."

Isabelle waited until they'd settled, then said, "Felix gave us a way out of the wedding. If we want to take it."

"Yes!" Hugo shouted, leaping to his feet. "We do! We absolutely do!"

"Be quiet!" Isabelle hissed, grabbing his arm and pulling him back down.

When he was seated again, Isabelle told them what had happened. Both reassured her that Felix would come back, and both felt that using the money to leave Saint-Michel was the only way to stop the wedding.

Isabelle listened to them, but still felt uneasy with the decision. "There might be one other way out," she said.

"Go on," Tavi urged.

"I could use the money to rent rooms for us right here, in Saint-Michel," Isabelle offered. "If we do that, Hugo and I still wouldn't have to marry, but you and I and Maman would have shelter."

Tavi crossed her arms. "Yes, let's rent rooms. Smack in the middle of the village, if possible," she said. "It will make it so much easier for Cecile and the baker's wife and whoever it was that burned our house down to call us *ugly* and throw things at us. Why, we can have our windows broken every day!"

Isabelle, stung by the sarcasm, tossed her a dirty look.

"Tavi's right. The people here won't forget. And they'll never let *you* forget," said Hugo. "Start over, Isabelle. Somewhere new. That's what Felix wants for you. It's why he gave you the money. Can't you see that?"

Isabelle knew Hugo was right. And so was Tavi; the abuse would never end if they stayed here.

"It will be hard getting to Italy, Tavi. And once we're there, we'll have to live frugally to make the money last. One room for all of us. Few pleasures or luxuries," Isabelle cautioned.

Tavi shrugged. "It might be hard, but it won't be bad. For me, at least," she said. "In fact, it will be wonderful. Every bit as wonderful as life here, on the farm, has been. Maybe even more so."

"*Wonderful?*" Isabelle repeated, incredulous. "In case you haven't noticed, you've been living in a hayloft. Milking cows and cutting cabbages and digging potatoes all day long. What is wonderful about any of that?"

Tavi examined her work-roughened hands. "My gowns are burned, my satin shoes and silk corsets destroyed. Parties and balls are a thing of the past. Suitors no longer come to my door. The world calls me ugly and stays away."

Isabelle's heart ached at her sister's words, but then Tavi raised her head and Isabelle saw that she wasn't sad; she was smiling.

"And so the world sets me free," Tavi said, her smile deepening. "The days are hard, yes. But at night I have a candle and quiet and my books. Which is all I've ever wanted. So, yes. *Wonderful*. Don't you see? A pretty girl must please the world. But an ugly girl? She's free to please herself."

"All right, then," Isabelle said, swallowing the lump in her throat. "We'll go."

Tavi grinned. Hugo threw his arms around her. And then the three of them immediately set about making a plan.

Isabelle would not hear of leaving Nero behind, so she, Tavi, and Maman would ride to Italy. She'd managed to salvage two saddles from the stables when the Maison Douleur burned; Hugo said she could take an old one of theirs, too. They would sleep at inns along the way but would need to buy food, canteens for water, and oilskins, in case it rained. New dresses, too, as theirs were little more than rags, and warm things for the cooler weather. It was September now; it would be well into autumn by the time they arrived at their destination.

Isabelle had moved the other two horses she'd rescued from the slaughter yard to the pasture at the Maison Douleur to make Madame happier. They had filled out on the sweet grass there and had built up a bit of muscle. Tavi could ride one,

Maman the other. Martin would have to stay behind. Isabelle choked up at the thought, but he was too old to make the trip.

"I'm not going unless you swear on your life to take good care of Martin," she said to Hugo.

"I will."

"*Swear*, Hugo, or I'll stay here and marry you!"

Hugo swore, quickly and vehemently.

Tavi estimated it would take them four days to assemble their supplies, which meant they could leave on Friday—one day before the wedding. The girls would take turns going to market with Hugo and shop for provisions while they were there. They decided to say nothing of their plans to Maman—who could not be trusted to keep secrets—Tantine, or Hugo's mother. Avara and Tantine would likely be furious when they learned that the wedding was off and might make Isabelle and her family leave the farm before they were ready.

They rose and left the horse stall, and the stables, together. They were resolute, determined to go about their chores and keep to their routines in order to raise no suspicions.

They had no idea as they walked out into the bright afternoon that someone else had been with them in the stables. Had they once looked up, they would have seen her, a black-haired girl sitting in the rafters, her thin legs dangling.

Watching. Listening.

Eating spiders.

Ninety

Isabelle stared up at the ceiling beams of the hayloft.

Maman and Tavi were asleep, she could hear their steady breathing, but she couldn't sleep, no matter how hard she tried. Even though she was only wearing a thin chemise, she was sweating. It was hot. The air was still. She'd tossed and turned for the last several hours, unable to get comfortable.

Sighing, she got up, crossed the room, and sat down on the floor by the hayloft's open doors, hoping a breeze might blow in to provide some relief.

The moon was nearly full. Its rays fell over the farm, illuminating the fields and orchards. The pond and pastures. The chicken coop. The dairy house. The woodpile.

And, to Isabelle's surprise, a fox. She was sitting on the chopping block, next to the ax, her tail wrapped neatly around her feet.

"Your Grace," Isabelle said, nodding to her.

With a sinking feeling, she realized why Tanaquill had come. "You've heard, haven't you? You know I'm leaving."

The fox nodded. The gesture was small, quick, yet in it Isabelle read the fairy queen's displeasure and disappointment.

Isabelle bent her head, ashamed. "I found two of the pieces," she said. "I found Nero. And I'll never let anyone take him from me again. I found Felix . . . just in time to lose him again." Her voice caught. The tears she held back all day came, and this time she couldn't stop them. "He's not coming back, Tanaquill. No matter what Tavi and Hugo say. He's too gentle to drive a bayonet through another human being." She wiped her eyes with the back of her hand. "Ella is the third piece, isn't she? I tried to see her, tried to tell her that I'm sorry. But I didn't. And now I'll never get the chance."

She raised her head; her eyes found the fox's again.

"I failed, I'm afraid. I didn't get all the pieces. Is that why my heart hurts so?" She pressed her palm to her heart, anguished. "Something inside it gnaws and gnaws, and sometimes I think it will never stop, that it will torment me until I'm in my grave. What is it, this pain? Do you know?"

The fox made no reply.

"Ah, well," Isabelle said with a broken laugh. "I guess I was never meant to be pretty, and ugly girls don't get happily-ever-afters, do they?" She went silent for a moment, then said, "Thank you for your gifts. The sword and shield saved my life. It looks like I'm not going to find out what the seedpod does, but I'd like to keep all three if I may. To remember you. And the linden tree. And home."

The fox nodded. And then, in the blink of an eye, she was gone.

Isabelle knew she would never see the fairy queen again, and the knowledge was heavy inside her. She would never see the Wildwood again, or Saint-Michel. The uneasiness she felt about leaving deepened into a certainty that leaving was wrong. But she knew what Hugo and Tavi wanted. Felix, too. And the decision was made now; she would have to go through with it.

"What else can I do?" she asked the darkness.

That's when a face, small and furry, appeared in the open doorway.

Ninety-One

Isabelle scrambled backward, frightened.

Then she saw it was only Nelson, dressed in his customary pearls.

"You gave me such a scare!" she scolded in a whisper, so as not to wake anyone. "What are you doing here? And how did you get those pearls back? I gave them to the diva!"

Nelson thrust out his paw. He was clutching a small piece of paper, folded over several times.

Isabelle took it from him and unfolded it. Swirls and curlicues of gold ink decorated the border. In the centre was an invitation, written in a swooping script.

His Excellency the Marquis de la Chance
requests your presence at the Château Rigolade
for the premiere of his new theatrical extravaganza,
*An Illustrated History of the World's Greatest
Military Commanders*.

"How strange," she said slowly. "That's the title of a book. One I owned a long time ago." She looked up at the monkey, perplexed. "How can that be?"

Nelson looked away. He fingered his pearls.

"When is this happening? Tomorrow?"

Nelson grabbed the piece of paper back and shook it in Isabelle's face. She looked at it again, more closely this time. At the very bottom was one word: *Now.*

Isabelle squeezed her eyes shut. "This is a dream. I'm dreaming. I *must* be," she said.

She opened her eyes. Nelson was still there. He grabbed a lock of her hair and pulled it so hard that she yelped.

"Fine. I'm *not* dreaming," she said, extricating her hair from his grasp. "But it's the middle of the night. And the château is miles away. And it's a *château* and the marquis is a marquis and he'll have invited other people. And they'll all be very important and beautifully attired. I have one dress, and it's full of holes. I can't go. I'd only be an embarrassment."

Nelson regarded Isabelle; then he regarded his pearls. He heaved an anxious sigh, unhooked his necklace, and handed it to her. Isabelle was deeply touched. She had a feeling those pearls meant the world to the little creature.

"You'd let me borrow them? Really?"

Nelson looked longingly at his treasure, now clutched in her hand. Isabelle could see he was struggling with his decision, but he nodded.

"All right, then," she said, hooking the pearls around her own neck. "Let's go."

She was off to see a play. At a marquis's estate, with a monkey, in the middle of the night.

"I *am* still dreaming," she said as she pulled her dress on over her head. "At least I hope I am, because if I'm not, I've lost my mind."

Ninety-Two

The moon lit the way as Nero carried Isabelle and Nelson over meadows and hills to the grounds of the Château Rigolade.

They'd taken a shortcut and emerged through the woods at the back of the château. Isabelle was surprised to find that the building was completely dark.

An eerie yellow light was emanating from another part of the property, though—the clearing behind the château. Isabelle remembered that that was where Felix had built the marquis's theater. She turned Nero towards it.

As they drew close to the structure, Isabelle saw that it was footlights casting the glow. They illuminated the stage, with its red velvet curtains and its garlands of fresh roses twining across the arch.

Strangely, the stage itself, and the grounds around it, were deserted. Isabelle had expected dozens of dazzling people talking and laughing. Jewels bobbing on swells of cleavage. Hair rising like swirled meringue. The rustle of silk. Gilded chairs set out in rows.

But only a single chair stood in front of the stage. A chill shuddered through her. *It's as if the marquis was expecting me, and only me*, she thought uneasily.

Nelson jumped down from her shoulder to Nero's rump to the ground and scampered off. Isabelle got down, too, then walked past the chair to the foot of the stage.

"Marquis de la Chance?" she called out.

He didn't answer. No one did. Isabelle realized that she was in a strange place, in the dead of night, alone.

"I think we'd better go back," she said to Nero.

That's when a man in a mask stepped out from behind the curtains.

Ninety-Three

Isabelle backed away from the stage warily. Her hand tightened on Nero's reins.

The man bowed to her. Isabelle relaxed as she realized it was the marquis. Though he was masked and in costume, she recognized his long braids. He straightened, then began to speak, in a deep, resonant voice.

Greetings to you, honored guest.
We're here at Chance's own behest.
Tarry now.
We beg you, stay.
Indulge us as we give our play.

These are not the tales you've heard
In spoken verse, or written word.
Of kings and emperors,
Warlords, knights,
Slaughtering enemies in their sights.

These are tales little told,
Of generals mighty, rulers bold,

Whose courage, cunning,
Wit and skill,
Were partnered with an iron will.

Heroes all, but most unknown.
Reduced by time to dust and bone.
Yet on this stage,
They live again.
Such power has our playwright's pen.

Hear their stories, all but lost.
Watch them rise and bear the cost.
Some will lose
and some will win.
Sit now. Watch our play begin.

As the last words left Chance's lips, the footlights blazed high, startling Isabelle so badly that she stumbled backward and fell into the chair. The curtain rose. Trumpets blared. Drums pounded. Cymbals clashed. Isabelle clutched the arms of the chair, her heart thumping. She looked around for Nero. In her fright, she'd dropped his reins. She soon saw that he was only a few yards away, unperturbed by the noise, happily munching the marquis's lawn. His calmness calmed her. She turned back to the stage.

The curtains had opened to reveal a book. It was standing upright and was at least eight feet tall. *An Illustrated History of the World's Greatest Military Commanders* was written in huge letters on the cover.

Did the marquis know she'd owned a copy of that book,

and that it had meant the world to her? Or was this all just a coincidence?

As she watched, entranced, the cover slowly swung open. Pages turned, as if flipped by an invisible finger, then stopped. The book stood open to the chapter on ancient Rome's most esteemed generals. And then a door, cut into the page, opened and a man dressed in a leather breastplate and short cloth skirt stepped out of it. On his head he wore a steel helmet with a red plume. In his hand was a fearsome sword.

Isabelle recognized him. He was Scipio Africanus. She'd looked at his portrait, and pored over his story, a thousand times.

The pages turned again, and Scipio was joined by Achilles. Then Genghis Khan. Peter the Great. And Sun Tzu. All were dressed and armed for battle. Together they strode to the front of the stage, weapons raised, shields aloft.

The Roman spoke first, delivering his words in a booming stage voice.

I, Scipio, brave and strong,
Waged a battle bloody and long,
Against my foes on Carthage's plains.
Their defeat was proud Rome's gain.

Next came Achilles.

In war's own furnace I was forged,
And on my enemies' blood I've gorged.
A son of Ares, made for glory,
All quake to hear Achilles' story.

Then it was Genghis Khan's turn.

A Mongol conqueror without equal
A warrior king, a god to his people—

"Oh, *enough!*" declared a voice from offstage.

Isabelle looked for its source. She saw the curtain at the right ripple, then heard sharp, indignant footsteps. A few seconds later, a woman emerged from the wings.

She was slender and straight-backed, with vivid red hair styled high on her head. A stiff lace collar framed her face. She wore a white gown embroidered with pearls, emeralds, and rubies. In one jeweled hand, she carried a bucket of paint; in the other, a brush.

Peter the Great stepped forward. He puffed out his chest. "Who are *you*, madam?" he demanded.

"Elizabeth I. Move," she said, waving him and the others aside with her paintbrush.

Flabbergasted and sputtering, they did as she bade, half shuffling to the right side of the stage, half to the left.

Elizabeth walked through the path they'd cleared and up to the towering book. She kicked the cover with a well-shod foot. It slammed shut. Then she dipped her brush into the bucket, crossed out the word *History*, dipped the brush again, and wrote *HER STORY* in its place.

Ninety-Four

Isabelle sat forward in her chair, mesmerized.

"This wasn't in the book," she whispered.

As she watched, Elizabeth walked to the front of the stage and addressed her.

"I am the daughter of England's Henry VIII," she said. "I was a disappointment to him because I was not the son he wished for. I survived his neglect, my half-sister's hatred, attacks on my country and attempts on my life, to become the best monarch England has ever seen." She smiled smugly, then added, "Or ever will."

The book receded. The footlights blazed again. The actors playing Scipio and his fellows crouched low, using their hands to cast shadows of horses and knights on the walls.

A din rose of shouted commands, shrill whinnies, a fanfare. There was a cannon blast, a flash of light, and then the theater's left wall fell flat to the ground with a boom, followed by its right. The back wall fell next, carrying the arch with it. And then, before Isabelle's astonished eyes, the shadows came to life. Warhorses in chain mail stomped and snorted. Officers sat astride them. Soldiers massed next to them, carrying bows, pikes, swords, and halberds. The oak-sheltered clearing became an army camp on the banks of the River Thames.

And Elizabeth, standing in a gown only a moment ago, now rode in on a white charger, wearing a steel breastplate. She held her reins in one hand, a sword in the other. Her red hair streamed down her back.

"Tilbury camp, 1588!" she shouted at Isabelle. "The Spanish king sends his Armada, the most powerful naval force in the world, to invade my country. His nephew, the Duke of Parma, joins him. They have fearsome warships, troops, and weapons." She grinned. "But England has *me*!"

She spurred her horse on and rode to her troops.

"My loving people!" she addressed them. "I am come amongst you . . . being resolved, in the midst and heat of the battle, to live and die amongst you all; to lay down for God, and for my kingdom, and my people, my honor, and my blood, even in the dust!"

As Isabelle watched, spellbound, the Thames swelled into a roiling blue sea and a naval battle commenced. Swift English warships fired broadsides at the Spanish vessels. Cannon boomed. Ships burned. Smoke billowed. When it finally cleared, the Armada had been routed. England was victorious.

The scene changed. Bells pealed as Elizabeth rode through the streets of London. Roses were strewn in her path. She reached Isabelle and dismounted. A groom led her horse away, the cheers died down. "The victory was England's greatest, and mine," Elizabeth said. "But there are more battles. More wars. More victories. Not told in any book."

She waved her hand. Trumpets blared. And then a woman

walked out of the trees towards her. And then another. And another. Until there were dozens. Scores. Hundreds. When they had all assembled, Elizabeth introduced them one by one.

"Yennenga, a Dagomba princess," she announced, and a young Ghanaian woman, wearing a tunic and trousers of woven red, black, and white cloth, stepped forward. She was carrying a javelin. London gave way to lush plains. Two lions walked out of the tall grass and sat at either side of her.

"I commanded my own battalion and fought against my country's enemies," she said. "No one could match me on a horse."

She threw her javelin high. It pierced the night sky and exploded into a silvery fountain of shooting stars.

Isabelle could hardly breathe, she was so excited. All her life, she'd been told that women rulers were only figureheads, that women did not fight or lead soldiers in war. She stood on her chair, the better to see these remarkable creatures.

"Abbakka Chowta," Elizabeth said as a young woman from India wearing a pink silk sari walked to the centre of the stage. "A woman who shot flaming arrows from her saddle, a woman so brave she was named Abhaya Rani, the fearless queen."

Abhaya Rani nocked an arrow into the bow she was carrying, aimed for the sky, and released it. It burst into brilliant blue flames. She smiled at Isabelle. "I fought my country's invaders for forty years. I was captured but died as I lived, fighting for freedom."

Isabelle thought her heart might burst. One by one, queens, pirates, empresses, and generals from all the corners of the world told their stories, bowed their heads, and left the stage.

They were not pretty, these women. Pretty did not begin to describe them.

They were shrewd. Powerful. Wily. Proud. Dangerous.

They were strong.

They were brave.

They were beautiful.

Finally, after what felt to Isabelle like only minutes, but was actually hours, only Elizabeth was left on the stage.

"Strange, isn't it, how stories that are never told are the ones we most need to hear," she said, then she bowed, too, and walked off into the darkness.

Isabelle realized the play was ending. "No," she whispered hungrily. "Don't go."

The marquis, still wearing his mask, reappeared. In one hand, he held a heavy silver candlestick with a flaming taper in it. He stepped forward and began to speak.

Now our queens have told their stories,
Of battles won, of conquests, glories.
But power is a treacherous thing,
Its bite is sweet, its kiss can sting,
And, unless I'm much mistaken,
It's never given, always taken.

Each queen was once a girl like you.
Told who to be and what to do.
Not pretty, not pleasing, far too rough.
Lacking, less than, not enough.

Till wounded subjects, anguished dead,
Mattered more than things that others said.
Then, like a flag, her will unfurled.
Go now, girl. Remake the world.

The marquis bowed. He raised his candle to his lips and blew it out.

Most of the footlights had burned out, a few still glowed faintly. In their light, Isabelle could see that the marquis and his players were gone. The stage was empty and silent. All Isabelle could hear was the sound of her heart beating.

The spell of the play was broken. Isabelle looked around and realized she was still standing on the chair. She stepped down, her hands clenched. The excitement and wonder and sheer joy she'd felt only moments ago ebbed away. Grief, agonizing and deep, filled the void it left.

"Why show me this?" she shouted wretchedly to the darkness. "Why show me something I can never have? Something I can never be?"

No one was there. Isabelle was talking to herself.

She unhooked Nelson's pearls from around her neck and placed them on the seat of the velvet chair where he would be sure to find them.

A moment later, she and Nero were galloping back over the marquis's grounds. Just before she disappeared into the woods, Isabelle looked back. At the ruined stage. The dark château.

"Damn you," she whispered. *"Damn you."*

Ninety-Five

Tavi stretched tall, then bent to unknot her skirts.

"When I leave here, I never want to see another cabbage. As long as I live," she said.

Isabelle agreed with her. The day in the field, harvesting under the hot sun, had been long and exhausting. Isabelle's dress was soaked with sweat. Her boots were filthy from treading in the black dirt. She was looking forward to dunking herself in the duck pond, and later, falling into her hayloft bed.

She'd been tired all day. Last night had been unrestful. She'd had such a strange dream. Nelson had appeared in the hayloft. Then she'd taken a midnight ride to the Château Rigolade, where the marquis and his friends had presented a play.

The dream had felt so real, but it wasn't. It couldn't be. All those women . . . leading armies into battle, fighting for their realms . . . a fantasy cooked up by her vivid imagination, that's all. A fond childhood wish.

"You need a pistol. We didn't think of that. You're three women traveling alone."

Hugo, who had been working one field over digging potatoes, had joined Isabelle and Tavi. His words dispelled the lingering images of Isabelle's dream.

"If there are three of us, then we're not alone," Tavi said.

Hugo looked at her as if she were an idiot. "You don't have a man with you. Of course you're alone. You can buy a secondhand pistol in the village while we're at the market tomorrow. Use some of Felix's money. You'll need gunpowder and bullets, too."

Tavi picked up her knife and the basket she used to carry cabbages to the wagon. Isabelle did the same. Hugo rested his spade on his shoulder, and together the three walked to the barn, talking about their secret plan the whole way. Isabelle and Tavi would leave in three days, and there was still a good deal to do.

As they rounded the side of the farmhouse, Isabelle's head was bent towards Tavi; she was concentrating on what her sister was saying. Her gaze was on the ground.

Had she been paying more attention, she might've seen the signs of trouble up ahead.

The many hoofprints in the dirt.

The blur of blue uniforms by the stables.

The tall, imperious Colonel Cafard eyeing the horse that had been brought from the pasture on his command.

A black horse. Her horse.

Nero.

Ninety-Six

It was only when Isabelle rounded the corner of the barn that she realized something was very wrong.

Nero was in the yard in front of it, wearing his bridle. He was wild-eyed and rearing. A young soldier was struggling to hold on to his lead.

"Let go of him!" Isabelle shouted. She ran to the man and snatched the lead from his hands.

The soldier hadn't seen her coming. He stumbled backward, startled, and fell on his rear end. There were others with him. They hooted and laughed. Tantine, Avara, and Maman were standing together nearby, worried expressions on their faces.

"Looks like the girl's even feistier than the horse!" one of the soldiers shouted. "Maybe she needs a good crack across the backside, too!"

Isabelle whirled on him. "*Too?* Did you hit my horse, you jackass?"

The soldier stopped laughing. His eyes turned mean. "Maybe she needs a good crack across the mouth," he said. "And maybe I'm just the one to give it to her."

"Isabelle!" Tavi called out, alarmed. She'd caught up with

her. Hugo was close on her heels.

But Isabelle didn't hear her. She was focused on her adversary. Still gripping Nero's lead, she took a step towards the man.

"Maybe you are. Get a crop. I'll get one, too. We'll find out." When the soldier made no move, she cocked her head. "Scared? I'll make it a fair fight. I'll tie one hand behind my back."

A ripple of laughter rose from the others.

"Hey, isn't she one of the ugly stepsisters?" the one who'd fallen on his backside called out.

"It's her. She's ugly all right," said the one Isabelle had challenged.

The familiar shame seared Isabelle, but this time she didn't blush. She didn't lower her head. She looked him in the eye and said, "Every bit as ugly as a man who beats a defenseless animal."

"Isabelle, *please*!" Tavi hissed.

Isabelle ignored her. "Why are you here? What were you doing with my horse?" she asked her antagonist.

Another man, one wearing a bicorne hat and black boots that were so shiny, he could see his own reflection in the toes when he looked down at them—which he did quite often—stepped forward. "I'm afraid he's my horse now, mademoiselle," he said.

Isabelle looked him up and down. "Who the devil are you?" she asked, tightening her grip on Nero's lead.

Tantine was immediately at her side. "This is Colonel Cafard, Isabelle, the officer in charge of the army camp near the village."

"That doesn't give him the right to take my horse," Isabelle said.

"Actually, it does," the colonel said. "The army is short of mounts. They're the first thing the enemy shoots at. We're commandeering any sound animal we can find."

"By whose orders?" Isabelle asked, panic rising inside her.

"The king's," the colonel replied, clearly growing tired of the exchange. "Will that do?"

"Enough, Isabelle!" Tantine hissed. "Give the creature up before we're all hauled off to jail!" She pried the lead from Isabelle's fist and handed it to a soldier. Then she pulled her away. "We're at war, you foolish girl!" she scolded.

Isabelle twisted free of her grasp. She ran to Cafard, ready to plead, ready to drop down on her knees and beg him not to take her horse. Let his soldiers laugh and jeer. She didn't care. All she could see in her mind's eye was her beloved horse falling on a battlefield, his side ripped open by a bullet.

"Please, Colonel," she said, pressing her hands together. "Please don't—"

And then Tantine was beside her again, sinking her fingers into Isabelle's arm, her grip as strong as iron. "Please don't let Volkmar win," she said, drowning her out. "Use the horse to defeat him. We are honored to help our king."

Cafard gave her a curt nod. Then he strode off towards his own mount, a cowed-looking chestnut mare. The horse shied slightly as he swung himself into his saddle. Isabelle's expert eyes swept over the animal, looking for a reason. She soon found it. There was blood on the mare's sides, behind the stirrups. She looked at Cafard; he was wearing sharp silver spurs. Isabelle's heart lurched.

"Colonel!" she cried, running after him.

Cafard turned. His brittle smile couldn't hide his irritation. "Yes?"

"Please don't use spurs on him. He listens if you're kind to him. And he'll do anything for an apple. He loves them."

Cafard's smile thinned. "My men love apples, too. They rarely get them these days, yet they still do what I tell them." He nodded at Nero. "That creature is a horse, mademoiselle, and he will be treated like one. Intractable animals must be made tractable."

Nero whinnied loudly; he tossed his head, trying yet again to tear the lead away from the soldier holding it. When that didn't work, he spun around and kicked at him.

An image flashed into Isabelle's head. Of Elizabeth on her white charger. Of Abhaya Rani, shooting flaming arrows from astride her mount. Neither woman would have let *anyone* take her horse.

"He's hungry, sir," she said. "He usually gets his supper now. If you let me feed him, he'll be manageable for the trip to your camp."

Cafard looked at the unruly horse, and at his men stumbling over themselves as they tried to get him under control.

"You have ten minutes," Cafard said. Then he barked at his men to hand the horse over to her.

Isabelle whispered to Nero to calm him. Head down, she led him to the stables.

Had the soldiers seen the determined set of her mouth and the fire in her eyes, they never would have let her.

Ninety-Seven

Isabelle walked to the barn at a normal pace. To do anything else would raise suspicion.

The barn had two large doorways—the one she and Nero had just passed through, and one directly across from it—which led out to the pasture. A large open area spanned the space between the two doors. To the right of it were horse stalls; to the left, stanchions for the cows.

Isabelle walked slowly, veering a little to the right, as if she were going to lead Nero into a stall. As she did, she cast a casual glance over her shoulder. Three of the soldiers were talking to the colonel. A few were milling about. One was watching her. She caught his gaze; he held it. She wiped her eyes, hoping to appear as if she were crying. It worked. The soldier, embarrassed, turned back to his companions.

Within seconds, she and Nero were through the far door. She tensed as they walked out of the barn, expecting to hear shouts or the sound of footsteps. But it was quiet. No one had seen them.

An old milk can stood under the eaves of the barn. Isabelle used it as a mounting block. Once on Nero's back, she knotted the loose end of his lead into his halter. It would serve as reins. There was no time to get proper ones, or his bridle and saddle. When she was finished with the knot, she quietly urged Nero forward. He was across the hardpan that separated the barn from the pasture in a few strides.

Isabelle knew that as long as she kept the barn between herself and the soldiers, they could not see her ride off. Anger, blind and beyond reason, drove her. Nero was *hers*; she would not allow Cafard to take him.

She gripped his improvised reins and clucked her tongue. As if he understood her purpose, Nero jumped the wooden fence that enclosed the pasture and landed almost noiselessly in the grass.

Isabelle touched her heels to his sides, and he was off. Within seconds, he reached the far side of the pasture. He sailed over the fence again, and then they were streaking across a wide meadow to the forest. She looked back, just for an instant, as they reached the treeline. No one was after her. Not yet. She probably had another minute or two before Cafard told one of his men to see what was taking her so long, but it was already too late; they'd never find her. They didn't know the Wildwood like she did.

Isabelle faced forward now. The woods were dense, and navigating them commanded all her attention. Her hands were shaking, her heart pounding.

She was headed to the Devil's Hollow.

Ninety-Eight

Some people are afraid of the forest; others only feel truly safe under its dense, sheltering canopy.

Isabelle was among the latter. The sights and scents of the forest were familiar and comforting to her. She had spent the happiest days of her life in the Wildwood.

After she and Nero had escaped, they'd ridden hard through the trees for a good half hour to put distance between themselves and Colonel Cafard; then Isabelle had dismounted, unknotted the makeshift reins, and walked the horse. Dusk was falling as they reached the path that would take them into the Devil's Hollow, a forlorn wooded canyon. Isabelle wanted to be down in the Hollow before dark. The path was treacherous when you could see it; suicide when you couldn't.

The Wildwood covered the gently sloping south side of a small mountain and abruptly gave way to the mountain's craggy, cliff-laden north side. The narrow path to the Hollow zigzagged down the north face, obscured in parts by thorny, scrubby shrubs. It snaked through rocks and boulders at the bottom, and ended at a river. It had once been used by travelers to Saint-Michel, but as the village had grown, and the roads leading to it had improved, the path through the Devil's Hollow had fallen out of use. The old wives of Saint-Michel said the place was haunted.

Isabelle and Nero picked their way carefully down the path and through the rocks. When they finally reached the river, Isabelle's stomach growled loudly. She realized that she hadn't eaten anything since noon, and it had to be nearly eight by now. Nero hadn't eaten his nightly ration of oats. Nor would he, for she hadn't packed any. She had no food and no money with which to buy some. Felix's money was back in the hayloft. So were all the provisions she and Tavi had managed to assemble. She reached into her pocket, hoping against hope that she'd stuffed a crust of bread in it. Instead, her hand found Tanaquill's gifts. The seedpod pricked her fingers.

Something else pricked her, too—her conscience. She was walking slowly to make sure Nero could find his footing, but now she stopped, racked by an agonizing uncertainty.

"What have I done?" she said aloud.

She'd been so determined to save Nero's life that never for a second had she considered what impact her rash actions might have on anyone else's. She'd tricked a colonel of the French army. What if he took his wrath out on her family? Or the LeBenêts and Tantine?

Isabelle saw that she'd let her anger drive her actions, once again. Just as she had with Ella. The baker's wife. The orphans. She'd been selfish. She didn't want Nero to die, but there were mothers, wives, and children who didn't want their sons, husbands, and fathers to die, either. Men were giving their lives to the fight; Felix might well give his.

Groaning, she buried her face in Nero's neck. She wanted to be a better person. She wanted to change, yet here she was, endangering people who needed her, running away from her responsibilities.

"I have to go back," she said, her heart heavy. It was the right thing, the only thing, to do.

It was just as those words left her lips that she heard the voices, drifting towards her across the river, from deep within the trees.

She stood perfectly still, listening. Fear plucked at her nerves. Were the old ones right? Was the Hollow haunted? Or could it be a band of outlaws or deserters?

Or maybe the voices belonged to Cafard's men, out hunting for her? No, that wasn't possible. There was another way to get to the Hollow, but it involved a long ride around the mountain on a narrow, rutted road. It was unlikely his soldiers could have gotten down it so quickly.

Isabelle waited for the voices to speak again, but Nero's breathing was the only sound she could hear.

"Stay here, boy," she said, looping his lead over his neck.

She ventured closer to the water and looked across it. In the dying light, she could make out the far riverbank, and dense line of trees along it, but nothing else. Here and there leaves rustled, but that could be the breeze. Just when she'd convinced herself she'd imagined the voices, she heard them again. And then the strong smell of tobacco wafted to her.

Isabelle had never seen a ghost. She did not know much about them, but she was certain of one thing: Ghosts did not smoke cigars.

Ninety-Nine

Nelson crept quietly through the partly open window.

He dropped down to the bench underneath it, then threw an anxious glance back at Chance.

"Go!" Chance mouthed at him from outside the window. "Fetch the map!"

He could see it, open on Fate's table, from where he stood; the skull at the bottom was as black as ebony.

Fate, busy digging in her trunk, her back turned to the window, didn't see the little creature scamper across the floor.

But Losca, roosting on top of the wardrobe, did.

With an ugly shriek, she launched herself at him. The monkey jumped from the floor to the bed. The raven wheeled about and flew at him again. Nelson rolled across the bed, dodging her, then threw himself on her back.

Fate whirled around. Her eyes went to the tangled animals.

"What on *earth*—" she started to say, but a high, rusty screech cut her off. It was the hinge on the casement window. Chance had just climbed through it. He rushed to the table and the map lying rolled up upon it. But Fate got there first. She stood in front of it, blocking him, a long silver stiletto in her hand.

"Step aside. I don't want to fight you," Chance warned.

A viscious smile twisted Fate's lips. She snapped her wrist and a split second later, the stiletto was flying straight at his heart.

Chance leapt to the right. The stiletto sank with a *thuk* into the wall behind him. He was about to advance again, but at that instant, a fox leapt through the window. She lunged at the fighting animals. The monkey, terrified, catapulted himself into Chance's arms. The raven flew high, circled the room, then landed back on top of the wardrobe.

Growling and snapping, the fox jumped onto Fate's table. With a sweep of her tail, she sent Fate's inks flying. Bottles smashed on the floor; lurid colors seeped into the cracks between the boards. She jumped down, and a few seconds later, a woman stood where the fox had been, clutching the map in her hand.

"Enough," Tanaquill said, tucking the parchment deep within the folds of her cloak.

"That map is mine," Fate said, starting towards her. "Give it to me."

Tanaquill bared her teeth, snarling. "Come, crone. Take it," she dared her.

Chance stepped forward. "Keep the map, Tanaquill. But help Isabelle. Save her."

"The girl will make her next move herself. Neither of you will make it for her. There is only one person who can save Isabelle now . . . Isabelle."

With a swirl of red, she was through the open window and gone. Fate and Chance were left standing by themselves.

Chance pulled the stiletto out of the wall. He handed it back

378

to Fate. She put it down on the table, then looked around the room, at the havoc Tanaquill had wreaked. Losca was already down off the wardrobe, in her human form, cleaning up the broken glass.

"I have a bottle of port," Fate said with a sigh. "At least the fairy queen did not break that."

"A good vintage?"

"I am too old to drink bad ones."

Chance rocked back on his heels, weighing her offer. "I *do* enjoy a good port."

Fate crossed the room and dug in her trunk once more. A pair of hand-blown goblets emerged. A porcelain platter. The port. A box of dried figs dipped in dark chocolate. Roasted almonds flecked with salt. A hunk of crumbly Parmesan wrapped in waxed cloth.

"Do something useful," Fate said. "Pull the chairs up to the fire."

One chair, short with soft cushions, was already near the fireplace. Chance pushed it closer; then he carried over the wooden chair that stood by the table. He spied a stool and positioned it between them. Fate arranged the treats on the platter and set it on the stool. She poured two glasses of port and handed one to Chance.

"This changes nothing," she cautioned. "No quarter asked—"

"None given," Chance finished.

"The skull is jet black. I doubt she will survive the night."

"As long as she still breathes, there is hope," said Chance defiantly.

Fate shook her head, muttering about fools and dreamers, but the two ancient adversaries sat down by the fire and enjoyed a brief truce in their eternal war. They drank a toast to foolish humans, who stumbled and fell, made more wrong choices than right ones, who broke their own hearts again and again but somehow managed to do one or two things right, fine port and good Parmesan among them.

And out in the darkness, the fox ran, carrying the map in her mouth. Across the fields and over the stone walls she loped, through the tall grass and the brambles, until she came to a burned-out ruin and the linden tree that stood by it.

She dropped the map down into the hollow at the tree's base, then turned and sat, watching and waiting. Her thoughts were silent, known only to herself. But she sent them Isabelle's way.

Stop burdening the gods. Stop cursing the devil. They will make no path for you. They gave you their dark gifts: reason and will. Now you must make your own way.

What's done is done. Whether to you, or by you, and you cannot change it.

But what's not done is not done.

And there, both hope and hazard lie.

Believe that you can make your way. Or don't. Either way, you are right.

Every war is different, yet each battle is the same. The enemy is only a distraction. The thing you are fighting against, always, is yourself.

One Hundred

"I'll be right back, Nero. Stay here and don't budge," Isabelle whispered.

She wanted to know who was in the Hollow. It was close to Saint-Michel and her family, and outlaws and deserters were dangerous. One had stolen from her and almost killed her.

Isabelle knotted her skirts up and waded into the water. Luckily it wasn't too high, only up to her knees. Her boots were getting soaked, and the slipper Felix had made for her, but she didn't remove them and leave them on the bank. Without them, she moved slowly, and she might need to run. When she reached the other side, she scrambled up the bank, which was steep and loamy. She grabbed gnarled tree roots to pull herself up it. She was careful to be quiet as she climbed, not wanting to alert anyone to her presence. As she reached the top of the bank and peered over it, she sucked in a sharp breath. Before her were tents, hundreds of them. Not in neat rows but dotted over the ground. They were made of dark cloth and blended in perfectly with the trees.

Then she saw men. They were wearing uniforms. Talking in low voices. Cleaning rifles. Sharpening bayonets.

There must be a thousand of them. Are they the king's army? What are they doing here? she wondered.

Snatches of conversation drifted over to her, but they were so broken, they made no sense.

After a few minutes, though, she was able to piece the fragments together, and they did. And then terror squeezed the breath out of her.

The men were an army, yes; but not the king's army.

They were Volkmar's.

One Hundred and One

Isabelle dashed for cover behind a large tree, her heart thumping.

After a few seconds, she peered out from it and bit back a cry. One of the soldiers was heading right for her, a glowing cigar clamped in his teeth. Had he seen her? She ducked behind the rock again, trying to make herself as small as possible.

The man stopped just short of her hiding place. Then he planted his feet in the dirt and relieved himself. Isabelle didn't move; she didn't breathe.

While he was still hosing down the other side of the tree, several of his fellow soldiers called to him. Isabelle heard the name Volkmar over and over. The men's voices were low but excited.

Finally, the soldier buttoned his trousers and rejoined his friends. Isabelle's entire body sagged with relief. She risked another peek at the enemy's camp. Every soldier was hurrying from his tent to the centre of the camp.

Why? she wondered. *What's happening?*

Isabelle knew she should run. She should get away while she had the chance. What could she possibly do? She was alone. Defenseless. Just a girl.

Like Elizabeth, a voice inside her said. *Like Yennenga. Abhaya Rhani. They were just girls once, too.*

She stepped out from behind the tree and, crouching low, made her way between the tents into the heart of the enemy encampment.

Inside her, the wolf stopped gnawing. He became still. Tensed. Ready.

One Hundred and Two

They were gathered in a large circle, several rows deep.

A man was standing in the centre, speaking. Isabelle couldn't see him—the soldiers blocked her view—but she could hear him.

If someone sees me . . . If I'm caught . . . , fear yammered at her. She silenced it and tried to figure out how to get closer.

There was a boulder up ahead of her. She would be able to see over the men if she climbed it, but if one of them turned around, he would see her, too. Then she spotted a pine tree. Its lower branches were bare, but the upper ones were thickly needled. If she got up high enough, she could see without being seen. A tent, wood-framed, larger than the others, stood near the tree. It would block her from view as she made her way up the trunk.

It had been years since Isabelle scaled a tree, but it came right back to her. She made her way up through the branches easily and silently, just as she had when she and Felix were pretending to climb the mast of Blackbeard's ship. Higher and higher she climbed. When she was certain no one could see her, she slowly pressed down on a branch, lowering it slightly to give herself an unobstructed view.

Several lanterns had been placed in the centre of the circle. The light they gave illuminated a man wearing a tricorne hat. His dark hair, shot through with gray, was tied in a ponytail underneath it. A traveling cloak swirled about him as he moved. He was tall and broad-shouldered with a commanding stride. A scar ran down one cheek. Lantern light glittered in his violent eyes.

Volkmar, she said silently, her heart nearly shuddering to a stop.

He's here.

One Hundred and Three

Isabelle sat motionless, watching as Volkmar talked.

He was telling his men to attack Saint-Michel. They were going to slaughter every last person in the village, like they'd done in Malleval. That's why there were so many of them.

Volkmar finished talking and swept his arm out before him. As he did, another man appeared. He stood at the edge of the lantern's light, flanked by half a dozen of Volkmar's soldiers.

Isabelle's hand came up to her mouth. *No*, she thought. *God help us, no.*

It was the grand duke.

Dread bloomed in her belly; its dark vines twined around her heart. Volkmar's forces had taken him. They must've ambushed him as he was coming or going from Paris to Cafard's camp. How else would they have captured him? What were they going to do with him? Torture him? Execute him? He was one of the most powerful men in the realm. Only the king outranked him.

As Isabelle watched, breathless, Volkmar von Bruch strode up to the grand duke.

And embraced him.

One Hundred and Four

Isabelle felt as if she were made of ice. Her heart had frozen. The blood was solid in her veins. Her breath was frost. If she moved a muscle, she would shatter.

The grand duke, who was sworn to protect king and country, was in league with Volkmar von Bruch. Volkmar, who had slaughtered thousands of French soldiers. Who had burned towns, killed fleeing people.

Isabelle thought of her family. Felix. Her village. She thought of Remy, and the silver cross he'd given her, and his friend, Claude, and all the other young soldiers who might never go home again.

She watched, stone-faced, as Volkmar's soldiers raised their fists in a noiseless salute to their leader and to the grand duke. She watched as the soldiers walked back to their tents, the fire of war glowing in their faces, as Volkmar and the grand duke made their way to Volkmar's tent—the tent at the base of the very tree she was in—and sat down in the two canvas chairs in front of it. She watched as a young private appeared with lanterns, a box of cigars, a decanter of brandy and two crystal glasses.

The fear was gone. Isabelle felt only one emotion now—a cold, lethal fury. It didn't control her now, though; she controlled it. She let it help her instead of hurt her.

Slowly, she climbed down the tree, as silent as a shadow, lowering one bare foot to a branch, then another, without disturbing so much as a single pine needle.

Lower and lower she climbed, until she was only a yard above their heads. And then she listened.

"To France's new Lord Protector," Volkmar said, touching his glass to the grand duke's. "As soon as I defeat the king, the country will be mine and you will rule it for me."

Smiling, the grand duke bowed his head. Then he handed Volkmar a rolled parchment. "A gift."

Volkmar took it, broke the red wax seal—the king of France's seal—and unrolled it.

"A map . . ." he said, his eyes roving over the document.

"Showing the size and location of every battalion the king has left."

"Well done!" Volkmar exclaimed. "This will make hunting them all down much easier." He took a deep swallow of his brandy. "Is everything in order for tomorrow?"

"It is. You will attack Cafard's camp at dusk. He just sent four regiments to Paris and has only one left. After you kill his remaining troops, go to the field hospital and kill the wounded. I've no use for them. Leave Cafard alive, of course, and take him prisoner for appearance's sake. We'll reward him when the war is over. He's been a loyal ally."

Volkmar looked at the map again. "The civilians of Saint-Michel . . . will they put up a fight?"

The grand duke chuckled. "With what? Wooden spoons? I've been riding up and down the countryside, asking them to donate any weapons they had to the war effort. They're completely defenseless."

The young private, Volkmar's manservant, appeared again. Volkmar handed him the map and asked him to take it inside his tent, then bring them some food.

"I want to move swiftly on the king's other garrisons as soon as we're finished in Saint-Michel. Take them one by one until we get to the king himself," said Volkmar.

"I say take the king first. He'll surrender and that will break the spirit of any surviving troops."

"What if he doesn't?"

"He will. I'm certain of it. Don't forget that we have a very valuable bargaining chip."

Volkmar arched an eyebrow. "You're not terribly fond of your young sovereign, are you?"

The grand duke's expression soured. "The king is a fool. He had his pick of princesses from esteemed royal houses and he married a kitchen girl. He allows her to persist in her idiotic missions—caring for the wounded, housing orphans in the homes of the nobility—when it would be so much less of a burden on the crown's coffers to simply let them die. My own château is swarming with peasant brats." He shook his head disgustedly. "The king has demeaned the crown. While he fights in the field, a lowborn girl sits on the throne of France. Worse yet, the heir to the throne will have the blood of a commoner running in his veins."

"That's not a worry," Volkmar said. "The king's days are

numbered. He will not live long enough to sire a child."

The grand duke drained his glass. "Unless he already has."

Volkmar was silent as he leaned forward to pour more brandy for his guest. Then he sat back in his chair and said, "I can have no heirs to challenge my claim to the throne. You know what that means."

The grand duke took a sip of his drink, then lifted his eyes to Volkmar's. "It means the queen must die, too."

One Hundred and Five

Isabelle climbed up to a higher branch and sat down, her back against the trunk, her hands wrapped around smaller branches, her feet dangling.

It is said of great commanders that their blood runs cold in the fiery hell of battle. That the cannons' roar, the screams of the dying, the smoke and sweat and blood, only serve to sharpen their perception, the better to see where advantage lies.

Isabelle felt that clarity now.

She was in a tree, only yards above two bloodthirsty men who would kill her without a second thought if they were to discover her, yet she sat quietly, calmly considered her options, and determined the way forward.

Volkmar wanted to kill the king, and the queen, too; she had to find a way to stop him. She could try again to get to Paris and see Ella, or to get to the king and tell him what she'd learned, but she had no idea how she would do that, or if either of them would believe her if she did somehow manage to gain access to them.

A memory surfaced in Isabelle's mind now, like a fish jumping in a lake. She was back at the Maison Douleur. Blood dripped into the dirt from her maimed foot. The grand duke was walking towards Ella, carrying the glass slipper on a velvet cushion when he suddenly stumbled and dropped it. Isabelle remembered the sound of it shattering. It was an accident, he said. Except it wasn't. He tripped on purpose; she'd seen it.

Because he didn't want Ella to marry the prince. Because she wasn't highborn. She wasn't good enough. Ella, who was kind and good. Ella, who was more beautiful than the sun. With a few cold words, the grand duke had defined her and dismissed her.

Then Isabelle heard another voice: the old merchant's voice. He had done the same thing to *her*. He'd called her ugly. Defined her before she ever had a chance to define herself. In the space of a moment, he'd decided everything she was and ever would be.

But now Isabelle saw something she'd never seen before—that the merchant hadn't acted alone. He'd had an accomplice—she, herself. She'd listened to him. She'd believed him. She'd let him tell her who she was. And after him, Maman, suitors, the grand vizier, Cecile, the baker's wife, the villagers of Saint-Michel.

"They cut away pieces of me," she whispered in the darkness. "But I handed them the knife."

The merchant's voice still echoed in her head. Others joined it.

. . . *just a girl* . . . *ugly little monkey* . . . *ugly stepsister* . . . *strong* . . . *unruly* . . . *mean* . . .

Isabelle sat, listening to the voices, trying so hard to hear her own.

And then she did. *The map*, it said. *You have to get the map.*

The voice was not shrill or fearful. It was clear and calm and seemed to come from the very core of her being. Isabelle recognized it. When she was a child, it was the only voice she'd ever heard. It had never led her astray then, and it didn't now.

If she got the map, she could stop Volkmar's attack. She would read it, then ride like the wind to the closest loyal army encampment. The camp's commander would certainly want to know how she'd come into the possession of a secret map with the king's seal on it. She would tell him, and he would send his troops to Saint-Michel's rescue. She had until tomorrow, at dusk. That's when Volkmar was going to attack.

Volkmar's servant had put the map inside his tent. Isabelle knew she had to get into the tent, snatch it, and get out again. Looking down, she saw that Volkmar and the grand vizier were still deep in conversation. Volkmar's servant had set up a table for them outside the tent and had brought them supper. They weren't even halfway through it.

It's now or never, she thought, then she climbed the rest of the way down the tree. Crouching low, she crept to the back of the tent. She listened for a moment, to make sure no one was inside it; then lifted the canvas flap and ducked under it. A large campaign table stood in the middle of the space. Spread across it were quills, an inkpot, letters, a telescope . . . and the map.

Her heart leapt. *You can do this*, she told herself. *Just take it and go.*

She'd been so focused on finding the map that her eyes had gone straight to the table instead of sweeping around. As she dashed towards it, a movement to her right caught her eye. She stopped dead, her heart in her mouth.

There, sitting on a canvas cot, her wrists bound, her mouth cruelly gagged, was a girl. Isabelle's eyes widened. She took a step towards her.

Then she whispered one word.

"Ella?"

One Hundred and Six

Isabelle half dropped, half skidded to her knees by the cot. She fumbled the knot out of Ella's gag.

"Isabelle!" Ella whispered, choking back a sob.

"What happened? How did you get here?" Isabelle whispered back, horrified to see her stepsister tied up like an animal.

"The grand duke," Ella said. "He and his guards were supposed to be escorting me to a manor east of Saint-Michel. I was going to see if it could house war orphans. Halfway there, we turned off the road. He ordered his men to bind me and bring me here. Volkmar—"

"I know," Isabelle said grimly. "I heard him and the grand vizier talking. I'm going to get the king's map. Then we're going to leave."

"How, Isabelle?" Ella asked. "There are hundreds of soldiers in this camp!"

"I got in. I can get out."

"But my restraints . . ." Ella lifted her hands. She tried to say more but dissolved into sobs again.

Isabelle took her face in her hands. "Listen to me, Ella," she said sternly. "You need to trust me. You have no reason to, I know, but I'll get you out of here. I promise. I—"

"Where is that blasted boy? No matter, I'll fetch it myself . . ." a voice bellowed.

It was coming from right outside the tent. And it belonged to Volkmar.

One Hundred and Seven

Simple is the opposite of hard, Isabelle thought. *Easy is also the opposite of hard. But simple is not the same as easy. Not at all. I bet Tavi has a theorem for that.*

Isabelle was babbling to herself. Silently. To calm her crashing heart. To force her lungs to pull air in. To distract herself from the fact that Volkmar von Bruch's big black boots were only inches from her face.

What she had to do was simple—get Ella and herself out of here—but it was far from easy. And Volkmar coming into the tent had just made it ten times harder.

The instant she'd heard his voice, she put the gag back on Ella. Then she dived under the cot and pulled her skirts in after herself. She froze, barely breathing, as he opened the tent flap and walked in.

"Ah, Your Highness. Comfortable, are we? No? Well, you won't have to endure it for much longer. Tomorrow the grand duke and I attack your husband's encampment and barter your life for his surrender. Of course, I have no intention of upholding my end of the deal. But don't worry. Neither of you will suffer. The men on my firing squad have excellent aim."

A very valuable bargaining chip, the grand duke had said.

That chip was Ella.

Isabelle's hands knotted into fists. She could smell Volkmar—alcohol, sweat, and the greasy mutton he'd just eaten.

"Now, where is that brandy?" Isabelle heard him say. Then, "Ah! There it is!"

Volkmar left the tent. In a flash, Isabelle was out from under the cot and on her feet. She unknotted Ella's gag again, then found a dagger on the table and used it to slice through the ropes binding her wrists and ankles. Ella stood unsteadily.

"Walk!" Isabelle whispered. "Get the feeling back in your feet! Hurry!"

While Ella took a few steps, Isabelle snatched the map off the table and rolled it up. As she did, a document that had been lying underneath it caught her eye. It was another map—one that showed the locations of Volkmar's troops. Isabelle's pulse raced as she saw it. This would turn the tables on Volkmar and that viper of a grand vizier.

She rolled the second map around the first one, then silently beckoned to Ella. The two girls slipped out of the tent the way Isabelle had come in. Once outside, Isabelle held a finger to her lips and listened. The camp was quiet. The gathering for Volkmar and the grand duke had broken up. Most of the soldiers were in their tents—most, but not all. Some still moved between the rows. Isabelle could hear them talking.

When she was certain no one was nearby, she took Ella's hand and started off. Staying low, they hurried, ducking behind the tents, careful to avoid any twigs, eyes peeled for movement. They had to double back and find a new route when a tent flap opened and a soldier put his boots outside, and again when they nearly ran out in front of a group of men smoking under a tree.

Scared, disoriented in the deepening darkness, Isabelle nonetheless managed to work her way towards the outskirts of the camp. Just as they reached the edge of it, though, an alarm was raised. Terse voices quickly spread the message that the queen had escaped and must be found. Crouched behind the same tree that had hidden Isabelle when she first discovered the camp, they watched as soldiers hurried out of their tents, clutching swords or rifles. Then Isabelle grabbed Ella's hand and blindly ran to the riverbank. Half skidding, half stumbling, they made their way down it.

When they reached the water, Isabelle hiked her skirts with one hand, held the maps up high above the water with the other, and waded in. Ella, who was wearing delicate silk shoes, took them off, gathered her skirts, and followed. The river rocks were treacherous. After taking only a few steps, she slipped on one and fell. As she went down, she lost her grip on her dainty shoes and the fast-flowing water carried them away. Drenched, weighed down by her wet clothing, she struggled to her feet, lurched after her shoes, and fell again.

"Leave them!" Isabelle hissed.

Ella's falls had made loud splashes. Had anyone in the camp heard them? Isabelle anxiously wondered. She stuffed the maps down the front of her dress to keep them dry, nervously glancing back at the bank. Then she walked to Ella and held out her hand. Ella took it. Isabelle pulled her up, and together the girls carefully picked their way over the stones.

They were halfway across the river, when a harsh voice rang out.

"Stay right there! Hands in the air! Don't move or I'll shoot!"

One Hundred and Eight

Isabelle couldn't see the man shouting the orders. She couldn't see anything. Soldiers were shining lanterns in her direction, blinding her. She tried to shade her eyes with her raised hands. She could hear dogs barking and snarling. Rifles being shouldered, triggers cocked. Her stomach tightened with fear.

And then a voice said, "Ah, there you are, Your Highness. I was wondering where you'd got to. And who have we here?"

"Lower the lanterns, you fools!" the grand duke ordered.

His soldiers did so. Isabelle lifted her hands above her eyes.

"It's the queen's stepsister. The girl who cut off her toes." That was the grand duke. "I recognize her."

"I recognize her, too," said Volkmar. "We met in Malleval." His eyes glittered darkly. "Now we can finish what we started there." He made his way down the riverbank.

He can't kill us both, not at the same time, Isabelle thought. *And it's dark. The soldiers aiming at us might miss.*

"Run, Ella, *run*!" she whispered. "Nero's on the path to the Wildwood. You can make it."

Ella began to weep. "I won't leave you," she said.

"No need for tears, Your Highness," Volkmar taunted. "I'm

401

not going to kill *you*. Not yet. Just your ugly stepsister. You should thank me for that."

He pulled his sword from its scabbard. The sight of it shocked Isabelle into remembering that she had a sword, too. And a shield. Instinctively, she reached towards her pocket, where she kept the fairy queen's gifts.

"Keep your hands up!" a soldier shouted. "Or I'll shoot you dead!"

Volkmar reached the bottom of the bank and stepped into the river. Isabelle's insides turned to water. Fear threatened to overwhelm her, but before it could, she felt a sharp pain on her thigh. She looked down. Her pocket was bulging. Curved black thorns were sticking through the fabric of her dress.

The seedpod! she thought, hope leaping inside her. *Tanaquill's last gift!*

But Volkmar saw it, too. "What do you have there?" he barked.

The seedpod grew bigger. It pushed through the fabric, shredding it. The bone and walnut shell fell into the river. "No!" Isabelle cried. Desperation gripped her. All she had left was the seedpod. Maybe it would turn into a weapon, too. If only she could get it.

But as she watched, the pod burst open. The seeds, which were red and shiny and as big as marbles, all fell into the water and sank. Then the husk fell in and was swiftly carried away. Her last hope disappeared with it.

Volkmar was close now. Isabelle knew that he would kill her here and let the river take her body. Then he would use Ella to carry out his ruthless plan. Their lives were lost. Saint-Michel was lost. Everything was lost.

He raised his sword, ready to swing it. Ella screamed. Isabelle braced for her death.

But the blow never came. Because an instant later, Volkmar's sword went flying through the air.

And then Volkmar did.

One Hundred and Nine

"Isabelle, what's happening?" Ella asked, her voice shaking with fear.

"I—I don't know, Ella," Isabelle said, reaching for her hand again.

A vine, as thick as a man's thigh, had risen up out of the water, thrashing violently. It had caught the blade of Volkmar's sword and launched it into the treetops; then it had slammed Volkmar against the riverbank. Thorns, some a foot long, sprouted from the vine. They'd carved red stripes in his chest.

"Blackbriar," Isabelle whispered. Just like the vines that grew on the trunk of the linden tree, the vines from which Tanaquill had plucked the seedpod.

As Isabelle watched, another vine rose out of the water, and then another and another, dizzyingly quick. Until there were dozens of them. Reaching, spiraling, they cracked like whips, catching rifles, launching snarling dogs, knocking soldier after soldier to the ground, forcing the grand duke back. As they writhed, their thorns caught, tangling them.

Some of the vines had shot up in front of the girls, others were rising behind them.

"We're going to be trapped!" Isabelle shouted. "Come

on, Ella, run!"

She pulled her stepsister after her. Ella stumbled over the slick rocks, tripping, stubbing her toes, falling to her knees. Each time she fell, Isabelle hauled her up again until finally they made it to the other side.

As they staggered out of the water, panting, Isabelle looked back. The blackbriar vines had twisted together to form an impenetrable wall, twenty feet high. She heard commands being shouted behind it, guns firing, dogs barking, but nothing could get through. She and Ella were safe. For the moment.

"We have to go," Isabelle said, still gripping Ella's hand.

"What is that thing, Isabelle?" Ella asked, staring at the blackbriar wall.

"Tanaquill's magic."

Ella turned to her, smiling. "You found the fairy queen?" she asked excitedly.

"She found me. I'll tell you all about it later. We can't stay here."

"Isabelle, how did you find me?" Ella asked as they hurried through the brush. "What were you doing in Volkmar's camp?"

Isabelle didn't know where to start. "I was running away. On Nero," she began.

"*Nero?* But Maman sold him."

"I got him back. But Madame LeBenêt—our neighbor, remember her? The house burned down—"

"*What?*"

"We were living in her hayloft, and she wanted me to marry Hugo—"

"Hugo?"

"So that Tantine would give him an inheritance. But I don't love Hugo. And he certainly doesn't love me."

Ella stopped dead. She made Isabelle stop, too. "How did this all *happen*?" she asked, upset.

"There's no time, Ella," Isabelle protested, glancing back the way they'd come. "I'll tell you later. I'll . . ."

Her words trailed away. She'd been so focused on getting Ella out of the camp, she'd had no time to think of anything else. Now the enormity of the danger they were facing hit her. The grand duke was a traitor, in league with Volkmar, and Volkmar's troops were hidden in the Devil's Hollow, and Ella knew everything. Volkmar and the grand vizier would try to stop her at all costs. She and Ella might not make it to safety. They might not make it out of the Wildwood, or even up the path. This might be her only chance to tell Ella what she needed to tell her.

So she did. She told her everything that had occurred since the day Ella had left with the prince. About Tanaquill. The fire. The marquis. The LeBenêts. Tantine's ultimatum. And lastly, Felix and his note, and how Maman had destroyed it and caused them both so much pain.

"Things would have been so different, Ella. If we'd run away like we planned. If Maman hadn't found his note and destroyed it. *I* would have been different. Better. Kinder."

"Isabelle . . ."

"No, let me finish. I need to. I'm sorry. I'm sorry for being cruel. For hurting you. You were beautiful. I was not. You had everything, and I'd lost everything. And it made me so jealous."

Shame burned under her skin. She felt helpless and exposed saying these things, like a small desert creature, tumbled from its den and left to die in the sun. "You wouldn't know what that's like."

"I might know more than you think," Ella said softly.

"Can you ever forgive me?"

Ella smiled, but it wasn't the sweet smile Isabelle was used to. It was bitter and sad. "Isabelle, you don't know what you're asking."

Isabelle nodded. She lowered her head. The fragile hope she'd felt when she'd told Ella that she was sorry had just been shattered. She had found her stepsister, found another piece of herself that had been cut away, but it didn't matter. There would be no forgiveness, not for her. The wounds she'd inflicted were too deep. Tears spilled down her cheek. She had not known that remorse could feel so much like grief.

"Isabelle, don't cry. Please, please don't cry. I—"

Ella's words were cut off by the sound of barking.

Isabelle's head snapped up. "We need to get going," she said, wiping her eyes. "We need to find a safe place for you."

"Where?"

"I don't know. I'll think of something. The important thing is that we get you there without getting shot. All right?"

Ella nodded. "All right," she said.

Isabelle gave Ella her hand. Ella took it and held it tightly. The two girls started running again.

For their lives.

One Hundred and Ten

Isabelle threw a pebble at the window.

It hit a pane of glass and fell back to the street.

She was standing in front of an old stone building at the edge of Saint-Michel. Looking nervously up and down the dark street, she picked the pebble up and threw it again. And once more. And finally, the window opened.

Felix leaned out in a linen shirt that was open at the neck, holding a candle and blinking into the darkness.

"Felix, it's *you*!" Isabelle said breathlessly. He'd told her he lived over the carpenter's workshop, but she wasn't sure she'd had the right window.

"What are you doing here, Isabelle?" he asked, bleary-eyed with sleep.

"Can we come in? We're in trouble. We need to hide."

"We?"

"Felix, *please*!"

Felix pulled his head inside. A moment later, he was at the workshop's gate with his candle. Isabelle met him there. She pointed across the street. Ella was standing in the wide, arched gateway of a stonemason's yard, holding Nero's reins.

She hurried towards them.

"That's Ella," Felix said to Isabelle. "As in your stepsister. As in the Queen of France."

"Yes."

"I forgot my trousers. The queen of France is standing at my door, and I'm in my nightshirt." He looked down at himself. "With my knees showing."

"I like your knees," Isabelle said.

Felix blushed.

"I do, too," Ella said.

"Your Royal Highness," he said.

"Ella will do."

"Your Royal Ella-ness," he amended. "I'd bow, but . . . uh, this nightshirt's a little on the short side."

Ella laughed.

Felix ushered them into the workyard. Then quickly took Nero around the side of the shop to the stables at the back. After giving him a drink and putting him in an empty stall, he returned to the workyard and locked the gate. Moving quickly and quietly, he led the two girls through the workshop and up a narrow flight of stairs to his room. After he'd put his candle down on the small wooden table in the centre of it, he snatched his breeches from the footboard of his bed and awkwardly stepped into them.

"Sit down," he said, motioning to the pair of rickety chairs on either side of the table. Ella did so, gratefully, but Isabelle couldn't. She was too agitated; she paced instead.

"You're bleeding," Felix said, pointing at Ella's bare foot.

A cut snaked across the top of it. He got her a rag and some water to wash it, then handed her a pair of battered boots.

"My old ones," he said. "They're too big for you, but they're better than nothing." He turned to Isabelle. "So what did you do?"

"What makes you think *I* did something?"

"Because you always got into trouble and Ella never did," Felix said, taking an oil lamp down from a shelf.

As Ella, exhausted, closed her eyes for a few minutes, and Felix removed the glass chimney from the lamp, Isabelle told him what had happened. Anger hardened his expression as he listened.

"After we escaped from Volkmar, we made it up the path and rode through the Wildwood," she said, finishing her tale. "I didn't know where else to go. I can't go back to the LeBenêts'. Cafard's men may be waiting there for me. I'm sorry, Felix. I didn't mean to drag you into this."

"Don't be," Felix said. "I'm glad to help you and Ella. I just don't know how." As he spoke, he tipped his candle to the lamp's wick.

"I don't know what to do, either," Isabelle said, sitting down across from Ella. She moved things aside—chisels, knives, wooden teeth—leaned her elbows on the table and rested her forehead in her hands. "We've got to get the maps I stole, and Ella, to the king's encampment," she said. "We have to prevent Volkmar from attacking Saint-Michel. But how? Soldiers will be out looking for us."

"Volkmar's men?" Felix asked.

"I don't think so," Isabelle said. "He won't risk showing himself. Not yet. Not until he wipes out Cafard's troops. It's the grand duke we have to worry about. No one knows that he and Cafard are in league with Volkmar. No one but Ella and me. He may have ridden out of the Devil's Hollow back to Cafard's camp to send out search parties. If he finds Ella, she's done for."

Felix trimmed the lamp's wick, now burning brightly, then replaced the chimney. As the light illuminated the large attic room, Ella gave a little cry. Not one of fright or horror, but wonder.

"What is it?" Isabelle asked, lifting her head.

And then she saw them.

Standing on the narrow shelves that lined the walls, on the mantel, on a dresser, in rows under the narrow bed, and jumbled into several crates and a large harvest basket, were carved wooden soldiers.

"My goodness, Felix. There must be *hundreds* of them," Ella said, standing up to admire them.

"Just over two thousand," said Felix.

Isabelle walked to a shelf and picked one up. He was a fusilier, complete with a torch. He looked war-weary and haggard, as if he knew he was going to die.

"These are beautiful," said Ella.

Felix, who was now heating up a pot of cold coffee over some glowing coals in the small fireplace, shyly thanked her.

"You must've been working on them for years," said Ella.

"Ever since I left the Maison Douleur."

"You put a lot of emotion into them. I can see it," Ella said. "Love, fear, triumph, sorrow, it's all there."

"It had to go somewhere," Felix said, glancing at Isabelle.

Ella winced, as if his words had cut her. She abruptly rose from her chair, cupped her elbows, and walked to the window. The she whirled and walked back again, as if she was trying to get away from something.

"Ella? Are you all right?" Isabelle asked.

Ella started to reply, but her words were cut off by the sound of hooves clopping over the cobblestones. It carried up from the street and in through the open window. Felix, Isabelle, and Ella traded anxious glances.

"Soldiers," Isabelle said tersely. "What if they're going door to door?"

Felix risked a glance out the window. The tension in his face softened. He smiled. "Not soldiers, no," he said. "But maybe saviors."

One Hundred and Eleven

Isabelle was out of the door and down the stairs in no time.

She'd rushed to the window to see what Felix was talking about and had spotted Martin. He was pulling a wagonload of potatoes. Hugo was in the driver's seat. Tavi was sitting next to him.

Isabelle ran in front of them, waving her arms. "Why are you in the village so early?" she asked. It wasn't even dawn yet.

Tavi explained they had to go to the army camp first, deliver the potatoes, return to the farm, milk the cows, and then bring another load to the market.

"Colonel Cafard was so furious when you took off that Tantine made him a gift of the potatoes. To help the war effort. And to keep him from throwing us all in jail. My mother was up fuming about it half the night. Thanks a lot, Isabelle," Hugo said.

Isabelle ignored his grousing. "You've come in the nick of time," she said. "We need you."

"Who needs us?" Tavi said, looking around.

"The village of Saint-Michel. The king. All of France. And Ella."

"*Ella?*" Tavi echoed.

"Enemy soldiers are trying to kill her. And me."

She quickly explained what had happened since she'd left them. Tavi and Hugo listened; then Tavi, eyes sparking with anger, said, "We have to stop them. They can't do this. They *won't* do this."

"Come upstairs. Hurry," said Isabelle.

Tavi climbed down out of the wagon and rushed to Felix's room. Hugo quickly tied Martin to a hitching post and followed her.

"Ella, is that *you*?" Tavi said as she entered the room.

Ella nodded. Tavi's habitually acerbic expression, the one she used to keep the world away, softened. Her eyes glistened. "I never thought I'd see you again," she whispered. "I never thought I'd get the chance to . . . oh, Ella. I'm sorry, I'm so sorry."

"It's all right, Tavi," Ella said, reaching for her hand.

"Hello, Ella," Hugo said shyly, staring at the huge, battered cast-offs she was wearing. "Should I bow or something?"

"Maybe later, Hugo," Ella said.

"We need to get Ella and Isabelle out of here before the whole village wakes up," Felix explained, handing out cups of hot coffee. "What if we hid them in the wagon, under the potatoes, and headed to a camp that's loyal to the king?"

"According to the map I stole, the nearest one is fifty miles away," said Isabelle. "Martin wouldn't make it."

Ella had released Tavi's hand; she was sitting at the table again, looking out of the window, a troubled expression on her face. Hugo said, "Could we use Nero?"

Isabelle shook her head. "He's never pulled a wagon. He'd kick it to pieces."

Ella covered her face with her hands.

For the second time, Isabelle noticed her distress. "Ella? What's wrong?" she asked, putting her coffee down.

"You are all so kind to me. So good," Ella replied, lowering her hands. "Isabelle, you saved my life. But I . . . I don't deserve your kindness."

"Don't be ridiculous," Isabelle said. "You deserve that and more. You—"

"No, *listen* to me!" Ella cried. "You apologized to me, Isabelle, back in the Devil's Hollow, and now you have, Tavi. And that was brave of you both. Very brave. And now it's my turn to be brave. As I should've been years ago." The words came out of her mouth as if they were studded with nails. "Isabelle, earlier you asked me to forgive you and I said you didn't know what you were asking. I said that because *I'm* the one who needs to be forgiven."

"I don't understand . . ." Isabelle said.

"The note," Ella said, her voice heavy with remorse. "The one Felix left for you in the linden tree. You said Maman found it and destroyed it, but you're wrong. *I'm* the one who found it. I took it and burned it and ruined your life. Oh, Isabelle, don't you see? I'm the ugliest stepsister of all."

One Hundred and Twelve

Isabelle sat down on Felix's bed. She felt as if Ella had kicked her legs out from under her.

Ella had destroyed the note. Not Maman. *Ella.* No matter how many times Isabelle repeated this to herself, it still made no sense.

"Why" she asked.

"Because I was jealous, too."

"Jealous? Of whom?" Isabelle asked.

"Of *you*, Isabelle. You were so fearless, so strong. You laughed like a pirate. Rode like a robber. And Felix loved you. He loved you from the day my father brought you, Tavi, and Maman to the Maison Douleur. He was my friend and you took him away."

"I was still your friend, Ella. I was always your friend," Felix said, wounded.

Ella turned to him. "It wasn't the same. I didn't jump over stone walls on stallions. I didn't race you to the tops of tall trees." She looked at Isabelle again. "You and Felix were always having adventures. They sounded so wonderful and I couldn't bear it. Couldn't bear that he liked you better than me. Couldn't bear to be left behind. So I made sure I wasn't."

Isabelle remembered how upset Ella would get when she and Felix rode off to the Wildwood and how relieved she always was when they returned. *I should be angry. I should be furious,* she thought. But she wasn't—just deeply, achingly sad.

"I was so sorry afterward," Ella continued. "When I saw how miserable you were. But I was too afraid to tell you what I'd done. I thought you would hate me for it. But then everything changed between us and you hated me anyway."

Ella got up, crossed the room, and sat down next to Isabelle. "Say something. Anything," she pleaded. "Say you hate me. Tell me you wish I was dead."

Isabelle exhaled loudly. Raggedly. As if she'd been holding her breath not for seconds, or minutes, but years.

"It's like a fire, Ella," she said.

"What is?"

"Jealousy. It burns so hot, so bright. It devours you, until you're just a smoking ruin with nothing left inside."

"Nothing but ashes," Ella said.

Isabelle closed her eyes now and sifted through those ashes.

Everything would have been different if Ella hadn't burned Felix's note. She wouldn't have lost Felix. Or Nero. She wouldn't have lost herself.

She thought about the day Felix left, and the years that had come after. The music tutors and dancing masters. The dress fittings. Sitting for hours at her needlework, when her heart longed for horses and hills. The excruciating dinners with suitors looking her up and down, their smiles forced, their eyes shuttered as they tried to hide their disappointment. The aching loneliness of finding that nothing fit. Not dainty slippers or stiff corsets. Not conversations or expectations, friendships or desires. Her entire life had seemed like a beautiful dress made for someone else.

"I'm sorry, Isabelle. I'm so sorry," Ella said.

Isabelle opened her eyes. Ella's hands were knotted into fists in her lap. Isabelle reached for one. She opened the fingers, smoothed them flat, then wove her own between them.

She was sorry for so many things. She was sorry for her mother who had always looked to mirrors for the truth. She was sorry for Berthe who cried when she was mean, and Cecile who didn't. She was sorry for Tavi writing equations on cabbage leaves.

She was sorry for all the grim-tale girls locked in lonely towers. Trapped in sugar houses. Lost in the dark woods, with a huntsman coming to cut out their hearts.

She was sorry for three little girls who'd been handed a poisoned apple as they played under a linden tree on a bright summer day.

One Hundred and Thirteen

Ella stood.

She crossed the room and knelt by Tavi's chair.

"I'm so sorry, Tavi," she said. "What I did hurt you, too."

"It's all right, Ella," Tavi said, rising. She pulled Ella up and hugged her. Isabelle joined them. The three stood for a moment, locked in a fierce, tearful embrace.

Then Ella turned to Felix. "I need to apologize to you, too," she said, reaching for his hand. "Your life would also have been different if I hadn't stolen the note."

"Oh, Ella," Felix said, taking her hand. "I'm sorry you thought I wasn't your friend any more."

Ella turned to Hugo next. "You wouldn't even be here now if it wasn't for me," she said to him. "In this room. In this mess . . ."

Hugo shrugged. "Actually, my life kind of got better. The last few weeks, with you two around"—he nodded at Isabelle and Tavi—"have been really awful but exciting, too. I mean, what did I have before you came? Cabbages, that's about it. Now I have friends."

Isabelle hooked her arm around Hugo's neck and pulled him into the embrace. He tried to smile, but it came out like a grimace. He hastily patted Isabelle on the back, then extricated himself. She knew he wasn't used to affection.

"We should go. We have to find a way to get Ella to safety and the maps to the king," Hugo said. "And that's going to become a lot harder once the sun is up."

"We'll need an armed escort," Tavi said hopelessly. "Our own regiment. No, make that an entire army."

Isabelle was quiet. She was slowly walking around Felix's room, eyeing his shelves. His bureau. The mantel. Then she turned to the others and said, "We don't need to find an army. We already have one."

"We do? Where is it?" Tavi asked.

Isabelle picked up a carved wooden soldier from a shelf and held it out on her palm.

"Right here."

One Hundred and Fourteen

Hugo blinked at the little soldier on Isabelle's palm. He forced a smile.

"You can lie down, you know. On Felix's bed. If you're tired, you can rest," he said.

Isabelle shot him a look. "I'm not tired. Or crazy, which is what you really mean. I'm serious. There's a fairy queen. She comes and goes as a fox and lives in the hollow of the linden tree. She has strong magic."

"A fairy queen . . ." Hugo said, raising an eyebrow.

"It's true, Hugo," Ella said. "She came to me one night when my heart was broken and asked me what I wanted most. I told her, and she helped me get it. How else do you think I got to the ball?"

"I've seen that fox," Felix said. "When I was a boy. Her fur is red like autumn leaves. She has deep green eyes."

"She turned mice into horses and a pumpkin into a coach," said Ella.

"She could enchant these carved soldiers and turn them into real soldiers. I *know* she could," said Isabelle. "All we have to do is get them to the linden tree."

"But how?" Tavi asked, turning in a slow circle. "There are so many of them."

"Two thousand, one-hundred and fifty-eight, to be exact," Felix said.

"We would have to find cases or trunks to put them in. Do you have any?"

"No, but we have plenty of coffins," said Felix. "I bet two of them would get the job done."

"We could use Martin and the wagon to transport them," Isabelle said. "We'd just have to unload the potatoes."

"Then let's unload them," Ella said decisively. "We have an enemy to defeat. A king and a country to save. And traitors to capture." She smiled grimly. "And then hang, draw, and quarter."

Both of Hugo's eyebrows shot up. He scratched under his cap. "You're different, Ella. You're not the girl I remember. I guess it's true what they say. What doesn't kill you—"

"Makes you the queen of France," Ella finished. "Let's go," she added, glancing out Felix's window. "Hugo's right. It's going to be a lot harder to sneak two thousand soldiers to a fairy queen in broad daylight."

One Hundred and Fifteen

Felix opened the gates to the work yard, and Hugo backed the wagon into it as quickly as he could.

Working together, the five unloaded the potatoes, heaping them on the ground. It was decided that they would load the coffins into the wagon first, then carry the wooden soldiers down from Felix's room in crates, baskets, bedsheets—anything they could find.

The coffins were simple, slender pine boxes, not terribly heavy. Felix and Isabelle picked the first one up by its rope handles, carried it out of the shop, and set it down on the wagon's bed. Felix pushed it, trying to get it to slide in neatly under its seats, but it wouldn't go. It seemed to be blocked by something. He was about to push it again just as Hugo and Tavi appeared, carrying the second coffin.

"Wait! Felix, don't!" Hugo cried. "You'll let it out!"

"Let what out?" Felix asked, confused.

"The sweaty dead dog," Hugo said as he and Tavi slid the second coffin into the wagon.

"There's a dead dog in the wagon?" Ella asked confused.

"No, it's a cheese. Tavi invented it. It's in a box under the seats," Isabelle explained.

"It smells so bad, I can't get rid of it," Hugo said. "Be careful, you really don't want to knock the lid off."

He climbed into the wagon, shoved the wooden box over to the left side of the bed, then slid the first coffin in next to it. Isabelle pushed the second one in. They just fit.

Everyone worked together to bring the soldiers downstairs. Soon, both coffins were full. As Felix secured the lids, tapping a few nails into them to keep them from sliding during the trip, Isabelle went to the stables to see Nero. She would leave him there, hidden away, to keep him safe. If Cafard saw him, he would take him, and she did not want a traitor to have her horse.

She scratched Nero's ears, kissed his nose, and told him to be good. She didn't know if they would make it to the Maison Douleur, or if she would see her beloved horse again after tonight. As if sensing her distress, Nero nudged at her with his nose. She kissed him again, then hurried away without looking back. Nero watched her go, blinking his huge, dark eyes; then he gave the stall door a good hard kick.

The others, except for Felix, were already in the wagon by the time Isabelle rejoined them. She climbed in and settled herself on the back seat. Tavi and Ella were up front. Hugo, in the driver's seat, guided Martin out of the work yard. Felix closed the gates, then swung up beside Isabelle.

Hugo cracked the reins, and Martin trotted down the dark street. Isabelle looked up. The moon was still high, but the sky was beginning to lighten. Worry shriveled her insides.

"Volkmar's men are only a few miles away, and what are we doing?" she said, turning to Felix. "Hauling tiny wooden soldiers off to a magical fox who lives in a hollow inside a tree. That sounds like the craziest thing yet in a night full of crazy things. Ella says she told Tanaquill what her heart wanted. And Tanaquill granted it to her. Do you think it will work?"

Felix looked at Ella, nestled in between Hugo and Tavi. Then he took Isabelle's hand and held it.

"Maybe it already has," he said.

One Hundred and Sixteen

The old farmer, bleary-eyed and grizzled, raised a hand in greeting.

Hugo did the same, and their two wagons passed in silence.

They'd made their way out of Saint-Michel without seeing another soul. Ever since they'd left the safety of Felix's room, Isabelle had felt as if iron bands were wrapped around her chest. As they started towards the gentle hills that lay beyond the village, she finally felt as if she could take a breath, as if they might actually make it to the Maison Douleur.

Until Hugo swore and pointed up ahead of them. Isabelle could see the old church silhouetted on top of the hill in the thinning darkness. On the road next to it, riding fast, was a group of soldiers.

"If we stay calm, we can get out of this," Tavi said.

"How? They're going to recognize Ella right away," Hugo said.

He's right, Isabelle thought. "Ella, change places with Felix," she said. "They might not see you so well if you're sitting in the back. Tavi, you come back here, too. We'll put Ella between us."

They quickly rearranged themselves, but it wasn't enough, and they knew it. Ella still shined like a star.

Felix pulled a brightly printed handkerchief from his pocket. "Wrap your hair up," he said.

Hugo handed her his glasses. "Put these on, too."

Ella did as they bade her. The three girls were sitting on an old horse blanket that had been folded over to cushion the seat. Tavi pulled it out from under them and draped it around Ella's shoulders. Isabelle spotted a clod of dirt by her feet. She picked it up, crushed it, then rubbed it on Ella's soft hands, working it into her knuckles and nails so that they looked just like her and Tavi's rough ones.

"This might just work," Tavi said.

Felix, his eyes straight ahead, grimly said, "It had better. They have rifles."

A few minutes later, the soldiers approached them, riding two abreast. Isabelle's nerves were as taut as a bowstring.

Hugo nodded solemnly to the first riders. The men looked him and his companions over but didn't stop. The two lines moved quickly by. Isabelle saw that they wore the uniforms of the French army. They were Cafard's men, they had to be. Thankfully, the grand duke was not among them. The riders' commander brought up the rear. He, too, peered closely at them as he trotted by.

Keep going, Isabelle silently urged him. *Nothing to see here.*

"Halt!" the commander suddenly bellowed to his men, turning his horse around.

Isabelle's heart dropped.

"Let me do the talking," Tavi said quietly. "I have an idea."

"*You* have an idea?" whispered Hugo, his hands tightening on the reins. "God help us all."

427

One Hundred and Seventeen

"Why are you about at this hour? Where are you going?" the commander demanded, looking at Hugo.

But it was Tavi who answered him. "Where are we going? Where *would* we be going with two coffins in the back and the churchyard just up ahead?" she shrilled. "It's hardly a mystery, Sergeant!"

"It's *Lieutenant*. And it's very early in the day to be going to the cemetery."

Tavi gave him a contemptuous snort. "Death doesn't keep bankers' hours. My husband here"—she slapped Hugo's shoulder—"must be in the fields by sunrise. My brother-in-law, too," she said, nodding at Felix. "My sister and I just lost two brothers to this blasted war. Their bodies came home yesterday. One was a married man. Now my sister-in-law here"—she gestured to Ella—"is a widow with three small children."

Ella lowered her head and sniffled into the horse blanket.

"They have no one to provide for them. My husband and I must take them in," Tavi continued. "Four more mouths to feed when we've barely got enough for ourselves. So, Lieutenant, if you are satisfied now, can we move on? Bodies don't keep in the heat."

"The queen is missing," said the lieutenant. "The grand duke fears she's been kidnapped. He's given orders to stop anyone who looks suspicious and to inspect all wagons."

Tavi laughed out loud. "The queen is a great beauty, lieutenant. Who is a beauty here? Me, in my old dress? My sister in hers? Or perhaps my four-eyed sister-in-law?"

Ella looked up. She squinted through Hugo's eyeglasses. The lieutenant's gaze passed right over her.

"Let me see your feet. Each of you ladies," he said. "It's well-known that the queen has the daintiest feet in all the land."

One by one, the three girls showed the lieutenant their feet. Isabelle's were big, her boots filthy. Tavi's, too. Ella's were absolutely enormous in Felix's old, battered boots.

"Now, if you're finished harassing a grieving family . . ." Tavi said.

Hugo made ready to crack his reins, but the lieutenant held up a hand.

Now what? Isabelle wondered, panic rising in her.

"You could be smuggling the queen in those coffins," the lieutenant said. He directed two of his men to the back of the wagon. "Open them up!"

Isabelle was paralyzed by fear. She glanced at the others. Felix's shoulders were up around his ears. Hugo was saucer-eyed. Tavi had turned pale, but she hadn't given up.

"This is a desecration!" she shouted. "Have you no shame?"

The two soldiers selected for the task glanced uneasily at each other.

"That was an order!" the lieutenant barked at them.

429

The soldiers dismounted from their horses.

"The bodies are several days old!" Tavi protested. "Must our last memories of our loved ones be an ungodly smell?"

An ungodly smell.

With those words, Isabelle's paralysis broke. She knew exactly what to do. She turned around and faced backward, pretending to watch the soldiers. As she did, she snaked her right hand under the seat. Her fingers found the wooden box there. Slowly, carefully, she wedged them under the box's lid.

Anticipating that the coffin lids would be nailed down, as coffin lids always are, one of the soldiers pulled a dagger from his belt to pry them off. He shoved the blade in under one of the lids and levered the handle. A few nails screeched free of the wood. As they did, Isabelle made her move.

She slid the lid off the wooden box and unleashed the sweaty dead dog.

One Hundred and Eighteen

The carnage was magnificent.

The horses shrieked. Three of them threw their riders. Some of the soldiers lost their suppers. Even the lieutenant turned green.

Isabelle, Tavi, and Ella, sitting right over the rank abomination, felt their eyes burning from its fumes. Tears poured down their cheeks, making them look even more like the bereaved family they claimed to be.

Tavi saw her advantage and took it. Standing up in the wagon, she shook a finger at the lieutenant. "You should be *ashamed* of yourself, sir!" she shrilled. "Disturbing the dead! Upsetting mourners! Making a poor widow weep!"

"For God's sake, seal it up!" the lieutenant thundered, his hand over his nose.

The soldier who'd pried up a corner of the lid now frantically hammered it back down with the butt of his dagger.

"I've half a mind to tell the good Colonel Cafard what you've done," Tavi continued. "We are not kidnapping anyone. We are poor, grieving folk trying to bury our loved ones!"

"My apologies, madame. Drive on!" the lieutenant said, waving his hand.

Hugo nodded, then clucked his tongue. Martin trotted off. Isabelle, still facing backward, quickly slid the lid back over the dead dog. It lessened the stink, but Hugo urged Martin into a canter nonetheless, in an attempt to outrun the lingering fumes. A few minutes later, they crested the hill, leaving the soldiers behind them.

When they'd made it down the other side, Hugo stopped the wagon. He leaned forward, breathing heavily. His hands were shaking.

"That was very, very close," Felix said, a tremor in his voice.

"We don't know if that's the only patrol. We should keep going," Isabelle urged.

Hugo sat up, having caught his breath. "I need my glasses back. Before I drive us off the road."

Ella handed them to him. "Thank you, all of you. You saved my life," she said.

"It was Tavi," said Hugo. "She made that thing."

Tavi shook her head modestly. "It was Leeuwenhoek."

"Who?" Ella asked, as Hugo started off again.

"It's a long story. I'll tell it to you one day. If we live long enough," Isabelle said grimly. Hugo coaxed Martin into a canter again. As he did, one of the wagon's wheels caught a pothole and jounced Tavi to the edge of her seat.

Ella grabbed hold of her, then took her hand to keep her safe. She took Isabelle's hand, too. As the wagon sped through what remained of the night, neither Isabelle, nor Tavi, nor Ella let go.

One Hundred and Nineteen

The stars were fading as Martin trotted up the drive of the Maison Douleur to the linden tree. Before Hugo had even brought him to a halt, the others were out of the wagon.

An inquisitive whinny carried through the grounds. Isabelle knew it was one of the two rescued horses that now lived in the pasture. Martin whinnied back. Ella stared at what was left of the mansion.

"I'm sorry, Ella. It was your home. Long before it was ours," Isabelle said.

"I don't miss it," Ella said. "I hope all the ghosts escaped when the walls fell in."

Felix and Hugo had already carried one of the coffins to the base of the linden tree. Felix pried the lid off with a knife he'd tucked into his pocket.

Tavi and Isabelle carried the second coffin. Felix pried the lid off that one, too. Then they all turned to Ella.

"How do we do it?" Felix asked her. "How do we summon Tanaquill?"

"I—I don't actually know," Ella said. "Isabelle, do you?"

Isabelle felt a flutter of panic. "No," she said. "I can't remember exactly what I did."

Ella took a deep breath. "Let me think . . . I remember walking to the linden tree after everyone had left for the ball. I was so upset. I wanted to go more than I've ever wanted anything. With my whole heart. And then suddenly, she just appeared."

"A tall woman . . ." Felix said with a shiver in his voice.

"Yes," said Ella.

"With red hair and green eyes and sharp teeth."

"How do you know that?"

"Because," Felix said, pointing past them to the ruins. "She's already here."

One Hundred and Twenty

Tanaquill walked out of the shadows.

She wore a gown made of black beetle shells that gleamed darkly in the moon's waning light. Her crown was a circlet of bats. Three young adders curled around her neck; their heads rested like jewels on her collarbones.

Tanaquill addressed Ella. "I did not expect to see you back here. And certainly not in the company of your stepsisters. All you wanted when last we spoke was to get away from this place. Now you return?"

"I would not be here, standing in front of you, if Isabelle had not rescued me from a traitor's plot. If Octavia had not thrown my enemies off my scent. I owe them my life. Now Isabelle needs your help, Your Grace."

Tanaquill circled Isabelle. She placed a sharp black talon under her chin and lifted it.

"Have you found all the pieces, girl?"

"Yes, Your Grace. I-I think so. I hope so," Isabelle said.

"And now that your heart is whole, what does it tell you?"

Isabelle looked down at her clenched hands. She thought of Malleval and tears of anger welled in her eyes. She thought of the grand duke coolly arranging the deaths of his young king and queen. She remembered the sweet weight of a sword in her hand.

"It tells me impossible things," she whispered.

"Do you still desire to be pretty? Say the word and I will make it so."

Isabelle looked up at the sky for some time, blinking her tears away. "No," she finally said.

"What is it that you wish for, then?" Tanaquill asked.

"An army," Isabelle replied, meeting the fairy queen's eyes. "I wish to raise an army against Volkmar and the grand duke. I wish to save my family, my friends, my country."

"You ask a great deal," Tanaquill said. "Nothing comes from nothing. Magic must come from something. Coaches can come from pumpkins; that is child's play. But an army? That is far more difficult. Even I cannot make a private out of a pebble, a major out of a mushroom."

"We brought you these," Isabelle said, hurrying to the coffins. She picked up a figure—an officer holding a saber across his chest—and put it in Tanaquill's hand.

Tanaquill regarded it. She cocked her head.

"Please, Your Grace," Isabelle said. "Please help us."

Tanaquill's deep green eyes caught Isabelle's. Held by their gaze, Isabelle felt as if the fairy queen could see deep inside her. Tanaquill stepped back, raised one hand high, and swirled it through the air.

A breeze rose. It turned into a wind. And the wind curled in on itself, spinning in a widening gyre.

Isabelle's pulse quickened as the wind whirled the figurines

436

out of the coffins and spread them across the lawns, the gardens, the paddocks and fields.

When the coffins were empty, the wind stopped.

And a new sound rose.

One Hundred and Twenty-One

Isabelle felt the ground under her feet rumble and shudder.

Creaks and groans and sharp, shattering cracks were heard—the sounds trees make in a violent storm. Isabelle looked out over the hills and fields, illuminated now by the dawn's first light.

Felix's tiny carved figures were growing.

Isabelle's heart beat madly as she watched them. Wooden bodies drew breath. They stretched tall, heads back, arms open wide to the sky. Wooden cheeks flushed with color. Blank eyes ignited with the fire of war.

Shouts carried across the fields as sergeants ordered men into formation. Isabelle heard the heavy metallic clunks of rounds being chambered and rifles being shouldered. A sea of blue uniforms flowed around her.

Two horses jumped the paddock fence and galloped to Tanaquill. As the fairy queen stroked them and spoke to them, Isabelle realized that they were the two she had rescued. They looked nothing like their former selves. Their coats gleamed; their manes rippled. They huffed and blew and raked at the ground, impatient for their riders.

Tanaquill stepped back as two men—lieutenants, Isabelle reasoned, judging from their uniforms—claimed the horses. They swung up into their saddles easily, lengthened their reins, then turned to Isabelle.

"Our general, mademoiselle. Where is he?" one of them asked her. "We await our orders."

Isabelle craned her neck. She looked past the lieutenants. Out over the garden. The paddocks. Searching for their general. He would be tall and powerful. Scarred from his many battles. An intimidating man with a fierce bearing.

But she didn't see him.

"Where is he?" she asked, turning to Felix. "Where's the general?"

"Isabelle . . ." Felix said, shaking his head. "I—I didn't carve one."

One Hundred and Twenty-Two

"Felix, what do you mean, you didn't carve one?" Isabelle asked, panicking.

"I was going to carve him at the end. I'd finished the soldiers and all the other officers—I just didn't get to the general."

"What are we going to do?" Isabelle said.

"What about the marquis?" Tavi asked. "He would make a good general."

"Yes! The marquis!" Isabelle said, turning to Tanaquill. "I'll go fetch him. It won't take long. It—"

"There's no time," Tanaquill said, cutting her off. She pointed at the enchanted army. "Look at them."

The soldiers' movements were becoming stiff and jerky. Their color was fading. Their eyes were dulling.

"What happening to them?" Isabelle asked, distraught.

"They are warriors. They exist only to fight. If they have no general to lead them into battle, their fire fades. The magic dies."

Isabelle's panic bloomed into terror. She couldn't lose this army. It was the only chance Ella had. The only chance their country had.

"What about Felix? Or Hugo? Can you transform one of them into a general?" Isabelle asked.

She turned to the boys, expecting to see Felix wearing a uniform, to see Hugo with a sword, but they remained exactly as they were.

"What's wrong? Why didn't anything happen?" she asked.

"That is your wish, not theirs," Tanaquill replied.

Isabelle turned to the two boys. *"Please,"* she begged them.

"Isabelle, I'm a *carpenter*. I haven't even reported for training yet. I'd get these men killed," Felix said.

Hugo shook his head; he stepped back.

Isabelle pressed the heels of her hands to her head. "What can we do?"

Tanaquill circled her again. "What is your heart's wish, Isabelle? Its truest wish?" she asked.

"To save my queen, my king, my country," Isabelle babbled madly. "To save innocents from being slaughtered."

But again, nothing happened.

"To give these fighters a general who is brave. Who's a true warrior. Who will give everything to the fight—his blood and tears. His body and soul. His life."

Tanaquill stopped in front of Isabelle. She pressed a taloned hand to her chest.

Isabelle could hear her heart beating, louder and louder. The sound was crashing in her ears. Filling her head.

Tanaquill's voice cut through it like thunder. "I will ask you one last time, Isabelle—what is your heart's desire?"

One Hundred and Twenty-Three

Isabelle tried to speak, to form words, but her heart was pounding so loudly, the sound filled her throat and they wouldn't come.

She closed her eyes and a thousand images swirled through her head. She saw herself as a child, happy and free. Before she was told that she was less than, that all the things she loved were the wrong things.

She saw herself flying over fences on Nero. Galloping over fields, the mud flying from his hooves. She saw herself climbing to the top of the linden tree with Felix, imagining the branches were the rigging of a pirate ship. Fighting duels with a mop handle. Fighting off a hungry wolf from the chicken coop with nothing but a broomstick.

Those childhood images vanished and others came. She saw herself fighting against Maman. Against dull boys she wouldn't have willingly spent ten minutes with, never mind a lifetime. Fighting against the endless dreary days of teacups and cakes, fake smiles and small talk.

Isabelle saw now that she'd been fighting her entire life to be who she was.

With anguish, and hope, and yearning, she asked her heart how to win that fight.

And her heart answered.

She covered Tanaquill's hand with her own.

And Tanaquill, smiling, said, "Yes."

One Hundred and Twenty-Four

Isabelle opened her eyes and looked around.

Tanaquill had stepped away, into the shadows under the linden tree.

But Tavi, Ella, Felix, and Hugo were frozen in place. They were staring at her. Tavi was smiling. Ella was wide-eyed. Hugo was openmouthed. Tears were spilling down Felix's cheeks.

Isabelle looked down at herself and caught her breath.

Her worn dress was gone. She was wearing leather breeches, a tunic of chain mail, and a gleaming silver breastplate. In her hands she held a finely made helmet. The weight of her armor, and the drag of her sword at her hip, were sweet to her. She felt taller, stronger, as if she were no longer made of blood, bones, and tender flesh, but iron and steel.

A high, fierce whinny echoed across the gray morning.

Isabelle turned and saw a black stallion cantering up the drive. He was wearing a blanket of mail and a silver faceplate. He looked fierce and majestic, a horse fit for a warrior.

He slowed to a trot, then stopped in front of Isabelle and snorted. Isabelle laughed. She patted his neck.

"He was shut in a stall. In a stable in the village," she said, turning to the fairy queen. "How did he get out?"

Tanaquill shrugged. "Kicked the door down, I imagine. You know what he's like."

Isabelle walked around to Nero's left side. Hugo held her helmet while Felix boosted her up into the saddle. Tavi and Ella gathered close.

The lieutenants sat up tall in their saddles, awaiting orders. All across the grounds of the Maison Douleur, in its fields and meadows, soldiers stood at attention.

It was dead silent as they waited, their eyes on Isabelle.

"I'm afraid," she whispered, squeezing Felix's hand. "I don't know how to do this. I've never been a general."

"You know the most important thing," Felix said. "You know how to be brave. You've always known that."

"You know how to outmaneuver the enemy," Ella said. "You got us here."

"You know how to fight," Tavi said.

"You're the worst girl I've ever met, Isabelle," Hugo added, with touching sincerity. "You're so tough and stubborn, you give me nightmares."

Isabelle gave him a tremulous smile. "Thank you, Hugo. I know there's a compliment in there somewhere."

"Go now," Felix told her, releasing her hand. "And then come back."

Hugo handed Isabelle her helmet. She took it, then bowed her head to the fairy queen. "Thank you," she said, with a catch in her voice.

Tanaquill nodded. "What was cut away is whole again," she said. "The pieces of your heart are restored. The boy is

445

love—constant and true. The horse, courage—wild and untamed. Your stepsister is your conscience—kind and compassionate. Know that you are a warrior, Isabelle, and that a true warrior carries love, courage, and her conscience into battle, as surely as she carries her sword."

Isabelle put on her helmet. She drew her sword from its scabbard and raised it high. Nero stamped at the ground. He turned in a circle and pulled at the reins, eager to be off. The muscles in Isabelle's arms rippled. The sword's silver blade gleamed.

A cheer rose, a war cry from two thousand throats. It rang out over the land and echoed through the hills. Isabelle smiled, reveling in the thunderous sound.

"Soldiers!" she shouted as it died down. "We march on a fearsome enemy this morning! He murders our people, he plunders our villages and towns, lays waste to our fields. He has no claim to our lands. Greed and bloodlust are all that drive him. He and his fighters are without mercy. Their hearts burn with the flames of conquest, but ours shine with the light of justice. We will surround the Devil's Hollow. We will fight him there, and we will vanquish him!"

The roar that rose then was the sound of a hurricane, a tidal wave, an earthquake. It rolled on, an awesome force that nothing could stop. The soldiers were mesmerized by Isabelle. They would have marched into the depths of hell and fought the devil himself had she asked them to.

"For king, and queen, and country!" Isabelle shouted.

She touched her heels to Nero. He reared, hooves battering the sky, then lunged forward, bolting for the stone wall and the field beyond. Her lieutenants rode after her. Her soldiers followed.

Isabelle rode tall in her saddle. Her color was high, her eyes were flashing.

She was fearsome.

She was strong.

She was beautiful.

One Hundred and Twenty-Five

The moon had faded. The stars had all winked out.

Tanaquill's work was done.

She watched, a half smile on her lips, as Felix, with his dagger, and Hugo, with an ax he pulled from a chopping block, followed the troops, determined to fight with them.

Ella and Tavi clambered back into the cart and started down the drive to what was left of their stables. Tavi planned to stow the cart there, put Martin in the pasture, and hide in the chicken coop with Ella until it was safe to come out.

As the wagon trundled off, two figures emerged from behind the ruins of the mansion. One was an elderly woman, dressed all in black; the other a young man in a blue frock coat and suede breeches.

"She did it. I had my doubts," Tanaquill said as the two figures approached her. "The girl is brave. Far braver than she knows."

"I've come for the map. It's mine," said Fate. "You must return it to me."

"You should give it to me. I won the wager," said Chance.

Tanaquill faced the crone. "Isabelle's life will no longer be mapped out by you." She turned her green eyes on Chance.

"Nor will it be altered by you," she said. "Her life is a wide-open landscape now, and if she survives the day, she will make her own path through it."

As Tanaquill spoke these words, she pulled Isabelle's map from the folds of her cloak. She tossed it high into the air and whispered a spell. The map dissolved into a fine, shimmering dust and was carried away on the breeze.

Fate and Chance watched it disappear, then turned to the fairy queen, full of protests. But she was gone. They saw a flash of red as a fox leapt over a stone wall. Their gaze followed her as she loped through the fields and over the hills. She stopped at the edge of the Wildwood to glance back at them once, then vanished into the trees.

There *is* magic in this sad, hard world. A magic stronger than fate, stronger than chance. And it is seen in the unlikeliest of places.

By a hearth at night, as a girl leaves a bit of cheese for a hungry mouse.

In a slaughter yard, as the old and infirm, the weak and discarded, are made to matter more than money.

In a poor carpenter's small attic room, where three sisters learned that the price of forgiveness is forgiving.

And now, on a battlefield, as a mere girl tries to turn the red tide of war.

It is the magic of a frail and fallible creature, one capable of both unspeakable cruelty and immense kindness. It lives inside every human being ready to redeem us. To transform us. To save us. If we can only find the courage to listen to it.

It is the magic of the human heart.

One Hundred and Twenty-Six

The scout brought good news.

The wall of blackbriar rising up from the river, thick and impenetrable, was still there.

"Good," Isabelle said quietly. "That walls off the southern edge of Volkmar's camp and blocks any chance of escape up the mountain into the Wildwood."

As she spoke, she sketched a diagram of the Hollow in the dirt with a stick. Her lieutenants stood clustered around her, watching as she drew the camp, hidden in the hollow's centre.

"We need to surround the other three sides and block off *all* escape routes," she continued, drawing an arc from one edge of the blackbriar wall to the other and enclosing the camp within it. "Divide the troops in two. One half goes to the west, the other to the east. They meet here, where we are now," she said, tapping her stick at the diagram's northernmost point. "Be quick. Be silent. Send the signal as soon as you're in place. Go."

Isabelle had brought her troops out of Saint-Michel, around the Wildwood, and down a long, rutted road to the border of the Devil's Hollow. They had marched double time the whole way, but the sun was rising now, and they no longer had darkness as their ally. Isabelle had maintained what she hoped was about a two-mile distance between her troops and Volkmar's camp, to keep them from being seen or heard, but she knew the chances of their being spotted increased with every moment that passed.

If that happened, she would lose the asset of surprise. She believed that her troops outnumbered Volkmar's, but Malleval had shown her what the enemy was capable of. Isabelle knew she would need every advantage she could get. Until the signal came, she would be on tenterhooks.

The lieutenants rode to their troops and gave their orders in low, urgent voices. Immediately the soldiers disappeared among the trees. They were made of wood. They were creatures of the forest, and as they moved into place, they became one with it again, making no more noise than a branch creaking in the wind, or leaves whispering in the breeze.

Isabelle nodded to a young, wiry private. He saluted her, then climbed a tall pine tree behind her, a spyglass tucked inside his jacket.

Twenty minutes passed. Thirty. Isabelle had given orders that each company send a man up a tree with a piece of red cloth. The man was to wave it when all the members of his company were in place. Forty minutes went by.

She tightened her grip on her sword. *What is taking them so long?* she wondered tensely. Nero tossed his head but made no noise.

Just when she thought her taut nerves would snap, she heard it—a hawk's cry, made by the young private high in the tree above. That was the signal. The red flags had all been sighted. Everyone was in place.

Isabelle lowered her head. *Elizabeth, Yennenga, Abhaya Rani, be with me*, she prayed. *Give me cunning and strength. Make me fearless. Make me bold.*

Then she lifted her head, raised her sword, and shouted, *"Charge!"*

One Hundred and Twenty-Seven

The grand duke never saw Isabelle coming.

After she and Ella had escaped, he'd ridden to Cafard's camp to order search parties out after them; then he'd returned to Volkmar's camp, where he'd spent the rest of the night. He'd been in his tent, shaving in front of his mirror, as Isabelle had been fanning her forces out along the edge of the Devil's Hollow.

He'd been buttoning his jacket as she took her place at the head of them.

He was sitting at a campaign table, slathering butter on a slice of toast, as she and her fighters descended.

Shouts and screams brought him to his feet. He heard gunshots. Horses whinnying. A jet of blood spattering across the wall of his tent. The wet *thuk* of a blade being driven home.

He grabbed his scabbard, buckled it around his waist, and ran out into the fray. The camp was in chaos. Isabelle's soldiers were swarming through it, savaging Volkmar's troops.

"My horse! Bring me my horse!" he bellowed, but no one answered his command. Men were falling all around him. The air was filled with the white smoke of gunpowder. The grand duke's hand went to the hilt of his sword, but he never got a chance to draw it. His last sight was of a girl on a black stallion, an avenging fury bearing down on him. And then Isabelle drove her blade into his chest, straight through his treacherous heart.

He fell to his knees, a crimson stain blooming across his jacket, an expression of surprise on his face. Then he toppled forward into the dirt.

Isabelle did not stop to exult, for she took no pleasure in killing, but rode on determined to do more of it. Soldier after soldier fell under her slashing sword. Her men swirled through the camp like a raging, flood-swollen river, some fighting with swords, others with bayoneted rifles. They set fire to tents, destroyed paddocks, freed horses, smashed wagons.

Though they'd been surprised, Volkmar's men quickly rallied. They were formidable soldiers who were fighting for their lives, and they put up a strong counterattack. But Isabelle was fighting for the lives of her countrymen and she fought like a lion, urging Nero on, deeper and deeper into the camp.

She'd just run her sword through an officer who'd been aiming his rifle at one of her lieutenants when she heard hooves behind her. Turning in her saddle, she saw a rider bearing down on her. He wore the uniform of the invaders. There was a sword in his hand and murder in his eyes.

Someone's just walked over your grave, whispered Adélie's voice.

Had he?

Here, in the Devil's Hollow, she would finally find out.

Isabelle whirled Nero around.
Came face-to-face with Volkmar.
And let the wolf run free.

One Hundred and Twenty-Eight

Blue sparks flew into the air as the two swords clashed.

Volkmar was bigger, he was stronger, but Isabelle was nimble. She parried his blows with her blade, blocked them with her shield.

On and on they fought, their horses churning the dirt around them, their shouts and grunts and oaths mingling with those of their soldiers. Volkmar hammered against Isabelle's shield, making her left arm shudder. He had run out of his tent without armor. Isabelle deftly thrust her sword at his unprotected head, opening a gash in his cheek, but neither was able to deliver a killing blow.

Then Volkmar reversed direction and swung his sword at Isabelle's back, catching her with the flat of his blade. The force of the blow sent her sprawling out of her saddle to the ground. The impact knocked her helmet off, but she managed to hold on to her sword.

Volkmar jumped down from his mount and advanced on her. Dazed by her fall, Isabelle didn't see him coming. But as he raised his sword, one of Isabelle's soldiers, fighting only a few feet away, shouted a warning.

The blade slashed through the air. Isabelle rolled to her right, trying to get out of its way, but its tip bit into her left calf. She screamed and scrabbled backward across the ground with her good leg,

Volkmar ran at her and kicked her in the side, behind her chest plate. There was a crunch of bone. Blinding pain. She fell onto her other side, gasping, her sword underneath her.

"Get up, you little bitch. Stand up like the man you think you are and face your death."

Isabelle tried to get up. She struggled to her knees. Volkmar backhanded her savagely across the face, knocking her to the ground again.

Isabelle's entire body was made of pain. She struggled to see through its red fog. Volkmar was nearby, circling, playing with her before he killed her.

"Pick up your sword! Come at me!" Volkmar shouted at her.

Spitting out a mouthful of blood, Isabelle raised her eyes to his. He was holding his own sword across his body to protect his gut. She knew that her only chance was to somehow get to her feet, then get him to lower his blade.

But how? she wondered.

Appear weak when you are strong, and strong when you are weak, came the answer.

"Thank you, Sun Tzu," she whispered.

"Please," she begged Volkmar. "Don't kill me."

Her enemy smiled at the fear in her eyes, at the pain in her voice. "Oh, I *will* kill you. But not just yet," he said.

His arm relaxed slightly, his blade dipped a little.

With effort, Isabelle pushed herself to her feet, then tried to hobble away, dragging her wounded leg behind her.

Volkmar circled, taunting her. He'd already counted her among his kills. He had no idea that she had fallen off horses a thousand times and knew how to bury her pain. He did not know about the duels she'd fought under the linden tree as a child. How she'd practiced with scarecrows at the LeBenêts'. How she'd learned to parry and thrust, to feint, fall back, then strike. He could not see that she was feinting now. Her wound was bleeding badly, but it was not deep. The kick he'd delivered to her rib cage hurt like hell, but she had not lost her breath, her will, or her courage.

Panting, grimacing, one hand pressed to her side for effect, Isabelle stood, her head bent in supplication. She was leaning on her sword, using it as a crutch. Making it look as if she was helpless, her weapon useless.

Though her gaze was down, she could see Volkmar's feet and his sword. The tip was only an inch or so above the ground now. He walked towards her.

Closer, she urged him. *Just a little bit closer . . .*

"You're a good fighter, I'll admit. For a girl," Volkmar said, only a few feet away now. "But you're too rash to be a great fighter. You have more courage than common sense."

Closer . . . that's it . . .

"The grand duke told me about you. And how you maimed yourself to marry the prince." He chuckled. "I'll bet you surprised *him*. I saw you kill him. It was a lucky thrust, of course. But still. I'm sure he never expected to see you back here, and at the head of an army, no less. He never expected much at all from a plain girl pathetic enough to cut off her own toes."

Closer . . .

Isabelle tightened her grip on her sword. She took a deep, steadying breath, then slowly raised her head.

"No, of course not. Why would he? Why would you?" she asked. "But I don't cut off toes anymore . . ."

And then, with an earsplitting cry, she swung her blade high and sliced cleanly through Volkmar's neck.

"I cut off heads."

One Hundred and Twenty-Nine

The door to Isabelle's carriage opened.

She stepped out and strode purposefully up the sweeping marble stairs that led up to the palace's tall, gold-washed doors. Soldiers lined both sides of the stairs. They snapped her a salute; she returned it.

This was a special day. Isabelle could barely contain her excitement.

Two footmen opened the doors for her, another ushered her inside. The grand foyer, all marble and mirrors, was illuminated by a thousand candles flickering in crystal chandeliers. As she walked through it, she thought about the first time she had come to the palace—with Tavi and Maman for the prince's ball.

Her heart clenched as she recalled how they'd left Ella at home, sobbing in the kitchen. Isabelle had been wearing a stiff silk gown then—trimmed with glass beads, festooned with lace. Her hair had been piled up on her head in an absurd bird's nest of a style. As she'd entered the palace, she'd caught a glimpse of herself in a mirror—and had hated the girl who'd looked back at her.

She passed that same mirror now and stopped, just for a few seconds, to look at her reflection. A different girl gazed back now—one whose bearing was confident, who stood with her head high. This girl wore her hair in a simple braid. She was dressed in a close-cut high-necked jacket of navy twill, and a long, matching split skirt that allowed her to ride with ease. Shiny black leather boots peeked out from its hem.

Underneath her uniform, a white bandage was wound tightly around her torso to help with the pain from the ribs Volkmar had broken when he'd kicked her. A line of stitches ran down the outside of her left calf where he'd opened a jagged gash with his sword. The wound was healing nicely. A field surgeon had stitched it closed after the Battle of Devil's Hollow.

That fight had been bloody and long, but Isabelle had won it. She and her forces had descended on Saint-Michel next, where they'd removed Colonel Cafard as commander and locked him up. Then she'd headed for the king's encampment.

She'd had the map showing the whereabouts of the rest of Volkmar's troops. She'd attacked them one after the other, winning three more battles before she even reached the king. Once she'd arrived at the king's camp, she'd explained who she was and why she'd come, and then she'd given the king Volkmar's map, and his own—as proof of the grand duke's treachery. Together they'd routed the rest of the invaders.

Tanaquill's magic was strong. It hadn't ended at midnight like the enchantment she'd made for Ella but had faded slowly. After each battle, when it came time for the dead to be collected and buried, none could be found. None of Isabelle's soldiers, that is. Those whose task it was to comb the fields after the fighting found only the bodies of Volkmar's troops, and sometimes, strangely, a small carved wooden figure tangled in the grass.

The blackbriar wall had sunk back into the river after the Battle of Devil's Hollow. Isabelle had returned to the linden tree, knelt down, and tucked a medal that she'd been given for valor into the hollow.

"For you," she said, bowing her head. "Thank you."

A footman, hovering at Isabelle's elbow, cleared his throat now, pulling her out of her memories. "General, the king and queen are waiting in the Grand Hall," he informed her.

Isabelle nodded and followed him. He led her down a long corridor, to a pair of gilded doors. Giving them a mighty push, he entered the palace's Grand Hall and announced Isabelle's name.

At the far end of the hall, seated on golden thrones, were King Charles and Queen Ella. Lining both sides of the room, three rows deep, were the noble heads of France, dozens of courtiers, ministers, officials, and friends.

As Isabelle proceeded down the centre of the room towards the royal couple, she saw Hugo and his new wife, Odette. Tavi was there, in her scholar's robes. At the queen's urging, the king had decreed that all the universities and colleges in the land must admit female scholars. Maman stood next to her, beaming at this duke and that countess. She had apologized to Ella, they had reconciled, and she now spent her days in the palace gardens, talking to royal cabbage heads.

Felix was there, too, and Isabelle's heart danced when she saw him, dressed up in a new jacket. The man to whom he'd sold the wooden soldiers demanded that Felix return his money, but the king had been so grateful to Felix for making the army that had saved France, that he paid the man back himself and gave Felix a scholarship to Paris's finest art school. Felix was busy every day learning how to sculpt stone, but he made time to ride with Isabelle every evening in the king's own forest.

Isabelle had reached the king and queen now. She stopped a few feet away from them, bowed her head, and knelt.

The king rose. A gloved servant stood nearby holding a gleaming ebony box. He opened it, revealing a heavy golden chain of office nestled in black velvet. The king lifted the chain out of the box, walked to Isabelle, and put it over her head. He settled it on her shoulders, then bade her rise and turn to face his court.

"Lords and ladies, citizens of France, we are all here today because of the courage and strength of this young woman. I can never repay her for all that she's done. And I will never part with her. I have come to rely upon her wise counsel. Her bravery and strength inspire me with hope as we move from the destruction of war to the golden days of peace. I have made sure she will always be by my side. At meetings of my nobles and ministers, and, should it ever come to it again, on the battlefield." The king smiled at Isabelle, then said, "Good people, I give you France's bravest warrior . . . and my new grand duchess."

The applause was deafening. Shouts and cheers echoed off the high stone walls.

Isabelle's heart beat strongly—with joy, with gratitude, with pride—as she looked at the faces of all the ones she loved.

Ella joined Isabelle and the king, and together they walked down the steps to greet the court. Well-wishers mobbed Isabelle.

463

Family and friends hugged and kissed her. Nobles wanted to hear her recount her battles. Ministers asked for her thoughts on the state of fortifications along the border.

The attention was dizzying. She stepped back for a moment to ask a servant for a drink. As she did, she saw another face in the crowd. And for an instant, it felt as if time had stopped and the king and queen, and everyone in their court, had been frozen in place.

The Marquis de la Chance smiled. He was tossing a gold coin in the air. He flipped it at her. She caught it. Then he doffed his hat and disappeared into the press of people.

Isabelle watched him go, clutching the coin tightly in her hand.

She never saw him again.

She never forgot the day she'd met him, or how his friends had told her to want to be more than pretty. She never forgot Elizabeth, Yennenga, Abhaya Rani. She wore his gold coin on a chain around her neck until the day she died. But the thing she treasured most was the memory of his smile, a smile that was a wink and a dare. A wild road on a windy night. A kiss in the dark.

A smile that had given her all she'd ever wanted—a chance. A chance to be herself.

Epilogue

The boom of the large brass knocker, so rarely used, echoed ominously throughout the ancient palazzo.

The mother looked up from her work. Candlelight played over her face. "Are we expecting visitors?" she asked.

"Who is it?" the crone barked at a servant.

The servant scuttled to the map room's huge double doors and opened them, then he hurried down several flights of stairs to the street doors.

A man was standing on the threshold, dressed in a brown velvet frock coat. His long black braids hung down his back. A large satchel was slung over one shoulder. A monkey was perched on the other. The servant gave the man a dark look, but he ushered him inside and led him upstairs.

"You had to bring your blasted monkey," the crone said, as the man walked into the map room.

"Nelson's very well-behaved," Chance said.

"You have an odd idea of good behavior," the crone commented. "What can I do for you?"

Chance pressed a hand to his chest, feigning offense. "Do for me? I've come only to enjoy the pleasure of your company, not to beg favors," he said.

The crone gave him a skeptical look. "Our contest ended in a draw. I do not have to give you any maps."

"And I am still allowed to visit my three favorite ladies in their beautiful palazzo," Chance said, flashing a charming smile.

"If I allow you to stay, you must promise that you will not steal any more maps."

Chance solemnly held up his right hand. "I promise," he said.

The crone waved him inside and bade him sit down at the long worktable. The servant was sent to fetch refreshments. Other servants, cloaked and hooded, moved silently down the long rows of shelves that contained the Fates' maps.

Chance put his satchel on the floor and sat. He turned to the little monkey and patted him. "Hop down, Nelson," he said. "Stretch your legs."

"Don't let him go far," the crone warned.

"He won't. He'll just play around my feet," Chance assured her.

The servant reappeared with a bottle of port, four glasses, and a tray of fine cheeses. When everyone had been served, the crone asked, "To what do we owe the honor of your visit?"

"Truth be told—"

"I doubt it will be," said the maiden.

"—I felt bad about my last visit. It was a bit rushed. I left so abruptly."

"Thieves usually do," the crone said.

"I wanted to make amends, so I brought some gifts,"

Chance finished.

"I believe that's what the Trojans said to the Greeks," the mother observed.

Chance bent down and opened his satchel. One by one, he pulled presents out of it. "Pearls from Japan," he said handing a small suede sack to the maiden. "Silk from India." He gave a bolt of shimmering crimson cloth to the mother. "And for you"—he handed the crone a velvet-covered box—"black opals from Brazil."

"These are generous gifts, thank you," said the crone. Then she gave him a knowing smile. "I still say you want something in return."

"No. Nothing," Chance said innocently. He smiled, waited a few beats, then said, "Well, perhaps *one* small thing . . ."

He dipped into his bag again and placed three small bottles on the table.

"Here are some inks I made especially for you," he said. "Perhaps you could try them out. That's all I ask. Here's *Moxie* . . ." He pulled out a bottle containing an ink the shimmering teal blue of a peacock's tail. "This one's *Guts*." That one was a fleshy, intestinal pink. "And my favorite, *Defiance*." He held that up to the light. It flared red and orange in the bottle, like liquid fire.

The crone gave the inks a dismissive wave. The mother eyed them suspiciously. But the maiden picked up *Defiance*, swirled it in the bottle, and smiled.

As she did, a noise was heard from deep within the towering rows of shelves. A sound like an entire shelf of maps falling to the floor.

The crone's eyes narrowed. "Where's that monkey?" she demanded.

"He's right here," Chance said, bending down to the floor. He picked up the little capuchin, who'd been sitting by his satchel, and placed him on the table. The monkey looked at the crone. He blew her a kiss.

The crone's scowl deepened. A servant hurried to see what had caused the noise, then reported back that some maps had, indeed, fallen to the floor. He suggested that the shelf had been overloaded and assured the Fates that the problem was being fixed. The crone nodded; her scowl relaxed back into a frown.

Chance drained his glass, thanked the Fates for their hospitality, then he said he must be going. He cinched his bag and picked it up. Nelson jumped onto his shoulder.

The crone accompanied him to the map room's doors. As they said their goodbyes, she suddenly took hold of his arm. With something almost like pity in her voice, she said, "The girl—Isabelle—she was an exception. Do not ask more of mortals than they can give."

"You are wrong. They have so much to give. Each and every one of them. More, sometimes, than they know."

Fate released his arm. "You are a fool, my friend."

Chance nodded. "Perhaps, but I am happy."

"In this world, only a fool could be."

A servant led him out of the map room, and back down the stairs to the street. Chance stepped outside, then turned to thank the servant, but he was gone. The doors were already locked behind him.

Chance tilted his face to the dark sky, happy to see the

stars and the moon, happy to be out of the gloomy palazzo. Nelson, still on his shoulder, pointed to a group of colorfully dressed people who were loitering nearby in the glow of a street lantern. Chance hurried across to them.

"Well?" said the magician, raising an eyebrow.

"She made me promise I wouldn't steal anything," Chance said. "I honored it."

The magician's face fell. So did everyone else's.

Then Chance opened his satchel. Three monkeys jumped out, chattering gleefully. Nelson chattered back.

"She didn't make *them* promise, though," Chance said, cracking his rogue's smile.

He opened the bag wide, so his friends could see inside it. Nestled on the bottom, slightly squashed by the monkeys, were a dozen rolled maps.

Laughing, Chance took the magician's arm; then they and their friends ran down the sidewalk into the ancient city, into the crowd, into the beautiful, sparkling, full-of-possibilities night.

Acknowledgements

Stepsister is a story I've wanted to tell for years. That I finally get to is because of many wonderful people and I can never thank them enough, but I'm going to try anyway.

Thank you to Mallory Kass, my awesome editor, for her intelligence, huge heart, sense of humor, and affection for ugly stepsisters, balky horses, high-strung authors, and other difficult creatures. Isabelle and I are so lucky to have our very own Tanaquill in you – minus the sharp teeth and talons!

A huge, heartfelt thank you to Dick Robinson, Ellie Berger, David Levithan, Tracy van Straaten, Lori Benton, Amanda Maciel, Rachel Feld, Lizette Serrano, Lauren Donovan, Alan Smagler and his team, Elizabeth Parisi, Maeve Norton, Melissa Schirmer, and the rest of my Scholastic family for your incredible enthusiasm for *Stepsister*, and for your lovely welcome to my new home. A very special thank you to Jane Harris, Emma Matthewson, Jenny Jacoby, and the whole Hot Key team for bringing the story to my UK readers. It all means the world to me.

Thank you to Graham Taylor and Negeen Yazdi at Endeavor Content, Bruna Papandrea at Made Up Stories, and Lynette

Howell Taylor at 51 Entertainment, for working to bring *Stepsister* to film. I am so proud to be partnering with all of you, and so excited for what's to come. A huge thank you to film agent Sylvie Rabineau at WME, and Ken Kleinberg and Alex Plitt at Kleinman, Lange, Cuddy & Carlo, for your excellent counsel and guidance.

Thank you to my wonderful agent, Steve Malk at Writers House, for believing in *Stepsister*, and all my stories, and me. Wherever you go, go with all your heart, Confucius tells us. I get to tell stories, to follow my heart every day, because I have Steve as my traveling companion on the writer's journey. Thank you, too, to my foreign rights agent, the amazing Cecilia de la Campa, for bringing *Stepsister* to readers across the world.

Thank you to illustrator Retta Scott for the Big Golden Books' Cinderella. Thank you to my grandmother Mary for reading it to me five million times. Thank you to Pablo Picasso. His saying "I am always doing things I cannot do. That's how I get to do them", inspired a similar remark from the Marquis de la Chance when he first meets Isabelle, and has always inspired me.

Thank you to my lovely family – Doug, Daisy, Wilfriede, and Megan – for reading early versions of the story and giving me valuable feedback and encouragement. An extra thank you to Doug for the cool tagline. Thanks most of all for putting up with me, guys. You teach me every day what real beauty is all about.

Thank you to the fairy godparents – to the countless generations of storytellers who told the ancient tales to sleepy-eyed children gathered around the fire at night, and to the collectors like Jakob and Wilhelm Grimm who preserved them in writing. Because of these elders, the old stories endured, as vital and relevant today as they were centuries ago.

Fairytales were so important to me as a child. They still are. They're entertaining, instructive, and inspiring, but more importantly, they're truthful.

The world conspires in a thousand ways to tell us that we're not enough, that we're less than, that life's one big, long party on the beach and we're not invited. Dark woods? What dark woods? Wolves? What wolves? Don't worry about them. Just buy this, eat that, wear those, and you'll get on the invite list. You'll be cool. Hot. Liked. Loved. Happy.

Fairy tales give it to us straight. They tell us something profound and essential – that the woods are real, and dark, and full of wolves. That we will, at times, find ourselves hopelessly lost in them. But these tales also tell us that we are all we need, that we have all we need – guts, smarts, and maybe a pocketful of breadcrumbs – to find our way home.

And that brings me to my last thank you – it's to you, dear reader. Thank you for loving words and stories as much as I do. Thank you for your lovely posts and emails. Thank you for being part of my own fairytale. You are everything I ever wished for.

**HOT
KEY
BOOKS**

Thank you for choosing a Hot Key book.

If you want to know more about our authors
and what we publish, you can find us online.

You can start at our website

www.hotkeybooks.com

And you can also find us on:

We hope to see you soon!

theo

AMANDA PROWSE is the author of nineteen
novels including the number 1 bestsellers
What Have I Done?, *Perfect Daughter* and *My
Husband's Wife*. Her books have sold millions
of copies worldwide, and she is published in
dozens of languages.

Amanda lives in the West Country
with her husband and two sons.

www.amandaprowse.org

9030 00006 2188 0

theo

Amanda Prowse

HEAD
ZEUS

First published in the UK in 2018 by Head of Zeus Ltd
This paperback edition published in 2018 by Head of Zeus Ltd

Copyright © Amanda Prowse, 2018

The moral right of Amanda Prowse to be identified as the author
of this work has been asserted in accordance with the
Copyright, Designs and Patents Act of 1988.

All rights reserved. No part of this publication may be
reproduced, stored in a retrieval system, or transmitted in any form
or by any means, electronic, mechanical, photocopying, recording,
or otherwise, without the prior permission of both the copyright
owner and the above publisher of this book.

This is a work of fiction. All characters, organizations,
and events portrayed in this novel are either products of
the author's imagination or are used fictitiously.

9 7 5 3 1 2 4 6 8

A catalogue record for this book is available from
the British Library.

ISBN (PB): 9781788542128
ISBN (E): 9781788542050

Typeset by Adrian McLaughlin

LONDON BOROUGH OF WANDSWORTH	
9030 00006 2188 0	
Askews & Holts	11-Oct-2018
AF	£7.99
	WW18008799

I dedicate Anna and Theo to you, my readers.

Alexandra Ackroyd, Christopher Ackroyd, Ardelle Acosta, Lindsay Adams-Riley, Sharon Aldom, Lynette Alexander, Sarah Allen, Kirsten Amis, Melanie Anderson, Julie Antidormi, Flora Arbuckle, Christine Archer, Karen Aristocleous, Breda Arnold, Kim Arthur, Michelle Ascott, Gail Atkins, Janet Atkins, Deanna Atkinson, Julie Aylott, Jean Bailey, Joanne Baird, Sharon Baker, Kim Bakos, Sharon Bartlett, Tina Batt, Irene Beattie, Teresa Beedom, Alison Beesley, Sue Bellwood, Laura Bendrey, Leila Benhamida, Katherine Bennett, Brenda Bent, Sarah Bernarde, Ritu Bhathal, Parminder Bhogal, Elaine Binder, Madeleine Black, Marie Blair, Melissa Borsey, Samantha Borthwick, Ann Borthwick, Sonia Boston, Carolyn Bott, Andrea Boulton, Lori Boyd, Allison Boyle, Barbara Boyles, Shirley Bradbury, Sylvia Braden, Mandy Brandon, Carmel Breffit, Rachel Brewer, Melanie Brookes, Sarah D. Brown, Ann Browne, Sarah Bulley, Larissa Bunn, Rebecca Burnton, Ella Burrows, Rachel Bustin, Juliet Butler, Heather Byers, Georgia Calvert, Karen Campbell, Kyle Cann, Julie Caseberry, Timea Cassera, Louise Chamberlain, Jackie Cheal, Lynda Checkley, Kellie Clarke, Nicolas Theo Cocking, Marsha Coffer, Jane Collins, Lynda Cook, Mary Coombs, Sandi Coombs, Maxine Coote, Heather Copping, Maddy Cordell, Nonie Gail Cornelison, Isla Coull, Kellie Cowles, Stephanie Cox, Lorraine Coxon, Marcia Cramer, Jacqueline Crookston, Eleanor Rose Cunliffe, Rachel Curwen, Lydia Cutland, Michelle D'arcy, Alison Da Silva Barros, Angela Daly, Cindy Dando, Wendy Davies, Deborah Davies, Louise Davis Smith, Joan Dean, Susan deJong, Judy DeLong, Theresa Dempsey, Val Depledge, Ellen Devonport, Susie Dixon, Virginia Dogar, Shannon Dolgos, Jay Dor, Liz Dorrington, Catherine Downie, Mary Dragon, Heather Drew, Debra Drewett, Michelle Driscoll, Susan Duko, Helen Durman, Allison Earnshaw, Lucy Edwards, Alex Edwards, Jo Egerton, Margaret Ellis, Emily Ellis, Maria Ellis, Loo Elton, Sarah Farmer-Wright, Katherine Feeney, Debra Feldman, Karen Flint, Pam Flynn, Rhiannon Fox, Lin Fox, Emy-Kay Fox, Kerry Foyle, Suzanne French, Belinda Fry, Madge Fuller, Cheryl Gale, Heather Gannon, Barbara Gardner, Amanda Gardner, Tricia Garrick, Lesley Gibbs, Audrey Gibson, Joanna Gibson, Lisa Gillingham, Jemma Gish, Vanessa Goethe-Farber, Ange Goldsmith, Saymme Gowanlock, Chantelle Grady, Mary Grand, Jamie-Lee Grenfell, Jane Griffiths, Karen Haggerty, Greta Halliday, Lorraine Harkins, Jemma Harper, Molly Harper, Bev Harris, Rachel Hart, Diana Hattersley, Jean Haylett, Sharon Healey, Natalie Heighton, Anne Henshaw, Andrea Hewings, Sharon Hill, Trish Hills, Mary Holder, Patricia Holderness, Loraine Holland, Kaisha Holloway, Beverley Ann Hopper, Ann Hopwell, Aisha Hussain, Rose Hutton, Sandra Isaac, Jennifer Jeffers, Rhiann Johns, Nikki Johnston, Kate Jones, Merith Jones, Shirley Jones, Marie Judd, Jenny Just, Shannon Keating, Lisa Keeney, Joanne Kendall, Kirsty Kennedy, Jeannie Kershaw, Kim Kight, Jackie King, Sally Kirton, Sue Kitt, Cheryl Koch, Julie Kouiret, Colette Lamberth, Lori Lassiter, Maria Lee, Emma Lee, Janice Leibowitz, Catherine Lindsay, Caz Linley, Leonie Lock, Rhonda Lomazow...

... Samantha Long, Russell Lowe, Anne Lynes, Annie Mackenzie, Donna Maguire, Isobel Main, Claire Manger, Trudy Mardon, Dawn Marsden, Kelly Mason, Amy Mason, Daisy May Mason, Becky Matthews, Emily Maurice, Claire Mawdesley, Kris Mayer, Caitriona McCafferty, Fiona McCormick, Lynda McDonald, Linda McGovern, Suzanne McGuckin, Philippa McKenna, Bridget McKeown, Theresa McLaughlin, Jane McLaughlin, Kamini Mehta, Susan Melia Hill, Julia Merrick, Pauline Mertens, Anna Meyer, Kathryn Milazzo, Jen Mitchell, Jacqueline Morley, Mary Morling, Estee Moscow, Suzannah Mountney, Catherine Mulcair, Mary Murray, Andrea Napier, Kathryn Naylor, Paul Neaves, Anne Nee, Lynn Needham, Gabi Nesbit, Christine Newton, Teresa Nikolic, Nicky Nobbs, Lauren Jae Nommik, Kristina Noren, Kathryn Norris, Miriam O'Brien, Rosemary O'Hare, Louise O'Gorman, Linda O'Shea, Joanne Owen, Chris Owens, MaryAnne Pardoe, Helena Parker, Anna Parsons, Holly Partridge, Morag Paterson, Carol Peace, Emer Peel, Jaqui Petar, Jackie Phillips, Mary Picken, Christine Playle, Cat Plummer, Jacqi Ponsford, Andrea Porteous, Jane Power, Priya Prakash, Keena Pratt, Janette Pring, Judy Quigley, Gabrielle Reed, Victoria Reeve, Nadine Reynolds, Beverley Richards, Val Ridley, Rachel Ritchie, Irene Ritchie, Deborah Roberts Mendoza, Joanne Robertson, Sandra Robinson, Kate Rock, Bex Roncoroni, Sue Rouse, Deborah Ruddle, Fleur Rudland, Lorraine Rugman, Michelle Ryles, Kathy Sackett, Suzanna Salter, Irene Sampson, Fiona Sanders, Belinda Saunders, Bev Saxon, Debbie Scarpari, Donna Schechner, Janette Schwar, Jacqueline Sefton, Carly Sefton, Jo Selby, Michelle Shapiro, Justine Sharp, Ann Sharp, Gail Shaw, Bridget Shelley, Nicole Shepperson, Paula Short, Sarah Sigsworth, Eliana Silva, Claudene Silverman, Kathryn Sinclair, Sophie Skelton, Julia Skinner, Andrea Slade, Rebecca Sloan, Brenda Smith, Miriam Smith, Sandra Smith, Julia Soakell, Nicola Southall, Paul Southall, Judith Spencer, Alison Spurrell, Collette St Romaine, Susan Stafford, Helena Stanbury, Claire Stanley, Sian Steen, Judith Stevens, Laurel Stewart, Claire Stibbe, Kay Sturgess, Kerrie Sullivan, Lainy Swanson, Jane Tanglis, Deborah Taylor-Bryant, Vicci Thomas, Wendy Thomson, Linda Tilling, Jayne Timmins, Isabelle Timmins, Beth Toale, Jayne Tomkinson, Pam Travis, Jaime Trotter, Sam Tulloch, Joan Fox Turned, Cal Turner, Persephone Turner, Allison Valentine, Peter Valleley, Luschka van Onselen, Karen Vanderputt, Samantha Vanderputt, Liz Vasquez, Kate Vocke, Wendy Waddington, Leanne Waldman, Judith Walker, Jodi Wallace, Katie Warburton, Sue Ward, Sharon Washbrook, Lisa Washington, Gisele Waterman, Sarah Watts, Su Waymont, Pauline Wearing, David Welham, Tami Wells Silva, Cassandra wengewicz, Pat Werths, Mary Westwood, Lynsey Wheater, Julie Whitaker, Mandy Wilds, Jo Wilkes, Nic Williams, Catherine Williams, Carla Wilson, Einat Winter, Megan Wishnowsky, Penny-Sue Wolfe, Karen Woodman, Paula Woods, Sarah Woods, Jane Wright, Emma Lucinda Ellen Yarnell, Charlie Ydström Nilsson, Donna Young, Jessica Young, Abby Zimmel.

Thank you for coming on this journey with me.

One

Theo felt the swirl of nausea in the pit of his stomach. He swallowed and looked to his right, along the length of the lower playing field, calculating how long it would take to run back to the safety of the building should the need arise. He knew that Mr Beckett, his housemaster, would be watching from his study, peering through the wide bow window and rocking on his heels with his hands behind his back. He pictured him staring, stern faced, monitoring his every move. 'You go immediately!' he'd said angrily. 'And you undertake the task assigned to you. And I want you to think, boy, think about what you have done! Yours is not the behaviour of a Theobald's boy! And I won't tolerate it, do you hear?'

And Theo had gone immediately, trying to ignore the fear that was making him shake and the sting of tears that threatened, knowing that neither would help the situation. He stared at the dark, weatherworn patina of the wooden door in front of him. Even the thought of making contact with the infamous man in the crooked cottage made his heart race fit to burst through his ribs. He'd heard terrible stories about the cranky ogre that lived within. Theo could only take small breaths now and his skin pulsed over his breastbone. Raising his pale hand into a tight fist, he held it in front of his face and closed his eyes before bringing it to the oak front door, tapping once, twice and immediately taking a step back. The wind licked the nervous sweat on his top lip. It was cold.

There was an unnerving silence while his mind raced at what he should do if there was no reply. He knew Mr Beckett wouldn't believe him and the prospect of further punishment made his stomach churn.

Finally, a head of wiry grey hair bobbed into view through the dusty little glass security pane.

Theo swallowed.

'Who are you?' the man asked sternly as he yanked open the door and looked down at him.

'I'm... I'm Theodore Montgomery, sir.' He spoke with difficulty. His tongue seemed glued to the dry roof of his mouth. His voice was barely more than a squeak.

'Theodore Montgomery?'

'Yes, sir.' Theo gulped, noting the man's soft Dorset accent and the fact that he was not an ogre, certainly not in stature. But he did look cranky. His mouth was unsmiling and he had piercing blue eyes and a steady stare.

'Now there's a name if ever I heard one. And how old are you?'

'I'm... I'm seven, sir.'

'Seven. I see. What house are you in – is that a Theobald's tie?' The man narrowed his eyes.

'Theobald's, yes, sir.'

'So you are Theodore from Theobald's?'

'Yes, sir.'

'Well, that's some coincidence.'

Theo stared at the man, not sure if it would be the right thing to correct him and tell him that, actually, it was no coincidence.

The man nodded, looking briefly into the middle distance, as if this might mean something. 'And you are here for MEDS?'

'Yes, sir.' He tried to keep the warble from his voice; it was his first time in 'Marshall's Extra Duties', a punishment that fell somewhere between detention and corporal punishment. He was grateful to have avoided the sting of his housemaster's cane, at least.

'Is this your first time?'

The man, who smelt of earth and chemicals, lifted his chin and seemed to be looking at him through his large, hairy nostrils. They reminded Theo of a gun barrel, but one with grey sprigs sprouting from it. The man was old and looked more like a farmer than a master, the kind of person he'd seen up in Scotland when his father had taken him grouse shooting on the glorious twelfth. He shuddered at the memory of that weekend, having found nothing glorious about it. He hadn't liked it, not at all, and was still ashamed of how he'd cried at the sight of the birds' beautiful mottled plumage lying limply in the gundog's mouth. His father had been less than impressed, banning him from the shoot the next day. Instead, he'd had to sit in the car for eight hours with just a tartan-patterned flask of tea and a single stale bun. There'd been no facilities, so he had to tinkle on the grass verge. It was a chilly day and his shaky aim had meant he'd sprinkled his own shoes. Thankfully, they'd dried out by the time his father returned.

3

'Yes, sir.' He nodded, sniffing to halt the coming tears.

'Well, for a start, you can stop calling me "sir". I'm not a teacher. I'm part groundsman and part gamekeeper. My name is Mr Porter. Got it?'

'Yes, sir. Mr Porter, sir.'

Mr Porter placed his knuckles on the waist of his worn tweed jacket and looked Theo up and down. 'You're a skinny thing, reckon you're up to picking litter?'

Theo nodded vigorously. 'Yes, sir. I… I think so, sir. I've never done it before.'

'Don't you worry about that, it's as simple as falling off a log. You ever fallen off a log, Mr Montgomery?'

'No, sir.'

'It's Mr Porter.'

'Yes! Sorry…' Theo blinked. 'Mr Porter, sir.'

Mr Porter shook his head in a way that was familiar to Theo, a gesture that managed to convey both disappointment and irritation. Again, an image of his father flashed into his head. Theo offered up a silent plea that Peregrine James Montgomery the Third, Perry to his friends, would not get to hear about this latest misdemeanour. Theo had been a Vaizey College boy for a little over three weeks. His father had been not only head of Theobald's House, but also captain of the cricket and rugby teams, earning his colours in his first term. His were big shoes to fill. '*Don't you let me down, boy!*' His father's words rang in his ears like rolling thunder.

Mr Porter broke his chain of thought, emerging from the house with a large black bin bag and a pair of gardening gloves.

'Here, put these on.' He tossed the gloves in Theo's direction. They landed on the ground. Theo cursed his inability to catch and scrabbled for them on the path before shoving them on. They were miles too big, sitting comically askew on his tiny hands.

'Follow me.' Mr Porter marched ahead, striding with purpose. Theo noted that his feet seemed disproportionately large for his small build, though that might have been because of his sturdy green gumboots. He wore a flat cap in a different tweed to his jacket, and a burgundy muffler fastened around his neck.

'Keep up!' he called over his shoulder and Theo broke into a trot, his knees knocking beneath his long grey shorts.

They continued in silence for ten minutes, long enough for Theo's body to have warmed up and for his cheeks to have taken on a flush. It was only four in the afternoon, but dusk was already nudging the sunshine out of the way. Theo liked this time of year, when the air smelt of bonfires and at home an extra eiderdown was placed on the foot of his bed against the chill of his room.

'Here we are then,' Mr Porter barked as they neared the edge of the field and the narrow lane that led to the older girls' boarding houses.

'The wind blows a stiff northwesterly...' He used his chunky fist to draw the shape of the wind in the air. 'And the litter gets picked up like a mini tornado and carried along until it meets this hedgerow, and this is where it gets stuck.' They both stared at the hedge. Mr Porter took a breath. 'I suppose you're wondering why it matters that the odd rogue crisp packet or strip of newspaper gets lodged in the hawthorn?'

Theo hadn't been wondering any such thing. His primary concern was in fact whether or not his fingers would get snagged on the spiky branches. But he nodded anyway, because it sounded like a question.

'Well...' Mr Porter bent down and placed his gnarled hand

5

on the top of the hedgerow. 'Come nesting time, this rather sorry-looking tangle will be home to birds. I've seen blackbirds, dunnocks and wrens all making nests here, nice and cosy for their eggs. They need to do all they can to get the environment right for their little families to flourish. Do you think they want to get their heads caught in a crisp packet? Or read what's happening in the *News of the World*?'

'No, sir.'

'Mr Porter.'

'Sorry. No, Mr Porter, sir.'

Mr Porter blinked. 'So we have a responsibility to pick up the litter and discard it sensibly and safely. And the headmaster and Mr Beckett both see this as a good way to punish boys who break the rules.'

At the mention of Mr Beckett, his housemaster and the man responsible for school discipline, Theo's bowels shrank.

'Why are you here, Mr Montgomery? What *odious* crime did you commit?'

Theo looked down at the damp grass and his cheeks flamed with embarrassment. He didn't know what odious meant, but he could guess that it wasn't good.

'Someone, erm, someone did a pee in my pyjama bottoms.'

'Oh.' Mr Porter stopped dead and pulled his head back on his shoulders. Clearly this was not the response he'd been expecting. He looked at Theo. 'Why would someone do that?'

'I… I don't know.' Theo blinked. 'Maybe they didn't do it on purpose. Maybe they were too scared to get up in the night in the dark and so they went back to sleep even though they knew they needed the bathroom and when they woke up in the morning it was too late, it had just happened.'

'I see.' Mr Porter sighed and gave a small nod. 'How did they try and dispose of the evidence?'

'They stuffed them down the back of the big radiator in Matron's study and when the radiator came on, it was a really bad stink.'

'I bet it was.' Mr Porter sniffed the air, as if considering this. 'How did they know they were your pyjama bottoms?'

'They had my name sewn in.' Theo kept his eyes on the grass.

'Of course they did.' Mr Porter rubbed his chin sagely.

Theo kicked at the soft mud with the toe of his black shoes and scrunched up the plastic bag in his hand.

'Well,' Mr Porter began, 'if you ever find out who did it, you can tell them two things. Firstly, if they're ever going to commit another crime, best be sure not to leave any items of clothing with their nametape sewn in at the scene.'

Theo nodded. This seemed like good advice.

'And secondly,' Mr Porter said slowly and kindly, 'you can tell them from me that there is never any reason to be afraid of the dark. Everything is just as it is during the day, like a room without the light switched on, and any talk of ghosties or ghouls is poppycock. Those things don't exist. They're just the stories some boys use to frighten others.'

Theo looked up at the man with the crinkly eyes, red cheeks and hairy nostrils.

'Don't you forget that now,' he said.

'I won't, sir.'

'Mr Porter.'

'Yes. Sorry, sir.'

★

Theo made his way across the quadrangle with something of a spring in his step. He wasn't quite sure if it was down to relief that the o-d-i-o-u-s chore was now over or the fact he'd enjoyed litter-picking far more than he'd expected. There was something about Mr Porter that he liked – the man was far from scary once you got used to him. Granted, he looked a little odd with his wild hair and peculiar smell, but Theo had found his company to be the most pleasant he had experienced so far at Vaizey College. He tried to remember what the man had said about ghosts, that they didn't exist.

'Poppycock!' he said out loud, liking the word.

'What was that, Montgomery?' It was Magnus Wilson, also a Theobald's boy, two years older and a whole head taller, who called across the walkway.

'I... I'm...' Theo knew what he wanted to say, but nerves again rendered his tongue useless.

'"I'm a faggot" – it's quite easy to get out,' Wilson yelled, and the two friends either side of him, Helmsley and Dinesh, laughed. 'Where have you been? You weren't at tea,' Wilson asked in a manner that told Theo he expected an answer.

Theo felt anger and fear ball in his gut like a physical thing. He wanted to shout back, but he didn't have the confidence or the words. 'I've been doing MEDS,' he whispered.

'Ha!' Wilson laughed. 'With Porter, the old homo? Where did he take you? Up the back alley?'

His friends snickered.

Theo shook his head. 'No, but near the back alley, to... to the hedge.'

The boys' roar of laughter was deafening. Theo had no idea what was so funny and now he was embarrassed as well as frightened. He wanted to cry but knew that was the worst thing he could do. Instead, he bit the inside of his cheek until it hurt. The taste of iron and the seep of blood into his mouth was the distraction he needed.

'Heard you pissed the bed, is that right?' Wilson said.

'No! It wasn't me!' Theo kept his eyes down and willed his heart to not beat quite so loudly, for fear of them hearing it. His legs swayed, as if they belonged to someone else.

'Good afternoon, gentlemen,' Mr Beckett offered crisply as he swept by with his hands clasped behind him and the cape of his black robe billowing, bat-like, as he moved.

'Good afternoon, sir,' all four boys said with their heads lowered.

'Prep should be your main focus at this time of day, not loitering in the quadrangle. So off you go!'

The three bigger boys jostled each other as they ran off towards the dorms.

I want to go home. I just want to go home. Theo closed his eyes and concentrated on not saying the words out loud. If he did, he'd probably land himself in more trouble than he could cope with.

It was now Thursday, the day Theo longed for. This was the day each week when just before bedtime he was allowed to call home. Having waited all day in eager anticipation, he lined up outside his housemaster's study along with the other boys in his year. One by one they were called in and handed the telephone. It was, as ever, ringing by the time it was deposited in his hand, giving him less opportunity to plan what he wanted to say.

Actually, this was a lie, he knew exactly what he wanted to say, but he was more concerned about what he *could* say while under the watchful eye of Mr Beckett, or Twitcher, as he was known among the boys on account of his left eyelid, which blinked rapidly and seemingly with a will of its own.

'Perry Montgomery.'

The booming sound of his father's voice answering the call sent a stutter to Theo's throat. He wanted to be brave, wanted so badly to make his father proud, but it was hard when he was fighting back tears and what he really wanted to say was, 'Please, Daddy, let me come home! I hate it here and if you let me come back, I promise I'll be good. I'll try harder not to cry on the grouse shoot. I miss you so much! Let me come home!'

But of course he would never do this, especially not with Twitcher sitting only three feet away.

'Daddy, it's me, Theo.'

'Ah, Theo old boy!' His father sounded pleased to hear from him and this alone was enough to lift Theo's spirits while at the same time causing more annoying tears to gather. 'One second. I'll fetch your mother.'

And just like that, his father was gone.

Theo wanted to talk to him; he always wanted to talk to him. The trouble was he never had anything of interest to say, and even if he had, his father didn't have the time to hear it. He remembered summoning up his courage before walking out to the garage in the summer, determined to talk to his dad. The sight of him holding a chamois leather in his big hand, preoccupied as he buffed the paintwork on his pride and joy had left Theo flustered. 'I... I...'

'For God's sake, spit it out!' his father had yelled, and Theo had turned on his heel, embarrassed, and hotfooted it back up to the safety of his bedroom. He'd sat on his bed and stared at his tiny, sausage-like fingers, wishing that he could be grown-up with big hands like his father's, certain that when that time came, when he had hands like his dad's, he would know exactly what to say.

Today was no different. In fact, trying to think of 'chitchat', as his mother called it, was even harder with an audience. He pushed the earpiece close to his head and could hear his father's voice. He pictured him standing in the lamplit hallway as he called into the dark recesses of their grand Edwardian house. 'Stella! It's the boy on the phone!'

Theo knew his call was being timed and he cursed the silent seconds while his mother made her way to the phone. *Hurry up! Hurry up!*

Finally, he heard the rattle of her charm bracelet.

'Mummy?'

'Hello, my darling!' she breathed. 'How lovely to hear from you!' She sounded surprised and he swallowed the urge to remind her that it was Thursday, of course she was going to hear from him! But he knew that it would be a waste of time as well as a waste of words. 'What did you have for supper?' She always asked this.

'Erm, we had steak-and-kidney pie, but I picked the kidney out, although one bit got through and it was yucky.'

'Oh, Rollo, that's Daddy's favourite! Don't tell him or he'll be very jealous!' she trilled, before screaming loudly, 'Waaaagh! Oh my good God – I called you Rollo!' This was followed by a series of great gulping guffaws that lasted many seconds.

Theo waited until it passed, then whispered, 'Yes, you did.'

'Oh good Lord above!' she shrieked. 'How could I possibly have called you Rollo? I am a terror! Although that's quite funny in itself, if you think about it, as Rollo is a terrier!' She howled loudly once again.

And Theo had to admit that if time were not of the essence and if there hadn't been so much he needed to say and reassurances he needed to hear, being called by the dog's name would indeed be very funny.

Help me, Mummy! Please help me! Read my thoughts: I want to come home, I am so sad here. Please, please let me come home! Theo screwed his eyes shut and hoped that his pleas might float through the ether and reach her. He liked to think they had this psychic link that stretched all the way from his school in Dorset to the family home in Barnes.

'Darling, I'm still chuckling! I only made the slip because Rollo is on my mind. He's been a bit of a scamp, let me tell you. He got out of the garden and caused absolute havoc in Mrs Merriton's rabbit run. Created quite a stir. He was only playing, of course, but the poor rabbit looked fit to have a heart attack. I told him, "No sausages for you, naughty Rollo", and do you know, he looked at me as if he knew he'd been a bad boy. So of course that *melted* my heart and I gave him some sausage anyway, but don't tell Daddy! He says I spoil him.' She whispered the last bit.

'I won't tell Daddy.' He felt a small flicker of joy at this shared confidence.

'Anyway, very much looking forward to seeing you for exeat, only a few weeks now.'

Twitcher stood up and tapped his watch face. Time was up. Theo felt the pressure to say something, to get something across, anything! 'I saw a hedge...' He took a breath. 'Where... Where birds lay their eggs and it's very important that we don't let crisp packets gather in it or they might get their heads stuck.'

'Theo, you're such a funny little thing!'

He thought about his mum's parting words as he lay under the taut white sheets on his bed later that night. *I am a funny little thing, but I don't want to be.* He turned his face into the pillow. Unseen in the dark dorm, he was finally able to give in to the tears he'd kept at bay all day.

* * *

Theo regularly hid during lunchbreak. Not literally – there was no climbing into small spaces or standing still behind cupboard doors, although he'd considered both. No, his hiding was subtler than that. He became adept at loitering and looking purposeful, reading and rereading noticeboards slowly, as if engrossed, stooping to painstakingly tie and retie his shoelaces, or sitting endlessly in a toilet cubicle while killing precious time, willing the clock to go faster. And if he had to move on, he walked with a resoluteness to his step and an expression that suggested he had a mission on his mind. This was all very exhausting, but it was unavoidable because he had no one to talk to and nowhere to sit. Try as he might, he couldn't understand how all the boys in his house and all the girls in his form had friends who they could talk to, sit with and eat with, or even just read next to in silence. How come he didn't have one single friend?

What's wrong with me? It was this question that haunted him.

Walking across the quad, he spied Wilson and his cronies, Helmsley and Dinesh. All three were in their games kit, coming from the squash courts to the right. His heart jumped and his palms began to sweat at the prospect of an encounter. Averting his eyes, he broke into a light jog, pretending he hadn't seen them as he made his way along the field. He carried on jogging until he found himself outside the crooked cottage where Mr Porter lived. The man himself was sitting on a bench attached to a slatted table similar to the ones he'd seen in the garden of the Red Lion pub, where his parents took him sometimes for Sunday lunch when he was at home.

Theo stared at Mr Porter and hesitated, trying desperately to think of a reason for being there, uninvited, in front of his path during lunchtime.

Mr Porter looked up briefly before returning his gaze to the fiddly task that seemed to be occupying him fully. 'How good is your eyesight, Mr Montgomery?' he called out.

'It's good.' Theo glanced up the field to see if Wilson had followed and breathed a huge sigh of relief that he hadn't. His gut muscles unbunched.

'In that case, you can help me with this.'

Theo clenched and unclenched his hands, unsure whether it was okay to enter Mr Porter's garden.

'Well, come on then, lad, you can't help me from all the way down there now, can you?'

He didn't need telling twice. He walked up the short path and stopped at the table, on top of which he saw piles of small, brightly coloured feathers, shiny glass beads and thin strips of wire.

'What… What are you doing?' he asked softly, wanting to know but not wanting to be a nuisance.

'I'm making fishing flies. Do you know what they are?'

Theo shook his head and took a step closer.

'You can sit down.' Mr Porter nodded at the bench on the opposite side of the table.

Theo sat on the edge, feeling the rough texture of the untreated wood against the underside of his legs. He watched, fascinated, as Mr Porter took feathers into his nimble fingers and bound the ends with an almost invisible twine. He worked slowly and carefully, wrapping them into little bundles.

'That looks like an insect.'

Mr Porter sat back and shook his head. His expression this time was one of surprise. 'Well, I didn't realise you were so smart.'

Theo's face split into a smile. He let the compliment slip under his skin, ready to warm him on a cold night at the end of a bad day.

'That's exactly what it's meant to look like – an insect! This "fly", as we call it, bobs on top of the water and will help me catch game fish, like salmon or trout. It tricks the fish into thinking they're getting a tasty bug.'

'But really they're getting this fake bug!'

'Exactly.' Mr Porter winked.

'I've never been fishing. Apart from with a net in a rock pool, but I don't know if that counts,' Theo mumbled, wary of saying the wrong thing. 'I caught a starfish once, well, half a starfish. It was dead.'

Mr Porter shook his head sympathetically. 'Sure it counts. But what I do is very different to rock-pooling. I like nothing more than to stand on a riverbank, or in the river itself, feeling the flow of the water, and watch the sun dappling the surface with light, birds fluttering overhead – and with a flask of tea and a sandwich or two in my pack. That's where my happiness lies.' Mr Porter smiled and closed his eyes briefly, as if picturing just that.

'Do you catch many fish?' Theo found it easy to think of what to say because he was interested.

'Nope. I hardly ever catch a fish. Truth be told, I'm not as keen on the catching bit as much as the standing bit.'

'It... It...'

'Spit it out, lad!' Unlike his father, Mr Porter issued this familiar instruction in an encouraging voice and with a crinkle-eyed smile. This had the opposite effect to normal and instead of clamming up, Theo continued calmly.

'It seems like a lot of trouble to go to if you don't catch any fish – couldn't you just buy some from the shop?'

Mr Porter leant back and laughed. Slipping his fingers up under his tweed cap, he scratched at a bald patch on his head and Theo saw that the skin there was a shade or two lighter than his face. 'Well, yes, I'm sure I could buy some, but shall I let you into a little secret?'

Theo nodded.

Mr Porter looked at him and spoke levelly. 'The best thing about fishing is the stillness, the quiet. And the one thing I have learnt, possibly the most important lesson of all, is that when you're still and quiet, that's when your thoughts get ordered, when your mind sorts out all of its problems and when you're able to see most clearly. Don't ever underestimate the value of stillness.'

Theo digested his words.

Mr Porter placed his hands on his greasy lapel and turned it over to reveal a delicate turquoise-and-gold-feathered fly with a blue glass bead attached to a safety pin. He ran his fingertip over it. 'I wear this here to remind me of just that. If ever my head is too busy or the world feels like too big a place for me to find my corner in it, I run my fingers over this and it reminds me to seek out the stillness.' He looked directly at Theo. 'Do you understand what I mean by that, lad?'

Theo nodded, even though he only half understood.

'Now, if you want to help, sort these feathers into piles for me. Group them by colour.' He tapped the tabletop with his square finger.

Eager for a job, Theo swung his legs over the bench and began pulling the little feathers apart, grouping them into colour-coordinated piles. It was fiddly work.

'When did you learn to do this?' he asked in his high voice.

'In the war. I fought some of my war in Italy and that's where I learnt to fish.'

'Did you fire a gun?'

'No, we just used rods and bait same as everyone else.' Mr Porter chuckled.

'I didn't mean to fish – I meant to get the baddies.' He blinked, unsure of whether the topic was off limits, as it was with Grandpa, who'd been in a place called Burma and had, according to his parents 'had a terrible war'. This phrase intrigued him, as he couldn't picture a war that was anything but terrible.

Mr Porter paused what he was doing and stared at him. 'That's the thing, Mr Montgomery. I did my duty for King and country and would gladly do so again.' He straightened his back and tilted his chin. 'But as for "baddies", as you call them... I only saw people. People in all shapes and sizes, but people just the same. War is a terrible thing and sometimes you might think you've got home scot-free, might think you've got away with things, but you haven't. You never know what's waiting for you around the next corner or even at home. There is always a price to pay. It's as if fate waits in the wings to rip the heart out of you and it's then you realise your war will never be over.'

Mr Porter took a big breath. It was only when he continued making his fly that Theo took his cue to continue chatting.

'How did you know who the baddies were then? How did… How did you know who to shoot?' He looked up, wary of entering unchartered territory.

'As I said, I didn't do much shooting, but the enemy, if you will, were pointed out to me by my commanding officer long before I ever set foot on foreign soil and before I met a single one of them. I was told to identify them by the uniform they wore. But therein lay the problem.' Mr Porter leant in, and Theo was thrilled at the possibility that he might be sharing a secret. 'I considered my commanding officer to be a baddy. I was unsure of his judgement – he was no more than a boy himself, just a few months free of his mother's apron strings and a bit of a bully, and yet he held my fate and the fate of many others in the palm of his young hand. That made it hard for me to trust him. Whereas some of the fellas who wore a different colour uniform to me, baddies if you will, well, close up, they had similar faces to those of my mates. We were all as scared and desperate as each other.' He let this hang. 'And let me tell you this, Mr Montgomery, those that didn't make it home were mourned by their families just the same, goodies and baddies alike.'

Mr Porter gave an odd little cough and his eyes looked misty, so Theo knew it was time for quiet. And that was all right with him. He was happy to have somewhere to sit and someone to sit with, though he would have found it hard to fully explain how or why Mr Porter's garden felt like a refuge from loneliness.

The two worked in silence until the sound of the school bell echoed along the field.

'That'll be the end of lunch then,' Mr Porter muttered without lifting his eyes from his fishing flies.

Theo gave an involuntary sigh. 'I'd better go back up to school.'

'Here.' Mr Porter pulled a slim navy tube from his jacket pocket and handed it to Theo.

'What is it?'

'What does it look like?'

Theo scrutinised the object in his palm. 'A pen!'

'Ah, appearances can be deceptive! Look.' Mr Porter took the fake pen from him and twisted the lid until a beam of light shone from the nib. 'It's a torch. I thought you might be able to give it to that boy you know. The one who you thought might be afraid of the dark. You see, with this in his possession, he can get up in the night and go to the bathroom without fear and that might stop him pissing in your pyjamas.' He gave a small chuckle.

'We're... We're not allowed torches.' Theo ran his fingers over the gift. He felt torn, desperately wanting to keep it but painfully conscious that it would be contraband.

'Of course not – that's a rule I'm perfectly aware of. But that's not a torch, is it? It's a pen!' He smiled.

Theo rolled the marvellous gift in his hand. 'Yes! It's a pen.' He beamed. 'Thank you.'

'You are most welcome.'

Theo swung his legs out from under the bench and started to walk up the path. Turning back, he called over his shoulder, 'Mr Porter?'

'Yes, Mr Montgomery?

'It... It was me.'

'What was you?'

'It was me that pissed in my pyjamas and hid them behind Matron's radiator.'

Mr Porter looked startled. 'Well, I never did! But here's the thing: you never have to lie to me, and I will never lie to you, how about that? Deal?'

'Deal.' Theo twisted the pen cap and smiled at the thin stream of light that shone into his palm.

Two

Theo had just finished another unsatisfactory Thursday phone call with his mother and was making his way from Mr Beckett's study. He was in a world of his own, struggling with the latest wave of homesickness and desperate for his first exeat, when quite unexpectedly Twitcher grabbed the top of his arm, pulling him back into the room.

His housemaster bent low and spoke directly into his ear. Theo could smell his piquant breath; he tucked in his lips to avoid inhaling it.

'I have to say, I find it quite troubling that you can never think of anything informative to share with your parents, Montgomery. Listening to your weekly call is painful. Your father was head of house here! He's a good man, paying a small fortune to turn you into a Vaizey boy, and yet you don't have the courtesy to let him know how the 1st XV are doing or that the quadrangle race record was broken by Danvers only last week? These things *matter*, especially to an OVB.'

At the mention of the Old Vaizey Boys, Theo's insides curdled. His father held regular and horribly loud dinner parties for other members of this esteemed club and the deafening noise of their reunions always floated up the stairs to his room. He had spied on them through the keyhole once. They were all dressed in dinner jackets and bow ties in their old house colours, and they were banging their palms on the white tablecloth and belting out a tuneless song about port and knickers, taking it in turns to swig the dark red wine from a silver cup.

'But I think that's the problem in a nutshell.' His housemaster's booming voice pulled him back to the present. 'I don't think these things *matter* to you.'

'I... I...' Theo's mouth was having trouble catching up with his brain. This happened sometimes.

'Tell me...' Mr Beckett let go of his arm and walked towards the study window, which had an unusually good view along the field and all the way down to the crooked cottage. 'Why do you hang around with the ground staff?' His eyelid twitched as he clasped his hands behind his back.

Theo shrugged. 'I don't know, sir.'

'Let me put it another way. What is the nature of your relationship with Porter, the groundsman?'

'He... He's my friend. Sir.'

'Your friend!' Twitcher guffawed. 'Good God, man, don't you have any friends your own age?'

'No, sir.' He felt his cheeks colour at the admission.

Mr Beckett stopped dead and turned, an expression of disbelief and disdain on his face. 'None at all? Not one?'

'No, sir.' Theo's shame wrapped around him like a heavy cloak, dragging him down.

Twitcher took a deep breath and spoke over Theo's head, as if he were invisible. 'Do you know what I think when I see a boy who, in a school of over six hundred pupils, in an environment where friendships flourish on and off the sports field, and where connections are made that can last a lifetime, still finds himself on his own?'

'No, sir.'

'I think it can't possibly be the other five hundred and ninety-nine or so who are at fault. The odds are simply too high. I believe there has to be a reason for your isolation, and do you know what that reason is?' He lowered his eyes to meet Theo's.

'No, sir.'

'Weirdness.'

Mr Beckett was silent for a second, letting the horrible word with all its negative connotations sink in. 'I've seen it before and will no doubt see it again. You have a weirdness about you, Montgomery, and weirdness is something that the other pupils, in fact all humans, fear more than anything. It's like a disease and, believe me, it's contagious. That's why weirdos stick together in toxic little huddles, backs to the wall, eyes wide, waiting to see who might be picked off next.'

Theo wanted badly to cry, but doing so in front of Mr Beckett would be asking for trouble. Twitcher did not like weakness. On or off the field.

'Do you want some advice?'

'Yes, sir.' Despite his housemaster's hurtful words, Theo looked up with genuine hope, feeling a flash of excitement that there might be a cure for his toxic condition. Because what Theodore Montgomery wanted more than anything in the whole wide world was not to be weird!

He wanted a friend, a proper friend of his own age.

Mr Beckett leant in closer. Theo cocked his head so he could take in every detail of the advice that just might prove invaluable.

'Stay quiet and stay out of sight. Become invisible. Go to ground and try not to take root.'

It was a strange thing, but as Theo turned his face into his pillow that night and waited, he was surprised to find that there were no tears. It was almost as if this wounding was so deep, so visceral, that he was hurt in a place beyond tears.

I'm weird. Weird. The word tumbled around his head until sleep claimed him.

⋆ ⋆ ⋆

There was a burble of excitement all through the school: everyone got to go home for three whole days and they weren't due back at school until Monday. Theo had packed a day ago and now sat by his bed with his tan leather suitcase at his feet and his eyes glued to his watch, waiting for the minute hand to tick again, each cycle taking him closer to the comfort of his father's car and escape. His leg jumped and his heart raced; the moment could not come soon enough.

And then, like a vision, there she was, standing in the doorway – his mother. Her floral scent permeated the air, red lipstick shone from her pale face and her impossibly long dark eyelashes fluttered upwards. She looked… She looked beautiful. Soft, pretty and familiar in an environment that was none of those things.

'Theodore!' She giggled in her high-pitched way, which sounded to him like the tinkle of glass.

At the sight of her, his reserve disappeared and he ran into her, gripping her tightly about her waist, inhaling her smell with his head buried against her chest.

'Darling! Now that's quite a welcome. How lovely.' She patted his head before easing him away by his shoulders, turning the whole embrace into something a little embarrassing. 'Come on, Daddy's in the car. We don't want to keep him waiting, do we?'

Theo lifted his small suitcase off the ground, letting it bang against his skinny leg with every step.

'If it isn't Mrs Montgomery!' Twitcher called from his open study door in a loud, happy voice.

'Well, hello you!' she shouted back.

Theo shrank, not sure if his mother or indeed anyone was allowed to talk to his housemaster in such a fashion. Apparently she was forgiven, as Mr Beckett trotted out from behind his desk and held her in a tight hug, smiling in a way Theo hadn't seen before. He noted with a twinge of envy that their hug lasted at least twice as long as his had.

'So good to see you!' Mr Beckett beamed.

'You too, darling.' His mother gripped Twitcher's forearms with her dainty hands and stared into his face.

She called him "darling"! Theo looked over his shoulder with trepidation, checking no other boys were around to witness this. But he was the last to be collected, so he was quite safe.

'So are we seeing you at Le Mans? Tiffany has had the house redecorated apparently and is very keen for us all to go and admire it. I've been assured that the plumbing actually works now!' His mother spoke with her hand resting on Twitcher's chest; it was a gesture so intimate, it made Theo's heart race and his stomach flip. He thought he might be sick.

He wanted to hurl his suitcase to the floor and shout out, 'He's mean to me, Mummy! Don't be happy to see him! He says I'm weird, and I hate it here! I hate it! Please don't be his friend.

Be on my side!' But of course he didn't, because he was seven and he had neither the confidence nor the wisdom to know when to shout.

'Do you remember the great bathroom fiasco?' his mother continued. 'Poor Gerry, he's still mortified, by all accounts. I have this image of him running onto the veranda starkers and with a scalded bottom! I shouldn't laugh really.' She hid her mouth with her hand and laughed anyway.

'God, don't remind me. I still haven't recovered from last year!' Mr Beckett bellowed and the two laughed like old friends.

'Oh, please don't be boring, Becks, I'm counting on you. No one, but no one makes a Manhattan like you do.' His mother dipped her head and spoke with lowered lashes.

'Stella, you know that where you are concerned, flattery will get you everywhere.' He winked. The phone rang on his desk. 'Duty calls,' he shouted as he made his way back into his study. 'Love to Perry!'

'Of course. Come on, Theo.' She walked ahead and clicked her fingers.

As he skipped to heel, he wondered if once again she might have got him confused with Rollo the terrier.

He waved at his father, who'd parked the shiny dark blue Aston Martin V8 across two parking spots reserved for staff. This was another reason for Theo to feel anxious.

'Mind the paintwork!' His father winced as he approached with his suitcase. He sprang from the car, placed his lit cigarette in his mouth, popped the boot and lifted the luggage with such ease that Theo's arms seemed to weaken in protest.

His father ruffled his hair as Theo climbed into the back seat. He liked the weight of his dad's palm against his scalp and could feel its heat for a while after. The car smelt of leather, cologne and cigarettes and Theo hoped he wasn't going to be sick.

'All set?' his father asked, looking at him in the rearview mirror. His mother buckled up in the front and twisted the chunky green glass bangle on her wrist.

Theo nodded.

'God, I bloody love this building!' His father beeped the horn and whooped as they drove out onto the lane. 'Spent the best years of my life here, and when I come back, it's like coming home! I don't want to wish your life away, Theo old son, but I can't wait for you to feel like this!' He beeped the horn again.

His mother turned round and pulled a face at Theo. It made him smile, but it was a fake smile. He knew he was never going to feel anything other than hatred for the whole place.

His mother ran her arm along the back of the leather driver's seat and toyed with the lick of dark hair that curled at his father's neck. 'I saw Becks. He's moaning about last year's Le Mans hangover, sounded like he might be wimping out of the trip. Can you believe it?' she drawled, reaching into her clutch bag for her cigarettes.

'Tell him to man up! For God's sake.'

'I did, more or less. He's such a darling. He won't miss it, of course. I think he's teasing, fishing for compliments.' She lit her cigarette and in a well-practised motion flipped the gold Zippo lighter. It closed with a loud thunk.

Theo stared out of the window, watching the hedgerows whiz past. He pictured the wrens, blackbirds and dunnocks that would make them their home when the time came and hoped they wouldn't get their heads stuck in an old crisp packet or a strip of newspaper. He patted his pocket to make sure his trusty pen torch was where he could find it.

As they left Muckleford and continued along twisty Dorset lanes, heading towards London, Theo listened to his parents chatting and laughing and playfully slapping each other's hands away from the radio dial. He liked being in their company but he wondered if he should cough, remind them that he was there. Just as he was considering this, his mother turned to him.

'Have you had supper?'

Ignoring the growl of hunger in his gut, he smiled at her, not wanting to be any more trouble than he already was, interrupting their busy lives to travel down to Dorset and bring him home. 'I'm fine,' he lied.

'Thank God for that!' She giggled, resting her hand on her husband's thigh. 'I'm not sure what we have in?'

'You are a crap wife! The crappest!' his father yelled in jest.

'Don't listen to your father, Theo. I am an exceptional wife! I can't help it if cooking and food shopping and all that stuff bores me rigid.' They both laughed. 'Ooh!' She raised her index finger to indicate that an idea had occurred. 'I think I have some cheese in the fridge and a tin of crackers in the larder – that'll do. We'll make a meal of it, bottle of plonk, none for you, Theo, but some of Edith's chutney... We could even eat by candle-light!' She laughed, turning to him briefly before reaching for another cigarette.

It felt like an age before the car pulled into the gated driveway of their grand red-brick home in Barnes. No longer laughing, the three had travelled for the last hour in silence, his father gripping the steering wheel with white knuckles.

Now his father tutted as he alighted from the car. His face

was thunderous, his anger coming off him in waves. 'Out you jump,' he instructed, his tone curt and his eyes blazing.

Theo clambered out on wobbly legs. The fresh air was a welcome tonic.

'I'm very sorry, Daddy.'

'So you said, and it's not your fault, but a bit of notice would have been nice and no amount of sorrys is going to get rid of that bloody smell.'

Theo looked at the dark stain on the pale brown leather where his vomit had splashed. 'Shall I wash it for you?'

'No!' his father barked. 'For God's sake don't take a scourer, or detergent or in fact anything to the leather, you'll only make it worse.' He ran his hand through his hair.

'He's only trying to help!' his mother called across the wide bonnet.

His father pinched the bridge of his nose and Theo knew he was angry with him. The whole horrible journey home had burst the happy bubble that had filled him up all day. He'd been so excited about coming home, but now he felt nothing but awkward and embarrassed, and rather than enjoying his exeat, he was already dreading the drive back to school, knowing that the combination of cigarette smoke and winding roads might have the exact same effect on the return journey. The only thing he was dreading more than the drive back to school was arriving there.

His mother climbed the steps to the front door and as she put the key in the door he heard Rollo's bark.

'There he is! There's my baby boy!' she said in a baby voice that sent a tingle of envy through him. 'Look! It's your brother! Theo's home!' She lifted the lithe Jack Russell and waved a paw in Theo's direction.

His father jogged up the steps in his brogues, bent forward, kissed Rollo's nose and muttered something to his mum. The occasional word floated down to Theo and made his tummy hurt. 'Fucking smell... vomit!... bloody expensive... idiot!... what the fuck is wrong with him?'

Theo went inside and climbed the stairs. Ignoring the stabs of hunger, which seemed almost insignificant now, he sat on the end of his bed. The pale green and pink floral carpet he'd always hated had been vacuumed ahead of his visit, but the place was still thick with dust. The room had been decluttered. Gone was his collection of Matchbox cars, which had once filled an entire bookshelf, and his *Rupert the Bear* annuals were missing too. There was a new reading lamp, a mahogany sideboard and a flowery chair that he hadn't seen before. These items had probably been brought up from the basement, where his grandpa's furniture was stored.

He unbuckled his suitcase and pulled out his pyjamas, red-striped and edged with white piping. They smelt of school and because of that he was loath to put them on. He'd forgotten that his bedroom could be quite noisy with the traffic on the road between their house and the river and the shouts of people returning home from the pub. It would take a bit of getting used to after the quiet of Vaizey College and all that countryside.

He slipped between the cold sheets and laid his head on the flannelette pillowcase. He liked its soft bobbles; they comforted him and reminded him he was home. Curling his feet up under his bottom to try and get warm, he reached into his discarded blazer for his pen torch and, twisting it on, fired shafts of light up towards the ceiling. A thousand million particles of dust danced in the beam; he disturbed them with his fingers before settling into the dip in the mattress where the springs had gone a little slack.

'What's that you've got?' his mother asked from the doorway.

'It's my pen torch. My friend gave it to me.'

'Oh, Theo, I'm so pleased you have a friend! Well done you. Is he nice?'

'Yes,' he whispered.

'What's his name?'

'I... I don't know.'

His mother snorted her laughter. 'You don't know his name? You are a funny little thing.'

You don't need to keep saying that to me. I already know!

'I don't want to go back to school, Mummy.' He switched off his torch and toyed with the silky edge of the wool blanket.

'Yes, you do! It's a wonderful school, with wonderful opportunities for you.'

He stared at her and for the first time her full smile had the opposite effect to the one intended. Instead of reassuring him that things were okay, he knew that even though she might be listening, she didn't actually hear him, and that made him feel invisible.

'I hate it there.'

'No, you don't, not really. Everyone feels like that when they first start – ask Daddy or Uncle Maxim. Even Grandpa felt like that in his junior years! And they grew to love it, all of them. They would all say their time at Vaizey was the best time in their whole life and look at some of the amazing things they've done. And you are a Vaizey boy – it's in your blood! Goodness me, you're even named after Daddy's house.'

'I wish I wasn't named after Daddy's house. I wish I was called

John. And I don't have any real friends,' he whispered, carefully placing his torch on the bedside table.

'Well, making friends takes two, you know! You have to make the effort, put yourself out there a bit, chat!'

'What should I chat about?'

'Oh, for goodness' sake, Theo! You're being a wee bit silly! You *know* what to talk about!' She sounded irritated now. 'Sport? School subjects? Good God, the weather? Anything!' She threw her hands in the air before sweeping across the room to his bed and kissing him firmly on the forehead.

He fought the temptation to reach out and pull her to him, clinging on as if his life depended on it. Instinct told him that she might think that was a wee bit silly too.

'You're probably just tired. Things will iron out, you'll see, they always do. Now then, I need to go and let Rollo out for his night-time tinkle. Sleep well, John.' And with her delicate laugh floating in the air, she closed the door.

Theo did his best over the weekend to keep quiet and stay out of his father's sight. Every time he thought about being sick in the car, he felt like crying. This was not how he had envisaged his time at home, not at all. His parents had got their weekends in a muddle and had invited the Drewitt-Smiths over to dinner, even though it was his special Saturday night at home. While the adults squawked laughter from the dining room and popped in periodically for bottles of wine from the fridge, he sat in the kitchen with the portable TV for company. He watched *Dad's Army* when the picture wasn't too fuzzy and ate chicken pie with mashed potatoes and green beans while Rollo sat on the seat next to him. Theo petted him and fed him tiny morsels of chicken.

'You can stay here with me if you promise not to make a noise,' he whispered. Rollo laid his head on Theo's leg. 'Do you ever think about running away, Rollo? I do, but I don't know where to go. And I don't like the dark.'

It was as he lay in his bed, wide awake and staring at the ceiling while the adults screamed their laughter below, that a sad realisation came to him. He didn't want to be anywhere, not at school, not in the back of his father's car, where cigarette smoke and fast corners had made him sick, not in the cold kitchen with the fuzzy TV, where there was no one to talk to, and certainly not in this bedroom filled with antiques from his grandpa's house. And that left only one question: if he didn't feel comfortable anywhere, then where was he supposed to be?

Relieved that he'd made it back to school without vomiting, Theo knew he had to be brave. He felt sick at the prospect of not seeing his parents for another six weeks and even sicker at the thought that he'd been looking forward to the exeat for so long and now it was over. In truth, it hadn't gone as he'd hoped. He tried to quash the ache of disappointment.

As they left, his mother kissed him warmly on the forehead and hugged him too tightly; his father ruffled his hair briefly, before looking at his watch and clapping his hands together.

Theo watched the car drive away, waving until they were completely out of sight, in case they could see through the scratchy hawthorn hedge.

'Who are you waving at, homo?'

And there they were, the torturous words that marked his return. He'd been praying for a gentle casing back in, but no.

Theo whipped round to see Wilson standing with muddied knees in his hockey kit, twirling his stick in the air and catching it with one hand. He felt torn, knowing that to leave the question unanswered might invite further attacks and yet to answer without knowing fully what a homo was would leave him wide open to ridicule.

'I was waving at my... my parents.' He cursed the wobble to his bottom lip.

'My parents! Boohoo! But at least I've got old Porter the homo to keep me warm!' Wilson mimicked Theo's voice and pretended to cry.

Theo dug deep, ignoring the taunt. Recalling his mother's advice, he plucked a desperate piece of small-talk from the swirl of nerves in his stomach. 'I... I quite like hockey!'

'You *quite* like hockey? Well you'll never make a team, because you can't run with a stick and your hand–eye coordination is shit – you can't even catch a bloody ball!' Wilson jeered.

While Theo tried to remember what had come next on his mother's list of suggestions – was is the weather? – Wilson walked towards him and raised his hockey stick, making as if to strike him at close range. Theo flinched and covered his eyes, awaiting the full force of the blow. His reaction sent Wilson into fits of laughter.

'You, boy!' The bellowed words echoed off the old walls.

Theo looked up to see Mr Porter pushing a wheelbarrow full of compost along the path.

'You! Mr Wilson!' Mr Porter barked, his finger extended in Wilson's direction.

Theo's blood ran cold as Wilson slowly turned on his heel and walked back to where Mr Porter stood in his plaid shirt and corduroy trousers held up by leather braces. His sleeves were rolled above the elbow, revealing his brawny arms.

'Did I see you with a hockey stick in this area? Because that's against the rules. It should have been put away at the end of the session and I would hate to have to recommend you for a detention.'

'Then don't,' suggested Wilson calmly.

Theo didn't recognise the voice Mr Porter used. If his usual voice was like warm, soft toffee, this one was like cold, sharp glass.

'Here's the thing, Mr Wilson. You need to be very careful that you respect everyone in your path, as you never know where they'll pop up again. And, trust me, the path we walk is long and winding.'

Wilson smirked. 'Got it – long and winding.' He nodded and turned back to walk across the quad.

'Did he hurt you?'

Theo shook his head.

'Did you have a good exeat?'

Theo shook his head again.

'Want a cup of cocoa?'

This time he nodded and fell in step beside Mr Porter.

Mr Porter heated some milk in the green enamel kettle that sat on the stove top and with mugs of hot cocoa in their hands they sat side by side on the bench, looking out over the cottage garden and the field beyond. Their breath sent plumes of vapour up into the air. Mr Porter liked to be outside in all weathers, as if he was most at home there, surrounded by nature.

'What's a homo? I think I know, but I'm not sure,' Theo asked as he sipped the warm froth from his drink.

Mr Porter placed his mug on the table and twisted a little so he could look Theo in the eye. 'It's a horrible word, and like all horrible words, if used enough it will make the person who says it ugly on the outside as well as on the inside.'

Theo nodded.

'What do you think it is?' Mr Porter eventually asked.

Theo looked up at him, kicking his legs back and forth. 'Um, I think it's a boy who loves other boys.' He scratched his nose.

'Yep, that'll do. And if a boy loves another boy, that's just fine.'

'They call you "homo".' This Theo offered in the spirit of their pact that they would never lie to each other.

'I know.' Mr Porter picked up his cocoa and slurped it.

'Are you a homo?'

'No, I am not and if I were, as I said already, that would be absolutely fine. Let that be the last time you use that word.'

'I'm sorry.' Theo looked into his mug.

'It's okay, you weren't to know, but now you do, do not say it again.' This was said in the voice that was more sharp glass than soft toffee.

'I won't.'

There was a moment of quiet. Then Mr Porter said, 'I love girls, if you must know. Well, one girl, to be exact.'

'What's her name?'

'Her name was Mrs Porter, or Merry to me, and she *was* merry and beautiful.' Mr Porter twisted the worn gold band on his finger.

'Did she die?'

Mr Porter coughed, nodded and pulled his white handkerchief from his top pocket. He blew his nose and dabbed at his eyes. 'Something in that compost must have got to me.'

And there it was again, the quiet.

'I told my mother about you and she asked me what your name was and I didn't know. Apart from Mr Porter, I mean.'

'My name is Cyrus.'

'Cyrus,' Theo repeated, trying it out. 'Doesn't it make you angry when they call you a name like the one I'm not allowed to say any more?'

'No, it doesn't.' Mr Porter rubbed at his stubbly chin.

'Why not? It makes me angry when they call me names.'

'It doesn't make me angry. It makes me sad. Because, like you, they're only children and they do that because they're afraid and I don't like the idea of anyone being afraid. In fact I fought a war so that no one would be afraid.'

Theo pictured his pen torch. 'What are they afraid of?'

'Who knows, Mr Montgomery? Not being heard, having their own secrets discovered… But it's best to learn to rise above the things they say and the things they do, otherwise a man can spend his whole life fighting, and I reckon we've all had enough of fighting.'

Theo nodded to show that he understood, even if he didn't.

'Having said that, are you familiar with Gandhi? He was a fine man and he said something similar to this: "Where there is only a choice between cowardice and violence, I would advise violence."'

Theo shook his head. 'No, I haven't heard of him.'

Mr Porter took a deep breath. 'Well, I'm beginning to think it might be time you did.'

'Why did Mrs Porter die?'

'Oh, now there's a question I ask myself every hour of every day.'

Theo and Mr Porter stared ahead and sipped their cocoa. That wasn't even close to a satisfactory answer, but Theo could tell by the set of his friend's face, and the silence, that it was the only one he was going to get.

Three

Theo sat in the hundred-year-old library, where the smell of old books danced up his nose. Hunched over his geography textbook, he folded his slim, toned arms and became engrossed, keen to learn about how the earth's crust, its shell, was divided into tectonic plates and how they'd shifted over the last two hundred and fifty million years to form continents and mountains. It was incredible, a reminder that his place in the world was as nothing by comparison.

'Two hundred and fifty million years...' he whispered.

He ran his finger over a map showing the edges of the shifting plates and realised it made sense that this was where there were more volcanoes.

A scream of laughter came from behind him, breaking the silence of the library. He looked round quickly to see Wilson, now in the fifth form, with his cronies Helmsley and Dinesh on either side, chatting to the fourth-form girls. It appeared to be the same interaction, as ever, Wilson leading the pack and the girls flicking their long hair over their shoulders and gently thumping him, a chance for contact. Theo hated the way Wilson had grown his fringe, trying to look like Simon Le Bon, he hated his cockiness, and he hated his friends; in fact he hated most things about him. This had been the case now for the last seven years, ever since Wilson had singled him out in his first weeks at Vaizey College. Theo had learnt to ignore him and continued doing his best to remain invisible, as instructed all that time ago by Mr Beckett, but it wasn't always easy.

Mr Porter reminded him regularly that people who were mean like Wilson had something dark growing inside them and were to be pitied. Theo tried, he really did, but he couldn't help wishing the dark thing growing inside Wilson would just get on with it and suffocate him, anything to get him out of his life and ease his torment. At the start of each new school year, Theo prayed that Wilson might back off, get bored or, shamefully, find a new victim. His bullying was relentless, and Theo had to be permanently on guard. It was exhausting and distracting.

At fourteen, Theo had lost his gangliness. He was tall, slim rather than skinny, and muscular thanks to his running and gym regimes. Everything about him was well proportioned, and with his square jaw and thick hair it was clear he was on the way to becoming a handsome young man. Not that he saw this. He avoided mirrors and kept himself to himself, preferring a quiet life. He was a loner and could only see himself as the weedy boy with the nervous stutter and pallid complexion. Outside of studying, his sole preoccupation was to try and keep his weirdness at bay.

'What are you looking at, Montgonorrhea?' Wilson fired this latest moniker in Theo's direction, before looking at his group to make sure his comment had been properly appreciated.

Theo hadn't realised he was still looking in their direction. He redirected his gaze back to his book, his pulse racing. Closing his eyes, he offered up a silent prayer that they would leave him alone. This he did without conviction; if prayers were all it took, his torment would have abated long ago.

'Quiet, please!' The elderly librarian looked up from her desk and put down her mug commemorating the engagement of Prince Charles and Lady Diana.

'Sorry, miss, it wasn't us, it was Mr Homo here.' Theo glanced up as Wilson stood and pointed in his direction. 'He's making a proper racket and we're trying really hard to study.'

Theo felt the burn of several pairs of eyes fixed on him and a hot prickle spread across his skin.

The girls placed their hands over their mouths to stifle their giggles.

The librarian stood up. 'Right, Mr Homo, gather your books and leave!' She seemed oblivious to the snickers that rippled around the room. 'I will not have disruption in my library. There are people trying to work. Off you go!' She made a shooing sign towards the door.

Theo knew there was no point protesting and, besides, he wanted to be as far away from Wilson as possible. He gathered his books, as instructed, and made his way along the corridor, walking slowly down the wide stone stairs, trying to kill time, practising the art of hiding in plain sight. Even so, despite his best efforts at purposeful dawdling, he arrived at his English class ten minutes early.

He hovered in the classroom doorway and leant his palm on the frame, content to stand and stare. For sitting in the seat next to his was the most beautiful girl he had ever seen. She seemed to be whispering to herself as she ran her hands over her skirt. Her thick flame-red hair hung around her face and her peachy skin was dotted with adorable freckles. Her eyes were green and her nose was tiny and snub. He looked around the classroom to see if it was a set-up, another joke at his expense, but she was alone.

Theo walked slowly forward, mindful that he had only minutes before his classmates arrived and introduced him as the school weirdo.

He pulled out his chair and tried to order the jumble of words flying around inside his head. But before he'd had the chance to construct a comprehensible sentence, she spoke to him.

'Hi there, I'm Kitty.' She smiled warmly and waved at him, even though they were close enough to speak, and he liked it. It was the nicest welcome he'd received in a long time.

'I'm Theo.' He sat down and stared at her face.

'Well, you're going to have to help me out here, Theo. You know when a girl is a million miles from home and is smiling as though she has it all figured out but is actually just very scared, wondering how to fit in at a new school this late in the term?' She dipped her eyes, her tone sincere, her Scottish lilt most attractive.

'Uh-huh.'

'Well, I am that girl.' She laughed softly and leant in closer, laying her fingers briefly on his arm, with the lightest of touches.

Theo's limbs jumped and a jolt of pleasure fired through him. He wouldn't have been surprised to find that her fingers had burnt right through his flesh.

Kitty continued, whispering now. 'Actually, that's not strictly true. I'm a warrior like my mum and that means I can get through just about anything.' She sat back in the chair and rested her hand on the desktop. Theo had a strong desire to place his on top of it. Kitty the warrior carried on. 'Mr Reeves told me to sit here and then left me all alone. He seemed a bit odd.'

'I guess.' Theo nodded. 'And people fear people who are odd, weird. They think they're toxic, contagious.' He blinked.

'I suppose we do.' She gave a small laugh and it was abundantly clear that this beautiful, confident girl was not one of life's weirdos. 'I was going to give it five more minutes and then run and hide somewhere, but then you turned up. You just might be my knight in shining armour.'

He liked this idea very much. 'I'm not usually this early. I was working in the library...' He let this trail, not wanting to recount or even recall what had happened only minutes earlier. 'It's a coincidence, really. Out of all the people that might have turned up early... I'm a Montgomery, so you must be...?'

'Oh! Oh, I see!' She smiled when she caught his thread. 'I'm a Montrose. So that explains the seating.'

Theo loved that she was smart.

'I think I can get through this, Mr Montgomery, with you by my side. What was your first name again?' She was so close now that tendrils of her thick hair were brushing his shoulder, vivid orange against the navy of his V-necked school jersey. It took all of his strength not to reach out and touch them.

'My name's Theodore, but everyone calls me Theo.' *Not that they call me anything really, as no one talks to me, but I don't want you to know that and right now you don't and I feel like someone else and that's brilliant.*

She twisted her head to look at him. 'Theodore? Let me guess... after Mr Roosevelt? I must confess, I can't think of any other Theodores right now!'

'Actually, no.' His face broke into a wry smile, but he made sure his lips covered his teeth, which he had neglected to clean that morning. 'I was named after Theobald's House. My father was a Theobald's boy and my grandfather too, in fact all the men in our family came here, but I think my mother drew the line at Theobald and so Theodore was the compromise.'

'That's crazy!' She put her hand to her cheek and he noticed a kink in her left forearm, a slight bend that meant her hand curved ever so slightly to the left. Imperfect and therefore, to him, perfect.

She continued, either unaware or uninterested in his scrutiny. 'So your family are, like, Vaizey College through and through?'

'I guess.' He shrugged, pleased to have impressed her a little and sad that it was based on a lie. It might have been true that in the past the Montgomery men were Vaizey to the core, but his hatred of the place meant that line ended with him. It felt to Theo as if his awkwardness at the school was like a loose thread and that each time it got pulled it left another little hole in his father's reputation as well as his own. It was a huge weight to carry. 'I sometimes wish I was named after Roosevelt instead.' This was as close as he could come to admitting how he felt about the school. 'It would be easier and quicker to explain.'

'And is that a Rudyard Kipling novel I see in your bag?' she asked in her soft voice as she peered at the green cloth spine.

'His poetry actually. For prep.' Not that he'd started it yet. He was, in truth, dreading it. *I mean... poetry? What's the point?*

'We have a lot of it in the library at home, you must know some of it already?' Her eyes blazed with enthusiasm.

He looked at her and in that moment wished beyond every-thing that instead of maths equations, tectonic plates and the properties of light, all the things that had held his attention over the last term, it had been the poetry of Mr Rudyard Kipling that he had studied. To have been able to recite just a single line from one of his poems would, he knew, have made the greatest impression on Miss Kitty Montrose. And he wanted to impress her. He wanted that very much. Instead, he hesitated and confessed with a flush of embarrassment to his cheeks. 'I'm afraid not. I haven't really read any yet.'

Her smile faded a little and her brows knitted. But she quickly regained her equanimity. 'Well of course, why would you? My boyfriend is the same. He only reads comics, if you can believe that!' She shook her head and reached for her textbook.

Theo felt his stomach bunch as if he'd been punched. This was the very worst news imaginable – not that Kitty's boyfriend only read comics, but that she had a boyfriend at all. A surge of something thick seemed to clog his veins, making his limbs feel leaden and his head light. He hated the boy, even if he had no idea who he was.

'You have a boyfriend?' he mumbled weakly.

'Yes.' She nodded. 'My cousins are already here at Vaizey – Ruraigh and Hamish Montrose…'

Theo nodded. He knew them of course and with this information came a sickness in his gut. Her cousins would no doubt fill her in on all of his quirks, laughing, probably, as they did so. And, just like that, the crackle of confidence that had flickered into life when Kitty had considered him her knight in shining armour, was now extinguished. He watched her beautiful mouth move and half listened to the words that came out.

'They always bring their friends home for the holidays, and he's one of their gang, so we kind of met a while ago. He's a fifth former,' she said with pride. 'Angus Thompson, do you know him?'

Theo could only nod as he pictured the confident, athletic Thompson, a full two years older than him, good-looking in a New Romantic kind of way, and captain of the 1st XI. His heart sank. He stared ahead, almost unable to look at Kitty. *I wish I was Angus Thompson. I wish I was anyone other than Theodore Montgomery.*

'Are you sporty?' she asked, as if she'd read his thoughts.

He shook his head. 'Not really. Are you?'

'Swimming, that's my thing. I love to swim. My dad always says that one day I'm going to develop gills behind my ears!'

Theo watched, fascinated, as, at the mention of her dad, her eyes narrowed and for a split second there was a look of longing on her pretty face. Could it be that she too came from a home where she felt like a guest and with parents who made her feel like an encumbrance? Oh, to have someone to discuss this with – it would make things so much easier to bear.

'I'm finding being here harder than I can say,' she said.

Theo's heart lifted. 'I understand that.' And he truly did.

She sighed. 'My mum and dad are my best friends really. God, I know how naff that sounds, but they are. We do so much together and I would rather be with them than do anything else. Do you know what I mean?'

He nodded vacantly. *Of course she's not like you, idiot.* He cursed the very idea. *Look at her, she's perfect.*

The moment the bell rang at the end of class, Theo gathered up his books and headed off to find Mr Porter. He knew the man's routine as well as his own and figured that he'd be up at the cricket pitch on this sunny day.

'Now what's that face for?' Mr Porter placed his hands on his lower back and stood up slowly from where he'd been crouching. He made his way to the other side of the crease, where he bent down again and with his little white dabbing stick filled in the gaps in the line.

Theo sighed and began stripping the bark from a twig he'd found on the path. 'Do you know any of Rudyard Kipling's poetry?' He thought it might be easier to learn a poem off Mr Porter than try and find an appropriate one in the book he had in his bag.

'Can't say as I do.'

'Dammit.' Theo tutted.

'I see someone's got a cob on today.' Mr Porter laughed. 'Poetry's not really my thing. I might have recited the odd ditty to my comrades during the war, but none that's fit for your tender ears, Mr Montgomery.'

For the umpteenth time that afternoon, the name and image of Angus Thompson came into his head. A fine name for a fine scholar and sportsman. 'I wish I wasn't named after Theobald's House, a place I hate. It annoys me.'

'Well, don't let it,' Mr Porter said, keeping his eyes on the white line as he continued dabbing it with paint.

Theo huffed. As if it was that easy.

'When you met Mrs Porter, did you like her the first time you saw her?'

'Ah, so that explains the face.' Mr Porter rocked back on his haunches and looked away to the horizon. 'Yes, I did. I liked her the very second I saw her and I loved her until the very last.' His eyes crinkled in a smile.

'Did you tell her you liked her?'

'Oh no. Not at first. That's not how it's done. You have to be subtle, get to know a lady and win her over.'

Theo snorted. He had never won anything in his life, let alone a prize like Kitty Montrose. 'I just wish...' He kicked at the ground.

'You just wish what?'

'I wish I could be someone else.'

'And who would you like to be, might I ask?' Mr Porter's knees creaked as he stood up. He looked Theo in the eye, easy now they were of a similar height.

'Anyone,' he said quietly.

'Here's the thing, Mr Montgomery. There isn't a single pupil in this school, or any other, come to think of it, who hasn't wished for the same at some point. Everyone wants to be taller, thinner, smarter, funnier, faster, less afraid, you name it! I've known you for a very long time and I can tell you that you are one of the best people I know. You have heart!' He placed his fist on his chest. 'And if you can find the confidence to follow your heart, which one day you will, you will be happy and that's the greatest gift you can give yourself.'

'How do I win a girl over?' he asked. These life lessons were all well and good, but time was of the essence.

Mr Porter reached up under his cap and scratched his head. 'Well, it depends on the kind of girl she is. You might be able to impress her with gifts and expensive treats, but therein lies a problem, because if she's the kind of girl that's *impressed* by gifts and expensive treats, the kind of girl who won't pay her own way, then I would say she isn't the girl you want, even if you think you do. But if you can make her laugh and she can make you laugh in return, oh boy, that's the nicest way to live.' He gave a small chuckle.

'Did you and Mrs Porter make each other laugh?'

'Every day, Mr Montgomery, every day. Spending time with her…' He looked into the middle distance, his expression wistful. 'It was like the sun was out, even when it was raining. She was my sunshine.' He chuckled. 'It's important, those little things that bind you, and they're often found in the mundane. There are some men, Mr Montgomery, who are like a glass of champagne – exciting, glamorous – but you don't want to be a glass of champagne.'

'I don't?'

'No. You want to be a cup of tea.'

Theo stared at Mr Porter. 'I think I might like to be a glass of champagne!'

Mr Porter shook his head. 'No, you don't. Champagne is for high days and holidays – people don't always have a fancy for it. But a good cup of tea? There isn't a day in the year when it isn't the best thing to have first thing in the morning. A cup of tea warms your bones on a cold day and can bring you close together as you sit and chat. You want to be a cup of tea.'

Theo smiled at him. 'You sound mad. Going on about tea and champagne when all I want to know is how to make a girl like me!'

'Aye, maybe so, but love makes you mad, that's a fact, and when it comes to affairs of the heart, I know what I'm talking about. Merry was…' He paused. 'She was perfect and yet she picked me.'

'Because you were a cup of tea.'

'Exactly.' He winked. 'I was a cup of tea.'

A burst of laughter filtered across the grass. It came from behind the wide oak tree, where a gaggle of his peers were sitting chatting, flirting and studying, enjoying the freedom of being fourteen and with only a couple of weeks left on the school calendar.

'Why don't you go and sit with them?' Mr Porter asked.

'Are you joking? They hate me!'

'They don't hate you! And if they do, then it's because they don't know you. You should give them the chance to get to know you and you can only do that by going and saying hello.'

'Mr Porter, I've been in their classes for seven years and they haven't once shown any sign of wanting to get to know me. And I know why – it's because I'm weird.' He held the twig in both hands and pushed on the middle with his thumbs until it snapped.

Four

The end of term arrived quickly and Theo was in his dorm packing his case for the summer break. He worked slowly, distracted as ever by thoughts of Kitty, the girl whose face sat behind his eyelids and pulled him from sleep in the early hours. He now longed for his English class, previously his least favourite subject, just for the chance to sit with arms touching and her scent filling his space with a cloud of sweetness. Under the ruse of reading the set texts and with his head propped on his arm, he was able to stare at her unnoticed, fascinated, while his heart ached with longing and regret that it was Angus Thompson whose name she wrote in a circle of hearts on her folder. He knew that if it had been his name so artistically inscribed, he would want for nothing else ever again.

'Get a move on, Montgomery. No one wants to be hanging around here after the bell, especially not for you!' The prefect, Xander Beaufort, hovered in the hallway, shouting his commands through the open door of Theo's dorm.

Theo got it. Being held up when everyone was keen to get their summer started would be bad enough, but being held up by him would be doubly annoying. For the good-looking and popular boys there was always some leeway, but for him there was no softening of the rules and no kindness.

Toxic...

Having tossed his belongings into his case, he buckled it up, then sat on the end of his bed and waited.

And waited.

And waited.

Once or twice he walked to the deep-set mullioned windows and watched boys and girls being swept into hugs by parents who seemed to be just as excited as their offspring, clapping and skipping as they herded them onto the leather backseats of Bentleys, Jaguars and a snazzy new Audi Quattro. But the cars had stopped coming a little while ago, and it was now painfully quiet. Theo looked up along the lane and over the hedge, where he knew the birds would have been hiding from the earlier cacophony.

'You still here?'

Theo stood up and faced Mr Beckett, as was the custom when addressed by a master. 'Yes, sir.'

'Parents collecting you?'

'Yes, sir.'

He felt the familiar rush of heat to his face that came whenever he sensed he was inadvertently doing or saying something wrong. His housemaster snorted his irritation and swept from the room. Theo again walked to the window and prayed they might come soon. *Please, Mum. Please hurry up.*

It was evident after a further hour that his parents had been horribly delayed. Mr Beckett reappeared, in worse humour than before and with two high spots of colour on his cheeks. Theo's spirits sank.

'Come with me. Bring your bag.' His housemaster pointed at the suitcase, his eye twitching furiously.

Theo knew it could only be bad news and wondered if his parents had crashed the car in the lanes. He pictured it: his mother slapping his father's hand away from the radio dial through the fug of cigarette smoke and then quite suddenly the car swerving sideways...

He followed Mr Beckett into his study with his stomach bubbling, prepared to hear the worst. To his surprise, he was handed the telephone. He held it to his ear and heard the echo of a voice far, far away, along with the squawk of birds and the shouts of a crowd in the background. It sounded a bit like a party.

'For fuck's sake!' His mother was roaring with laughter, carrying on a conversation with someone at her end, presumably. 'It's *not* funny!' Her raucous giggles suggested the exact opposite.

'H... hello, Mum?' he interrupted.

'Darling!' She shouted this loudly, as if surprised to hear his voice on the end of the phone. There was a slight delay on the line. He could hear the sound of water splashing and it seemed like there were a lot of people around; mixed-up chatter floated down the line. Her words carried the slight slur they usually had after she'd drunk alcohol. 'Darling, I am a terrible mother! Just terrible! Oh my goodness, Theo, what is there to say?'

'You bloody are!' he heard his father call out in the background. This was followed by another roar of communal laughter.

'Okay, so this is what's happened.' There was a pause and then the unmistakeable sound of his mother drinking from a glass with ice in it. 'Daddy and I got our dates in a muddle.'

'Don't fucking blame me!' Again, his father's voice called out, and again it was followed by a collective burst of laughter.

'Sssshhh! I'm on the bloody phone! Keep it down!' she yelled.

Theo felt his cheeks flame, not only because his mother sounded inebriated and was swearing, but also because he was in Twitcher's study, and because the call felt a lot like eavesdropping on her and her friends. He pushed the earpiece closer to his head, hoping this might muffle the sound.

'As I said, we got our dates in a muddle and didn't realise that it was *today* that you broke up and, well, there's no easy way of saying this, but we're in St-Tropez!' she squealed, as if the whole thing was uproariously amusing.

And maybe it was. For them.

'I… I don't…' Theo struggled to find the words that would smooth the situation. 'I don't know where that is,' he managed.

'The French Riviera, darling! And you are going to love it here!'

'How am I going to get there?' he whispered, gripping the phone in both hands.

'Now, we've been giving it some thought and plans are afoot! Fret not! We're sending a girl and a car to collect you from school tomorrow, she'll have your passport and she will drive you to the airport, where tickets will be waiting. Simply hop on a plane and Daddy and I will meet you at Nice airport.'

'What girl? And what should I do today? Everyone else has left.'

'Theo, listen to me, darling, you're a wonderful boy and we are all very much looking forward to seeing you tomorrow! Tata for now!'

The line went dead and Theo was engulfed in silence.

Twitcher broke the quiet, firing a question that indicated he had heard the whole exchange, and this made Theo's face even redder.

'So the problem is, where are you going to spend the night? School is effectively closed and I'm heading off any minute. Are you friends with any of the day boys who live locally?'

Theo shook his head.

Mr Beckett gave a deep sigh and Theo wished he could drop through the floor and disappear. He hated this feeling of being unwanted, a nuisance, even though he was well used to it.

'I do have one friend, I suppose.' He paused and blinked at his housemaster.

'There's no need to look so fed up. You shouldn't write off a place before you even get there. It might be wonderful – sea, sun, sand.' Mr Porter spoke as he pottered in the tiny cottage kitchen, reaching behind the faded floral fabric that hung in lieu of cupboard doors and delving into the creaky, bulbous refrigerator as he packed the khaki knapsack with slabs of pound cake and freshly made cheese-and-pickle sandwiches. 'There are many who've never left England's shores and would give their right arm to travel to the south of France—'

'They can have my ticket,' Theo interrupted. 'I hate sand.'

'Well, aren't you a ball of fun. And if you hate sand that much, my best advice would be, don't join the Foreign Legion!' Mr Porter chuckled.

Theo didn't get the joke and ignored it. 'I just don't like going on holiday. Well, I do and I don't. I'll be glad to be away from here.' He jerked his head in the direction of the main school building.

'Speaking for myself, I'm looking forward to the break. It's a hell of a lot easier keeping the grass in tiptop condition and the place litter-free when there's only the summer-school kids to contend with.'

'You don't know what it's like. You don't know what they're like!' Theo said, recalling his mother's slightly sloshed voice and the raucous background noise.

'You're right, I don't. But the fact is, you have to go tomorrow and the way I see it is you have two choices: you either jump into it and make the most of it, or you sulk and make yourself and everyone around you miserable.' He fastened the buckles on the bag and slung it over his shoulder. 'Come on then, let's get walking while we've still got the light!'

The two set off in the late afternoon with the sun still warm and the birds singing overhead. Theo knew it was Mr Porter's favourite time of day, in his favourite time of year.

'Can you help me with my English assignment?' he asked. 'I have to do this writing thing and it's really hard. I'm rubbish at that stuff. I just can't do it.'

'No such thing as can't.' Mr Porter stopped and turned to face him. 'I will, however, help you because I know that otherwise it will prey on your mind and stop you having fun when you're away, and that would be a rotten waste of a good summer.'

Theo felt a surge of affection for his friend, who was always so considerate. 'Thank you.'

'What's it meant to be about then, this assignment?'

'Oh...' Theo tried to recall the title. 'We have to write as if we're an animal and describe how we see the world. So a dog in a car, or a rabbit in a hutch or something like that.'

'Okay, I think I can manage that. Not a word to anyone, mind. They'd have my guts for garters if they knew I'd helped with your homework.'

'I won't tell anyone!'

'In that case I'll do a rough copy and post it to your room, then you can improve on it, use it as your template and make it your own.'

'Thank you.' Theo grinned. That was one less thing to worry about.

Mr Porter opened the kissing gate and set off down the bridle-way. Theo followed in his wake, inhaling the scent of freshly mown grass and dry, sun-scorched earth. They trudged on, across hard, dusty ground that was littered with stones and uphill via sloping fields, until with sweat on their brows and a shortness to their breath, they reached Jackman's Cross an hour or so later. Mr Porter came to a stop and sat himself down on a patch of lush green grass. Theo sat next to him and the two, now so comfortable in each other's company, were happy to stay there in silence for a bit.

'This is some view, eh?' Mr Porter said appreciatively.

Theo let his eyes sweep the broad fields of the Dorset country-side from left to right. Full hedgerows formed the boundaries and deer frolicked on the lower slopes in the pink haze of the evening sun. It was when their breath had steadied and their muscles were rested that he spoke.

'They... They forgot to pick me up,' he whispered, running his hand over the grass and cursing the thickening in his throat.

'So I believe.' Mr Porter rested his elbows on his raised knees.

Theo pulled at clumps of grass and threw them into the air. 'Kitty told me her mum and dad are her best friends.' He paused. 'I can't imagine that.'

Mr Porter considered this. 'It's my belief that there are many types of parent, each probably doing what they think is best.

My dad was raised under the philosophy "spare the rod, spoil the child" and because of his experience he never raised so much as a finger to me.'

'I don't think…' Theo swallowed. 'I don't think my mum and dad like me very much. Whenever I'm with them, I always feel as if they're just waiting for me to go back to school.'

Mr Porter glanced at him and gave a wry smile. 'Well, I'm sorry you feel that way. Have you ever considered that maybe they like you very much but don't know how to behave any differently? I mean, there's no handbook that arrives with a new baby – I don't know how we'd have fared.'

Theo looked at him. *You'd have fared brilliantly.* 'I wish I had arrived with a handbook,' he said, 'although I'm fairly sure my parents would have been too busy to read it.' He smiled at the laugh this raised in his friend. 'I do know that if I had a son, I would never forget to pick him up at the end of term. I wouldn't get in a muddle over exeat dates and invite friends over instead of cooking supper just for him. And I'd try to remember that he needs to eat more than cheese! And on phone-call night, I'd sit by the phone so that no time was wasted. In fact I'd never send him to a school like Vaizey College. I'd let him choose where he went to school. I'd let him be happy.'

Mr Porter waited until Theo had calmed before he answered. 'I understand why you're aggrieved…' He nodded. 'But here's the thing: everyone is different and some people can only repeat the choices their parents made because they're too scared to do anything else. I'm sure your parents meant no ill. They're probably just very busy people.'

Theo stared at him and shook his head, remembering their honesty pact. 'I just don't think it's good enough.'

Mr Porter sniffed and returned his gaze. 'Okay, I agree.' He wiped his hands on his trousers. 'You're right. If I had a son, I too would never forget to pick him up from school and I too would sit by the phone if I knew he was going to call. Happy now?'

'Happier,' Theo admitted. 'It's funny, the date of the start of the summer holidays has been in my mind for weeks and weeks, but I guess it just isn't important to them.'

'Well, as I said, they're very busy people, and—'

'Can't you just admit that it's shit?'

Mr Porter harrumphed his laughter and sighed. 'You're right. It's shit.'

Theo felt the twitch of a smile at the shared swearword, as well as relief that his anger was not misplaced.

A light evening breeze brushed over the hill.

'I've got you something.' Mr Porter reached into the breast pocket of his checked shirt and handed Theo a little gold safety pin. Attached to it was a delicate fishing fly of green and blue feathers, with a square red bead at the end.

Theo turned it over in his hand and stared at it.

'Now, I don't want to hear no more talk of being someone else. Be proud to be you, Mr Montgomery. Wear this somewhere discreet and use it like I do, as a reminder to seek out the stillness. That's where you'll find peace.'

Theo cursed the tears that spilled down his cheeks. He was fourteen now and there were lots of things that he didn't know, but he did know that big boys weren't supposed to cry.

'There, there.' Mr Porter patted him on the shoulder. 'No need for tears, not today, especially not with this view in front of us. This landscape should do many things, inspire you, calm you even, but it shouldn't make you sad.'

'Th... thank you.' Theo wrapped his fingers around the fishing fly and sniffed as he looked out over the magnificent vista.

'You're quite welcome, son. You're quite welcome.'

Theo stood in the front courtyard next morning as instructed and waited to be collected. His pulse raced at the prospect of what might happen if the girl failed to show up. He was certain they wouldn't let him go back to Barnes on his own, and another night on the camp bed at Mr Porter's was probably out of the question.

At a little after nine o'clock a red Mini pulled sharply through the gates as its horn let out a tinny beep. A blonde girl in jeans, black espadrilles and a worn, black, cap-sleeved T-shirt jumped out of the driver's seat.

'Theodore?' she asked, pointing at him, chewing gum and smiling at the same time.

'Yes. Theo.'

'I guessed it might be you – as you're the only person stood here with a suitcase and a face like a smacked arse!' She laughed loudly and bent double. 'Get in the car. That's such a cool name – Theo,' she wheezed. 'Are you all set?'

'Yes.' He placed his case on the back seat and climbed in after it.

'What are you doing? You think I'm a cab? Hell no! Get in the front!' she yelled as she slammed the driver's door and clipped in her seatbelt.

Theo reluctantly left the safety of the rear seat and settled himself in the front. No sooner had he shut the door than the girl drove back out through the gates at speed.

'What the fuck? That's actually your school? I've never seen anything like it! My school looked like a crappy old office block. I mean, seriously? It looks like something out of a Hammer horror movie.'

'It *feels* like something out of a Hammer horror movie.' He felt his muscles unknotting with every yard they put between themselves and his school.

'Ha! You're funny. I like that.' She twisted her head to the left to get a glimpse of him.

Theo smiled. He'd never been told that before and it felt nice.

'I'm Freddie, by the way, short for Frederica – named after my dad, the bastard, who did a runner when my mum was up the duff.'

'I...' Nervous of saying the wrong thing, Theo didn't know whether to apologise, sympathise or laugh, so he said nothing more. This girl was unlike any other he'd met.

'So how old are you? Twelve?'

'No.' Her guess both irritated and embarrassed him. 'I'm fourteen.'

'Christ, okay... Fourteen! I'm nineteen and you look a million years younger than me.'

Again, he decided that silence might be the best policy.

'So what's the deal here? Your parents *actually* forgot to pick you up? How whacked is that? I nearly pissed myself laughing! I guess it's lucky you're fourteen or whatever and not a baby. You could easily have been one of those kids whose parents leave them outside the supermarket and when they go back for them, they've been nicked.'

Theo stared at her, not sure which kids she was referring to but feeling a wave of concern for them nonetheless.

'Have they left you anywhere before?' she asked.

'I don't think so.'

'You don't *think* so? Jesus, what kind of people do that? It's hilarious! Completely off the scale!'

Theo didn't think there was anything funny about it. He stared out of the window.

Undeterred by his silence, Freddie continued. 'I have seriously never heard anything like it – how could they just forget to pick you up?'

'I don't know,' he admitted. 'They're very busy people.'

'I should cocoa, but that doesn't really cut it – how busy do you have to be to forget you have a kid?' She wrinkled her nose.

Far from taking offence, he was a little reassured by her being so shocked, feeling, as with Mr Porter's reaction, that it legitimised his own response. It made her seem like an ally of sorts.

'But I guess shit happens. So what music do you like?' Freddie rattled on without giving him time to reply. 'I love ABC. Do you know their stuff? They're brilliant. I'll let you borrow my tape if you like.'

'Thank you.' He found it hard to keep up. Freddie spoke so quickly and changed the subject without warning, not bothering to pause for breath.

'Have you got a girlfriend?' she asked suddenly.

His face coloured as he had just that second been thinking about Kitty. He shook his head. 'No.'

'What? You are kidding me? A good-looking boy like you? I would have thought you'd be beating them off with a stick!'

He shook his head again, wishing they could go back to talking about ABC.

'My boyfriend and I just finished. His loss. Cheating arsehole!'

She yelled this out of the window, as if the message might carry on the wind and land in the boyfriend's cheating arsehole ear. 'It's good though, in a way,' she continued, using brute force to crunch the gearstick through the sequence at every corner. 'I mean, if we'd still been going out, I wouldn't be here today.' She smiled at him. 'And this is an adventure!'

He wished she didn't feel the need to yell everything.

'Thank you very much for driving me to the airport.'

'No worries.' She grinned at him, still chewing her gum.

'I think my ticket is waiting for me, I'm not sure where, but I know I'm flying to Nice.'

'Yes, you wally, and I'm coming with you!'

'You're coming with me to Nice?' He twisted in the seat. 'Why?'

'Why?' she yelled. 'Because why not? And because it's the best fucking job in the world! I get to hire a car, pick you up, fly first class, sit by a pool for weeks on end and then fly you home! Hell, yeah!' She banged the steering wheel. 'The Riviera here we come!'

He wondered how this had been arranged. 'Do you know my parents?'

'Not exactly, but I used to nanny for the Mendelsohns?'

Theo shook his head. That name meant nothing to him.

'Charlie Mendelsohn used to work with your dad and then moved to Hong Kong a couple of years ago, and I looked after his kids when they were in London.'

'You're not my *nanny*?' Theo asked. That would be too much to bear.

'No, you dick!' She tutted. 'You're fourteen. I'm your companion.'

He looked out of the window and felt a familiar ball of rage and embarrassment growing in his stomach.

'Don't look like that! You seem mightily pissed off and I am far from the worst companion in the world.'

Theo ignored her, closed his eyes and rested his head on the juddering window. He decided to feign sleep.

Getting through to the departure area had left him flustered, but with his suitcase and Freddie's holdall whisked off on a conveyor belt, they now had two hours to kill. As they were debating whether to go and eat or find a place to nap, Theo spied Helmsley and his younger brother making their way through the banks of seats and heading in their direction.

'Oh shit!'

He didn't realise he'd spoken aloud until Freddie placed her hand on his arm.

'What's the matter? You look like you've seen a ghost.'

'Nothing, it's just a boy from school who… who…' He didn't know where to begin, how to phrase exactly just how miserable Helmsley and his best mate made his life.

'That guy?' She thumbed in Helmsley's direction.

Theo nodded quickly, hoping that he wouldn't be seen. 'Please don't speak to him! Please! He'll only tell Wilson!'

'Who's Wilson? Jesus, are you afraid of them?'

'I…' Theo still couldn't find the words. He sat down on a vacant chair and shrank back in the seat, wishing he was invisible, which made a pleasant change from wishing he was Angus Thompson.

Freddie, however, had other ideas. She sat down next to him

and began laughing loudly, so loudly that several people looked in their direction. Theo didn't know what to do.

It had the desired effect. Helmsley glanced across and grinned. Then he jabbed his brother in the ribs and the two made their way over. Freddie laughed again and placed her hand on Theo's chest. Theo's skin jumped beneath her touch. 'You are hilarious!' she shouted.

'Montgomery!' Helmsley called. 'We're off to Florida, where are you going?'

'Who the fuck are you?' Freddie turned suddenly to face Helmsley, who opened his mouth and faltered.

'I'm... a friend of Montgomery's.'

'Don't lie! If you were a friend of his you'd know not to call him Montgomery! Plus, if you were a friend of my boyfriend's, he'd have told me about you and he hasn't.' With that, she lifted her legs, stretched them out over both of Theo's and placed her hand in his hair.

Helmsley's eyes widened. 'I just wanted to...'

'Just wanted to what? Sod off!' she fired back.

Helmsley grabbed his brother by the shoulder and they walked off briskly in the direction they'd come from.

Astonished, Theo looked at Freddie. To his even greater surprise, she kissed him sweetly on the cheek.

'He looks like a right stuck-up prick.' Again, she made no attempt to lower her voice.

'He is.' Theo smiled at her, changing his mind about her in an instant. She was right, she certainly wasn't the worst companion in the world.

★

The drive from Nice to St-Tropez was fantastic. His mother kissed Freddie warmly on the cheek in the arrivals hall, like they knew each other, and thanked her profusely for bringing her son safely to her. Theo rolled his eyes at his new fake girlfriend. The way his mother spoke made it sound as if they had climbed mountains and trekked through the wilderness instead of sitting in first class and overdosing on cold lemonade and over-chilled chicken sandwiches. He put on the sunglasses that someone had left in the glove box of the black and burgundy Deux Chevaux and they drove along the winding coastal road with the top down and the warm wind blowing away the cobwebs. With no cigarette smoke to breathe in, his travel sickness was kept at bay. Theo felt good, in fact he felt *great*! He was away from school and, better than that, Helmsley thought that Freddie was his girlfriend!

'What are you looking so smug about?' His mother patted his thigh.

'Life!' he called out with his arms over his head.

'How marvellous!' His mother beamed. 'Does this mean I'm forgiven for getting in a muddle over the dates?'

'Of course you are. Shit happens!' He smiled, happy to get away with swearing in front of Freddie.

The three of them laughed out loud and Theo knew that how he felt at that exact second with the sun on his face and holding the attention of these two women was a moment to treasure, a moment when all good things felt possible. He liked feeling this way. He liked it very much.

La Grande Belle, the house his parents had rented for the summer, was both vast and beautiful. Its pale stone seemed to change colour depending on the time of day and bright pink bougainvillea clung to the walls, twisting round the ironwork of the Juliet balconies at the shuttered first-floor windows. These had the most beautiful views over the little village of Gassin. Theo stared out from his twin room at the sparkling azure swimming pool, the ancient olive grove and the sea beyond.

They had arrived during naptime and the rest of the party – various friends of his parents – had retreated for a postprandial siesta behind the carved wooden doors of their bedrooms. He was standing by his bed, trying to decide between unpacking and exploring, when he heard a loud splash. Running to the window, he saw that Freddie was already in the pool. Her blonde hair floated behind her, on top of the water, then she twisted and dived under again and everything but the pale soles of her feet disappeared. She bobbed up again, this time further along the pool. The water clung to her sodden T-shirt and black bikini bottoms. He watched, fascinated, as she pulled herself out of the water and lay cruciform and panting on the marble slabs. He ducked down out of sight, his heart beating very fast, and wondered what Kitty, the swimmer, would look like in her bikini.

Wary of discovery and unable to take his eyes from Freddie's slender form and the droplets of water shimmering on her skin, he sat by the window and tried to control his breathing. He wiped the slick of sweat from the dark, fuzzy down above his top lip and recalled the wonderful weight of her legs resting over his at the airport, and that sweet kiss on the cheek…

'There you are, boy!'

His father's booming voice made him jump. He hurriedly stood up and raced over to the bed, where he fiddled with the buckles on his suitcase – anything to occupy his shaking hands and distract his roving gaze, busy with the image of a semi-dressed Freddie.

'Sorry about the mix-up, but no harm done, eh?' His father

laughed, strode forward and patted his back, as if they had simply ordered the wrong milk or inadvertently jumped a queue. 'We had planned to pop back and collect you, but time kind of ran away with us. You know how it is. The days and nights merge into each other out here.'

Actually, Theo didn't know 'how it was', but he smiled anyway, wanting to get the holiday off to the best possible start. 'It's okay, Dad.'

'Good. Good.' His father beamed and wandered across to the window. 'Well, well, well.' He locked his fingertips together behind him and rocked back and forth as he stared down at the pool. 'Is that the little hottie that chaperoned you?' He turned to nod at his son. 'Goodness me, Theodore, no wonder you're transfixed by the view! I tell you what, if that's the welcome committee you get, I bet you want us to leave you behind every time.' He laughed. 'I have to say, I wouldn't mind where or when I was left if it meant I got to spend hours with that. Good Lord above, will you look at her?'

Theo stared not at the pool but at his father's expression. It sent bile rising into his throat. His father's eyes bulged and his mouth was slack.

'I'll let you get on.' He winked and left the room with a spring in his step.

Theo wasn't sure what bothered him most about his father's behaviour: the fact that his ogling of Freddie made him feel uncomfortable, jealous, even, or how it sent a tremor of sadness through him on behalf of his mother. It was a hard thing to explain. He continued to slowly unpack and, even though he had only just arrived, already saw the shiny veneer peeling from this beautiful day.

Having deliberated long and hard over what might be appropriate to wear, he decided eventually on tennis shorts and his gym shirt and then made his way downstairs. By now, at least half a dozen couples were sitting around the vast wooden outdoor table, which was illuminated by large pillar candles burning in glass lanterns. Some were sipping cold flutes of champagne, others enjoyed long cocktails, and all had the sun-kissed tans that came from spending days lounging by the pool.

'Here he is!' his mother called out and he felt the familiar awkwardness descend. 'For those of you who don't know, this is our son, Theodore – Theo to friends!'

'Ah, Theo, I hear they left you at bloody school? Unforgiveable, if you ask me! What kind of parent does that?'

'Oh do shut up, Pepe! Stop stirring!' His mother laughed and threw a cork at the man, who ducked and winked at him, to show it had all been spoken in jest.

'Darling, this is Pepe and Jemima, and then Leopold and Nancy...' She continued pointing out each couple as Theo nodded and mumbled 'How do you do?' knowing he would never remember who was who. 'Saskia and Konrad, Marcus and Pauly, Jennifer and Duncs – and Daddy and me you know!' She laughed and gave a small clap.

'Or does he? I mean, the poor sod hardly ever sees you, and don't forget, you did leave him in school!' Pepe shouted this loudly, and the whole group chuckled their laughter.

Theo pictured them sitting exactly like this during the phone call yesterday. How they must have laughed while he stood in Twitcher's study, waiting.

'Evening, everyone!' Freddie appeared, looking lovely in a

white strappy summer dress and with her hair wet around her shoulders.

'Ah yes, do come and join us, darling!' his mother called. 'This is Frederica, our guardian angel who gathered up Theo and brought him safely to my side.'

'I wouldn't mind being gathered up by Frederica!' Pepe yelled.

'Oh for God's sake, Pepe! Poor girl!' the group chorused, as Jemima, his wife, covered her eyes in mock shame.

The whole conversation made Theo's stomach flip with unease. He looked at his father, noting the way his eyes ran the length of Freddie's dress from over the rim of his champagne glass. Freddie, however, seemed unflustered and reached for her own glass of champagne before taking a seat next to his mother.

'What would you like to do, darling?' his mother asked loudly. It took him a second to realise it was him she was speaking to. He stared at her, not having the confidence to mention that he had thought he might like to sit at the table and join in. 'You could go and watch a bit of TV, might help your French?' She smiled. 'Or there's a whole stack of videos. There are snacks in the kitchen. Or you could have a play in the pool, it's still lovely and warm!'

Theo felt reduced. Dismissed. It bothered him that she didn't realise that not only was he too old to play in the pool but that there was no one to play with. He looked at the people seated around the table and wondered how it was that no matter where he was in the world or who he was with, he always felt like an intruder, a late arrival for whom no place had been set. And it felt horrible.

*

It was four days into the holiday and close to midnight when Theo was woken by shouts in the hallway. It took a beat for him to remember where he was. He heard his mother's voice and recognised the slight slur to her speech that meant she'd been drinking.

'Don't you give me that bollocks! I fucking saw you!'

His heart hammered at her words. He sat up in the bed, aware that his parents' fight would be heard by all of their friends. He closed his eyes at the thought, feeling the hot prickle of shame on her behalf.

'She's a kid, for God's sake!' his father barked. 'Give me some bloody credit!'

Theo hugged the white bolster to his chest.

'Give you credit? You make me laugh! I don't forget, Perry. I wish I could, but I don't bloody forget!' she yelled. 'You know what they say, that the clearest conscience is held by those who have the shortest memory! And that's you. You are like a fucking goldfish! But I'm not! I don't forget, ever!'

He heard his father make 'sssshhh' sounds, trying to contain his mum's outburst. Theo sensed the enforced silence in all the other rooms, as if, like him, everyone was listening with bated breath and ears cocked to see what would come next. And what came next tore at his heart: it was the sound of his mother weeping and howling with raw, animal-like distress, followed by the closing of their bedroom door.

And then nothing.

He lay awake, looking up at the dark, starry sky through the open balcony window and trying to quiet the nagging voice in his head that told him things were only going to get worse. Hopping out of bed, he grabbed his pen torch. It had gone through numerous batteries over the years and now sported a hairline crack, having been dropped onto the flagstones of the school bathroom in the dead of night. Mr Porter had fixed it with a well-placed spot of glue. Theo thought of him now, as he shone the beam up onto the ceiling of his grand bedroom. He pictured him asleep under the rafters of the cosy crooked cottage. 'Night, night, Mr Porter,' he whispered as he turned onto his side.

The days at La Grande Belle were bearable, pleasant even. Theo spent a lot of time alone, but unlike in Barnes, the weather was glorious and there was always plenty of food in the house. Fresh bread and croissants arrived every morning, pots of jam and chutneys lined the larder walls, and the fridge was packed with fragrant cheeses, cold cuts of ham and roasted chicken wings. He liked to eat his breakfast with the gang, listening to their chatter before setting himself swimming challenges throughout the day, seeing how far he could swim underwater and then how fast. He was a good swimmer and he enjoyed it. The solitude suited him and he liked the feeling of his body growing stronger every day. He noted new definition to his stomach and a broadening of his shoulders.

Freddie sometimes joined him, throwing coins or objects to the bottom of the pool, which they would race to retrieve. Occasionally she took him in the Deux Chevaux down to the harbourside for ice cream, or to the market, where they bought punnets of fat, soft peaches and brown paper bags full of fresh, sweet cherries. She was quieter in his company now than she had been on that first day; she kept her sunglasses on and smoked angrily, throwing the butts out of the car window, acting more like she had when she'd mentioned her arsehole boyfriend. He didn't blame her. Now that she'd got to know him, she probably realised what everyone else knew: that he was weird, and not funny after all.

The nights, however, were very different. When darkness fell, the tension rose as the wine flowed and the candles flickered. The air tasted the same as it did at school in the seconds before a fight and Theo didn't like it one bit, unable to fully explain the hostility he sensed lurking behind the humour. He spent most nights in his room with the balcony doors open, listening to the raucous chat and salacious gossip that was bandied back and forth across the table. At least he hadn't heard his mother crying again, and for that he was grateful.

That was until the night before he left for England. That night, all hell broke loose.

Theo had been in a deep sleep but woke to the sound of smashing glass. He sat up in the bed, fearing a break-in, but then realised he was at La Grande Belle and not at home in Barnes. The smash was followed by the deafening wail of his mother's sobbing, and then her loud shouts in a voice he hardly recognised.

'You fucking pig! This is it! This is it! I have put up with Shawna or whatever the hell her name was from the office and the horse woman from Crewe, and the bloody air hostess, all of them bitches! But this! This is the last straw, Peregrine. This is worse even than you cheating on me just after we got married, worse than you fathering that bastard boy, Alexander, worse than all of it!'

Theo's heart jumped into his throat and a massive roaring filled his ears. It was so loud that for a minute or so he couldn't hear anything else but his own blood pumping through his head. A bastard boy? His dad had another son? This fact ripped his heart, as tears began streaming down his face.

'I can't stand it!' His mum was shouting now. 'You're destroying me! We're here with our friends and she is just a kid!'

'Darling, you're overreacting. Keep your voice down, please!'

'Why should I? I will *not* keep my voice down! And don't you dare smile! Don't you dare! I will stop payments to Alexander, I will take the house and I will take your beloved cars and I will take Rollo and you will be out on your ear. I mean it. This is it. You can fuck off. I am done! It's over! It is really over, Perry.'

With his heart still hammering and his thoughts racing, Theo jumped up and watched from behind the shutter as his mother grabbed another bottle of champagne and threw it onto the marble by the side of the pool. It shattered. The green glass scattered like irregularly shaped marbles and the foaming liquid slithered into the pool. Looking to the left, he spied Freddie lying on a lounger, wearing her pants and what looked to be his father's dinner jacket. His mother continued her rant, lunging in Freddie's direction.

'And you – you little whore! You can guess again if you think I am flying you home. You are stuck here, but not in this house! Get out! Grab your nasty clothes and get out!' She was screaming now. 'I don't give a fuck if you have to *walk* home!' And she lunged forward again, seemingly intent on lynching Freddie.

Theo watched, horrified, as his father grabbed his mother roughly around the waist and manhandled her back inside. She shrieked and clawed at him, her hair falling over her face and her arms outstretched. Just before they disappeared into the house, she shouted, 'There are only two types of people, Perry:

those who cheat and those who don't. The number of times is irrelevant! The tenth time cuts just like the first.'

Theo sat on his bed and listened to the sound of his parents stumbling into their bedroom. He waited until silence fell and the night took on a new shade of darkness, the quiet broken only by the cicadas chirruping in the trees. It was hard to think straight. He had a brother, a half-brother who his mum hated. Alexander! That was a proper name, not like Theo. Why did his mum pay for him? What did she buy him? Did they take him home for weekends while Theo was safely away at school? There were kids at Theo's school who had complicated home lives, whose parents had gone off and had children with other people. But they didn't make a secret of it. What was he supposed to do with this information? His dislike for his father flared. What a horrible thing to do to his mum.

And suddenly it was as if a fog lifted. It was obvious! This was his chance to change his life! Theo now knew with certainty that his mum was unhappy. And so was he. The prospect of going back to school brought nothing but dread. He tightened the rope of his dressing gown over his pyjamas, took a deep breath and crept down the hallway and into his parents' bedroom.

His father was snoring lightly. His feet were sticking out of one end of the sheet and he was clasping the other end to the chest of his coffee-coloured silk pyjamas. Theo crouched down quietly and gently tapped his mother on the shoulder. She sat up and narrowed her eyes at him.

'What is it?' she whispered, looking to her right at her husband's slumbering form.

'I need to talk to you, Mum.' He reached for her arm and guided her from the bed and out onto the landing.

'What is it, Theo?' she asked again. Her gait was unsteady and her breath putrid with the odour of stale cigarettes and booze.

Theo gazed into her red, puffy eyes. His heart swelled with sadness that she had been made to feel this way. It took every ounce of his confidence and courage, but he looked her in the eye and in a lowered voice he told her, 'It's okay, I agree you should send Dad away, and you and I can stay in the house in Barnes and I can go to a local school and I will look after you, Mum. I will always look after you.' Theo had never meant anything more sincerely than these words, whispered on the landing of La Grande Belle.

His mother looked over the galleried landing and towards the great window. Moonlight streamed through it. She screwed up her face and he waited for the tears he expected would follow. But instead of crying, she burst out laughing. And once she began laughing, she couldn't stop. With her face all scrunched up, she tittered as if Theo's suggestion was the most bizarre, ridiculous and abhorrent idea she had ever heard. She looked at her son with a shake of her head and delivered the words that would lodge in his consciousness for the rest of his life. 'I love Peregrine! He is my heart, my soul, my life! And there is no one on this planet I would rather spend my days with!'

'But... But what about Alexander?' he managed.

With whip-like crispness his mother made herself abundantly clear. 'Do not ever, ever mention that name to me or anyone else again. Is that understood?'

Theo stepped backwards as if he'd been physically struck. Her words confirmed what he'd always dreaded: that he had no place there, not with her and not with them, not really. He realised then that no matter how bad things got between his parents or what foul infidelities his father committed, they were a couple, bound together through good and bad, and he was... He was alone and adrift. He swallowed and was overtaken by a great wave of sadness. He was nothing more than an inconvenience, a burden, so forgettable that they hadn't even registered when his school holidays had started.

He left his mother on the landing and shuffled back to his room, weighed down by embarrassment and tears. Walking over to the window he saw that Freddie was now sitting up on the sun lounger crying. Two long snakes of black make-up streaked her face. She looked up and they locked eyes. He stared at her and realised that his first hunch had been right after all: she was the worst companion in the world.

Five

Theo walked across the quadrangle with his suitcase under his arm. His trousers were a little high on his ankle and his blazer was tight across his back. A month of vigorous daily swimming at La Grande Belle had been good for his physique.

It had been a relief to travel back to the UK alone, leaving his parents to wallow in the unpleasant soup of their own making. He had said his goodbyes over breakfast, watching with barely disguised astonishment as his mother, her face hidden behind oversized sunglasses, sipped coffee and laughed at a remark Nancy made, while his father bit into a hot croissant and flicked through a copy of *Le Monde*. It was as if the previous night had not occurred, as if he'd dreamt the whole thing. Whereas he'd lain awake until dawn, replaying the row in his head like a movie, his gut twisting with anxiety. His parents seemed to have forgiven and forgotten and were now simply looking forward to another fun day on the Riviera. He realised that for them this was almost routine – the booze, the row, the hurt, the forgiveness – and it changed nothing. But for Theo, everything had changed. He'd made the extraordinary discovery that he had an illegitimate brother, Alexander. And, even more shattering, he'd learnt that his mother would choose his philandering father over him every time. That was a very bitter pill to swallow.

He thought of Kitty, wondering how they could possibly chat about the summer and how he might phrase the horror of his experience. She'd be full of the pleasures of having spent her holidays with her mum and dad. He thought of Freddie, who'd disappeared completely, and wondered if she was literally walking home. He couldn't help the flicker of concern for her wellbeing, despite what she'd done. Knowing now what he did about his father and recalling the way his dad had looked at Freddie on that first day, Theo saw her as a victim; troublesome, but a victim nonetheless.

Keeping his head low, he made his way towards the dorm with dread in his stomach and a head full of the events of La Grande Belle.

'There you are, sonofabitch.'

Theo stopped at the sound of Wilson's voice over his shoulder. *Oh please, no! Not now, not today.*

'Well, look at you with your lovely tan. Been sunning yourself, have you?'

Theo ignored him, hoping, though not believing, that if he stayed still and quiet, Wilson might leave him alone.

'I know you can hear me. Not so cocky now, are you, without a mouthy little whore to stick up for you. I thought not. Told you, boys.' Wilson laughed. 'Helmsley filled us in on how you gobbed off at him in the airport. Sonofabitch, who do you think you are?'

Who do I think I am? Good question. Theo's thoughts raced with images of his bulging-eyed dad and the cruel laughter of his mum. He turned slowly, preparing to reason with Wilson.

'What's that on your mouth? A caterpillar?' Again the boys guffawed into their hands.

Theo ran his index finger over his top lip and cursed that he'd forgotten to ask his parents for a razor and find out what exactly to do with it. He would ask Mr Porter.

'Is that all the rage in the gay clubs? Is that why you've grown it? To make your boyfriend happy?'

Theo shook his head. Tears of frustration threatened, which he concentrated on holding back; letting them flow would be the very worst thing.

Wilson dropped his sports bag at the feet of his chums and sauntered over, pushing his sleeves over his elbows. Theo knew what came next, but he couldn't think what to do. Ridiculously, his mother's advice came to mind. '*Oh, for goodness' sake, Theo! You're being a wee bit silly! You* know *what to talk about! Sport? School subjects? Good God, the weather? Anything!*'

He opened his mouth to speak, to try and use his smarts to defuse the situation. But Wilson's speed denied him the chance. He was fast. His first blow glanced off Theo's cheekbone, sending a searing pain whistling from one side of his brain to the other. It hurt. Theo's fingers curled into his palms.

'What's the matter?' Wilson bounced on the balls of his feet with his fists raised, as if he was observing the Queensberry Rules rather than brawling in the schoolyard. 'Too scared to hit me, faggot?' He rocked his head from side to side and jabbed a couple of mock blows before landing the third on Theo's left eye socket.

Theo winced and held a cupped palm over his face, cursing the tears that now spilled, as much in response to the pain as in frustration.

Helmsley and Dinesh skittered about like excitable pups. They darted around the two of them, shouting their approval and whooping and hollering as they cheered their leader on. 'Poof!' Dinesh yelled for good measure.

Theo tried to stand up straight, thinking that he should now speak, try to reason... The next blow caught him on the side of the head and for a second or two his vision blurred.

'What sort of bloke doesn't fight back? What the fuck is wrong with you?' Wilson spat. 'Is it like the homo code?'

Theo would have had difficulty describing the exact order of what followed. His fogged brain, a preoccupation with his injuries and a sense of disbelief made him a less than perfect witness.

He saw Wilson's head jerk sideways as something struck him on the side of the face with force.

'What the fuck?' Wilson yelled, in a high-pitched voice that Theo hadn't heard before.

What had struck him was a palm on the end of a brawny arm, belonging to none other than Cyrus Porter.

Wilson turned to face the groundsman and laughed, his face puce. 'I see how it is. Come to defend your boyfriend! So it *is* a homo code!'

Mr Porter slapped him again. His knuckle made contact with Wilson's mouth, whose lower lip split like an overripe tomato. Blood trickled over his chin and down his shirtfront.

'Fucking hell!' Wilson yelled and dropped to his knees, dabbing at the blood and rubbing his thumb over the pads of his fingers before bringing them up to his eyes, as if he needed visible proof. He remained kneeling, shocked and subdued by Mr Porter's intervention, stunned by the flow of his blood.

'What is going on here?' Mr Beckett's voice boomed across the quad.

Dinesh and Helmsley froze. Theo staggered backwards and tried to slow his breathing, which was now the only thing he could hear, loud in his ears. He glanced over at Mr Porter. The colour had drained from his face and he looked as pale as the ghosts he lived with.

The clock on the mantelpiece ticked insistently as Theo sat on the other side of the headmaster's desk and waited. Mr Beckett hovered, straight-backed, by the door, as if ready to stop any escapees, and Mr Porter stared out of the window. It occurred to Theo that this was probably a rare opportunity for Mr Porter to see his work from this vantage point: the cut grass, the trimmed borders and the immaculate playing fields.

'Mr Porter, I—'

'Best say nothing,' Mr Porter offered in a neutral tone, his head making a slight incline towards Mr Beckett.

Theo swallowed the words of gratitude and apology he wanted to share with his friend. They would keep.

Once the adrenalin had calmed, his face, and in particular his eye, began to throb. He looked down at the red stain on his right hand and flexed his fingers. He wasn't sure if the dried blood crusting the underside of his hand was his own or Wilson's.

The headmaster entered the room in a hurry. His robe billowed behind him and Mr Beckett followed in his wake like an impatient page. The head coughed and sat down hard in his leather chair. He let out a deep sigh, as if the whole thing was an inconvenience, before resting his elbows on the inlaid desktop and touching his fingertips in front of him to form a pyramid.

'I must say that I am at a loss, Montgomery.'

There was another pause. The sound of the clock was now quite deafening.

Mr Porter coughed, as if clearing his throat to speak.

'I will address you presently,' the headmaster snapped in his direction.

For Theo, despite everything he'd already gone through, this was the worst part of his day, hearing his friend Mr Porter spoken to with such disdain. He glanced at Mr Porter, who seemed to shrink. Theo felt like weeping at the reddening of the man's complexion. For him to be so humiliated when he'd only been trying to help, trying to stop Theo from getting a further beating. Mr Porter had defended him just as he'd defended his country. That was the sort of man he was.

The headmaster sighed again, his irritation apparent. Mr Beckett stood like a sentinel to his right, looking furious. Theo faced the two men and wished they would hurry up and get this over with. He wanted to be free to leave and to talk to Mr Porter out of earshot.

'I don't need to remind you that your father and your father's father both made head of house. They are Vaizey men, like myself. In fact your Uncle Maxim and I played in the 1st XV together. This fact alone is going to earn you a second chance.'

'Thank you, sir.' Theo barely hid the disappointment in his voice. He'd been half hoping for expulsion and permanent liberation.

'Not that I shall be easy on you, and nor indeed will Mr Beckett. It is obvious that you need a firm hand.' Theo looked up at them. It was laughable, the implication that until now they'd been soft on him. 'I don't need to tell you that yours is not Vaizey behaviour. Where did you think you were? A public house? The docks?'

'I don't know, sir.' He kept his eyes fixed ahead. 'It wasn't my fault.'

The headmaster exhaled loudly through his nostrils. 'In my experience, there are certain reasons why a boy might display such violent behaviour, especially when it is out of character, which I believe for you this was.' He sat forward in the chair. 'Mr Wilson, despite his injured state…' He fixed Mr Porter with a steely glare. '… was able to throw a little light on the possible cause of this scuffle.' He raised an eyebrow. 'Is there anything you would like to share with me?'

'No, I don't think so, sir.' Theo shook his head, trying to think what Wilson might have said. 'Just that it wasn't a scuffle.' That implied it had been a mutual thing, an altercation, almost playful, but Wilson's actions had been nothing of the sort. 'I would say that rather than a scuffle it was an attack. I didn't do anything wrong. I had only just arrived back and they called at me from across the quad—'

'Saying what, exactly?' Mr Beckett interjected.

'Erm…' Theo wondered whether to repeat the vile taunts, taunts that Mr Porter had taught him would make you ugly on the inside as well as the outside. 'They called me a sonofabitch. And then a faggot and then poof and homo, that kind of thing.' A blush spread across his cheeks. 'And then he called Mr Porter a homo.'

'I see.' The headmaster nodded and looked down at his hands, as if considering these words.

'And then he punched me. And he carried on punching me,' he levelled. 'I didn't punch him at all.'

'So it was an entirely unprovoked attack?'

'Yes.' Theo nodded with confidence.

'And Wilson attacked the groundsman too?'

Theo looked up at his friend and couldn't decide how best to answer. The words caught in his throat as he recalled their pact, made on a rough wooden bench many years ago. *'Here's the thing: you never have to lie to me, and I will never lie to you, how about that?'*

'Mr Porter is my friend. He... He was only—'

'It's a simple enough question,' the head interjected. 'Did Wilson attack the groundsman?'

'I...'

'Yes or no, Montgomery.' Mr Beckett joined in. 'Did Wilson hit the groundsman?'

Theo looked directly at the men, unable to hold his friend's stare. 'No,' he answered clearly. 'Wilson didn't hit him.'

The two masters exchanged a knowing glance and Mr Beckett breathed in and out through his nostrils.

'But Wilson was hitting me, he hurt me! And Mr Porter hates fighting, he says we've all fought enough, and he was only trying to—'

'Enough!' The headmaster held up his palm. 'You cannot possibly know what Mr Porter was or was not intending to do.' He took another deep breath. 'Mr Beckett, kindly escort Mr Porter to the staffroom. I would like to talk to Montgomery alone.'

Mr Beckett tilted his head in response and walked to the door. He opened it and stood back, waiting for Mr Porter. As he walked past, Theo caught the whiff of earth, petrol and real fires that he had so missed over the summer.

When the door closed behind them the head dropped his

shoulders and gave a small smile that softened his face. 'Now, Theo, is there anything else you might like to tell me about Mr Porter?'

'No.' Theo looked up, wondering what he might be getting at. He knew it was against the rules to loiter around Mr Porter's house during lunchbreak, as it was officially off school premises, but he'd been doing that for years and had never been taken to task over it. He remembered then that Mr Porter had agreed to do his English assignment for him. Had Wilson found it in the dorm? Was that what he was talking about?

'You have no secrets? Nothing that you would prefer to remain between the two of you?'

'No big secrets, only small ones...' Theo swallowed, remembering their agreement. *'They'd have my guts for garters if they knew I'd helped with your homework.'*

'Has Mr Porter ever asked you to keep anything... private?'

He turned to face Theo, who felt a flush of fear that his friend was going to get into trouble. He pictured his pen torch, given all those years ago and still serving him well. 'Nothing important, just something to help me, at night...' He swallowed.

The headmaster stood and walked around the desk slowly, before placing his hand on Theo's shoulder. 'I take the reputation of my school very seriously. Do you understand that, Montgomery?'

Theo nodded. Even though he didn't understand at all.

'Very well, you are free to go.' The head coughed again and sat back behind his desk, where he reached for his telephone.

Theo looked to his left but couldn't see Mr Porter anywhere. He walked to the dorm with the strangest of feelings; it was as if every pair of eyes in the school was on him. It wasn't until he got to his room and looked in the mirror that he saw the mess of his face. There was already a yellowy green bruise forming around his swollen eye socket and the white of his eye was scarlet. Touching the soft tissue, he wondered what Kitty Montrose would make of that.

Despite being the innocent party, Theo was gated, so it wasn't until the weekend that he was allowed to leave the confines of Theobald's House. He made an effort to order his thoughts and calm the anger bubbling inside him. Twitcher gave him a nod of acknowledgement as he walked from the dorm and for the first time Theo wondered if Mr Porter had been right about that Gandhi fellow. Had he been cowardly? Should he have fought back?

His cheekbone was no longer swollen, but the rainbow-coloured bruise left by Wilson's sharp fist had not yet disappeared. He walked purposefully along the length of the field, eager to thank Mr Porter for his intervention, keen to know what had been said and desperate to tell him about all the comings and goings at La Grande Belle. He was also hoping that Mr Porter would do what he did so well and help him make sense of what had happened, explaining Wilson's sudden violent attack and making him feel better about it all.

Jogging up the path, he knocked on the door and with his hands in his pockets called his usual greeting through the letterbox.

'Only me!'

There was no response. Theo ran through Mr Porter's schedule in his head. He should be home. He turned and knocked again, then made his way along the wall to the sitting-room window. Bringing his hand up to his forehead, he leant on the glass and squinted.

A pulse of shock rocketed through him. The room was bare! Gone were the books from the shelves and the cushions from the chairs; the mantelpiece was empty of the knick-knacks that usually sat there gathering dust. It was as if Mr Porter had never been there.

Theo raced back to the front door and barged it with his shoulder until it shifted and opened. He raced from room to room, ending up in the kitchen, where a green enamel kettle had once whistled on the stove and the radio had burbled with the gentle sound of the cricket.

As realisation dawned, Theo felt a physical pain in his chest. The knowledge that Mr Porter had gone was a sharp thing that now lodged itself in his skin. Sinking to his knees, his fists balled against his thighs, he howled a loud guttural cry that came from deep within.

'My friend! What am I supposed to do now?' he screamed as hot tears streamed down his face. 'My friend! I'm sorry! I should have said more. I should have told them to leave you alone! I'm sorry!' He yelled loud enough that the words might travel high and far, to be heard by his friend, who might or might not be sitting on the brow of a hill, letting his eyes sweep the broad fields of the Dorset countryside, where full hedgerows formed the boundaries and deer frolicked on the lower slopes in the pink haze of the evening sun.

Six

With no Mr Porter to turn to, Theo's last four years at Vaizey College passed slowly and miserably. As he was driven out through the school gates for the final time, he swore he would never return. No way was he going to be one of those Old Vaizey Boys like his father who met up every year for reunion socials and came back for sports days and fundraisers. It would have been different if things with Kitty had been rosier. But she was still with Angus Thompson, they were still the school's golden couple, and Theo had found out to his cost that it was far better for his mental health to simply keep out of her way. On his last day at Vaizey he hadn't said goodbye to her or anyone else.

Now, though, he was determined to try and start afresh. He'd got a place at University College London, and he and his parents had just arrived at his hall of residence, not far from the British Museum. They'd helped him carry his suitcase and stereo up to his room and had been there all of five minutes when Theo noticed his father pulling his jacket sleeve up over his watch and surreptitiously checking the time. He felt the familiar flush of unease at the realisation that his parents wanted to be elsewhere. He actually wanted them to stay, though he wasn't sure why.

It wasn't as if they hadn't left him many times before, throughout his school years, but this felt different. University was a big step.

From the corridor outside his room came the sound of two blokes yelling obscenities at each other. Theo cringed and glanced at his parents. It wasn't that the swearing bothered him per se – he'd heard far worse at school, often directed at himself – but watching his parents flash their fake smiles and speak a little louder, making out they hadn't heard, caused his anxiety levels to rise. They behaved the same way on the mornings after their own rows, acting as if nothing had happened. They were so proper most of the time, but when they were drunk they dropped all their airs and graces and swore like troopers, ignoring all the rules of acceptable behaviour that they'd drummed into him his whole life. The nasty, bitter arguments he'd witnessed at La Grande Belle had recurred with depressing frequency during subsequent exeats and holidays, but no one ever mentioned them and it was clear he was expected to carry on as if everything was fine. Theo had hoped that the three of them would get closer as he got older, that he'd be treated more as an equal and would no longer feel so nervous or unwelcome in their company. But it had been many years now since he'd felt comfortable running to his mother for a hug or speaking plainly about his emotions, and here he was at eighteen feeling increasingly ill at ease in their company.

His mother squeezed past the desk in her royal blue Laura Ashley frock and stared down at the street below. 'Good job you've got this double-glazing.' She tapped a slender knuckle on the window. 'Of course it looks absolutely ghastly, but it'll keep out some of the noise.'

'Yes.'

'Quite a nice spot though, really. Handy.' She smiled.

Handy for what, Theo wasn't sure, but he nodded anyway.

His mother looked back at him as if at a loss for what to say. She sighed and clasped her hands in front of her.

'We are going to be *late*, Stella.' His father widened his eyes, as if this were code. 'Besides, Theo probably wants to dive into his books or whatever it is students do all day.'

Theo clenched his jaw. His dad would not let it rest. A year ago, when he'd been filling out the application form at the kitchen table, his father had stopped en route to the fridge. 'I don't know why you're bothering, Theodore,' he'd boomed. 'We'll have you behind a desk in Villiers House in no time, and you don't need a fancy degree to do that, not when it's the Montgomery name above the door.' He'd huffed. 'A Vaizey education has always been perfectly sufficient, as your grandfather and your great-grandfather and myself have all demonstrated.'

Theo's insides had churned. 'Actually, Dad, I have thought about it and I would really like to go to university.'

'Anything to delay a hard day's graft, is that it?'

'No. I just like the idea of getting really good at something, becoming an expert.' He was determined not to work with his dad or for the family business and he knew that the only way to ensure that was to do a degree and then follow his own path.

His dad had stopped rummaging for the bottle of tonic and looked in his direction. 'An expert, eh? Oh good God! Don't tell me your bloody mother has finally managed to bend your ear about the law or, God forbid, medicine! Ghastly profession, full of egos and long shifts. Don't listen to her, she's as thick as mince, doesn't understand the business at all!'

Theo sat up straight. 'It's nothing to do with Mum.' He felt his cheeks colour, hating his inability to stand up for his mum in the face of his dad's relentless jibes. 'It's something I've been thinking about for a while.' He took a deep breath and then blurted it out. 'I want to study social science and social policy.'

His father laughed. 'You want to study *what*?'

'Social policy. It's about looking at social movements and ways to address social problems, help society. A lot of people that study it go on to be policy makers all over the world.' He grew quieter as his confidence ebbed.

His dad pivoted and placed his hands on his waist. His chin jutted sideways, which was a sure sign he was angry. 'Social problems, eh?' He gave a cold, hollow laugh. 'And tell me, Theo, what social problems have you ever encountered?'

'I... I...'

'I can hear it now.' His father guffawed and adopted a falsetto voice that made Theo's stomach bunch. 'I want to change the world! Even though I have only ever known the bloody best education, an education offered to the top ten per cent!' He shook his head in disgust. 'They'll laugh you out of town, boy!'

Theo's mind was racing. It was precisely because he'd seen the ten per cent in action that he wanted to do something that might help the other ninety per cent, but he kept this to himself.

His father returned his attention to the fridge. 'Just remember who pays for your education, boy. Social policy, over my dead body! I want to hear no more about it.' He grabbed the bottle of tonic, slammed the door and whistled as he made his way back to the drawing room.

This encounter had been followed by a tense week during which his parents weren't speaking to each other and neither appeared to be speaking to him. The impasse had ended when his mother had called to him casually from her bedroom. He stood at the door, inhaling the cigarette smoke that encircled her in a pungent cloud, her aqua silk housecoat spread around her on the bed like a pond. She narrowed her eyes at him and placed the novel she was reading face down on the bed. 'I've had a word with your father, darling. You can go to university if you want, but you'll have to study engineering, not social work or whatever it is you were on about. That's Daddy's condition, otherwise he won't pay. He says at least engineering might be of some use to the company.'

Engineering! Theo's heart sank. But it was better than nothing. And what mattered more than anything was that his mum had stuck up for him. That meant a lot. 'Thank you, Mum.' He smiled as he backed out of the room.

The blokes outside his uni bedroom had finally moved elsewhere and there was a sudden hush. His father coughed and rocked on his heels. 'As I said, we really can't be late, Stella. And Theo doesn't want us to hang around, do you?'

'No. I'm fine. I... I don't want to make you late.'

'If you're absolutely sure, darling?' His mother quickly acquiesced, just as she always did. 'I feel like we should stay and help you unpack your clothes or put up a poster or something?' She waved her hand limply towards the ceiling.

'I don't have that many clothes and I'm good for posters, thanks.' He scanned the blank white walls of his tiny room.

'Well, look...' His mother grabbed her cream pashmina from the back of the chair by the desk, gave a nod to her husband and smiled thinly. 'You have our number of course and it's not like we are far away!' She laughed. 'Call if you need anything, anything at all.'

He nodded. If anyone were to listen in on the conversations he had with his parents, they'd probably be touched at how loving his mum and dad sounded. What they wouldn't pick up on, though, were the stolen glances, the sighs, the hurried tone and the awkward pauses. It was these that spoke loudest to Theo.

After shaking his father's hand and accepting his mother's fleeting kiss on his cheek, he waved them goodbye and flopped down onto his bed. He noted how confined his room was and how bland. Actually, though, he didn't mind that. He was almost looking forward to being on his own in the middle of London, an invisible figure among the crowds, one of many, with no one to single him out as a loner, a weirdo. Almost subconsciously, he reached inside the neck of his sweatshirt and ran his finger over the fishing fly, pinned there.

Shivering, he felt suddenly cold and rolled himself into a sausage within the coverless duvet. Finally his time was his own: no bell was going to call him to study, to go to lessons or to have supper. He lay on the bare mattress and fell sleep.

A couple of hours later he was woken by a knock on his door. Startled, he took a sharp breath and quickly disentangled his feet from the duvet. He opened the door to find a tall, skinny, dark-haired boy with a bulky rucksack over his right shoulder and a toothy grin on his face.

The boy beamed at him. 'I'm your next-door neighbour,' he said, as if this were grounds for some special connection.

Theo thought of the countless boys he'd roomed next to at Vaizey – none had ever smiled at him like this. He looked at him nervously, wondering what he wanted, then dropped his gaze, waiting for the inevitable snide comment. None came. 'Right. I'm Theo,' he eventually offered.

'Did you say Cleo?' The boy took a step forward and squinted earnestly at Theo's face.

'Cleo?' Theo sprayed his laughter. 'Do I look like a Cleo?'

'No!' The boy laughed. 'I just thought that was what you said. I'm from Wigan!'

'What's that got to do with anything?'

'I don't know, man, I'm just freaking out!' He ran his fingers through his wiry hair. 'I'm in London and this is scary shit!'

Theo laughed. 'Well, I've lived not far from here my whole life, when I wasn't away at school, and I can assure you you have nothing to be scared of.'

'Thanks, Cleo.' The boy smiled, showing his large teeth. 'I'm Spud, by the way.'

'And I'm *Theo*.' They exchanged another smile. 'Is Spud your Christian name?'

'Kind of. My surname is Edwards and it started as King Edwards when I got to secondary school and within a year it was Potato Boy, and then Spud, and that stuck – even my parents call me it!' He chuckled. 'My school friends call my mum and dad Ma and Pa Spud – it's become a bit of a joke.'

'Spud it is then.' Theo hovered in the doorway, wishing he had a similarly witty anecdote about Ma and Pa Montgomery. He was badly rehearsed in what to do next, how to chat, though he did know that neither the weather nor sport were the answer. 'Anyway, I better unpack or something.' He pointed to the suitcase on the desk.

'Do you want to go the student union and get a beer later?' Spud asked, almost casually but with a flicker to his eyelid that suggested nerves. 'I mean, only if you haven't already got anything else planned. I'm not being pushy and I'm not trying to get invited, I just thought...' He ran out of steam, clearly flustered.

Theo nodded. 'Sure. A beer would be good.' He tried to sound cool, hoping to hide the explosion of nerves and excitement.

And just like that, Theodore Montgomery made a friend. A proper friend of his own age.

Holding their warm pints, served in plastic glasses, and with Van Halen's 'Jump' playing on the jukebox, the two took seats at the edge of the union bar. The furniture was dark, cheap and tatty and the walls, painted a deep red were covered with posters.

'So what are you studying?'

'Engineering. You?'

'Economics,' Spud answered with pride. 'Have you got brothers and sisters?'

'No, just me.' In the four years since that horrible night when he'd made the shocking discovery about his half-brother, Alexander, not a word had been said about him, and Theo hadn't told a soul. It wasn't that he dwelt on it, exactly, but it came into his mind sometimes. He felt nauseous at the thought of his dad cheating and lying to his mum. 'What about you?'

'Two sisters. One older, married with three kids, and one younger, still at school.'

Theo couldn't imagine having that many people in his life.

'We're just hoping my older one stops having sprogs and my younger one doesn't start too soon. Already at Christmas my nan has to sit at the table on the laundry basket with a cushion on top, and last year my cousin ate his lunch standing up!' He laughed. 'My mum says at this rate she'll be doing two sittings.'

Theo stared at him, trying and failing to picture the world he described.

'Have you got a girlfriend?' Spud kept the questions coming.

'No!' Theo laughed, despite himself. He tried to ignore the pull of longing in his gut as his thoughts turned to Kitty. 'You?'

'Nah.' Spud sighed. 'I saw a couple of girls at school, but nowt serious.'

'I liked a girl at school, but she had a boyfriend, so...' Theo shrugged.

'Well, you need to find a girl here and erase the memory of her!' Spud laughed. 'What's her name?'

'Kitty.' He swallowed. Even saying her name out loud felt like a big deal.

Spud raised his pint. 'To erasing Kitty!'

They clinked their plastic glasses.

'So you're from London?' Spud put his pint on the table and rubbed his hands together, whether with excitement or nerves it was hard to tell.

'Yes, but I went to school in Dorset.'

'Boarding school?'

'Yes.' Theo smiled. 'It would have been one hell of a commute if I was a day boy.'

Spud laughed loudly and Theo joined in. *That was funny. I can do funny!*

'I've never met anyone that went to boarding school.'

'You have now.' Theo sipped the pint. It was horribly bitter, left a nasty aftertaste and made him feel gassy. It would take some getting used to.

'God, living without your parents and being with your mates, it sounds mint. Was it like a party every night? Girls having pillow fights, midnight snacks, smoking out of the window?' Spud sat forward eagerly.

Theo gave a dry laugh. 'Not for me. I hated it, I really did.'

'Why?'

Theo considered his response, knowing how people feared the contagion of weird. 'I didn't like a lot of the people there. Some of them were right bastards.' He liked how easily he could talk to Spud. His new friend's kindly nature and their liberal consumption of booze made it possible.

Spud nodded. 'I suppose there are always going to be bastards. The trick is to avoid the wankers.'

'Yep.' He nodded. 'So what's Wigan like?'

Spud shrugged. 'Like anywhere else, I s'pose. I've never lived anywhere else, mind you. I mean, not like London! Nothing's like this place!' He giggled. 'We've got a good football team, a canal, shit shops, great pubs and even better clubs if you know where to look. People are friendly and that's about it. It's struggled since we've started losing the mines.'

'I'd hate to go down a mine. Can't imagine it – dark and cold.' He shivered.

Spud eyed him over the rim of his second pint. 'I guess most people would hate to go down into the cold and dark, but when that's the thing that's going to put bread on the table, you'd be surprised what folk'll do. My dad's a miner – like my grandad before him.'

Theo felt his face colour. He hadn't meant to be rude.

'I've never met anyone like you, Theodore.' Spud smiled. 'Have you ever been abroad?'

'Yes.'

'Have you ever been on a plane?'

'Yes!'

'Have you ever bought a single fag from an ice-cream van?'

'No!' It was Theo's turn to laugh.

'Have your mum and dad got a car?'

'Yes.'

'What kind?'

'My dad has a vintage Aston Martin.'

Spud nearly choked on his pint. He laughed and slapped the table. 'You, Theo, are the poshest person I have ever met.'

'I don't know if that's a compliment!' Theo pulled a face.

'It is what it is, my friend. It is what it is.' Spud shook his head and prepared to return to the bar for their refills.

That beer was to be the first of countless pints Theo and Spud drank together over the coming months, in pubs, bars and clubs across London. By the end of their second term, Theo had more than got used to the taste. Tonight he and Spud had gone out together as usual, and, as sometimes happened, they'd become separated a little after midnight.

Theo grabbed the hand of the girl he'd been talking to for the last half-hour and started running. 'Come on!'

'I can't keep up!' She giggled. 'I'm wearing heels!'

'Then take them off!' he yelled through his laughter.

The girl did just that, hopping, mid run, from one foot to the other and gathering her shoes into her hand. She gripped them like a pointy bowling ball and with Theo pulling her along she zigzagged down the pavement in just her tights, her fur bomber jacket and her blue suede mini skirt.

'Why are we running?' she asked between more giggles.

'Because I'm pissed and it seemed like a good idea!'

As they rounded the top of Inverness Street and turned right into Camden High Street he slowed and bent double, laughing loudly while he tried to catch his breath.

'You are fucking insane!' She laughed loudly too, then stood on tiptoes, reached up and kissed him full on the mouth. Her hand snaked under his shirt to find his solid chest. 'Did we really just run away from my mates?'

He looked back up the street. 'It would appear so.'

'Why did we do that?' She laughed.

'Because I wanted to get you on your own.' He grinned.

'You nutcase.' She kissed him again. 'So where now?' she whispered suggestively.

'My room?'

'Sounds like a plan.' She giggled some more and gave him a coy look from beneath her heavily mascaraed lashes.

The two walked with their arms across each other's shoulders, picking their way through litter, knotted black bin bags left underneath trees, prostrate clubbers and some market traders unloading their transit vans ready for their Sunday morning stalls. It was a typical Saturday night, or had been. Theo loved this time, just before dawn broke, the transition point between a good night coming to an end and a good day just beginning. They wobbled away into the dawn, stopping to snog where and when the fancy took them.

Theo put the key into the door of his building and turned to the girl. 'Ah, I should probably mention that it's my student room and I am not strictly allowed guests, plus my half-wit mate, who might or not have made it home before me, *might* be crashed out on my bed.'

'You share a room?' she asked, clearly unimpressed.

'No, we don't share a room, but he tends to fall wherever

is closest when he's pissed. He's not... how should I say it... boundary conscious.'

'Right.' She looked at him quizzically.

Theo paused and turned back to her. 'What's your name, by the way?'

'Mitzi!' She tittered.

'And I'm Rollo.'

'Rollo!' She laughed again. Theo prayed that she was really high and not just really stupid.

His room was a mess, although this was standard. It was no longer the kind of mess that could be fixed with a quick whizz round with a duster and a vacuum cleaner – it was way past that. The room was grubby and disorganised. A poster for the movie *Halloween* hung down from the sloping ceiling, its corner displaying a strip of yellowing Sellotape. Books and takeaway containers littered every surface and his bedside table was covered with the detritus of discarded joints, Rizla packets with the corners torn off to make roaches, thin strands of tobacco and an overflowing ashtray. An abandoned cereal bowl sat on the windowsill with a ring of sour milk clinging to the insides and soggy cornflakes stuck to the rim. Empty Sol bottles with shrivelled wedges of lime were lined up like skittles on the floor around the skirting board, and the air was stale with the tang of cigarette smoke and old food.

Theo took in the expression of disgust on Mitzi's face. 'It's the maid's day off.'

'Day off?' Mitzi curled her top lip. 'I think she wants firing.'

As Theo looked at her, at the dark rings of kohl around her eyes and her vacant stare, an image of Kitty popped into his head. Beautiful, clean, sparkling Kitty. There was a moment of awkward contemplation, in which he lost enthusiasm for her company.

'Do you know what, Mitzi?' He spoke calmly, rubbing at his stubble. 'I think we should call it a night. You shouldn't want to be here in this grubby room, with someone who's dragged you from your mates. You deserve better.'

'Are you kidding me?' She glared at him. 'You march me back to this shithole and now you're *dumping* me?'

'I'm not dumping you. I don't know you! And look, please let me pay for your cab, to wherever.' He reached into his back pocket and removed his wallet, peeling off a ten-pound note.

'What the fuck? You think you can pay me off?' she shouted as she slipped her red-heeled shoes back onto her now grimy stockinged feet.

'No! I'm just trying to be gentlemanly.'

'Gentlemanly? You are weird as shit is what you are!'

'So I've been told.' He blinked, sobering a little now and wanting nothing more than for her to leave so he could go to sleep. His messy bed had never looked more inviting.

'Morning. I think.' Spud walked past Theo's open door in a striped towelling dressing gown that was open, revealing his green underpants. 'Just off to the loo.' He scratched his hairy chest and yawned. 'God, don't remember much about the night. I think I lost you after Dingwalls. Are you coming in or going out, Theo?'

'Theo?' Mitzi screeched. 'You told me your name was Rollo!' This subterfuge was apparently the final straw for Mitzi, who snatched the ten-pound note from his hand and stomped off in her red heels. She turned at the end of the corridor to flip him the bird. 'Dickhead!' she yelled, loud enough to wake anyone who might have been sleeping off the night before.

'My bad,' Theo mumbled as he sank down onto his bed and closed his eyes.

'She seemed nice,' Spud called from the doorway. 'Your parents are going to love her! Are you thinking a spring wedding?'

Theo laughed despite his tiredness and turned on to his side. He needed sleep.

With Def Leppard's 'Animal' blaring out of the stereo in his room, Theo lay in the slightly rusted bath down the corridor. It was as good a remedy as any for his post-Mitzi hangover. The cold tap dripped constantly, leaving a mottled brown residue on the old enamel, but he had perfected a manoeuvre whereby he could turn on the hot tap with his toes, allowing him to languish in the bath for hours.

Spud banged on the bathroom door, pulling him from his day-dreams. 'How much longer are you going to be in there?' he yelled. 'I need a shit!'

Theo laughed. 'Getting out now!'

'Cool. Wanna come out and get pissed? Hair of the dog?'

Theo laughed at his mate's favourite and only suggestion when it came to socialising. 'Oh really, and forgo our usual seats at the opera? If you insist! Let's go via the takeaway first.'

An hour later they were both sitting on the low wall outside their nearest kebab shop. Theo bit into the kebab and simul-taneously took a swig from his can of pop.

'So who was that girl night last night? Thought you were going to see the French one you met?'

Theo shook his head, 'No, lost her number, kind of on pur-pose.' He pulled a face.

'I can't keep up.' Spud laughed and dug a small plastic fork into his polystyrene punnet loaded with heavily salted chips. 'Seems you are doing quite well in your quest to erase Kitty.'

'I was,' Theo paused, 'and then last night, I looked at Mitzi and thought about Kitty and I just wanted to be on my own.'

'A mere setback my friend.' Spud chuckled.

'I hope so, my social life is all I have to look forward to, bloody engineering!' he bit his kebab.

'I like my lectures!'

'It's all right for you, you love your subject. I hate mine!'

'So switch! You've only done two terms. Ben on the floor below us swapped from medicine to biology, it was easy and now he's happy. I mean, you'd probably have to work hard to catch up, but you work hard anyway. It's the answer. Life is too short, Theo old son, do what makes you happy!'

'I wish it was that straightforward,' Theo said with his mouth full, 'but my dad would go crazy.' It was a miracle he was at university at all and not chained to a desk in Villiers House.

Spud made as if he was answering a phone. 'Oh hello, yes. Right, I'll tell him.' He theatrically mimed replacing the receiver. 'That was the Universe on the phone. It said, "Tell your mate that this is his life, not his dad's, and he needs to do what makes him happy!"'

'You make it sound easy.' Theo took another bite, he was famished.

'I think it's as easy or as hard as you want it to be.'

'For you maybe. What would your dad say if you changed course?' He licked his greasy fingers.

Spud held his gaze. 'My dad doesn't care what I study, he just wants me to be happy and he is beyond chuffed that his son has got a place at university. It's a big deal for us. I'm the first ever on either side of the family to go and not just to any university – UCL, in that London!' He was making fun of himself, but Theo knew his humour masked a very real truth and he envied Spud that.

Seven

Spud had been right, as he often was. Switching degrees had been a doddle and Theo had thrown himself into his new course, attending lectures with pleasure and writing essays with gusto. The hardest part had been trying to tell his parents, but after one attempt he made a decision and kept his course change to himself. They hadn't exactly taken an interest in his engineering degree anyway, so why should this be any different? It was now the autumn term of his final year and he had already started looking at the jobs pages, keen to get on with his chosen career as soon as he graduated. He was particularly interested in housing policy, which was one of his specialisms.

It was rare that he slept through his alarm, but today had been an exception. He cursed the fact. It was vital that he get in on time for this morning's tutorial. His tutor had made it quite clear from the beginning: 'A degree from UCL cannot be coasted. A degree from UCL requires investment from you in the form of hard work and commitment and if the concept of industry and reward is something you do not understand, then might I suggest that a degree course here is not for you.' His dissertation was looming and today was the day set aside for discussing it with his tutor. It was important to Theo that he be the best he could, and regardless of whether he eventually managed to get his hoped-for 2:1, a good reference from his tutor would be enormously helpful.

'God, I hate being late!' Theo muttered under his breath as he raced from the flat in Belsize Park he shared with Spud and ran down the street. Jumping back onto the kerb, he tucked his shirt into the waistband of his jeans and looked the length of the road and back again, his eyes searching for a cab. 'Come on, come on!' he pleaded. He glanced at his watch. 'Shit!'

He started to half walk, half run in the direction of the UCL campus, watching eagerly for a cab as he went. Finally one swung into view. He jumped up and down, calling out 'Taxi!' with his arm straight up in the air. The cabbie flashed his lights and pulled over. Theo scrambled in, sat back and took a deep breath. He wished he'd had time to shower properly instead of doing only a quick spritz with a can of deodorant.

As the cab trundled along Eversholt Street and idled at the lights, Theo stared distractedly out of the window, mentally rehearsing the excuses he might offer to explain his tardiness to his tutor. And suddenly, there on the pavement, waiting to cross over, dressed in high-waisted baggy jeans, a cropped baby-pink sweatshirt and with a purple file in her arms, stood none other than Kitty Montrose.

'Stop the cab!' He leant forward and banged on the dividing screen.

The cabbie tutted and pulled over.

Theo thrust a note at him. 'Sorry! Keep the change!' he managed as he jumped out, desperate not to lose sight of her.

His heart thumped as he drew closer. He hoped he wasn't

mistaken. Many had been the time during the two and a half years since leaving Vaizey that his spirits had lifted at the sight of a red-headed girl, only to be disappointed when he got near enough to see that she was a poor imitation of the real thing.

He sidled along the pavement and watched her peer into the newsagent's window. He looked to his left and felt a spike of joy through his gut. It was her! No doubt about it. His jaw tensed and his mouth went dry. He tried to calm his thoughts, didn't want her to know he'd followed her – it *had* to look casual, a coincidence.

He willed her to go into the coffee shop, giving him a legitimate excuse to follow and bump into her in the queue.

'Hey, Kitty,' he practised in his head, 'fancy seeing you here!' He experimented with the face he would pull, sucked in his stomach and wondered how he should stand, how best to show off his height and broad shoulders.

'Oh my God! Theo? Theo!'

Her yell drew him from his thoughts. He looked and did a double-take for real, no time for rehearsals, as there she was not three feet away and she was smiling at him. He needn't have worried about feigning surprise; his shock at interacting with the girl who haunted his dreams was genuine.

'Oh my God! Kitty!' He beamed. 'No way!'

She rushed forward, dropping her bag and file on the pavement, and threw her arms around his neck. For a glorious second he knew what it must have felt like to be Angus Thompson, with Kitty's body pressed against his and her floral scent enveloping him like a gossamer cloth.

It felt bloody brilliant.

'What are you doing here?' she asked as she pulled away.

He slid his hands from her waist, where his fingers briefly made contact with her silky skin, and tried to hide the tremble to his limbs. 'Just on my way to uni. Exams are coming up, so I'm looking for a few pointers on my dissertation,' he said, with none of the urgency he should have felt.

'Oh God, it's *so* great to see you! Look at you!' She bobbed her knees, and he understood, because he too felt like dancing. 'Do you want to grab a coffee? Have you got time? I don't want to keep you.' She pointed over her shoulder with her thumb, to the coffee shop along the street. It had tables outside and a chalkboard detailing the cakes on offer and the soup of the day.

'Now?' His mind raced, weighing up the consequences of missing his tutorial against the chances of seeing her again, alone like this.

'Yes, now!' She laughed.

'Yep, of course, great!'

He fell into step beside her and it was a strange thing. He was twenty, working hard for his degree, living with Spud and, emboldened by booze, had spent time with a fair few girls, yet at that precise moment, walking along the street with Kitty by his side, he felt like he was fourteen again and just as clumsy. Even his natural walking pace lost its rhythm and he feared he might stumble if he didn't concentrate. He dismissed the several topics of conversation that flared in his mind, wanting to say the right thing, wanting to sound cool and yet interesting. His thoughts raged.

'I'm at college, not far from here.' She nodded into the distance. Her soft Scottish lilt hadn't disappeared and this made him happy. It would have been difficult to supplant the voice he heard in his daydreams.

'And you're studying journalism, right?' He tried to make it sound like he didn't know exactly what she was studying, as if he might have forgotten her plans laid out excitedly during one English lesson.

'Yep.' She nodded. 'Don't know if that's what I'll do finally, finally, but I'm enjoying it, so…'

'You're a long way from the Highlands,' he said, stating the obvious.

'I know.' She looked down. 'And I miss it so much. There are days when I have to stop myself throwing everything I own into a suitcase, jumping on a train, climbing into my walking boots and racing up a mountain to gulp down lungfuls of that beautiful clean air!' She closed her eyes briefly and he glimpsed the freckles that dotted her lids, just as he had remembered.

'Racing up a mountain or going for a swim.' He smiled.

'Oh, Theo, you remembered! Yes, I still love to swim.'

I remember everything: each word, each touch, each burst of laughter.

He studied her pale complexion and that tiny nose, half listening to her chatter about her course and her flatmates but at the same time taking in every detail of her, which he knew he would replay in the early hours whenever sleep evaded him. He watched her gather her cappuccino from the counter into her dainty hand and make her way past the tables to a vacant booth along the laminate-clad wall. He paid for the two of them, then followed with his can of 7up, remembering suddenly Mr Porter's words about girls who always assumed the man would pay: '*If she's the kind of girl that is* impressed *by gifts and expensive treats, the kind of girl who won't pay her own way, then I would say she isn't the girl you want…*' He swallowed the familiar mixture of guilt and sadness that hit him whenever he remembered Mr Porter and automatically felt inside his jeans pocket for the fishing-fly pin he carried whatever he was wearing.

'It is good to see you, Theo.' She studied his face and he felt himself blushing under her scrutiny. 'You look…'

'I look what?' He was curious and self-conscious in equal measure. He watched the words form on her lips.

'You look lovely.'

'Lovely? I'd prefer something a bit more rugged,' he quipped, tensing his arms into a he-man pose before sipping from the can. He was delighted nonetheless.

'Nope.' She shook her head. 'It doesn't work like that. You don't get to choose the words in my head and that's it: you look lovely to me.'

There was a second or two of silence while he let her words settle on him like glitter. They held each other's gaze without embarrassment, as if their shared history allowed for this intimacy.

'I've often thought I might bump into you, and I've kept a lookout for you, but you never go to any of the reunion events at Vaizey, do you?' Her words robbed him of the chance to respond to her compliment.

'No. I have absolutely no desire to go back.' He sat up tall in the seat, subconsciously showing her that he was now grown-up, different.

'But you should. They're good fun and it's nice to catch up with people.'

Theo struggled with how to respond, saddened and inexplicably angry that she felt affection for the place he'd detested, and wary of sharing his true feelings about their school. He didn't want the glitter to lose its shine. 'Only hell or high water would drag me back there,' he offered finally and firmly, hoping this was enough.

'I always liked sitting next to you,' she continued, seemingly oblivious to the depth of his feelings about Vaizey. 'I liked it very much. I remember how whenever Mr Reeves said something risqué or stupid we'd look at each other – that little glance that meant we both got it!' She threw her head back and laughed her beautiful laugh.

'He was so dull.'

'He was *so* dull!' She laughed again and he joined in. It felt good to share this. '"Page forty-three of the nominated accompanying text on *Othello*, please, ladies and gentlemen!"' She mimicked their English teacher's monotone warble perfectly.

'Oh my God, don't! That's too scary!'

'Shall we get some cake? I'm starving.'

'Sure.' He stood up.

'Just one bit, we can share.' She spoke matter-of-factly and he felt his heart might burst through his ribs.

The two sat in the booth with a slab of Victoria sandwich between them and two forks, jousting for the best bits of the disappointingly dry sponge. Theo didn't care that he'd missed his tutorial. He didn't care about much. He just wished he could bottle the hour and a half they sat there together, isolated from the real world, so he could carry it around in his pocket for the rest of his life. It was one of those rare, rare moments when there was nowhere else in the world that he would rather be.

'So, Theodore,' she asked sternly, 'have you learnt any of Mr

Kipling's poetry yet?' She dipped her chin and looked at him through her strawberry-blonde lashes.

Theo carefully laid his fork on the tabletop and took a swig of his lemonade to wash away the cake crumbs. He stared up into her green eyes and began.

'This is from "The Gipsy Trail".' He coughed. 'By Rudyard Kipling.

> *"The wild hawk to the wind-swept sky,*
> *The deer to the wholesome wold,*
> *And the heart of a man to the heart of a maid,*
> *As it was in the days of old.*
>
> *"The heart of a man to the heart of a maid—*
> *Light of my tents, be fleet.*
> *Morning waits at the end of the world,*
> *And the world is all at our feet!"'*

He had never imagined he might say the words out loud to her. He'd memorised the poem purely to plug the gaping hole in his knowledge, exposed that first day he'd met Kitty, and because the words seemed so apt.

Kitty's eyes glazed over with emotion, and so did his. They stared at each other in silence, and like the white spaces that allow an image to stand boldly on the page it was the silence that spoke loudest to him. It was a moment to be cherished. A moment in which to do something – when would he ever get another chance?

Her eyes were searching for something and her mouth moved, as if she was ordering the thoughts that hovered on her tongue.

She looked down into her lap and her voice when it came was hushed.

'That's beautiful.'

'You are beautiful. The *most* beautiful. I have always thought so. Always.' He offered this, not knowing where the courage to speak his mind had come from; it was as if the words tumbled out of their own accord.

He watched aghast as her tears fell. He focused on a solitary tear that slipped like glass over her cheek, magnifying the freckles as it travelled. He so wanted to wipe it away with the tip of his finger.

'Please don't cry! I'm sorry if I made you sad.'

'I'm not crying because of you, I'm crying because I have so much going on that sometimes I can't think straight.' Kitty sniffed and looked up at him.

Emboldened, he placed his hand over hers. 'Oh, Kitty, I'm sorry to hear that. Do you want to go and get something to drink that isn't coffee?'

Kitty nodded and managed a smile. 'I really would like to go and get something to drink that isn't coffee.'

The pub was quiet, not that this put a dampener on their day. Their boozing was frenzied: whisky shots followed pints of beer, and by early afternoon they were more than tipsy. Theo was fearless whenever he wore his booze cloak. Reaching for her hand, he pulled her to him and kissed her firmly on the mouth. He might have been part sloshed, but that kiss was as good as any he'd dreamt about. They parted and stood inches from each other, as if no words were needed. Theo reached for his bag and coat and watched as Kitty downed the last of her drink and picked up her file. Hand in hand, with Theo leading the way, they part ran, part walked to his flat in Belsize Park. They kissed on the stairs and again in the hallway and by the time he opened his front door, Kitty was pulling at his shirt, yanking it free from the waistband of his jeans.

'If you knew the minutes, hours, days, weeks I have dreamt of this moment, Miss Montrose.' He kissed her hungrily, guiding her to the bedroom.

'You are my knight in shining armour, remember?' Kitty slurred, hooking her hands around the back of his neck.

Theo felt the swell of joy in his gut. This was happening! Kitty was in his arms, in his bedroom and she was taking off his clothes...

Propped up on his elbow, he watched Kitty sleep. He was sobering up now and totally in awe of the beautiful girl lying on the pillow next to him. His face ached from smiling. He lay down next to her, suffused with an unfamiliar serenity. In his head, he made plans. *When you wake up I'll take you for supper, and one day we'll go to the Highlands together. I'll watch you swim and then I'll wrap you in a warm towel...*

Her eyes fluttered open and she smiled, stretching her naked arm over her head with abandon. 'Oh God, Theo!' She placed her hand over her eyes, as if the lamplight offended. 'What time is it?'

He glanced at the alarm clock on the bedside table. 'Nearly seven.'

'In the evening?' She sat up straight.

'Yes, in the evening!' He laughed.

'Shit! Oh Shit!' Kitty flung back the duvet and, unabashed by her nakedness, felt around on the floor for her hastily discarded clothing.

'It's not that late – I thought we might get some supper?' He moved the pillow beneath his head to get comfy.

'Supper?' She stopped ferreting on the floor and glanced at him. She looked stricken, and though her expression was hard to read, it was clear that supper was out of the question. She was squinting now, her brow furrowed in confusion and her top lip hooked with what might have been disgust.

Theo swallowed as a gut-churning quake of nerves and inadequacy burbled inside him.

'Theo...'

She faced him now, and he knew that whatever was coming next, he didn't want to hear it. His confidence collapsed and all of a sudden he was sitting in a puddle of regret and shame.

Kitty blinked rapidly and looked mournfully into her lap, her knickers in her hand.

Theo saw her eyes jump to her bra, jeans and top, locating them on the floor in case she needed a quick exit.

'I'm getting married.'

Her words cleaved open the quiet tenderness between them, peeling the beauty from the day, leaving him raw and feeling horribly foolish. He was that same fourteen-year-old boy all over again, his hopes newly dashed, just as they had been back in the classroom that first day.

What had you honestly expected, Theo, you weirdo? She's probably never given you a second thought, not really.

'You're...?'

'I'm getting married,' she repeated, a little louder this time.

'To Angus?'

'Yes, of course to Angus!' she snapped. She sighed. 'Sorry, but who else?' She stepped into her pants and bent down to retrieve her bra.

Rather than savour the sight of Kitty naked in his room, Theo looked away, almost wishing he could go back to longing for the sight of her nude because when he'd longed for her, wished for this chance, there'd still been hope.

'Who else indeed.' He ran his palm over his stubbly chin.

'I feel…' she began. 'I feel a little… uncertain,' she mumbled as she fastened her bra.

'Well, I guess that's something for you to discuss with your… fiancé.' The word was sour on his tongue. He sat up against the wall and watched her dress, torn between wanting her to go quickly and desperately wanting her to stay.

'I have to go. I'm late.' She shook her head, flustered, angry. Finally, she slipped into her trainers and made for the door.

She looked back over her shoulder. 'Goodbye, Theo.' She bit her lip and her expression softened into that of the girl he used to know. 'Today was lovely.'

'Lovely?' He wrinkled his nose at this inadequate description.

'Well, it was for me.'

And just like that, she was gone.

* * *

It was rare for Theo to cry in this way. If he ever had. Each gulped breath seemed to provide fuel for the next bout of tears. A salty mass sat in his throat, behind his eyes and at the back of his nose. He was utterly consumed by sadness. He wiped his face on his sleeve, then used his palms to mop up what he could, until there was no point and he just let his tears run off his chin and his snot snake down his face. Now that he'd started, he couldn't stop. Between sobs he let out occasional throaty growls, almost animal-like. A pain hovered in his chest, like indigestion. His heart hurt and his head ached.

Pushing his arms into a cradle on the tabletop, he laid his head on his forearms and found some relief in closing his stinging eyes in the darkness, crying quietly now. He didn't hear the key in the door.

'Mate!' Spud rushed forward, dropped his bag and without hesitation wrapped his friend in his arms. 'It's okay. Don't cry. What's happened?'

Theo allowed himself to be embraced, taking comfort from the unfamiliar warmth of another human so close. He opened his mouth to speak, but his breath stuttered in his throat and a new wave of hot tears formed. Instead, he pushed the letter across the table and watched as Spud held it close to his face, devouring every word.

Spud pulled out the chair opposite and the two looked at each other, both now at a loss for words. Spud reread the note and only then broke the silence.

'Jesus Christ.'

Theo nodded. *Yes, Jesus Christ.*

'When did this arrive?'

'Probably this morning. I just got it from the table in the hallway.' It was the communal dumping spot for all five flats in the building, a dusty place where mail, flyers and such forth gathered.

'Have you called her?' Spud asked.

Theo shook his head. 'I don't have her number, I don't know where she lives, plus I will do as she asks.'

Spud sighed. 'Oh, mate.' He picked up the letter and read it a third time, its neat script written in blue ink on white paper.

Theo didn't need to read it again. Each word was indelibly etched on his mind.

Hello, Theo,

I hope you're still at this flat. I have thought long and hard about whether to write and what to write, so here goes.

It was an unexpectedly joyful day when I last saw you. It was a day of escape and I want you to know that I have never done anything similar before or since. I hope you believe me when I tell you that it was special for me. I know how that reads and we both know that alcohol was the catalyst, but there are very few people on earth I trust in the way I trust you, Theo.

Theo, oh, Theo…

I'm pregnant.

I can only imagine what it's like for you to read these words. Perhaps it feels the same as it did for me, when I found out.

I thought you deserved to know. It is yours. I want to keep this baby and I'm still figuring out how to make it all work. The one thing I do know is that this is not the path for us, for you and I. We are not those people. I'm marrying Angus soon, in a few weeks, and he is aware. It's been horrendously difficult for us both. For this reason, I think it only fair that we have no further contact. If our paths should ever cross, please respect my wish for us to never mention this. I beg you, Theo. This is the only way I can build a life. Please.

I say goodbye now.

Your friend,

Kitty X

'A baby.' Theo shook his head.

'And she's told her bloke?' Spud asked softly.

'It would appear so.' Theo took a deep breath and forced the wobble out of his voice. 'I realised today that I know very little about her. The real Kitty and the one that has lived inside my head for all these years are probably very different people.'

'I'd say that's true.' His friend sighed. 'I mean, I know you've always had a thing for her, but she shagged you knowing she was about to marry someone, this Angus bloke, and she treated you like shit, just upping and leaving. It's not like it was a one-night stand, a mutual thing – she knew you had history.'

'But that's just it…' Theo coughed. 'It was a one-night stand – well, a one-afternoon stand, to be more accurate. It's just that one of us didn't know it.'

'She's not for you, mate, no matter what comes next. You deserve more, better.'

Theo looked at his friend. 'Well, I have no choice, do I? She's clearly cutting me out of the picture. If it's a toss-up between Angus Thompson or me as the best possible father for her child, why would she choose me? Even if it is my child.' Theo closed his eyes and heard his mother's anguished words. *This is the last straw, Peregrine. This is worse even than you cheating on me just after we got married, worse than you fathering that bastard boy, Alexander, worse than all of it!* That revelation had cut him to the quick – and now here he was in a similar position. He was no better than his dad! This thought was one of the hardest to swallow.

Theo stood up from the table and reached for the letter. He folded it and tore it and tore it again and again, then dropped the fragments into the pedal bin alongside last night's pizza crusts and a couple of old tins.

'Do you want to talk? Or go and get pissed?' Spud offered help in the only way he knew how.

Theo shook his head. He wanted neither. What he wanted was to go to bed and stay there.

He climbed beneath his duvet and ran his fingers over the pillow where her red curls had lain.

'I won't tell a soul. And I don't blame you, Kitty. You know I don't know the first thing about being a dad – I'd probably be even worse than my own father. Angus will do a fine job, I'm sure. I will never forget our afternoon together. It was lovely.'

Eight

Theo was aware of a hammering sound. He lifted his head from the pillow and laid it back down quickly. The room spun and he thought he might throw up. The hangover clearly hadn't finished with him yet. He pulled the duvet up over his naked shoulder and wished whoever was knocking would go away. All he wanted to do was stay there, in his room, hidden from the world. He had nothing to get up for and nothing to look forward to, and it felt easier not to bother. Today, just like every day since he'd received the devastating letter, he woke feeling utterly worthless, unable to shake thoughts of Kitty from his head, wondering how she looked, how she was feeling, whether she knew yet whether she was going to have a little boy or a little girl. His little boy or his little girl. Was she happy?

The same lines went round and round his brain: *I'm going to be a father, someone's father, the father of Kitty's child, but they'll never know me and I'll never know them.*

He pictured Kitty and Angus Thompson exchanging duplicitous vows and cooing over the baby. He pictured Angus being the best father, doing all the things he'd wished his own father had done with him; he pictured him teaching the child to ride a bike. It was torturous. But a promise was a promise: he would keep out of Kitty's life and there would be zero contact. It was best for everyone. It was fruitless to be so preoccupied with it all; he was nothing to Kitty and had absolutely no role to play. After all, what was he to her? Merely the boy she'd sat next to in class. The weirdo.

Depression had locked Theo in an endless cycle of self-doubt with nothing but a bleak dawn to look forward to each day. He hadn't been to a lecture or even on to the university campus since he'd received the letter. For weeks now he'd ventured no further than the corner shop or the pub. He no longer cared about his degree, or about anything much. Spud had tried to cajole him into going to his tutorials. He'd tried to persuade Theo that letting his studies slip wasn't going to help anyone and was a terrible waste not only of all the hard graft he'd put in so far, but of the exciting future they'd discussed. But Theo just couldn't see it.

He rolled over and stuffed his head under the pillow, but the banging on the door didn't let up. Eventually he sat up, rubbed his face and scoured the floor for some clothes to put on. He could hardly open the door in the nude, even if it was probably only Spud. Spying his dressing gown, he shoved his arms into the armholes and fastened the rope belt around his waist. The banging continued. He cursed the fact that Spud repeatedly forgot his keys.

'All right! All right! For God's sake, I'm coming!'

He yanked open the door, but it wasn't Spud on the step. There, in his trademark navy suit, his expression a mixture of disgust and disappointment, stood his father.

'It's three in the afternoon,' his father said coldly as he studied Theo, all but tapping his watch face with his index finger.

'Hi, Dad. I know. I...' He couldn't think of an excuse quickly enough. 'Come in.' He stood back and watched his father's eyes roam the place. 'Would you like to sit down?'

'Where *exactly* do you suggest I sit?' His father stared at the sofa, hidden beneath a pile of clothing, sauce-splattered plates, chip wrappers and a stack of study notes.

Theo looked at the mess and felt embarrassed.

'You look dreadful.' His father spoke without sympathy.

'I was just about to shower.' Theo gave a short laugh, trying to convey that it was no big deal: his greasy hair and unwashed body were easily fixed. He walked over to the kitchen area, lifted a plate from the sink and looked along the crowded countertop, trying to work out where to put it. At a loss, he shoved it back in the sink.

'You smell like a brewery.'

'That'll be the beer.' He knew this would have made Spud laugh; his father, however, just stared at him.

'Do you find this funny, Theo? This the sum total of your life on the planet so far? All that money spent on your education and this is it? Living in a shithole and sleeping the day away?' He turned his gaze slowly and pointedly around the messy room.

'I...'

'No, let me finish. An education such as you have had is an investment, a huge outlay by me to make sure you have a future. And if you think this is how I saw my investment performing then you are very much mistaken.' His father shot his cuffs and jutted his chin. 'A letter arrived at the house yesterday from UCL.'

Theo looked up.

'Yes, I already know you have missed assignments and yes,

I know that it is likely you will not graduate.' He shook his head. 'What a bloody waste! Did you think you could lie to us? Pretend everything was just fine?'

'N… no, I…'

'And before you go any further, I was also fascinated to learn that you are no longer studying engineering.'

Theo's bowels turned to ice. He'd almost forgotten his parents were unaware he'd changed courses.

His dad snorted his disdain. Theo decided not to ask who the letter had been addressed to; it seemed pointless and he felt gutless. He couldn't cope with the interaction, not today.

'I… I didn't want to lie to you, Dad, and I've worked really hard up until this year. My grades were good. And then…' He paused. 'Things have… kind of fallen apart for me a bit.' He rubbed his face.

'What do you expect – sympathy? You're hardly digging roads – you're writing bloody essays, sitting in lectures and getting pissed, how hard can it be?'

Too hard for me. Too much for me right now. She's having my baby, but she didn't want me, so she went away. 'It's hard for me to explain,' he began, feeling tears pool.

'Jesus Christ.' His father ground his teeth and placed his hands on his hips. 'Get a grip.'

Theo gathered himself. 'I… I've been thinking that maybe I should apply to do the year again, Dad. I can—'

His father held up his palm and cut him short. 'Oh no, Theo. That is not what happens next. Your student days are over.'

'But I'm good at it, Dad. I know that if I—'

'There are no buts! And there's no more money, no more turning a blind eye to your drinking, your slovenly ways and your bloody deceit. Social fucking policy!' He was shouting now and Theo was glad Spud was out. 'I could have predicted this,' he yelled. 'You are to pack up your things and come back to Barnes. You're going to work. You're going to work hard and you're going to work for me.'

'But, Dad, I—'

'There's no discussion. That's it!' His father lifted his arms and let them fall back by his sides. 'I expect to see you home by Saturday and if you don't show up by then, you're on your own. Is that clear?'

'Clear,' Theo managed, feeling powerless, afraid, and humiliated at his dad's ability to reduce him to this childlike state.

He watched his father navigate the empty lager bottles and full ashtrays on his way to the front door. As he gripped the handle, he turned round to deliver his parting shot. 'And for God's sake, shave before your mother sees you.'

Theo sat motionless on the sofa and waited for Spud to come home.

'Oh, well, at least you're up!' Spud said chirpily. 'This is progress indeed. What happened, did you wet the bed?'

In no mood for humour, Theo rushed out the words that had played in his head all afternoon. 'I... I've got to leave, Spud.'

'Got to leave what?'

'The flat. Uni. Everything.'

'What are you talking about, mate?'

'My dad was here.' Theo looked down, feeling swamped by the shame of having failed to stand up to his father or be honest with him. 'He says I have to go and work for him. He knows I'm not going to graduate. They sent a letter to my home address and he opened it.'

Spud sank down on the other end of the sofa. 'How do you feel about that?'

'Like a fish in a barrel. I can't see a way out.'

'It'll be okay, mate.' Spud gave him a sympathetic pat on the shoulder. 'You're in a bad place right now and maybe this is what you need.'

'How?' Theo raised his voice, angry not at his friend but at the feeling of utter hopelessness that engulfed him. 'How is this what I need?'

'As much as I don't want you to go, right now you're so close to the edge, you're only just surviving. Some structure might be good for you, give you something else to think about. There has to be more for you than this, Theo,' Spud said softly.

Theo nodded, unable to voice exactly how he felt or what he needed.

★ ★ ★

Stella Montgomery poured the thick black coffee into the china mug and set it on the breakfast bar. 'This is such an exciting day, darling!' she trilled.

Her cheerful tone grated on Theo's nerves. 'It is?' He bit into his toast and loosened the tie at his neck. It was three years since he'd worn a collar and tie and he'd forgotten how much it felt like he was being strangled.

'Daddy is very excited about taking you to work.'

'He has a funny way of showing it.' Theo sipped his coffee. 'And you make it sound like a day out, an adventure, but it's my whole life we're talking about here.'

'It is your life, of course, but it's right that you take an interest in the business that will be yours one day. And there's no better time to start than the present.' She lit her cigarette and took a deep drag, leaning back against the countertop. 'There are a million boys who would give their eyeteeth to be in your shoes! Goodness me, a lovely job with your father, and a lovely home here. There's no reason for you to feel fed up. And let's not forget that you failed university. It's not as if you have a stellar academic career beckoning – you didn't even finish!' She turned and flicked her ash into the sink and ran the tap to dispose of the evidence.

Her words were like a punch to the gut for Theo. 'I know I went off the rails a bit, Mum. I... I've been really low – not just fed up but... There was this...' Theo stopped himself right there as the memory of his mother's cruel laughter that night at La Grande Belle filled his head. She wouldn't understand about Kitty; he couldn't bear it if she trivialised how he felt and once again laughed away his upset. Better to stick to more neutral ground. 'I loved my course. I had a plan, kind of. I wanted to work in housing policy – you know, do something relevant – and I wanted to carry on living with Spud, my friend.'

He fought back his emotion at the mention of Spud, who'd looked so downcast as he'd taken down his posters and packed up his case ready for a new bloke to move in. A bloke like Wilson, or Angus Thompson or his half-brother Alexander, a decent bloke who'd be fun to be around and wouldn't lie in bed feeling sad the whole time. A bloke who would graduate and flourish. A bloke who would one day make a brilliant dad. Not a weirdo.

'What kind of a name is Spud?'

Theo finished his coffee and left the room, hating how Spud's name was the one thing his mum had taken from that conversation. Was this to be his life? This half life, doing what his parents told him instead of following his heart? Once he set foot in Villiers House, in this suit, he'd be as good as clocking on for life, and that would be that.

'What the fuck are you doing?' he asked the grey face that stared back at him in the bathroom mirror. Not for the first time, he wished he was someone else. He turned over the lapel of his suit jacket and pinned his fishing fly to the underside, just as Mr Porter had done all those years ago. He ran his finger over the delicate green and blue feathers and the square red bead. 'I'm sorry, Mr Porter. Sorry I didn't fight harder for you, sorry I didn't stand up for you. If I had that time again—'

A knock on the door made him jump.

'Leaving in five!' his father called, on his way down the stairs.

Theo bent forward and rested his forehead on the cold glass. 'I keep waiting for my life to begin. And just when I think it might, I'm hauled back to the start line. What would you say, Mr Porter? What would you say to make it all better?'

He closed his eyes and stood like that for a while, letting the cool glass chill his head, until his mother called from downstairs.

'Darling! Daddy's getting in the car!'

★ ★ ★

'So what's your role exactly?' Spud shouted as he speared the scampi, dipped it in tartare sauce and forked it into his mouth. The music was too loud to allow for easy conversation, just as the lighting was too low to allow you to fully see the grimy residue on the tabletop or the matted stickiness on the carpet tiles.

Theo rubbed his palms together. 'I don't really know.'

'You don't know?' Spud laughed uproariously. 'Only you, Theo, son, could have a job and not know what it is.'

'Well, I mean, obviously I know the title. I am currently in the valuation department in an assistant, junior, valuation role.' He sipped his warm pint.

'Sounds interesting.'

Theo ran his hand through his hair. He couldn't joke about it. He was still too raw at having messed up and been forced down a route not of his choosing. It felt like he'd been knocked out of a race at the last hurdle and it hurt.

'You should be happy you have a job and that you're not in an industry Thatcher's bent on dismantling. Plus it seems like the routine suits you – at least you're not sleeping the day away any more.'

'I guess. And I am feeling a bit better. There are days, though—'

'Oh, mate, there will always be days.' Spud, as ever, spoke wisely. 'Graduation was a bit of an event. My mum, dad, nan, sister and her bloke all came down, but we were only allowed two tickets so Mum and Nan sat with me and the others stood at the back of the hall. Mine was the only family to cheer when I went up to get my scroll.' He shook his head, clearly chuffed.

'Quite right too.' Theo liked that Spud hadn't shied away from discussing graduation like most people would have. Instead he'd brought it up early on, so that once aired they didn't need to feel embarrassed about it any more.

'I'm looking at doing telesales in some grubby office block on Tottenham Court Road. Commission only and proper shitty, but it'll pay the rent, I hope.' Spud grinned. 'And fingers crossed it won't be for too long, just till I figure out how I'm going to fund my master's.'

It had taken Theo years to fully comprehend that for most people there was a direct correlation between money and opportunities and that if you lacked the former you would likely have far fewer of the latter. But Spud had never held that against him. 'God, you're going to be one of these eternal bloody students while the rest of us work for a living!' Theo slapped the table and used his dad's voice.

The two of them laughed.

Theo sipped his pint. 'I sometimes feel like everything I want and everything I think will bring me fulfilment is dangling just out of reach.' He recalled the feel of Kitty's skin against his fingertips. 'Can I ask you something, Spud?'

'If it was anyone else, I'd probably say "no" to that question, as I'd expect it to be followed by a demand for cash, but as you're loaded, I'm going to go ahead and say yes, fire away.' He grinned and chased a chip around his plate to catch the last few breadcrumbs.

'Are you happy?'

'Right now?'

Theo shrugged. 'Not only right now but in general. Do you wake up happy? It always seemed like you did.'

'No, I usually wake up hungover in my pants and with a mouth like a badger's arse.'

'God, please can we just have one serious conversation!' He took a breath. 'I feel like… I feel like everyone else has got life sussed while I'm still trying to figure it all out. And it's not new – I've always felt like this. Even when I was young, it was like I couldn't work out how to be around other people or be like other people. I'd watch boys in my year planning for the weekend, the next break, the following term – always looking ahead and comfortable, as if life was a travellator and all they had to do was stand on it and grab whatever they passed, whatever took their fancy. But for me...' He looked up as someone in the corner laughed. 'I struggled just trying to figure out the day ahead and I couldn't look any further and if I did I could only see more of the same, nothing good.'

The edge to his voice made Spud sit up straight and place the fork flat on the plate. 'Am I happy?' He considered this, wiping his mouth with the back of his hand. 'I think so. I mean, I'm not unhappy, so I suppose I must be happy.'

The two men looked at each other.

'But is that enough?' Theo asked. 'To say your life is satisfactory because you're not unhappy – is that enough?'

'I think you might be overthinking things. And...' He paused and stared into his pint. 'And I think you might still be a bit depressed.'

Theo glanced up at him, noting the way Spud avoided his gaze. He guessed it had taken a lot for his friend to say this. 'Possibly, but I've always felt this way. Like I'm waiting for my good times to start, as if I might go round the next bend and see a big neon sign with "Get your happiness here!" – a destination that I will arrive at. But instead, no matter how far I travel, it feels like there are only more bends.'

The music quieted, as if giving Spud the floor. He leant in with his elbows on the table. 'So maybe you've *always* been a bit depressed. Is that possible too?'

Theo shrugged. 'I guess. But are people actually born like that, is that what you think? Or did it start when I got to school and the shit began to hit the fan?'

Spud took a big slurp of his pint and wiped the froth off his lips. 'I honestly don't know. But I do think a lot of it is about expectations. As you know, I come from Wigan and my dad's been a miner at the Golborne pit all his life – though it looks like that'll be coming to an end very soon, thanks to Maggie. As kids we were just happy that he had a job, happy that we got proper hot dinners. When I was eleven, ten miners were killed in an explosion down the mine and we were happy that Dad wasn't one of them. Right now my family is happy that I've been to university and that they got a day out in London to watch me graduate. I don't try to look too far ahead.' He downed the rest of his beer and placed the empty glass on the table. 'You, Theo, son, have had one hell of a lucky life. I'm not knocking you for it.' He held up his palm. 'You were no more able to control where and to whom you were born than I was. I also know that the shit with Kitty has knocked you for six, but I think sometimes—'

'You think sometimes what?'

Spud wiggled his tongue up around his gum, freeing bits of scampi that had got caught. 'Sometimes I think you're looking for perfect where perfect doesn't exist. It's important you look at what you've got and not at what you haven't.'

Theo raised his eyebrows and looked at his friend. 'I hear what you're saying, but I had such a crap childhood that I think it might have damaged my ability to feel happy. It's like my calibration is out.'

'Then you need to find a way to recalibrate yourself, mate, or you're going to have an unhappy adulthood as well. And in my opinion that would be a bloody shame.' Spud picked up his empty pint glass and stood. 'Same again?'

Nine

After eight years of working for Montgomery Holdings, Theo was well versed in every aspect of the family firm. The company bought land, built on it and acquired and renovated property in prime London locations, managing its portfolio to great effect. Because of its prudent, risk-averse strategy, the company's assets grew year on year. Theo found the 'profit before anything' mentality of his father and the rest of the board dispiriting, but in his quiet, unassuming way he had made it clear to staff and contacts in the industry that his values were more socially and environmentally oriented than those of his dad. He read articles on social policy and was drawn to the work of reforming organisations like the Joseph Rowntree Foundation, but he kept his head down, doing as he was asked and trying his best to fend off the depression that lurked inside him like a sleeping thing, curled and quiet but very much present. There was no denying he was still in his father's shadow and that rankled.

At least they were no longer sharing a house. Shortly before his twenty-fifth birthday, his mum had announced out of the blue that she and his father had bought him a lovely red-brick Edwardian house in Barnes and that Theo was free to do with it as he wished. The implication was that it should encourage him to find a wife and settle down to family life, but even if that wasn't on the cards, Theo was genuinely thrilled at finally gaining his independence. He could at last pursue his various flings without having to face a morning-after grilling when he didn't come home to his own bed. Not that there was ever anything much to tell. Few relationships made it past the second night together and none had lasted more than two weeks. Despite himself, the spectre of Kitty still haunted him, and the flash of red curls in a bar or on a dance floor was enough to make him do a double-take and step forward for a closer look.

Theo liked working in the City, close to the beating financial heart of the country, and he felt genuine affection for Villiers House, the handsome art deco building on Cheapside, a stone's throw from St Paul's Cathedral, which his great-grandfather had acquired in the 1920s. Theo appreciated the history of the building: each time he leant on the brass-topped handrails, curled his fingers around an ornate window latch or put his foot in one of the slight wells worn in the tread of the stone steps, he did so with a sense of connection to the relatives who had done so before him. Montgomery Holdings occupied the top floor, as it had since his great-grandfather's time, but the other six floors were rented out to financial trading companies.

Villiers House was mere yards away from several wine bars, and it was in these that he and Spud whiled away many an evening. But Spud was no longer free to stay out into the small hours, for fear of incurring the wrath of Kumi, his Japanese–American wife of three years. She wanted him home in suburbia at a reasonable hour, especially now that she was six months pregnant and not coping too well with the changes to her life. But, as ever, Spud appeared happy.

Theo noted that for the first time in their friendship, Spud seemed to be holding something back. He always shied away from giving specific details about Kumi's pregnancy and he quickly changed the subject when talk turned to his impending fatherhood. Theo presumed this was because Spud didn't want him to dwell on what he'd missed out on with Kitty. He loved that his friend was sensitive to this, but it had put the tiniest crack in their closeness. Spud was the only person on earth who knew he had a child; whether that child was male or female Theo still didn't know, let alone what their name was, but he did know that they would be turning eight very soon. He tried to picture them, tried to imagine the birthday party Kitty might organise for them, but he couldn't get beyond the dissatisfying image of a dark shadow of indeterminate features and size.

'Have you got the quarterly figures for Marcus?' Perry Montgomery stood in the doorway of Theo's office, impatiently tapping his signet ring on the wooden frame in double-quick time. His dark hair was now streaked with grey, but he still looked dapper.

Theo had been standing at his office window staring absent-mindedly down at the people scurrying back and forth on the pavement below. He turned now to answer his father. 'Nearly.'

'Oh good. I'll tell the board they can wait until nearly,' his dad shot back sarcastically.

The words flew across the room and almost choked Theo. As was usual, he averted his gaze.

'Could you be a little more specific or do you want me to ask Marcus to step in and give you a hand?' Perry's lips were set in a thin line and his eyes were fixed on the empty chair behind the desk, as if Theo had been caught shirking.

Theo's instinct was to dart back to his desk, take up the high-backed chair and start going through the spreadsheets, but he had a feeling that this false show of activity would only irritate his father more. He couldn't win. 'I don't need Marcus's help. I'm on it,' he levelled.

'Clearly.'

'I was just on my way out to grab some lunch – I'll do the figures the moment I get back. Can I get you anything?' He picked up his wallet from the corner of the desk and put his jacket on. The spacious office suddenly felt claustrophobic.

'Lunch?' His father's tone was so disdainful and was followed by such a lengthy sigh that as Theo walked past him he wondered if he'd accidently said he was going out dancing.

He decided to curtail his lunchbreak. Often he walked for a couple of blocks to clear his head, looked in the odd shop window or spent an age deliberating over the exact contents of his sandwich made freshly to order, relishing the change of scenery, but not today. His father would be watching the clock until his return.

London was hosting Euro 96 and the streets were uncomfortably rammed with football-mad tourists, many of them sporting their national colours. In the sandwich shop, Theo chose quickly, ordering the same as the woman in front of him to save on thinking time. He raced back to Villiers House, stepping into the road to avoid the throng of idlers who were clogging up the pavement and waving football scarves in the air.

'Hold the lift!' he shouted with his arm outstretched, brandishing the brown paper bag that contained the favourite sandwich of the lady who'd been ahead of him in the queue. He watched the doors begin to close, cursing his timing, but then felt a ridiculous sense of relief as he glided through the gap in the nick of time. Any win on a day like this was to be celebrated.

He took up a spot at the back of the lift and looked over at its only other occupant, a young woman with a dark bob who was standing in front of him.

'Sorry! I was trying to figure out which button might hold the doors, but they're all a bit worn,' she said, wrinkling her nose.

'Please don't worry about it.'

She glanced at him briefly over her shoulder and as her eyes swept his face he took the chance to do the same. She was not standard pretty, but she had an open face and a ready smile. *Great skin, bright eyes*. He liked the look of her. He liked the look of her very much.

'So, this is unusual.' Theo gave a small laugh as they took their seats in the snug of the Three Tuns. 'I meet you in a lift only this afternoon and now here we are. Cheers!' He raised his pint and clinked it against her small glass of white wine.

'You're a fast worker.' She sipped her drink, slurping from the top. 'I was really glad you asked me for a drink. Thank you.' She beamed at him openly.

'You're welcome. I'm really glad you said yes.'

Theo liked her lack of pretence, her down-to-earth manner. She made him feel relaxed. This was the exact opposite of the nervous state he usually found himself in on a first date.

The circumstances of their meeting had also been unusual. The creaky, sixty-year-old Villiers House lift had got stuck between floors, as it sometimes did, and when he'd realised that she was getting anxious he'd done his level best to distract her and keep her chatting. The more they'd chatted, the more interested he'd become and soon he'd forgotten they were waiting to be rescued by Bernie the maintenance man. He'd simply enjoyed finding out about the young woman, whose name was Anna. He'd been quite disappointed when the doors had finally slid open.

'So you live in Fulham?' he said now, trying to recall the various facts from their lift chat.

'Uh-huh, in a cupboard. Literally! My flat isn't much bigger than this table.' She rapped her knuckles on the surface as she placed her glass down and wiped her hands on her skirt.

She was unlike other women he knew. Nothing about her was pushy or presumptuous and she didn't seem to have any vanity or sense or self-importance. She wasn't one of the pouty, coming-on-to-him types he usually ended up with and neither was she sort of pretty, bright girl who expected to be adored – like Kitty. Theo realised that for the first time in as long as he could remember he was interested in someone. He was interested in her, Anna Cole with her shy demeanour and her cockney accent. He wondered how long Ned, the ex she'd mentioned, had been out of the picture and whether he'd been replaced. He hoped not.

'So you commute from Fulham? I come in from Barnes. I think the traffic in London is getting worse, don't you? It took me an hour to get over here in a cab from Paddington the other day. From Paddington! It might actually have been quicker to bloody walk.'

'I get the Tube to Mansion House usually, but sometimes I get off a couple of stops early and walk to Villiers House – to keep fit, you know.' She giggled. 'My friend Melissa's always going on at me to take up swimming or cycling, but I don't know how, do I, so that wouldn't be much good, would it?' She laughed again.

'You can't ride a bike?'

'Nope. Or swim.' She reached for her drink and sipped again.

'Anything else you can't do?'

She chortled. 'I think the answer to that is: considerably more than I can!'

He smiled, thinking of Kitty the swimmer, who might have grown her gills by now. *This girl...*

'Didn't you ever want to learn?'

'Which thing?'

'Both, I guess!'

'I suppose I did at one point, but swimming just felt wrong!' She wrinkled her nose with displeasure. 'And there was never any chance of me getting a bike, so I guess it would have been a bit pointless.' She tucked her hair behind her ears and seemed to consider this. 'But there *are* lots of things I wanted to do and didn't get the chance to – riding a bike was just one of them.'

'What things?' He was genuinely interested. He was attracted to her soft cockney accent and wondered where her thoughts had landed – she looked a million miles away.

Anna sighed and folded her hands neatly in her lap. 'Well, I would have loved to have gone to university. My grades were good enough, but...' She paused. 'It just wasn't possible.'

'Why not?'

She exhaled and hesitated. He guessed she was weighing up

how much to share on this, their first date. 'I was in care for part of my life and that kind of reduces your horizons, your expectations. The things I wished for were pretty simple, really. To stay safe, to keep out of the way of people who didn't like me... That sort of thing. I tried not to look too far ahead.'

Theo tried hard to mask his shock at hearing this. She'd been in care! He couldn't imagine it. They were from such hugely different worlds, but there was something about her that struck a chord. A sort of loneliness in her voice when she talked about her past, and a resilience.

'I can understand that.' He coughed to clear his throat, nervous about what he was going to confess, the shame of it; it was something he never normally shared. 'I went to university, but I didn't graduate.'

'Why didn't you graduate?' She held his gaze, her eyes steady and her expression non-judgemental.

'A number of factors. For a start I wasted the first couple of terms on a course I didn't want to be doing, engineering, when the thing that really interested me was social policy. So I switched, which was good, erm...' He faltered, searching for a way to phrase his story that wouldn't give too much away.

'Please don't tell me you were one of those students who couldn't possibly study until he had alphabetised his books and cleaned his whole apartment and made an apple pie! Whereas what you actually needed to do was get down to the studying! Or did you just get drunk and sleep?' She banged the table playfully. 'Was that it, Theo? Were you a lazybones?'

'Well, you're probably right about the avoidance tactics, though cleaning my apartment and making an apple pie are a little wide of the mark.' He smiled, thinking of how he and Spud had collected empty bottles of beer and lined them up around the edge of the room. He couldn't remember why they'd considered this to be a good idea. 'And actually I worked really hard, got good grades.' He paused.

'I feel a "but" coming on,' Anna said.

'And you'd be right.' He ran his tongue over his lips. Memories of that time were still painful.

'I kind of fell apart a bit.'

'Well, that happens.' She spoke softly. 'My brother had issues and it wasn't his fault, not really.'

She seemed to be close to tears and this new vulnerability made Theo's heart flex with tenderness and longing.

'I think we all go through things that shape us. I've always felt like an outsider.' She lowered her voice. 'I don't have tons of friends and I'm quite private. You just have to hope that when your time is over, you've lived a largely happy life, no matter that you had to dodge puddles of shit along the way.'

Theo laughed. 'I like that! And I myself have had to dodge some very large puddles of shit.'

'Does it bother you that you didn't graduate?'

Again, he liked her lack of guile. 'Not really, not now. Or maybe a little bit, sometimes.' He looked up at her. 'I'm definitely in the wrong job, though. I still daydream about working for social change, doing something that's not just concerned with maximising profits. I don't know...' He laughed to mask his embarrassment.

'Well, you're still young, you can do whatever you want. There's still plenty of time.'

'Yes.' He smiled at her. If only time really was the only barrier. 'I guess there is. Not graduating feels a little irrelevant now, but back then it felt like the end of the world.' He never wanted to go through that again – the taking to his bed and not wanting to wake up, the deep, black depression. 'I liked being a student, liked that life, but…'

'But life had other plans?'

'Actually, no, my father had other plans, but that's a whole other story.' He drummed his fingers on his thighs and reached for his pint.

'Well, I'm rather glad that your dad had other plans, or you would never have been in that lift and we wouldn't be sitting here now and there is absolutely nothing on the telly tonight.' She grinned.

'I'm glad to be a diversion.'

Anna smiled at him again, her beautiful, open smile. 'I think it's wonderful that you want to do a job that's for the greater good and not just chasing cash like so many people. I felt your kindness today in that lift. It made all the difference to me, more than you could know, and I get the feeling you can do anything you put your mind to, Mr Montgomery. There's something special about you.'

Theo stared at her, wondering if she knew what those words meant to him. She thought he could do anything he put his mind to! Him, the weirdo! Only she didn't make him feel like a weirdo. She made him feel… special.

'To puddles of shit!' She raised her glass.

'To puddles of shit!' he echoed and they both drank.

She wiped her mouth and reached for her purse. 'Same again?'

'I'll get them.' He made to stand.

'God, no!' She stood. 'You got the last ones. You should know I'm a girl who likes to pay her own way.'

★ ★ ★

'Hello, is this the correct telephone number for Mr Theodore Montgomery? Lover of Guns N' Roses, sore loser at Uno and lightweight when it comes to necking pints at speed?'

Theo laughed into the receiver. 'It might be. Who's asking?'

'My name is Spud and I used to be his best friend, but he seems to have gone to ground and the carrier pigeon I sent out has returned empty-handed, so I'm trying this number as a last resort.'

'Very funny.' Theo sat back in the chair behind his desk.

'How you doing, mate?'

'I'm…' Theo's grin pre-empted his reply. 'I'm great!'

'And does this or does this not have something to do with the mysterious Anna Cole you mentioned in our last chat?'

Theo laughed, loudly. 'What can I say? She's…'

'She's…?'

'She's bloody brilliant!'

'Bloody brilliant? High praise indeed. How long have you been seeing her?'

'Three or four weeks.'

Spud roared his laughter. 'That is funny! I know you know exactly and you're just trying to sound cool! "Three or four weeks!"'

Theo joined in the laughter. 'All right, you bastard. Four weeks to the day. Happy now?'

'Over the bloody moon!' Spud guffawed. 'You sound different.'

'I feel different,' Theo admitted. He looked up and out of the window. It was a grey day, but thinking of Anna made it feel like sunshine.

'So it's pretty serious?'

'I'd say so.' He grinned at the understatement. 'I feel like...'

'Go on! You feel like...?'

'I feel like she could be the one.'

'The one! Jesus, Theo, this is epic news!'

They both chuckled down the line.

'I'd say Operation Erase Kitty has finally been achieved. Took a little longer than expected, maybe, but we got there in the end.'

'It's completely different – real and brilliant and mutual!'

'So, sex good?'

'None of your business!' Theo smiled.

'That'll be a "yes" then. Met her folks?'

'No folks to meet. Both dead and she's pretty much looked after herself – she's a tough cookie, got her head screwed on.'

Spud exhaled slowly. 'Mate, I have to tell you that while that is undoubtedly sad, I have had Kumi's mum here for the last month, so the thought of hooking up with an orphan is pure genius.'

Theo laughed. 'That bad?'

'Worse. I made the mistake of reminding them that Kumi is not ill, just pregnant, and that millions of women give birth every day all over the world.'

Theo chuckled. 'What did they say to that?'

'I have no idea, but it was loud and furious and went on for a long time in Japanese. Both of them. In stereo. It might still be going on for all I know. Right now, I'd give my left nut for my wife to be an orphan. I'd give my right nut too, but Kumi already has that one in her purse. My life is over.'

'And yet you sound decidedly happy, considering your dire circumstances.'

'I am. Bit scared about the whole becoming a dad thing, but I am happy.'

'You're going to be a great dad.'

'Hope so. My parents keep calling me and asking, "What should we get for't baby? What do babies eat in Japan?" As if this child is going to arrive a fully fledged Japanese–American baby! They seem to forget that she's going to be half-Wiganer!'

Theo laughed, picturing the conversations with Ma and Pa Spud. 'I'm happy too,' he said, wanting to share this with Spud.

'Anna must be some girl.'

'She is, Spud. She gets me and she's a lot like me, even though we're from very different worlds. She kind of makes me feel better about stuff.' He sat forward in the chair.

'What stuff?'

'Everything, actually.'

There was a beat or two of silence and Theo knew what was coming next.

'We joke, but have you told her about Kitty, about… things?'

Theo closed his eyes briefly and felt the weight of the knowledge that he knew had to be shared. It sat in his heel like a sliver of glass that no matter how joyous the day or glorious the view, made its presence known with every step he took. 'No, not yet. It's hard to find the right time. It's a bit of a grenade and I don't want to spoil things.'

'I get that, and it's your call, but I think it'll be easier if you do it sooner rather than later.'

'You're right.' Theo rubbed his face. 'Anyway, mate, better crack on. Beer soon?'

'Yep, beer soon, and don't do anything I wouldn't!'

'Doesn't sound like you do much at the moment.' Theo laughed. 'Oh sod off!'

That evening, Theo and Anna sat in uncharacteristic quiet as the cab left the City and headed towards Anna's studio flat in Fulham. It was there, in her tiny, cupboard-sized space, that they did their courting. Little time was wasted on sleep; instead they laid the foundations for all that might come next. Both were high on what the future might bring.

Theo held her small hand and placed their knot of conjoined fingers on his thigh, where it rested comfortably. Tonight was the night. Spud was right: he had to confide in Anna about his child. But what if she despised him for it? Rejected him because of it? The prospect terrified him. The thought that his time with Anna might be coming to an end sent a shiver of sadness along his spine. His leg jumped with nerves.

They walked quietly up the stairs and into Anna's flat. Anna reached up to flick the light switch. Theo caught her wrist, knowing it would be easier to have the difficult conversation in the darkness. 'No, leave the light off, we'll just have the glow from outside.'

'I… I don't like the dark,' she stammered and his throat tightened.

'Me neither.' He laughed. 'But you've got me and I've got you, so we don't have to worry. Not tonight.'

'I don't worry, not when I'm with you. I don't worry about a thing. It's like everything is great in my world and it's the first time I've ever felt that way and I really like it!'

Theo placed his trembling hands on her face and Anna tilted

her head to receive his kiss. 'I... I feel the same,' he began, peppering his speech with light kisses on her face. 'It's like I know everything is going to be okay, because I've got you.'

'You have got me!' She beamed, nuzzling her cheek into his palm.

'There have been times when I was so sad...' He paused. 'No, more than sad – depressed. I have lived with depression,' he said frankly. 'My last terms at uni, they were hell.'

Go on, Theo, tell her! Tell her about Kitty and the baby! Tell her now! Get it out of the way!

'Oh, Theo...' Anna's voice trembled with compassion and for that Theo loved her more than ever. 'I'm sad you went through that.'

'I think I'm still going through it, I don't think it's really left me.' He bit his cheek. 'It engulfed me, knocked me sideways. I've come out of that phase, certainly, but it's like something that's always there, lurking just around the corner. I get the feeling it's never very far away.'

She nodded her understanding.

'But for the first time, I can see light and I guess that's why I don't feel as afraid of the dark.'

She met his gaze. 'You don't have to be afraid, not any more.'

Theo nodded. 'This thing that's going on with us, Anna...' He hesitated, wary of being the first to confess to the swell of love in his gut. 'I don't know what it is, but it's...' He exhaled.

'I know.' He could hear her voice smiling into the darkness. 'It really is.'

They kissed again and stumbled towards the bed at the end of her rather tiny living zone.

He did not want to break what they had – this, the most

perfect thing he'd ever been part of. This was not the time to tell her about a child he did not know, would never know; not the time to admit that his weirdness had led to Kitty rejecting him as the father of their child. No, this was the time to carry on falling for each other, for not worrying about a thing. He too had never felt this way about anyone and he too really liked it.

* * *

Theo looked at his reflection in the mirror of the office bathroom and stood tall. He took a deep breath.

'Would you do me the honour…?' He stopped. 'I ask this is in all sincerity…' He shook his head and coughed to clear his throat. 'Anna, from this day forth…' He felt the weight of the occasion, overly aware of the pose, tone and words required for asking this most important of questions. He had of course rehearsed before today, but now he was wondering if he should opt for something less formal. *Just make it count, Theo. Do it properly.*

It was a mere ten weeks since he'd met Anna Cole in the lift, but he knew with certainty he wanted to propose. Truth was, he'd known after one date and had spent the next few weeks looking for flaws, anything to test his suspicion that she was practically perfect. He shook his arms loose and turned his head until his neck cricked, surprised at how nervous he was. His mouth felt dry and his limbs were trembling.

Supposing she says no? What then?

If she said no, they'd be finished, they'd have to split up – they wouldn't be able to recover from that. The potential for disaster was significant, and that did nothing to allay his anxiety. He took another deep breath. Tonight, when he popped the question, it could be a beautiful moment; the start of a lifelong love, or it could be the worst of moments, the end of everything.

He could only liken it to standing on a cliff edge.

He entered the coffee shop with the advantage of not being seen and looked across at Anna, the woman he wanted to make his wife. The woman who loved him as no one had ever loved him and surely no one else ever would. The woman who, by loving him as she did, diluted his weirdness, robbed him of the 'loser' crown and turned him into the kind of chap that someone might want to marry. Anna made him feel like a man who was capable of becoming a husband.

As if confirmation were needed, her eyes fell upon him and her face lit up. He knew with certainty that there was no one in the world she wanted to see walk into that coffee shop more than him, and it felt amazing to be so wanted. To belong.

'So where are we going?' she asked, as, fifteen minutes later they settled into the back seat of a cab.

'I told you, somewhere special.' He smiled at her.

'I don't know if I'm dressed right.' She looked down at her work skirt and blouse.

'Don't worry. You look perfect.' He stared out of the window and tried to stem his nerves.

It wasn't until the cab drove over Hammersmith Bridge that the penny dropped and Anna realised he was breaking the code of a lifetime and was taking a girl back to his home. She looked at him with a knowing expression. He reached for her hand and the two sat quietly, each lost in thought.

For the hundredth time, he ran through in his head the many ways he might propose, wondering if it was absolutely necessary to go down on one knee, wary of making a fool of himself. After all, this would be a night they'd always remember. He swallowed – that thought did nothing to calm his racing pulse.

Theo paid the cab and retook her hand, guiding her along the gravel path, which crunched underfoot.

'Are you okay?' he asked, squeezing her fingers tightly.

Anna stared wide-eyed and he saw the grand façade as if though her eyes. She nodded up at him and that was how they stood for a second or two, in acknowledgement of the moment.

'Here we are.'

'Yes.' She bit her lip. 'Here we are.'

Theo fished in his pocket for his keys and gently pushed open the front door, elated to have finally found the woman he wanted to step over the threshold with.

It did indeed turn out to be a night Theo would never forget. Over a bottle of red, Anna talked freely about her life and her losses. There was no denying that to hear her story of losing first her mother and then her brother, Joe, who'd committed suicide, made him feel even more protective of her. And to top it all, she'd only recently discovered that the father she'd never met had also passed away. She talked fearlessly and frankly. Her story might have been too much for some, but for Theo it served only to bind them closer together.

Anna made no attempt to hide her tears. 'I feel like it's time,' she told him, 'and there is so much I want to say to you. I need you to *see* me.'

He nodded. 'I need you to see me too. There is so much *I* want to say.' He thumbed the skin on the back of her hand.

'We are from very different worlds,' she began.

'And I thank God for that.' He leant forward and kissed her gently on the forehead.

'I'm… I'm weird,' she managed, pulling away to look him in the eye. 'I've always been weird and I've had a weird life. A life I want to tell you about so that I don't have to worry about revealing it to you bit by bit. I think that's the best thing, like ripping off a plaster. I need to do it quick.'

Theo pulled her into his chest and held her tightly. 'Weird? Oh God, Anna, you have no idea…' He felt a bubble of relief burst inside his head. All these years, the toxicity of his weirdness had formed a barrier that kept other people at arm's length, and yet with Anna it was the very thing that joined them.

'I don't want to be on my own any more!' She raised her voice. 'I don't want to feel like sticks on the river! Like I'm being carried along, clinging on for dear life and hoping I don't drown.'

'I've got you, Anna. I've got you!'

'I've had enough, Theo. I'm tired. I'm so tired of being sad and being scared and lonely! So lonely!'

He kissed the top of her scalp and rocked her until she fell into a sleep of sorts. As she dozed, his confidence soared. They were meant to be together. She had to say 'yes'!

Later that night, after she'd woken and after more tears, more revelations, and more sadness about her family, her loneliness, Theo blurted out exactly what he was feeling, unplanned and heartfelt.

'I love you, Anna. I love you.'

'I love you too. I do, I really love you!'

They fell against each other, laughing, giddy in the moment.

'I always think you get the people in your life that you're meant to. I think we're meant to get each other.' Anna smiled.

'I think you're right. Two weirdos together!'

'Yes! Two weirdos with the lights left on.'

'I think…' Theo paused and reached for her hands, taking them both into his own. 'I think we'll get married and live here, together, just like this.'

This was very far from the formal proposal he'd practised so nervously and so many times, but it was no less perfect for it.

Anna couldn't halt the flow of tears that ran down her cheeks. 'Yes, Theo. I think we will get married and live here, together, just like this.'

Slowly he stood, pulled her up and guided her by the hand towards the staircase, towards a different life.

The next morning, as he came downstairs, he could hear Anna singing in the kitchen. He smiled. She was a little off key and hadn't quite got the words right. 'The things you do for love. The things you do for love!'

She was dressed in nothing more than his shirt and socks, and he stood in the doorway watching her fill the kettle, seek out tea-bags, rummage in the bread bin for a loaf and open several drawers and cupboards until she located butter knives, teaspoons and jam.

It was only when she turned to walk to the fridge that she saw him. She started. 'Oh! Theo!' She placed her hand on her chest. 'I was just trying to make breakfast. Is that okay?' She blinked, walked over and kissed his mouth.

'Of course it's okay. It's great.' He took a seat at the kitchen table and watched her navigate her way around the room, think-ing how brilliant that he would be waking every day for the rest of his life in her lovely company. 'I feel smug.'

'Me too.' She raised her shoulders and his eyes fell on her exposed thighs as the shirt rode up. She walked over and leant against him, kissing his forehead. It was as if she couldn't stop. He understood this constant desire for contact. It was new and exhilarating.

'Smug and peaceful.' He rested his hand on her bottom.

'And engaged!' She pulled a wide-mouthed grin and raised her eyebrows. 'Can you believe it?'

'Actually, yes, I can.' He chuckled. 'I'd planned what I wanted to say and everything – but then all my plans flew out the window and I got nervous and the words kind of tumbled out on a stream of red wine.'

'I wouldn't have had it any other way. It was perfect.' She carried on with her tea making, only returning to the table when she had two steaming mugs.

She took a seat opposite and held her tea in both hands. 'Do you know, I always wondered who I might marry. I think lots of little girls do and it feels strange that now I've found out. I mean, I hoped it would be you—'

'Did you?'

'Yes, from the first time I met you, I hoped it would be you, but now I *know* it is and it's wonderful!'

Theo couldn't stop grinning. He had never felt this special before – ever.

'I wish my mum had met you.' Anna sat very still.

'Would she have approved?' he asked cautiously.

Anna shook her head. 'Now that's a daft question. She would have loved whoever loved me of course.'

Theo wished he had the same level of certainty about his own folks. 'Well, my mum and dad are a bit challenging at times.'

He smirked at the understatement, wanting to manage her expectations.

'In what way?' She blew on her drink to cool it.

Theo swallowed. 'They're quite selfish, preoccupied with their social lives. And I guess the older I get, the more I question the way they parented me. I was desperately unhappy at school and they did nothing about it. It would have made my life easier if they'd taken more of an interest or given more of a shit.'

Anna reached out and laid her hand on his. 'I hate to think of you being unhappy. I absolutely hate it. I wish I'd been your friend. I would have loved you then too. Especially when you were depressed, Theo.'

'Thank you.' He kissed her fingers, swallowing his guilt; he *had* to tell her about Kitty...

'And if you get low again, I'll be by your side,' she offered softly. 'Sometimes it's enough just to know you're not going to have to face things alone, don't you find?'

Theo's smile was unstoppable as, yet again, realisation dawned that she'd said 'yes'!

'I sometimes think, though, that the rougher you have it, the more you appreciate the good stuff – almost like the nice bits are a reward.' She continued sipping her tea.

'That's a good way to look at things. I find it hard to rationalise. My parents used to act like every day was a party and the world was sharing a joke that I simply didn't get. But whenever I tried to explain how I felt, Mum and Dad would just laugh, as if I was making a fuss about nothing, as if I was the problem. The onus was always on me to fit in, not on them to help me fit in or give me guidance.' He smiled ruefully. 'I could have done with my mum teaching me the alphabet game like yours did, to distract me from my loneliness. It might have helped me get to sleep better those nights in the dorm at school. A... appalling parents! B... bloody awful school... Is that sort of thing allowed?' He shot her a cheeky grin.

Anna giggled and shook her head in mock despair. Then her expression turned serious. 'You're not the problem, Theo! You're wonderful! I think you're very brave to be so open about what you've been through. And it means a lot. I don't want there to be any secrets between us. It's important.'

He held her gaze, letting her words permeate and feeling his shoulders sag under the weight of the secret he carried. He took a deep breath.

'There is something I would like to tell you.' He gulped his tea and placed it down with a trembling hand.

'Go on.' She nodded encouragingly.

His heart was galloping. He exhaled. 'I'm not like my dad.' As soon as the words were out, he felt a punch of sickness in his gut, because he was like his dad! They had both fathered children and swept them under the carpet, unmentioned, a source of shame... He felt his face flash with heat and the room swam a little. 'He has often been unfaithful to my mum, including with a much younger girl, a kind of nanny to me during one summer holiday, when I was fourteen.'

'Shit!'

'Yes.' He sat tall in the seat. He felt a strange sense of relief that the truth still lay hidden, out of harm's way and unable to damage what they had, the love they shared. But there was also guilt that he was letting her down, already defaulting on her 'no secrets' request. He wiped the corners of his mouth and sat forward. 'I tried to tell my mum that I'd support her and look after her, but she just laughed! And then she more or less told me that I was irrelevant to her and that no matter what my dad did, she would always pick him.'

'Oh my God, Theo!' Anna raced around the table and laid his head on her chest, holding him tightly and rocking him slightly. It was the most sincere and wonderful hold he had ever known. 'You've carried a lot inside you and you've had a shit time, but you know what? You've got me now and I love you so very much and I always will and we're getting married! And everything is going to be wonderful!' She kissed him hard on the face.

He nodded and inhaled the scent of her. 'Yes, it is. It's going to be wonderful.'

'I look at this wonderful house, Theo, and I know it will be the most incredible place to bring up our children. Not because of how grand it is, but because we live in it and we will never let our children cry themselves to sleep and they will always know how much they are loved. I can see us eating family suppers around the table where we can all chat about our days without fear of ridicule or rejection. A safety net, a proper family! It's more than I ever thought I could hope for. Mrs Theodore Montgomery!' She laughed.

'Mrs Theodore Montgomery,' he echoed. Theo swallowed the uneasy feeling that despite how much he loved this girl, the proper family she yearned for was still something that felt beyond his capabilities.

Later that morning, while Anna was luxuriating in the bath, Theo sat down at the desk in his study. He couldn't stop thinking about Anna's alphabet game. He loved this quirk about her, the fact that anyone else would simply let their thoughts tumble, but not Anna: she took control and played the alphabet game, working her way through the letters until mental equilibrium was restored. He flipped open the lid of his vintage pen box, selected a pen and wrote 'A' to 'Z' in a column down the left-hand side of a fresh sheet of paper. He laughed, wondering what Spud would make of him doing this exercise. With his pen poised, he thought of all the things he loved about Anna, his Anna, Anna who was going to be his wife!

A...

He looked at the window and pictured the girl he loved, before writing in a bold script:

Here we go, Anna, my first ever attempt at the alphabet game...
A... Anna
B... beautiful.
C... courageous. So much more courageous than me.
D... determined.
E... eager.
F... funny.
G... gorgeous.

Ten

Theo crept out into the garden straight after breakfast, went round to the kitchen window and waved through the glass at Anna, who was peering at the rather unpromising-looking lemon tree she insisted on keeping on the windowsill.

Anna glanced up and shot him a puzzled look. She wiped her hands and came out onto the doorstep.

'What's that?' she asked, pulling her cardigan around her form and nodding in the direction of the shed.

'What does it look like? It's a bicycle!' he beamed, excited.

'Well, I can see that, but what's it doing in our garden?' She took a tentative step closer.

'I can't have a wife of mine unable to ride a bike!' He pulled the bike around and stood with the back wheel between his shins. 'And now that we have officially been Mr and Mrs Montgomery for, ooh, four months, one week and three days, the time has come to rectify this glaring defect. So come on! Hop on!'

'No-wer!' She shook her head, laughing.

'Come on, Anna! I am going to teach you how to ride this bike. It'll be fun.'

'No, you are not.' She bit the inside of her cheek. 'And it won't be fun. It'll be rubbish.'

'I thought it was sad that no one had ever taught you how, and it bothered me that you never thought you would have a bike. I intend to put both of those things right.' He reached forward and patted the leather saddle. 'And before you know it, we'll be biking all over the place with a flask of tea in your basket and a picnic.' He thought of Mr Porter and the delicious sandwiches packed into his knapsack.

'That is really, really sweet of you, and I love the idea of it, but I think you might be confusing me with someone out of an Enid Blyton novel. I can't do it. I will fall off. I'm useless at stuff like that.'

'How do you know if you have never tried?'

'Because, Theo, I twist my ankle if I wear heels, I trip up kerbs and I can't navigate a turnaround door!'

He looked at her quizzically. 'A revolving door?'

'Yes! See, I don't even know what they're called!'

'Come on, Anna, I won't let you go, I promise.' He beckoned to her gently and held her gaze as she walked from the step, down the path and towards the bike. He liked the way she ran her fingers over the green-painted frame and smiled, as if coming round to the idea.

'You got this for me?' She bit her lip.

'I did.'

'Thank you, Theo. You love me, don't you?'

'I do.' He felt the surge of love for her in his chest.

Anna moved a step closer and looked at the pedals.

'That's it! Now climb on.'

She did as she was told, gripping his shoulder tightly as she gingerly put one leg either side of the metal frame and placed her foot on one of the pedals.

'It's going to wobble, Theo!' There was no mistaking the slight edge of panic to her voice. 'I don't like it!'

'It will, yes, but I've already promised you I won't let you fall.'

He relished the way she looked at him so trustingly. It was lovely to hold her steady and see her almost literally steeling herself for the challenge.

'That's it,' he said encouragingly as she lifted herself up and sat back on the saddle, her feet on the pedals and her hands clenching the handlebars as if her life depended on it.

'Look at you, Anna Bee Cole! You're on a bike!'

'Don't let go!' she squealed. 'Please don't let go!'

'I'm going to hold you upright but we'll move forward, so the wheels will shift but I'll be holding you at the back, okay?'

'No!' Anna screamed. 'Not okay!'

But he did it anyway and he could tell she didn't know whether to laugh or cry as she sailed along with him gripping the back of her saddle.

'See, you're doing great!' He beamed. 'Now we're going to try the same thing but along the pavement.'

'Oh God! No, Theo, please, I might hit someone!' she implored, but without the conviction of someone who was truly afraid. This he took as a sign that she was more willing than she cared to admit.

He steered the bike along the path until it was lined up with the wall at the front of the garden. He started to walk, still guiding her from behind. Her feet kept up with the turning pedals and she began to laugh. 'I quite like it! Don't let go!'

'Don't worry! I've got you,' he called, running out of puff as the bike gathered pace.

Soon she was going too fast for him to keep up. He stood back and watched with pride as Anna trundled on down the pavement, too focused on pedalling to realise that he wasn't holding her saddle any longer.

'Woohoo! This is great!' she yelled. She turned to her left to smile at Theo, but he was a good few paces behind now, staring after her with a grin on his face.

He raised both hands and gave her a double thumbs-up – prematurely, as it turned out. The shock of realising that she was now riding solo proved too great for Anna. She wobbled and lost her confidence. The bike careered into a neighbour's garden wall and with a mighty clatter Anna toppled over, the bike landing on top of her.

'Anna!' Theo called, running to catch up. 'Are you okay?' He bent down, moving the bike with his hands and kneeling to examine her scuffed leg with the type of scrape and bruise usually seen on the knees of six year olds.

Anna looked up and kissed his chin, she was breathless, exhilarated. 'I am more than all right – I can ride a bike, Theo! I did it all by myself!'

'Yes, you did. You were brilliant. But I think we might leave it a while before we try skateboarding and swimming.'

'My poor bike, have I damaged it?' she looked up.

'Forget the bike. I'd be more worried about the damage to the wall!' he laughed.

The two kissed, as they sat on the pavement without a care in the world.

*

Springing surprises on Anna was one of the many little pleasures Theo had come to relish about his new life as a married man. The two had fallen into a happy routine, making even the most mundane of chores seem like fun. He felt optimistic about the future when he considered the genuine humour and friendship that bound them like glue. It was very different to the show of unity that his parents felt the need to portray. The loud laughter and almost rehearsed ribbing that was traded back and forth in front of their friends was more than a little staged. It was a nice feeling knowing that when he and Anna were in the car alone or about to fall asleep there was not going to be the roar of anger and resentment that might have simmered all evening and which he had heard his parents voice on more than one occasion. It was a new and wonderful feeling to be at peace.

He couldn't wait to tell her about the Maldives holiday he'd just booked to celebrate their first anniversary, but whether or not that would be the place to try and teach her to swim, he wasn't quite sure. He was certain she'd love the Maldives though – she'd never been to the tropics and he could practically hear her squeals of delight. That was part of the joy for him, seeing things through Anna's eyes. He would tell her that night, he decided, after their dinner date with Anna's friend Melissa and her husband Gerard.

'Yours was a cracking wedding,' Gerard commented, as he filled Theo's wine glass with a warm red. 'None of the usual shenanigans. It was simple and so much better for it.'

'Neither of us wanted anything flashy.'

'And pure genius in the choice of venue, a great lunch and then a short cab ride home in time for the football, job done. In fact I remember saying something similar to your mother who looked none too impressed!' Gerard laughed, loudly. 'I think I was wearing my champagne goggles, I then asked her who she supported.'

Theo laughed at the idea. 'What did she say?'

'Nothing, she stared at me as if she didn't have the faintest idea what I was talking about and reached for your father's arm.'

'That'll be about right. Cheers!' Theo took a sip, as Melissa arrived from upstairs.

'Hello my darlings! So good to see you both. Sorry I am behind as always. This little scrap is the biggest distraction; I don't know where the hours go. Do you want to hold him?'

Melissa waved baby Nicholas in his direction. Theo stared at the little boy in his pale blue sleepsuit and felt his face colour, as he wiped his hands nervously on his thighs. 'I'm not very good with babies.'

'Well, you'd better get good at it, pal, because trust me before you know it there will be the pitter patter of Montgomery feet in the house and you are going to wish you had paid better attention!' Gerard laughed. 'At least that's how it was in my case. One minute I am married to the biggest party girl on the planet, out all night dancing,' he lifted his wine glass in Melissa's direction, 'and the next I'm queuing in the all-night chemist for disposable nappies and nipple cream watching men who used to be me, trot along the pavement with the wobble of drink and a silly grin on their faces, and do you know what I envied the most about them?' Gerard waited for a response.

Melissa tutted, 'Oh not this again!'

'Yes! This again,' he winked at Theo, 'what I envied in them the most was not their drunken antics or the freedom they had to plan an evening on the town and actually leave the house, no, it was the fact that I knew these men were going home to sleep! Imagine that? Sleeping in a bed for longer than two and a half hours before a wailing monster squawks into the night and we all have to jump to attention.' He took a slug of his wine. 'I was plain jealous.'

'Poor Gerard.' Anna smiled at him.

'Poor Gerard?' Melissa shouted. 'It wasn't poor Gerard who was sliding off the mattress too tired to stand so a child could brutalise his once lovely chest! Don't you dare give him sympathy!'

'You love it right?' Anna asked.

Gerard scooped baby Nicholas into his arms and kissed his little face. 'I do, Anna, I love it more than I can possibly describe. And don't tell him this,' he lowered his voice to a whisper, 'but I'd get up to him any time of day and night, just to get the chance to spend five minutes with him. I'm obsessed.'

Theo felt Anna's stare across the room and hated her look of hope. It was proving to be the biggest bone of contention between them, her desire to start a family and his attempts at deflecting the issue.

It was as they drove home to Barnes that Anna again broached the topic, as he had guessed she would.

'Nicholas brings so much joy to their lives, doesn't he?' Her words sounded off the cuff, but he suspected she had been mentally rehearsing them since they had left.

'He does. But I also get the impression that they have given up a lot. I mean, Gerard was saying they hardly ever get the chance to go dancing or go out.' He let this trail.

'Oh God yes, I would hate for us to have to give up our dancing!' she laughed and he joined in, knowing they had never done this. 'I just feel so excited when I think about it, Theo. I can't help it.'

'I know you do, but there are lots of advantages to not having kids.' He squeezed her leg.

'Like what?'

'Well, the sleep Gerard mentioned, can you imagine not being able to sleep? That must be like torture!'

'I promise I will do every single night feed and you will not be disturbed. The advantage of having a big house is you can sleep in the spare room.' She smiled.

'I can think of other advantages.' He coughed, preparing to announce his big surprise.

'I get the feeling you are going to suggest sex?'

'Actually, I was going to tell you that I have booked for us to go to the Maldives for our wedding anniversary, but if sex is on the cards…'

He watched her turn in the seat and place her hand over her mouth. 'Oh my god! Theo! Really?'

'Uh-huh. Our own villa, luxury all the way.'

He heard her sharp intake of breath. 'Oh Theo, that will be wonderful, thank you. Thank you, darling.' She reached over and kissed his face. 'The Maldives.'

He listened, as she practised the sound of the place and couldn't help but notice the slight edge of disappointment to her tone, as if no amount of fancy travel could make up for what she wanted most. A baby. He swallowed the guilt that swirled on his tongue and put the radio on.

Eleven

'Well…' Spud popped the last of his scampi into his mouth and wiped his hands on the paper napkin before flinging it into the puddle of tartare sauce and breadcrumbs that sat in the middle of his plate. 'I have to say that for someone who's just returned from the Maldives, you look mightily down in the dumps! Did none of that sunshine and relaxed living rub off on you?'

'Not exactly.'

'Half your luck…! I think Kumi and I celebrated our one-year anniversary by sharing a tub of raspberry ripple and having sex. In fact…' He sipped his drink. '… that might actually have been the last time we had sex.'

Theo abandoned his grey burger and chips and pushed the plate away with a sigh. 'I just don't know—'

'Well, we both know that you *do* know, but you're just deciding whether to confide in me or not.'

Theo gave a wry smile. It was impossible to fool his best mate. 'Okay…' He took a slug of his drink. 'The villa was incredible, right on the water, with a deck and all the bells and whistles. Anna was so excited to be there and it was brilliant seeing her happiness – it was the first time she'd been somewhere like that.

And there was the usual champagne on arrival, blue sky, bluer sea…' He rolled his hand in the air. 'You get the gist.'

'I do and I can see why you'd be so miserable – it sounds bloody awful.' Spud sipped his pint.

Theo rubbed his hand over his face. 'I love her.'

'I know.'

'But it's the having-kids issue that keeps on cropping up.'

'It's going to, mate. You've been married a year, it's what she wants, and rightly or not, it's what others expect too. And it's a big thing, a pressure, the biggest inside a marriage, I would think – certainly it is in ours. Kumi is already pushing for number two and I'm still trying to get my head around the fact that number one is here to stay!'

Theo wasn't in the mood for humour. 'Anna thinks having a family will be the thing that cements us.'

'It might be,' Spud offered supportively.

'But I don't think so, not for me. I haven't learnt the things you did. The way you talk about your dad, like he's your mate, and all the experiences you've had together…' He paused. 'And now you're a dad too and you just take it all in your stride. I've had none of that – I wouldn't know where to start.' He fingered the fishing fly on his lapel, trying to calm his agitation.

'Everyone feels like that and, trust me, no matter how or where or by whom you were raised, nothing prepares you for having one of your own. You just have to try and figure it out as you go along. Kumi and I have had such different experiences, but I think that's what makes it work. Miyu will have balance.'

Theo shook his head and shifted uncomfortably in his seat.

'You're shaking your head like you don't believe me,' Spud said.

'It's not that I don't believe you, it's just…'

'Is it partly to do with Kitty and stuff?'

Theo gave a small sigh and looked towards the window, tapping his fingertips on the tabletop. He was someone who discussed land prices, wine, the weather, cars, politics, food and sport – not 'stuff'. He swallowed and spoke slowly. 'I know very few people who grow older with the express desire not to become a parent; some do, I'm sure, but I feel like an oddity, like I'm going against the grain.'

'But you are a parent!' Spud said quietly.

'Yes. But not in any way that anyone would notice, not in any way that counts! Fucking hell, I don't even know if my child is a boy or a girl. And I do know that the mother took one look at me and ran for the bloody hills!' He said this a little louder and more sternly than he intended and certainly than he was comfortable with. He wiped the corners of his mouth with his thumb and forefinger. 'I'm sorry, Spud, it's a subject I find difficult enough to fence with at home, let alone having to do it here in the pub too.'

'No need to apologise, mate. It's raw, I get it, but the fact that it makes you so mad means it is unresolved.'

'I guess.' Theo stretched out his legs and crossed his ankles.

'Have you told Anna about—'

'No.' Theo shook his head. 'How can I? I tried when we first got together, I've tried many other times and I did actually try again when we were in the Maldives, but... well, we were having a row, and she looked so broken already, so I chickened out and ended up telling her about my so-called brother Alexander. And she thought that was shocking enough.' He shook his head. 'Christ, she is so intent on becoming a mother, she even writes to her future kids! She's given them names, Fifi and Fox, and she scribbles notes to them, telling them all sorts. Who the fuck does that? It's the most enormous pressure.'

'I think part of the pressure is that you're keeping a secret that's directly related to what she wants most. Your kid with Kitty, not telling Anna and her drive to become a mum, it's all different parts of the same problem.'

Theo looked at his mate. 'You think I don't know that?' He nodded. 'But how can I have another child when there is already one in the world that I have nothing to do with?' The nerve in his jaw twitched angrily. 'I can't do it.'

'I think it's a shame. You have so much to offer a child.'

'You mean the money, the house.'

'No, mate.' Spud laughed. 'Not the money! It's not about that, although that helps. What you have to offer are all the good things that make you you. You're funny and smart, and you're kind, Theo, one of the good guys, and those are not bad qualities to pass on, to share.'

'Thank you.' He meant it. 'And you're right, no amount of money in the bank matters when the world feels like a hostile place.' He pictured himself as a child crying into his pillow. 'But what I don't have, I suppose, is the... the confidence.'

'You think I don't know *that*?' Spud countered.

Theo gave him a dry smile; his friend's humour was stronger than his own dark mood. 'Truth is, I've always been worried about turning out like my father, and then the Kitty thing happened and it made me exactly like him!'

'No, it didn't. He had his circumstances, of which you know very little, and you had yours. All your choices were taken out of your hands – you are *not* a bad person, Theo, quite the opposite.'

'I'm not sure Anna would see it as different.' Theo downed the rest of his pint and ran his fingers through his hair.

'You'll never know unless you tell her.'

'God, Spud, to hear her crying herself to sleep, and to have to answer her questions over and over as to why we can't have a baby, it kills me to know how much anguish I'm causing her. If she knew there was a child out there, my child, it would destroy her.'

Spud took a deep breath. 'I can't imagine keeping something so big from Kumi. And I really think Anna would understand. I think her joy at becoming a mum would outweigh everything else.'

Again there was a moment of silence as Theo considered his words. 'I spent days and nights trying to hide from the world, trying to make myself invisible. I can't put a child through that. I won't. And it's made me this... this...' He struggled to find the right words. '... this glass-half-empty kind of guy, no matter what. And yet Anna...' He shook his head admiringly. 'She had the very worst of starts but doesn't let it define her, in fact the opposite, she's nearly always sunny. Whereas me...'

'I think that with you, Theo, it's more about your ability to shake off past unhappiness, to recognise you're a different person now.'

'Or rather my inability.'

'Yes. Exactly.' Spud lifted his pint pot and wiped his beer tash with the back of his hand. 'Well, I certainly thought tonight was going to be more of a celebration.' He folded his arms over his chest.

'I'm sorry. You're right.' Theo clapped his hands. 'So, the big old U S of A! Mr Mega Job. Working in a thinktank, whatever that is!' He grinned. 'I can only picture humans in a giant fish tank with thought bubbles and all wearing goggles.'

'And that would mostly be correct. Kumi's getting my flippers and trunks ready as we speak.'

Theo noted the slightest twitch to Spud's eye. 'Are you nervous?'

'A bit, but as I often say to myself, the decision you make is always the right one – that way you remove the self-doubt and just bloody get on with it!'

'Amen to that.' Theo raised his hand for a high five, which Spud made a show of ignoring.

They both laughed, then exchanged a look, before Theo, embarrassed, jumped up. 'Same again?'

'Yup.' Spud drained his glass.

★ ★ ★

It was raining as Theo and Spud left the pub and emerged onto the Strand. Theo lifted his suit lapels and held them closed over his cotton shirt, letting his finger run over the little fishing fly that sat discreetly beneath. 'I can't believe you're going to the bloody States. I'm actually going to miss you.' He punched his friend lightly on the arm.

'You must promise to come and see us. Kumi and Anna can enjoy the delights of Washington and you and I can drink beer.'

'You always say that, but we'd get stuck with Miyu while they go off, meaning beer will become coffee. The last time we babysat, I ended up getting a makeover!'

Both men laughed at the memory of how Spud's daughter with her dad's help had gone to town with her face paints.

'You should be honoured that you're her favourite godfather.'

'I'm her only godfather!'

'Good point.'

Thunder rolled overhead and the rain got heavier.

'It's only a plane-ride away.' Spud nodded, a little choked.

'Yep.' Theo looked at the pavement, where fat raindrops bounced on the grey slabs. 'Who'd have thought we'd be standing here like this all these years after I first met you. I remember when you knocked on the door of my room in halls. I hadn't even unpacked. And there you were, skinny and geeky and you called me Cleo, said it was because you were from Wigan!' He laughed.

'I was panicking! You were the poshest person I'd ever spoken to and it threw me. My mum told me to knock on the door of my neighbours and ask if they fancied a beer. I was bricking it, but she said it was a failsafe.'

'Turns out Ma Spud was right.'

'She usually is. Christ, I thought it would be one quick drink, I never expected I'd still be lumbered with you thirteen years later!' Theo smiled at him. This move was a big deal. 'This is just the beginning, mate – we have a lot of years to cover yet and a lot more beer to consume.'

'Do you think they have scampi in Washington?' Spud scuffed his shoe on the wet ground.

'Probably. But I think it's called "scayumpee".' Theo tried out his appalling American accent.

The two stood awkwardly, using the banter to mask their sadness.

'Come here!' Spud reached out and embraced Theo warmly, hugging him a little more tightly than was comfortable. He released him and shook his hand firmly.

'I'll see you soon.' Theo coughed and slapped his friend on the shoulder.

'Yes, mate. I'll see you soon. And you know where I am if you need me.'

Theo raised his hand in acknowledgement, then turned and walked away.

He was glad of the rain. Somehow it helped dilute the emotion of their parting. He disliked the hollow feeling in his chest, which felt a lot like loss. Unwilling to go home just yet, he wandered past Charing Cross train station and stood on the corner, staring at Trafalgar Square. The bronze lions gleamed majestically in the downpour and the lamplight was hazy overhead as raindrops punctured the surface of the fountain pools. This was the London he loved, when the shiny façade and the crisp flags laid on for the tourists were removed and the beating heart of the capital was laid bare. Running his hand through his hair, he dusted the rain from his short crop and rubbed his face.

Get a grip, Theo!

It was as he ambled towards Whitehall, dithering over whether to go back to the pub and sink another pint alone or whether to trot down to the Embankment and walk along the river, that the number 53 bus drew up alongside him. Something about the shape of the figure in the window of the top deck made him turn and look up. It was a silhouette he'd carried in his mind since he was fourteen. There in the front seat, gazing into the distance, sat Kitty Montrose.

Theo quickly glanced down the street, searching for Spud, wanting to point her out, needing if not his mate's support then at least someone to share the moment with. His heart skipped a beat. Just the sight of her made his pulse race faster, taking him back to his unrequited teens and then that glorious afternoon together back when he was at UCL. But then came the stab to his chest and the memory of her letter.

If our paths should ever cross, please respect my wish for us to never mention this. I beg you, Theo. This is the only way I can build a life. Please.

I say goodbye now…

'What if, actually, it wasn't only your call to make, Kitty? Why did I not have a say?' he muttered under his breath.

As if on autopilot, Theo freed his hands from his pockets and broke into a run, looking ahead at the traffic lights and thankful that they were still on red. With his eyes trained on the bus, he collided with a group of men, all in suits and all, like him, looking as if they'd enjoyed one or two drinks after work.

'Watch where you're going, prick!' one yelled.

Theo lifted his hand over his shoulder. That would have to be apology enough; he didn't want to lose sight of the number 53.

Running and slipping in his smooth-soled brogues on the wet pavement, he raced up the street, overtook the bus and came to a halt at the next bus stop. His chest ached and he had a stitch in his side. He smiled at the driver as he boarded, flashing his travel card and holding the rail as the double-decker pulled away from the kerb. Slowly, slowly he trod the narrow stairs.

The bus was warm; gloved hands had wiped viewing portholes in its steamed-up windows and the air was pungent with the smell of damp wool. With only a couple of other passengers upstairs, Theo had a clear view of the back of Kitty's head. Her hair, still red, had dulled a little and she had lopped it off to shoulder length. Suddenly shy, he wondered how he might justify his presence there – what should he say? He also thought of Anna, waiting for him at home, and he swallowed his guilt at having chased the bus for a chance to say 'hi' to Kitty. How would he explain that?

Why was he so keen to see her again? He stopped in his tracks halfway up the stairs, taken aback at the spontaneity of his actions. He was hardly still holding a candle for her. No, it wasn't that – there was more anger in him now. He wanted... He wanted to show her that she'd misjudged him. Wanted to show her he wasn't the weedy weirdo she thought he was. Wanted her to see that he'd found happiness too.

He gripped the rail at the top of the stairs and hovered in the aisle.

Kitty turned towards the window and looked out at the dark street ahead. It was as he studied her profile and prepared what he might say that a child's head bobbed up into view on the seat next to her. At this, Theo's legs turned to jelly. A child! His child!

He quickly sloped down the aisle and sat down as inconspicuously as possible. His heart beat loudly in his ears and his knees shook. The child was wearing a woolly hat. It was red with a blue band, the kind that a boy or girl might wear. The child's shoulders were slight beneath its navy duffle coat. Theo recalled owning a similar coat at a similar age and felt a flare of joy at this tiny connection of sorts.

He was transfixed by the pair, noting their gentle interaction as Kitty bent her head to better hear the soft voice by her side. He was touched by the way she laughed gently, placing a hand against a cheek he couldn't see.

It was a surreal situation. The child had to be about ten. His child, his flesh and blood, now sat no more than twenty feet away, but oblivious. Theo glanced towards the staircase and was wondering if he should leave when all of a sudden the child knelt up on the seat and turned to face the back of the bus. Kitty, still looking forward, placed her arm across the navy duffle coat to ensure that her child wouldn't fall if the bus braked suddenly.

Theo's breath caught in his throat as he stared into the child's face – the face of a pretty, bright little girl. *A girl! A little girl!* His daughter. She had her mother's freckles and the same upturn to the tip of her nose, but her dark curly hair, her brown eyes and the shape of her mouth were his.

She looked like him!

He remembered Anna telling him how as a teenager she used to flag down taxi drivers on the off-chance, hoping that one of them would be her dad and thinking that she'd instantly know when she found him because looks and shared genes would make it obvious they were father and daughter. *You were right, Anna. I am looking at her and she is looking at me and I know, I just know...*

'Sit round now, please, Sophie.' Kitty spoke sternly, loudly.

Sophie! Sophie! The word rang in his head like a note. His daughter was called Sophie.

'I'm waiting to go round a corner.' Sophie gripped the back of the seat and leant out towards the aisle, her tongue poking from the side of her mouth.

Adventurous and fearless – a warrior like your mum.

'You are not going to do that, you'll fall, so please sit round now!'

Yes, keep her safe, Kitty, keep her safe.

Maybe she was drawn by his stare, or perhaps she too sensed

the shape of a face she'd known since she was fourteen. Either way, Kitty turned round and looked directly at Theo.

There was a moment of stunned silence before she placed a shaking hand over her mouth and blinked furiously. Floored by her reaction, having anticipated something different, Theo again looked towards the stairs, wondering now how to leave without making a fuss.

They were both frozen in shock, anchored to the spot. Theo looked from Kitty to Sophie and she did the same, their frantic stares joining the dots.

'Don't cry,' he whispered under his breath. 'Please don't cry. I won't cause any trouble. I didn't know she would be here.' She! Sophie...

Kitty pulled a tissue from her sleeve, dotted her pretty green eyes and wiped her freckled nose. She popped the tissue into the pocket of her voluminous mac and reached into the small space on the floor, from where she retrieved her handbag. Theo noted a wide gold band glistening on the third finger of her left hand.

The two continued to stare at each other. Then she stretched up and rang the bell. The bus slowed.

'Come on, darling.' With false brightness and a sense of urgency, she ushered Sophie from the seat, following close behind.

'Why did you press the bell, Mummy?' Sophie asked, her voice well-spoken.

The two stopped at the top of the stairs, only inches from him now, both swaying a little, waiting for the bus to come to a halt. They were within touching distance, these two who in another life, if things had been different, might have been his family.

It was eleven years since he'd last seen Kitty. He noted the creep of fine creases at the edges of her eyes and the fact that her lips had lost some of their fullness. He lowered his gaze and was drawn by the unmistakeable baby bump protruding over the waistband of her jeans. She cradled her stomach protectively. He gave a small smile, thankful that things had worked out with Angus and hoping they shared the happiness he and Anna enjoyed.

'Where are we going, Mummy?' Sophie laughed. 'We aren't at Blackheath yet.'

Blackheath – is that where you live? Are you heading home?

Kitty pulled her head back on her shoulders and narrowed her eyes at Theo, warning him to stay quiet. 'I want to get off now, darling.' He felt a spike of guilt at the tremor to her voice, the fear in her eyes. 'We can… We can get the next bus.'

'Why are we going to do that?' Sophie asked.

'Just because!' Flustered, she snapped at her daughter in the Scottish accent that had always sounded to his ears like the sweetest music.

He made as if to rise, indicating he would get off with them, but she gave a single vigorous shake of her head, her mouth set.

Theo hardly dared breathe. Kitty's tears gathered again, and she cuffed them with the back of her hand. He smiled at Sophie as she passed and she returned his smile with a curve to her lips that mirrored his own. Her dark, shining eyes fixed on his; eyes that were just like his.

He listened to the sound of their footsteps and Sophie's stream of questions, which continued until they were out of earshot. He placed his daughter's sweet voice in the middle of his memory, knowing he'd probably never get to hear it again. Craning his neck towards the window, he looked down onto the rain-soaked street and saw nothing but darkness.

The bus trundled on. Theo sat for some time before jumping off in an open spot on the outskirts of Blackheath. Unsure of where he was heading or even in what direction, he moved briskly with his hands in his pockets, thankful that the rain had eased and too preoccupied to notice the chill in the air. He looked up at the purple bruise of sky as thunder rumbled over the river in the distance. It felt like an omen. The storm he thought he'd outrun was in fact catching up with him. *I must tell Anna. I need to tell her about Sophie.*

Crossing a main road, he found himself heading in the direction of Greenwich Park. And just like that he was crying, sobbing so loudly and with such force it became hard to take a breath. He cried for the fact that his best mate was leaving London for Washington, he cried for Sophie, who would live a life without him, but most of his tears were for his beloved Anna and what he was unable to give her.

As the strength left his legs, he sat on the kerb, hardly aware of the traffic that flew past. He thought of his Anna, who would be padding around the house waiting for the sound of his key in the door. Beautiful, sweet Anna who had been through so much and deserved so much more than this. Anna, who would give anything to feel the swell of her belly under a mackintosh, her skin stretched with his child, growing inside.

I'm sorry, Anna. I am so, so sorry. I'm not good enough. You shouldn't have picked me. Kitty was right; fatherhood is not the path for me. I am not that person. You should have picked anyone but me.

Twelve

Theo flattened his tie to his chest and wiped the corners of his mouth with his thumb and forefinger, a habit he'd developed to clear away any stray bits of food or spittle. He knocked and entered his father's office, which was across the corridor from his own.

'Dad, I—' He stopped.

A dark-haired young woman was perched on the edge of the oval table where the board usually met. She abruptly uncrossed her legs and stood up. Her smile faded, as did his father's. Theo felt self-conscious and unwelcome. It was the feeling he often had with his parents, the sense that he was an unwanted guest for whom no place had been set.

'Sorry, I didn't realise you had company.' He kept his eyes on his father, noting the slight flush to the bulge of fat that had recently appeared above his dad's starched shirt collar. His father wore the glazed expression he always had when in the company of a pretty woman. Theo felt the first stirrings of nausea. 'I'll come back later.' He pointed to the door.

'No, not at all. Theo, this is Marta, our new intern. She'll be here for the next few months, learning about the world of corporate property. She has a degree,' he added, as if this was something of a surprise. Theo's father and his cronies were always wary of women who had both beauty and brains.

'Good for you.' Theo smiled in her direction.

Clearly confident in her position, she responded by pulling a face at him that in any other circumstances might have been childish, with the hint of a snarl to her top lip.

'Tell you what, Marta,' Perry Montgomery said, 'why don't you take an early lunch and we'll see you back here in an hour or so?'

'Thank you. See you in a bit.' She bobbed her head and left the room, letting her challenging gaze linger on Theo.

The two men waited until the door had closed behind her before resuming their conversation.

'She's *very* smart.' His father coughed.

'So you said.' Theo really was heartily sick of his dad's roving eye and disregard for his mum's feelings. 'You know, Dad, any of the heads of department would be happy to show Marta round. You're the chairman of this company, you don't have to be so hands on, especially with something that's of no real benefit.'

His father stared at him and licked his lower lip. His eyes darted round the room and he seemed to be deciding how best to respond. Then he sat forward with his hands in a pyramid on the leather-topped desk, apparently having chosen to ignore Theo's comment.

'What was it that you wanted to see me about?' He pointed to the chair.

Theo sat. 'I've... I've had an idea.' He felt his confidence ebbing.

'Go on.' Perry lifted his chin, listening.

Theo gave a nervous laugh, wary of beginning. 'This is going to sound a bit leftfield, but it's something I've been thinking about for a while, a slightly different direction.' He waited for an interjection, a loaded question, but it didn't come and so he continued. 'I want to buy an old spice warehouse in the Bristol docklands that's come up for sale. It's semi-derelict and surrounded by wasteland, but it's very close to the redeveloped town centre and the waterfront and I'm sure the whole area is going to explode, which means it will only go up in value.' He paused, again waiting for his father to comment, but he didn't. 'And while we have this beautiful property, while we're waiting for it to go up in value, I've thought of a way that it can do some good too, for the community.'

A slight smile crossed his father's lips. 'Some good for the community, you say?'

Emboldened, Theo sat forward and, leaning on the desk, he spoke with passion. 'As you know, Anna is a rare graduate of the care system. She's strong and special, she's a success story, but there are so many kids who come out of the care system and fall through the cracks, as if the jump is too big from care home to regular life.' He recalled Anna telling him about her former roommate, Shania, who'd apparently become homeless and an addict. 'I want to convert the warehouse into pods, not overly grand or over-engineered but studios that kids leaving care could live in until they're on their feet and working or studying or whatever. It would be the missing link in the care system and it could make a massive difference.'

'Bristol? What do you know about Bristol?' his father scoffed, rather missing the point.

Theo held his nerve. 'Enough to know that its property prices are rising by a healthy percentage year on year. The rise in equity would be commensurate with some of our lower rental gains in other areas where property values are stagnant. The warehouse would be a valuable asset, but mainly, Dad, it's the idea of providing these places for kids who need them, kids who are vulnerable. It's the chance to help turn them into adults with self-esteem, into good citizens. We win, society wins.'

Perry looked down. 'And can I ask, did you recite that from one of your textbooks?'

Theo shook his head and chose not to take the bait. 'I'm serious, Dad.'

'Warehouses?'

'Yes, once used for tobacco and spice storage mainly, built in the 1800s. They're crying out for renovation, they'd be perfect for the sort of loft living that's done so well in London's docklands.'

His father sat back in his chair. 'It's one thing building flats in the suburbs or remodelling old cinemas within the M25, but sending a crew down to Bristol, out of sight and out of reach? And doing so to satisfy some liberal touchy-feely do-gooder need? It feels like too much of a risk.' His father took a breath and sized up his son. 'You need to remember, Theo, that we have close alliances with the planners in London. Very close alliances.'

'Close alliances,' Theo was all too well aware, was code for the brown envelopes stuffed with cash that were routinely handed over in exchange for permissions granted. These turned risky investments into dead certs and grew the bank balances of petty officials in the process. He had been told long ago that that was just the way things worked.

He ignored his father's jibe. 'I get that, but this feels like an opportunity and I was thinking it might be good to get away from London, breathe some different air and follow my dream of making a difference.' He let this hang.

'You want to get away?' His father narrowed his eyes and set his mouth.

'Not get away completely, no, but venture elsewhere… try something new.' His nerves bit.

'Yes, Theo, of course, why didn't I think of it? Why would anyone risk investing only in London, one of the world's property hotspots since… for ever, when I could convert a warehouse into homes for junkies!' Perry was on a roll now. 'It's bloody genius! And anyway, what would Anna make of you swanning off to Bristol, eh? Wouldn't she rather you stayed here and grew that family of yours?'

Theo flinched. His parents did this, used Anna as a bargaining chip whenever the need arose, and yet they made very little effort with her most of the time. But, again, he decided not to bite. 'I wouldn't be swanning off.' He looked into his lap, unwilling to admit that in his father's expressions he saw more than a hint of amusement at the fact that his marriage, like the rest of his life, was, in his view, far from perfect. 'I'd be based here but overseeing the project—'

'I won't be taking it to the board.' Perry stopped him short, lifting his chin. 'I just don't think you have it in you, my boy. After all, your track record, flunking university and all that, doesn't really inspire confidence, does it? As for Bristol warehouses, well, we'll leave those for the carrot crunchers to get stuck into!' He laughed.

Theo met his stare, frustration bubbling in his gut. He wasn't willing to roll over just yet. 'Maybe if I showed you the site plans and explained my ideas—'

'I have given you my answer, Theodore,' his father cut in, 'and as far as I know, it is still my name above the door, at least for a few years yet.' He gave a nasal chortle.

When he'd got home that evening, all Theo had wanted was supper and sleep. But he'd returned to Barnes to find Anna in a highly emotional state. Her half-sister had just given her a photo of Anna as a baby in the arms of both her father and her mother and, unsurprisingly, Anna had been over the moon about it. Unfortunately, though, this had led on to another discussion about Anna's desperate desire for a baby of her own. And, as was so often these days, this had developed into a big row, with tears and recriminations and a sense that they were never going to see eye to eye on this.

It had been a testing evening at the end of a testing day and Theo was relieved to finally get in the shower and let the cascade of hot water soothe away some of his fatigue. It irked him more than he was able to admit that his father had given so little attention to his proposition. He'd put so much thought into his pitch, had spent hours working out exactly how to present it, and all for nothing. What sort of father relished making his son feel so insignificant? What sort of father made his son feel like a failure however hard he tried?

Thinking about his own father inevitably led Theo on to thinking about Sophie. Ever since he'd seen Kitty and Sophie on the bus, the image of the two of them had rarely been far from his thoughts. He heard Sophie's girlish voice as he fell asleep, he pictured her big smile and innocent dark eyes, and he saw Kitty's horrified expression, her speedy exit from the bus. The message had been loud and clear, and it hurt. It hurt him more than he was able to express, and even if he had felt able, with Spud in the States he had absolutely no one to express it to. He found it hard to concentrate and he was conscious of the fact he'd been more irritable with Anna of late, on a shorter fuse. He felt bad about the row earlier on – it wasn't Anna's fault, he knew that, but even so... He just couldn't face discussing parenthood right now, not with Sophie in his thoughts so much, and the warehouse project, and his dad's intransigence. The black shadow of depression seemed to be coming scarily close again.

Reluctantly Theo stepped from the shower and put on his sweatpants and sweatshirt. He didn't know if Anna had let Griff, their new Alsatian-cross rescue puppy, out for his night-time wee and he thought he might run him quickly round the block. The fresh air might help clear his head and perhaps then he'd have a better chance of getting some sleep.

Theo descended the stairs and ran through what he wanted to say to Anna. He didn't want to go to bed on a row and he loathed seeing her upset. The least he could do was apologise and explain how he felt about his dad's behaviour.

Griff was making a low growl, which was curious because as long as their beloved pup was within sight of one or both of them, all was usually right with his world. As if urged by a sixth sense, Theo quickened his pace, just in time to see Anna stumble backwards and tumble to the kitchen floor. *What the hell...?*

'Anna!' he yelled, racing to her side. She'd hit her head and seemed to be out cold. 'Anna! Anna!' he yelled again, his voice loud and panicky now.

Griff growled and yelped. Theo kissed Anna's forehead, her hair, put his ear next to her heart. He couldn't tell whether he was hearing something or not, he was too scared, his own heart was racing like a train. He wasn't helping. Inhaling deeply, he made himself calm down. He gently lifted Anna's right arm and held his finger against her wrist, checking her pulse. He made himself pay attention. The pulse was there. He gulped and sobbed, then yanked the blue linen dishcloth from the Aga door and folded it into a cushion between her head and the cold floor.

'It's okay, Griff, it's okay, boy!' He tried to reassure the pup, who stood alarmed and whimpering now, next to his basket. Theo grabbed his phone from the tabletop and dialled 999. 'Ambulance! I need an ambulance, please, quickly. It's my wife, she's collapsed…'

As soon as he finished the call, he opened the front door wide, then raced back to sit on the floor with Anna. He took her limp hand inside his and cooed to her, kissing her fingers and wiping her hair from her pale face. 'It's okay, Anna. The ambulance is on its way. They'll be here in a second, don't you worry.' He kept talking, as much to allay his own fears as to reassure her.

With one hand still clamped to Anna's, he reached for the pen and paper that was lying on the table, thinking it might be helpful to note down Anna's pulse rate before the paramedics turned up. He never got round to doing that, because the top sheet of paper had already been used. Anna had written one of her letters to her imaginary children, Fifi and Fox, presumably while he'd been showering. His breath caught in his throat as he read it.

Fifi and Fox,
Here it is.
    I have never been so close to giving up on my dream of you.
Never.

I sit here at the kitchen table, writing with tears trickling down my face at these words. It's a hard thing for me to write, and an even harder thing to imagine. But, like always, I have to try and carry on, find the good, because there is one thing I know with absolute certainty and it's this – if I give in to the deep, cold sadness that lurks inside me, if I submit to the lonely longing for the people who have left me and the things I can't have, then the darkness will take hold. It will fill me right up and it will drown me.

I can't let that happen. Because while I am here there is always hope. Know, my darlings, that life is worth living. Life is worth living! It's up to us what shape that life takes. I had reason more than most to let my life crush me, but I didn't let it. I fought against it. And I will keep fighting – fighting to find the happy in this good, lucky life I have made, this life I share with Theo.

I will keep positive. I won't give up. I won't.

Anna
(I hardly dare write Mummy – it feels a lot like tempting fate.)

Theo howled as he reached the last line. 'Oh, my Anna, I am so sorry! I am. I can't lose you! I can't! You are all I've got. You are the only one who understands, who loves me. Please don't leave me, Anna, please, I'm begging you…' He bent low and kissed her again, feverishly and repeatedly. 'Where the fuck is the ambulance?' he yelled towards the door. Every minute felt like an eternity. 'Don't leave me, Anna, please! I'll do anything to keep you alive, to keep you loving me! I'll… I'll have a child with you! We can do it! We can make Fifi and Fox, we can.

I can't bear for you to not have what you want. I don't know how I'll cope, but I will, somehow, and I will do it for you! I will do anything. Just please don't leave me.'

Finally Griff started barking and there came the sound of footsteps on the gravel path. Two paramedics, a man and a woman, both wearing green overalls, ran into the kitchen and gently eased his wife from his grip.

'Is... Is she going to be okay?' Theo swallowed, placing his hands on his hips and trying to keep it together.

The female paramedic looked up at him. 'Let's get her to the hospital, then she'll be in the best place.'

The next few hours were a nightmarish blur. Anna was whisked off into the inner reaches of the hospital and Theo was left in the visitors' room with only his thoughts and a plate of custard creams for company. His mind couldn't settle and he kept going over the last few weeks, trying to recall if Anna had shown any signs of being unwell. Had she mentioned anything, any pains or headaches? He wracked his brain. He'd been so wrapped up in planning the Bristol project, and there'd been Kitty and Sophie, and Spud leaving... He definitely hadn't been giving her as much attention as she needed. And then there was the baby thing. He kept replaying the words of her letter. There was so much sadness there, so much grief. He paced around the visitors' room, desperate to avoid the obvious conclusion but coming back to it again and again: had she collapsed because of their row, because she'd been so upset? He stopped in his tracks, stood up straight and made a decision. He'd made a pact as she lay on the kitchen floor and he would stick to it.

The nurse came in and she was smiling! Relief flooded through him.

'Your wife is comfortable now, Mr Montgomery. She's asleep, so you probably won't get much out of her for a few hours, but you're welcome to come and sit with her if you'd like to.'

Theo needed no second invitation. He sat beside Anna through the dawn and on into the morning, clasping her, sobbing intermittently, willing her to be all right. As soon as she woke, he told her what he'd decided.

'So, I've been thinking, Anna, I want to give you what you want. I will need your help, but we should go for it, we should have our baby. Our baby! I decided, last night when you were lying there on the floor, I decided that I'd been selfish and unfair and cowardly and that I couldn't bear not to have you with me and so I made a promise to myself that—'

'Oh, Theo!' She hoisted herself up in the bed and stared at him. 'You mean it?'

'I do.' He smiled. 'We can do it together, right?'

'Yes! Yes, my darling, that's right, we can do it together!' She reached for him and snuggled into his arms.

Not five minutes after he'd told Anna about his change of heart, her room started filling up with visitors, rather robbing them of the moment. Much to his surprise, in came Anna's friend Melissa, then Sylvie, the mother of her ex, and then his own mother. He was touched at their concern, but he worried that the party-like atmosphere might all be too much for Anna. In truth, though, she had beamed at all the new arrivals and it seemed they were just the distraction she needed.

He decided to leave them to it for a brief while. He took a minute to sit outside the room, relishing the moment of solitude and glad to be away from the hubbub. He leant against the wall and tried to stem the shake to his limbs. The medics had discovered an irregular heartbeat, which Anna had tried to dismiss with shrugs and glibly offered statistics. But he was less convinced, all too aware of her mum's shockingly premature death and keen to find out what could be done to prevent her collapsing again in the future.

He was relieved when the visitors finally left, traipsing past him and offering to help in any way they could.

Melissa kissed him firmly. 'Call me, let me know what she needs, anything at all, and I can be there in minutes.'

Sylvie wagged a nicotine-stained finger at him. 'You take care of her, lovely boy, and you take care of yourself!'

'I will.'

His mother hovered, waiting until the other two were out of earshot. 'Keep us posted, darling.'

'I will, Mum, and thank you for coming.'

'Not at all. An interesting bunch.' She looked towards Melissa and Sylvie.

Theo chose not to react; a hospital corridor was neither the time nor place.

Stella cleared her throat. 'It wants keeping an eye on, that heart thing.' She nodded towards the door of Anna's room as she looped her pashmina around her neck.

'Yes, I know.' He watched his mum sashay along the corridor towards the exit. 'And I shall keep an eye on my own heart too,' he muttered, 'because if anything happens to Anna it will break.' He took a deep breath, assumed an air of confidence and opened the door to Anna's room.

He took up the seat next to her bed and held her hand.

It was only a few minutes later that the consultant reappeared. He flipped the pages of his notes, then held the clipboard behind his back. 'We have all your test results, Mrs Montgomery.'

Theo sat forward in the chair, trying to remain calm. He was a lot more concerned than Anna seemed to be.

'As we discussed earlier, your heart is nothing to worry about at this stage, but with your family history we will keep an eye on it.'

'Thank you.' Anna squeezed Theo's hand and raised her eyebrows as if to say, *ha, I told you, nothing to worry about.*

'There was something else, however.' The consultant paused and Theo felt as if those five words had sucked all the air from the room. He felt lightheaded and nauseous, desperately afraid of what might come next. With good reason, as it turned out.

'We ran some blood tests,' the consultant continued, 'and your hormones are drastically out of balance. It would seem that you are in the middle of an early menopause.'

Anna slowly let go of Theo's hand and sat up in the bed. 'What does that mean?' she whispered.

'It means, Anna, that your fertility is coming to an end.'

'No more periods,' she whispered. 'No baby. Oh, Theo! No... no... baby. Not now. Not ever. Not... with you. Not with anyone.' She sobbed into her sleeve.

The consultant left almost immediately and the two of them sat there with the ramifications of this 'something else' spinning around them. It was like they were caught in a tornado that was ripping apart everything they thought they knew. It did so at speed and with such force it left them breathless.

'No, Theo! Please, no! It's all I ever wanted!' Anna cried

noisily, messily, clinging onto him as if for dear life. 'I wanted my babies. That is all I have ever wanted! Please, Theo. Oh God! Please, no!'

Theo had no idea how to console her. What could he say? What could he do? Only hours ago it seemed like they'd finally agreed to do this thing together, and she'd been so elated, brimming with joy at the prospect. But now... God, what a mess. The worst day of his life by far.

As he sat there with Anna wrapped in his arms, rocking her gently, he realised with surprise that he wasn't only desperately sad for her, he was sad for both of them. The idea of becoming a father had started to take root, and now that the possibility had been so brutally taken away, he felt deflated, denied the challenge. There had to be another way, didn't there?

They continued sitting there until Anna had calmed sufficiently and felt ready to pack up and go home. Theo made his way to the bathroom, leaving her alone for a few minutes, and decided to call his mother as he'd promised.

'Yes, Theodore?' His mother did this, always made it seem as if now was the worst possible time to phone her. It took him back to Vaizey, to when he was a small boy standing in Twitcher's study, praying that she'd pick up the phone.

'The consultant has just left and, er, we've had some bad news, I'm afraid.'

'Oh, Theo, dear—'

He sighed, swallowed, and blurted it out. 'We've just found out that Anna is going through an early menopause. So that means—'

'Yes, dear, I am aware of what it means.' She tutted disapprovingly, as if reminding Theo that it was not the done thing to discuss bodily functions and especially not women's health issues. A wave of embarrassment washed over him.

He pictured the note sitting on the kitchen table:

I have never been so close to giving up on my dream of you. Never.

I sit here at the kitchen table, writing with tears trickling down my face at these words. It's a hard thing for me to write, and an even harder thing to imagine…

Oh, Anna! My Anna! Coughing away his emotion, he decided he was after all in no mood to talk to his mother. A bolt of frustration shot through him. What had he expected – support, kindness? He was about to phrase his goodbyes when his mother interjected.

'I did want grandchildren eventually – what a shame. And I think Daddy is similarly minded. Not that we've discussed it, but I know he would like someone to carry on the Montgomery name and all that. Still, life is a long and winding road, as they say. Who knows what's around the corner?'

Theo's anger boiled. What she was she implying? That he would leave Anna and find a second wife to provide them with a grandchild? His skin prickled with fury and he could barely find the words. 'You are fucking kidding me!' was what he came up with, and with that he ended the call.

He paced the corridor, his stomach in knots of anger and grief, steeling himself to go back into the ward.

'How are you doing?' he whispered to Anna, who looked small and fragile sitting on the hospital bed. It was as if the news of her infertility had made her shrink.

She shrugged and bit her lip. Her eyes were swollen from all the crying and she looked wretched. Theo's heart contracted. It tore at him to see her like that.

He took up the seat by her bedside and again reached for her hand. 'I meant what I said earlier about making a pact when you were on the kitchen floor, when I thought...' He gulped. 'When I thought I might lose you.'

She turned her head towards him.

'I meant every word – that we should have a baby, that I will be a dad for you, with you.'

Her tears fell quickly and her voice when it came was barely more than a whisper. 'Bit late now,' she managed.

Theo's stomach churned. She was blaming him and he deserved it. But he would make it right. He would try and put his past behind him and do right by Anna. 'No, my darling! There will be a way. We'll find a way. We could... We could adopt! We could become parents that way – we could do it, we could!' He gripped her tight, hoping this might be something they could focus on. 'You know more than most how every kid needs a home. We might not be able to... to have a child, but we can help one. Give one a happy home, just like you've always wanted. We can teach it like your mum taught you – how to be strong, how to survive!'

'Or two.' Anna managed a small smile. 'Two kids.'

His heart leapt with relief. 'Yes, my Anna. Or two.' He placed his head on the side of the bed and offered up a silent prayer.

Thirteen

'You have a lock of hair sticking up.' Anna spat on her palm and ran it over Theo's scalp. He found this both revolting and demeaning and he ruffled his hair as soon as she'd finished. She tutted at him, playfully. He pressed the front doorbell and stood in the porch, waiting, with her arm resting through his.

'I can't believe you don't have a key to your family home. That's so messed up.' Her words hung in the air like the after-burn of a sparkler writing in the dark.

'Anna, as you well know, there's lots about my family that is messed up. Denying me entry unless I come with a semi-formal invite to dinner is just one of them.' He gave her a false grin.

'Okay, well, I'm keeping a mental note, and your messed-up family is definitely not something we should mention at our adoption interview, okay?' She looked deadly serious.

'Okay.' He sighed, already wary of doing or saying the wrong thing at their introductory meeting, scheduled for the following week. 'I can't believe you're making us do this.'

Anna laughed. 'Honestly, you sound like you're twelve! I am not making you do anything! I just think that whatever beef you have with your mum is not going to be resolved by sitting at home and brooding. It's important you fix it – life is too bloody short.'

He smiled at her, his brilliant wife who was being so brave, with the news of her infertility still only a few weeks old. He had only told her vaguely about hanging up the phone on his mother at the hospital, but not the reasons why. 'I know you're right, but we're not staying long.'

'Wow! You have no idea how much I'm looking forward to tonight.' Her words dripped with sarcasm.

They were silent for a beat or two.

'What are we doing? They do this – they turn us into crazies!' He turned to her, his tone conciliatory. 'Shall we just go home and drink wine and have sex? Why don't we say you've got a headache?'

'Why do I have to be the one with the headache? You have the bloody headache! And besides, if I have a headache then sex is most definitely out of the question!'

'Actually, Anna, if you carry on shouting at me like that, I might just well have one.'

'Ah, there you are!' His mum opened the front door wide and greeted them warmly, kissing them both on each cheek as if there was nothing amiss. She had clearly dressed for dinner and was looking chic in her high-waisted navy palazzo pants and a cream silk shirt tucked in to show off her slender frame. There was a string of pearls at her neck and her hair was scraped back into a French knot.

'Come in! Come in!' She ushered them eagerly into the rarely used drawing room, her eyes bright.

He and Anna shared a look of mild concern. It had been years since Theo had seen his mother make such a fuss.

His father was standing by the fireplace; flames roared in the grate and logs crackled comfortingly. He was holding a glass of whisky and resting his elbow on the marble mantelpiece, looking very much like a portrait in oils.

There was a man sitting in the wing-backed chair behind the door. He stood up and Theo's eye was immediately drawn to the bootlace tie around his neck. The man's jacket was cut long, his jaw-length hair was slicked back with oil and he sported a large, drooping moustache. Theo guessed he was in his fifties.

Anna strolled across the room and kissed her father-in-law on the cheek.

'How are you doing now?' Perry boomed. 'The damnedest thing!'

'I am doing well, thank you.'

Theo's heart flexed as Anna painted on a smile, burying her sorrow. He knew she was well-practised at putting on a brave face; it was something she'd had to do a lot through her childhood. The weeks since the devastating news about her infertility had been terribly hard for her. Theo had taken some days off and they'd spent most of the time going for long walks with Griff, distracting themselves, focusing on their playful pup instead. Bit by bit Anna had thrown herself into researching the adoption process. Once he'd returned to work, she seemed to spend most of her days calling people, making appointments, getting books on the subject out of the library. Their conversations at night became dominated by her findings. He was pleased for her, and excited too. It was such a relief not to be arguing any more. Now at last they were united, and they were even able to laugh again together. He kept his doubts to himself and tried not to dwell on them, but every so often they surfaced. How much would he have to disclose, and did he really want to raise someone else's child when he already had one of his own?

His mother almost skipped back into the room, pulling him back to the present and to the strange guest standing among them.

'So, Theo...' She clapped and flicked her fringe flirtatiously. The blush to her cheek was one he hadn't seen in a while. 'This,' she announced with clarity and a determined emphasis, 'is Pastor Julian.' She gestured towards him as if she were a hostess on a TV gameshow highlighting the many attributes of a fridge-freezer.

The man stuck out his hand at an odd angle, making the handshake awkward. Theo knew that his father would be sharing the same thought: *not the Vaizey way...*

'*Pastor* Julian?' he queried.

'Please, call me Jules.'

The man had a deep voice that Theo could easily imagine preaching sermons of fire and brimstone. He was aware of his father's stare and the two exchanged a look that bordered on comical. To share anything with his father felt like a win and he enjoyed the interaction.

'This is my wife, Anna.' Theo held out his hand and pulled her over to receive her own odd handshake.

'Nice to meet you,' she offered and, as ever, Theo was touched by her sweet nature.

'Ah yes, Anna. I was so very sorry to hear about your recent bad news.' Pastor Julian nodded sagely, as if he had the measure of Anna.

It irritated and bemused Theo that this man had been given the lowdown on their lives. He looked at his mother, wondering what the hell was going on.

There was a pause while all five glanced from one to the other, unsure of what came next.

'Do you have a… Is your church local?' Theo faltered, wary of causing offence. His parents had never shown even the slightest interest in any religion. The only time he had seen them in a church was at weddings, christenings and funerals.

'It's not a church so much as a shed. In Putney!' his father interjected, loudly and with a wheezy rattle of laughter. This was followed by the clink of ice as he brought the tumbler of whisky to his mouth.

'Your dad's right. I minister in Putney, but the truth is my church is anywhere people need it to be.' Pastor Julian spoke with his palms upturned, as if halfway through a magic trick and keen to show he had nothing secreted up his sleeve.

His dad rolled his eyes behind the pastor's back and Theo had to admit that he found the man's theatricals more than a tad amusing.

'If you don't mind me asking, how do you all know each other?' Anna asked the obvious and most interesting question, pointing at them in turn with her index finger.

'Mrs Montgomery is a valued member of my congregation.' The pastor smiled at Theo's mother.

'My mother, a member of your congregation?' Theo laughed, waiting for the punchline. He didn't have to wait long.

'That's right, Theodore, isn't it marvellous! Your mother has found Jesus!' his father boomed. 'And not just regular Jesus, not your common-or-garden, couple-of-hymns, sign-of-the-cross type Jesus. Oh no. This church is something very special. It is a kind of magic church. I don't want to steal her thunder, but this week she has in fact been chatting to Great-Aunt Agatha

– the fact that the woman's been dead for nigh on thirty years is neither here nor there. Isn't it marvellous? Pastor Jules has a hotline to heaven! Who'd have thought it? Could you see your way to asking my Great-Uncle Maurice where he buried the family gold?' He chuckled and took another sip.

There was an uncomfortable silence while everyone waited for this new insight to settle. 'And as if that wasn't revelation enough, she found Jesus in the darndest place. Tell him, Stella. Tell the boy where you were when you had your epiphany.'

'Daddy is trying to be funny, but, yes, I have found Jesus. Or rather he found me.'

'And *where* did he find you?' His father wasn't going to let up.

His mother lost a little of her colour and Theo felt sorry that she was being put under the spotlight in this way. 'He found me in… in Marks and Spencer's.' She stuttered slightly but held his gaze.

The atmosphere at the dinner table was strained, to put it mildly. Theo's mother ferried the vintage tureens that had graced her own mother's dresser to the table and fussed over every detail, checking the saltcellar and wiping a smudge from Anna's wine glass. Eventually she perched herself on the edge of her seat, as if waiting for her next instruction.

Pastor Julian took in the sumptuous spread, coughed and announced, 'It would be my honour to say grace.'

This, despite the fact no one had asked him. Theo looked at his father, fully expecting a disdainful response, but Perry merely sucked in his cheeks, swirled an ice cube in his tumbler and stared at Pastor Julian, as though trying to figure him out. His mother clasped her hands earnestly and Theo did his best to avoid Anna's stare, desperate not to give in to the laughter that threatened.

The uncomfortable silences between mouthfuls meant that every dropped fork and each clang of a glass against a plate seemed to deepen the embarrassment of everyone present. Everyone except Pastor Julian, who seemed more than at home as he repeatedly dug the silver serving spoon deep into the dish of mashed potatoes and ladled chicken gravy over the top with relish. 'So, Anna, Stella tells me you were in care?' he said casually, almost as an aside.

Again, Theo was irritated by the pastor's tone. He watched Anna's face carefully as she responded, ready to swoop in and save her if need be.

'Yes. Yes, I was. From my early teens until I was eighteen.'

'You seem...'

Anna paused, holding her fork mid mouthful, waiting to hear what came next.

'You seem incredibly calm, astute, if you don't mind me saying.'

Anna's response was cool and well delivered. 'Well, that's very kind of you to say, but in my experience, people who have been in care are many and varied in their personalities and circumstances. I think it depends where you lived, who you lived with and why you were there in the first place.'

'And that is of course true, but still, the statistics would suggest that a life in care can lead to criminality, depression, drug abuse...'

Anna swallowed her mouthful and stayed calm. 'Sadly that is what the statistics say, but I'm not really one for statistics, 83.4 per cent of which are apparently made up on the spot.' She smiled at Theo and he laughed quietly, feeling a rush of love for her. 'Take my roommate, Shania. She and I were from not dissimilar backgrounds, and she nearly fell through the cracks after she left care. She was homeless not that long ago, in fact. But now she is clean, healthy and pregnant! I saw her just the other week, as it happens, for the first time in a long while, and it was a pleasure to see her doing so well.' She raised her glass and took a sip in honour of her friend. 'The secret is having somewhere safe to go when you leave care. Like Theo's idea for dedicated studio-homes for kids in Bristol, trying to give them a proper chance. Wouldn't that be wonderful?'

Theo held her gaze, quite overcome by her very public support for the project his father had been so derisive about.

Perry took the bait. 'Well, if Theo feels that strongly about those poor kids, he should fund the sodding project himself. How about that?' He banged the table. 'Or is that what this adoption malarkey is all about? Another do-gooders' attempt to make a difference? Can't see it myself, bringing up someone else's sprog – you surely never quite know what you're going to get! And the idea of him looking after a baby!' He pointed at Theo. 'He had a goldfish once, won it at a fair, don't think it lasted the night!'

The colour drained from Theo's face and he looked over at Anna, aghast. He'd told his parents in passing that they were exploring the idea of adoption, but of course they hadn't had a proper discussion about it – about that or anything in that vein. His dad's words cut him to the quick and he hated that it might be doing the same to Anna.

'It's okay,' she mouthed at him. 'I love you.'

He felt like weeping.

Stella sighed. 'Perry, please! That's quite enough! Do carry on, Anna.'

Anna was silent momentarily and then, to her absolute credit, she continued. 'I don't let my past define me, but also I don't forget it. I have learnt a lot through all of my experiences, I hope. Some good and some not so good.'

Theo eyed her across the table. *I am proud of you, my strong, lovely Anna.*

'And you were in care on account of losing all of your family?' Pastor Julian just couldn't seem to let the topic drop.

Theo clenched his teeth, holding back his anger.

'Yes, but I do have a half-sister and -brother here and a cousin, Jordan, but he lives in New York.' She smiled. 'But obviously that's far away and so I don't see him nearly as often as I'd like.'

Theo's dad had clearly had enough. 'Just going to let Rhubarb out for a shit,' he announced, standing abruptly and dropping his napkin into his chair.

'Nice.' Theo smiled at Anna.

'So, Theo…'

He braced himself for whatever crap the man was about to spout.

'Your mother tells me you're a troubled man? That you have an admirable social conscience?'

He looked first at the pastor and then at his mother and this time did nothing to stop the laughter from escaping. He made no apology, just swiped at his mouth with his napkin. 'No.' He shook his head. 'I wouldn't say I was troubled. A little pissed off, maybe, bemused, embarrassed certainly, but troubled? No. Could you pass the peas, please, Anna?'

Anna handed him the unwieldy tureen.

Pastor Julian failed to take the hint. 'I can tell you that there is no shame in not having everything figured out. Your mother tells me that school was very hard for you.'

'Actually, let me stop you there. Firstly, I don't know you and secondly, even if I did, I would not be willing to discuss anything as personal as my childhood.'

'Pastor Jules is only—'

'Only what, Mum? What exactly is Pastor Jules doing here?' Theo shook his head with annoyance.

'Theo!'

'It's okay.' The pastor patted Stella's arm and wiped his mouth, returning the napkin to his lap. 'I understand that when there is a lot unsaid, the messenger is often the one who is attacked. It's understandable.'

Theo glance at Anna and said, without attempting to whisper, 'Anna, did you say you thought you might have left the gas on? Do we need to leave *now*?'

They exchanged a look and he felt another flush of love for her. It felt good to have an ally in this shitty situation.

The pastor sat forward and stared at Anna. 'I am a messenger, Anna, and I have someone here that is trying to talk to you. His name is Jim. No...' He closed his eyes and held out his hand with his fingers splayed. 'James. Or John?'

Anna gasped. 'My brother?' she whispered, her face white. 'Joe?'

'That's enough!' Theo raised his voice and glared at the pastor. Stella sat forward, looking cross, but Pastor Jules ignored Theo and continued. 'He says it wasn't your fault. He says he is sorry. And I can hear music... Let me see...' He cocked his head to one side, as if to hear it better.

Anna was almost whimpering now and Theo was incandescent with rage. What was this man trying to prove? How dare he upset Anna like that? 'I said, that's enough!' He slammed his cutlery down onto the table and stood, stopping Pastor Julian in his tracks. With eyes blazing he reached for Anna's hand.

Anna, as if in shock, stood too, her legs wobbly.

'Okay…' Theo reached out with a shaking hand and addressed his mother. 'I have no idea what the fuck is going on, but I want no part of it, not for me and certainly not for my wife, who has been through quite enough recently. Thank you for an interesting supper. It's been a blast.'

'What do you mean? We've only just started eating, you've hardly touched your food and I made tipsy pudding!' his mother whined.

'Trust me, Mum, I've more than had my fill. Come on, Anna. Say goodbye to Dad for us.' He placed a hand on Anna's back, guiding her along the hallway until they were outside, standing in the cool night air.

'What on earth…?' Anna gave a nervous laugh. Slipping her arm through his and bending over to laugh some more, this soon gave way to tears, which she swiped with her sleeve. 'I don't know why I'm crying.'

Watching her try to be brave tore at his heartstrings. 'I do, and I'm so sorry, Anna, that was truly awful.' He scuffed his sole on the pavement, trying to release some of the tension inside him. 'Are you okay? Did that scare you?'

'I honestly don't know what to think,' she levelled. 'It did scare me and I hated it, but at the same time, what if he really can do that?'

'Trust me, he really can't do anything, it's utter bollocks!' Theo shook his head.

'But it sounded like he knew things… About Joe… About… the music box he stole maybe? I've never told anybody about that except you,' she whispered. 'You didn't tell…?'

'Oh Anna, my lovely Anna.' He placed his hands either side

of her head and kissed her face. 'I've never told a soul, of course I haven't.' He hated what that vile man had dredged up. 'Do not give that so-called pastor a moment of consideration. It's a trick, and a cruel, dangerous trick at that. He was just fishing – it was all so bloody obvious, he just lobbed out some random names and hoped to get lucky.'

She nodded, and he could read the disappointment in her eyes. It was indeed the cruellest trick. Who wouldn't want to talk to someone they'd lost?

'Where did that guy spring from?' she asked.

'A shed in Putney apparently.'

'But how come your mother hooked up with him? It's nuts!' She twirled her fingers by her head, emphasising the craziness. 'I didn't even know she was religious!'

'Neither did I. And of course I have no problem with that if she has genuinely found faith, but *that guy…*'

'I know, right – *that guy*!'

Theo shook his head. 'I got the feeling she liked him.'

'I should say! Inviting him for dinner, sharing intimate details of her *troubled* child.' She pinched his cheek affectionately.

'No, seriously…' He pulled away a little. 'I mean, *liked* him. She seemed giggly and a bit besotted.'

'Two words I never would have associated with your mum.'

'Exactly.'

'Maybe it's a late mid-life crisis?'

'It's something all right.' He sighed.

'Okay…' She paused. 'Pastor Julian – another thing definitely not to be mentioned at the adoption interview.'

'On that we are agreed.' He nodded. 'God, I'm starving.'

'Me too. Chip shop?'

'Yes!' He grinned. 'Chip shop.'

They trod the pavement arm in arm, each pondering what they'd just been through.

'But just supposing—' Anna began.

'No, Anna,' he interrupted, 'there is no "just supposing". As I said, it is complete and utter bollocks.'

'I know,' she said quietly. 'I just wish it wasn't.'

An hour later, with the White Stripes CD playing, vinegar-stained chip paper littering the sitting-room floor, Griff asleep in the kitchen and a bottle of wine sunk, the two of them lay next to each other on the rug.

Anna ran her fingers over his chest and kissed his mouth. 'Troubled or not, I do love you, Theo, my little goldfish murderer.'

'Thank you for that. And for your information, the bloody thing died of natural causes, pretty much before I tipped it from the bag into the bowl. And also for your information, I love you too.'

She reached down and unfastened his belt.

'Wait a minute.' He grabbed her wrist. 'Do you think we should say grace first?'

Anna howled her laughter and climbed on top of him, kissing his mouth and running her hands over his chest.

He kissed her back, happy for the joy of contact and the happy abandonment of sex, which had been missing of late. In a paused moment they stared at each other.

'I love you, Theo. I really, really love you.'

He reached up and used the pad of his thumb to brush the sweet mouth that had uttered these words so sincerely. 'I love you too.'

'I can't stop thinking about it...' she began.

'Thinking about what?'

'That adoption might be the thing for us!'

And just like that, Theo's carefree mood was nudged out of the frame by the flicker of self-doubt he just couldn't shift. He was determined to try and make Anna happy, it was all he wanted, and he was going to give this adoption meeting his very best shot. But what if he really was destined to turn out like his parents? What if in twenty years' time their own child came round for the dinner party from hell? What if he simply wasn't father material, just as Kitty had surmised?

Fourteen

The ringing of the doorbell woke Theo, and then came the sound of Griff barking loudly in response. He opened first one eye and then the other. It was 9 a.m., late for them, and as always on weekends it was a joy not to have been roused by the alarm. Anna sat up and rubbed her face. 'Who's that?' She groaned, reaching for the glass of water on her bedside table.

Theo didn't reply, unable to think of an answer that wasn't obvious or a little sarcastic, considering he hadn't yet opened the front door. He threw his sweatshirt over his head and pulled on his pyjama bottoms.

'Mum! Hello.' He couldn't remember the last time she'd turned up at the house without calling first. It was usually when she needed a favour, like the dog walking or plants watering while they were away.

She was clearly agitated, fingering the pearls at her neck and blinking rapidly. Without any pleasantries or preamble, she began. 'I feel you let me down terribly last night, Theo!' She'd raised her voice and was speaking pointedly, as if the words had been cued up, waiting to be released. Judging by the dark circles under her eyes, she'd probably been mulling them over since the early hours.

'Come inside, Mum. Please.' He stood back with his arms wide, then glanced up the pavement as she marched in, to see if any neighbours were taking an interest. They weren't.

'I mean it. You let me down and you were rude!'

'Please calm down.'

'Calm down?' Stella continued at the same pitch. 'It was important to me! I wanted it to be a pleasant evening. You all knew that. I went to a lot of trouble.'

'I...' Theo struggled to know where to begin, torn between voicing his concerns about her and giving in to the anger that was brewing inside him.

'Morning, Stella. Would you like a cup of tea?' Anna had come downstairs in her dressing gown. Theo appreciated her soft, placatory tone, which felt like balm on their hot-tempered exchange.

'No, I do not want a cup of tea. I want an apology!'

'Right. Well, I'll pop the kettle on anyway.' Anna ran her hand over Theo's waist as she passed, a tactile show of support for which he was grateful. The happy glow of their union still clung to their skin and it would take more than his cranky mother to dampen it.

He followed her into the kitchen and his mother came on behind. Theo and Anna exchanged a knowing look.

'I mean it.' Stella's tone was accusatory. 'How often do I ask you for anything?'

'Quite often actually.' He kept his tone level.

She ignored him. 'My faith is now a big part of my life and all I asked was that you be civil to Pastor Jules, a guest in my home! My friend! A man of God! And you couldn't even find the decency—'

A man of God? He swallowed the many unfavourable comments that sprang to mind. 'Whoa there! I think, Mum, that we just need to slow things down a bit here. Firstly, it might have been an idea to call me, talk to me, and let me know about this big change in your beliefs so that I was a little bit prepared. And secondly, the man's a charlatan. He went way over the top last night, he was invasive and out of line.'

Behind his mother's back, Anna pulled a disapproving face at his frankness.

'That's what Pastor Jules says people with closed minds and people who don't have his vision will say.'

Theo pinched the bridge of his nose. 'Well, how bloody convenient. He's right, I don't share his vision and I don't share his moral code. How dare he say those things to Anna, how dare he? And I'm furious that you put her, put us, in that position.'

'Well, if you had stuck around and not marched out halfway through dinner, you might have learnt how his gift works.'

'Christ alive, his gift? Really?' He took a breath. 'You are free of course to do as you see fit, whatever is right for you – fill your boots!' He let his arms fall to his sides. 'But telling a complete stranger personal things about *my* life, about our life, aspects *I* would not want shared—'

'He's not a complete stranger to me!' she shouted.

'Well, that much was obvious.' Theo folded his arms across his chest.

'Have you been speaking to your father?' She shot him an anguished look.

Theo laughed. 'Since when did I speak about anything with

Dad? Ever? And while we are on the subject, he was horrid last night, just casually trashing our adoption plans – can he not see that it's important to us? I know it's too much to hope that it might be important to him. It's the same with my bloody plans for Bristol!'

'Oh, please, not that again!' Stella took a deep breath and pushed her thumbs into her brow, as if trying to relieve the pressure.

'Yes, that again. And for the record, Mum, you can't just come in here and wake us up with a row and then get mad when it doesn't go your way. You and Dad have always seemed to think that it's okay to put me on display when it's called for, but it's been on your terms and this is just another example of that. What you did last night with your crazy new friend and his parlour tricks was bloody disgraceful!'

'Don't swear,' she snapped. 'I haven't forgotten the way you cursed at me on the phone the other week – is it your new thing?'

'"Bloody" is not swearing. Shit, arse, bollocks and fuck, now *that's* swearing.' He regretted the outburst the moment it had left his mouth.

She looked at him with her mouth agape.

'Your tea, darling.' Anna handed him a mug and rested her hand briefly on his shoulder, a reminder to calm down.

He took it sheepishly and sipped, letting his pulse settle. 'I'm sorry,' he whispered.

The slight nod of Stella's head indicated an acceptance of sorts.

'But here's the thing, Mum. You have drunk, sworn, smoked and God knows what else for my whole life and then after one hour in the company of Pastor Putney, you expect me to just go along with the whole Julie Andrews charade? And worse still, he's fooling you – I don't think he's what you're looking for. I really don't. And I think he might be dangerous. Do you think you're being forgiven for all the bad stuff you've ever done and said? Is this a way of wiping the slate clean? Because I get that you might want to, but I'm not sure this is the right way.'

His mother shook her head. 'No, it's not that at all. I know that I'm not without faults, without sin, but it's more than that – I like the stillness, the quiet of the church, and the ceremony. It makes me feel better.'

Theo remembered how he used to lie in the dark at school with such longing in his gut, so desperate to return home that it physically hurt, and how it was made far worse because no one at home gave a shit.

'Watching you close your eyes in prayer as though it was the most natural thing in the world, even though you've never been a churchgoer, seemed a bit bonkers,' he said. 'And as for communicating with the dead...'

'It's not bonkers.' His mother stood her ground. 'And believe me when I say I wish I could go back and do a lot of things differently. In a sense, now I can – it's like being born again.' A smile flickered around her mouth.

'Oh, for God's sake, what next? A baptism?'

And then to his horror and acute embarrassment, his mother started to cry, properly cry, with a heave to her chest and a shake to her shoulders. Her mouth twisted and her eyes flamed.

'Stella, come and sit down.' Anna shepherded her to the kitchen table and helped her settle. 'I'm going to go and have my bath.' She winked at her husband, purposefully leaving them alone.

Theo sat opposite his mother and waited until her great gulping sobs had abated.

'I *like* feeling this way.' She sniffed. 'I *like* listening to Pastor Jules and what he thinks about life and I *like* the way he listens to me.' She pointed at her chest. 'I am a person too, and what I say and what I want has never been considered. Never.'

Welcome to my world... Theo buried the thought.

'I have never been heard!' Stella shook her head.

He felt the stirring of sympathy and tried to imagine living each day in the shadow of his father. He replayed some of the million ways his father deliberately made him feel worthless. He adopted a softer tone. 'I get it, Mum, I do, and if going to church is something you want to do and you get something out of it, then it can only be a good thing, but do you have to go to *that* church?'

'You know nothing about it!' she replied. 'You have made up your mind based on what – ten minutes in Pastor Jules's company? Why do you think that's okay?'

He swallowed the words that rattled in his mouth, took the path of least resistance and conceded. 'You're right, Mum, I probably could have been more civil. What I think about Pastor Jules and his shed in Putney stands, but for embarrassing you, I am sorry.'

His mother sat still, letting his apology percolate. She straightened her back. 'Daddy is being so horrible to me about the whole thing – he finds it all most amusing. He doesn't understand that I need the calming space to keep sane.' She curled her fingernails into her palm as she spoke. 'I need the quiet contemplation of prayer to get my head straight.'

'*Possibly the most important lesson of all is that when you're still and quiet, that's when your thoughts get ordered, when your mind sorts out all its problems and when you're able to see most clearly. Don't ever underestimate the value of stillness.*' Mr Porter's words came into Theo's head; he heard his distinctive accent and felt a smile forming at the vivid recollection of that conversation.

'I do understand, Mum.' He spoke softly. 'But I wouldn't be doing my job, would I, if I wasn't looking out for you, making sure you were safe and that there wasn't something I should be doing to make you happier.'

Stella reached across the table and placed her hand over the back of his. 'You have always been a good boy.' She gave a long, slow blink that looked a little like a prayer and smiled at him.

Theo suspected that she, like him, was picturing that night in the upstairs corridor of La Grande Belle when he had summoned all of his courage and had tried to act as her protector.

★ ★ ★

Anna fidgeted in the plastic seat, adjusting the cuffs of the blouse she had deliberated over for almost an hour. 'I want to look smart but motherly, trustworthy but fun – which do you think, Theo, the pale blue or the white?' She had held the hangers out alternately.

He had stared at her, trying desperately to get in the swing of it but knowing the biggest barrier to their adoption plans would probably not be which shade of blouse she chose but something far more fundamental. *Please let me get it right*, he urged himself, over and over. *We need this.*

They'd already had a massive row about where his priorities lay. The Monday morning after the Pastor Julian dinner, Theo had gone into work with his dad's snide aside running on a loop through his head: '*If Theo feels that strongly about those poor kids, he should fund the sodding project himself.*' He was damned if he was going to let his father reduce him to tears over something he cared so much about, just like he'd done to his mum and her new interest in all things religious. Before he had a chance to think better of it, Theo had called the Bristol agent and bought the warehouse – funded the sodding project himself, lock, stock and barrel. Anna had been furious when he told her: she worried that his attention was no longer one hundred per cent on their adoption plans (probably true) and that tying all their money up in this gamble of a project endangered their future security (also probably true). It hadn't exactly made for the most peaceful run-up to the adoption meeting. And to make things worse, Anna's pregnant friend Shania had just asked Anna to be her birthing partner in a few months' time. Theo was pretty sure that the experience of seeing her friend give birth would not be helpful and he was dreading the upset that would surely follow. Why did things have to be so damn complicated?

But here they were nonetheless, sitting on a couple of narrow seats along a plain wall in a waiting room that was probably no different from the waiting rooms of countless other municipal buildings. He could feel waves of excited energy coming off Anna. 'Don't be nervous,' he whispered. 'All it will take is five minutes in your company and it'll be blindingly obvious to anyone that any child's life would be infinitely better with you in it.'

He saw relief spread slowly across her face. 'Thank you for saying that, Theo. With you by my side, I think I can do anything!'

'Exactly.' He smiled at her.

'Mr and Mrs Montgomery?'

Anna shot up and grabbed his hand, marching him into the office. The woman used her foot to hold the door ajar as she beckoned them in. Theo took in her stocky build, the muted tones of her mustard and green skirt and the blunt cut of her grey hair. A neat, square woman in her mid sixties, she wore stout lace-up shoes and looked more like a dog walker than an adoption official, not that he'd tried to paint a picture of her beforehand, but if he had, this wouldn't have been it.

'Come in.' She gestured with her open hand towards the bland, sparsely furnished room. Bar a table in the centre, six leggy, school-type chairs and a set of royal blue vertical blinds, there was little else. No distractions.

'It's good to meet you, Mr Montgomery. I am Mrs Wentworth.'

'Theo, please.' He felt a small flicker of embarrassment that she didn't extend the same courtesy, then smiled as he caught her eye, desperate for her to like him, to approve.

'And Mrs Montgomery.' She shook Anna's hand.

'Anna, please.'

'Please, do sit down.'

He watched Anna deliberate over where to sit, as if this too might be part of a test. He wished she would relax. He was, as ever, immaculate. It was important to him, this first impression. He hitched up his suit trousers, twisted his signet ring, straightened the Windsor knot of his pale blue tie and adjusted the lapels of his jacket, running his thumb along the silk underside and taking courage from the feel of his fishing fly. Then he coughed to clear his throat.

'So, all we're going to do today is have a chat. I can tell you about the process that you're considering embarking upon and it's a chance for you to ask any questions you might have before you make that decision. How does that sound?'

'It sounds wonderful!' Anna fired back, sounding to him like the try-hard girl in school, keen to get the answer right, desperate to be picked. It tore at his heart, because he knew she was perfect. Perfect for him and perfect for any child that might need a home. But then again, maybe she was right to be this way; maybe it was the little things that would make the difference. He thought about getting stuck in the lift with her that day, three years ago, a little thing on a seemingly insignificant day. A day, no, a minute that had changed his entire life. And hers.

Conscious of Mrs Wentworth's scrutiny from the seat opposite his, he became hyper aware of his every facial tic. He found himself trying to suppress the flurry of thoughts that swirled in his mind, as if her incisive gaze could penetrate deep inside his brain. What if she could see his doubts, what if she could tell he had a big secret in there, had deceived Anna for all these years? What if she somehow intuited that he already had a child and therefore shouldn't be allowed to take on someone else's?

He inhaled and shook himself out of this stupidity – it seemed his mother wasn't the only gullible one in the family. Mrs Wentworth was some sort of social worker, not a psychic!

Mrs Wentworth smiled and rested an elbow on the arm of her chair. 'I can tell that you're a little nervous, and that's perfectly understandable, but there is really no need.'

'I guess that's because it's so important to me.' Anna jumped in again with the textbook answer.

'And that I understand, but this really is just a chat.'

'Okay.' Anna exhaled. 'I will try.'

'And what about you, Mr Montgomery? How are you feeling about this?'

He didn't like the slant to her head, as if she really had seen something in him that might be a tick in the wrong box. He held her gaze. 'Er… I'm a bit nervous too, I guess. It's more the fear of the unknown for me, I think.'

'Would you like to expand on that a little?'

'Er… I don't know.' He paused, feeling like an idiot. He decided to change tack. 'I just wish Anna would show you her true self, because she's—'

'I am being my true self!' Anna shot back, cutting him short.

'I didn't mean it in a negative way, I was only thinking that you are perfect and you don't need to perform.'

Mrs Wentworth raised her pen. 'What do you mean by "perform", exactly?' This had clearly caught her interest.

And, awkward though it was, that exchange turned out to be the least uncomfortable of the day…

They drove home in a fug of hostility distilled from all the words left unsaid and bubbling under the surface, waiting for release.

'How do you think—'

'Don't talk to me, Theo.' Anna raised her palm. 'Don't say anything!'

He took her advice and kept quiet.

It was she who broke the silence, a few minutes later. 'Did you deliberately try and sabotage the whole interview? Was that your game plan?' She shook her head, muttering something acidic but inaudible.

'Of course not! I got flustered, I—'

'What was all that about me performing? It made me sound like a fake!' she yelled.

'I was only trying to say that the real you, the everyday Anna, is more than good enough to adopt a child and that you didn't need to be so on edge!'

'The everyday Anna? And who is that exactly? I *was* being myself! Not that Mrs Wentworth would believe that, not now! Jesus, Theo!'

'I just—'

'No, don't say anything!' She turned and pointedly stared out of the window, staying like that for another good few minutes.

'Then she asked you a basic question, Theo! Basic! "Why do you think you would make a good parent?" And you... you just... Urrrrgh!' She shook her head and looked furious.

Theo's mouth went dry at the recollection.

'Why do you think you would make a good parent, Mr Montgomery?'

Twisting in his seat, he'd seen the image of Sophie smiling at him on the bus and then Kitty's face, horror-struck at the prospect of any interaction, and his confidence had evaporated. *Why do I think I would make a good parent? I don't, not really! I'm not sure I could be. I am weird, toxic, useless.* He then heard his father's voice, loud and clear: '*The idea of him looking after a baby!*'

And then he'd given his stupid answer, mumbled from cracked lips. 'I don't...'

'You don't think you *would* make a good parent?' Mrs Wentworth had prompted.

He'd sensed Anna sitting ramrod straight in the seat next to him, her words a decibel higher than her normal speech, her tone urgent. 'He'll... He'll be great. He's just nervous! He's kind and he listens and he has a good, good heart...'

Her rapid and heartfelt defence only made him feel worse. He shook his head. 'No, I was going to say, I don't know exactly, but I will try very hard.'

Glancing across the car now, he noted his wife's set expression, the tension in her jaw. Her hand was clamped over her mouth as if to prevent her from saying the wrong thing, the hurtful thing.

I want so badly to be the man you want me to be, Anna. I want us to adopt, but I don't know how to jump through hoops and be the smiley, untroubled father you have in mind. I don't know how! And that's the truth.

Fifteen

'Your dad's asking for the projection figures on the Deptford development.' Marta stood in the doorway to Theo's office, clinging to the frame with her red, talon-like fingernails, her lips painted to match. She tapped the toe of her black stiletto on the floor impatiently.

She bothered him.

'I'll give them to Marcus.' He spoke without looking at her again, keeping his eyes on the unopened envelope that had just been delivered to his desk.

He heard her sigh as she closed the door. Sitting back in his chair, he tried to imagine working as an intern and feeling confident enough to treat the chairman's son with such disdain. Was that how everyone saw him – a walkover?

A few seconds later she opened the door again. 'He says, can you—'

'Look, I'm sorry, Marta,' he said, cutting her short, 'but if my dad wants to speak to me, he is capable of coming in here himself and if he isn't, he can use this.' He picked up the telephone and held the mouthpiece towards her. 'And if for whatever reason neither of those things are possible, then you too can use the phone and call me. I'm trying to concentrate here and that's a little hard to do when you keep popping through the door like a bloody cuckoo clock.'

He wasn't sure why he was so irritable, or where his confidence had come from, but the way Marta pursed her glossy red lips and slowly walked backwards told him that he'd got the message across. And it felt good.

He picked up the brown envelope. His heart beat a little too quickly and he felt lightheaded. He breathed deeply, trying to quash the surge of excitement. This was it, the letter from the planning office in Bristol. He ran the pad of his thumb over the postmark and slid his finger under the gummy flap. The single sheet was officious, peppered with words, dates and departmental logos, all in red, but the only thing that drew his attention, was the single sentence informing him that planning permission for his twenty-four self-contained studio units had been APPROVED. He read and reread the word, feeling a fire of achievement in his belly – and this was before he'd shifted a single brick.

He contemplated calling Anna but instantly decided not to. He felt disinclined to argue with her today or hear the inevitable disappointment in her voice. The fallout from the adoption meeting was still tarnishing things between them and it took the edge off what should have been a day of celebration.

Sitting back in the leather chair, it felt as if his bowels had turned to ice. It wasn't just that all their money was tied up in this pile of vintage bricks; he'd also paid for security, started clearing rubbish from the site and engaged the best architect he could find. It felt like he had a mountain to climb and, much worse, it felt as if he was climbing it alone.

He sighed and leant back, feeling the tilt at the base of the chair as he stared up at the same ceiling his forefathers must have stared at many a time, plotting and scheming to build up the business. He closed his eyes.

'Are you asleep?' Marta woke him with her question.

'No!' He let the seat tilt forward again, aware of dampness on his chin. He had drifted off and he must have been drooling, but there was no way he was going to admit to either. He wiped his face with the back of his hand.

'It looked like you were sleeping to me.'

'Did you want something?' he asked, recalling their conversation about using the phone not an hour since.

'Yes. I've been to sent to ask if you're coming in for the quarterly review? It's just that everyone's waiting to start.' Her blouse gaped open to reveal a lacy camisole and she stood there with her right hip sticking out and her hand resting on it, as if striking a cover pose. It made him feel uncomfortable.

He'd forgotten that the quarterly review was today – he'd been too distracted. 'I'll be in in a minute.' He hurriedly opened the file on his computer that would provide him with the information he needed to share with the board.

'You might want to…' Marta touched her own fringe.

The moment she left, he checked his reflection in the window and cursed the wayward flicks of thick curl that stuck up vertically around his face. He used his fingers as a makeshift comb and tried to calm them. With his laptop under his arm, he gulped down the cold coffee sitting in the mug on his desk and winced at the bitterness, then crossed the hallway.

His father's terse glance at the wall clock did little to assuage his anxiety.

Theo felt only semi-present, nodding as reports and updates were given slowly and methodically, a stream of numbers and information in which he had only the vaguest interest. All he could see was the letter of approval from the planning department, as if it was tattooed on the inside of his eyelids. His mind whirred with all the possibilities.

'Theodore?' His father's voice drew him into the proceedings.

'Yep?' He straightened his tie and sat up in the chair.

'Sorry, are we keeping you from something more important?' Perry Montgomery asked. 'We are waiting for your input.' He nodded at the men assembled around the table.

'Yes. Of course.'

He tapped the keyboard, trying to find the damn spreadsheet, unsure of where they were up to and what had been said. 'Sorry, just give me a moment.' His face flared with embarrassment.

'If my son is a little distracted, it might be because he is fixated on buying a property in Bristol, would you believe! He wants to drag us down the M4 and get involved in *social housing* or some such.' A strained chortle rippled around the room.

Theo heard the laughter. It felt the same as it had that day in the library at Vaizey College. '*Right, Mr Homo, gather your books and leave! I will not have disruption in my library. There are people trying to work. Off you go!*' He felt a jolt in his gut and before he knew it he had closed the lid of his laptop and was standing.

'Actually, it was more than a fixation, it was a sound business proposal. But I can see there's no point in regurgitating the details here and now. As it happens, I believed in it and so I bought it, a little while ago now.'

He enjoyed the look of surprise on his father's face.

'Well, well. Interesting.' His father nodded and tapped his fingertips in a pyramid at chest height. 'Can we now get back to the task in hand?'

Theo looked at the gathered group and felt a shiver of dislike. These men were his father's cronies. In a sudden moment of clarity he decided he no longer wanted to be part of the gang. 'I'm sorry,' he mumbled, before buttoning up his jacket and leaving the room.

'Finished already? That was quick,' Marta called out as he walked past her desk and into his office.

He ignored her. Standing at the window, he looked down at the pavement, as he was wont to do, drawn by the hundreds of dark suits traipsing up and down, presumably every one of them trying in their own way to make their mark.

I'm thirty-one years old, not a boy. It's time, Theo. Time to do something different. He thought of Mr Porter, pottering in his front garden, sitting at the table, taking brightly coloured feathers between his leathery fingers and turning them into something wonderful. He felt beneath his lapel where his gift of a fly on a safety pin nestled.

I wonder if you're still alive? How old would you be now, dear friend? If you were nineteen in 1944, blimey, you must be in your seventies. I always thought of you as an old, old man back when I was at school, but you weren't all that old, were you? Just grey-haired and dealing with all life had thrown at you. I am sorry, I will always be sorry. I should have done more, said more... I didn't realise until it was too late and you were gone.

The door of his office flew open, pulling him into the present. He closed his eyes briefly and steeled himself. His father was the only one who came in like that, without introduction or forewarning, making the point this was his building, his company and that they had to play by his rules. It had the effect of making Theo feel like a guest, keeping him on his toes, and this too was familiar.

'Well, well, well, that was quite a display.' Theo noted the hint of amusement in his father's tone. 'When you have calmed down, do you think we might be able to continue with our meeting? There are six good people sitting around a table waiting for you to deliver your report. The report you are paid to deliver. They're not used to being kept waiting and I'm not used to having to explain away such unprofessional behaviour. So if you don't mind...' His father gestured towards the door.

Theo stayed by the window and shook his head briefly. His limbs were trembling. 'I received a letter today from the planning department in Bristol. They've approved my plan for the warehouse.'

He wasn't sure what he wanted from his father by way of response. Good advice? A little bit of support?

His father sank down into the chair on the other side of the office and crossed his legs. His eyes were bright, his stare challenging, and there was a nasty smirk on his lips. 'Well, what a surprise!'

Theo had imagined this moment often, but it didn't feel half as good or victorious as he'd anticipated. He paced behind his desk. 'How can you sit there as my father and not be happy that I've succeeded in something? Would it kill you to give me a bit of reassurance? Why do you always make it feel like I've lost!'

'Is that what you're after, boy? A pat on the back? A medal? Trust me, I know good men who've received medals for doing great things...'

Theo stared at him, dumbfounded.

'... and you haven't succeeded at anything yet. Buying a pile of bricks and turning them into something are two entirely different skills. And your business model is flawed!' He was yelling now, wiping spit from his damp lower lip with his handkerchief. 'That challenge, however, now sits firmly on your shoulders, but it's not important, not to me. My loyalty is here with the company my father and grandfather built.'

Theo got the picture. He had let them down, all of them. 'If you'd given me room to move within Montgomery Holdings, then maybe I wouldn't have felt the need to do something outside. But you've never valued me, you've always assumed the worst, treated me like a failure without giving me the chance to prove otherwise.' He faced his father and placed his hands on his waist.

'So this is my fault now?' His father chuckled. 'I am the reason you need to throw all this away?'

His dad's laughter was like a punch to Theo's already fragile confidence. His temperature flashed hot. He was furious. 'You could say that.' He breathed heavily, unable to list the many ways his father had hurt him and let him down.

'Is that right?' Perry sat back in the chair. 'Have you ever looked at it from my perspective, Theodore? I was overjoyed to get a son – *a son*!' He balled his fist, as if he'd won the jackpot.

Theo desperately wanted to ask if he was his father's first or second son – just how old was Alexander? But this was neither the time nor place.

Perry continued. 'I tried to coach you, influence you, tried to lay the foundations that would turn you into the man I wanted you to be. But, Jesus Christ, you never even picked up a fucking rugby ball! I used to place one in your hands and try, but you simply weren't interested.'

Theo could just about see the funny side of this. Was this what his old man's disappointment boiled down to – his lack of interest in the game of rugby?

Perry wasn't done. 'Why couldn't you have been like every other Vaizey boy, the sort I grew up with, men I loved and admired? Was it too much to ask for you to try and fit in a bit, find one thing in common with everyone else – just one thing? Even as a toddler you were always running off to hide behind you mother's skirts like a nancy boy. What was the matter with you?'

Theo stared at his father, wondering how much of his unhappy childhood to dredge up, not wanting to make things harder for his mother than they already were. The air between them was thick. The shadows of their words crept into the cracks in the ceiling and hid between the drawers of the desk. They weren't going to disappear any time soon. He took a deep breath and rounded off the sharp edges of his response.

'I don't think there's anything wrong with me. And I don't think not having an interest in a particular sport should be the thing that defines whether I'm a man or not.' His voice was calm. 'And actually, Dad, if I found you hard to approach as a toddler, if I preferred to run to Mum, was that my fault?' He let this sink in and saw the faint twitch to his father's left eye. 'Sometimes trying to force a square peg into a round hole results in it breaking. But I didn't break.' *Not quite.*

His father stared back at him with the beginnings of a smile on his face. He was hard to read sometimes. 'I like your frankness,' he said. 'And I have to say, knowing that you actually had the balls to follow through with something that caught your eye, this Bristol business, knowing you had the nerve to follow your instinct, is bloody marvellous! That, Theodore, is what makes a businessman.'

Theo felt the strength leave his legs. He had waited years to be thrown even a crumb of congratulation by his father and here, at this moment of exhaustion and in the face of his triumph, here it was. It was sickening to him just how overjoyed he was at his old man's self-styled compliment.

Perry had more to say. 'Following your heart, that's what it's all about. Not following orders or toeing the line. It's about challenging those orders and carving your own path. That's when things get really interesting.'

Theo opened his mouth to respond to this, but his thoughts were three steps ahead and he was as shocked as his dad when he gave them voice.

'I'm leaving the company, Dad. I'm setting out on my own. I can't do this any more and I think putting space between us can only be a good thing, a healthy thing.'

The smile fell from his father's face and something close to hurt flickered in his eyes. Far from feeling triumphant at having gained the upper ground for the first time in his life, Theo instead tasted the familiar guilt, this time tinged with fear.

'Be bold, Theodore.' His father stood, straightened his cuffs and held his son's gaze before he left the room. 'Always be bold.'

* * *

Anna laughed loudly into her fist before grabbing a piece of kitchen roll and wiping her nose and mouth. 'For real?' She gazed at him and refilled her wine glass. 'You've quit your job?'

'Yes. For real. I'm going to find a way to make that site work and when I've found the magic formula, I can repeat it. I can make an honest living while changing lives, Anna.' He took a slug of beer from the bottle in his hand.

Anna shook her head in disbelief as she paced round the kitchen. 'Did our conversation about openness not resonate with you at all? And what about the adoption process?'

'Yes, it resonated! It's not like I planned it. It was one of those spur-of-the-moment things. Dad was pushing and I—'

'Oh God, Theo!' She placed her hands in her hair, looking and sounding exasperated. 'Don't you see that you don't have the luxury of making spur-of-the-moment, unplanned decisions! You are married – to me! I'm not saying don't do it, don't follow your heart, and I'm not saying I don't admire what you're trying to achieve – I do! But we should have discussed something as fundamental as this!'

'I know, and in the cold light of day, away from the office—'

'How are we going to pay for the build and the house bills while it all gets going? How are we going to show we've got the stability and security to support a child?'

He hated the way she managed to turn his project into something fanciful, impossible, less a plan than a whimsy. 'I don't know yet.'

'Well, that's a good start.' She sighed. 'My wages won't cover our fuel bills, much less anything else.'

'I've already told you that I've never seen either of our contributions as anything other than all going into the same pot. We're a team.' He hoped the subtle reminder that he had pretty much funded their entire life together might be a prompt for kindness and understanding.

'A team?' She shook her head. 'It takes more than simply saying the word to make it the truth.'

'I need you to support me on this, Anna.'

'And I needed you to commit to the adoption!' She took a deep breath. 'It's not like I have any choice, is it? You've already jumped.'

The telephone in the kitchen rang. Anna rushed to the counter-top and lifted the receiver in anger. She shot a look at him from across the room.

'Yes?' she answered sternly, before closing her eyes. 'Oh, sorry, Stella, I thought it might be a sales call. Yes, I'm fine. No, not at all, I'll just grab him for you.' She laid the phone on the surface and left the room.

Theo held the receiver and spoke slowly. 'Hi, Mum.'

He was greeted by the sound of his mother crying. Her words were off rhythm, burbled amid the breaks for her tears. 'I don't... I don't know what to say to you! Daddy told me... and I thought it was a wicked joke. I could never have imagined you walking away from everything that the Montgomerys have built up over the years! I just don't understand it, Theodore! Why? Why would you do this to us?'

He sighed and pinched the top of his nose. 'Because it's time. And I'm not emigrating or abandoning you and Dad, just trying a new career path, that's all.'

'That's *all*? You are our only son and heir! How can you say "that's all"! I have prayed for you all afternoon. I asked Pastor Jules to pray for you too.'

Well, that's all my problems solved! He bit his lip, angry that once again she was talking to the greasy pastor about his private life. 'Look, Mum, I'll be happy to discuss this when you're calmer, but there's no point going back and forth like this when you're so upset.'

His mother changed tack, her voice now clipped. 'Daddy says you need to collect your things from the office and you need to do it tomorrow!' And with that she ended the call.

Theo reached into the fridge for another beer. He knew that this edict came from her and not his father, a way to vent her hurt, and it took him right back to his school days, when he'd felt like a pawn in the middle of whatever drama had been unfolding between them. This only served to reassure him that he'd made the right decision.

'Well, this is going to make tomorrow's birthday celebrations interesting.'

He turned and looked at Anna, having quite forgotten that tomorrow was his birthday. His head felt like it might explode.

Sixteen

The next day, Theo slept late, uninterested in his day of supposed celebration. He took Griff for a run and did his best to stay out of Anna's way until she left to meet Shania for a hospital appointment, part of her duty as birth partner. He waited until early evening before making his way into town, knowing that by six o'clock his father would be at his club and the seventh floor would be mostly deserted.

He let himself into his office, flicked on the desk lamp and scanned the room. He would always view Villiers House and his time in it with nostalgia. It was after all where he'd met Anna. Opening his leather sports bag, he took a couple of social policy books from the windowsill. This made him think of Spud. What wouldn't he give for a pint with him right now, today of all days, when things with Anna were tense and he'd just taken his great leap into the unknown. Spud would have been full of good, practical advice.

He picked up a picture of himself and Anna on their wedding day with Big Ben and the Houses of Parliament as the backdrop. Pausing to run his fingertips over her beautiful face – *Oh, my Anna* – he then placed the lot into the bag and, rummaging through the drawers, retrieved his various bits and pieces: a mini desktop golf set, a Christmas gift from Anna, three spare ties, and several travel books purchased spontaneously from Stanfords during lunchtime jaunts up to Covent Garden.

He heard a sound coming from the corridor outside and looked up. With his heart thudding, he crept across his office floor, glancing around for something he might use as an impromptu weapon. He swiftly gave up on the idea – the thought of having to bash someone made him feel sick. He'd never been good at all that macho stuff; his plan had always been to run should the need arise.

Out in the corridor, he was surprised to see a thin shaft of light coming from under the boardroom door. He opened it an inch or so and narrowed his eyes.

The first thing he saw was a bottle of champagne on the table and two half-empty glasses. The second thing he saw was his father, sitting on the edge of the table. His shirt was undone, and he wasn't alone. Marta was, as ever, looking suitably alluring in red lipstick and some sort of very revealing black lacy garment. Unseen by either of them, he watched his father lunge forward and grab Marta's slender wrist, yanking her to him; his other hand held the back of her neck as she slid against him.

And just like that, Theo arrived at a place that he knew was a beginning and an end, a destination to which he'd been running ever since that holiday on the Riviera, if not before. He looked down at his palm and fingers and balled them into a fist. As a boy, he had once longed for the big hands of his father, hands he had seen drag his mother from the edge of a pool in a drunken rage, hands he had seen wrung together in frustration at his own many acts of perceived ineptitude. It wasn't until this moment, however, as Marta lifted her foot and rested her heel on the wall for leverage, that Theo finally acknowledged the grown-up hands of the man he had become. And they were honourable hands, hands that had to put things right.

He slammed the door against the wall and watched them both jump. Marta let out a small, theatrical scream and clasped her blouse over her near-naked form as she fled the room. His father, however, took his time, seemingly unflustered; he smoothed his hair and buttoned up his shirt before casually reaching for his glass of champagne, sipping it as Theo walked closer.

Is this bold enough for you, Dad?

'Well now, do you have permission to be here, as an ex-employee? Don't we have to change the locks or something?' his father asked with something akin to amusement in his voice.

'I thought I might hit you.' Theo wiped the sweat from his top lip with a trembling hand. 'But, unlike you, I have enough regard for Mum not to put her through that.' His voice was steady but his breath came in bursts.

'Well, there's a shock, you choosing the sissy-boy way out!'

Theo bit the inside of his cheek and tasted the iron seep of blood on his tongue. 'I feel sorry for you, Dad.'

'Don't.' Perry emptied his glass and put it down sharply.

'No, I do.' Theo held his stare. 'You are a sad old man. Do you think Marta would be the slightest bit interested in a pot-bellied old boozer like you if you didn't own the company?'

'And do you think I give a shit?' His dad laughed, his arms wide open. 'Have you seen her?'

'I remember the way you looked at Freddie at La Grande Belle – it was revolting, predatory.'

'Who the fuck is Freddie?'

She had clearly been expunged from his dad's memory, probably like countless others. That horrible holiday had proved so pivotal in Theo's life, but to his father it was nothing. It was Theo's turn to laugh. 'I guess it must be easy to forget all the women you've had, every one of them just another distraction, a game you play with no regard to the damage you're causing.'

'You think I'm unique? Get real, boy! You think your mother and I should sit around watching good documentaries in our slippers, drinking cocoa into our dotage?'

Theo ignored him. 'Let's talk about Alexander.' He spoke the name clearly, loudly, the name that usually hid at the back of his mouth, whispered only in the solitary darkness. 'Do you remember his mother? What damage did you do her, and him?'

A flicker of surprise crossed his father's face and it felt good to have the upper hand.

'Yes, Dad, Alexander. Is he younger than me? How did that feel, knowing that expensive Vaizey education was being wasted on me while he was living God knows where in God knows what situation?'

Perry was smirking now. 'You think you're so clever, Theodore. You think you have it all figured out.' There was a moment of hesitation while the two men stared at each other. 'But here's the thing.' His dad took a step towards him. 'Alexander did have the benefit of a Vaizey education. He was a couple of years older than you. How do you think I knew about your woeful performance on the rugby pitch? Your fucking weird antics with the gardener? Did you think I was psychic? No, Alex told me. Alex who works in the City, Alex who is a bloody success!'

Theo felt as if he'd been punched in the gut. His body folded and he gripped the table for support. 'He... He was in my school?'

'NO! He was in MY school!' his father roared. 'A Theobald's boy of course! Xander Beaufort.'

Theo's mouth dropped open. Xander Beaufort! He struggled to recall the boy's face, but he remembered that he'd been a prefect at Theobald's and he hadn't cut Theo any slack. 'Did… Did he know about me?'

'Of course he bloody knew about you!'

Theo felt as if the room was spinning. His father reached for his jacket. *You win, Dad, you win. I am done.*

'You see, Theo, life is about planning, it's about putting things in place so that all the bits of the jigsaw fit together. The fact that you are starting to see the whole picture is, I suppose, inevitable.'

'Did… Did Mum know Alexander was at Vaizey?'

'What do you think?'

Theo felt winded by the revelation. He'd felt helpless and inadequate that night at La Grande Belle all those years ago, but this took it to another level. He'd said only recently that despite his father trying to force him, a square peg, into a round hole, he hadn't broken. But that was then. Now he felt quite broken.

Perry walked around the table and made for the door. 'Oh and happy birthday, Theodore. Save some cake for me!'

Theo left the office and stood in the street, breathing in the cold evening air and trying to clear his head. The depth of his father's duplicity took his breath away and, try as he might, he couldn't stop thinking of Sophie, and Kitty, and Anna. *Like father, like son.* Was he really so different from his dad? There was only one person he wanted to talk to right now, but sadly he was in Washington DC. He saw he had a missed call from

Anna, probably wanting to know where he was, but instead he pressed the button to speak to Spud. Given the time difference, he wasn't surprised to get an automated answerphone; Spud would be working.

'Mate, it's me.' He took a deep breath. 'It's my birthday, but that's not why I'm calling. I feel like I'm falling apart. I told my dad I knew about Alexander and...' He paused. 'Well, it didn't go how I thought it might. It's made me think about my situation. I don't ever want Anna to feel how I felt tonight, to find out I have a little girl, a child in this world who doesn't know me... I'm gabbling. Call me when you get this. I need to talk to you, Spud.'

He hung up the phone and hailed a cab to take him home.

Trying to quash the turmoil that swirled inside him, Theo straightened his tie and paid the cabbie before running up the steps to the front door. Taking a deep breath, he tried to erase the previous hour. He didn't want the image in his mind of his father and Marta together, nor the memory of his father laughing at him. The revelation about his brother was still hard for him to accept. It felt like a bad dream. All he wanted was a drink, a shower and an early night. He hated his birthday, always had. He found the whole celebration a little forced and pointless, not to mention embarrassing. Anna, however, felt differently. It distressed her that his parents had been all but indifferent to his birthdays as a child and he knew she'd want to make a fuss today, as she always did, a sort of compensation for past lacks, with the obligatory opening of presents, a steak dinner and a fancy cake. To deny her the joy of organising these little celebrations felt mean. Although, right now, he'd never felt less like celebrating.

He let himself into the hallway and dropped his keys on the dresser. The house was darker than he'd expected – almost pitch black, in fact. He was grateful for the glow of the street light that filtered through the sitting-room window and cast an intricate flickering pattern over the hall floor.

'Oh God, please not a surprise party,' he whispered, ditching his jacket. He couldn't face having to make small talk with Anna's clutch of girl buddies and their other halves, with whom he had zero in common, or, worse, having to deal with his mother, knowing what he now knew and listening to the excuses for his father's absence: '*Daddy's been caught up at the club... Dad's at a planning meeting... Your father's gone to an auction...*' He'd heard them all.

He fixed an expectant expression and opened the door with gusto. The sight that greeted him took him aback.

There was no party. No steak dinner, no gifts and no cake. The room was eerily quiet and cold. Even Griff sat with his muzzle on his extended paws, as if in contemplation.

Instead of a crowd brandishing blowers, standing under a homemade banner and wearing elasticated conical hats, there was just Anna, sitting alone at the kitchen table in the semi-darkness. As his eyes adjusted to the low light, he could see that her hair had been pulled back into a messy ponytail and that she'd been crying. Her eyes were red and swollen and she was rolling tiny sausages of shredded kitchen roll between her fingers.

'What's going on?' he asked, looking around the room for clues as to her state of mind but finding none.

'Please sit down, Theo.' Her voice was small, cracked.

'What's the matter? Are you okay? Has something happened?'

She waited until he was seated before reaching for her phone. She laid it on the table between them and played her answer-phone messages. 'You have one message,' the robotic voice informed.

Theo braced himself and cocked his head, waiting to hear what devastating news had made her so upset. Something to do with Jordan maybe? He mentally began planning her trip to the States, wondering how quickly he could get her packed and on a plane to New York. He slid his fingertips towards her hand, hoping that physical contact might bring some comfort. Anna flinched, quickly pulling her hand beneath the table and resting it in her lap.

The moment the message began, he knew.

His head swam, his stomach dropped and his mouth went dry. His heart was racing fit to burst as the bile rose in his throat.

'Mate, it's me. It's my birthday, but that's not why I'm calling. I feel like I'm falling apart. I told my dad I knew about Alexander and, well, it didn't go how I thought it might. It's made me think about my situation. I don't ever want Anna to feel how I felt tonight, to find out I have a little girl, a child in this world who doesn't know me... I'm gabbling. Call me when you get this. I need to talk to you, Spud.'

This was how his beloved Anna had learnt of the secret he had tried so hard to keep from her! After all that time spent fretting, plotting, dissembling... The countless restless nights worrying about whether it was better to tell her or not to tell her, waiting for the right time, the time when the news would do the least damage to her, to them. And that time had now been forced upon them, dropped like a bomb on their future.

It had all boiled down to one slip of a finger on an answerphone message.

'You have a little girl?' she rasped.

'Yes.'

'You're a dad.' She swallowed, shaking her head. 'Is Kitty her mum?'

He closed his eyes and nodded. God, this was worse than he could ever have imagined. She was sure to be jumping to horrible conclusions. Christ, why hadn't he listened to Spud? Why hadn't he come clean with Anna in their first weeks together? They could have got it all out of the way early…

'I knew it. I always kind of had this feeling about her, the way you looked when you told me she was just some girl from school, the way you changed the subject when her name came up. You were always so evasive. I just knew.'

And there it was – the damage was done. Damage he might never be able to undo, however hard he tried to convince her.

'Do you… Do you love Kitty?' she asked quietly.

'No, not at all. I was infatuated with her at school, but no.' He shook his head.

The two of them sat quietly, on opposite sides of the kitchen table, in close physical proximity but miles and miles apart.

He tried again. 'I don't have any relationship with either of them, Anna. None at all. And I didn't plan it – it just happened,' he whispered. 'It was long before I met you, a one-time thing, and I was told in no uncertain terms that I was not to make contact because, unlike you, Kitty knew that I would be a shit father and a fucking useless addition to any child's life!'

Anna shook her head. 'Don't you fucking dare! Don't you dare compare me with some woman you had a one-night stand with who doesn't know you like I do! Don't you dare suggest that it is for reasons *she* came up with that *I* have been denied motherhood! You are my husband!' Her voice squeaked, sounding raw with sadness. 'You've been cheating on me since the day we met.'

'I have not!'

'Yes, you have, Theo.' She was cool now, her voice barely quivering. 'Lying through omission and lying by keeping a secret, a big secret!'

'I haven't lied to you, Anna. Not intentionally. I might have held back, but—'

'Held back? You have a *child*!' She laughed, wiping her nose with the back of her hand. 'Have you any idea what it's like living with you?' She looked up. 'You have never given yourself to me, not fully. I have tried to be content with the little bits of you that you cast at me like pieces of a puzzle. And I scamper to catch whatever you throw because I love you.' She broke off, crying again. 'I love you so much, but every time you give me a new piece of you, you take away an old piece and I now know that I can never, ever complete the picture of you. Never. And as if that wasn't punishment enough, I find out you have a little girl. A little girl you share with a woman who isn't me, a little girl you phoned Spud to discuss while I was running around trying to make a party for you, collecting a fucking cake!'

'Anna, I… I wish I had told you. I do! But every day, every month that passed made it seem harder and harder to come clean.'

'Well, bravo, Theo.' She clapped. 'But I doubt you would have "come clean", as you put it, if you hadn't misdialled that number today.'

He looked away and both knew this to be the truth.

★ ★ ★

Creeping up the stairs, he trod with caution into their bedroom, a room in which he now felt like an intruder. He snatched items off hangers and rummaged in the drawers like a thief, only half conscious of what he was doing, wishing he was somewhere else, someone else. Eventually, with his suitcase in his hand, he walked slowly back downstairs to say goodbye.

Anna glanced up at him and his heart tore to see how wretched she looked. How had it come to this?

'I don't know what's happening, Theo. I don't know if we're ending, and I don't know what to do.'

'I'm sorry, Anna. I love you.'

'Please don't keep telling me that you love me – it's like wiping away the blood after you've cut me. It doesn't help the hurt or excuse the act, not even a little bit.'

He hovered awkwardly by the fireplace and stuttered out his plan. 'I've decided to go to Bristol. I need to see to some things there anyway, and I need to sort my head out. I'm sure you do too.'

'I'm sad, Theo, but I'm not surprised.' Her voice was a harsh croak. 'I've been waiting for this conversation since we went to the Maldives. I think deep down I knew then that we were on a timer.'

'You did?'

Anna nodded. 'I think possibly since the day we married. I mean, I was never right for you as far as your parents were concerned – I don't speak right, I don't know the wrong and right way to do things and I never went to that bloody school they bang on about.' She gave a false laugh. 'And for someone who cares as much about what others think as you do, especially your shitty parents, whose approval you still crave...' She let this hang.

'Don't say that.' He choked back another wave of sobs. He hadn't even had the chance to tell her about his earlier confrontation with his dad, or Marta, or bloody Xander Beaufort.

She followed him into the hall as he unhooked his coat from the newel post and ferreted in the pocket for his car keys. He bent towards her with arms slightly open, unsure whether or not to hold her, both of them instantly and painfully aware of how in such a short space of time the boundaries had shifted between them, to the point where he no longer felt able to take his wife in his arms and offer comfort.

'Just go, Theo! Fuck off to Bristol or anywhere else!' She jumped up and ran to the front door, holding it ajar, standing with her jaw clenched, waiting for him to pass.

'Anna, I... I can't be the man you need me to be.'

'So you've said.' She wiped away a stray tear. 'And actually, tonight, for the first time ever, I am starting to believe you.'

Theo headed west in a daze, driving on autopilot, his head swimming with hurtful snippets – *you've been cheating on me since the day we met*' – his heart aching so much he didn't know if he'd even make it to Bristol. He heard the long beep of an angry horn and was momentarily blinded by the flash of headlights on full beam. He swerved to retake the inside lane, unaware that he had drifted through lack of concentration. He swallowed, slowed his speed and took a swig of the coffee he'd picked up at the service station. He shook his head and put the radio on, desperate for something, anything, to distract him from the noise that filled his head.

Seventeen

Theo woke a fraction of a second before his alarm. He rubbed the grit from his eyes and lay back against the soft pillow, breathing deeply, knowing this was how best to shrug off the memory of the nightmare that lurked. He flexed his muscles against the cool sheet, a little damp with his sweat, and clicked on the lamp, careful not to wake Anna. He glanced across to where her sleeping form lay... but of course she wasn't there. This was not their bedroom at home in Barnes, this was the hastily secured bedroom of a budget hotel beside the river in Bristol. The place where he'd spent the last couple of weeks. By day he paced the docks, taking in the majesty of his red-brick warehouse and wondering how his life could have gone so spectacularly wrong in such a short space of time. By night he covered his ears with the spare pillow to block out the shouts of revellers coming and going at all hours, students mainly, pouring out of the famous Thekla nightclub, a former cargo ship which was moored opposite.

Contact with Anna had been minimal, each conversation curt and to the point. She wasted no time on pleasantries, and the lack of kindness in their exchanges deepened his sadness still further. *What did you expect, Theo?*

But despite his torturous dreams, today was going to be a good day, and that was enough to encourage him into the bathroom at such an ungodly time of the morning.

A couple of hours later he was pacing the arrivals hall at Cardiff airport with eager anticipation, checking his phone repeatedly. It was while he was distracted by the noisy reunion of a mother and daughter to his right that a familiar voice called out, 'Mate!'

Spud wrapped him in a big hug. They only ever embraced before or after significant time apart; to do so at routine hellos and goodbyes had never crossed their minds when they were younger, but now that they lived on different continents, it would probably become the norm. It was over six months now since they'd last seen each other.

'Liking the sideburns.' Theo pointed at Spud's hair. 'Even if I can spot a bit of a grey fleck. Very distinguished.'

'Got to do something to keep down with the kids,' Spud said, laughing.

Theo grabbed the folded suit carrier from his hand.

'You can mock my smattering of grey, but I see you're going a bit thin on top there.' Spud stood on tiptoes, an unnecessary charade as he was taller than Theo, and peered at his friend's crown.

Theo ran his palm self-consciously over his pate. 'Probably! The month I've had, nothing would surprise me.'

Spud patted his back, brotherly and affectionate. 'Glad you've not opted for the comb-over. Better to just get rid, as you have. Nice and short.'

'Thank you for that advice, Mr Sassoon. And it's not that bad! Any other comments on my appearance?'

'Not that I can think of – you're looking good, Theo, been working out?' Spud patted his own flat stomach.

The two laughed and Theo was grateful for how easily they always picked up where they'd left off, no matter how long they'd been apart. 'So, a whole five days in Blighty, eh?'

'Yep. Been in London the last two days – where you clearly were not – and now it's here for three days, for a conference and back-to-back meetings, but at least they're in beautiful Wales, which makes it slightly more bearable. If nothing else, I can look out of the window and enjoy the view. Thanks for coming to get me, by the way.'

'No worries. It's a good chance for a catch-up, otherwise wasted if you were sitting in a cab. And it's no distance from Bristol.'

Spud flashed him a thin-lipped smile when he mentioned Bristol. They had much to discuss, but that could wait.

'And of course you can take time out of your day as you're now your own boss! Must be great to do what the hell you like.' Spud grinned and punched Theo lightly on the shoulder.

'Oh yes, mate, I am living the dream.' Theo grinned. 'Only a couple of weeks in and I am indeed my own boss. Not a penny of income, rising costs, dwindling savings, loneliness, self-doubt, one single employee, and the only thing stopping me from jacking the whole thing in and going for a long swim off a short pier is the fact that I still, in some tiny crevice of my mind, believe that what I am doing might just be the right thing.'

'Well, as a wise man once said, the decision you make is always the right one.'

'It was you that said that!' Theo tutted.

'And I was right.'

'So, a good flight from town?' Theo asked as they made their way across the car park.

'Is there such a thing? I hate it. Sitting high above the clouds in a tin can. Planes are nothing more than a necessary evil for me, a way to hop across the pond and get around.'

'How are Kumi and the kids?'

'All good. Really good, in fact. Miyu is talking as well as walking now and she bosses me around when Kumi is otherwise engaged – they're like a tag team! And I swear to God they agree with each other on anything I am opposed to on point of principle, ganging up on me – my life is not my own and when her granny is around, I have to deal with the three of them!' The big grin on his face belied his words. 'I am secretly learning bits of Japanese so I can listen to what they say about me without them knowing. It's been illuminating.' He nodded.

'What do they say?'

'Essentially that I am not only stupid but I might actually be the most stupid man ever to grace the earth, like perennially stupid.'

'I don't think the stupid have Master's degrees and I don't think they use the word "perennially".'

'You might be right.' Spud chuckled. 'Tom is a sweet baby, the opposite of his sister in every way. If she is a tornado, Tom is a gentle breeze.'

Theo flipped the boot of his new black Mercedes SL. 'So you prefer Tom?'

Spud stared at him as he unloaded his bags from the trolley to the boot. 'You don't prefer one of your kids over the other!' He laughed.

'You don't?' Theo was only half joking.

'No! God, they're just different!' Spud shook his head and ran his eyes over the sparkling metallic paintwork of the car. 'Flipping heck – this is a beast! And if this is the car you get with no income, then sign me up!' He rubbed his hands together at the prospect of a ride.

'A legacy from Montgomery Holdings, mine for the next eighteen months, and then the way things are going, it'll probably be Shanks's pony. Want to drive?' Theo held up the keys.

'Mate, I am jetlagged, out of practice at driving on the left and more used to an automatic minivan – think I'd better pass. But I won't pretend I'm not insanely jealous and insanely excited at the thought of doing so!'

Theo slid onto the cool leather and watched his friend do the same in the passenger seat.

'Oh, she's a beauty! What's the most you've got out of her?' Spud clapped. 'Kumi would never let me have a car like this, even if we could afford it.'

'Well, Anna doesn't drive it.' He had mentioned Anna, done the thing they had seemingly been keen to avoid until the time was right.

'How's she doing?' Spud asked soberly, as if only now remembering that there were more important questions to ask than what top speed Theo had managed in his awesome car.

Theo concentrated on fastening his seatbelt and starting the engine, which purred. 'I don't know, is the truthful answer...' He raised his hands and let them fall. 'Our conversations are very formal and I don't know what she's thinking. Christ, I don't know what I'm thinking!'

'It must feel like you're in limbo.' Spud gave him the words.

'It does.' He gave a glum nod and looked straight ahead, unwilling and unable to discuss this further right now.

Spud lowered his voice, his words sincere. 'It will get easier. Everything will become clearer. You know that, don't you? It just needs time.'

Theo gulped down the embarrassing lump that sat in his throat. He looked across at his friend, who now ran his palm over the hand-stitched leather of the console. The temptation to open up to him properly before they'd even left the car park was strong. 'So where first?' He coughed. 'Celtic Manor – that's where you're staying, right?'

'Yes, and as long as they have good coffee, take me there. Right now I can think of nothing better.'

Theo shook his head in mock disgust. 'And to think we used to drink beer with our cornflakes every morning!'

'We used to do a lot of things.' Spud laughed. 'And at least one of us had a lot more hair!'

Theo pressed the stereo into action and the familiar strains of Guns N' Roses' 'Sweet Child O' Mine' filled the car.

'Oh, mate! Yes!' Spud began his impromptu air-guitar routine, while Theo banged the steering wheel as though it were a drum. They might have been two grown men with responsibilities, travelling in a high-end executive car from the airport, but for the five minutes of the song, they were nineteen again, scruffy and living in their grotty flat in Belsize Park, where the plumbing was leaky and they mostly slept or hung out in their underpants.

It was late by the time Theo arrived back at his Bristol hotel. He settled back on the bed and opened his laptop, dialling up for an internet connection. His email pinged repeatedly. He glanced up at the ceiling, imagining he was in the kitchen in Barnes, and smiled fondly at how Anna used to get irritated if any noise filtered up the stairs. He thought about Griff the puppy and felt a wave of longing for that house and those in it. He looked at the phone and considered calling, but another stilted exchange with Anna was the last thing either of them needed.

He liked working there in the quiet at that late hour. Catching up on emails from planners, architects, the team at the council and Jody, the young woman he employed remotely as his right hand. It was a world away from his plush office in Villiers House. He shook the image of his father and Marta from his head. Jody had emailed him the CVs of candidates who'd made the first and second cut for the role of project manager, to oversee the renovation – someone with more building experience than him. Theo smiled. If only he'd studied engineering!

He yawned, scratched his stubbly chin and gave the CVs only scant consideration, wondering if he really wanted the egg and cress sandwich that had been warming in his briefcase since he'd picked it up on the way back from dropping off Spud. As he debated how hungry he was and prepared to call it a night, his attention was drawn to one CV in particular.

'It can't be.'

He swallowed, sat forward and squinted at the screen. His pulse quickened as he clicked on the attached document. There it was: confirmation that Mr Magnus Wilson, of Bath, former pupil of Vaizey College and with a whole list of qualifications and achievements to his name, was asking Theo for a job. Not that Wilson would have known; there was nothing at a glance to link Theo to the company. Theo's reaction to seeing Magnus Wilson's name was surprising. Even now, more than a decade later, he felt a stab of discomfort at the memory of the boy who had made his school life hell. His leg jumped as if he was back in Theobald's House.

Sitting back on the bed, he thought long and hard about what to do. Would it be a good thing to see Wilson again or was it better to let sleeping dogs lie? He pictured the way Wilson had stood triumphantly after beating him up, his eyes showing no remorse.

Theo was unnerved. Instead of going to sleep, he reached for his briefcase and grabbed the slightly squashed sandwich. He was hungrier than he thought. He tried to stem thoughts of Wilson, already looking forward to meeting up with Spud again the next day.

The two men sat at a table in the sticky-floored pub in Wood Street, Cardiff.

'So are you going to interview him?' Spud asked through his mouthful of scampi.

'I honestly don't know,' Theo said. 'What would you do?'

'I'd be tempted to, just to get a look at him, and the vile, vengeful part of me would want to take him so far in the process and then let him down in a withering way.' He pretended to twirl an invisible moustache in a villainous manner.

'You don't have a vile and vengeful part, that much I do know.' Theo held his mate's gaze.

'True, I'm an old softie, but I like to think that if there was a call for it, I could do mean and macho.' Spud laughed and sipped his pint. 'Ah! I tell you what… crap food and a warm pint, I have missed home!'

'I'll bet. So do they have scayumpee in Washington?' Theo chuckled.

'Yes, but they call it "shrimp" – go figure! Not that I'm allowed to eat it. Kumi watches what I eat.' He pulled a face.

'So you are going for a pud?'

'Absolutely!' Spud grinned. 'I've got my eye on a hefty rum baba with extra cream.'

Theo shook his head in disgust.

'It's bothered you, hasn't it, this guy popping up after all this time.'

Theo sniffed. 'It has. You know how you have those people in your past who just…' He balled his right hand into a fist and punched it into his left palm. 'They have that ability to get under your skin because the memory of them is so powerful. It doesn't matter that years, decades have passed – he was a thorn in my side for so long.'

Spud paused, placing his pint on the tabletop. 'It does you no good to harbour those thoughts. They cause stress and stress is not something you want building up inside. You've got enough going on right now.'

'Haven't I just.'

'So, this move to Bristol, is it permanent?' Spud asked, his tone neutral.

'I don't know.' Theo looked towards the window. 'I know we both need a bit of space to get our heads straight, but I don't know if she wants me back, and I don't know if I can go back.'

'That's a lot of "don't knows".'

Theo nodded. 'Anna wanting a baby has always been the

biggest thing for her, and so to find out about Sophie...' He paused. 'It's knocked her for six and it's all my fault. If only I'd told her on our first date... But the longer I left it, the harder it became and there was always a reason not to bring it up.'

'Because you were scared to.'

'Yes, I was scared to and now I'm scared of what comes next.' He sighed. 'I want Anna to be happy, she deserves happiness more than anyone, and I wanted to be the one to make her happy. But now...? I'm not sure if I can.'

'And the Kitty situation?'

Theo coughed. 'No change. I have no part in her life. She doesn't want me to muddy the water for either of them, and I get it.'

'My advice would be to let it go, let a lot of those memories go, the ones that trouble you.'

'I know that, but what if I can't let them go, what if they're ingrained in here...' He tapped his forehead. '... springing up when I least expect them to?'

'I'd say you need to find a way to let them go, try harder.'

'The problem is...' He sniffed and exhaled, trying to compose himself. '... that right now I am very, very unhappy. And I shouldn't be. In truth, I am sick of it, mate, weary with being this sad.' He sighed for the umpteenth time. 'I had everything and I was loved.' He pictured Anna, again. 'But it's like I have nothing and it's... it's been this way for my whole life. I've been good at hiding it at times, but I'm aware of these fault lines running through my mind, and what leaks out of the cracks is sadness.' He clenched his jaw. 'And I've always felt that one jolt of fear, one huge knock and those lines might open up and I might fall into the abyss.' He looked up at his friend.

'Like when you got that letter from Kitty about Sophie,' Spud said, 'and you seemed to give up. I was worried about you then. Mind you, I'm worried about you now.'

Theo gave a dry smile. 'I know that if I fall, I might never resurface. I've faced depression many times, felt it breathing down my neck, and it's a hostile place to live and a place I never want to go to again. And I've always refused to talk to anyone about it. I took some pills and battled through. And it got better, a little.' He clenched his fists. 'But the state I'm in now feels different, it doesn't feel like depression, it feels like failure.'

'It's not failure – it's life.'

Theo shrugged. 'I guess. I'm just thinking of the times when I have been happy. The moments, often quite brief, when I was with someone I wanted to be with in a quiet place.' He thought of falling asleep next to Anna under a canopy of fairy lights in her tiny flat, and of the night spent on a camp bed in the front parlour of Mr Porter's crooked cottage with the smell of wood smoke and kerosene permeating the walls. 'This means I am capable of happiness, right?'

'Yes, absolutely, and that's really important.' Spud spoke plainly. 'Knowing when you're happy and what it was that made you happy is like learning the code.'

Theo nodded, feeling an overwhelming sense of longing for his wife.

'You're a good man, Theo, you always have been, and you're one of the very few people I trust. You're brilliant – I just wished you believed it.'

Theo blinked at his friend. 'I tell you what I wish: I wish we had another pint.'

He raised his empty glass, doing what he did best, skirting over the sentiment, making light of the moment and swallowing the howls of distress and regret that rumbled in this throat.

★ ★ ★

Theo revved the engine and slipped the gearbox through its paces. He was edgy. Not even Guns N' Roses on the stereo could lift his sense of apprehension. Having deliberated long and hard over what suit to wear and which shirt, he looked at his reflection in the mirror, satisfied with his appearance at least.

The traffic was heavy coming out of Cardiff, where he'd just dropped Spud at the airport for the first leg of his journey back to the US. As he crawled along the M4 towards Bristol, he began to lose his nerve. He put in a call to Jody.

'How's it going?' she said when she picked up, knowing he had to be at the hotel in Bristol by 11 a.m. to interview the two final candidates.

'Yep, good. Anything to report this morning?' A small part of him hoped for a cancellation, a change in plans that would mean he could peel off at the next junction and go and find some breakfast. *What were you thinking, Theo? What part of you thinks this is a good idea?*

'No, nothing to report. We're all good,' Jody chirped.

'Righto. Well, have a good one and I'll call you later.'

He ended the call and watched as the traffic miraculously vanished, leaving him plenty of time to make his appointments. He turned up the volume for 'Sweet Child O' Mine' and hit the gas.

★

Theo stood and shook the hand of Phil Marshall. 'Thank you for coming in. We'll be in touch.' He smiled as the man got to his feet and buttoned his suit jacket.

'Thank you for seeing me and if you need any more information or have any other questions, then just shout.'

'We will. Once again, thanks for coming in today, Phil.'

'My home phone is best – I'll be on it all day. So…'

'Yes.' Theo sensed Phil's desperation. 'Thank you.'

He watched him reluctantly leave the room; it was obvious he wanted to stay there and work on Theo until he said yes. He thought of Spud and the way Miyu wore him down. He smiled at the image of his browbeaten buddy, trying to picture him holding court on Capitol Hill, advising senior politicians on fiscal policy with confidence and then going home to try and negotiate bedtimes with a headstrong little girl.

He felt a new and unwanted pang of regret over Sophie, tried to imagine going home to her. Spud's words filled his head. '*My advice would be to let it go, let a lot of those memories go. It does you no good to harbour those thoughts.*' Theo wished it were that simple. He was going to miss his mate.

He stood and walked across the spacious top-floor meeting room of the city-centre hotel, taking in the waxed wooden floor, comfortable leather furniture and painted brick walls. He liked the nautical overtones, the porthole mirrors and the over-sized rope-wrapped lanterns, approving of the nod to Bristol's maritime heritage. They were a welcome distraction as he waited. He swallowed the bile that rose in his throat and wiped his sweaty palms on his trousers.

He was nervous. Very nervous.

He stared out of the window onto the cobbled courtyard

beneath and tried to slow his breathing, thinking of how best to approach the meeting and wishing he was somewhere else. His eyes scanned the far wall to see if there might be another way to leave, a different exit, but there was none. He glanced at the door and tried to imagine Wilson walking through it. His stomach jumped when he realised that at any moment that was exactly what would happen.

There was no way he was going to give Wilson a job. No way on God's earth, but the temptation to see his tormentor again, now that he had the upper hand, was one Theo could not resist. He had already decided to be gracious and kind, to be the better man. What he wanted more than anything was not revenge, nor even to gloat; he wanted answers, answers that might help keep his nightmares at bay. Not that he would ever have admitted this to another living soul. He now wondered if Wilson would even recognise him. It occurred to him that it was most unlikely that he haunted Wilson's dreams in the way Wilson did his.

Theo made his way back to the desk, fingering the CV that sat in front of him, taking in the few facts: married, three children, aged thirty-four. It seemed almost impossible that that amount of time had gone by. It was as he read further that the door creaked and in walked a man Theo would have passed in the street without recognising. It was only his eyes that marked him out as the Magnus Wilson of old.

Shorter than Theo had remembered, and slighter, Wilson sported a dark, close-cropped beard and had been liberal with his eau de toilette. He smiled and walked forward with his hand outstretched, mimicking the many masters who had taught them that this was the Vaizey way. '*Make an impression, boy!*

Hold eye contact! Command the room!' 'Magnus Wilson,' he announced as he neared the desk.

Theo drew himself up to his full height and liked the advantage it gave him. He too held out his hand and met Wilson's gaze. As they shook hands, he saw the faint hint of recollection cross Wilson's brow; he was clearly trying to place the face, no doubt running through the database in his head, attempting to find a match.

'Theodore Montgomery.' Theo nodded and released the man's hand.

'Christ alive!' Wilson smiled broadly and opened his mouth, seemingly uncertain of what to say. 'Theo?'

'Yes.' He sat.

'Good God! We were at Vaizey College together!'

'Yes, we were. Please sit down.' He spoke with an air of indifference, indicating the chair and watching as Wilson took up the seat.

'How long is it since we've seen each other?' Wilson shook his head in surprise.

'A long time.'

'I can't believe it! Did you know it was me?' Wilson glanced at the CV sitting on the desk.

'I did, but only just before you arrived,' he lied.

Wilson shook his head. 'This is nuts, Theo! I can't believe it. It feels crazy to ask how you've been, with so much water under the bridge. How would we start?'

'How indeed.' Theo wasn't sure if Wilson was playing nice, had forgotten their violent relationship or simply didn't give a shit. Either way, he kept his guard up.

Wilson carried on. 'I went to a couple of the OVB reunions,

but they weren't really my thing. I know a couple of the lads that still go, but I've not kept in touch with many people.'

'I would have thought the reunions would have been right up your street.' Theo sat back in the chair.

'Are you kidding? An army brat like me? I only had a place because the military were paying the fees and there were plenty who never let me forget it.' Wilson shook his head. 'I always felt like an unwelcome guest.'

Theo stared at him, shocked to hear Wilson describe his feelings for Vaizey in the same terms he himself used. 'I didn't know that. You certainly didn't let it show.'

'Yep, it's true. My mum left my dad when I was a toddler, which now I have kids myself I cannot begin to fathom, not at all. I don't remember her.' He shook his head. 'Even though my dad wasn't an officer – officers' kids routinely went to Vaizey – the MOD helped him out and so it was boarding school for me while he was in the army. He was often on tour and it was deemed better for me than going into care, and better for my dad, of course.'

In care, like my Anna, like the kids who will benefit from this project.

Wilson continued. 'I used to spend the holidays with my old nana in Dorchester. For me it was like two worlds colliding: one minute I was roaming the privileged halls of Vaizey College and the next I was sharing a bunk bed with my cousin and doing paper rounds to get cash. I even had two voices – my school voice and my home voice.' He shook his head. 'I always felt split, like I didn't belong in either world, not really. In fact I don't think I properly became me until I met my wife, Julie.' He licked his lips. 'God, I am over sharing. Please put it down to nerves and the fact that we have history.'

Theo noticed that his voice now was a mixture of the two worlds, not overly posh and overbearing as it had been, but softer, more pleasant.

'Are you nervous?'

'Yes, of course! I want this job and I can't decide whether our school days makes it more or less likely that I will get it, if I'm being honest.' His eyes settled on Theo's face and Theo watched his Adam's apple rise and fall.

'You treated me quite badly at school.' Theo spoke the words slowly, a watered-down version of the long diatribe he had practised countless times over countless years. But today, with Wilson sitting in front of him, this measured approach seemed more appropriate.

'I did, and I remember it.' Wilson nodded. 'I remember us fighting.'

Not fighting – you beat me up.

'You came back from the summer break looking tanned and happy and I'd been stuck indoors for the best part of two months, staring at a rainy window, and my dad had only just gone back on tour and I was pig sick with jealousy.' He smiled at Theo like they were old friends reminiscing, which only served to confuse Theo more.

A jolt of nerves fired through his gut, the reminder of not only the fight but that summer at La Grande Belle. 'I can assure you I might have been tanned, but I was far from happy and even if I had been, that was surely not sufficient grounds for beating me up.'

'No question you are absolutely right. I was a little shit to you. A proper little shit.' Wilson chuckled, as if they had shared a joke. 'Theo…! Well, I never.' He spoke his name fondly. 'I was made house prefect just before you arrived…'

A Theobald's house prefect. Like Xander Beaufort – my brother.

Wilson coughed. 'Anyway, I was cleaning Twitcher's study one day when he took a call from admissions to say that you were arriving. I was earwigging and heard him say you were a close family friend. Oh my God! We were all panicking, convinced you were going to be a right snitch, running to your dad's mate, spilling our secrets.'

Theo shook his head. 'I don't think I'd even met Twitcher until I started school.'

'I hated you so much!' Again, Wilson's tone was warm, almost affectionate.

'Why? Why did you hate me?' Theo sat forward and rested his arms on the desk, keen to understand why he'd been the target, what exactly he'd done to incur Wilson's wrath.

'Are you kidding? There you were, jetting off on a plane in the holidays. You had everything I wanted. The best I could hope for was making cakes with my nana in her little kitchen and eating cheese on toast, squashed next to her and my cousins on the sofa. I'd never been on a proper holiday, much less on a plane!'

Theo pictured this and knew that he would have loved to have spent time in a cosy house, eating cheese on toast on a crowded sofa.

Wilson was still talking. 'You were rich, like mega rich, and I had to put up with a second-hand uniform out of the lost-and-found box. And your dad used to turn up in that sweet navy blue Aston Martin.' Wilson whistled. 'She was a beauty – I remember it now, it was the talk of the school. And your mum...!' He smiled. 'I don't want to sound disrespectful, but your mum was smoking hot! And how she fussed over you – I think we were all a bit jealous of you.'

Theo laughed. 'Yes, that car was a beauty.'

'*Fucking smell... vomit!... bloody expensive... idiot!... what the fuck is wrong with him?*'

'But remember, that's my mother you're talking about!'

'I know! I know!' Wilson placed his hand over his mouth. 'But she was something else. We knew you had a flash house in London – the rumours swirled. God, you even had old Porter to keep an eye on you at school, and he gave it to me with both barrels every time I saw him. He cuffed me one right on the head.' He rubbed his temple, as if the pain still lingered. 'I was shit scared. Scared of him and scared of getting another one if my dad found out. You had it all, Theo, and I had nothing, and I found it hard to stomach. It wasn't personal. I was just a messed-up kid. A very messed-up kid who was missing his mum.'

'I guess that's easy for you to say, but it was *very* personal to me,' Theo levelled.

Wilson nodded. 'I can imagine, and the thought of anyone treating my boys how we treated you...' He shook his head. 'I am sorry.'

The two men sat, letting the apology hang between them like a bridge. Theo visualised Mr Porter and heard his words as he reprimanded Wilson. '*Here's the thing, Mr Wilson. You need to be very careful that you respect everyone in your path, as you never know where they'll pop up again. And, trust me, the path we walk is long and winding.*'

Theo smiled at the irony. *Isn't it just...*

Wilson sat forward. 'Would you like to see a picture of my family?' Without waiting for a response, he pulled out his wallet, holding up a slightly faded image of a homely blonde woman flanked by three young boys. 'My oldest, Joe, only nine but plays good rugby!' He nodded with pride at the photo. 'And the other two are Max and Ben. Ben is our surprise. We'd agreed to stop at two, but you know what these women are like – persistent! – and after a bottle or two of Lambrusco, she took advantage and got lucky.' He laughed.

Theo pictured Anna and felt sadness on her behalf. She too had been persistent but hadn't got so lucky.

'What about you, Theo, any kids?'

'No. No kids.' *Apart from you, Sophie... Apart from you, and to deny you cuts me to the quick.*

'Oh, I'm sorry.' Wilson folded away his wallet and it occurred to Theo that those who did have children, Spud included, could only see his supposed childless state as regretful.

'So, about the job...' Theo coughed and brought the meeting back on track.

'Oh God, I'd almost forgotten why I'm here. Excuse me while I switch into professional mode.' Wilson sat up straight and adjusted his jacket lapels. 'I have a lot of experience on projects like this. Last year I worked on a similar build in Hereford – vast industrial barn conversions that were made into holiday studios, but a similar principle. I control budgets, oversee materials, the whole shebang.'

Theo cast his eyes over Wilson's CV and tried to think of an appropriate question.

He drove down the M4 with a peculiar feeling of peace. Seeing Magnus Wilson had helped draw a line under the years of persecution and given him greater insight as to why things had happened as they did. It wasn't that he forgave Wilson, not at all, but he came away from their encounter with a better understanding, and he hoped to build on that foundation. He smiled at the metaphor, then put in a call to Jody.

'Evening, boss, you heading back to London?'

'Yes, I've got the bank meeting tomorrow and I need to do a few personal things. I'll let you know how it goes.'

'Does this mean we can guarantee my pay for the next few months?'

'Yes, if the loan gets approved. Otherwise I shall give you a glowing reference for whoever is lucky enough to employ you next!'

'You are too kind,' she said. 'How did it go today?'

'It was good, actually.'

'Have you made a decision?'

'Yes. Yes, I have.' He smiled. 'And assuming we get the funding, we are good to go. Can you get me Phil Marshall's number.'

Night fell as he reached Barnes. Heading there had been a spur-of-the-moment decision as he'd hit London. A quick drive past his house had revealed nothing. The hall lamp was on, but the curtains were drawn. He'd hoped to see Anna in the street, on her way home or walking Griff, and in his mind he'd played out how he might make their meeting look casual, but she was nowhere to be seen. He decided to pop in and see his parents. He hadn't spoken to his mother since his resignation and he wanted to smooth things with her at least.

He parked up, rapped on the door and waited while his parents flicked on the various lights and slid the many bolts to allow him entry.

'Theo! Is everything okay?' His mother gripped the thick shawl at her neck. Her immediate concern indicated that their angry call was now at the back of her mind and he was thankful.

'Yes, just thought I'd pop in and see you.' He walked forward and grazed her cheek with a kiss.

'Well, this is most unexpected!' She smiled nonetheless and ushered him into the sitting room, shuffling a little in her slippers.

'Theo, is everything okay?' His father roused himself from his chair; he had clearly been dozing. There was no particular animosity in his tone, nothing to indicate that this was their first meeting since the damaging encounter in the boardroom at Villiers House.

'Yes, I was just passing. Well, kind of.' He sat on the sofa.

His father stared at him quizzically. 'How's the Bristol thing doing?' He reached for his glasses and rested them on his bulbous nose.

'Good. So much red tape.' He nodded, wanting to give only the minimum of detail, which was as much as his father deserved. He noted the change to his father's once athletic frame, the slight bowing under the extra weight. His mother, in contrast, had lost the curves that had apparently so enraptured his peers and was now reed thin. Theo recalled the way Wilson had admired her. He yawned and rubbed his face; it had been quite a day.

'Daddy and I were just having cocoa, darling. Here's yours.' His mum handed him a mug.

'Thanks.' He took it gratefully between his palms. 'I was in Bristol today, interviewing. I met up with an Old Vaizey Boy – he was on the shortlist for the position of site manager. Magnus Wilson?'

'Magnus Wilson,' his mum repeated, tapping her mouth with her finger. 'That name rings a bell for some reason.'

'Was he a Theobald's boy?' his father asked, loudly.

'Naturally, Dad. Theobald's through and through.'

His father's face split into a grin of pure joy and he clapped his hands. 'Well, good for you, Theo! Good for you! How was he?'

'Good. Yes, good, I think.'

His father sat forward in the chair. 'It's wonderful to share those memories, isn't it? A unique experience, I've always found, and it binds you for life.'

'Yes, I would have to agree.' Theo smiled ironically and sipped his cocoa, knowing he would always be mystified by the esteem in which his dad held the place. It had felt so important to share the news with his father, but at the same time he hated that at some level he still sought his approval and, worse, that it was all wrapped up in that bloody school. 'I have a meeting with the bank tomorrow, to sort a business loan, funding for the renovation and so forth. Fingers crossed.' He remembered his conversation with Jody and sincerely hoped he wasn't going to have to let her go.

'You don't need a loan, darling – you're still a shareholder of Montgomery's and you can use company money.' His mother spoke matter-of-factly.

'I...' He looked at his father – this hadn't occurred to him. He wasn't sure but thought there might have been a flash of something like regret in his dad's eyes.

'Your mother is right. Loans cost money. That's just basic, boy. Don't borrow if you don't have to. Speak to Marcus, he can go through the funding. And you should take offices at Villiers House too, and claim your start-up costs, that makes it

270

tax-efficient. Have you considered registering as a charity? There are tax breaks to be had there too, means you'll have more to plough back in where it's needed.'

'Thank you.' He meant it, sincerely.

'Don't thank me! It's not a case of thanks, it's a matter of birthright!' his father boomed.

And right there and then, the moment seemed appropriate. 'There's something I'd like to tell you.'

His mother peered over the rim of her glasses. 'Are you referring to the fact that you have been lodging elsewhere?'

'I wasn't, actually, but you've heard that Anna and I are taking a break?' He didn't know how else to phrase it.

'Oh yes, dear. I mean, it's none of our business, of course, but gossip spreads like wildfire in Barnes.'

Theo bit his tongue, knowing it spread like wildfire because she liked to set the kindling and apply a match. 'Yes, well, we're apart right now, regretfully, but we'll see.' He sipped his cocoa, a taste that took him back to childhood, to school. 'As I say, that wasn't what I was referring to.'

'Oh?' He had her interest.

He took a deep breath. 'The reason I fell apart in my last year at university was not because I was being lazy or partying too hard – it was because I was depressed.'

'I think we rather gathered that.' She sniffed.

'Yes, but maybe not the reason why.' He paused. 'I fathered a child. I have a child, a little girl.'

His mother gave a gasp and slopped her cocoa onto the arm of the chair. His father remained unnaturally still, alert, waiting to hear more.

'She's not so little now,' Theo continued, keeping his gaze on his mug. 'I'm not in her life, but Anna knows, and I don't really know why but I wanted to tell you. It felt important. No more secrets.' He caught his father's eye.

'A granddaughter?' his mother asked with a wistful air. She placed her cocoa on the table by her chair and reached for her handkerchief. 'And does the child have a name?'

Theo nodded. 'Her name is Sophie.'

'Sophie,' his mum repeated, taking the corner of her handkerchief to blot whatever was in her eye.

His father picked up the remote control and turned up the news.

After saying goodbye to his parents, Theo grabbed his briefcase and checked into the local pub, where the rooms were overheated and the floors creaky. His phone buzzed.

'Hey, mate.'

'Hey! You home?' He tried to picture Spud's whereabouts.

'Nearly, thank God. How did it go?'

Theo smiled, knowing that Spud had probably spent most of his day envisaging Theo's great showdown with the school bully. 'Better than I thought it would, actually.'

'Did you punch him over the desk? Kick his shins? Nick his lunch money?'

'No!' Theo laughed. 'You've been watching too many of Miyu's cartoons.'

'You might be right.' Spud sighed.

'It was weird. I got really worked up before he arrived, I was nervous, but I don't think I would have recognised him, to be truthful. I realised that the boy I pictured doesn't exist, not any more – and he hasn't for years. If anything, he looked—'

'Looked what?'

'I don't know.' Theo huffed. 'Ordinary. Not like someone that would pose a great threat or be the total bastard that he was as a kid.'

'Well, people can and do change.'

'Some, yes. If anything, I felt quite sorry for him.'

'Bloody hell! You did?'

'Yup.'

'And did he recognise you?'

Theo recalled the way Wilson had eyed him over their handshake. 'Yes, almost instantly, and he wasn't embarrassed or overly contrite. I think his memories have a different filter. He made the whole school thing and his behaviour sound like they were par for the course, and I realised that for him they might well have been. I don't think he had the easiest time as a child, but for very different reasons to me.'

'So what did you do, send him packing? Spit in his eye?'

'Actually, no.' Theo loosened his collar and spun his keys on his finger. 'I chatted to him civilly. Not a punch was thrown.'

'You were civil?'

'Better than that – I was almost chummy.' He closed his eyes and held the phone away from his ear while Spud laughed loudly, as if this was the punchline he'd been waiting for.

'I'm proud of you, Theo.'

'Thanks. You don't think I'm a mug for not challenging him more?'

Spud's laughter again filled the gap between the oceans.

'What are you laughing at?' Theo asked.

'Oh, mate, I am sitting in a cab, it's late afternoon, traffic is horrendous and I have a mountain of work to do. I've got emails pinging in left, right and centre. And all I want is to be at home with a cup of coffee, but instead I'm heading to a toy shop because I promised Miyu a Sylvanian Families tree house and there wasn't one at the airport, surprise, surprise. I'm on a mission to keep a promise when there are a million things I should and would rather be doing, and you ask if I think *you* are a mug? Still, the joys of parenthood, huh?'

'I guess so.'

'Ah, shit, bad choice of words. How are things? Have you seen Anna?' Spud adopted a softer tone.

Theo opened the rickety sash window and looked up at the night sky, listening as a duck squawked and landed on the water. 'No. I haven't seen her. Did you ever wonder if you were accidentally living someone else's life? You know, like when there's a mix-up at the hospital and people get the wrong kid?'

'No, I never felt like that.'

There was a beat of silence while both waited for more. Neither took the lead.

'I need to go, Spud, I need a leak. I'll call you back later in the week.'

'Okay, but what happened with the Wilson bloke? How did it end?'

Theo took a deep breath and gave a small laugh. 'I gave him a job.'

Eighteen

Theo had been living in the little flat in Bristol for six weeks. He kept it bare, wary of making it feel like home as that would have given it a permanence that he feared. There were no pictures on the walls, no crockery or cutlery in the cupboards and no landline. He preferred to treat it as he had the hotel not too far from the flat, nothing more than a base. Just until...

It had been strange to wake up in his childhood home in Barnes that morning, and not for the first time in recent weeks he'd come to with a start, wondering where he was. He fastened the towel around his waist and stared at his reflection in the bathroom mirror.

The call from his mother the previous day had shocked him and the sense of disbelief hadn't lessened. It was a strange time, a day he'd always known would come, but one he'd assumed would be far into the future, giving him a chance to mentally prepare. He could only imagine how Anna had coped, having had to deal with something similar when she'd been nothing more than a little girl. His heart flexed for her.

He was yet to feel the sadness that he'd anticipated; right

now he was simply exhausted by the weight of the news. He guessed this was shock. He felt floored, angry even, as his brain struggled to accept the finality. His nerves twitched and his limbs jumped, as though surprised. He felt cheated; he'd figured he'd have more time. At the back of his mind a fantasy had hovered for longer than he cared to admit. It was one where he and his father sat in front of a roaring fire, pints in hand, as they gave each other the floor and spoke openly about their clashes and their differences before hopefully arriving at a place that resembled calmer waters, if not understanding. He knew it was ridiculous – he was a grown man, and how many people reached his age without considering the inevitable loss of those they loved? But Theo had, as ever, felt in some way immune.

There was so much he had yet to say to his dad, so many conversations started but not finished. Worst of all were the apologies that had danced around them over the years. Both men had failed to reach up and grasp the words, unable, for reasons deeper than he could fathom, to make peace. The wounds of their recent battle, where harsh and hurtful truths had been exchanged in the boardroom, had healed a little, but the skin that wrapped them was thin, new and still tender.

And now it was too late. It was all too late.

He stared at his reflection, wiping the steam from the mirror with his hand, and wondered what else was slipping beyond his reach faster than hc realised.

Two memories were proving especially hard to shift: his dad leering at Freddie from the bedroom window of La Grande Belle, and his dad trying to hide his anger when Theo had thrown up in his Aston Martin. Both events so long ago now and yet still stuck on replay in his head. Spud's good words of advice came to him once more: '*Let it go, let a lot of those memories go, the ones that trouble you.*'

If only it were that simple. He wished he could replace them with something more agreeable, like the Christmas morning from his childhood when he'd watched as his Dad tore open yet another pair of socks before throwing the packaging at his mum, who ducked and giggled, trying not to spill her breakfast Bellini. Or the time he'd spied the two of them through the crack of the kitchen door, dancing with each other, both in their pyjamas and neither with any clue that he was looking. But it was the negative memories that persisted. His father's face livid: '*The idiot!... What the fuck is wrong with him?*'

'It's a good question. What is wrong with you?' he asked the face that stared back. He jutted his chin and ran the back of his fingers over his neck and face, taking in the deepening furrows on his brow.

He shaved, dressed slowly and made his way downstairs. The sound of Stella's sniffing filled the air. He was ashamed at how much the noise grated his bones. It was more than he wanted to deal with. He resisted the urge to put the radio on and dilute the atmosphere with something, anything, unsure of the correct etiquette in this situation. He watched her make cups of tea as a distraction and wipe the sink and countertops with a bleached dishcloth, going over and over the same pristine surfaces, until, spent, she sat slumped. Her usual upright posture was bowed under the weight of her grief. She drew random shapes with her finger on the tabletop. She looked... She looked old.

'Are you going to say something at the service?' she eventually managed, looking up. She blew her nose into a paper tissue and balled it into her handbag.

'I hadn't really thought about it. Would you like me to?'

'Of course I'd like you to! It's very important. And you have six days to think about exactly what.' Her voice cracked, the sandpaper vowels rasping in a throat raw with distress. She resumed her invisible doodling.

'Sure.' He nodded. 'If you think that's a good idea.'

She rolled her eyes, as if the answer should be evident. 'And I think we should go and see him. Together.' She stared at him, her eyes brimming.

He felt the rise of nausea. 'Do you… Do you think that's wise, Mum?'

Her reply was instant, her voice shrill. 'It's not about what's wise, it's about what's right! I *have* to say goodbye to him. My husband, my darling husband…'

'But you said goodbye to him at the hospital,' he reminded her, keeping his tone neutral, 'and he won't know if you go and see his… his body or not.' Saying the word 'body' felt both disrespectful and uncomfortable, reducing his father to a thing. A thing that was now gone. This thought hit him with force in the centre of his breastbone. 'I just don't want you to be upset by seeing him after he's passed, that's not how he would want you to remember him, and I don't think it's healthy that your last image of him might not be a pleasant one.'

'I don't get to choose, Theodore! I can't help what I find, but I *will* do the right thing by him.'

'But that's just it, Mum, who says it's the right thing? There is no right thing. There is only what's right for you. You don't have to do anything you don't want to. I just think—'

'I don't need to know what you think!' Stella raised her voice. 'Don't be like him! Don't tell me what to think or what I can or can't do!'

Theo took a deep breath. 'I'm only trying to look out for you, Mum. Even though this is the worst possible thing that could have happened, try not to forget that we are both going through it and I am trying to make it the best it can be for you. Because I love you.'

'Well, good.' She reached into her handbag for her packet of cigarettes. 'Because the right thing for me is going to see your father before he is laid to rest, and the right thing for you, as his only son, is to come with me. Okay?'

She jammed the cigarette into her mouth, once pretty and full, now pulled thin and puckered with creases which fanned out from her top lip. She held the lighter to the end of the cigarette. It had the usual effect of making him want to smoke, which annoyed him as much as it tested his reserves.

He threw open the kitchen window.

'It's already quite cold in here,' his mother snapped, gathering her fur stole around her narrow shoulders with her cigarette-free hand.

'Yep, but I don't particularly want to breathe your cigarette smoke, so what are we going to do?'

He folded his arms across his chest, holding his position. He watched her draw on her cigarette and wondered how many mothers, when told by their child at a time like this that they loved them, would have answered that they loved them too... He left the room, rubbing his temples to try and alleviate the first signs of a headache.

The funeral felt flat, predictable, and after Theo had given his rather rushed eulogy, his mind wandered. In the lead-up to the day, he had suspected, in fact hoped, that the service at St Mary's might be the point at which he'd experience the full force of his grief. He wanted to succumb to the tsunami of emotions that he figured must be bubbling inside him somewhere – but no. Instead, he remained almost dazed by the proceedings, unable to relate to the outpouring of grief from his mother, which made him feel more than a little uncomfortable. He had assumed she'd be more contained, a quality she had always admired in her peers, but, as so often, it seemed that such rules only applied to other people.

The speeches were numerous and heartfelt, given by glum-looking old men who stared out over the congregation from the lectern. He suspected they were considering their own fates as much as they were mourning their friend. Several Old Vaizey Boys spoke of a man who was smart, successful and benevolent. But as for the principled family man whose door was always open, Theo hardly recognised that description.

He remembered something Spud had said long ago, when as students they'd strolled round Highgate Cemetery, drunkenly searching for the grave of Karl Marx. '*I wonder where they bury all the shitty people? I've only ever seen gravestones for the good, the beloved and the wise. Do you think there are any that say "My husband was an absolute arsehole"?*' They'd giggled at the thought. He wished the memory hadn't popped into his head right now. Spud had sent a simple card of condolence with a simple message: *Ever onwards and upwards, my friend.* Theo coughed and returned his attention to the service.

Back at his parents' house for the wake, Theo grabbed a drink and, turning, saw Anna walking in. *My Anna.* A smile crept over his face; his default setting whenever he saw her was happiness. She looked beautiful: make-up-free and neat in her black dress with a white crocheted collar. He saw her bite her lip and knew she was feeling nervous. He walked towards her.

'Hey, you.'

'Hi, Theo.' She reached out and squeezed his arm, and he fought the temptation to sweep her into a hug and hold her tight.

'How's Shania doing?' He searched for common ground and was rewarded with the beginnings of a smile.

'Good. Getting close to due date – she's going to be such a great mum. Did you get my card?' She spoke quietly.

'I did, and thank you. And thank you for bringing Mum food and checking on her, she did mention it.' He had studied her words of condolence, scouring them for any hidden note of forgiveness, any hint of a possible reconciliation, but finding none.

'Not a problem. Of course.' She looked down. 'I was genuinely sorry to hear about your dad. I don't think any of us were expecting it. I mean, of course you never are, but you know what I mean.'

'I do, and thank you.' He hated the formality with which he had offered thanks three times in as many minutes.

'How are you doing?' She placed her hand on his chest, a gesture that brought a lump to his throat.

'I'm...' He lifted the tumbler in her direction, as if that might be explanation enough.

'I thought it was a nice service.'

'Yes, it was.'

'And let's face it, Theo, it could have been so much worse.' She pulled a face.

'In what way?'

She leant towards him and he inhaled her particular, intoxicating scent, somewhere between clean laundry and summer. 'Your mum might still have been going through her Jesus phase, which would have meant that Pastor Jules, he of the legendary bootlace tie and magnificent tash, might have been conducting affairs from a shed in Putney.'

Theo laughed, feeling instantly self-conscious that he should find anything funny today but at the same time so glad they could chat like this. 'God, I'd almost forgotten about him! But at least she'd have been able to chat to Dad and find out where he left the key for the shed.' He laughed, recalling some of the pastor's excesses. 'That was some night.'

'Yep.' She gave a faltering smile, as if the mention of a good night inevitably led to thoughts about the bad one, when he had walked out and she had let him. 'Anyway, I'm sure you have to mingle.' She stepped backwards and it took all of his strength not to reach for her and pull her close.

Saskia, his mother's friend, closed in. 'Come on, Theodore, eat up.' She held up a foil platter of bite-sized morsels, all pink and sitting on something crunchy, the sight of which made his stomach lurch.

'I'm okay, thank you.'

Saskia winked, then continued on her mission. 'We have no space in the freezer – I need to make sure everyone in the house consumes at least one of these. Or it will be doggy bags – really, not the done thing!'

The kitchen felt like the safest place to hide, among the

lavender- and mothball-scented crowd of well-wishers. From somewhere in the middle of the throng, his mother let out a loud cry. He looked over to see Nancy, another friend of old, supplying her with tissues and a steady forearm on which to lean. He pushed his way through to where Nancy seemed to have hemmed her in. His mother glanced up at him with an expression of relief.

'Theodore, you remember Nancy?'

'Yes, of course. Hello, Nancy.' He smiled at the woman, whose orange lipstick and green eye shadow reminded him of the crude makeover Miyu had given him with her face paints. 'Thank you so much for coming.'

'I wouldn't have missed it. Peregrine was a dear. Besides, we go way back, your parents and I. I think the last time I saw you, Theo, was on the Riviera – you were no more than a tiddler.' She wagged her finger at him, as if he still merited no more than tiddler status. 'I remember Leopold thought you were a fine young man, not at all giddy-headed like some of a similar age, my own included.' She sighed.

He was embarrassed that this woman and her husband had been present at La Grande Belle. The whole gang must have been aware of his father's drunken infidelity. He felt his face colour. They probably knew a lot more besides. He pictured Xander Beaufort, whom he had half expected to attend today. Poor Alexander, just another aspect of his father's past to be smudged into the background until no one could see it clearly.

His mother seemed indifferent to what her peers did and didn't know. He wondered if it was the fog of old age that coated anything unpleasant with a veneer of acceptability or whether it was simply a deterioration of the memory that meant events were not so sharp, so damaging. Or, of course, it might have been that she now didn't give a shit. His smile faded to a watery imitation.

Nancy raised her voice, as if this might make her point more valid, or perhaps it was that she was used to addressing her friends whose hearing was on the wane. 'I was just saying to your mother that I think it would be a good idea if she went to speak to someone.'

'And I have told Nancy that I have no intention of doing anything of the sort.' Stella spoke determinedly.

'Well...' Nancy gripped her elaborate, bead-encrusted handbag to her chest. 'That's what you say now, but when Leopold died I went to speak to a therapist. It helped me enormously. I needed to make sense of it all, and talking things through made a difference.'

'Darling, I really don't think that kind of thing is for me.' His mother gave a sharp nod, signalling an end to the topic.

Nancy, however, had other ideas. 'And I didn't think it was for me either, and I have to admit, I *was* okay for a while, but when the fuss of the funeral had died down and Douglas and the grandchildren had gone back to Zurich, I was at a loss. I needed to talk to someone who wasn't family and who was going to listen and help me stay on track. And she did. She was wonderful. I really owe her so much – it's hard to explain. Her name is Miss Garcia and she is based in Bloomsbury.'

'Oh, I can just see me popping off to Bloomsbury each week! It's hardly convenient!' his mother scoffed. 'Thank you, Nancy, but no.'

'Well, I shall leave her card on the side here. She is very expensive but worth every penny. She's clever, and all I know is that when I was at my lowest point, she helped me find happiness.'

Nancy's words had a profound effect on Theo. He wondered if it was possible, that there really could be someone, a clever someone, who could help him sort his muddled thoughts, help him find the equilibrium he so craved. He pictured it in that second, his happiness as a rainbow-striped thing hiding under a bed or lurking in the back of a cupboard behind long-forgotten boxes...

'Theo?'

He turned at the sound of Anna's voice and raised his eyebrows in reply.

'I'm off.'

'Right.' He wished they were alone; there was so much more he wanted to say. But as he was ordering his thoughts and summoning the courage to voice them, she called to his mother.

'I shall speak to you soon, Stella.' And just like that, she was gone.

★ ★ ★

It felt strange walking into Villiers House again, knowing he was now the last Montgomery in the place. And for possibly the first time, he considered what his parents meant by birthright – would all this be Sophie's? How would that work – a letter like the one Anna had received from her unknown father, Michael Harper, sent after his death? The thought was as depressing as it was cowardly.

He walked past the desk once occupied by Marta, suppressing the unease he felt at the memory of his last sighting of her, and smiled at the young man sitting there.

'We were all very sorry to hear about your father.'

'Thank you.' He stared at the man, trying to recall his name from when they'd been introduced, a while ago now.

'Stephen.'

'Yes, sorry. Thank you, Stephen. My memory...' He tapped his head, as if that was all the explanation required. 'My mind's all over the place at the moment.'

'I can only imagine. Marcus said you'll be taking over your dad's office when you're ready and so I just wanted to say that if there's anything you need or anything we can do...'

'Thank you.'

Theo opened the door to the big room. It smelt of his dad, of woody cologne and nicotine, with a hint of peppermint and whisky, the former used ineffectively to mask the latter. He opened the window and welcomed the cold breeze that whipped around the furniture. The uncomfortable coolness seemed to help clear his thoughts. Settling back into his father's chair felt illicit. He ran his palms over the cracked leather of the arms where the old man's hands had rested over the years, and still his reaction was subdued.

Pulling open the top drawer, he touched his fingers to the black and white picture of his father in his cricket whites. He was kneeling on one knee, one of a team of eleven: two rows of smiling, bright young things, wearing striped cricket caps that proudly displayed their house colours and with the Gothic architecture of Vaizey College providing the impressive back-drop. Anyone could see that those fortunate young men would go places. Theo felt a stirring of sadness, but it was Mr Porter he pictured, bending low and painting the cricket crease with a stubby paintbrush.

'Can I get you a hot drink or anything?'

Theo hadn't heard Stephen come into the room. He popped the photograph back into the drawer and stood, adjusting his jacket. His finger lingered on the feathered talisman that always brought him comfort.

'No, thanks, Stephen. I'm only popping in. I'll come back soon. I need to...' He ran his hand through the air in an arc, hoping this might hint at all the things he needed to do but was currently unable to voice.

'Where shall I put this?' Stephen bent low with a bundle of mail in his hand.

'Oh, just here on the desk is fine.'

'I've given all the corporate stuff to Marcus. These are more personal.'

'That's fine.' Theo smiled and watched Stephen walk slowly out of the room.

He blew out through bloated cheeks and flicked through flyers for executive car services and an offer from the golf club his father and the rest of the board played at. Lastly, he picked up the magazines from the bottom of the pile. A building magazine, several devoted to classic cars or classic boats, past editions of which cluttered up the windowsill in his parents' downstairs bathroom, and there at the very bottom a copy of the *Old Vaizian* with the outline of the most beautiful school buildings plastered all over the front. Theo had never subscribed, being far from interested in anything anyone old or new at the school had to say. For some reason, call it nostalgia, call it sixth sense, he pulled it from the plastic covering and flicked through the glossy pages.

His heart fluttered as his fingers splayed to hold two pages open.

There was a picture of the crooked cottage, pretty much as he remembered it bar a new roof and a fresh lick of paint on the front door and windows. It surprised him, the wave of emotion that broke over him. He lifted the page to his face and read: *Mr Cyrus Porter, former groundsman of Vaizey College, passed away...*

He rolled the magazine, placed it in his pocket and grabbed his car keys.

Nineteen

It felt strangely emotional to wake to the feel of a hard bolster beneath his head. Theo had arrived at the old-fashioned B&B on the outskirts of Dorchester the night before, exhausted, and had slept with the deep-set window slightly open. The chill air, cold bedding and quiet Dorset countryside placed his memories back at Vaizey College. He lay back on the mattress with his arms locked behind his head and wondered, as he did every morning, how Anna was doing. He reached for his phone, hesitated, then placed it back on the nightstand, nervous of calling to say he was thinking of her, mulling over whether or not it was a good idea, aware of how such a small thing had now become so much more complicated.

He showered, then declined the kind offer of breakfast that was, said Mr Whittaker, the portly owner of the establishment, now being kept warm on a hot plate on the Aga, given the late hour. Theo had no appetite and decided he would grab a coffee later. Hitching his bag onto his shoulder, he gave his thanks and offered praise for a night well spent.

'Actually...' He hesitated, twisting his brogue on the patterned hall carpet. 'I don't suppose you could point me in the direction of a good sports and tackle shop?'

A couple of hours later, with the boot of his Mercedes full to bursting, he pulled the tag from his new, waxed-cotton hat, which sat askew on his head, a size too small, and punched in a call to Jody, who was fast becoming his most valuable asset.

'Just to let you know, I won't be in today or tomorrow and maybe not for the rest of the week.'

'You okay, boss?' She cut to the chase.

'Yep, I'm fine. I'm handing you the reins. Keep me posted if you need anything and I'll phone in when I can. Stephen is taking all calls at Villiers House, but do check in with him.'

With Wilson running the build and Jody's remit now extending into all operational areas – she excelled at just about everything she did – the team was coming together nicely. Theo's dreams were becoming a reality. His worries were now giving way to a sense of pride and excitement, as if he could see the finished building and all that it would achieve. And it felt good.

He pumped the gas on his sleek Mercedes and headed off into the countryside. With his window down, he breathed in lungfuls of the clear Dorset air.

It was two full days later that Theo stomped the mud from his boots and climbed into the comfortable front seat of his car before making his way back along the lanes to the homely B&B with the white bolster pillows that he'd been dreaming about.

Bathed now and with a cold beer in his hand, he went down to the library, fancying a read to distract his thoughts.

'Well, good afternoon to you, Mr Montgomery.'

Mr Whittaker the owner was kneeling by the grate, restacking the log pile and filling the coal bucket from the scuttle. 'Nice to have you back, sir. Been off exploring? I saw the wellies outside!'

'I have actually spent the last couple of days thigh-deep in cold water in the middle of bloody nowhere with a fishing rod and a box of warm sandwiches for company.'

Mr Whittaker chuckled loudly. 'Fishing, eh? Did you enjoy it?'

'No.' He shook his head. 'I absolutely hated it. I was cold, miserable and bored witless.'

'Well, I guess it isn't for everyone.'

'I'll give that a true.' He laughed. 'Anyway, thought I'd grab a novel.'

'Be my guest.' Mr Whittaker indicated the shelves and shelves of dusty books, which again made Theo think of school.

Maybe it was a subconscious decision. Theo hadn't planned on going near his old school, but like a scar that screamed to be itched, and given that it was almost en route to St Barnabas' Church, Wrendletown, he couldn't stay away. Slowing the car, he approached with caution, not intending to stop but figuring he would simply have a quick look and drive on. He was surprised to feel none of the angst he associated with the place. It was just a building after all, and a pretty building at that. He thought of Wilson, busily at work on the Bristol project and doing a fine job. It was a revelation that the more time he spent with him, the more he liked him. It was an odd thing to admit that they were slowly building a bridge between colleague and friend.

He pulled the Mercedes across the entrance to the car park, whose gates his father had driven through in his beautiful Aston

Martin on many an occasion. The sense of nostalgia left a lump in his throat. He knew that Peregrine James Montgomery the Third, of Theobald's House, Vaizey College, would have been delighted to see his son returning to the place he'd held so dear.

A car beeped behind him. He looked into his rearview mirror at a man trying to pull in from the lane. Theo raised his hand in acknowledgement and drove forward into the car park. The silver Range Rover rolled past and parked up next to him, disgorging two boys in full games kit. It made him smile, how only a blink ago that had been him, albeit without the enthusiasm these two now showed for getting to their match.

He watched a woman, bent over, struggling with a cardboard box as she lifted it from the boot of an old Golf. And as she straightened he felt his stomach shrink around his bowels.

It was Kitty.

'Jesus Christ!' He swallowed and looked behind him, keen to make a hasty retreat, unable to cope with another painful encounter, unwilling to deal with a rerun of the 'stay away' glare she'd fired at him on the bus. But with the Range Rover tight behind, he was hemmed in. Trapped.

Becoming aware of his stare, Kitty looked up, blinked and squinted, before placing the cardboard box on the ground and walking over. His heart raced and he was unsure of what to do or how to explain his presence. He didn't want a scene, especially not here – he didn't want any more bad memories to heap onto those that already held him captive. He rolled down the window.

'Theo! Oh my God! Theo, it *is* you! I don't believe it!' she called out with something closer to delight than distress, her fingers lying flat against her chest.

'Hello, you.' He beamed, studying her. 'I didn't want you to think…' He ran out of words, not sure what he was apologising for. The image of her on the bus was still crisp in his mind; the way she had implored him with her eyes to stay away.

This was different, felt different. She looked well and wasn't tense in the way she'd seemed then. She stared at him, seemingly at a loss for words. He climbed slowly from the car, aware of his slightly crumpled suit and the mud clinging to the soles of his shoes.

'So which is it – hell or high water?' she asked slowly, her hands on her hips.

'What?' He was confused and embarrassed that he hadn't picked up the thread.

'I seem to remember you saying that those were the only two things that would ever drag you back here to Vaizey.'

She took a step towards him, her face now only inches from his, as if this was the most natural thing in the world and this was exactly the right distance to have between them. But whereas once he might have held his ground, drinking in every bit of her, today he took a step backwards.

'Yes, I probably did say that.' He smiled and shoved his hands in his pockets. 'If you must know, I've been fishing and I'm about to gatecrash a funeral, if you can believe that.'

'Oh I believe it.' She grinned.

'And what about you?' He jerked his head towards the school, expecting Angus to pop up from somewhere at any moment. He decided that he would shake Angus's hand firmly, smile, and meet his eye – getting to know Wilson really had been helpful in laying his school ghosts to rest.

'Just dropping off.'

'Where's Angus?' he asked, looking over her shoulder towards the quad.

'How should I know? On a golf course probably.' She shrugged. 'Did you think we were still together?'

His gut lurched. 'Are you not?'

'No, not for a while. But it works – we share the kids' care and we are quite good friends now, better friends in fact than we ever were when we were married.'

'So that's good?'

'Yes, it's good!' She laughed again. 'Angus is... with a new partner and happy.' She nodded and gave a thin smile. 'So it's all good!' A flicker of nerves seemed to have disturbed her casual demeanour. 'So you're off to a funeral?'

'Yes. Mr Porter's, actually, who used to be the groundsman here.'

'Oh, I remember him! He had a lovely crinkly smile.'

Theo was happy that she remembered this about him. He pictured Mr Porter standing not far from where they were now, with a wheelbarrow full of compost.

'I must admit, I never had you down as the huntin' and fishin' type! What did you catch?'

'Nothing.' He raised his hands and let them fall as he looked skywards. 'Absolutely nothing. I actually went for the stillness, the quiet.'

'Stillness and quiet – that sounds like bliss. Sometimes I can hardly hear myself think.' Theo noted the creasing of her brow. 'Actually, that's not fair, I think I keep busy to stop from thinking.' She bit her bottom lip and he got the impression that she rarely confessed to this.

'Kitty, I've spent the last few years overthinking and it turns out it wasn't actually very good for me.' He nodded.

'Well, good for you, Theodore Montgomery.' Kitty leant a little further in, her voice now barely more than a whisper. 'It is *so* good to see you.'

'It's good to see you too.'

'Are *you* still married, Theo?' Her enquiry was casual.

'Yes, Anna's great – greater.' He looked at the ground, flustered.

'"Great – greater"? Gosh, you really didn't pay attention in Mr Reeves's class, did you! That is terrible English!' She threw back her head and laughed.

He laughed too, glad of the joviality, which erased any nervousness.

There was a beat of awkward silence as both of them allowed their façades to slip.

'That letter I sent...' she began, taking a deep breath.

Theo nodded. What could he say?

'It was a very difficult time for me.' She shoved her hands in her pockets and held his gaze.

'It became a very difficult time for me too,' he acknowledged, quietly.

'I never in a million years imagined... after that one time...' She pulled a face as if the words were physically painful. 'I was about to get married... There was so much going on in my head.' She tapped her forehead.

'You don't need to explain. I've spent a lot of hours thinking it through and I get it. I totally see why you didn't want anything to do with me, didn't want me in our... your child's life. Why would you? I'm hardly good father material. I had nothing to offer.' *Weirdo...*

'Oh my God, Theo, is that what you thought?' Tears filled her eyes.

He nodded.

Kitty shook her head, her mouth twisted as if she was trying to stop herself from crying. 'No! No, it wasn't that at all. I've never hidden the truth from Sophie – or Angus. Quite the opposite. You, Theodore, are the kindest, sweetest, gentlest friend I ever had. You are smart and funny and any child would be lucky to have you in their life, so lucky. It was never about you! It was only ever about me. I couldn't see any further than what I was going through. I robbed you.'

An inexplicable feeling of weightlessness came over Theo. He exhaled and leant back on the car, fearing that if he didn't, he just might fall. 'But... But then on the bus...' He faltered.

Kitty shook her head. 'Angus and I were falling apart, I was pregnant with Oliver, and little Soph...' She smiled up at him. 'It would have been too much for Soph right then, and too much for me.' She sniffed. 'I am so sorry, Theo. I was young and stupid and frightened when I wrote to you, and if I could—'

'Mum! Mum, have you got my hockey stick?'

Kitty whipped her head round and smiled through her tears at the confident girl striding towards them.

'Why are you crying?' Sophie wrinkled her nose with embarrassment.

'I'm not.' Kitty swiped away her tears and pulled her daughter towards her. She took her face inside her hands and kissed her nose. 'Sophie, this man... This is...' Emotion stopped the words from forming.

Theo stepped forward and held out his hand.

The young girl with the clear skin, dark curly hair and brown eyes placed her hand confidently in his palm. 'Hello.' She smiled. 'I'm Sophie. Sophie Montgomery Thompson.'

Theo didn't often feel the need to give thanks, but as he parked the car and looked up towards the heavens, he closed his eyes. 'My name! She has my name! My daughter, my little girl, Sophie – what a wonderful, wonderful, thing!'

Gathering himself, he wondered if he had come to the right place. There were very few cars around and the beautiful moss-covered Norman church looked strangely quiet. He couldn't help but compare the scene to his father's funeral, when clusters of well-dressed mourners had stood outside the church in Barnes, dabbing at tears and shaking hands with gusto. He flattened his suit lapels and adjusted his tie before pushing on the heavy arched wooden door. There was only a handful of people inside. A couple of elderly folk were already in situ in the front pews and one or two others, men mainly, had taken seats further back. Theo only glanced at them, avoiding eye contact, feeling like an interloper on this sad day.

A keen-looking moon-faced vicar walked over and handed him a single-page order of service. Theo took it and nodded his thanks. As he gazed down at the black and white photograph of Mr Porter he felt a rush of emotion. He coughed to clear his throat and sat up straight, unable to take another look for fear of losing control in public, in front of strangers. The old man in the picture, 'the Fishing-Fly Guy', as Anna called him, looked thinner and very old, but his smile and the crinkle of kindness around his eyes were exactly the same. He was wearing a tweed cap and Theo pictured him raising the front and scratching his head, deep in thought, revealing the dark tan line across his brow.

Music began to play. Theo stood and smiled to hear the

faint strains of Elgar's 'Nimrod' coming from the speakers as the simple wooden coffin was wheeled up the aisle. The music was most fitting, Theo thought, as he recalled snippets of their conversation about Mr Porter's wartime service: '*We were all as scared and desperate as each other. And let me tell you, those that didn't make it home were mourned by their families just the same, goodies and baddies alike.*' For the second time that day, Theo's tears threatened.

The vicar followed the coffin to the altar, then stood in front of the grand brass lectern and spread his arms.

'Welcome, all, to St Barnabas on this sad day when we say goodbye to Cyrus. But I would like to remind you that it is also a happy day, as we celebrate his long life.'

Theo looked around and counted the congregation. There were only thirteen of them in total, and that bothered him. He wondered how different today might have been, how crowded the pews, if Mr Porter's wife, Merry, had lived and they'd gone on to have children, even grandchildren. He thought then of his own dad, who also never got to be called Grandpa, and again his whole being was filled with the image of Sophie.

The vicar continued. 'Cyrus Porter was a man who liked to garden.'

As Theo listened to him reading from his crib sheet, he thought how shabby that was – how hard would it have been to learn a few things by heart?

'He liked to garden and indeed won first prize three years running for his marrows in the village harvest festival competition. He had been a soldier in his youth and fought in France, before taking up the post of gardener at the prestigious Vaizey College, a much revered establishment in our county.'

Theo felt a flash of heat on his skin and, as if powered by something bigger than him, he stood and shuffled to the end of the pew. He walked steadily down the aisle, aware that all eyes were on him as his shoes, now wiped clean, clip-clopped on the tiled floor. He approached the lectern, looking first at the vicar and then at the elderly men and women in the front pew.

'It wasn't France.' He leant in.

'I'm sorry?' the vicar asked with a tense, fixed smile.

'Mr Porter fought his war in Italy. That would have mattered to him. It would have mattered a lot.'

'I'm so sorry.' The vicar coloured. 'I can only go on the information I've been given.' He held up the flimsy sheet of paper that for Theo only added insult to injury.

'Might I?' He nodded at the lectern.

The vicar looked towards an old woman in the front pew, who looked bemused but nonetheless gave a slow nod.

Theo took the vicar's place and gripped the side of the brass stand.

'My name is Theodore Montgomery. Mr Porter was the groundsman at Vaizey College and that's where I met him.' He cursed the tightening of his throat and coughed before resuming. 'He was so much more than that, however, to a young boy who needed a friend, who needed an ally and an escape. He taught me...' Theo was only vaguely aware of the tears that now coursed down his cheeks. 'He taught me more about life than anyone else, before or since. His voice has lived in my head since I was a boy, giving me advice long after I lost contact with him.' At this he felt a stab of pain as sharp as it had been on that day he'd found the crooked cottage empty. He bowed his head and wiped his face with the back of his hand, seeing himself as a fourteen-year-old falling to his knees and howling. '*My friend! I'm sorry!*'

'He was so much more than the groundsman of Vaizey College, so much more than a man who grew prize marrows.' He paused again to regain what composure he could, but his eyes flamed and his tears spilled.

He reached for his suit lapel and turned it over to reveal the small gold pin decorated with a fishing fly of green and blue feathers above a square red bead.

'He was like a father to me.'

He gripped the sides of the lectern as the breath stuttered in his throat and the tsunami of emotion that had been swelling inside him for so long now found its release. The hush in the church was broken by the creak of a pew near the back. A portly man in his late fifties stood and walked forward until he reached Theo's side. He turned over his lapel to reveal a similar fishing fly and shook Theo's hand before turning to the assembled mourners and speaking through a mouth contorted with emotion.

'He was like a father to me too.'

And then a third man came forward; his fishing fly sat proudly on his shirt. 'He was like a father to me,' he offered in a rich Middle Eastern accent.

Then up came a fourth, a fifth, a sixth and a seventh, all of them standing in a line behind the coffin of the man who had scooped them up when they had needed him the most and cared for them when kindness had been in short supply. Their collective tears turned to laughter as they stood shoulder to shoulder, the now grown-up sons of very, very busy people.

Each had thought they were the only one.

'Seemingly Cyrus was a most wonderful man!' The vicar stood next to them, giving words to the air of celebration that now filled the church. 'How very lucky you all were to have him guide you when you were at your most vulnerable.'

'Yes.' Theo nodded, still unable to stem his sadness. 'Very lucky.'

It no longer mattered that there were only thirteen people present. The love those thirteen felt for Mr Porter could have filled a cathedral built for a thousand mourners.

Later, as he threw dirt into the freshly dug hole that had received his dear friend, Theo felt a strange sense of elation.

'Mr Montgomery?' a voice called from the church path as he was making his way back to the car.

'Yes?' He turned to stare at the elderly woman from the front pew, who was supported by a nurse on one side.

'I'm Nelda, Merry's sister,' she explained in a rasping voice. 'Cyrus was my brother-in-law.'

'Yes, of course. Hello!' He shook her hand warmly; the skin was paper thin and cool beneath his touch. 'I'm sorry if I...' He pointed towards the church, feeling a little awkward now, in the daylight, that he had taken centre stage without invitation.

'No, don't be sorry.' She shook her head and smiled at him. 'Cyrus would have been so very proud, touched, I know. I have something for you. He didn't leave any instructions, but my son found an envelope in a box and it has your name on it. Truth be told, I wouldn't have known where to begin if you hadn't shown up today – I would probably have discarded it. But that's by the by, because here you are.'

'Yes, here I am.' He smiled. 'Where is it, the envelope?'

'Back at his house. Only five minutes' drive.'

Theo followed Nelda's Ford along the winding lanes until they came to the village of Marlstonbury. Having left the nurse in the pub, he and Nelda made their way slowly across the village green, Nelda holding onto his arm.

'I'm glad the rain held off. It's turned out nice after all.' She waved her stick towards the sky.

'Yes, it has. Is your son here today?'

'No, he had to go back to Glasgow – that's where he lives now. So far away. I do miss him.'

He thought of Spud.

'Here we are, at Cyrus's house.' She pointed ahead and there, next to a paddock, sat a small cottage, not quite crooked but not far off. 'Not quite sure what we'll do with it – sell it, I suppose.' Nelda pulled out a key from her handbag and opened the front door.

Theo stepped into the narrow hallway. The peculiar aroma – of earth, smoke, oil and wood – instantly took him back to the day when, at seven years old, a cottage like this had provided him with a refuge, a home.

'Do you know, I once slept in the little house Mr Porter lived in at Vaizey College. It was in the grounds of the school and it was very much like this. I felt safe and cosy and I remember thinking how lovely it must be to wake up like that every single day of your life. I was about fourteen.'

'Did you not have parents?' she asked matter-of-factly.

'I did, yes, but they were... they were very busy people.'

She gave a nod of understanding.

'How did Merry die? If you don't mind me asking.'

Nelda inhaled sharply, as if the event was still fresh or at least still hurt as much as ever.

'It was a terrible thing for us all. She was my older sister and she was an adventurer. It's a sad story. She was a newly qualified nurse and got caught in a bombing raid on Liverpool during the war. She was injured but didn't die. My family were of course overjoyed that she'd survived, but we didn't understand just how badly she'd been damaged. She was very quiet, stoic and I like to think she hung on to see Cyrus home safe, but she was never properly well again and she died three weeks after he came home from Italy. I was always glad they'd had that short time together.'

'I'm sorry.'

'Long, long time ago. Another world.' She patted his arm before wandering into the adjoining sitting room.

He let his eyes scan the shelves crammed with books, recognising many of the dusty knick-knacks and ornaments that sat in a row on the mantelpiece. He looked through to the tiny kitchen and there on top of the cupboard sat the green enamel kettle. He again cursed the tears that gathered.

'Here we are then.' Nelda held out her hand. In it lay a cream-coloured envelope with his name inscribed on the front in handwriting he recognised.

'Thank you,' he whispered.

Nelda bent forward and held him in a loose hug. 'He would have been so happy to hear what you said today. And who knows, maybe he did?'

Theo smiled and considered this.

He abandoned his car in Muckleford just as the sun broke though the clouds and set off along the bridleway, climbing steadily. The track opened up and he trod the incline with his hands in his pockets until eventually, with his breath coming in short bursts, he reached Jackman's Cross. His chest heaved and the cool wind stung his skin. The view was every bit as breathtaking as he remembered from his walk there with Mr Porter. He let his eyes rove the horizon, taking in the spires of distant churches and the glorious swathe of green fields. Tucking his mac beneath his legs, he sat down on the damp earth of the hill and reached into his pocket for his letter.

The envelope opened with ease, the old glue having yellowed and turned quite brittle. Carefully, he extracted a lined sheet of A4 paper, torn from a gummed pad. The top line read:

The World through the Eyes of a Blackbird
by Theodore Montgomery.

Oh my God! My homework assignment!

Theo paused and took a deep breath, exhaling slowly before holding the paper up to his face and reading it. He devoured the first two paragraphs with a tremble to his lip and a clamp around his heart. But it was the final few lines of the third paragraph that really made him smile. His tears fell as the wind lifted his hair and his spirits.

As I make my way over fields and lakes, marvelling at the changing landscape below me, I realise that what I learn year on year is what makes me stronger. With strength comes confidence and with confidence comes the ability to be the master of my life, to own my happiness and to make the changes necessary to be the best I can be. And that is why I sing! I sing loudly! Letting the world know that I might be small in the scheme of things, I might be just a bird, but what do I bring to the world? I bring this, my own unique song.

Theo sat for some minutes with tears in his eyes until he felt able to do what he'd been wanting to do for a very long time. He lifted his phone from his pocket and with a sense that time was chasing him, he dialled the number for home.

'Hello?'

'Anna?'

'Theo! Oh my God, I've been so worried about you. Radio silence is never good! Are you okay?'

'I'm...' The strength of his emotions made speech almost impossible. 'I'm more than okay,' he managed.

'Well, that's good to hear.' Her relief was palpable. 'I... I found your note in the study. Your list – your mum told me where to find it and I love it!'

He could hear the joy in her voice and it warmed him. 'You did?'

'I did! I really did. You alphabetised me! You did my game.'

'I tried.' He laughed. 'It was a long time ago, but I wanted so badly to get it right. I wanted you to know how much I loved you, how much I love you.'

'Oh, Theo, it's perfect. It...' There was a hesitation and Theo thought he heard a sob. 'It... couldn't have been written by anyone but you, Theo. Only you know me that well.'

It was Theo's turn now to try and mask his sobs.

'I've missed you so much, Theo, and it seems such a waste, all this... being apart.' She sniffed down the line. 'I love the things you wrote about me. They've made me happy.' The sound of another sob. 'H for happy...'

'I want to make you H for happy, Anna. I really do.'

There was a pause, then Anna changed tack. 'Are you outside somewhere?' she asked.

'Yes, I'm on the top of a hill looking at the whole wide world.'

'Are you drunk?' she asked. 'You sound… different. More… emotional. Has something happened?'

'I'm not drunk, no, but I do feel as if a mist has lifted. That's the only way I can describe it. I went fishing and then I went to Mr Porter's funeral, and I even visited Vaizey College, and something strange has happened to me… I feel like I can see clearly for the first time.'

'In what way?'

Her tone was heartbreakingly hopeful, and he pictured her clutching the phone to her ear, wondering what on earth he was going to say next.

'I met Sophie. I met her, Anna, properly met her – totally by chance – and she is incredible. And I want you to meet Sophie. I want to grow up, Anna. I want the responsibility of being the best husband I can possibly be. I'm not going to let the past shape me, not any more. Someone…' He swallowed. 'Someone whose opinion I valued above all others—'

'Let me guess – Mr Porter, the Fishing-Fly Guy?'

'Yes!' He laughed. 'The Fishing-Fly Guy. He's just told me that I need to be the master of my own life, to take charge, be confident and watch the changes. I need to cut away the shadows of my childhood.'

'Oh my God, he is right, Theo, he is absolutely right, and you can do it, *we* can do it! I have Shania and the twins here and, oh, Theo, seeing those two new lives begin to blossom, it's such a pleasure and a privilege. You will fall for them just as I have,

I know you will. Your Fishing-Fly Guy is absolutely right, my love – the universe is a marvel.'

'Yes, it is, and I want us to discover it together, my Anna. My love. I'm coming home. I'm coming home to make a plan. We should try and be parents, Anna, just like you've always said we should. No ifs or buts. There are kids that need guidance, kids like you and kids like me. We will try our very hardest and one way or another we will make our family. I'm going to be a dad, and you are going to be the best mum ever.'

'Theo...' she managed. 'My Theo.'

'I'll be there as soon as I can. I'm coming home.' He spoke quickly. 'I am sorry, so sorry, that I held back, that I didn't give you all of me, but I will make it up to you, I promise. We have time – we have all the time in the world. Mr Porter was eighty when he died – that means we aren't even halfway through! My Anna, we're going to live the best life!'

His energy was infectious. 'My Theodore, you have no idea how happy I am right now. Drive safely. I love you!'

'I love you too.'

'And I will be waiting for you, right here. Griff and me.'

Theo placed his phone back in his pocket and looked out towards the hedgerows, where blackbirds, dunnocks and wrens were busy feeding their young and keeping their nests nice and cosy, doing all they needed for their little families to flourish.

He stood and reached for the keys in his pocket.

'I'm coming home, Anna! I'm coming home.'

Epilogue

2002

'There you are! Thank goodness. I was about to send Griff out with a little barrel of brandy around his neck to come and find you!' Anna shouted as Theo walked through the front door.

He watched her disappear from view, scooting across the tiled floor in her socks, heading towards the fridge while holding a dish laden with some goodies she had no doubt been prepping for most of the afternoon.

Griff barked his approval at Theo's homecoming and, as ever, it made him smile. His faithful friend.

'Where on earth have you been?' she called.

'I've been walking along the river.' His voice was calm, steady.

'I don't blame you, escaping the madhouse.' She smiled. 'You're nervous,' she whispered.

'I really am. I went out mainly to call Spud, but he just said I needed to pull up my big-boy pants and get on with it.'

She laughed. 'Wise advice.'

Walking slowly into the kitchen, he felt his heart swell with love at the sight of the Easter table, beautifully set with sparkling glassware and polished silver cutlery. The radio was burbling away in the background and the sumptuous smell of roast lamb wafted from the range. Anna was going to so much trouble.

She pulled the blue linen dishcloth from where it hung on the range door and wiped her dainty hands on it. 'You don't have to be nervous, Theo. It's all going to be fine, I promise. You are surrounded by people who love you.' She stood on tiptoe and kissed his mouth.

'Anna...'

'Yes, love?' She scooted in the opposite direction, off to fetch a small spoon from the cutlery drawer.

'Thank you.'

'For what?' She looked up at him with a wrinkle at the top of her nose.

'For making it easy. For being you.'

She beamed, batting away the compliment. 'I'd do anything for you. For us.'

'We need kitchen paper in here!' came the shout from the sitting room.

Anna grabbed the roll and walked briskly in response to Shania's call. It was a sight of near chaos that greeted her. Joshua and David, her twins, now boisterous toddlers, were running off the effects of several Easter eggs, chasing each other around the sofa. One or both had inadvertently knocked over Stella's rather large gin and tonic, which had been perched on a side table. Samuel, their dad, smiled awkwardly. 'Sorry, Anna.'

'Don't be daft! I love having them here. And, trust me, when you four are all back in St Lucia in a few days' time, I will be longing for the sound of them running around, trashing our home!'

Shania laughed and smiled at her friend, knowing it was the truth.

'In a few days, you say? Well, there we are,' Stella shouted, her expression indicating that the exit of these little human wrecking balls couldn't come soon enough.

'I was just telling Shania that the sooner she gets these kids hooked on TV, the more life she'll get back.' Melissa pointed at Nicholas and Isabel as if to prove her point. Both lay on their tums with legs kicked up, chins on upturned palms, staring at the TV screen.

'I'm doing my level best to keep them away from the TV.' Shania sighed.

'Well, good luck with that!' Standing in front of the fireplace, Gerard, Melissa's husband, raised his wine glass in a show of support. 'Although I guess if I lived in an island paradise, I might find things to do other than watch rugby on TV.'

It was Samuel's turn to laugh. Theo thought he looked smug, happy, and this feeling he understood only too well. 'Come and see us any time – you know that. We love having guests.'

'Do I have to bring this lot or can I come alone?' Gerard ducked, trying to avoid the cushion expertly hurled by his wife.

Shania looked up at Anna and Theo and smiled broadly. 'All these joys await you, you lucky things! Any more news from the adoption agency?'

Theo glanced at Anna and winked at her. 'Well… we've officially passed the "suitable parents" test, apparently, so the next step will be when the agency calls us with a possible match.' He grinned. 'We've asked to adopt two kids – siblings, if possible. We might even get twins, like you guys! So we'll be wanting lots of tips, that's for sure.'

'Oi oi! There's a cab just pulled up!' Sylvie shouted from the chair by the window, a position she liked to occupy, being perfect for watching the comings and goings of the street. As usual she had her slippers on her feet and a mug of tea in her hands and was ready with a running commentary.

Theo looked at Anna, noting the almost imperceptible nod of her head. *I've got this...* He gripped her hand and the two walked into the hallway and threw open the front door.

'Aaaagh!' Anna screamed and ran down the path to meet her cousin Jordan, who looked immaculate in his navy Crombie and with a soft grey cashmere scarf knotted at his neck. 'Goldpie!' She jumped into his embrace and he twirled her around with his arms clamped around her.

'I love you so much!' he yelled to the sky.

Levi, his partner, shook his head with barely disguised embarrassment and walked towards Theo with his hand outstretched. 'How you doing, Theo?' he offered sedately.

'Good, good, Levi. It's great to see you.' He took Levi's hand into both of his.

'Where is he?' Jordan shouted as he plopped Anna onto the floor.

Theo braced himself as Jordan ran at him, almost knocking him sideways, and wrapped him in a tight hug. 'Have you missed me?' Jordan squeaked.

'More than I can say.' Theo screwed his face up as Jordan planted a kiss on his cheek before releasing him.

'Are Lisa and Micky here?' he enquired after Anna's half siblings.

'Not yet, they're having lunch with their mum and then coming over later. Don't worry, you'll see them. Be warned, Kaylee is hoping for a singing lesson!' Anna grimaced.

'Bless her, it would be my pleasure. Are the babies here?' Jordan clapped.

'They are, but they're not babies any more – they're three and running around like loons after too much sugar.'

'Oh goody!' Jordan trilled. 'That is *exactly* how I plan on spending today!'

Theo ushered the new arrivals into the sitting room and Anna followed with a cold bottle of champagne and two glasses.

'Everyone!' Theo called the room to attention. 'Most of you already know, but this is Jordan and Levi!'

Sylvie dragged her attention away from the window. 'Oh, the Americans! Aren't you two a couple of erm... a couple of...' She clicked her fingers as if the word evaded her.

It seemed to Theo that the room held its collective breath, wondering what the word might be and considering when it would be appropriate to jump in.

'Actors!' Sylvie shouted.

'Yes!'

'Actors!

'We act!'

'Actors!'

Laughter rippled around the room.

'Not that well known, I would suggest, if my son finds it necessary to tell us their names. I don't think Humphrey Bogart or Robert Redford would have to be similarly introduced!' Stella downed what was left of her G&T.

Anna was just opening her mouth to reply when the front doorbell rang.

'Oh my God!' She put her hand over her mouth and pulled up her shoulders. Theo's heart sang to see her joyful anticipation.

Untying her pinny, she threw it over the back of a chair and ran her fingers through her hair.

'Come on – together.' He reached for her hand and the two of them walked slowly down the hallway, side by side.

Theo opened the door.

There was a split second of silence as they all allowed the enormity of the moment to sink in.

It was Kitty who made the first move, as she walked in. 'Hello, Theo! Good to see you. And Anna, so lovely to meet you.'

Theo watched as the two women held each other in a brief but sincere embrace. He felt nothing but relief.

'You too.' Anna smiled. 'I feel as if I know you already, I really do.'

'Same.' Kitty nodded.

The two women turned and stood next to Theo and all three stared at the teenage girl hovering nervously on the doorstep.

'And you must be Sophie.' Anna, his beloved Anna, took the girl's hand and guided her into their home.

Sophie nodded, embarrassed, awkward and a little overcome.

'This is quite a day for you, for us all,' Anna offered with her customary kindness, and Theo felt another rush of love for her.

'Hello, Sophie.' He smiled at the beautiful girl and felt as if he was dreaming. *Here she was, in their house!* He had to curb his instinct to rush ahead, give her a key!

'Hi...' Sophie hesitated. 'I don't really know what to call you.' She looked over to her mum.

'Whatever you're comfy with, darling.' Kitty winked at her girl.

It was permission of sorts and Theo was thankful. 'Theo is fine,' he managed, his voice full of emotion.

'Or Dad-Theo,' Anna suggested without embarrassment. 'I know you already have a proper dad – Angus – but as someone who grew up with no one I could call Dad, I can only imagine how wonderful it might be to be able to say that to two people.'

Sophie beamed at Anna. 'Yes, you're right.' She looked at Theo. 'Hi, Dad-Theo.'

'Hello, Sophie,' he repeated, just for the sheer joy of being able to address her by name.

Anna placed her hands on Kitty and Sophie's backs and ushered them towards the sitting room. 'Now, be warned, the house is bursting at the seams and we are an eclectic bunch, but everyone is very much looking forward to meeting you.'

'I'm looking forward to meeting them.' Sophie spoke with confidence. 'And I'm used to eclectic bunches. My family – my... my other family – we're all really weird.'

'Then I think you're going to fit in just fine.' Anna laughed.

Theo gulped down the tears that gathered and gazed at the girl who looked a lot like him. His tears, however, were for his wife, his beautiful Anna, who had given him the biggest gift in the world.

She made him feel like an ordinary man and not in the slightest bit weird; the kind of man, in fact, who was capable of being a dad.

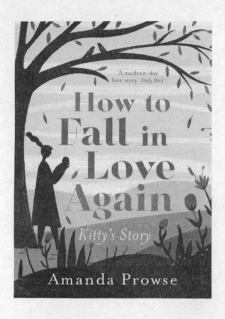

Is it ever too late to find your soulmate?

Kitty Monrose is packing up her house. Under this roof, she's
seen her children grow up, her grandchildren arrive,
and her marriage come and go.

She had always hoped for more.

Then Kitty meets Theo, an old flame. Can they find a way to
fall in love again? Or is it too late for them both?

This is Kitty's story.

Turn the page for an exclusive preview of
How to Fall in Love Again.

One

'Kitty,' her mother called from the stable yard, 'come back here right now! You are not to go near that pony again today. I've told you twice!'

'But why can't I go with you and the boys?' Kitty stomped her little riding boot on the cobbles and stuck out her bottom lip.

'Because.'

'That's not an answer!' Kitty bellowed, hitting the leg of her jodhpurs with her crop.

'Well, it's all the answer you're going to get, my little love. Now go into the house and scrub up and ask Marjorie for some tea and sandwiches. We won't be too long.'

'But, Mum, Marjorie smells of dog and even though you say you won't be too long, I know you will. It's not fair! I ride better than Ruraigh, just ask Daddy, and Hamish is a crybaby. And I never cry!'

Her mother rubbed her brow, the soft leather of her riding glove squeaking across her fair, freckled skin. 'For the love of

God, Kitty, why do you have to question everything! Why can't you for once just do as I ask, just *once*?'

Kitty shrugged inside her Fair Isle sweater and wondered the same thing. She knew her mum, always keen to be doing something, was constantly saying, 'To sit idle is a waste of a day, a waste of a life, and who wants that?' Not Kitty, that was for sure. Her fidgety nature meant she completely understood her mum's need to be on her way, but her mum appeared to have forgotten how much Kitty hated having her wings clipped. And it felt horrible.

She might have only been seven years old, but Kitty knew that her compulsion to query everything was not something her six classmates shared. She had overhead Miss Drummond saying to the priest, 'That young Kitty Montrose, she has wings on her feet and the devil on her tongue – it's a full-time job trying to coax her into staying in her chair!' This description had filled Kitty with happiness, though she suspected the other girls in her class would have been upset in her place. With wings on her feet, she now knew she could outrun Ruraigh and Hamish, her cousins, no matter that they were a whole one and two years older than her. They might have known words she didn't, occasionally teaching her the odd one, but she wasn't going to let them beat her at everything, no way.

'I'm meeting everyone on the ridge – we're going for a hack, and I'm already late.' Her mother sighed. 'We want to catch the last of the light.'

'Please, Mum! I love riding up there,' she whined.

'Well, you shouldn't love riding up there, it's way too steep for your pony, and the weather comes in quickly. It's not safe.'

'If it's not safe for me, how come it's safe for you?'

'Because I'm a grown-up. And remind me, why am I still here having this conversation?' Her mum walked forward, leading the tall horse.

'But Daddy said I was a natural,' Kitty said in desperation.

'Your dad's an idiot!'

Kitty knew her mum didn't really think he was an idiot. She watched the two of them after supper each evening, sitting in the library while she played in front of the fire. Her dad would rub her mum's toes as they drank cocoa or whisky and giggled, sometimes whispering when they thought she couldn't hear.

She stuck her chin out and pulled her most endearing face. 'Please, Mumma!'

Fenella Montrose ignored her pouting daughter, stepped up onto the mounting block and swung her leg over the muscled back of Ballachulish Boy. 'Go and find Marjorie. I shan't tell you again, you wee scamp!' she shouted, but with a flash of love in her eyes and the twitch of a smile around her mouth. She gathered Balla's reins loosely, making the lightest contact between her hands and the bit, then clicked her tongue against the roof of her mouth and gently squeezed his girth with her lower legs. Horse and rider walked serenely out of the yard.

A ball of rage swirled in Kitty's tummy as her cheeks turned pink.

'Kitty? Kitty, hen?' Marjorie called from the deep front porch of their vast grey house, Darraghfield. 'There's soup, sandwiches and cake when you're ready!'

Late afternoon was Kitty's favourite time of day. As the sky turned purple, softening the outlines of the deep glens and rolling Highland hills around them, the lights of the main house would come on one by one, reminding her of an advent calendar

3

with each little window opening to reveal a secret.

'Kitty! Kitty!' their housekeeper called, her tone becoming more exasperated.

Using the shadows, the little girl wove her way across the cobbles, darting this way and that to stay hidden, looking back over her shoulder until she felt the scratchy straw of Flynn's bedding underfoot.

'Sshhhh! Flynn, we're on a secret mission.' She held her finger up to her lips and told her pony not to make a sound. 'We're going to follow Mummy and her friends out and come home before them and they will never know we've been gone. Don't worry about Marjorie, she can watch *Crossroads* in peace in the kitchen.'

With her two red plaits bouncing up and down, Kitty trotted Flynn across the cobbles, out of the yard and along the lane. She looked up at the darkening sky and breathed in the late-afternoon air, which was heavy with moisture and the sweet scent of moss. With a wide smile of satisfaction, she walked her pony across the field; clumps of tall thistles and lichen-covered rocks littered the wet grass, making the going a little tough along the sharp incline. Bending forward, she patted her pony's flank with the flat of her palm. 'You're such a good boy, Flynn! I love you.'

At the top of the field they broke into a canter and it was only when Kitty looked back down the sweep of the bank towards the house that her smile faded. It was further away than she'd anticipated and suddenly the path wasn't where she thought it would be. She'd forgotten that this side of the ridge fell into darkness first, as the sun dropped behind the towering conifers along the summit.

'It's okay, Flynn. Don't be scared, boy. We'll just go down very slowly and go home – we'll be back on the lane before you know it. I think it's too late and too dark for a baby pony like you to be out all on your own.'

Kitty's heart was beating loudly and droplets of sweat had broken out above her lip. Her hands felt clammy against the reins and in the half-light the trees and hedgerows harboured the sinister shapes of monsters and ghouls. The two of them went forward with caution; Flynn's steps were hesitant, and Kitty's breath came in short bursts.

'Don't be scared, Flynn!' She swallowed. 'It's only the dark and we're nearly home. We'll get you settled and I'll go and watch TV with Marjorie in the—'

Kitty didn't see the large red hind and her baby feeding on the lower slope of the field, but Flynn did. He whinnied, bucked and raised his two front legs, skittish on the slippery bank, before throwing Kitty down hard.

It was a shock to view the world from such an odd angle when only seconds before all had been well. She screamed as she tumbled. A pain in her arm drew all her attention as she lay on the grass, finding it hard to catch her breath. Flynn, now free of his rider, raced off as fast as his little legs would take him, in the opposite direction of the house. She heard his canter fade into silence.

Kitty cried loudly, glad at first that no one was around to hear. Then she fell into some kind of sleep, the soft moss and grass as her mattress, the damp earth soaking her clothing and the crescent moon peeking at her from behind the dark bruise of dusk.

'Kitty!'

The call was faint to start with. She thought she might be dreaming, but the uncomfortable ache to her body told her she was awake. Slowly opening her eyes, she tried to sit up, but the pain in her arm and shoulder made moving impossible.

'Kitty!'

It was louder this time, closer, and then came beams of light, swinging up and down the field from powerful torches. She raised her good arm and flexed her fingers as best she could before replying quietly, 'Here,' and then again, louder, 'Here!'

'Kitty!' There was an almost hysterical edge to her mother's voice. 'Oh, sweet Lord above!'

She closed her eyes and heard the flat, heavy thud of footsteps running across the ground to where she lay, accompanied by shouts and the metallic jangle of lanterns and torches. Her body softened a little. They'd found her.

'Oh, darling! Oh, my baby!' Her mother sobbed. 'Are you hurt?'

'No,' she managed. Even in her dazed state she knew to lie so as not to make her mother any more anxious.

'Now, Kitty Montrose, what have you been up to?' Her dad's soft, calm tone made her smile, despite her discomfort. His big bald head, and hands as wide as pans came into view as he crouched down beside her. Just knowing he was there made everything feel a whole lot better.

'I wanted to ride with everyone up on the ridge, and…' Her face scrunched up as the left side of her body throbbed.

'There now.' He smoothed her wispy fringe from her clammy forehead. 'You need to breathe and try and relax your muscles, and remember that you're a warrior, like your mum.'

Kitty nodded. She never forgot. *A warrior, like my mum.* It made her special. Strong.

'Let's get you inside and warmed up.' Her dad bent down and Ruraigh swung the torch over her form.

As the beam of light fell across her left arm, her mother screamed. 'Oh my God! Her arm! Stephen, will you look at her arm!' Then came the sound of Hamish being sick into the grass.

'Don't look down, Kitty.' Her dad leant in close and spoke firmly, yet calmly. 'Keep your eyes on my face and we'll get you to the hospital and they can patch you up and you'll be good to go.'

She could hear the fear in his voice, and despite being told not to look, he had piqued her curiosity. She lowered her eyes and stared at her arm. It looked odd to say the least – it was broken, clearly, and stuck out from her body, twisted at a very awkward angle. It was scary to see something so familiar so bent out of shape and, strangely, once she'd seen it, it hurt even more. 'Fuckaduck!' she screamed, before giving in to tears of fear.

Despite the dire circumstances, Ruraigh laughed and Kitty wondered what was so funny about the word that he and Hamish had taught her only yesterday.

Moving Home

2018

Kitty let her eyes rove across the mountain of sealed boxes stacked neatly along the back wall of the landing, their contents summarised in scrawls of thick black marker-pen. More still were lined up in the bedroom, with others dotted around the kitchen. Every room of the four-storey Victorian terrace in Blackheath, London had been dismantled; the fittings and fixtures had been plucked off walls and gathered from shelves, cloaked in bubblewrap and secreted away inside the cardboard boxes, ready to emerge in their quite different new home. It felt odd, packing up a lifetime of memories. She hadn't banked on it being so emotive, but with each new box filled she felt swamped by recollections. Some of her happiest times had been spent in this house, playing with the kids when they were little, on the sitting-room rug that now stood, rolled and bound with tape, waiting in a corner. And she'd had some of her saddest times here too, curled up in the chair in the sitting room, waiting for the next big showdown, crying silently and wondering how she'd got it all so wrong.

Kitty had no idea she had so much stuff.

Lots of it belonged to the kids, admittedly. She had unwittingly become the custodian of the crap they didn't want in their own homes. Everything from ski gear to boxes of books, camping equipment and even a spare rabbit hutch – God only knew where that had come from! Not that she minded, not really. Having their things around her allowed her to believe at some level that they still lived there, and that in itself was a comfort.

Moving house, however, was a good chance for a clear-out. It forced her to investigate long-abandoned corners and dusty cupboards that bulged, mostly with rubbish. It was surprising that after years of taking up precious space in her home, the value of certain things was no more than the fact of their having been around for a long time. She sent the clutter to the tip without too much consideration. At least where they were moving to was big, with plenty of storage. Although, last she'd heard, certain individuals already had their eye on several of the outbuildings, which would apparently be perfect for a woodworking studio, a workshop and a potting shed, if she remembered correctly. She smiled at the image of them set up and cosy in a family home; the giddy swirl in her stomach was that of a teenager and not a fifty-two-year-old woman. She rather liked it.

It was early morning. Sophie, who had popped in as promised to help with the lifting, called down through the open loft hatch. Kitty was grateful for her stopping by.

'Are you ready, Mum? This is getting heavy.'

Kitty stretched up her arms and steadied herself against the aluminium ladder, which felt none too secure. 'Yes, drop it! The anticipation is killing me!'

'Here it comes.'

Kitty braced herself and gathered the sturdy plastic box into her arms, which were still strong, muscled. Sport, and swimming in particular, had proved to be the kindest thing she'd done to her body over the years.

'What's in it?' Sophie called from within the dusty confines of the loft.

'Give me a chance! Good Lord, are you this impatient with your pupils?' She laughed, trying to imagine her daughter in her role as teacher, a department head, no less.

'I am, actually – they're all petrified of me.' Sophie laughed.

'Poor them.' Kitty smiled with pride.

She lugged the box across the narrow landing and heaved it onto her bed, before pulling it open and showering the duvet with dust. As she peered inside, her heart fluttered and she felt a whoosh of excitement in her chest. She looked up at her daughter, who now stood in the doorway of the bedroom. 'Oh, Soph! Oh, how lovely! These are my old photographs. Mainly from when I was little, and a few from school, I seem to remember.'

'Ooh, marvellous – snapshots from debauched parties and your misspent youth, I hope?' Sophie rubbed her hands together and flopped down on the bed next to her mother.

'Hardly!' Kitty laughed. 'More likely me in the swimming pool or playing Scrabble with your grandad – that kind of thing.'

She ran her fingers over the collection of images, some dog-eared and others sporting the sticky ring of a carelessly placed glass of squash. Some were in black and white, others had gone sepia-toned where the colours had faded. But every one of them took her back to a particular place in time; she could recall the decor, the time of year, even the scent of summer grass or winter fires.

'I know you all snap away now on your phones quite frivolously, but in those days photographs were only taken by a sturdy camera and they felt quite important. They were printed and some even got framed and made it onto the mantelpiece, and they were always hung on to; they were precious things. Not like now when you have thousands of them sitting on that tiny screen and you delete them willy-nilly.'

'Yes, but we get to choose the best pictures, edit them, even, so we wouldn't end up with something like this!' Sophie held up a picture of Kitty as a small child in a hand-knitted Arran jumper. Her hair stuck up at odd angles and her eyes were half-closed. The whole image was blurry. It was less than attractive.

'True! But I like the authenticity of it. That's exactly what I was like – a bit boisterous, too fidgety to sit still for a camera and always wearing jumpers like that. I was probably eager to get to my pony or to run off somewhere.'

She delved into the box and pulled out another image of her with her head close to the beautiful broad forehead of a pony.

'Oh, Sophie!' She sighed, turning the image outwards so her daughter could see. They both laughed. 'Will you look at that! That is a look of pure love!'

She had written on the back: *Kitty Dalkeith Montrose aged nine and a half with Flynn.*

'I love how I've given my full name lest there be any doubt!' She peered more closely at the picture. 'You can't see it here, as my arm is hidden, but I had just come out of hospital. I remember being desperate to get back to Darraghfield. I think this was after the fifth operation on my arm. I hated being away from home, the food was terrible and there was a very strict ward sister who put the fear of God into me, put the fear of God into all of us! She was revered through-out St Bride's – you remember St Bride's, don't you? The local cottage hospital up there.'

'The one where Nana went sometimes...?'

Kitty nodded quickly and continued. 'Your nana and grandad would come and visit me for an hour every night. That was all they were allowed. They'd take a painted green metal chair from a stack by the door, just the one, mind, as per Sister's rules, and take turns sitting on it. And they'd try and make me laugh, cheer me up, right up until the five-minute warning bell for the end of visiting time, and then your nana would sob. She cried so easily...' Kitty paused, close to tears herself now, at the memory of her mother.

'She'd weep and go on about how I might have been killed that night, when I was seven, but I always thought she was exaggerating. I do know I hurt my arm so badly that it took six operations over about four years to get it to this.' She held out her arm, which was far from straight, far from perfectly fixed.

'Funnily enough, the thing that bothered me most was that I'd been promised a shotgun for my tenth birthday and I was so looking forward to it, but I knew that with my wonky arm I wouldn't be able to shoot straight. The idea of not being as good a shot as Ruraigh and Hamish... God, that was more than I could bear. They teased me so much.'

'Even then?' Sophie smiled.

'Yes, even then.' Kitty shook her head and was surprised by how maudlin she felt. 'Just talking about the hospital takes me back to that room – I can smell the antiseptic in the air and remember the layout of the ward.' She ran her hand over the bone that was permanently bent. 'I've been told that if I'd been taken to a bigger hospital, with specialist surgeons and all that, you'd never be able to tell I'd hurt my arm.'

'Instead you were probably sawn open by a rank amateur at the cottage hospital who was over the moon to be dealing with something other than frostbitten fingers, haemorrhoids and babies with croup.'

'Probably something like that.' She smiled.

'I rather like your wonky arm, Mum. It's just another thing that makes you unique.'

'Oh God, Sophie, is that the kind of cliché you offer your students?'

'Only the shit ones who need a bit of bolstering.'

'You are funny.'

'I've got to go.' Sophie glanced at her watch, then back at her mum. 'Do you know, I've never seen you this happy. It's wonderful.'

Kitty looked up at her. She was overjoyed that her daughter approved of this new beginning. 'Thank you, Soph. I love you.'

'Love you too. Don't bother coming down, I'll see myself out. I expect you'll sit here for some time working your way through those.' She nodded towards the box of photos.

Kitty pressed the one of her and Flynn to her chest. 'I wish I had time, but this old house isn't going to pack itself up.'

'Will you miss it, Mum?'

Kitty took a second or two to formulate her response. 'I will miss the happy memories that I have of you and Olly being little, and I'll miss Blackheath's lovely shops!' She smiled, briefly. 'But I think I'm overdue this change and it will be good to live free of all the ghosts that lurk in the drawers and cling to the curtains.'

'But you don't regret *everything*, do you? I mean, you can't, it's too much of your life.'

'Oh, Soph, not only do I have so much to feel thankful for, but I try to regret nothing. It feels pointless. I do wish I'd had more courage at times. I wish I'd listened to my instincts. But regrets...? Not really.'

A letter from the publisher

We hope you enjoyed this book. We are an independent publisher dedicated to discovering brilliant books, new authors and great storytelling. If you want to hear more, why not join our community of book-lovers at:

www.headofzeus.com

We'll keep you up-to-date with our latest books, author blogs, tempting offers, chances to win signed editions, events across the UK and much more.

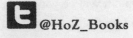 @HoZ_Books

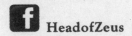 HeadofZeus

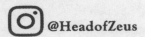 @HeadofZeus

🦜 HEAD *of* ZEUS